CIPHER'S WRATH

CIPHER'S WRATH

THE COLLISION

BOOK 2

T. M. CLAYTON

Podium

For Henry

Cover design by Tom Edwards

ISBN: 978-1-0394-3843-9

Published in 2023 by Podium Publishing, ULC
www.podiumaudio.com

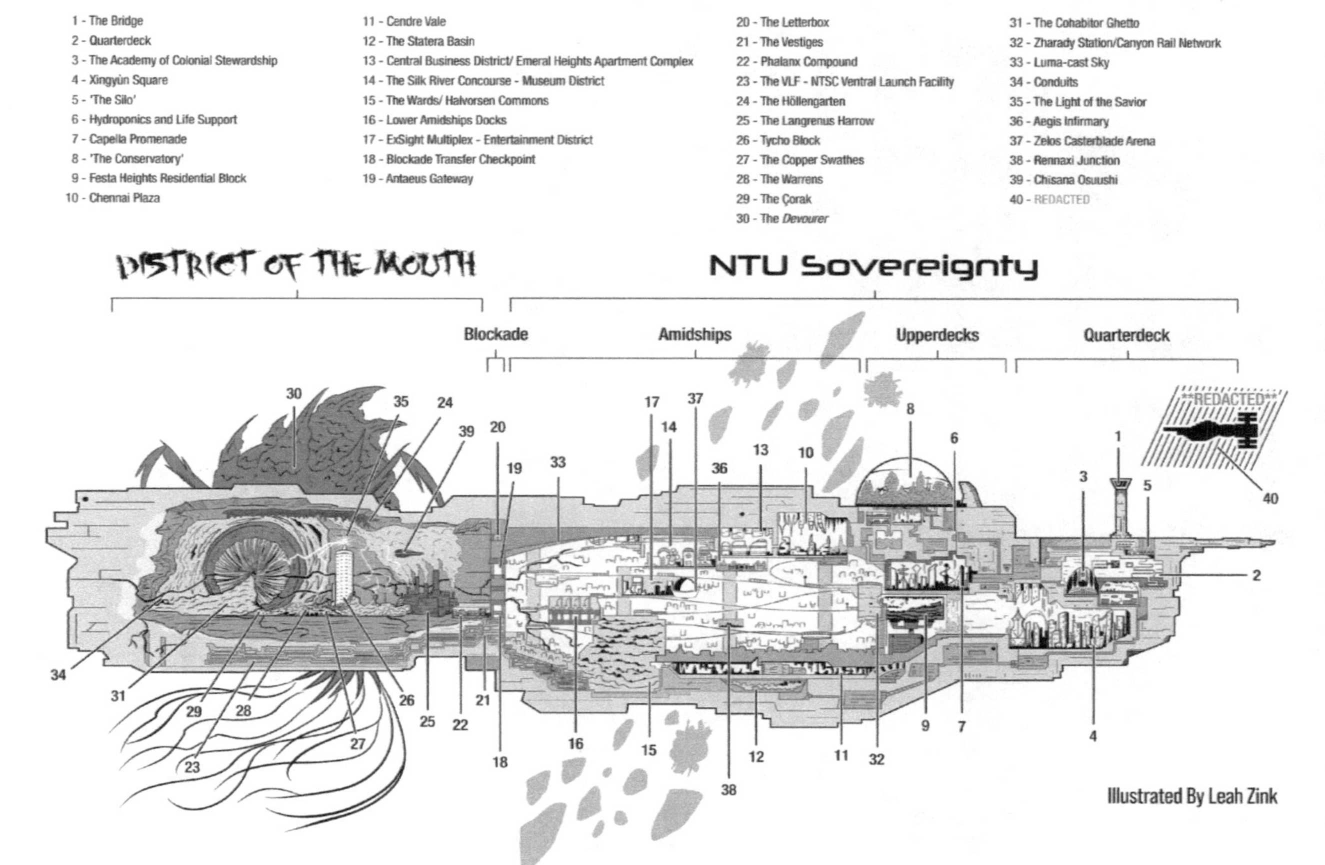

1 - The Bridge
2 - Quarterdeck
3 - The Academy of Colonial Stewardship
4 - Xingyùn Square
5 - 'The Silo'
6 - Hydroponics and Life Support
7 - Capella Promenade
8 - 'The Conservatory'
9 - Festa Heights Residential Block
10 - Chennai Plaza
11 - Cendre Vale
12 - The Statera Basin
13 - Central Business District/ Emeral Heights Apartment Complex
14 - The Silk River Concourse - Museum District
15 - The Wards/ Halvorsen Commons
16 - Lower Amidships Docks
17 - ExSight Multiplex - Entertainment District
18 - Blockade Transfer Checkpoint
19 - Antaeus Gateway
20 - The Letterbox
21 - The Vestiges
22 - Phalanx Compound
23 - The VLF - NTSC Ventral Launch Facility
24 - The Höllengarten
25 - The Langrenus Harrow
26 - Tycho Block
27 - The Copper Swathes
28 - The Warrens
29 - The Çorak
30 - The Devourer
31 - The Cohabitor Ghetto
32 - Zharady Station/Canyon Rail Network
33 - Luma-cast Sky
34 - Conduits
35 - The Light of the Savior
36 - Aegis Infirmary
37 - Zelos Casterblade Arena
38 - Rennaxi Junction
39 - Chisana Osuushi
40 - REDACTED
DISTRICT OF THE MOUTH
NTU Sovereignty
Blockade
Amidships
Upperdecks
Quarterdeck
REDACTED
Illustrated By Leah Zink

THE
CONSERVATORY

1- COHP Atrium
2- Loading Bay
3- Khadija's Green
4- Amphitheatre
5- Stone water fountain
6- Kid's Play Area
7- Rainforest Biome
8- Tropical Greenhouses
9- Wildflower Meadows
10- Orchard
11- Botanical Gardens
12- Beech Glade Complex
13- Learning centre
14- Bistro restaurant

15- Function room
16- Gift shop
17- Butterfly greenhouse
18- Europan Memorial Autumnal Arboretum
19- 'Shimmer' cafe
20- Bandhavghar Reservoir
21- Wetlands Aviary
22- Operations Cabin
23- Polytunnels / Herb garden
24- Pentagonal maze
25- Running track / Tennis courts
26- Desert biome
27- Cactus gardens
28- Artifical cave system

CIPHER'S WRATH

PROLOGUE

Yusef Lei-Ghannam had not yet been born when the NTSC *Novara* departed from the Lunar Shipyards of Old-Earth. Nor would he live to see the colossal arc ship arrive at her destination: a tiny, green speck orbiting a star in the distant Hephaestus Cluster, yearningly named Pasture by his ancestors. He bore no resentment regarding these two facts; as a captain serving midway through the centuries-long voyage, he measured himself not by metrics of valor or tactical prowess. Like his predecessors, future history would judge him by his capacity for patience and endurance instead. By the end of his career, he aspired to have achieved four decades of dutiful, if notably unremarkable, service to the New Terra Union. There would be no war stories told in his name of hard-fought victory or narrowly averted cataclysm; no glasses raised, nor songs sung of his unmatched mettle or military skill. No . . . The *Novara*'s cargo was far too precious for those charged with its protection to end up the subjects of legend . . .

With its dying breath, Earth sent its doomed children catapulting across the stars in a vessel equipped with the technology to bend and distort the very fabric of reality, compressing mind-boggling distances to decrease a travel time that would have spanned a hundred generations down to just a mere few. The nature of ripple-space traversal meant that if any transmissions were coming from Old-Earth, they could not be received; they'd be scrambled and deflected by the powerful gravitational pulses emitted by the *Novara*'s ripple drive—the last pitiful whispers of a moribund civilization diffused like vapor in the wind.

In the deafening radio silence, it was far safer to assume that the ship's complement of two million—descendants of the original undertakers of the expedition—were the very last of mankind: the human remnant. Above all else, Yusef considered himself their shepherd, their anointed protector. The precarious existence and, indeed, the increasingly uncertain future of his species rested squarely on his shoulders, and so he could not allow himself to become slack or complacent in the tedium of his duties. In earnest, it gave him comfort, because another twenty-four-hour cycle without incident meant the looming specter of extinction had been successfully thwarted for one more blessed day.

The bridge of this metropolis-sized arc boasted a grandiosity befitting its monumental importance. In his mind, there were none more so in the history of aerospace engineering. An enormous, rotatable control tower protruding from the dorsal hull; he had always likened it to a grand opera house—somewhat less gilded, but magnificent nonetheless. The helm platform functioned as the podium from which he conducted his ensemble of engineers and systems analysts in the orchestra pit. Rows of New Terra Space Corps, or NTSC, personnel occupied desks in the arcing auditorium, overseeing everything from life support and aquaponics to civilian-sector transport and communications. Then, there were the dual stages, where the performance itself took place . . . Through opposing movie screen–sized viewports, the vast expanse of space spilled into the bridge in all its shimmering, undulating majesty, the ripple drive warping the surrounding light like pebbles dropped in the crystal-clear waters of a quiescent lake.

He had once seen a centuries-old photograph taken from the top of a New York skyscraper, captured before ravenously rising sea levels claimed the lower echelons of the city. The staggering vista unfolding before him bore a striking resemblance, the heavens replaced by a roiling ocean of liquid mercury, that hulking aggregation of glass and concrete now the monolithic shape of the *Novara*, a slumbering behemoth in an eternity's repose.

He stood at his post—an unflinching pillar of authority—his silver hair fashioned in a military crew cut that perfectly framed a face etched with deep wrinkles, the harsh lines of his decorated NTSC uniform sharpening his rigid physique. Some of his bolder subordinates would occasionally joke that he could install a statue of himself atop the helm platform and no one would be any the wiser. He took it as a compliment, for it meant they appreciated his commitment to keeping a steely, watchful eye over his kingdom, never wavering in his vigilance, nor his dedication to the safety of his subjects. It had always been meant in good spirits, and nothing seemed to boost morale quite like his ability to take humor made at his expense in stride. If he felt they were becoming too distracted from their duties, he would occasionally request his bihourly status report thirty minutes ahead of schedule, just to keep them on their toes . . .

"Fission reactors are at eighty-seven percent output, sir," Lieutenant Commander Castaneda promptly advised. "Ripple drive is operating at maximum efficiency. Relative velocity factoring in time dilation is currently zero-point-three luminal . . . The weather's perfect."

Only on a handful of instances had a report ever come back with variances in information: minor reactor fluctuations, gravitational disturbances, or solar radiation spikes as they passed nearby stars. The *Novara*'s architects built her to be self-sustaining and fully autonomous—perfectly capable of staying the course in the contingency of such events. Admittedly, Yusef's only responsibilities were to observe and assess, which he had been doing for sixteen hours when he felt a heavy weariness creeping in around his mental fringes. Deciding the time had come for some well-earned rest, he gladly handed command of the helm over to Acting Captain Roccille and started toward his private quarters. He stopped dead in his tracks as an emergency klaxon sounded its grating, blaring song. He didn't immediately recognize the whining tone; its originating console had fallen into such disuse since the *Novara* left the Sol heliopause that it hadn't been manned in decades: the local navigation and traffic console, or LNAVT for short. The nearest engineer—a clean-shaven lad fresh out of the Academy—rose from his station and headed over to investigate. Relaying the warnings appearing on screen, his face turned ashen, voice low and grave. The noise scratching at Yusef's eardrums was, in fact, a collision alarm, warning that the *Novara*'s forward sensors had detected a sizable mass obstructing her path—smaller than a planetary body, larger than an asteroid. But in a universe where everything was constantly in motion, the mass was suspiciously stationary . . .

Yusef pulled up his wristwatch interface and summoned the projection of a three-dimensional star chart; a luma-cast cosmos filled the bridge with a preponderance of virtual stars, hanging in the air like the cinders of a raging fire frozen in time. The *Novara* appeared as an arrowhead, her trajectory an undeviating, orange streak.

It doesn't make any sense, he thought, narrowing hawklike eyes as he consulted the map, the tiny depiction of his twenty-kilometer-long chariot hovering just before his nose. For several years, the *Novara* had been scudding along the vast, interstellar nothingness between Sigma Tau and Vurri-389, and their predicted course suggested she would do so for several more . . . By all accounts, there should have been nothing this far out of system but compound gases and dust. He stared intently through the forward viewport at the coruscating tunnel of mirrors racing by. If the *Novara*'s robust instrumentation was to be believed, *something* lurked in the blackness ahead, lying in wait to turn this great vessel and her charge of two million souls into a cloud of smoldering particles. The *Novara* existed in *real* space only intermittently due to her semi-spatial means of propulsion. Even still, a collision at their current relative velocity would result in the atomization of the ship, putting a swift and silent end to the human remnant.

His options at this late juncture proved limited at best: Disengage the ripple drive and decelerate, adding years or perhaps even decades to the voyage because of the time it would take to accelerate back up to 0.3 luminal. Or execute an evasive maneuver that would cause an unmanageable influx of broken bones and whiplash injuries to Aegis Infirmary, having subjected everyone aboard to extreme g-forces. Neither solution proved particularly appealing, but with the unknown object drawing ever nearer, little time remained for deliberation.

With much reluctance, Captain Yusef Lei-Ghannam brought the *Novara* up to black alert; he would be the first in history to do so, which was certainly *not* the legacy he had hoped to leave behind. All the way from bow to stern, people were directed to cease operations and brace themselves—for what, exactly, he couldn't advise: sudden deceleration, abrasive lateral g-forces, or— if it came to it—impact . . .

Deciding on the best course of action, he began initiating ripple drive shutdown protocols when the young lad, who had now assumed executive control of the LNAVT console, gave another startling update. The object had begun moving toward them, and they no longer had the time nor the distance to do anything about it . . .

As the bridge succumbed to calamity, Yusef calmly turned his attention to the viewport, hoping to catch a glimpse of this accursed incubus—whatever it was—before it brought about the annihilation of the ship that was the only home he had ever known and the countless souls he had sworn an oath to protect. But he could scarcely make sense of the sight that awaited him: titanic, segmented tentacles, breaching through the silvery boundaries of ripple-space and lunging toward the hull. He traced the structures to their originating point: a black, amorphous mass approximately a third the size of the *Novara*—a vessel appearing both engineered *and* organic in its composition. It was a leviathan, a gargantuan man-of-war jellyfish dredged up from the nightmares of some long-forgotten Gothic impressionist, its massive hull a sinister mountain range with only the scantest suggestions of purpose in its design. Intentions hostile, it reached out with a battery of gruesome, hooked appendages, latched onto the *Novara* and dragged her like a hideous anchor. Somebody in the orchestra pit brayed something about failing structural integrity—somewhat redundant information, given the discordant symphony of howling agony, resonating along the ship's immense superstructure, proved all he needed to know that she was buckling under the tormenting strain of opposing forces.

Emergency fail-safes soon kicked in; an almighty jolt arrived as the ripple drive automatically disengaged, aggressively ripping the *Novara* back into real space. He knew from his contingency training that what followed was a phenomenon known as "entropic reconstitution": seconds stretched into tortuous minutes, an indeterminable passing of time resulting from the abrupt cessation of temporal distortion. He scraped himself off the floor and returned to his station, gasping in astonishment at the breathtaking view of the cosmos stretching on before him, the stars serene and still in a way he had never before seen them, stippled like frenzied flecks of white acrylic paint across a canvas of flawless black. Naturally, the moment of tranquility did not last; the alien abomination had tumbled with them into real space, and bore down on the *Novara* once more. Yusef's forebears had prepared for every eventuality—an attack by an unknown enemy aggressor was chief among the long list of possible disasters that could befall the expedition. As such, the *Novara*'s builders had outfitted her with more sharp sticks than the ventra-class dreadnoughts used during the Lunar Colony rebellions: several tower-sized kinetic rail gun emplacements ran in succession along her spine while a massive particle burst cannon, designated as the main battery, occupied her underbelly.

"Are we weapons ready?"

"Main battery control are already tracking the target, sir. Ready to fire in five, four . . ."

The entire bridge quaked as the rail guns proceeded to hammer the alien monstrosity with a sustained bombardment of boulder-sized projectiles. Successful impacts tore chunks of semiorganic matter off its surface, ghastly ribbons of fluid and viscera spiraling off into the abyssal emptiness beyond. Yet, the abomination persisted undeterred. It reeled in its wretched tendrils, bringing into view the vortex of jagged spears occupying its bow, poised to devour its hopelessly ensnared prey.

Not if I have anything to say about it . . .

Staring into that monstrous maw, Yusef felt a whirring crackle of static in the air as the main battery charged, the substantial power draw required to fire a single shot causing the lights throughout the *Novara* to flicker and dim. All hands braced as a thunderous explosion rocked the superstructure. Through the viewport, a phosphorescent bolt of energy cleaved the black asunder and struck the enemy vessel directly in its main bulk. The shot passed straight through its fleshy form and out the other side, carrying on into infinity.

A roar of triumph erupted from the staff on the bridge as they reveled in this small victory. Indeed, from first appearances the strike had proven highly effective; the enemy ship faltered, releasing its grip and drifting away spewing a sinuous nebula of Gaia-knows-what from the grizzly wound inflicted on its outer shell. But their celebrations proved premature . . . It soon recovered, renewing its assault with vicious resolve. Using its serrated tentacles as ice axes, it shambled around to the lower-aft section of the *Novara* before unleashing a salvo of retaliatory fire; brash, arcing streaks of plasma rained down, piercing the *Novara*'s hardened, nanocarbon exterior as easily as if it were constructed from tissue paper. The damage reports came in thick and fast. Fission reactors: offline. Ripple drive: offline. Main thrusters: offline. It was a surgical strike of devastating precision, clearly not meant to destroy its foe but to completely immobilize her, rendering her helpless for whatever grim fate it had in store.

"Where is my fighter support?" Yusef screamed, his calm and composed facade steadily disintegrating. An encouraging sight answered the manic inquiry: three kestrel squadrons launching simultaneously from the dorsal fighter-deployment facility, known as the Silo. The fighters, vanguard of the *Novara*'s defense efforts, swooped low in attack formation, peppering the enemy vessel's surface with a hail of sidewinder and flak cannon fire. They proved nimble enough to avoid the continuous volleys from its energy weapons as well as the ponderous swipes from its seemingly endless array of menacing appendages. They had just about pushed it back with sustained fire when it reared up like a cobra, baring its terrible cyclone of fangs, and plunged into the *Novara*'s starboard hull. Like a parasite, it clung to the side of the ship, locking its jaws and digging in deeper with every futile attack run made by the defending kestrels.

"Hail Wing Commander Luekazs and ask him where the hell my remaining fighters are!" Because there were still only *three* squadrons engaging the enemy and no sign of the additional *four* that should have already deployed from the Ventral Launch Facility.

"We've lost all communications with the VLF, sir," Castaneda replied darkly. "It appears the facility may have been targeted before any of them could launch. The units currently starside are all we have available."

As if it had heard that last, harrowing exchange and connived to rub salt in their wounds, the leviathan set its own swarm of fighters loose into the void—ferocious interceptors that engaged the kestrels with extreme prejudice and merciless efficiency, sweeping through them in a tide of destruction that left none alive in its wake.

Thus began the great despair of the human remnant, the dream of planting roots in alien soil and beginning anew cruelly snatched away by this new nemesis. Reports came in from the aftmost regions of the ship that the *Devourer*, as it soon came to be known, had started feasting, burrowing like a mole into the *Novara*'s superstructure and picking her apart from the inside out. It sent a tangled riot of elongated proboscises digging through her meat, tapping into water and protein stores, and sucking them bone-dry. Both fission reactors had been irreparably damaged during the conflict, leaving aquaponics without the energy resources to resupply the purloined reserves. Perhaps even *more* concerning was the subsequent shutdown of power and life support throughout the ship. One by one, entire sectors became uninhabitable, causing mass migrations of terrified citizens that inevitably resulted in the dangerous overpopulation of confined spaces. The sudden breakdown in infrastructure caused an eruption of civil unrest, including ship-wide looting, protests, and riots. As resources dwindled, a murmuration of dissent rippled throughout the increasingly disillusioned bridge crew. The source of the growing controversy: Yusef's private preserve of cryogenically frozen materials and produce—namely, the whiskey and honey he kept for hot toddies on special occasions; the mountains of herbs and vegetables grown in earthen soil, as well as the spices, sea salt, and jasmine rice used in his frequent culinary expeditions. Over the years, he had even amassed a veritable treasure trove of precious metals and cultural artifacts—utterly useless to the starving population, but then, greed needed no incentive in times as desperate as these.

Rightfully so, his staff began to quiz why it should be right for a captain to hoard such a bounty given the severity of the crisis. But what could he do? Handing his collection over to the public would result in a bloodbath, and merely continuing to hold it would only push hungry looters to storm the bridge in an effort to seize them. Reluctantly, he had his cherished stock loaded into a shuttle and jettisoned into the night leaving no temptation for himself, nor for those who might think violence an appropriate means of repatriation.

Now, some weeks after the battle had concluded, the reason the *Devourer* had chosen to refrain from destroying the *Novara* during their fateful encounter became apparent: it was a leech, and she, its host—a bloodsucker that conspired to drain the life essence of its prey until left no more than a withered, desiccated husk, presumably before moving on to its next hapless victim to continue its cosmic campaign of insatiable consumption.

Yusef had imagined many ways in which the expedition could have gone disastrously awry: catastrophic hull rupture; some unforeseen failure with the ripple drive that sent two halves of the ship to opposite ends of the galaxy. But never this—this slow and grueling death, forced to watch as his people succumbed to asphyxiation while they tussled and warred for diminishing provisions.

It was never supposed to end this way.

Still standing at his usual spot atop the helm platform—the lights continuing to dim and the air growing thinner by the hour—he couldn't help but become enraged by the sight of the Conservatory: the bright, glass dome protruding from the dorsal hull, housing the plethora of botanical gardens comprising the Center of Horticultural Preservation. With people struggling to breathe, he hardly deemed the gardens an *essential* expenditure to be kept online, especially considering the inordinate power requirements needed to maintain its advanced irrigation and atmosphere conditioning. But for reasons that evaded him, the ship's architects, in their blind faith, had locked all control for the installation behind an infuriatingly stubborn virtual intelligence, one programmed with the churlish personality of the long-dead gardener herself, Amara Thaddeus. So, try as he might to reroute power from her pet project into life support in a desperate bid to keep the air circulating, he simply did not have the permissions.

"Your request is denied, Captain," Amara's synthesized but no less brusque voice droned through the bridge speakers. "I have my directives; the gardens *must* be kept operational—even though crisis. And you do not have the authority to tell me otherwise."

"I am Captain Yusef Lei-Ghannam of the NTSC *Novara*, protector of the human remnant; there is no higher authority in the universe!"

He didn't make a habit of asserting dominance in such an uncouth manner, but never had he been made such a fool out of in front of his subordinates. The only saving grace was that there would be no one alive in a hundred years to remember him as *the captain who spent his last few days bickering with a robot.* These conflicts were pointless and always ended up the same way: with the defiant VI repeating a phrase of admittedly stirring, but no less aggravating, poetry.

Nature's first green is gold,
Her hardest hue to hold.
Her early leaf's a flower;
But only so an hour.
Then leaf subsides to leaf.
So Eden sank to grief,
So dawn goes down to day.
Nothing gold can stay.

Nearly two months had passed since what came to be known as the Collision. The dust had settled, and the scale of the devastation had now made itself painfully evident. The death toll was incalculable; Yusef didn't know the precise figure, but estimates were that a third of the *Novara*'s population had perished in the battle and subsequent disarray. With air and resources reaching critical levels, the remainder would follow suit within a matter of days. Communication throughout the vessel remained fragmented at best, but what little information he possessed suggested that the *Devourer* had begun excavating a cavernous chamber in the abandoned stern section of the ship. The ripple drive, main thrusters, aft reactor, centrifugal dampeners—essentially any means of propulsion had been gouged out and consumed. The human remnant were stranded light-years, eons from solid ground, cast adrift in an ocean of nothing, imprisoned by their parasitic captors . . .

Reports arrived of *beings* finding their way into the ruins of the *Novara*—wandering bipedal entities that, unlike the warship they arrived in, did not appear hostile. Then again, neither had they made any attempt to communicate. Humanity's first contact with an alien civilization and the creatures seemed wholly ambivalent to their hosts. Yusef didn't think he'd have the chance to encounter one before he perished, but then, he didn't have any real desire to do so. He had kept himself well-versed in first-contact protocols since bumping into other travelers along this light-year-spanning voyage had always been a remote possibility. But since his own people were on the cusp of extinction, he didn't see the point in wasting his final hours as captain trying to forge diplomatic relations, especially not when the aliens had claimed so many lives . . .

Yusef had chosen to relieve the bridge crew from their duties so they could spend their final moments with their loved ones, hoping the gesture would provide some semblance of comfort. Alone on the bridge, he sat slouched in his great-grandfather's armchair, having dragged it from his private quarters up onto the helm platform. Skeletal ribs lay bare beneath the unbuttoned blazer of his uniform, his breath condensed before his face in the plummeting temperatures, crystallizing in his hoary, unkempt beard. He felt himself drifting off—to sleep, or perhaps something more permanent. As the final tenuous strands of consciousness began slipping through his mental fingers, power suddenly returned to the bridge. He shielded his eyes as the main fixtures flared to life, his pupils dilating as a fluorescent glow seared his retinas. A tremendous roar arrived as the air filtration engaged, blessing his wheezing lungs with freshly circulated atmosphere. A sweet symphony of beeps and whirs followed as the instrumentation around the helm awoke from its slumber, the *Novara* gradually coming back online, system by system.

Struggling to hoist his frail frame out of the armchair, he staggered toward the systems overview console. Naturally, his first assumption was that the team of engineers tasked with restoring reactor functionality had made some miracle breakthrough. However, all sensor readouts pointed to it being still very much inoperable, which made little sense given power output had somehow reached an astonishing 130 percent. Addressing his personal interface, he navigated to the security directory for the engineering decks. Fortunately, one of the reactor chamber's survey cameras remained intact, although the imagery shown made little sense to his tired eyes. Before the Collision, the forward fission reactor had resembled a colossal donut forged from platinum, suspended in the center of a vast cavity by an intricate framework of struts and braces. It appeared now as a charred whorl of mangled metal, silhouetted against a backdrop of infinite emptiness visible through a gaping fissure in the *Novara*'s hull. The damage inflicted during the *Devourer*'s assault was so extensive and irrevocable that no amount of repairs could salvage it, and yet, the twisted wreckage seemed strangely aglow. Lances of electricity jumped from its crumpled frame to conductive surfaces, the camera feed shaking from the heavy vibrations resonating from its inexplicably active core.

A gasp escaped Yusef's cracked lips as his eyes fell on the cause of this perplexing reawakening; one of the very same tentacles that had spent the last two months siphoning the *Novara*'s life force had *integrated* with the reactor, coiling around its decimated structure like a boa constrictor around its victim. But instead of consuming, the serpentine behemoth had somehow reanimated it, restoring power to the *Novara*'s core systems, and bringing her back from the brink of death . . .

He straightened his posture, spine cracking and popping like a monotonal xylophone, shoulders stiff and aching from prolonged inactivity. He felt a surge of conviction inflating his chest, the contention and despair that had hung over him with such heaviness all but immediately alleviated. Staring into the feed, it dawned on him that, although entirely incomprehensible, the *Devourer*'s intentions may not have been as *final* as he had first assumed. The cynic in him hypothesized that it was in the mammoth parasite's nature to keep its host alive, enabling it to continue feeding for as long as possible. This wasn't salvation by any measure. But, having resigned himself to the reality that his days as captain had come to their sorry end, it appeared his people had been given a second chance, and he felt resolute in his belief that they would need a captain *now* more than ever . . .

Eamon Wyatt could think of few places more perilous to find himself traveling through as a wanted man than ExSight Multiplex. The *Novara*'s buzzing sports and entertainment district took the form of a glitzy, subterranean boulevard, nested beneath the museums and galleries of the Silk River Concourse. Famed as the single most overcrowded area on the ship, its myriad casinos, music venues, and virtu-sim arcades drew thousands of visitors even on a quiet day. The facility's main attraction was Zelos Casterblade Arena—where venerated titans of the *Novara*'s most popular sport went head-to-head in a high-adrenaline riot of competitive airborne athleticism. Fans had flooded in from all areas of the ship for the long-anticipated clash between three-time Phantom Streak champions, the Amidships Stingrays, and the scrappy underdogs battling their way up the leaderboard, the Cendre Vale Razorbacks. This would be the most anticipated sporting event in recent history, as evidenced by the landslide of rabid fans shuffling along the main vestibule toward the arena.

A smarter man in Eamon's precarious position would have been making every effort to avoid a hot spot of such notoriety, but *he* had opted to use the vibrant hustle and bustle to his advantage. With its sleek architecture and faceted, azure-blue surfaces, ExSight Multiplex had been struck down by a terrible technicolor affliction, commandeered by the garish, contrasting colors of the opposing team's regalia. As if scribbled to life by a toddler wielding a fistful of mismatched crayons, the unruly horde paraded to their holy temple garbed in casterblade bobble-hats, scarfs, and jerseys, representing either the Stingrays in purple and black, or donning the green and gold synonymous with the Razorbacks. Banners and flags bobbed up and down overhead, emblazoning a chaotic collage of crests and insignias that, he hoped, would baffle even the most sophisticated of automated security cams.

Eamon had taken extra precautions to ensure he didn't stick out like a sore thumb among the writhing mass. Earlier in the day, he had latched onto a particularly rowdy group of supporters who had chosen to prepare for the big game by pounding an impressive number of syn-beers in a nearby bar. He had ponied up a small fortune acting as the sole financier of the revelry—usually, all that was required to have oneself declared a "solid dude" and warmly welcomed into any brotherhood. The one the others nicknamed Rusty, likely on account of his magnificent, ginger facial plumage, had offered up his oversized Stingrays jersey in heartfelt thanks—not Eamon's preferred choice of team, but he had happily accepted. His new friend had then dipped fingers coated in greasy nacho powder into a pot of purple face paint and applied clumsy streaks to his cheekbones, chin, and forehead. Perfecting the ensemble with an "I heart NVRA" cap—*borrowed* from a local souvenir stand—and he looked all but unrecognizable—a point he found himself immensely thankful for when he rounded a corner with his boisterous comrades and came face-to-face with his own wanted poster, projected on a repulsor-suspended billboard hovering lazily over the crowd.

Eamon Wyatt is wanted for the murder of Administrator Madeline Vargos. He is considered armed and extremely dangerous and should not be approached if spotted. Notify Phalanx if you have any information.

Extremely dangerous, he echoed internally. *Now you're just flattering me.*

Seeing his own haggard mug plastered across every pane and public terminal throughout the *Novara* had proven his least favorite part of living as a fugitive. Perhaps back in his Phalanx Academy days, he might have been considered something of a heartthrob—bronze skin, square jaw, chiseled physique, and all the trimmings. But that definitely wasn't the case anymore, so the supremely unflattering *armed and dangerous* shot now flooding the feeds—with his scruffy fur-collar jacket and almost black, bedraggled hair—left him feeling even more uncomfortable than being hunted for a murder he didn't commit . . .

"Hey, look!" Rusty half belched, pointing at the billboard with a syn-beer bottle gripped loosely in hand. "Eamon Wyatt—ain't that the cop from Halvorsen Commons—the one that got his own partner sacked for killing a leech?"

Eamon locked eyes with the oblivious moron, probably pushing his luck but thinking it too amusing not to. Besides, the last time they saw his face without all the war paint was something like five or six beers ago, and any effort to tag him with their Echo wearables—personal tech integrated with the *Novara*'s preeminent social media platform—would be impeded by the scatter lenses sitting irritatingly over his corneas, identifying him instead as one Abraham G. Shepherd.

"Yeah, that's the guy," he answered. "Wasn't *just* his partner, though: there were a whole bunch of enforcers who had to resign because of those allegations—even the division chief was implicated." And it took considerable effort to repress the bragging undertone creeping into his voice regarding that last point. Thankfully his new friends were too drunk and gullible to see through his pathetic facade.

"Bastard!" Rusty hissed. "Novarian heroes hung out to dry just for doing their bit for the union . . . Too bad Vargos didn't jettison his traitor ass while she still had the chance; the guy's a menace to society."

Eamon let an artful grin touch his zebra-striped lips. "You're right about that."

A drone of disgruntled voices rippled through the crowd as those passing beneath the billboard expressed similar sentiments, a thousand bloodlusting eyes dissecting his enlarged, luma-cast face. He was no stranger to facing public scrutiny, but his wrongful implication in the death of the administrator had elevated him from social pariah to public enemy number one . . .

Just keep your head down for long enough to get a warning out about the grenadiers, he told himself. *If the battle-mechs aren't already under Harmony control, then they soon will be. The insurgents will use the machines to incite bloody revolution, and the* Novara *will be thrown into a conflict that'll make the Antonelli Expansion look like a ruttin' pissing match.*

The tricky part: getting the ear of an official who wouldn't immediately sell him out to Phalanx, who held enough sway to kick up a fuss about the situation but didn't sit so high up the food chain they were potentially involved in Vargos's conspiracy to engineer civil war. Thankfully, he knew just the man, but accessing this individual in a time of such heightened security, prompted by the troubles in the Mouth, had proven easier said than done. In truth, the game would serve as a welcome distraction from the scenes of encroaching war seeping like feculent smoke through the blockade. Beneath the roar of eager crowds, Eamon detected fear and resounding uncertainty—exacerbated, no doubt, by the New Terra News Network's shameless vivisection of the feeds coming in from the conflict beyond the blockade, showing only harrowing glimpses of robed cohabitors stalking the ruins of the increasingly war-torn region. Soon, citizens of the NTU would have to face the uncomfortable reality that there were humans among the insurgent forces too, fighting side by side with the aliens, emboldened and united in their shared struggle against their oppressors.

Strangely, having uncovered the staggering degree of corruption blighting the Administration, Eamon found himself in stark agreement that the time had come for a shake-up. But the reckoning Harmony had planned would come at an incalculable loss of life—and it was ingrained in his very DNA to prevent that at all costs.

Two androgynous statues heralded the entrance to Zelos Arena, fashioned from bronze and sculpted in evocative combat poses. While they didn't detail the protective padding and visors normally used by casterbladers, the frenetic essence of the sport had been captured perfectly. Passing between them, the crowd funneled through a bulwark of security scanners, where armed Phalanx enforcers vigilantly watched the rabble, probably none expecting to find the administrator's purported murderer marching flagrantly by looking like a psychedelic eggplant. Eamon started his tipsy flock off chanting "Stingrays! Stingrays!" to achieve just the right degree of disorderly behavior to blend in without drawing too much attention to himself.

Clear of security, they entered a large foyer featuring a multitude of various grub and merchandise stands. This large space connected the two adjoining ends of a corridor, which ran in a circular loop around the circumference of the arena. Casterblade, unlike the handful of alternative sports that had escaped Sol with the human remnant, was not played on a two-dimensional plane. Unbound by the archaic concepts of up and down, players skated through the air on repulsor blades in a massive, zero-gravity sphere, encircled like Saturn by rings of tiered bleachers, from which the audience watched. Around the sphere's equator, where the view proved optimal, Novarian high society could enjoy the game in luxurious private boxes, comfortably segregated from the rowdy common folk. It was in one of these boxes Eamon hoped to find his old partner, a man called Fenn Haken, who had apparently done relatively well for himself following his expulsion from the Glow Enforcement Agency for stomping a cohabitor to death during an unsanctioned interrogation. In retrospect, the entire thing had been a complete farce; the top brass only demanded Fenn's resignation to appease public outcry stemming from concerns over rising interspecies enforcer brutality. After his ousting, the man was covertly employed as an internal affairs investigator for an accounting firm under the corporate branch of the Administration.

I guess this is what you get for murdering an unarmed suspect in cold blood, Fenn: a handsome promotion and a lifetime season ticket for a Zelos Arena VIP box. I just hope you learned your lesson . . .

Confoundingly, Fenn was perhaps one of the least-suited candidates for internal affairs in the history of Phalanx. The man was impatient, hotheaded, held little regard for rules and due process, and had not a modicum of common sense between those cauliflower ears of his. Eamon had been in the process of submitting a reluctant request for a new partner when Fenn decided to channel his frustrations with his many shortcomings through his bootheel into the skull of a restrained cohabitor. On the surface, it didn't make a lick of sense that Vargos had wanted the unpredictable assclown keeping an eye on the books, but then again, if she had needed a useful idiot who could quite easily overlook the substantial amount of nunits presumably required to subsidize a terrorist organization beyond the blockade, she could probably have done a lot worse . . .

Eamon had no idea how the man would react to his old partner showing up unannounced. Right up until that terrible night in Halvorsen Commons, the two had been close friends. They shared a great deal of history together, and despite his abysmal performance when it came to paperwork, Fenn *did* have his moments—usually when things *didn't* go to plan. He had saved Eamon's skin on multiple occasions, from pulling his hide out of dangerous firefights to the time he took the rap for totaling their cruiser during a botched pursuit. They'd been through a lot, and it was for that reason Eamon had to believe that, even after all the recent unpleasantness, Fenn would at least let him speak his piece.

Or maybe he'll just kick your ass and hand you straight over to the authorities . . . I guess we'll soon find out.

First, he had to find a way of getting into the man's private box undetected, so he advised Rusty and the others to go and find their seats while he went to replenish from the bar. Sadly, the boys would go thirsty, as they had now fulfilled their purpose; if they ever saw him again, he'd either be getting marched out in cuffs or wheeled out in a body bag . . .

Thanks to Fenn's relentless peacocking on the Nov-Net, Eamon already knew the general location of his private box. The boastful idiot was hardly subtle about his love of the finer things in life and had no issue flaunting his recent successes on his Echo-feed, normally popping a bottle of syn-champagne with some model or influencer hanging off his arm.

Eamon had studied the background of some of those images and extrapolated the location of his box to be somewhere around the back right quadrant of the arena, down near one of the irises through which players entered the play space—perfect for scrounging autographs or collecting used sabers after a game to scalp for profit, which was right out of Fenn's playbook.

Keeping his head down with the brim of his cap low over his brow, Eamon skirted around the access corridor, pushing his way through the ebullient herd, the air practically fizzling with anticipation for the game. Occasionally, the crowd parted to let the arena's army of service bots roll through. The machines appeared as silver trash cans ambling along on spherical, multidirectional wheels, issuing polite, synthesized thank-yous as people moved aside. Programmed with delivering refreshments from the bar to the patrons in the private boxes, their glass-domed heads laid bare a tantalizing array of exclusive cocktails and snack foods notably unavailable from the regular vendors.

One of the machines bumped into the back of Eamon's leg, cordially pardoning itself before chiming an impatient request to clear the way. On its serving tray, it carried an immediately recognizable beverage—one he'd seen ordered at just about every dingy watering hole on the *Novara* that would willingly entertain such an abomination: a strawberry daiquiri garnished with a single, hydroponically grown ghost pepper. He could think of only one individual insecure enough about his masculinity to order the ghastly concoction—as if incinerating one's throat and taste buds was necessary penance for consuming such a sweet and fruity libation. He had no doubt that following the service bot would lead him straight to Fenn Haken.

The door to Fenn's box slid open automatically as the robotic server arrived. It trundled into the room, opened its domed head like a mechanical beak, and allowed Fenn to retrieve his order. Eamon waited for it to cruise back out into the corridor before quietly darting through the entrance as it sealed shut. Fenn sat forward, occupying one of the sofas, with his elbows resting on his knees, the rounded outline of his head highlighted by the neon shades of pink and blue pouring in through the observation screen. He had let himself go in recent years, which Eamon knew was incredibly hypocritical of him to remark on considering his own declining physique. He remembered Fenn as being built like an upside-down pyramid, with broad shoulders tapering down to a thin waist and stick-thin legs that looked barely able to support the heft of his hulking upper half. He still had the biceps to win an arm-wrestling match with a cohab, by the looks of it, but his gut now practically bulged out of his striped, button-down shirt, his stubborn reluctance to admit that the time had come to move up to the next size or two was abundantly evident.

Through the observation screen, the game raged on. Casterblade consisted of two teams battling for dominance of the inside of a gravityless globe— a kaleidoscopic ballet of twisting, lunging aerobics. Players used elongated sabers to strike a cylindrical puck, sending it bouncing chaotically around the arena. The sabers cast localized hexagonally shaped fission fields. Points were scored by batting the puck into the enemy team's net—glowing, diamond-shaped apertures situated at the pole of each hemisphere. Players could boost off one another to perform incredible tackles and defensive interceptions, use their repulsor blades to loop and waltz through the air, wholly unconcerned by the shackles of Newtonian physics. A truly astonishing spectacle. Eamon almost wished he had the time to pull up a seat and watch, leaving all the impending ugliness until *after* the game.

"How are we doing, Fenn?" he asked, almost out of force of habit.

Barely able to pry his attention away, Fenn partially glanced over his shoulder. "Hard to say; Stingrays are really coming out swinging. Must know we're gunning for the title."

Then came a moment of abrasive realization as it dawned on the man that he was not, in fact, sitting in his apartment den five years ago, watching the Saturday night game with his old partner as they had done countless times before. He spun around sharply, his V-shaped jaw tense and jutting forward, furious, protruding eyes piercing and still.

"Wyatt?" he asked, cautiously rising to his feet and keeping a steady distance. That hesitation soon gave way to anger, as he strode forward and grabbed Eamon by the shoulders, the two grappling and shoving one another in an unwieldy display of confused emotion. It wasn't obvious at first whether they were hugging or fighting, but then the fumbled uppercut Fenn planted on Eamon's jaw took away any uncertainty from the matter.

"What the hell are you doing here, rat bastard?" Fenn demanded, holding him up against the wall by the scruff of his neck. "You're supposed to be in the Mouth where leech-sympathizing reprobates like you belong! You got a lot of nerve showing up like this."

Tasting blood, Eamon coolly replied, "You're still pulling your punches, Fenn. If you wanna hit me, then hit me."

He forcefully released himself from the man's grasp, leaving him watching on in wrathful bemusement as he retrieved a syn-beer from the minibar and flopped exasperatedly into one of the sofas.

"I was in the area and thought I'd come and watch the game—for old time's sake . . . Looks like this new gig of yours has some pretty nice perks. Good to know where egregious use of excessive force gets you in life."

Fenn sidestepped in front of him, peering down over a crooked nose that told of numerous hard-won bar fights. "You've got ten seconds to explain yourself before I beat the shit out of you, just like I promised I would if you ever showed your face again."

Eamon took a candid swig from the beer bottle. "Believe it or not, I'm here cuz I need your help."

Fenn threw his head back and gave vent to a sardonic laugh. "Help? Help with what: laying low after you went and bludgeoned the administrator to death? I know you always hated that old crone, but damn, I'm not sure she deserved that . . . What was it that she ended up nailing you to the wall for in the end? Lemme guess: Drinking on the job?"

Eamon pursed his lips and shook his head. *Not exactly, but then again, not far off.*

"I don't kill people in cold blood, Fenn; that's much more your style . . . Trust me, Vargos had it coming, but it wasn't yours truly who did the deed."

Fenn shuffled in impatience. "So . . . You're being framed? Spare me, will yah? I wasn't born yesterday. You know how cliché that shit sounds in our line of work?"

"This isn't about self-exoneration; it's way bigger than that . . ." He paused, knowing the next words out of his mouth could only be perceived as the desperate ravings of a madman, the last resort of a murderer on the run in a hapless bid to prove his innocence. *Still gotta try.*

"All the shit going on beyond the blockade," he began. "The unrest, the attacks on the Phalanx Compound: Vargos was behind *all* of it. She was out-sourcing terrorism—cooked up a whole ruttin' insurgency to put the fear of the Abyss into her constituents, making sure no one thought twice about her blockade refortification bill and subsequent deployment of the grenadiers . . . She had Anaya Lahiri killed to keep it under wraps, and you better believe she had a crack or two at me as well."

"Ludicrous," Fenn breathed, blurting the word once more in a voice rising with annoyance. "You've gone off the fuckin' deep end if you think I'm gonna believe for a second the administrator was bent . . . I'll go ahead and presume you don't have a shred of evidence to back any of this insane notion up."

Eamon shook his head, the weight of defeat pulling his gaze to the floor. "Vargos was nothing if not thorough when it came to covering her tracks; she didn't exactly leave me a smoking gun. But you know I ain't crazy, Fenn— self-righteous, foolhardy, maybe, but not crazy . . . That's why you *need* to believe me. Because something big is coming—something that could change the *Novara* forever . . . I wouldn't be standing here risking my neck if I didn't think there was a serious threat to public safety."

Fenn nodded with the same patronizing aplomb as someone humoring a rambling drunkard in a bar. "OK. Let's say I believe you: Vargos is the big bad villain behind the whole conspiracy. If she's dead, then mission accomplished, right? What could this big threat possibly be?"

Beyond the observation screen, the Razorbacks' striker performed an incredible aerial backflip and backhanded the puck into the Stingrays' net. The VIP box rumbled with a chorus of applause, affording Eamon a brief moment to prepare his next words. *If you're gonna believe anything I say, Fenn, please let it be this.*

"The grenadiers have been compromised . . . The people Vargos charged with the destabilization of the Mouth betrayed her, and now they have everything they need to bring down the blockade and stage a military coup. The garrison stationed at the Phalanx Compound *must* be deactivated and recalled for emergency maintenance or a lot of innocent people are gonna die."

Fen slapped his thigh in scornful glee. "Lei-Ghannam! You must really think we're stupid, huh? So, we turn off the grennies, and then what: the leech army rolls up the Canyon like a damn tsunami to harvest us all? Does that about sum it up, old buddy?"

"Please," Eamon begged, disgusted by his own groveling cadence. "There's too much at stake for you to see me off empty-handed . . . I don't know if redemption is something you want, or if it's something you even think you need, but this could be your opportunity to make things right."

The man swatted a hand dismissively, lips curled in disapproval. "Even if I *did* believe you, what makes you think I could do anything about it? You know I'm just an internal affairs investigator, right? Don't exactly have the grenny kill switch under my desk."

Eamon lifted Rusty's jersey, revealing the ragged whorl of partially healed scar tissue streaked across his lower abdomen like a patch of fibrous roots.

"I'm a dead man walking, Fenn. The administrator might be pushing up daisies but that doesn't mean the marksmen she sent to hunt me down are gonna let up any time soon . . . I know I really put our friendship through the wringer, but you know damned well I couldn't let what you and the others did to that bug and its cipher stand."

He felt a pleading expression tug at the contours of his face as he gazed up at his old partner. The moment had a strangely nostalgic quality to it, as though he were just a boy, seeking help and advice from an older brother who, despite all the bullying and torment, the noogies and painful wrist burns, was still his guardian—his stalwart protector.

"I'm out of options here. I get that you don't have the authority to set the wheels turnin' yourself, but you can get a message out to someone who could . . . Please, you owe me that much at least."

Fenn offered a wistful smile, seeming for a fleeting moment like Eamon's words might have gotten through. Then, he raised his hand, showing a feather gripped in his palm and the pulsating screen of the outbound emergency call he had already placed through to Phalanx. Doubtless, they were listening to the entire conversation, and already en route . . .

He pursed his lips, crafting a look that telegraphed *This hurts me more than it hurts you*, then said, "I'm sorry, old buddy. But the only thing I owe you is a head start . . ."

Eamon backed away, listening intently to the sounds of squeaking boots and stifled movement arriving from beyond the door—the unnerving, controlled quiet of a tactical armed enforcer squad preparing to breach and clear. He glanced around the box, frantically searching for an alternative way out; there was only one by his reckoning, but by no means would it be a discreet exit . . .

Bidding Fenn a profanity-riddled farewell, he picked up a metal barstool and hurled it at the observation screen, shattering it with a single blow. He took a running jump and dove into the zero-gravity bubble that lay beyond. The casterbladers skidded to a halt on their physics-defying repulsor blades, hanging still in the air as he careened into their domain, the arena's sphere of floodlights scintillating in the surrounding nebula of broken glass.

Beneath the collective gasp of the audience, he heard the enforcers bursting through the door into Fenn's private box.

"Phalanx! Freeze!" But the inertia from the jump meant he couldn't stop, even if he wanted to. Suspecting their orders were shoot to kill, he reached out and snatched a saber from the nearest player, wrenching it over his shoulder like someone flagellating themselves. He tucked his knees into his chest and activated the saber's fission field, casting a protective shield over his back. Panic engulfed the arena as the enforcers opened fire, the rounds ricocheting off his improvised turtle shell in denticulated strobes of white-hot light. The enforcer in him wanted to spin around and lambast the impulsive idiots for recklessly opening fire in an area packed with civilians, but doing so would only afford them an opportunity to take him out. The concussive force of the rebounding projectiles accelerated his aimless drift, pushing him to the far side of the arena where he just managed to catch a guardrail and hoist himself into the bleachers. His stomach lurched as he transitioned from weightlessness into the *Novara*-standard 0.9Gs, feeling a wave of nausea and disorientation as he took a second to right himself. Had any of the nearby spectators possessed the sense to pile on him and put him under citizen's arrest, it would have been over there and then. Thankfully, nobody took the initiative, or they were all too chickenshit. So, while everyone clamored for cover, he bolted for the exit and headed back out into the encircling corridor.

This side of the arena looked clear of any Phalanx presence, but the entire facility would undoubtedly be swarmed within a matter of seconds. Nearly colliding with one of the ambling server bots, he cut into a dingy labyrinth of staff-only passageways and found his way through a service tunnel back out into ExSight Multiplex.

Ducking and darting frantically through the throng of moviegoers and virtu-simmers, he found a secluded alleyway to stop and catch his breath.

But his quiet refuge turned out to be not as vacant as first perceived. He felt the presence of a tall, ominous figure looming in the shadows behind him. He had the innate sense that they had been waiting for him or, perhaps, had been stalking him since he first entered the multiplex. But before he could turn to identify them, there was a flash of sudden movement. He felt the crack of a blunt object strike him on the back of the head. Then, blackness took hold, and the world fell silent.

TWO

Several weeks had passed since Tobias Cole Edevane left his comfortable life in the Upperdecks to permanently join the crew of the *Assurance*. So far, his time serving under Captain Delilah Holloway had been an enlightening, if also hectic and exhausting, affair. The ship's welding designation meant they were often needed starside within a moment's notice, as the crew typically had little to no warning as to when a rupture in the *Novara*'s disintegrating hull might occur. Throw into the mix that the ship and everyone on it were now wanted by merciless kingpin Vidalia Drexen—or "the Governor" as he had proclaimed himself—and life as a spacer had proven decidedly more turbulent than he had anticipated . . .

With no prior shipboard experience, he kept himself busy in whatever capacity he could, which, for the most part, meant keeping the ship's magma cannon loaded with scrap metal and flexing some of his culinary skills in the galley. But with the captain now unable to dock for fear the Governor's Monarchs would be waiting to exact revenge, he couldn't help but grow increasingly frustrated at the stagnation of their circumstances. After all, he hadn't signed up with Delilah's crew to be a cabin boy; with its covert route through the Savior's core, the *Assurance* had proven to be the perfect vessel for his efforts to resume his mother's humanitarian work in the Mouth, which became all the more crucial as the conflict beyond the blockade continued to escalate . . . Bloody skirmishes had broken out all over the district. The Copper Swathes were now almost completely under Harmony control as the insurgents pushed Drexen's mob farther into the outskirts. The fighting had encroached into the Cohabitor Ghetto, where there were presently twenty-plus vulnerable children holed up whose safety had rapidly become his number one concern. He and Delilah had already butted heads regarding his proposal of mounting a rescue mission to evacuate the previous residents of

Juniper Sanctuary, but even the captain's infamously austere bearing couldn't deter him from suggesting it a second time . . .

"I think it's admirable you're ready to risk your life pulling those scamps out of the fray," she responded, peering at him with scrutinizing brown eyes over a mug of herbal tea as she sat sidesaddle in the copilot's seat on the bridge. "But I can barely guarantee our own safety right now—let alone offer shelter to twenty-plus orphaned children . . ."

"But you've seen the level of devastation in the Mouth," Tobias asserted, lingering in the bridge entrance wearing a black nylon fiber bomber jacket. With disheveled, brown hair and thick stubble encrusting his aquiline jaw, he looked a far cry from the debonair son of a councilman but felt more himself than ever before. "I'm well-aware a scrap trawler isn't really a suitable place to run a shelter, but surely keeping them here on the *Assurance* would be far better than the alternative. This isn't just about salvaging my mother's legacy; I dread to think what will become of them if we choose to simply do nothing."

"You don't think it keeps me up at night, too? But Vidalia isn't playing around here; we destroyed one of his most lucrative operations going down into the Vestiges to rescue Isaac—not to mention seriously injuring three of his people and stealing those hydro-ionizers. The second we make landfall, he's gonna turn our LZ into a smoking blast crater, and getting ourselves obliterated won't do those junies any good at all now, will it?" She set her mug down on the control pedestal and stood up to meet his eye level. "I know you want to help, but honestly, the best thing you can do for them right now is to keep working on honing your hyper-resonance with Null . . . Remember what Wyatt said: interspecies tensions are reaching a boiling point. There aren't many other ciphers who can boast diplomatic competencies and insider knowledge of the Administration like you. That's why we *need* you putting the work in; it's imperative we understand each other—now more than ever. Otherwise, it'll come to war, and I don't know if the *Novara* can survive another Antonelli Expansion."

Annoyingly, he knew she was right, but something felt grossly irresponsible about spending all his free time meditating in a dark room while a humanitarian crisis played out beyond the blockade. Besides, he struggled to imagine how any kind of diplomacy could result from what he had experienced in attaining resonance with Null so far. The cohabitors' extrasensory means of communication, which for some baffling reason fate had gifted him innate comprehension of, seemed more like telepathic interpretive dance, or playing a game of psychedelic charades than conversation—far too fluid and imprecise to be used as a suitable mode of dialogue for cross-species peace negotiations, with so much room for error and misinterpretation. He openly acknowledged, however, that such an assumption might merely stem from the nascent state of his abilities, recognizing that greater finesse and sophistication could potentially emerge through further practice. So, he concurred with the captain and thanked her for her counsel, suspecting she had given him more sage advice in these few short weeks than he had received in twenty-two years of life in the Upperdecks.

Since upgrading his status from convicted felon to bona fide crewmember, he had been relieved to leave behind the days of sleeping on a grimy foldout bed in the cargo hold. Null and Mercy had graciously invited him to bunk with them in their quarters, which had been set up in a disused storage area situated toward the rear of the ship, positioned directly above engineering. He recalled a time when his fraught mind required no less than absolute silence to drift off to sleep; now, he found the loud, continuous roar of the *Assurance*'s thrumming fission reactor intensely soothing, as well as strangely conducive to lulling him into a heightened state of receptivity. It felt like floating in a sensory deprivation tank—a white noise magnetosphere deflecting any and all external interference.

Few things might have repulsed him before his resonant awakening more than the prospect of sharing a room with a cohabitor, but cohabitation on such an intimate scale had proven vital for the development and refinement of his fledgling abilities. Moreover, Null made for a surprisingly good roommate: ae was quiet, tidy, and respectful of property and personal space. He wasn't sure if ae slept in the same way humans did, but ae certainly didn't snore. Despite aer enormous size, ae took up remarkably little room, spending most of aer time dangling upside down from a support girder using aer digitigrade legs, rocking back and forth in peaceful contentment. It perplexed him to think of just how little direct interaction he had had with Null, considering it felt as though their two souls had been bound in the ether: their personalities, their hopes, their fears, even their moods—the more they attained resonance, the more bleed-through occurred, their powerful empathic bridge allowing a melding of their emotional and experiential essences; two individuals gradually coalescing into one.

Another unforeseen side effect, or perhaps utility, of resonance, was the transferal of memories. Tobias had over two decades worth of experiences from which to draw from: a creditable childhood growing up with his beloved sister, Hazel, where they were well-provided for, if somewhat neglected by their career-obsessed father; his teenage years were spent utterly inseparable from his best friend, Caleb Callaghan, and their time studying together at the Academy of Colonial Stewardship. Bizarrely, the connection he shared with Null meant aer memories were now his, too. His mind swelled with an inscrutable pastiche of knowledge and experience, like recollecting a past life that he'd never actually lived. Much of what he could access made little sense to him, but still, the memories felt just as lucid and impactful as any of his own. He remembered the terrible, chafing growing pains of his chitin exoskeleton forming as he morphed from larval stage into adolescence; the years of hunger and hardship as he fended for himself in the Cohabitor Ghetto, watching helplessly as many of his fellow Prey were taken by disease and famine. He remembered the fear and fascination he felt upon meeting a human for the first time—a human who, confusingly, was his own mother, who had come from beyond the blockade to assist at a time of great desperation, disabusing him of the apprehensions he had felt toward the frail, fleshy aliens by showing unexpected kindness.

He recalled a transformative period of academia in which he had been granted access to the vast habitat chamber located *within* the Savior's core, known as the Magnanimous Hollow. There, he learned from who he interpreted to be a techno-shaman—one fluent in the sacred ways of the Savior's physiology and the exciting frontier of splicing its engineered flesh with human technology. He remembered his recent disappointment and confusion upon learning that this esteemed educator, whose cipher-given moniker was Absence, was now in league with Harmony, using aer knowledge to craft weapons of destruction and wage war against the NTU. He too endeavored for a brighter future for his people, but not at the cost of innocent lives . . .

Nominally, he recalled crossing paths with a small, fragile human whose colors were white and whose essence sang of innocence and generosity. This human was called Mercy, and he recalled his unbridled joy upon discovering that he could attain resonance with her, and the trepidation stemming from the realization that doing so put him within the cruel and inescapable clutches of Vidalia Drexen . . .

Null had laid bare the book of aer life before him, their two stories now inextricably interlaced. He knew that, just as *he* had been given intrinsic comprehension of aer character, so too could ae now comprehend his. There were no secrets; no deceptions; ae knew all too well what his opinion of aer kind had been up until recently, ae knew of his involvement with Bhaltair Abernathy's human supremacist movement and of his unforgivable actions in the Langrenus Harrow. And yet, of the vibrant tapestry of emotions he could sense radiating from within, animosity and resentment were not among them. Either ae was the single most understanding and forgiving being in the universe, or the Prey were biologically incapable of holding a grudge.

* * *

Upon arriving in their quarters, Tobias found Null and Mercy already deep in resonance, dousing the dingy space in the resplendent effulgence of their emissions, their eyes like tiny portals into a dimension forged from pure light. Hanging like a bat from aer metal branch, Null placed a paw on aer thorax and then motioned it toward him—a gesture of acknowledgment and appreciation.

You are before me, and I, before you.

He reciprocated the greeting, mimicking its intricate nuances as best he could as he moved toward his bunk.

"You are back." The delicate cadence of Mercy's voice came floating to him from across the room. The girl sat cross-legged in her own bunk with hands cupped in the swathes of white gown fabric pooled in between her thighs. She held in her palms her brass, crescent-moon-shaped pendant, its embedded microemitter luma-casting the image of a smiling man with the same sunken eyes and thin lips as her. Tobias didn't know the identity of the stranger, but guessed from how frequently he saw her staring into those glassy, projected eyes that it was someone she held very dear . . .

"I am," he replied, changing course, and taking a seat on the edge of her bunk. "Just had to speak to the captain about something."

She smiled faintly, then dipped her head in consternation. "I was hoping we could take a moment to discuss what took place last night . . ."

Tobias felt his insides churn in discomfort and embarrassment; he had been dreading this conversation and had spent the day avoiding it as best he could. Because what *did* happen, exactly? To an outside observer, it probably would have looked like nothing more than a bout of awkward, fumbling heavy petting, but he deemed the truth far stranger . . .

Humans couldn't attain resonance with one another; the empathic connection enabled by the Savior's light was reserved exclusively for interspecies communication. But with Tobias's hyper-resonance—something exceedingly rare that meant he could read *any* cohabitor as opposed to just one as usual—he and Mercy had discovered that, by simultaneously linking with Null, they could essentially use aer as a conduit, enabling the transfer of concepts, impressions, and emotions between them. Like a signal amplifier, Null channeled and enhanced their two empathic essences, sculpting aer own exaggerated rendition of either party and relaying it to the other in an arresting psychic performance.

At some point during their experimentation, they realized the phenomenon had a particularly intense effect when it came to physical sensation. Even so much as stroking the inside of one another's arm resulted in euphoric pleasure, the lust and excitement usually attributed to intimacy multiplied tenfold by the feedback loop generated by Null.

Mercy had flawless, porcelain skin, a slender physique, and perfectly pleasant features, but Tobias couldn't say he felt particularly attracted to her or that there was any real chemistry between them. He suspected the feelings, or lack thereof, were entirely mutual, and yet, they had *both* found themselves caught up in the moment. What started out as pushing the boundaries of resonance soon escalated into something a lot less scientific. Nothing *too* explicit had transpired between them, but it had been enough to leave the pair feeling incredibly sheepish the following day . . .

"Yeah . . . that," he uttered, rubbing the back of his neck awkwardly. "I was kinda hoping we could just call it a one-time thing and let it lie . . . You know: heat of the moment."

Mercy exhaled in relief, visibly releasing the tension in her spine. "We are in agreement then . . . Do not mistake my meaning: I'm not saying it wasn't enjoyable or . . . enlightening. But a three-way ciphership is already complicated enough without bringing intimacy into the equation. We must consider that Null is just as much of a participant; carrying on any further would be to continue to involve aer, which I don't believe is fair."

Mercy reached out and touched his shoulder, briefly catching his gaze with wide eyes set in deep hollows. "And . . . I would appreciate your discretion in the matter, as well."

He pressed a finger to his lips to signal his compliance and understanding, knowing exactly who it was she didn't want word getting back to . . .

"This is the last we'll speak of it; you have my word . . . The training you and Null are providing means everything to me. I've still got so much more to learn, and would hate to jeopardize it by doing something that could negatively impact our friendship . . . So, yeah . . . Let's try and keep things *metaphysical* going forward."

"Nebula," she thanked. "But know that there is nothing you could do that could threaten our friendship. The bond the Savior has created between the three of us is profound. I doubt we have even scratched the surface of what is possible yet . . . There is much we can teach you about resonance, but I also believe there is a great deal we can learn together, too."

She glanced down at her locket, seeming to realize that it had been open throughout the conversation, the projection of the mystery man watching the exchange with his permanently solemn countenance. She promptly closed the trinket and pursed her lips, seeming unwilling to address the obvious elephant in the room. Tobias conveyed with a smile that he had no intention of pushing her on the subject.

"Do you ever get confused?" He asked. "About memories, I mean . . . There are times when I'm having to stop and ask myself, 'Did this happen to me, or did it happen to Null?' The lines are really starting to blur, especially when I'm dreaming. One minute I'm somewhere familiar—in the academy dorm or my father's Emeral Heights apartment—then I open a door and find myself walking down a dark passageway, somewhere deep inside the Savior. I know it sounds ridiculous considering I've only just recently stepped foot beyond the blockade; I'm just getting mixed up about whose experiences it is I'm experiencing."

Mercy gave a thoughtful pause, perhaps struggling to put into words something she had likely only ever thought about before. "There will come a time when you realize making such distinctions is redundant. If something happened to one of you, then it happened to you both. Null's memories are yours now, and you may use them to guide your decisions in the future just as you would your own . . . Remember: you are not simply viewing the contents of your resonant partner's mind through a looking glass: it is an exchange. You take something with you and leave a piece of yourself behind. That's why hyper-resonance like yours is so incredible; your mind is a sponge that can absorb memories and experiences from a much deeper well than an average cipher. And the reach of your influence can extend much further too. You may even leave your imprint on cohabitors who were never fortunate enough to have found a cipher. Truly, you are an ambassador for the human remnant."

He scoffed playfully. "No pressure . . . Let's just hope it's the more honorable parts of my character that are rubbing off and not my less-desirable attributes."

Null dismounted from aer inverted perch, using aer hulking arms to flip themselves upright and land on powerful talons. With ponderous footsteps, ae approached, staring down with four pairs of almond-shaped eyes aglow, filling Tobias's nostrils with a pheromone that he had decided smelled a little like vanilla. He felt a sudden bolstering of his constitution, pride, and determination flourishing within. An image took shape in his mind of an alien flower with strange, elongated petals and an aggregation of bulbous nodes running up its thorny stem. Like watching a time-lapse, the specimen began as a shriveled, colorless weed, soon brought to life by the accelerated touch of spring, unfurling and blossoming as its dull, brown shades transmuted into vivid orange and turquoise. The words "growth," "development," and "improvement" arrived on his tongue—loose translations of an unfamiliar concept that had firmly taken root in his chest.

Mercy placed two fingers on her temple, tilting her head slightly as she joined them in resonance. "We see what lies inside of you, Tobias. There is no facet of your personality that you should feel ashamed to share. For a long time, you were led astray by external forces, but your essence *is* and always has been noble. Your crimes were guided by your compassion for others, as there is nothing you would not do for those you love. And now that the veil of fear and ignorance obscuring your vision has been lifted, your capacity for love has increased infinitesimally . . . The ability to grow from one's experience is among the most revered qualities in Prey culture; only by adapting to their environment and their circumstances did they survive the Apex for so long. They will rejoice to know of your story . . . You must not hide from your true self; instead, wear your journey as a badge of honor so that others might follow in your footsteps."

Tobias glanced at Null, knowing that, although ae had zero comprehension of human language, the words were just as much aers as they were Mercy's. To unenlightened eyes, cohabitors could appear stoic and emotionless, but the well of their wisdom had proven bottomless, their propensity for spirituality unrestrained by scientific understanding. In their minds, no such distinction existed; comprehension of the natural world *was* comprehension of one's own being, the Savior's light, not just a method of communication, but a blueprint for consciousness itself—a map detailing the web of awareness connecting all sentient life in the universe.

Tobias was a babe in the murky woods of these alien concepts; they came to him from Null like messages in a bottle, written in a language he could not yet speak. But with every new day, he received another piece of the puzzle, the path to full apperception of the Savior and all its mysteries now tantalizingly clear.

Tobias felt the galley's coffee synthesizer calling out to him as it often did following prolonged resonance. There were many wondrous things to cherish about the Savior's gift, but he had no love for how severely drained it often left him. Temples throbbing, he brewed himself a mug and took a load off on one of the old sofas in the lounge, but any hope of having a moment to himself to recharge was dashed when Isaac Verhoeven crept out of his dark corner and approached.

Since Tobias's tempestuous introduction, the crew of the *Assurance* had been warming to him nicely. *Amazing how easily one can repair a relationship by cooking a few hearty communal meals.* Isaac, however—the ship's engineer—had proven an exception, only seeming to regard him with more contempt as the days went on. At first, the constant acrimony stemmed from the irreconcilable political and philosophical differences between them, but he now suspected it had more to do with how much time he had been spending with Mercy . . . It was no secret Isaac had started developing a fondness for the girl; in the rare instances she wasn't by Null's side they could be seen cozying up together, flirting, play-fighting, and whispering into each other's ear. The closer they grew, the more protective of her he became, which meant directing more and more hostility Tobias's way. Tobias had little patience for playground politics and wouldn't normally have entertained such petty behavior, but last night's *mishap* had left him feeling horrendously guilty about the whole situation.

Isaac loomed over him, the sleeves of his orange jumpsuit tied around his waist, his oil-stained vest encapsulating a pale, emaciated physique. The sandy-blond hair draped across his forehead partially obscured his eyes, but Tobias could still see those cloudy cataracts—the telltale mark of a severe glow addiction.

"You got a second to talk?" Isaac worded it as a question, but Tobias suspected it of being more of a demand.

"What's on your mind?" He replied, doing a piss-poor job of feigning ignorance.

"I wanna know what it is you're really doing with Mercy in there." Isaac began pacing back and forth like a caged animal. "I mean . . . What's so special about this training that it has to be done behind closed doors?"

Tobias had to bite his tongue, almost wanting to spill his guts and get the unpleasantness over with. *Honestly, we were doing exactly what you think we were. But it was weird, there was nothing to it, and it's over now. So, punch me in the face as hard as you can so we can call it even and move on.*

But doing so would stand in direct contradiction to what he had promised Mercy, so he slapped on a face of dubious surprise and politely refuted the insinuation, which, of course, only served to exacerbate Isaac's growing irritation.

"Do you think I'm a complete idiot?" the engineer growled. "I may not know all that much about resonance, but I know what I heard last night coming through the ventilation duct in my quarters had *nothing* to do with talking to cohabitors."

Feeling a flush of incensement, he stood up to meet Isaac's furious gaze. "You're right. You don't have a clue what you're talking about, so maybe we should end this conversation before it gets ugly."

"Oh, I was counting on it getting ugly," Isaac retorted acidly, squaring his shoulders and compensating for his unthreatening stature with a baleful expression. "You might have convinced everyone else on this ship that you're a stand-up guy. But you won't fool me, you two-faced, silk-talking scum sucker . . . There's no way the son of an Upperdecks politician could possibly know what's best for a girl like Mercy, so why don't you do her a favor and leave her the fuck alone!"

Tobias batted Isaac's finger away as the prick jabbed it into his shoulder. He truly had no interest in fighting for Mercy's honor but couldn't in good conscience tolerate such vitriolic slander. "Mercy's perfectly capable of deciding what's best for herself," he answered. "And anyway, it turns out what *really* floats her boat is scruffy, glow-addicted grease monkeys—the binary opposite of me in every conceivable way. So, whatever you *think* you heard last night, I promise you've got nothing to worry about."

Baring fangs, Isaac looked ready to start throwing fists when Teodora Brižan blew into the galley in a hurried whirlwind of knitted syn-wool and industrial hardware. She padded on bare feet past the feuding pair and slammed her luma-puck down on the island countertop, her metallic-blue hair glistening in the golden tones of the loading Sinegex Systems interface as it appeared in the air before her.

"If you two meatheads can spare five minutes from tryna rip each other's throats out then would yah kindly join me over here on the grown-up's table so we can talk shop?"

Isaac shot Tobias a fierce glower, telegraphing *this isn't over*, before dutifully joining the salvage specialist in the galley. "You got something?" he asked, taking on a considerably more measured demeanor.

"What I've got is potentially the biggest score in the history of salvage, but if you're too busy measuring your struts over there then by all means, we can leave it for the next crew to swipe."

Isaac shook his head. "*Assurance* is running on fumes; we need every break we can get right now."

"Good, cuz it just so happens I mighta found us one."

Teo began navigating through menu screens with sweeping arm movements, bringing up a map of local space and zeroing in on a remote location in the outer reaches of the Debris Belt.

"What is it?" Tobias asked, catching a simmering look of disapproval from Teo as he joined her side. Disapproval, or . . . jealousy. After all, if Isaac had heard what happened last night, then it stood to reason that she had too . . .

"That," she said, turning her attention to the pulsing crosshairs marking the target destination. "Is Captain Lei-Ghannam's private preserve."

THREE

Eamon jolted awake to stabbing pain as the canvas bag covering his head caught on his chin stubble. Cold steel met his exposed wrists, which were bound tightly behind his back with what felt like electrical tape. His heartbeat drummed loudly in his ears, accompanied by a throbbing ache radiating from the back of his skull. Fighting through the pain, he pieced together his frantic escape from Zelos Arena into the neon-soaked back alleys of ExSight Multiplex. But then a disconcerting void swallowed any memorable detail beyond that . . .

The air in his confined space felt uncomfortably close, saturated with the pungent odor of cleaning chemicals. He could only surmise that he had been struck over the head and forcibly hauled to a janitor's cupboard, tucked away in some secluded maintenance passage. The pressing question remained: By whom? Clearly, the enforcers who had pursued him in the arena had been given authorization to terminate him on sight; they would have had little desire to waste time conducting an interrogation before carrying out their orders. Drexen's Monarchs were a possibility, but he reasoned the Governor almost certainly had his hands full fighting Harmony for supremacy of the district. It seemed unlikely the man would want to sidetrack himself by resuming their cat and mouse rivalry when his focus *and* his resources were needed elsewhere. Only one option remained, and as he watched a blurry silhouette move toward him through the sweat-logged lattice of fibers draped before his nose, he felt certain he knew to whom it belonged . . .

The room's fluorescent tube fixtures smeared his retinas with ugly green light as one of his captors forcibly removed the bag from his head. His pupils took a moment to adjust as his squinting gaze met a pair of strikingly familiar eyes—beautiful, upturned eyes like pearls crested by halos of sienna-brown. They seemed somewhat muted now, their arresting color drained by his complete incomprehension of the person that lay beyond them. Where once he had known warmth and keen intelligence, he now saw only malice and deceit; they were windows into a dark room in which a predator lurked—one proudly wearing the skin of someone he cared for dearly and using that friendly face to coerce him into lowering his guard . . . Jyn Sato, if that was even her real name—incognito terrorist leader and DMED's newest marshal—stood before him with a guileful smile and a hand on her hip. Her petite-but-hale physique was encased in a tight, black bodysuit, buried beneath a hooded cape colored the same muddy gray as the robes donned by her acolytes. A network of prominent veins framed her soft-angled face, crawling up her neck and fanning out from her eyes like lightning forks frozen under her beige skin: the scars of her since-renounced faith laid bare for all to see. Holding her gaze, an unpleasant concoction of clashing emotions steeled upon him: terrible grief, mainly, as he mourned the plucky, tenacious sprite he had spent the better part of three years fostering a partnership with. Then, anger and chagrin upon the realization that it had all been for nothing . . .

Was any of it real? he pondered bitterly: the ride-alongs, the stakeouts, the downtime spent in their favorite watering holes, and the painfully gradual evolution from snarky banter to admiration and, eventually, genuine affection—had it really all been just a sham? Eyeing the ferocious insurgent leader standing before him, it certainly seemed that way . . .

Repressing his growing indignation, he switched his focus to the other individual present in the room, unfamiliar with the sullen-faced man currently leaning against a storage rack in the far corner. Practically oozing acrimony, the stranger cut an imposing shape. His tall, brawny frame was mostly concealed under mounds of mottled cloth but telegraphed by his square jaw and broad neck. His black skin appeared cracked and dry, covered in a rind of crimson residue that Eamon knew from firsthand experience to be the result of exposure to heavy bloodfall. Once dry, the substance took some serious scrubbing to wash off. Although, curiously, many mouthians had taken to letting it cake on their skin, wearing it as a symbol of their patriotism—their veneration of the *Devourer* and all its blessings manifested physically on their flesh. Jyn's companion was likely one such loyalist, the braided cornrows zigzagging across his scalp similarly discolored by the scarlet downpour. The degree of staining combined with the stranger's signature Harmony garb meant Eamon could safely extrapolate he was dealing with a fanatic: a true believer in the Composer's mission, and one of the same foot soldiers presently waging war on the streets of the district, forcing nonbelievers out of their homes and setting the territory ablaze in the fires of retribution.

Better tread carefully with this fella . . .

"Oren," Jyn finally said, maintaining eye contact with Eamon but addressing her accomplice. "Cut him free."

Oren's snarling expression became one of concern. He stood up straight, slowly unfolded his arms, and in husky, sonorous tones, replied, "Are you sure that's a good idea? This man was the marshal, no? Seems like an unnecessary risk."

"I know him," Jyn replied, sotto voce. "He's no threat . . . Please, do as I ask."

Wouldn't be so sure about that, Eamon mentally rebuked while Oren produced a fission-edged blade from the sheath strapped to his leg and used it to cut the bindings tied around his wrists.

Jyn let a forlorn smile tug at the corners of her lips. "You have no idea how happy I am to see you, dude."

Eamon rubbed the back of his throbbing skull "Sure got a funny way of showing it."

She winced. "Yeah, I'm sorry about the theatrics. We couldn't risk letting you get away. I'm not sure you're aware just how much you've rattled the hornet's nest; it's a miracle you're even alive right now—what with the amount of heat on you. Good thing *we* got to you before anyone else did."

Eamon scoffed. "Saved by the exalted Composer. What a stroke of ruttin' luck."

Oren spun around to Eamon's rear, placed an abrasive hand on his shoulder, and held the blade near his neck. "Heretic!" the brute hissed. "You are addressing the Composer, the Will of the Savior; she who will quell the dissonance and blaze a path to salvation. Watch your tongue before I cut it from your mouth and stuff it down your throat!"

"Will you cool it already, Oren?" Jyn interjected, pinching the bridge of her nose exasperatedly. "We didn't come all this way to kill him."

Oren reluctantly resheathed his blade and resumed his brooding silence in the corner.

"And why is that, Jyn?" Eamon asked, feeling a hot rage rising in him. "Why weren't those poor refugee bastards at the blockade spared from righteous slaughter, too? Or those trainee pilots you swatted outta the sky like mosquitos? How about the folks in the Mouth caught up in the crossfire between you and Drexen as we speak? What makes *me* so different from any of them?"

Jyn let her shoulders sink in a surprising display of humility. "Look . . . I'm not gonna stand here and feed you a load of exculpatory bullshit. There's blood on my hands—I've got no disillusions about that . . . But maybe if you'll let me, I can provide some context that might help you understand why things played out the way they had to."

"You're welcome to try, Deputy. But honestly, I reckon you should just let Skippy here gut me, cuz I doubt there's anything you can say that'll deter me from wantin' to bring you to justice."

She leaned forward, appropriating a condescending smirk. "It's 'Marshal' now, actually . . . We'll probably save a lot of time here if you go ahead and tell me what you know already, then I can fill in the blanks."

Eamon reached into the imaginary pocket where his ciggys would have been stored, were he wearing his aviator jacket and not a stolen casterblade jersey. Dropping his hand in disappointment, he sighed, then began, "Well . . . I did as much digging as I could with my Phalanx privileges revoked. Imagine my surprise when I discovered it wasn't a *complete* crock of shit you sold me. Sure enough, you *did* manage to escape ritual sacrifice and left the Church of the Abyss when you were just a sprout. Ran as a Mouth rat for a spell before ciphering up with a cohab vendor known as Absence. Ae was arrested for possession of stolen tech and charged under the Illegal Salvage Act of 94 AC. You hired a couple amateur mercs to try and bust aer outta custody; needless to say, it didn't go so well."

Oren began fidgeting in his skin, growing increasingly vexed by the blunt nature of Eamon's retelling of his prophet's saga. Eamon leaned forward on his knees, squared his shoulders, and wondered just how much insolence he could get away with before the thug finally snapped. "This is where the trail gets hard to follow, unless, of course, you got a nose as good as mine . . . After the failed prison break is when you ended up on the administrator's radar. Once she found out about your hyper-resonance, she cut you a deal: Absence's life in return for your service. Ae was allowed to continue aer work splicing human and *Devourer* tech as long as the results could be weaponized and ended up in her possession. Meanwhile, she tasked you with forming this bogus insurgency and starting a proxy war, the goal being to ensure Vargos got all the public funding and approval she needed to refortify the blockade and strengthen the segregation of the district. She planted you in DMED to keep an eye on me and I, being the gullible idiot I am, took her glowing recommendation in good faith." He allowed a stern bearing to overcome him, searching her eyes for the slightest intimation of empathy or remorse. "She's had a gun to your head ever since, forcing you to do her dirty work in exchange for sparing Absence . . . That was until you decided you weren't her dancin' monkey no more and used your prototype tech to reprogram her own grennies to assassinate her. Now, you're using the powers and resources she afforded to wage war on her behalf to bring down the union." He shrugged blithely. "That's about all I got. How am I doin' so far?"

Jyn gave a sarcastic slow clap, which seemed remarkably out of character. Then again, what did he really know about her *true* character anyway? "Not bad," she smarmed. "You always were wasted behind that desk . . . Although I do need to make a couple of small corrections . . . Firstly, there's *nothin'* bogus about this insurgency. Harmony as a movement existed long before Madeline sank her claws into it. Mouthians are sick of living in fear, sick of oppression, sick of the inequitable distribution of wealth and the resources the Savior provides us. It was only a matter of time before people began rising up. All the administrator needed *me* to do was bring order to the chaos. A revolution is nothing without a leader. But, unified under one voice, Harmony could become exactly the threat she needed to stoke the fires of fear and ignorance." She furrowed her brow, umbrage weighing her expression. "Secondly, you really think I would have inflicted so much pain and suffering on so many of my people just to save my own skin? You know I'd happily throw myself on the pyre before any one of them."

"So why didn't you, Jyn?" Eamon asked coarsely. "Because it occurs to me you probably could have saved a whole lotta lives had you done just that."

Eyes downcast and steeped in shadow, she recited, "Sacrifice the few to save the many . . . This had *nothing* to do with Vargos holding a gun to my head or keeping Absence safe. My only goal was to convince her she had my full compliance, biding my time until I finally had the opportunity to play my hand." She came down to a squat before him, appropriating an air of sincerity that, instead of pacifying him, only served to boil his blood.

"You were right, Wyatt—right about everything. I hated that I had to leave you chasing your tail for so long. Vargos was corrupt to the damned-Abyss core—quite happy to wreak interminable suffering on the inhabitants of the Mouth to secure her position of power . . . And now that she's dead, I can run Harmony *my* way. The death, the destruction, the unnecessary civilian casualties—it all ends now. Everything we do, we do to ensure the success of our mission—nothing more."

Eamon's head nearly spun off his neck with how forcefully he shook it. "I'm sorry, Jyn, but when your mission is to topple a ruling government, you're kiddin' yourself if you think you can achieve it without causin' considerable collateral damage. There are over a million people bowside of the blockade: they're not all evil. They're not *all* your enemy."

Jyn's manner soured, her plump lips shriveling into a stifled frown. She straightened her back, seeming to recede under her hood. "Of course, not . . . But this is a storm that's been brewing for a century, and anyone who chooses to stand in its path can expect themselves to get swept away."

He waited a beat, giving her a sideways stare. "Even me?"

"Even you . . . But it's not gonna come to that. I wasted so much breath trying to stop you from hurling yourself into situations that were way above your pay grade. Because a marshal who actually gives a shit about the plight of the Prey is worth a helluva lot more to the Mouth alive than dead. Getting Madeline to fire your ass was the only way I could keep you out of harm's way, and it was a damn sight better than how *she* would have preferred to deal with you." Jyn stood up, offering her hand in a gesture of truce, seeming to naively expect him to hungrily accept it and blindly rally to her cause. "Now, *I'm* the one asking *you* to jump into the fray, but this time, with me right alongside you. Together, we can put an end to the tyranny of the NTU and build a brighter, fairer future for all on the Coalescence." A wanting expression took her, impressing the image of a child begging for forgiveness from angered parents. "Isn't that what you want? Isn't that all *both* of us ever wanted?"

He left her hand lingering in the air, repeating the word "Harmony" with a face as though he'd just bitten the inside of his cheek. "The same terrorist cell I nearly got myself zeroed ten times over tryna smoke out of the district? You really think I'm gonna just forget everythin' you've done and, what, swear fealty?"

A frown of disappointment consumed her delicate features. She retracted her hand, turning her shoulder in annoyance. "Understand this: the Harmony you've been chasing was a work of fiction, conjured up by a wicked, old bat whose entire political strategy hinged on the population fearing the emergence of pan-species society."

"Harmony might be a work of fiction, but the crimes you've committed are as real as the fleas on Abraham's neck. Coming forward now doesn't bring the scores of innocent people you murdered in the name of emancipation back to life."

"Composer!" Oren furiously blurted. "You *must* allow me to cut this craven ingrate down. None can treat you with such disrespect and be allowed to draw breath."

She raised a hand to silence the man, staring at Eamon with eyes girdled by webs of captured electricity. "Believe whatever you want, Wyatt, but *don't* try and get in my way. I'm not somebody you want to make an enemy of."

Eamon saw Oren preemptively place his hand on the hilt of his blade, and something told him that *this* time, should the brute reiterate his desire to use it, Jyn might not stop him. Fearing that continuing down his path of defiance and insolence would only result in swift execution, he showed his palms and forced a disarming smile. "I won't cause trouble, Jyn, but I don't want any part of your holy war. You wanna throw the *Novara* into chaos? Fine, but I'm not about to help you do it."

Jyn breathed a sigh of relief that, harrowingly, suggested she had fully intended to kill him had he not given her at least *some* measure of cooperation. "I guess that's as much as I can ask for . . . Still, I know how much you hate sitting on the sidelines. There are ways you can help without getting *involved* involved, you know?"

Ears pricking in intrigue, he watched as she reached into a pocket hidden beneath her flowing cape and produced a luma-drone: a small, one-turbine copter with a microemitter embedded in its chasse. She cast the device into the air with a flick of the wrist, its tiny blades whirring to life as it stabilized itself before coming to a stationary hover in the center of the room. Its microemitter bathed the gloomy space in glimmering shades of gold and cyan, luma-casting the life-sized, three-dimensional projection of an aging man with a stony-faced expression wearing a highly decorated NTSC uniform. Eamon stood up, bringing scrutinizing eyes in line with those of the avatar. "Admiral Jasper Coombs?"

Jyn nodded. "By removing Vargos, we cut the head off the serpent. But this serpent is a hydra, and the head it's growing in her place is far uglier, and I dare say, has much sharper fangs . . . Coombs is the one pulling the strings now. Vargos's death resulted in a political vacuum. That pompous ass, Councilman Edevane was next in line to succeed, but with his unexpected resignation, the council are scrambling to determine new leadership, and in all the disarray, Coombs is gradually seizing power. And remember, he's a military man; if he succeeds, there'll be curfews, martial law, armed enforcers on every junction and communal hub, and that's only bowside of the blockade; Abyss knows what fresh hell will become of the Mouth . . ."

Eamon felt a sinking feeling in his chest, dismayed at finding himself somewhat aligned with Jyn's concerns.

She continued. "My intel says Coombs was in cahoots with Administrator Vargos—literally and figuratively in bed with her."

He grimaced. "Thanks for that image."

"I know—gross. The pair of them orchestrated this whole charade. Although, where Madeline was focused on the socio-political impact of Harmony, Jasper is more concerned about the acquisition of tech. His whole angle is using the hybridized technology Absence has been developing to reinforce *Novarian* defenses. You saw firsthand what this shit can do when we assaulted the blockade; imagine Phalanx enforcers armed to the teeth with the same spliced weaponry we have in our arsenal . . . You mentioned the ambush that wiped out those trainee pilots. That was a weapons test—authorized and overseen by the admiral himself. Absence created those modified kestrels, but Coombs deployed them, and you better believe he's got his scientists reverse engineering them right now so he can mass-produce his own."

Eamon shook his head in hopeless disbelief. "Well . . . this sounds like just about every shade of FUBAR imaginable . . . Still mystified as to what you think *I* can do about it."

"Nothing . . . Leave Coombs to us . . . He's not a politician like Madeline; he doesn't care about approval ratings or public opinion. It won't be all smoke and mirrors like it was with the administrator. He'll rule with an iron fist. It'll be a totalitarian regime, and all *we* can do is cut at his heels and try'n stay one step ahead of him."

She tapped a few keys on her wristwatch. Jasper's projection fizzled out of existence, replaced by the luma-cast depiction of a young woman with brown hair tied up in a tight military bun, her uniform adorned with markedly fewer badges and commendations.

Eamon made a grunt of recognition. "Hazel Edevane—the councilman's daughter."

Jyn's eyes fell to the floor, the faintest suggestion of regret present in her distant stare. "Hazel was the sole survivor of the weapons test," she morbidly explained. "One of the last things Madeline did before I killed her was repri-mand me for a lack of due diligence. They didn't want there to be any loose ends, and although Coombs cares little for what people think about his meth-ods, he can't have it getting out that he was directly involved in the slaughter of five NTSC pilots. The public outrage would be too much, even for him . . . Vargos wanted me to kill Hazel if she ever recovered from her injuries; I pre-dict Jasper will be planning on doing the same."

Eamon studied Hazel's features, finding her narrow-set eyes and gently sloped nose remarkably similar to those of her brother, Tobias—the *other* Edevane kid he'd had recent dealings with.

What is it about this damned family that just seems to attract trouble?

"Why are you telling me this, Jyn?" he asked. "Conscience got the better of you?"

"Hazel *must* live to tell her story," the Composer divined. "If she dies, then the truth dies with her. Harmony may not be able to defeat Coombs in a stand-up fight. Abyss knows we'll try, but we don't exactly have numbers and firepower on our side. If there's *anything* we can do to undermine his advan-tage, then we must act upon it. Hazel's testimony would be a major blow to his position, which means she must be kept alive at all costs."

"I see . . . So, it's not because there's a lil girl's life at stake that you want me to intervene, but because doing so will give you an edge against the admiral."

Jyn turned to Oren and held out her hand expectantly. After a moment of disgruntled hesitation, the man produced a firearm from beneath his robe that looked identical to the spliced handgun Eamon had recovered following the attack at the Phalanx Compound. Oren handed Jyn the weapon and she, surprisingly, passed it to Eamon. He held it in his hand, the sight of its gruesome, organic modifications inducing a wave of nausea, as though it had been dipped in a bucket of rotting entrails and left to bake for a few hours under the radiance of the Höllengarten.

"Keep her safe, Wyatt," Jyn commanded. "Do it for whatever reason you think is right, even if it's just to save a life . . . Either way, you can't let Coombs get to her first. Understand?"

He wrapped his fingers around the pistol's grip, repressing the urge to toss it away and douse his hands in gallons of bacterial sanitizer. He glanced at Jyn, giving a nod of comprehension. He didn't honestly know what the future held in store for them—probably nothing pleasant. Their story, he feared, could only end in tragedy. But figuring that out would have to be put on the back burner for the time being. Right now, he had a new purpose: save the girl.

Jyn gave a heart-wrenching smile that reminded him of . . . well, her—who she *used* to be, anyway. "There's just one more thing."

Seeming as though he had been champing at the bit for this very moment, Oren sprang to life, grabbing both of Eamon's arms and locking them behind his back, then sweeping him off his legs and forcing him back into the chair. Before he even knew what was happening, the bag had been pulled back over his head. He heard the pair make a hurried exit, then silence fell . . .

Arms unbound, he removed the bag from his head, surprised and elated to find Abraham, his trusty canine companion, sitting at his feet, looking up with glistening, chocolate-brown eyes, head tilted to the side. The loving mutt vaulted into his lap and began affectionately licking his jaw with his sandpaper tongue. Eamon wrapped his arms around him and buried his face into the brindled fur of his neck. "Hey, boy! Where in the stars have you been?"

FOUR

The *Assurance* maintained position approximately ten klicks beyond the outer edge of the Debris Belt. On the bridge, Captain Delilah Holloway sat in the copilot's seat, absently watching the steam rising from her mug of loose-leaf tea as it bloomed in the glow of the countless blinking lights bespeckled across the helm. Ordinarily, little soothed her nerves more than the sight of that colossal nimbus of wreckage as it waltzed beyond the windshield. Parking up this far out often felt like finding refuge from the increasingly tumultuous reality of life aboard the *Novara*. Of course, "holding position" didn't quite describe their current situation as accurately as "dead in the water." With the pitiful dregs of fuel remaining in the hydrogen tanks now reserved exclusively for powering life support, staying put was the only option the crew had at their disposal. The endless night, in all its abyssal emptiness, suddenly felt oppressively claustrophobic—less like a sanctuary and more like a tempestuous ocean, the *Novara* a lonely island inhabited by a pack of hungry wolves, waiting for their next meal to wash up on their shores . . .

In recent days, she had developed an almost slavish obsession to watching the numbers tick down on the core systems panel, the ship's depleting resources gradually drifting into critical territory. Atmospheric pressure had now dropped to a worrying 85 percent, and the fission reactor had spun down to zero just several hours prior. She likely would have had to bite the bullet and return to the docks of Lower Amidships to face whatever awaited them, were it not for the fortuitous arrival of some much-needed assistance . . .

Through the windshield, against a gently rotating backdrop of scrap metal and stars, another ship hung motionless in the black. The *Etherow in Spring* was a cancer-class salvage vessel, which Delilah had always likened to a giant, legless crab—a lenticular, ovoid shell with two mechanical pincers mounted on either side of the cockpit; the pincers were used to tear debris into smaller chunks to be sucked into the hold via the gravity funnel occupying its snub bow. Favoring function over appearance or maneuverability, the *Etherow* had been purpose-built for its salvage designation, unlike the *Assurance*—a balaener-class hauler originally designed for atmospheric flight, which Delilah had clumsily retrofitted for weld and salvage following her acquisition. The old girl may not have been quite as efficient at sifting through the refuse of the Collision, but she was fast, quiet, and a damn sight easier on the eyes . . .

From an outlet on the *Etherow in Spring*'s hull, an elongated hose twisted and looped in the weightlessness of space, trailing toward the *Assurance*, and disappearing behind her nose cone, its probe end plugged into a socket beneath the cargo bay. Given most vessels in the fleet generally operated within a fifty-kilometer bubble of the *Novara*, remote refueling operations like this were uncommon but not unheard of. In Delilah's case, it was the kiss of life that would bring her crippled ketch back from the ineluctable grasp of the deep, and she knew she would be forever indebted to her valiant rescuer, as much as the woman would probably be disinclined to accept it . . .

Just forward of the helm, an emitter luma-cast Captain Thea Rebbeckis's image via comm-link, as she sat in the utilitarian cockpit of her ship. An irascible woman with piercing, green eyes and freckled skin, her explosion of frizzy, chestnut hair could barely be contained by the fabric headband encircling her crown. Her fetching features were marred by heavy bags under her eyes telling tales of many a sleepless night—the likely culprit of which was cradled into her bosom in a material sling, quietly and contently nursing from her exposed breast. Sitting in the pilot seat with his shoulder turned, Kahu Heperi had taken to making an almost burlesque show of *not* looking at the woman's projection, playing solitaire on one of the consoles embedded in the pedestal beside him.

Chivalrous old fool.

Delilah felt a pang of sadness as she traced the gentle curve of the baby's head, strangely, mourning the loss of someone who had never existed. Relationships, children, family—her mission to acquire a welding ship to make sure *nobody* had to meet the same grim fate as Micah Verhoeven ever again hadn't allowed for such things. That wasn't to say that she didn't desire them; certainly, in her younger, more idealistic days she had assumed that would be the natural course her life would take. With her parents incorrigibly dedicated to serving the union, she yearned to forge the tightly knit family unit that she herself had been deprived of, which probably explained why, on a subconscious level, she had such a habit for rounding up strays and recruiting them to her crew. Still, she wasn't sure it compared to having a family of her own . . .

There hadn't been anyone romantically in the picture since, well, ever—not that a man was an essential component in having kids on the *Novara*. To ensure the provision of ample genetic diversity in the event of a catastrophic loss of population, the vessel boasted masses of cryogenically stored eggs and semen, should a population bomb be required to colonize Pasture. Procreation was really as simple as filling out a few forms. What prevented Delilah from doing so were her concerns over what quality of life she would be able to provide. Weld and salvage was gritty, dangerous work, affiliating her with a glut of unscrupulous mercenaries and profiteers. And if Eamon Wyatt's prediction of imminent civil war was accurate, then she couldn't say what kind of world she would be bringing a little one into. It seemed a reckless endeavor to spawn someone into existence just to satiate her own maternal desires. Thea, however, clearly didn't share those same apprehensions . . .

"What is he now?" Delilah asked, shaking off her malaise. "Two months?"

"Ten weeks," Thea corrected, hoisting the little spud into a better position to feed. "Ten glorious weeks of shitting, barfing, and screaming. Little bastard was struggling to latch on for a while, but I think he's gettin' the knack now."

"I don't remember you saying if he had a father or not. I mean, obviously, he *does*, but do you know who it is?"

"Abyss knows," laughed Thea, the strident tones of her voice humming through the bridge speakers. "Some bum with no hope of getting his golden ticket aboard the *Novara*; saved his bloodline by sending his spurt rocketing across the stars instead." She dipped her chin to kiss her baby's forehead and softly cooed, "Because daddies who died two hundred years ago can't stick around to complicate things for us, can they? It's just you and me forever and ever."

"Got enough juice in the tank to initialize the reactor," Kahu cut in abruptly, seeming increasingly uncomfortable with the topic of conversation. "Get ready for point-eight Gs and full atmos."

The fuselage creaked and groaned as the *Assurance* took a yawning breath and awoke from her slumber, the beeps and whistles of her systems coming online like a morning chorus of birdsong. Delilah felt her posture shrivel and her arms grow heavy as the artificial gravity returned to normal levels. "Thanks, Thea. You've really done us a solid here."

"No, I haven't," the woman countered, the lines of her face crumpling into an unsmiling expression. "This isn't me helping you out; I'm just repaying the debt I owe you after you helped me through all that nasty business with Wolf Engstrom . . . We're square now . . . Nebula? I don't want you calling up asking for any more favors."

Wolf Engstrom . . . Delilah hadn't thought about the cretin in some time. Thea had been serving as a hand aboard the man's grub runner several years back. Being the pretty young thing she was, he, like any weak-minded man, had inevitably taken a liking to her, but affection soon became an obsession. *Captain's orders* quickly devolved into possessive, predatory behavior. Thea never disclosed exactly what degree of abuse the man subjected her to but would show up at the harbor master's weekly safety briefings looking more timid than an antelope in the company of lions, sometimes with bruises on her neck or ligature marks on her wrists, her vivacious spirit well and truly broken. Wolf's crew were a bunch of degenerates—so much so that Delilah had genuinely feared what confronting him would mean for Thea's safety. However, she just so happened to know that it wasn't only food Wolf used his ship to transport. After informing then-detective Eamon Wyatt about the situation and tipping him off about Engstrom's trafficking of alien narcotics, the GEA raided his hauler and found a massive shipment of glow caps stored in the hold, ready for delivery to the Upperdecks. Wolf and most of his posse were put away on smuggling charges while Thea received immunity due to her cooperation, as well as her being more of a prisoner than a participating crewmember. Among mountains of contraband, Eamon additionally recovered huge amounts of hidden lucre, which he made sure was subsequently *misplaced* during the checking-in of evidence. Coincidentally, this happened to be around the same time Thea mysteriously came across a large sum of nunits—enough to buy a ship and blaze her own trail as captain of a reputable salvage outfit. That, thankfully, had been the end of it, but while Delilah was glad to have helped, and had only done what she thought was right, Thea sparing a little fuel to get the *Assurance* up and running again seemed scarcely enough to make them even in her estimation . . .

"Nebula," she conceded. "Just needed a jump start; we'll be outta your hair in a split."

Thea dropped her shoulders, seeming unprepared for Delilah's amiability in the matter and, perhaps remembering just how bad a scrape she had pulled her out of. "I'm sorry, Lilah," she said. "It's just, you're damaged goods now . . . Since you started working for Drexen, and what with all these rumors floating around that you've got a leech serving on your ship—I could get kicked out of the Captain's Guild just for talking to you." She zipped up her jumpsuit and rearranged the sling into snooze mode. "It's not just my own skin I gotta think about now, yah know?"

"We ain't working for that crook no more," Kahu put in, able to return to the conversation now that the *goods* had been securely stowed. "You think if we were he'd be going to such crazy lengths to hunt us down. What's the bounty he's got out on us now anyway: fifteen-k?"

"Twenty-five," Thea answered soberly.

"Shit . . . Think I would have taken it."

Through the windshield, Delilah saw the *Etherow in Spring*'s mechanical pincers rotate and snap as Thea manipulated her auxiliary controls. "Reckon I could leave a few nasty marks with these bad boys, but I'd have to be real stupid to go toe-to-toe with a fearless vet like you, Heperi."

"Smart kid, this one," Kahu snickered, twiddling the ends of his rebellious mustache.

"Damn straight," boasted Thea. "Problem is, stupid would be an understatement concerning some of the other skippers in the fleet. Doubtless, *someone* will be fool enough to take a run at you."

"We'll be ready for them," assured Delilah, but her conciliatory tone apparently left Thea unconvinced.

"What's your plan here?" the woman riposted briskly. "Because you can't hang out in the Debris Belt forever. And I don't know if you'll ever be able to return to the Lower Amidships Docks now that the Governor's taken them over."

Kahu's weathered face became a map of the same shock and unease that Delilah had done a much better job of suppressing.

"Don't tell me you didn't know?" asked Thea, shaking her head at their perplexed expressions. "First it was just a few Monarchs sniffing around your docking bay and asking questions. But word has it the Governor isn't doing so hot in the battle for the Mouth. He's lost a lot of turf to the leech insurgents, and now he's seizing every inch of territory he can get his hands on on this side of the blockade. Phalanx don't seem the least bit concerned about what goes on down in Lower Amidships—not after what happened to the administrator; didn't so much as bat an eye when Monarchs forced their way into the control tower. Now, the swines are demanding protection money and charging exorbitant berthing fees. Honestly, it's looking pretty bleak."

"Can't imagine the harbor master's jumpin' for joy about this," Kahu submitted. "The Captain's Guild ain't exactly the Governor's biggest fans."

"I doubt he's got much of an opinion at all, considering those sadistic bastards marched him up to the fission field and tossed him out into the night . . . Don't get me wrong: I never much liked Iver Polakorski but I'm not sure he deserved a spacing."

Delilah let an unintentional gasp escape her lips, causing Thea to angrily reiterate the words, "What's your plan?" growing frustrated by her apparent naivety to the gravity of the situation.

Of course, Delilah *did* have a plan, but disclosing to a fellow salvage skipper that she had potentially uncovered the location of Captain Lei-Ghannam's fabled preserve would be a supremely stupid move. Whosoever successfully recovered Yusef's lost treasure trove would find untold riches and a permanent place in the pantheon of scrap captains, giving any prospecting bounty hunters just one more reason to track them down.

Obviously, money and accolades mattered little to Delilah—no amount of nunits could help dig them out of the hole they found themselves in. What *she* sought was the leverage a prize of such historical significance would garner with the Administration. The only other docks large enough to berth the *Assurance* were, after all, the Phalanx-controlled ones situated just below the *Novara*'s bridge. Her hope was that she could use the valuable stash as a bargaining chip to negotiate for shelter and amnesty until the situation with Vidalia blew over . . . *if it ever did.*

The one potential snag with this grand scheme of hers was, of course, Null. Flagrant lockdown violations the Administration would surely overlook, but harboring an enemy of the NTU was a whole different kettle of fish.

Cross that bridge when we come to it . . .

It took no less than a bald-faced lie to placate Thea's concerns for their safety—some arbitrary nonsense about a friend in the Upperdecks with access to an airlock who had offered them sanctuary. With remote refueling complete, Thea retracted the probe hose back into the belly of her ship and prepared to take her leave. "Is it true?" she asked, tempering her voice so as not to disturb her sleeping charge. "About the leech I mean. Do you really have one on your ship?"

Delilah answered by switching the comms feed from the bridge to the cargo bay, where Null had begun helping Teo prepare her EVA equipment for the upcoming extraction. As the girl lifted her leg to slide into the pressure suit, she lost her balance and tumbled backward. Null burst into action and caught her with chitin-plated arms. Ae lifted her off the ground with astonishing ease and lowered her into her workwear like a gorilla tenderly handling its adopted kitten offspring.

"Stone the crows," Thea rasped, half-amazed, half-repulsed. "Wing Commander Heperi, I find it hard to believe *you* of all people signed off on this. I mean, I know the *Assurance* isn't technically yours anymore but . . . really?"

Kahu gave an ambivalent shrug as he ritualistically fired up the impulse thrusters. "Ah, the bug's alright. A helluva lot more competent than some of the lazy schmucks who've served on this old crate over the years. Plus, you think there's anyone else on the *Novara* who could challenge *me* in an arm-wrestling match? It's nice to finally have someone aboard who can actually put up a fight."

*   *   *

We can trust Thea, Delilah told herself, simultaneously ordering Kahu to wait for the *Etherow in Spring* to leave sensor range before departing. She had every confidence Rebbeckis wouldn't intentionally sell them out, but the *Assurance* and her crew were renowned for digging up high-ticket salvage that other outfits might consider too dangerous or difficult to extract. If word got out they'd been lingering in the Debris Belt with obvious intent, it could raise suspicions, and the last thing they needed was a kettle of vultures swooping down and snatching the score from under them.

Once the scopes were clean, Kahu fired up the thrusters and vectored toward an especially desolate region of the belt known as the Boneyard. Like sailing through arctic seas in which the icebergs were behemoth chunks of dormant, organic machinery, this dense cluster of disunited *Devourer* material had gone largely untouched since the Collision, due to there being very little demand for exo-salvage, not to mention the litany of superstitions spacers held about it being a haunted void, where hapless crews fell prey to the cortege of vengeful alien spirits who lurked there, never to be seen or heard from again.

Salvagers made a point of giving it a wide berth, but Delilah knew that with Eamon's hybridized tech now hitting the black market, that would soon change, and she had to ensure *her* operation was the tip of the spear in the inevitable gold rush that would soon follow. It was for precisely this reason Teodora had been performing detailed composition scans for Null's technical analysis when she detected something unexpected: a whisper reaching out through time from the faded pages of ancient history . . .

"There's probably a dozen old jump shuttles floatin' around in this crypt," asserted Kahu, switching on the *Assurance*'s external floodlights, the ominous megaliths of sinew-fused metal, adrift outside, rendering their surroundings in perfect darkness. "What's got the mouth rat all giddy about this one? Seems like a bit of a stretch to presume it's old Yusef's stash."

Eyes milk-white, Isaac sat in the copilot's seat with his knees tucked into his chest, leaning forward with busy hands scurrying across the surface of his pane. There had been some discussion already concerning the logistics of retrieving the invaluable cargo. While Teo prepared for an EVA assessment, he was in the process of downloading reams of technical schematics from the Nov-Net in the hope of remote piloting the shuttle and docking it with the *Assurance*'s airlock. "The signature of the transponder ping Teo picked up suggested it came from a lupus-class bunker shuttle," he explained. "Only a handful were ever manufactured—famously issued to the highest echelons of *Novara* command before the Collision. Most of them were lost or presumably stripped for tech and parts. The only one known to have survived is on display in the aerospace museum on the Silk River Concourse. Then, of course, you've got Captain Lei-Ghannam's."

"Yeah, and we all know what that lunatic did with his. Guy *must* have had a few bats in the belfry to jettison all that good spirit."

"I don't think he had much of a choice," Delilah interjected, perched on a ledge by the windshield feeling a flutter of unease as she gazed out at the nearest clump of wreckage, its asperous, ice-encrusted surface morphing eerily as the floodlights caught its many jagged protrusions. "What with hordes of hungry looters trying to break down the bridge bulkheads. Remember, this was before the *Devourer* restored the *Novara*'s remaining fission reactor. People honestly thought it was the end-times; spacing it was really his only means of keeping the peace in those final days."

"Nawh," Kahu drawled. "Best thing woulda been to crack open all that ancient firewater and have a huge end-of-the-world party. Go out with a bang."

"Well, it's a good thing he didn't. Otherwise, it wouldn't have been waiting here all these years for us to come and find it."

Kahu applied gentle pressure to the flight stick, rolling the *Assurance* sideways to clear her left wing of a wedge of debris that looked unnervingly like a giant rib cage. "True," he conceded. "My old man always used to tell me it was just a myth, that if it *did* exist then the shuttle's inertia would have taken it out into the deep void, way beyond the range of any ship in the fleet. But I always knew it was here . . . Used to keep my eyes peeled whenever me and Tala got sent out to do sweeps of the Debris Belt. Used to daydream about finding it, retiring early, and buying us one of them fancy duplexes up in Festa Heights, living out our golden years in high society and dying fat, drunk, and filthy rich together."

The old pilot issued a hearty laugh that quickly degraded into a biting silence. Turning introspective, he dipped his battle-weary face into his chest and let his ash-gray, matted dreadlocks obscure his eyes. It was a reaction Delilah had seen many times before—the Tala effect, as she had come to know it. Over the years, she had managed to piece together a fragmented understanding of the past trauma Kahu remained so reluctant to unburden himself of. Tala was a scout pilot who flew a condor in the squadron he commanded back in the glory days. Their relationship wasn't a romantic one, as far as she could tell, but more like the love that exists between siblings, Kahu often adopting a big brother persona on the rare occasions he spoke of her. She, like many other NTSC pilots, died during the Antonelli Expansion, but there was something about the circumstances of her death that had left him deeply traumatized. Clearly, it wasn't just grief: guilt and shame lay behind those tortured eyes, a sense of culpability, as if, at least in some way, he felt responsible for whatever happened to her. The truth of it would, unfortunately, remain a mystery; the old dog could get fairly loose-lipped after one too many syn-rums, but this particular point in his history was a nut that not even the most potent of serums could crack.

She reached over and touched his shoulder. Thinking the words, *You picked a hell of a time to go catatonic on us*, she asked, "Everything OK?"

He shook off his brooding reticence like a dog shaking off fleas. "Peachy, Skip . . . We're comin' up on the Mouth rat's coordinates now. Lei-Ghannam's shuttle should be comin' into view."

Sure enough, an object materialized in the brash glare of the floodlights—a craft resembling a door wedge fashioned from porcelain with a wide, black-tinted windshield and a single impulse thruster recessed into its stern. Like the pearl of an oyster, it had been encased in a frozen shell of *Devourer* detritus, completely hidden from anyone not already privy to its location.

"What's goin' on up there?" Teo's voice buzzed through the ship-wide intercom as she prepared to cycle the cargo bay airlock. "Is it here? Did we find it?"

"We sure did, kiddo," Delilah confirmed. "Looks like you and Null just saved our bacon. Are you ready to get outside and start your assessment? We need to know if it's pressurized and whether there's any residual power in the core. Last thing we want is to trigger a meltdown."

The girl returned a chipper, "Can do, Cap," before turning on her helmet audio and blessing the bridge with the crackly, lo-fi tones of her latest twentieth-century music obsession: a dark, chugging, rhythmic piece that built to a rousing crescendo, with melancholy lyrics about "breaking the chain."

The radar suddenly lit up with several unknown contacts that seemed to bounce and ricochet around the *Assurance* like pinballs.

"Don't worry about that," Kahu reassured. "There's some weird magnetic property to the alloy in this *Devourer* shit that sends the scope wackadoo. Probably why you hear so many ghost stories about this place."

He engaged the inertial dampers to bring the *Assurance* to a gentle stop fifty meters from the target. Reaching up to the overhead instrumentation panel to silence the chiming proximity alarm, he continued, "Don't see why we gotta faff around with all this remote piloting malarky. I've seen the girl cut through nanocarbon like it was gelato with that fission cutter of hers. Why not just pop the cork and ferry the booty into the cargo bay like we normally would?"

"The second we expose whatever's stashed in there to the vacuum it becomes worthless," Delilah answered. "Gotta think of it like a time capsule: the better we can preserve it, the more valuable it'll be to us."

"Plus, if there *is* pre-Collision booze in there," Teo began over the comms. "And it *ain't* stored in a hermetically sealed container, it'll boil in a second if we let the black in on it."

Kahu sat back in the pilot seat with his hands behind his head. "I should probably leave the finer details to the experts then, ey?"

"Think that'd be best," joked Delilah, resting her head on the electrical cabinet behind her. "It's just nice to finally be getting some work done. I really needed a distraction from the whole Vidalia situation."

"Yeah, I'm right there with you, Skip . . . If I had to spend another minute sittin' around listening to any more teen drama, I might have had to take a trip to the airlock and let the black in on myself."

"Teen drama?"

"Oh, you know." He nodded coyly at Isaac, the lad making stifled grunts of frustration as he struggled to integrate the shuttle's systems with the *Assurance's*. "Grease Monkey's got a thing for Bug-Eyed. The Mouth rat likes the Upperdecks kid, but he's been knocking boots with Bug-Eyed. Now the Grease Monkey wants to kick the shit outta him."

A distorted squall of shock exploded through the bridge speakers, Teo's sudden fury like a solar flare hammering the exterior of the ship.

"Shut your mouth you crazy old drunk," Isaac scolded, eyes still furiously glued to his pane. "You don't know what the fuck you're talking about."

"Sure . . . Last night sounded like a ruttin' nature documentary but *I'm* the crazy one."

Finding an incredibly inopportune moment to join the conversation, Tobias arrived on the bridge.

"Wow," he gasped, staring out through the windshield at their discovery. "So, you really found it?"

"Sure did, lover boy," Kahu replied, beckoning the lad over with a wave. "Lay thine eyes upon Captain Lei-Ghannam's treasure trove. I know you're stinkin' rich already, but I hope you're ready to get even stinkin' richer."

Looking like the humble twin brother of the obsessively groomed cavalier who joined the crew only several weeks prior, Tobias moved beyond the helm to peer out through the windshield, a look of perplexity sweeping across his unshaven face.

"That's *not* Lei-Ghannam's shuttle, Captain."

"The hell it isn't," blurted Kahu, almost falling out of his seat in surprise.

Delilah folded her arms and engaged the boy in a harsh stare as he turned to face her. "What makes you think that?"

"Well, the shuttle he famously jettisoned was a lupus-class—an incredibly rare range of luxury bunker shuttles, but that one out there is a Vulpix

R-40. I know because my father recently bought one just like it, you know, for emergencies."

"Of course, he did," Teo berated through the comms.

Furrowing his brow, Isaac blew an exasperated sigh. "I hate to say it, Captain, but I think he's right. The shuttle's encryption doesn't look anything like what I was expecting—far too modern to be pre-Collision."

"That don't make any sense," Teo said, silencing her helmet music, a note of uncertainty trickling into her voice. "The ping I detected definitely had a lupus-class signature."

"You weren't wrong about that," Isaac asserted. "But there seems to be a mismatch, almost as if someone physically swapped out the transponder."

"But why in the Abyss would anybody wanna do that?"

Delilah felt a pit in her stomach, the obvious answer to Teo's question dragging her entire constitution as though a malfunction had sent the sub-deck gravity emitters into overdrive. "To lure us into a trap . . ."

An emergency klaxon shrieked from somewhere on the main control pedestal. Kahu went rigid, muscular hands jolting back to his workstation. "You gotta be kiddin' me," he bellowed. "Skipper, the shuttle's self-destruct just armed itself. Brace for impact!"

Seconds later, a silent explosion unfurled like a blossoming rose of fire beyond the *Assurance*'s nose cone, followed by an almighty shock wave that violently shook the fuselage and knocked the vessel reeling off-kilter. Delilah shot a horrified glance at the feed coming in from Teo's helmet cam. The girl had only been a few meters out of the cargo bay when the blast struck, sending her careening back into the belly of the ship and crashing with a guttural "Oomph." She clambered to her feet and punched a glowing red button on a nearby panel, sealing the cargo bay doors and beginning the repressurization sequence.

Delilah staggered to the rear of the bridge, gripping the faded leather of Kahu's seat to steady herself behind him. "Report!"

"She's rattled, Skip," the old pilot replied, grappling with the flight stick to wrest back control. "But nothin' she can't handle."

"Just surface damage," Isaac confirmed. "Nothing structural. Hull integrity still in the upper nineties."

"How about you, kiddo? Any broken bones?"

"I'm alive, Cap," Teo spluttered over the blare of atmosphere rushing into the hold. "But shoot, if that didn't knock the wind outta me."

Feeling palpable relief, Delilah ordered Tobias to help the girl up to the med cubby, handing him a breathing respirator from the emergency locker before seeing him off in case of pressure loss. *We're not out of the woods yet.*

Kahu pitched the *Assurance* up and turned the vessel back on herself. Then, through the V-shaped windshield, two ominous shapes materialized in the darkness, hanging unnervingly still amid the constant motion of the Debris Belt. The first vessel she recognized as the *Esarhaddon:* an accipiter-class gunship, decommissioned by the NTSC and redesignated for bounty hunting. Taking the form of a shallow, oblique pyramid with smoothed corners and edges, the *Esarhaddon* bore an uncanny and frightening resemblance to the head of a snake, the two hard-point emplacements mounted on either side of its upper hull like wide, predatory eyes. Its new owner, Djoser Kern, was a small man of even smaller mind—a much-maligned Phalanx reject who made up for what he lacked in stature by commissioning the most fearsome ship in the fleet and using it to track down rogue captains who had fallen foul of the law. Delilah had never before been in water hot enough to warrant his attention; clearly, his code of ethics wasn't as superior as he projected, if it allowed for taking work from a criminal magnate like Vidalia Drexen . . .

Like a giant butane tank with a semicircular cockpit fixed haphazardly to its starboard side, the unmistakable profile of the *Segregator* skulked on the *Esarhaddon's* right flank—a pugnator-class freighter once captained by the late Jonah Sinclair, now under the command of his younger brother, Edmund: a mendacious, volatile man who made his older brother seem polite and well-balanced by comparison, here no doubt seeking revenge for Delilah's involvement in his death.

"Clever bastards," Kahu forcefully whispered, seeming genuinely impressed by the ingenuity of the trap they had just wandered into. "Lured us out here with that phony transponder signal, knowing all this *Devourer* crap would send the radar haywire. Crept up on our rear without us even suspecting a thing. Gotta hand it to 'em: that was one helluva bushwacking,"

"I'm glad you're impressed, but do you think you could focus on coming up with a way to get us out of this?"

A chime sounded from the comms console indicating they were being hailed. "Let's not make this any harder than it has to be, Holloway," Djoser Kern's brassy voice droned through the bridge speakers. "Submit to boarding and hand yourselves over peacefully."

"Screw that noise," came a second voice, this one perhaps even more unpleasant on the eardrums than fingernails scraped across a chalkboard. "This uppity bitch killed Jonah. And you know she's got a leech on that ship, right? I say we waste 'em."

"Absolutely not!" Djoser rebuked, appropriating the tone of a teacher castigating an unruly student. "Vidalia expressly stated he wants them alive."

Delilah leaned over Isaac's shoulder and thumbed a switch on the comms console. "I'm surprised to see an esteemed member of the Guild taking on work from the Governor, Djoser." An attempt to rattle the man, since he was famously ousted from the Guild by the other members who could scarcely tolerate the dishonorable nature of his pursuits.

"Oh please," he replied. "For twenty-five-k I'd work for the leech queen bee. Now for the last time. Submit! If we all play our cards right, then nobody needs to get hurt here."

"And do you think Vidalia will show us the same leniency once you hand us over to him? We either die here in the belt or die at the hands of his Monarchs. Which do you think is a worse way to go?"

"I'd like to not die at all if that's an option?" Kahu murmured.

Through the windshield, Delilah saw Djoser arming his hard points: two gimbal-mounted harpoon guns locking into position, each loaded with a barbed, three-meter-long, nanocarbon javelin that would make even the most seasoned whalers of maritime history jealous. Once fired, the menacing spears would pierce the *Assurance*'s hull and tether her to the *Esarhaddon* via unbreakable, braided-steel cables. The hauler's retrofitted impulse thrusters were some of the most powerful on the market, but no match for the sheer force Djoser's bounty hunting behemoth was undoubtedly capable of.

"You should have thought about *that* before you decided to cross him," the man grimly suggested.

Movement drew Delilah's gaze to the *Segregator*'s ugly, rounded nose cone as a magnetic rail gun deployed from a hidden compartment and target-locked the *Assurance*. Such armaments were strictly prohibited for civilian use since commercial ships were permitted defensive countermeasures only. But that didn't appear to have deterred Jonah from gearing his grub runner up for war . . .

"Disarm your weapons, Sinclair!" Djoser nagged. "You let your trigger finger slip here and you can kiss our reward goodbye."

"I don't give a shit about the money," Edmund hissed. "All I care about is making sure this traitor is made to pay. So, if I see that scrap trawler so much as flinch, I'm blowing her out of the sky."

Leaving the pair to their oddly public, open-channel domestic dispute, Delilah squeezed Kahu's shoulder and gave him the nod—the one that told him, *I hereby give you permission to do whatever insane, reckless thing you need to get us out of this predicament.*

Grinning, he cracked his knuckles and engaged the ship-wide intercom. "Everyone get strapped in and prepare for high G."

Yanking the flight stick to the left, he rolled the *Assurance* on her side, making her profile much harder for gimballed weapons to track. True to his word, Edmund fired a round from his illegal rail gun, the brilliant projectile screaming past the windshield and missing the fuselage by no more than a few meters. The old pilot then slammed the throttle forward, threading the *Assurance* through the dangerously tight space between the *Esarhaddon* and the *Segregator* and leaving them in the dust. Although the pursuing ships were fast traveling along a straight trajectory, they would be cumbersome to turn; Kahu had bought them some time, but not much.

Opting to remain in the Debris Belt, he slalomed in and out of the wreckage to create as much obstructed distance between them and the idiots behind them as possible. But it wasn't long before Djoser and Edmund caught up, both plowing through with tireless resolve, their robust hulls unscathed by the swamp of metal refuse occupying their path.

An explosion ripped through the fuselage as Edmund's next round successfully connected. "Impact!" Isaac yawped, the engineering console lighting up like Capella Promenade. "Shit! Hull's compromised; we're venting atmosphere!"

"Can you isolate it?" Delilah asked, straining her voice over the deafening wail of emergency sirens.

"Negative! The round struck us just above the galley. I need to get out there and patch it up! Kahu, you have to get us clear ASAP!"

"I'm workin' on it!" the old pilot answered, biting his tongue in concentration. He yanked the flight stick again, aggressively vectoring toward the *Novara*'s stern. Strapped into the jump seat at the rear of the bridge, the sudden change in velocity threw Delilah to the side, her seat belt cutting painfully into the skin of her neck. Kahu then maxed the throttle and accelerated away, forcing her body into the wall, the assailing g-force ripping the air from her lungs, the weight bearing down on her chest like a ton of bricks.

A suffocating sheet of hopelessness descended upon her as she confronted the absolute futility of fleeing; traversing increasingly exposed space, they became fish swimming in open water with hungry sharks following in their wake, frenzied by the fresh scent of their blood. They had no safe ground to go to: not the docks, not the Mouth. Their only option was to run until the fuel ran out, or until Edmund Sinclair targeted the fission reactor and triggered a meltdown of explosive magnitude. Neither choice proved particularly enticing, but both were considerably better than leaving the lives of her crew to the mercy of Vidalia Drexen, of which the man had demonstrably little to show. She would initiate the *Assurance*'s self-destruct sequence before allowing that terrible fate . . .

The outline of the *Novara* drifted to the starboard side of the windshield; she felt a cautious flitter of hope as Kahu's intentions became clear. He planned to reach the NTU perimeter—the negotiated boundary between NTU and *Devourer* airspace. With her nonhuman crew member aboard, the *Assurance* had been granted indefinite permission to cross that threshold, but any other vessel that dared trespass into the *Devourer's* protected airspace would be met by its ferocious interceptors. Djoser and Edmund would have no choice but to break off or face inevitable annihilation.

A second impact rocked the fuselage, cruelly snatching away her fleeting spike of optimism. This one she heard more than felt—a grating screech of metal accompanied by nowhere near as much concussive force as the one prior. Seconds later, sudden deceleration wrenched her body forward, slamming the contents of her abdomen against her rib cage.

"That rat Djoser just harpooned us!" Kahu spluttered, half-choked by his seat straps. "Got us hook, line, and sinker!"

The second javelin overshot them, skimming beneath the cargo bay and off into the Abyss, its steel cable coiling after it like a sewing needle threaded to the end of a spring. Kahu pushed the throttle as far as it would go, but the hauler strained in raucous agony to free herself. Speared by only a single harpoon, the old pilot still had some forward thrust, but it felt adjacent to a donkey pulling a bull by fishing line. Gazing through the windshield, Delilah could just make out the ring of flashing buoys encircling the *Novara* and delineating the edge of NTU space. *We're so close!*

Her first "Isaac," came out as a hoarse whisper, the second only just audible over the cacophony of blaring alarms and venting atmosphere. "Divert everything you can to the impulse thrusters. Take power from life support if you need to. We have to get past that perimeter!"

The artificial gravity went first; she felt sweeping relief as the weightlessness lifted her out of her seat, availing her of the raging vibrations caused by the desperate tug-of-war. Lighting, life support, fission reactor noise cancellation—as further systems went offline, she felt the power of the impulse thrusters increasing, the *Assurance* gradually finding the strength to pull away.

As Djoser launched a tirade of insults over the comms, Edmund swung the *Segregator* around to their bow, rail gun primed to fire. Delilah couldn't see the man's sinister grin through the tinted-glass canopy of his bridge, but knew inherently that it was there . . .

Not even the zero-g could save her from the succession of bone-shattering impacts that followed. The *Segregator* pummeled the *Assurance* with a brutal volley of magnetically catapulted shells, punching through the hull and making synthesized Swiss cheese of the fuselage. She had no way of knowing the status of Teo, Tobias, Null, or Mercy, and could only hope the incoming rounds had missed them, and that they had had the sense to pre-emptively put on their breathing apparatuses.

Pulling his own mask over his mustache, biceps rippling and bulging beneath his burgundy flight suit, Kahu pushed with all his weight against the throttle, the perimeter buoys outside edging ever nearer. Then, he seemed to recede. Sinking into his seat, his eyes widened at first in surprise, then shock, then terror. Tremors surged through his body, pulling trembling hands away from the flight controls as if hot to the touch. Delilah couldn't tell at first what had caused the bizarre reaction, but then, beyond the unshapely profile of the *Segregator*, she spied the source of Kahu's growing agitation: interceptors—the *Devourer*'s dreaded fleet of defensive fighters, racing out to meet them like a swarm of hornets. Only recently had they learned, thanks to Null and Mercy's insight, that the crafts were, in fact, unmanned drones, no longer piloted by cohabitors as had been the case during the Antonelli Expansion but controlled by the *Devourer* itself. Tobias had attested that this was almost definitely *not* common knowledge, which in Delilah's estimation amounted to either an egregious intel oversight on the part of the NTSC, or another mendacious alternative truth propagated by the Administration. Still, knowledge of their true nature seemed to do little to hamper the sheer terror they wreaked upon Kahu. He had planned for precisely this outcome but apparently failed to prepare himself for the reality of coming face-to-face with his age-old enemy once again.

"No," he whispered, then again in a pleading whimper. "Break off . . . Break off!" He placed his face in his hands, dreadlocks clutched tightly between fingers, voice breaking into a tremulous shout. "Break off Tala! You gotta break off now! You're too close. Tala! Break off before it's too late! Don't let them get in range. Break off now!"

Delilah unbuckled herself from the jump seat and floated over to the helm, using Kahu's headrest to maneuver around until she was all but straddling him. As the *Esarhaddon* began dragging them back into NTU space, Isaac leaned over from the copilot's seat and slammed the throttle forward to maintain positive thrust.

Apparently unaware of the welcome party approaching his rear, Edmund continued his vicious and disorganized assault. The portside impulse thruster took a direct hit, pulverized in an instant by a lethally accurate shot from the rail gun, which Delilah hypothesized might just have been possessed by the vindictive ghost of Jonah Sinclair himself. Stars spiraled through the windshield as the *Assurance* fell into a barrel roll, her trajectory thrown off by the uneven thrust.

"Snap the hell out of it, Heperi!" Delilah pleaded, slapping the man's face repeatedly, as if trying to wake him from a drunken slumber. But it was no use: the old fool was utterly transfixed, gawping with horrified eyes at the nearing flap of interceptors, muttering increasingly distressed and unintelligible nonsense about his long-dead squadmate. Try as she might, she couldn't free him from the ravenous quicksand of those memories. They had consumed him, and no amount of pounding on his chest nor screaming in his face could bring him back to reality.

She glanced despairingly over her shoulder to find Edmund's rail gun now pointed directly at the *Assurance*'s bridge, its elongated barrel disgorging blue sparks as it charged another round. But the obliteration she imminently expected never came; before Edmund could take the shot, the interceptors arrived—dozens of pebble-shaped objects, no larger than a swoop in size, with a smooth, glossy finish as if eroded over eons by wind or wave, almost imperceptible against the black of the endless night, if not for the faint, orange aurora enveloping each craft. With startling synchronicity, they formed a perfect sphere of evenly spaced points around the *Segregator*, much like the network of rudderless geostationary satellites orbiting the now-dead Earth. The *Assurance*'s sensors detected no particle burst, no plasma fire—no weapons discharge of any kind. The *Segregator* simply dematerialized, dissolving like sugar in water, taken apart on a submolecular level, and dispersed as atoms into the void. Edmund's anguished shriek lasted only a moment before fading to silence; it was as though he had never even lived, erased from the past, present, and future by the *Devourer*'s autonomous antiexistence engine.

Kahu's hysterics only worsened as he watched the disintegration unfold, the war-tested veteran now clutching onto his captain like a terrified child. She had long suspected the man of suffering from severe post-traumatic stress disorder, but the blubbering caterwauling he now exhibited left no question about the matter. *Did he watch the same thing happen to Tala?*

Needless to say, Djoser witnessed the fate of the *Segregator* and immediately broke off, cut loose the cable attached to the javelin still lodged in the *Assurance*'s fuselage, and retreated to safety.

"This isn't over, Holloway," he threatened over the comms as he sped away. She didn't doubt the man but could take solace in the fact that, for now at least, they were in the clear.

With the crew alive and accounted for, Isaac took control of the *Assurance* and used what little piloting skills he possessed to vector the crippled ship toward the *Devourer*. He had managed to isolate what hull ruptures he could with the systematic opening and closing of bulkheads but couldn't stem the venting atmosphere. They now had only one remaining option: head through the *Devourer*'s core and land in the District of the Mouth for repairs—a region that, if the NTNN was to be believed, had now been completely engulfed in conflict. She only hoped that the Governor would be too busy fending off Harmony to notice their arrival. Because otherwise, there would be things far worse than war waiting for them in the district.

FIVE

Jyn Sato recruited a handful of her most elite fighters and ventured into the war-ravaged streets of the Copper Swathes. After three long weeks of bloody skirmishes, the Mouth had been all but captured, with only a few remaining pockets of Monarch resistance scattered throughout the district. Passing ransacked storefronts and blackened chassis of burned-out vehicles, Oren Castegar led the way down a heavily embattled thorough-fare, his sharpened gaze scanning the shadows for any Monarch assassins who might be lying in wait hoping to put an abrupt end to the conflict with a single perfect shot. As Jyn's sworn protector, the Red Scythe, as his affiliates knew him, had argued with an assertiveness she would tolerate from no one else that traveling on foot constituted an unnecessary risk—especially when they had several of the Governor's rapid aerial personnel transports (known as raptors) at their disposal. With the sporadic pangs of marksman fire ringing out in the distance, his concerns had not been without merit. But after her conversation with Eamon Wyatt, she thought it important to subsume herself in the havoc her campaign had caused; to look fleeing residents dead in the eye and truly understand the misery and suffering her efforts had wrought upon them. Like a trapped animal gnawing off his own limb to survive, Vidalia's retaliation had become more frenzied and destructive as further territory slipped through his fingers, but she couldn't deny the truth that it was her own provocations that had precipitated the violence. She gazed across the rust-colored rooftops of the Copper Swathes at the blockade's immense edifice, resolute in her belief that, although tens of thousands inhabited this chasmic chamber, it should never be considered a home: it was a prison and war . . . merely the unavoidable cost of liberation. Eamon likely didn't see that now, but in time he would . . . or at least, she desperately hoped so.

Gather intel and derail or otherwise hinder any investigation into govern-ment involvement with insurgent activity. Those had been Madeline Vargos's orders upon Jyn's infiltration of DMED, and she had followed them to the letter right up until the moment she could finally break free from the administrator's chains. At no point had she planned on allowing herself to develop attachments—especially not to the very man she had been directed to keep tabs on. But Eamon's rugged charm, fearless outlook, and immutable dedication to justice had left a profound impact on her. She couldn't help but lament that she didn't have him by her side. After all, the need for subterfuge, her cruel masquerade, had since faded. She could finally lay herself bare to him—scars and all—and together, they could take the fight to those who had wronged them both so terribly, guiding all accepting of the Savior's light to a brighter future, and laying waste to any who dared resist. For now, it was just a fantasy because she couldn't say with any degree of certainty that he didn't still plan on killing her and putting an end to everything she had worked so hard to build. But *if* there was a chance she could convince him otherwise, help him see that Harmony were more than just a militia—then she had to take it. Otherwise, Eamon would become an obstacle. And not even someone she cared for so deeply could be allowed to stand in the way of her mission . . .

With a manic array of hand gestures that she only partially understood, the Red Scythe rallied the team at the foot of a crumbling wall, its surface pocked and punctuated by a crazed hail of bullet holes. Jyn peered around the corner into the deserted courtyard that lay beyond—a space she had loitered in with a ciggy and syn-coffee countless times before, now almost unrecognizable due to the haphazard fortifications strewn about like an abstract art installation crafted from reclaimed metal.

The DMED precinct house stood at the far side of the courtyard—a squat, four-story building with several rooftop landing pads for the department's fleet of aerial patrol vehicles. Squinting through the smoky haze lingering in the uncomfortably muggy air, she spied the double-door entrance leading to reception. It had been barricaded with a collage of blue and white bodywork, no doubt stripped in a panic from one of the older cruisers and hastily welded to the building's exterior cladding.

"They're hunkered down tight in there," she said, removing her hooded cape to reveal the button-down shirt and Kevlar vest that, not so long ago, had been her daily attire, reluctantly slipping back into her obsolete camouflage. "I'll go in alone first, see if I can't get them to lay down their weapons peacefully."

Skin encrusted like a rind of Martian sand, Oren shimmied up beside her, eyes still vigilantly tracing their surroundings. "We will do as you command, Composer . . . But are DMED not cut from the same cloth as the

Administration? Why should we not treat these heretic pigs with the same prejudice as the other oppressors?"

"This doesn't need to be a bloodbath," she answered. "These are good people; they've always had the district's best interest at heart, even if they're technically on Admin payroll."

A cohabitor who had been named Nix by aer cipher plodded toward her, emissions simmering. Ae effortlessly attained resonance and flooded her mind with a torrent of concepts, emotions, and imagery that she interpreted, *Allow one of us to go in your stead. Do not needlessly endanger yourself by confronting them without an escort. We cannot bear to lose you.*

She reached out and touched the hardened chitin plating of aer neck, singing a silent melody of gratitude and reassurance. Meeting the eyes of each of her comrades, she translated her empathic response into the dull, colorless modality of spoken language. "I know this crowd; they trust me. But the second they catch sight of *any* of you that may no longer be the case. I don't want this to end up in a shoot-out if it doesn't have to, so let me see if I can't talk them down first."

She tapped on her chest, signifying the microemitters clipped to each of their robes. "Activate your luma-shrouds and stay out of sight . . . Intervene *only* if and when I give you the signal."

"Yes, Composer," they chanted in unison. "Quell the dissonance."

"Quell the dissonance."

Like candles extinguished by a whip, Oren, Nix, and the others vanished from sight, rendered invisible by personal luma-cast stealth bubbles that reflected their surroundings—a relatively fringe technology, adapted from the stolen specs of Vidalia's luxury yacht, which hung over the district hidden inside its own illusionary sphere. With her retinue of phantom bodyguards following closely in step, Jyn crossed the dangerously exposed courtyard and approached the precinct house with her hands raised in the air, the acrid miasma of a recent firefight filling her nostrils, the glowing warmth of the Höllengarten beating down on her shoulders.

"Who goes there?" a hoarse voice called out from behind the barricade.

"Open your eyes, Keller, you stupid bastard. It's me!"

"It's the marshal!" said another voice, this one belonging to someone decidedly happier to see her. "Quick, Let her through!"

Like stage curtains forged from steel, the barricade parted, creating an opening just large enough for her to enter the premises. She stormed through reception exuding the precociousness and tenacity synonymous with the fictional iteration of Jyn Sato the DMED staff were familiar with—a force of nature imbued with enough grit and determination to ensure that, although some may have been unhappy about it, none had formally opposed her expedited rise through the ranks.

The uproarious atmosphere usually present in the bullpen had been hijacked by an oppressive stillness, the tension in the air as crushing as the intense pressures of the ocean deep. Deputies Keller, Kirst, and the team of enforcers and pencil pushers comprising the rest of the department staff had turned the spacious office into a fort, stacking desk cubicles up against the wall to barricade the windows and creating an inner safe zone with the remaining furniture. The contents of the armory lay in disorganized heaps in the center of the room—DMED's own stock of assault rifles, vipirinae SMGs, and a collection of confiscated firearms from the evidence locker were propped up against several ammo crates. They had even set up a makeshift medical area complete with a bed and a few preemptively deployed emergency trauma kits. To the best of her knowledge, neither of the factions currently tussling for power of the district had exchanged fire with anyone in the precinct house: neither Harmony nor the Governor's Monarchs. The building itself existed within the boundaries of a nonverbally agreed upon neutral zone. But judging from the level of armaments her old colleagues were preparing to make use of, they had yet to be made aware.

"Lei-Ghannam. You guys gearin' up for your own Battle of the Aristarchus Plateau or what?" but the catalog of frowns evoked by the comment suggested the staff were in no mood for Lunar Colony rebellion–based humor.

Deputy Keller was the first to pipe up. *No surprise there.* Looking as if operating on about three hours of sleep, with bags slung like purple hammocks beneath worried eyes and pallid skin matching the ash blond of his neatly shorn hair, he stood up from his perch near the mess table, thumbs hooked through the loops of his bulletproof vest.

"You got some nerve showing up telling jokes after going AWOL on us for four days. Did you forget you're supposed to be the marshal or something?"

As far as welcomes go, it was about as polite as she had come to expect from the man. After all, he made no secret of the utter contempt he held for her, almost to the point where she actually respected his forthrightness on the matter. Given his long tenure with the department, his many grievances stemmed from her speedy promotion from desk jockey to head deputy and then marshal, regularly citing that it was only due to Eamon's *having the hots for her* that she had been favored over him—nothing to do with his blistering incompetence or the fact that he botched just about every assignment given to him, of course.

In marked contrast to Keller's hostility, Deputy Maylenne Kirst looked all but ready to reach out and pull Jyn into a relieved embrace. "Last we knew you were out in the Cohabitor Ghetto helping coordinate the evacuation," the senior deputy said. She was a woman who had taken Jyn in like a doting aunt and proudly watched her ascend the ranks far beyond even her own career prospects. "When we heard Harmony had forced their way into the *Devourer*, we assumed you'd been killed or captured," she continued, wrinkled face blanched, SMG gripped in trembling hands.

"I'm sorry I left you all waiting," Jyn conceded. "It wasn't fair to keep you outta the loop, but I've been busy putting fires out all over the district"— a bald-faced lie, considering it was mainly she who had been setting them. "And it hasn't exactly been easy getting around. Drexen's mounted a bunch of auto-turrets to the deck of his yacht; turned it into a goddamn hovering antiair battery. He's swatting anything that's not flying Monarch colors outta the sky. Not even the Höllengarten harvesters are safe."

"One came down in the Warrens," Keller explained morbidly. "That rotten son of a bitch has got absolutely *no* regard for human life . . . or nonhuman, for that matter." He dropped his shoulders, swapping his supercilious attitude for a more earnest tact. "What's your plan here, Jyn? Because there's people dying out there by the dozens and something don't feel right about sitting on our asses waiting for the fight to come to us?"

"My plan?" Jyn repeated, one eyebrow raised. "The plan is we get the hell outta Dodge."

A susurration of shock and disapproval rippled around the room—not the reaction she had been anticipating, considering how terrified and exhausted they all looked. *Perhaps I've underestimated them.*

"You can't be serious," said Maylenne. "Turn tail? With everything that's going on?"

"We aren't prepared to fight a war," Jyn affirmed. "And frankly, neither are we expected to. It's easy to forget since we have our own jurisdiction, but at the end of the day, DMED operates under the umbrella of Phalanx, and by extension, the Administration. The top brass don't want us throwing our lives away for no good reason, so they've arranged transfer through the blockade for you *and* your families; even the Mouthborn among us who don't explicitly have NTU citizenship status have been given approval to cross the checkpoint."

"And how do you suggest we get to the Phalanx Compound?" One of the enforcers catechized from his watch post near a window. "The second we step foot outside this precinct house we're all dead!"

"Well, that's part of the reason I've been gone for so long," Jyn explained placatingly. "The truth is I've been parlaying with the Composer; trying to resolve the biggest damned-Abyss diplomatic incident since the Expansion.

She agreed to grant us safe passage to the compound if we lay down our weapons and surrender. She doesn't want things turning ugly any more than we do."

The temperature in the room seemed to plummet, winds of doubt sweeping through the bullpen and leaving her audience in the bleak clutches of suspicion. She had spent the better part of three years working to earn their trust, and in the span of a few blundering and unconvincing sentences, it appeared she had seriously jeopardized it.

A tumult of disapproval broke the silence, followed by several curt requests for clarification.

"What do you mean? The Composer is a terrorist; she can't be trusted! This is an outrage!"

Keller's voice cut through the clamor like a clap of thunder. "So *that's* where you've been: fraternizing with the enemy! You really think we'd be prepared to make a pact with that witch, leave the people *supposedly* under our protection at her mercy just to save our own asses? You've gone too far this time, Jyn; Eamon *never* would have stood for this."

"Yeah, well Eamon ain't here, is he?" Jyn replied, pinching the bridge of her nose. *You damned fools. I'm trying to save you.*

"You say that like you didn't have anything to do with it." Keller stepped forward, bringing his flaring nostrils inches away from her forehead. "Thing is, I always knew there was something fishy about you: little COTA reject shows up outta nowhere with *zero* prior enforcer experience and gets promoted to marshal in her first three years? I don't buy it for a second." He flicked his furious gaze around the room, setting piercing eyes on each of his colleagues one by one. "Don't you oblivious idiots see what's happening here? Jyn hasn't been negotiating with Harmony; she *is* Harmony. *She* saw to it that Eamon got the axe so she could take over the department and terrorize the district with minimal DMED interference. Now she finally wants rid of us but is too chickenshit to get her hands dirty." He met her eyes again, pressing the stock of his assault rifle against his shoulder, positioning her chest firmly between the iron sights. "Well, we *ain't* gonna roll over for the likes of you. You really want us gone? Then suck it up and kill us yourself!"

Jyn showed her palms, leaving her own weapon holstered so as not to further inflame the situation. "Gotta be careful making those kinds of accusations, Keller. I'd hate for people to think you're cracking under the pressure . . . Don't suppose you've got any evidence to back this insane hypothesis up?"

"It just so happens I do! Since *you* seemed hardly interested in picking up the investigation into the Composer after Eamon's extradition, I decided to start doing a little digging of my own. I have a source *inside* Harmony who indicated to me that the insurgent leader is a hyper-resonant *and* that she's marked by the Church of the Abyss. How many people in the district do you think fit that profile, Jyn?"

Not so incompetent after all . . .

His steadfast conviction looked to be rubbing off on the others, so she made one final attempt to talk him down off the ledge. Even Maylenne appeared to be subscribing to the man's denunciative ravings, staring at her from across the bullpen with the dolorous expression of a child who had just learned the truth about the Winter Solstice Elf.

The allegations were not without merit, of course: Jyn *did* want DMED out of the picture, although executing them wasn't something she found herself prepared to do—not because she didn't have the stones; the irritating truth was that she genuinely cared for them, and if she couldn't get the blabbering half-wit to shut his mouth soon, then he would force her hand.

Seeming as though his mind had been made up, Keller tightened his shooting stance. She, in turn, raised her hands and made two interlinked rings with her thumbs and middle fingers, moving them in a steady, circular motion above her head. To users of the ancient and relatively unchanged universal sign language, the gesture meant *harmony*; for Jyn and her followers, it simply meant *green light*. A chorus of horrified gasps erupted from the staff as a glistening veil of crimson cascaded from Keller's neck, his throat slashed by an invisible knife and opened like a zipper. A chilling visage of death, the Red Scythe disengaged his luma-shroud and materialized behind the deputy, who fell to his knees, thrashing and gurgling as he clutched his bisected esophagus. One by one, the rest of Jyn's accomplices appeared around the bullpen having crept in after her unseen—ghoulish apparitions springing into existence, each with a hybridized rifle trained on a separate target, greatly outnumbering those of the department staff brandishing weapons.

Jyn crouched low over Keller as he convulsed on the floor. She reached out and placed a hand on the breastplate of his vest, meeting his eyes as the final attenuated filaments of life slipped away. "I'm sorry, old friend. I wish you could have just listened to me." She stood up, keeping her gaze firmly on the now-motionless body lying at her feet, a pang of guilt tearing through her chest as she imagined the judgmental eyes of Eamon Wyatt scouring her from afar, watching in disapproval as the very thing she had promised him *wouldn't* happen inevitably did. *But what could Eamon possibly know about what it takes to win a war? What does he know about sacrifice; about having to make tough decisions that get people killed when the lives of ninety thousand hang in the balance?*

As noble as his intentions were, he had only witnessed a sanitized sliver of the hardships people faced in the Mouth, hardly making him the authority on deciding what level of collateral was acceptable to free her people from purgatory.

Dismissing Wyatt's imaginary objections, she lifted her head to address the room. "I had hoped no blood would need to be spilled today, but Keller left me with no other option . . . I suggest anybody who doesn't want to join the deputy drop their weapons immediately."

The staff did as advised—some without hesitation, others with visible reluctance. An especially hot-headed enforcer named Chet outright refused to relinquish his, but that soon changed when Nix took two hulking talon steps toward him and aggressively jabbed the muzzle of aer burst rifle into his sternum. Reeling, Chet threw his firearm clattering to the ground, turning his stare submissively to the dark pool of blood gathering around Keller's head—a truly gruesome scene, but necessary to deter them from considering taking up arms against her. They likely didn't understand it now, but through Keller's sacrifice, *they* had been given a second chance.

"Now listen closely," she commanded. "I imagine many of you will want to kill me—makes perfect sense why that might be the case. But know that attempting to do so would not be smart, nor conducive to living a long and healthy life." She scanned the faces of her old colleagues, witnessing a diverse spectrum of emotional responses: grief, anger, betrayal—none so intense as Deputy Kirst, who stood sobbing uncontrollably with her face buried in her hands. Strangely, little had tested Jyn's resolve up until that point more than seeing Maylenne cry . . .

"The administrator is dead," she declared. "She fell by Harmony's divine sword . . . Vidalia's forces are teetering over the edge of annihilation; we saw to that, too . . . Next, we move on the blockade, and when that happens, Phalanx will turn the District of the Mouth into the seventh circle of hell to try and put a stop to us . . . There's no tricks here; no deception. I am *urging* you to flee while you still have the choice . . . To any of you who wish to join us in our fight for freedom, justice, and security for *all* on the Coalescence, then we would welcome you with open arms." She glanced down at Keller's corpse a final time, silence ringing out in the space between her words, her audience as captivated as they were utterly petrified. "But make no mistake: this is a reckoning, and anybody who chooses to oppose us will face the same fate as the man before you . . . Submit to Harmony and you will live, pledge your allegiance, and you will transcend . . . Resist, and suffer the consequences."

SIX

yn stood alone on a metal gantry, suspended across the center of a room with steeply chamfered arrises and gray cushioned surfaces. Dim spotlights ran in concentric rings around her, shining up from below and dappling through the laser-cut grating beneath her feet. A burning stench invaded her nostrils—a smell like ozone or singed arm hair redolent of something she couldn't quite place, her surroundings spawning feelings of familiarity and comfort, underpinned by the lurching sense of doom inhabiting her every fiber . . .

Glancing down at the vibrant collection of beads and sumptuous cloth scattered around the footbridge, it dawned on her that she stood not just in a room, but an airlock—reclaimed by the Church of the Abyss and transformed into a place of worship, dressed at present for ceremony.

This is my rite of passage, she thought, the intoxicating nearness of the Divine and Everlasting Night inspiring an overwhelming sense of awe. *I am to be baptized in the Abyss, my body and spirit given over to the one great emptiness so that it may live in my heart for the rest of my days and until our ascension to the Grasslands of Pasture.*

In mere moments, the elliptical bulkheads occupying the wall before her would open and the cosmos would reach in and pull her into its cold embrace, permeating every iota of her unworthy being. She felt a gush of excitement; finally, her chance had come to prove her faith to her family and fellow congregants. She would be reborn anew, her soul sewn into the seraphic tapestry interweaving all life throughout the universe.

But before her excitement could reach its euphoric pinnacle, a wave of unease crashed violently upon her mental shores. She raised her hands before her face, finding the skin on her arms embossed by intricate patterns of black, protuberant veins, reaching up toward her shoulders and neck. *This can't possibly be my rite of passage,* she thought, *for I already bear the mark of someone baptized in the Divine Abyss . . .*

Perplexment spiraled into panic with the realization that her wrists and ankles were free instead of bound with safety tethers, as was customary for the proceedings in question. Her imminent exposure to the vacuum of space was only meant to be very brief—as long as the human body could withstand without succumbing to ebullism or hypoxia. Without the necessary bindings, she would be consumed, dragged beyond the threshold into the merciless black and forever lost to the void, a lonely mote of frozen organic matter adrift in an infinitude of nothingness.

She spun around in futile hope that the airlock entrance might still be open, but only further despair awaited her as she found the blast doors to her rear sealed shut. Through a honeycomb arrangement of pentagonal-shaped portholes, she saw her family watching her growing alarm: her two younger brothers, Haneul and Tae-hyung, screamed her name in tears, their anguished cries failing to reach her through the thick panes of glass separating them. Her parents stood beside the boys, dressed in their Church of the Abyss regalia: indigo cassocks flourishing black collars detailed with intricate silver embroidery. In stark contrast to her brothers' distress, her mother and father had a look of blissful contentment about them, sharing a wistful smile with their hands clasped in prayer, perfectly at peace with what would soon transpire. Only then did the horrifying truth of Jyn's situation dawn on her, arriving in her fraught mind like a funeral procession to its destination.

This isn't a sacrament: it's a sacrifice . . .

Spinning warning lights transformed the airlock into a disorienting carousel of flashing orange and contorting shadows. The bulkheads opened with such speed that they seemed to disappear, jettisoning her like a shell from a cannon into the endless night, the force of the ejection ripping the air from her lungs. Like plunging into a pool of ink, the gulf lurking beyond the ancient confines of the *Novara's* hull smothered her senses; there was no light, no sound—just Jyn, alone with the crushing silence and the utter desolation taking root in her chest.

I'm alive! she thought, feeling like a rag doll in a tumble dryer, her sense of up and down, light and dark cruelly snatched away. *Why in the stars am I alive?* She posed the question to herself not in relief, but in dismay, for the Divine Abyss, in its wrath, had seen fit to bestow upon her a fate far worse than asphyxiation: a dizzying and unending tumble into the depths of oblivion, never to know the sweet release of death but, instead, cast adrift for all eternity.

She let out a scream, which by all accounts she shouldn't have been able to do in a vacuum, but she did anyway, with such volume and force she thought it might split her throat or rupture her eardrums. Strangely, the sound became dampened, muffled—its sharp edges softened as if heard through five feet of concrete. She felt an unusual sense of detachment from it; though her vocal cords strained painfully, the sound seemed to resonate from elsewhere, surrounding and enveloping her like a silk blanket. Gradually, it transmuted into the canorous swell of an orchestral string section, each symphonic breath a wave of soothing warmth, lulling her into an increasingly relaxed state. The reason the ethereal music put her so at ease was that she recognized it: Beethoven's Symphony no. 9: Adagio molto e cantabile, performed in D minor by the Hellas Basin Symphony Orchestra—an all-time favorite, and in her humble opinion, one of the most enchanting and emotionally moving classical pieces ever written.

The exquisite melodies caught her like a butterfly in a net. She began to sink lower and lower, the inescapable hand of gravity pulling her from somewhere beneath, eventually depositing her into the cradling arms of an old corduroy sofa. She recognized the antique's musty odor and the feel of its coarse, threadbare material beneath her fingertips. It instilled in her feelings of home and safety, although she soon came to realize that these emotions stemmed not from the sofa itself, but from the individual she found herself sharing it with . . .

She brought her head to rest on the chitin-encased shoulder of the cohabitor slouched beside her. Ae nuzzled her cheek with the tip of aer snout in a reciprocation of affection. Lighting the fires behind her eyes, she journeyed deep into aer psyche, allowing the tide of aer emotional and experiential essence to wash over her. Ae sang a silent melody of admiration and valor, aer keen intellect and steadfast dedication cutting through the darkness like the beacon of a lighthouse. In a strange and unfamiliar place, she found refuge in aer imposing physique and comfort in aer nurturing and protective way. Ae took her in when all else had abandoned her; ae gave her purpose and offered her the guidance and direction she craved so fervidly. *But who are you?* she thought. Searching the labyrinthian hallways of aer mind for an answer, ae presented her with a response in the form of a single concept: *absence*, meaning, *the Prey do not have language, so I do not have a name.*

Then "Absence" is precisely what I'll call you.

The scenery shifted from an abyssal expanse to a teeming marketplace. Jyn and Absence sat together beneath the canvas awning of a spare-parts stall, its shelves overflowing with miscellaneous tech and chaotic bundles of wiring. Before them, resting atop a cabinet made from imitation wood, sat the source of the sanguine music: a vintage turntable built into a leather-bound suitcase, sporting a rose-gold tonearm and pitch dial. She watched the gentle rotation of the record platter, allowing the sound waves to soak through her skin and seep into her soul. Through resonance, the profound emotional reaction the music elicited in Absence bled through into her own, culminating in an overpowering mélange of awe, sorrow, and joy. She felt the childlike wonder the glorious tones engendered in aer; with no knowledge or understanding of human orchestral instrumentation, no frame of reference with which to identify *any* of the sounds ae could hear, it felt to aer, and through resonant extension to Jyn, like pure magic.

Then, before the long-departed orchestra could build to their triumphant crescendo, the turntable gratingly began looping the same few discordant seconds, the needle head bobbing up and down as it became stuck on a warped section of vinyl. Jyn found watching the motion bizarrely entrancing, lured like a moth to the flame deeper into a disquieted transfixion, the skipping audio like a cage entrapping her mind. She finally managed to break free her gaze, finding herself no longer sitting on the sofa but now kneeling down on a cold, steel-plated floor. A lightning bolt of anguish tore down her spine, the hairs on the back of her neck standing on end as she beheld the horror manifesting before her. Arms and legs shackled in place, Absence lay on an inclined gurney positioned at the center of a sterile chamber. Sharpened medical implements hung like rows of metal teeth from hooks on the wall, the array of power tools strewn about the floor suggesting the space had been outfitted for something far more sinister than surgery. A man wearing a mask, an apron, and blue nitrile gloves stood at aer side, using a pair of heavy-duty bolt cutters to pry apart a section of the chitin of aer left bicep, twisting and tearing aer exoskeleton apart for what seemed like little other than senseless mutilation. The cohabitor wailed in agony from the breathing orifices in aer neck, rattling the entire chamber with aer fruitless efforts to break free. Jyn felt the nauseating cracks and pops of aer iridescent shell breaking apart with such horrific visceral clarity it was as though the torment was being visited upon her, too.

"Stop," she pleaded, rising to her feet. "You're killing us . . . Please, stop! You're killing us!"

Lunging forward with arms outstretched, her hands collided with the shimmering meniscus of hard light projected like a barrier across the entrance to the chamber. She slammed her fists repeatedly against the fission field, every impact sending painful jolts of energy screaming up her wrists and into her chest. But the man performing the procedure cared little for her desperate pleas for mercy, continuing his gruesome work with callous disregard.

Absence dolorously turned aer head to face her, defeated, despondent, aer emissions as dim and flickering as dying candlelight, aer beautiful carapace a jagged, mangled corrugation. She tried again to break through the fission field, pounding her fists until her heels were bruised and raw. It felt like suffocation, the oppressive weight of helplessness like a hand gripped around her throat, a wretched anchor dragging her beneath the surface and down into the icy depths of despair.

Then, a hand reached in from somewhere beyond, shaking her forcefully by the shoulder. Dazed and disoriented, she jolted awake to the sight of Oren Castegar looming over her bed, his blue eyes like lucent baubles in the gloom of the encampment barracks.

"Our enemies need not waste their efforts sending their assassins to kill you," he said, standing at her bedside bare-chested, the layer of scarlet residue caking his muscular torso cracked like a parched desert terrain. "These nightmares of yours cause so much distress that I fear one day you might snap your own neck in your sleep."

Jyn propped herself up and massaged her aching forehead, the harrowing imagery still seared into her psyche. "They're not nightmares . . . They're more like echoes, memories—sometimes mine, sometimes Absence's, all mixed up and amplified as if looped through a megaphone."

Oren rarely exhibited zeal for anything other than smiting heretics, so he gave a creditable nod to acknowledge, but register his disinterest in, her sleeping woes.

"You managed to get about four hours in total . . . Nix came by wanting to speak with you about something, but I sent aer away."

She touched his hand, thanking him for both his vigilance *and* his patience.

"Your thanks are unnecessary," he answered in deep, growling tones. "I know how dangerous unconscious resonance can be for a cipher. Your mind is a train that will run away and derail if left to its own devices."

She nodded soberly. "It's a risk we can't afford to take. If any unwitting Prey come within resonant range while I'm out, it could result in fatal synaptic overload . . . I'm just grateful to have someone to watch over me, or else I really could injure myself."

With arms as broad and coarse as redwood tree trunks, he delicately helped her up, fetching her hooded cape from the footlocker at the end of her bed.

"You are the one true Composer, the Will of the Savior and messiah to my people. It is my duty to ensure that no such fate can befall you . . . Besides, I am accustomed to having to protect the sleep sanctity of those I hold dear . . . There was a time when I had done the same for Xander . . . Before . . ." He trailed off, averting his gaze.

Before he killed himself, Jyn mentally completed the sentence. She carried her thoughts back to a time before Harmony, when her fight for liberation had been limited to Absence alone, and not all ninety thousand inhabitants of the Mouth. But as it had turned out, ae was not the only nonhuman dissident incarcerated beyond the blockade for crimes against the NTU. There had been another whose freedom she managed to secure by selling her soul to Madeline Vargos. Xander Castegar, Oren's older brother and longtime collaborator, had been the closest thing Harmony had to a director before the administrator hijacked the movement and installed Jyn as his successor. More political agitator than insurgent leader, his disruptive anti-union demonstrations had caused enough of a nuisance to incur the wrath of the Quarterdeck autocrats. Because of his notoriety and constant presence in the media, however, Xander proved nigh untouchable, but the same could not be said for his cohabitor counterpart . . .

Zilch, as he had named aer, was imprisoned for subversion in his stead, and subjected to the same horrific torture that Absence had endured. Tragically, ae succumbed to aer injuries shortly after aer return to the Mouth, hurling Xander into a catastrophic spiral of grief and depression from which he never recovered. Because there was nothing more painful to bear for a cipher than the loss of their resonant partner . . .

The cracks in Oren's stoic facade began to show, sadness pulling at the corners of his brown lips. "That selfish coward," he seethed. "I will never forgive him for abandoning us like that, for giving up hope when we needed him most."

Jyn dipped her head into his eye line to catch his stare, placing a hand supportively on his shoulder. "Xander didn't die by his own hand; we must never forget that . . . Like Zilch, and like countless others, he was murdered by the union, by the sinners languishing in the Upperdecks who seek to exploit, oppress, and enslave our people . . . We can never bring back what those monsters have taken from us, but I promise you this: we *will* make sure our kin didn't die in vain."

As if an omnipotent hand reached in and flicked the reset switch on the back of his neck, Oren squared his broad shoulders and recovered his infamously surly demeanor.

"Our enemies will wish they had accepted the light of the Savior. We will destroy the blockade, eradicate the Administration, and blaze a path to salvation!"

Jyn smiled like a proud mother, moving her hand up from his shoulder to softly cup his cheek.

Some would argue Oren's dedication to Harmony had crested dangerous levels, that his allegiance had developed into something closer to fanaticism. But she knew it was only his means of coping with Xander's death: by channeling his grief into the cause. She saw it as a strength rather than a weakness, taking solace in the fact that, no matter what happened, no matter who sought to bring their machinations against her, she always had his abiding devotion and lethal skill set in her arsenal. Though he might occasionally question her decisions, he would never betray her nor refuse an order. Save for Absence, she could think of no one else with whom she could trust so implicitly. And when the list of people who wanted her head on a platter grew by the day, that was something she didn't take lightly.

Once Jyn fully roused from her slumber, Oren disclosed that the reason for Nix's visit had been to pass on a summons from Absence, which, at a time when their respective roles in the organization strived only to pull them further apart, exclusively happened when ae had something important to discuss.

Not wanting to keep aer waiting, they exited the barracks and headed out into the encampment proper—a cluster of compact modular buildings, complete with an armory, an infirmary, a vehicle repair bay, and a combat information center. These same prefabricated structures would have been used to house the first colonial settlers had the *Novara* successfully completed her expedition to Pasture. But fate, as it were, had a different purpose in mind . . . Ciphers knew the vast habitat chamber in which Harmony had erected this forward operating base and temporary settlement as the Magnanimous Hollow—a rough interpretation of the emotions and concepts the Prey attributed to it. Jyn craned her neck to survey the enveloping cavity, likening it to the interior of a magnificent cathedral carved into a mountain of obsidian. Lambent moss grew in dramatic sweeps of glowing orange around the cavernous walls and ceiling, scintillating in the vitreous surfaces and bathing the ring of yurts, built around its perimeter, in the same coppery haze as the Höllengarten.

It was here, deep within its immense, biomechanical shell, that the Savior protected and provided for the Prey after uplifting them from ruin. The space reverberated with the drone of a thousand bleating, trumpeting cohabitors, the warm air suffused with the rich, woody pheromone they exuded when they felt content and relaxed.

The Hollow was their ancestral womb, the primordial cave in which they weathered the storm of the endless night after escaping an eon of predation. For Jyn, just standing in a place of such historical significance inspired overwhelming feelings of reverence and humility; though she had only recently taken her first steps inside, her own personal association with this place stretched back for the better part of a millennium. A little-known gift of hyper-resonance was the granting of access to not only the memories of those she achieved resonance with but to the memories of their ancestors too, a daisy chain of knowledge and experience passed down like an heirloom through the generations. It was precisely this evolutionary mechanism that had allowed the Prey to survive the Apex for so long. A caveat of sentience, she had come to believe, was a level of instinctual ineptitude. Just as a human would have insufficient skills to build a nest or spin a web without extensive prior tuition, the Prey relied on this cascade of wisdom, built on the success and failures of their forebears. to evade and defend against their ancient enemy. Every cohabitor was, by their very nature, an expert historian, and resonance afforded Jyn that same vicarious hindsight. She could cast her mind back centuries and recall with striking lucidity the sights, smells, and sensations of being uprooted from her world and chased across the cosmos. She remembered the biting ache of starvation, her four stomachs growling as her new host struggled over decades to meet the dietary requirements of her species. And she remembered the fear and uncertainty she felt as every new paradise the Savior delivered her to subsequently burned in the ravenous fires of the hunt. She saw and felt these things as vividly as if she had experienced them in person—the trials and tribulations of an entire people, inscribed like a subliminal encyclopedia onto the parchment of her mind. It was the primary driving force behind her compulsion to fight for their deliverance; she knew firsthand what they had been through, the challenges they had overcome. To see such a noble, courageous, and spiritual people relegated to the fringes of society in the name of old wounds spurned a vengeful tempest in her belly. She knew in her heart that humanity and the Prey could live in harmony together, that they could thrive as equals in true pan-species society. But not willingly would the oppressors beyond the blockade relinquish their cruel monopoly on the Savior's blessings. Until they could be removed from power, the bright future she envisioned could be no more than a fantasy.

Jyn had done some terrible things in her time since assuming the role of the Composer: she had killed people, turned the home she loved into a war zone, and even forced many Prey from their most hallowed ground—the stubborn loyalists who refused to accept Harmony rule. She wasn't blind to the suffering this campaign had wrought, nor ignorant of the innocent lives lost in the pursuit of freedom, and the countless more that would surely follow before her mission was done. But this, unfortunately, was the cost of deliverance. War loomed like a dark cloud on the horizon—inevitable, as Eamon had once lamented.

No, she decided. *Not inevitable: necessary.*

Just beyond the boundary of the encampment lay a bustling staging area. Here, several of the Governor's appropriated raptors hovered on idling repulsor pads, each cutting the fearsome, chrome-black outline of a giant rhinoceros beetle. The fifty-strong elite strike force known as the Choir busied themselves near the vehicles, training in hand-to-hand combat and preparing an arsenal of hybridized weaponry in anticipation of the upcoming operation, the decisive advance that would see the Governor's toxicity expunged from the Mouth once and for all. Wearing brown cape coats over slim-fit polycarbonate body armor, they stood to attention as Jyn and Oren passed through, pressing their forearms together vertically before their faces and chanting "Savior's blessings," and "Quell the dissonance." This group of fearsome warriors was among the most devoted of Jyn's acolytes, their unquestioning faith matched only by their thirst for vengeance, their unrivaled skill in combat and militaristic obedience undoubtedly the primary contributing factor toward Harmony's many victories in the fight against Drexen. Incorporating humans and cohabitors of a varying degree of tenure, some were even grizzled veterans heralding from *both* sides of the Antonelli Expansion, now fighting side by side, having discovered their resonant compatibility during the decades of conflict in the Mouth. Ancient history tells of bloody civil war in which brothers were forced to take up arms against one another. And yet, during the Expansion, brethren were unified on the battlefield, their petty differences evanesced in the light of the Savior.

Of the five Phalanx defectors who had since pledged fealty to Harmony, three fought alongside their Prey counterparts. With their empathic link providing enhanced combat awareness and their intimate knowledge of the enemy they faced, they would be the tip of the spear in the impending offensive against the NTU.

"The Choir are ready to deploy," Oren reported. "Give them a target and they will strike fast and true."

Jyn kept her reply subdued so that only he could hear, humbly bowing her head to her adoring disciples as she passed. "The Governor has been allowed to keep his pestilential hold on the district for far too long . . . We may have successfully cleansed the streets of his Monarchs, but our people can never truly know what it means to be free while that viper looms overhead . . . Their target is his yacht . . . I don't want it destroyed; just do whatever we have to do to rid it of its infestation. It must stay airborne for the advance on the blockade."

Oren flashed an uncharacteristic look of concern. "But how can we commandeer what we cannot see, Composer? The coward hides like a vole beneath his luma-cast veil. And with the antiair battery he has affixed to the deck, a straightforward aerial assault can only result in failure."

"Absence has a plan," she reassured. "Every day, ae gets one step closer to unlocking the true potential of the signal . . . Whatever countermeasures Drexen has in place to thwart us, they won't matter."

"I hope you're right," he muttered, turning solicitous as he eyed the battle-scarred commandos grouped around them. "The Choir will gladly die for the cause, but that doesn't mean we should throw their lives away needlessly."

Jyn reached out and touched his hand, feeling the grainy texture of the bloodfall residue covering his skin. "Have faith in the Savior, love . . . Absence and I aren't making this up as we go along. Every decision we've made, every action we've taken, has been done heeding the guidance given to us through the Pyre . . . It hasn't led us astray so far; there's no reason to suspect it will now."

"I do not mean to cast doubt," Oren clarified, dipping his gaze in a slight show of submission. "It is no small feat, how far we have come. But we cannot allow our triumphs to cloud our judgment. A reckless decision now could cost us everything; I only want to make sure you are certain this is the right move."

"I'm certain: as sure as the night is everlasting . . . Call it prophesy or prescience—whatever you want—just know that you can trust me on this. Drexen's time is up . . . Today, the Glow Syndicate falls."

They left the staging area and ventured into a series of interconnected pathways that cut through the uneven terrain of the Magnanimous Hollow and fanned out like a web from its center. Through shared ancestral memories, Jyn could personally recall digging out this network of shoulder-high trenches many centuries prior—an effort by the first Prey inhabitants to carve out a home in this strange and unfamiliar environment, contending with the pullulating mounds of coagulated ink that seemed to dominate the ground.

Taking a dizzying succession of lefts and rights, she mused that this circuitous maze would have been all but impossible to navigate were it not for the spectral ribbons dancing overhead—billions of glowing spores, condensed into individual streams of light, meandering from the outer walls of the cavity and inward to its core.

Ciphers knew the bright nucleus where the luminant strands converged as the Pyre, doubtless because of its uncanny resemblance to a raging inferno. Simmering over a structure distinctly reminiscent of a cauldron, this concentrated particle storm was, as far as she understood it, the Savior itself—a twisting, churning mass of pure, cosmic consciousness; a celestial higher power possessing its colossal machine husk like a poltergeist. Though its true nature remained a mystery, its qualities of nobility and altruism were easy to perceive. It defended and cared for the Prey, it had given Jyn and many others the gift of resonance, and—despite the constant aggressions demonstrated by the NTU—it persisted in sustaining the lives of the million-plus beyond the blockade who demonized it with such vehemence.

It had *more* than lived up to its name in her estimation and, as they left the trenches, she felt a faint smile touch her lips, feeling its benevolent radiance kissing her cheeks, beckoning her closer like a wise elder, eager to soothe her woes and impart the knowledge accrued in its eons of existence. Contrastingly, she saw Oren's brutish frame shrink, her stouthearted bodyguard and master assassin reduced to a quivering boy by what lay before him. It wasn't an unusual reaction—quite common, in fact. Because, for all the feelings of wonder and veneration the Savior inspired, it also inspired fear—fear stemming from finding oneself in the presence of something incomprehensibly alien, unfathomably powerful, and possessed of a technology that, for all intents and purposes, might as well have been witchcraft.

She knew that for the *uninitiated* it could be an unsettling experience; for her, any aversions had since been nullified by the astounding revelation that she had the power to communicate with it . . . Historically, the Savior's role in resonance had been limited to an impartial observer, initiating the connection but never directly involving itself in the discourse. The final endowment afforded Jyn by her hyper-resonance, however, was the ability to establish a direct line of contact, in effect, enabling a rudimentary form of telepathic dialogue.

In practice, it felt about as legible as attempting to communicate underwater with tin cans and string, leaving far too much room for guesswork and interpretation. Nevertheless, it was this unique ability that had earned her the title of the Will of the Savior among her adherents: the one it entrusted to relay its warnings, advice, and aspirations.

Even now, as Jyn and Oren stepped out onto a fibrous basin that acted as the iris encircling the pupil of the Pyre, they were swarmed by people begging for the latest word from the Savior or offering messages of thanks and appreciation to be passed along. A young couple even presented their sickly newborn daughter, tearfully begging for Jyn to persuade the Savior to use its healing light to cure her ailments.

"I'll see what I can do," she assured them, knowing full well that any such request would go unheeded. The Savior's mission was the extrication of entire species; it harbored little concern for the plights of individuals. But, like worshippers of any other deity, it was her people's belief in the possibility of personal miracles that spurred them on, that gave them hope when all else was lost. Cruel or not, she took it upon herself to propagate and nurture their delusions, because those without hope had nothing to fight for . . .

"Make way!" Oren's booming voice cleaved the crowd of hopefuls asunder, clearing a path to Absence's workshop. Situated on the opposite side of the Pyre, a mountain of eviscerated bio-machinery stood as a grand, if slightly repugnant, monument to the cohabitor's many years of invention and experimentation. Aer growing interest in hybridization manifested as a visible increase in the density of human tech present in the pile, becoming more prevalent toward its peak like narrowing layers of sedimentary rock. A structure resembling the concert shell of an auditorium occupied a flat at the very summit—a meshwork of recycled computer components glued together with a glistening secreted residue. A kaleidoscope of electric figments composed of thousands of blinking LEDs flitted like butterflies across its surface, the synapse of an artificial neural network firing in frantic, but clearly coordinated entropy.

Jyn and Oren ascended a flight of steps comprising a succession of metal plates lodged like surgical staples into the compacted viscera. At the top, they found Absence toiling among a huddle of storage crates, workbenches, and terminals, reams of indecipherable code cascading synchronously across the array of surrounding monitors.

A congregation of cohabitors lingered around the perimeter, rocking gently from side to side, seeming as if both studiously observing a lecture *and* reverently attending a sermon. Because Absence was *more* than just a teacher: ae was an engineer, a xeno-biologist, a philosopher, and a religious leader combined into a single role, aer chosen field existing at the unlikely intersection between fringe science, philosophy, and theology.

Many adolescent Prey strived to glean aer unrivaled comprehension of the Savior's anatomy, often as part of a ritual pilgrimage, charging themselves with inventing or discovering some new way to better the lives of their people as they came of age.

Absence, however, over the years had become far less receptive to constantly having a gaggle of mythering onlookers watching aer every move and would occasionally perform an abrupt threat display to ward them off. Jyn struggled to discern whether this increasingly aggressive behavior was merely a symptom of aer growing older and grouchier, or an unfortunate result of empathic trait transferal . . . Hyper-resonance was so rare that no definitive scientific study had yet been carried out to fully explore its capabilities. And yet, she had grown more and more convinced that certain personality traits belonging to her parents were beginning to rub off on Absence, sticking to aer resonant essence like pollen to a bee. The more memories of early life she shared, the more ae seemed to exhibit her father's explosive temper and her mother's curt and fastidious personality—a far cry from the gentle, endlessly patient soul who had all but adopted her after she absconded from COTA.

Good thing ae hasn't inherited their infanticidal levels of religious fanaticism, too . . .

On this occasion, *she* found herself on the receiving end of aer irascibility. Ae drummed aer talons into the ground, raising aer hackles as she and Oren approached. Like static behind the eyes, she felt their empathic bond fizzle into existence; a tirade of interrogatory queries regarding her whereabouts arrived on her tongue, accompanied by a furious flurry of red and white mental flashes.

"Will you get off the damned ceiling? I was sleeping, OK?" she groused, habitually relaying her retort of empathic indignation into Union Standard, which she usually did for the benefit of any nearby humans. Life and death decisions were often made through the medium of resonance, and she felt it important to air the conversation aloud so nothing could be misconstrued or lost in translation.

In response, she felt Absence's irritation transmute into regret over the ungracious welcome ae had given her. Ae huffed concededly, then placed a paw to aer thorax before motioning gently toward her. *You are before me, and I, before you.*

She reciprocated the gesture and joined aer beneath the domical framework, casting a doleful glance at the damaged and time-worn chitin of aer aging exoskeleton. The sections that had been removed during aer incarceration had never properly regrown, a grizzly ravine of purple-gray scar tissue and mutilated plating excavating its way from aer shoulder down to aer pelvic carapace. Larger cracks that left fleshy areas covering vital organs exposed had been plugged with the use of a fusible cermet; the metallic branches creeping across aer torso reminded her of something her uncle had called "Kintsugi"—the ancient practice of repairing broken pottery with lacquer and gold.

Oh, uncle. I know we didn't always see eye to eye, but I swear by the Divine Abyss, those neofascist thugs will suffer for what they did to you . . .

Oren moved toward a large object positioned just beyond the workstation and concealed beneath a blue tarpaulin.

"Absence had us extract this from an abandoned NTSC hanger deep within the Vestiges," he explained, ripping the sheet away to reveal an MX-8 auto-turret, the dual Gatling barrels mounted on either side of its armored chassis cutting the intimidating profile of a charging bull.

"We pulled it off an old accipiter-class gunship . . . The vessel had two other hardpoint mounts but they had been pillaged before we got there . . . Though we didn't encounter any Monarchs, we found the remnants of one of Drexen's capping plants. It's safe to assume the missing turrets are the same ones he is using to defend his yacht."

Jyn tilted her head in focus, the details of Absence's plan beginning to take shape through a combination of resonance and intuition.

"We took the ground from him," she replied. "With a little faith, we can take the sky."

A simple idea had manifested in her mind—one she had insufficient technical basis to prove, but now believed without any doubt. There existed an order of functional similarity between the neural cortex of a grenadier and the guidance matrix governing the automated turrets. Absence's means of reappropriating the dissemination signal to bypass the Administration's hardware encryption could potentially be used to turn Drexen's antiair battery against him . . . *Genius.*

Leaving Absence to prepare a demonstration of this breakthrough, she turned her attention to the source of the raspy, labored breathing emanating from just outside the workshop. Her gaze settled on a topless middle-aged man, sitting slumped with his wrists bound behind his back, tied to a metal pole that had been dug into a ledge overlooking the Pyre. He had been badly beaten, his bare chest bruised purple and black, a garnet curtain of clotted blood hanging from his misshapen nose and draped over his chin. He strenuously lifted his head as she approached, quickly averting his gaze in shame, defiance . . . fear.

Oren gave the captive man—named Heston Aldrich—a hard kick to the thigh.

"The sentries at the gates caught this rat trying to escape the Hollow," he explained. "They nearly executed him on site, but I thought you might want to have words first."

Heston spat a mixture of saliva and blood on the ground near Oren's feet, then glared up at Jyn with bloodshot eyes. "I think we understand each other perfectly well."

"I disagree," she replied, raising a halting hand to prevent Oren from kicking the man a second time for the show of insolence. "Of all the people who I thought I might have to worry about plotting against me, your name was honestly at the bottom of the pile . . . You and Rien are two of our best medics—together, you've been keeping Harmony healthy since Xander was in charge . . . I'm struggling to understand what happened that made you want to go flapping your mouth to DMED?"

"Do you know what they call us beyond the blockade?" Heston asked in a choked voice, staring distantly. "They call us terrorists, insurgents—they think we're nothing but vicious murderers, and they're right. They're absolutely right."

Jyn crouched down to meet his eye level. "And why should slaves care about the opinions of their masters? Every revolution in history has been tarnished under the same brush. Calling what we're doing an insurgency is just another means of keeping us down."

He shook his head, chest and shoulders convulsing as he struggled to regulate his breathing. "This stopped being about liberation a long time ago: it's about vengeance . . . You promised us a better future, but all you've managed to do is get people killed. Your psychotic reign of terror won't be over until you've butchered every poor idiot on the *Novara* who refuses to submit to your ideology." He spat blood again, his entire body now shaking in either terror or fury. "*Someone* had to try and end this madness. I didn't want it to be me, but I wasn't left with much of a choice. Once I found out that you were doubling as a deputy for DMED, I had to get a warning out to someone who could put a stop to you."

Jyn let out a sigh of disappointment, standing to her feet and staring down at the defiant whelp with a look of contempt. "Well, Oren just opened up your contact's neck all over the floor of the precinct house, so a fat lot of good it did in the end. Keller wasn't a bad guy, and by choosing to involve him in this little plot of yours, you might as well have held the blade yourself."

A mechanical discord of gears and servo motors juddered behind her as Absence powered up the automated turret. She turned on her heel to find the behemoth rotating ninety degrees, left and right, scanning its environment for potential hostiles. Disconnected from the targeting computer of its accipiter-class host, and not to mention the fact that it was built for ship-to-ship combat and *not* an antipersonnel weapon, it subsequently failed to find any.

"What will you do with Rien?" Heston asked over her shoulder, his voice quiet and timorous. "Ae didn't have any part in this . . . P . . . Please . . . do whatever you want with me but don't punish aer, too."

Jyn turned to face him. She crouched low and hooked her hands under his clammy armpits, pulling him up to his feet and propping him against the metal pole.

"I know ae wasn't directly involved," she reassured, initiating her bond with Absence and bathing the man's sweaty, bloodstained features in the amber luminescence of her emissions. "However, ae *is* guilty of trying to keep your disloyalty from me, and with so much at stake, complicity is just as serious as committing the crime itself . . . Unfortunately for you both, there can be no secrets when it comes to hyper-resonance. I only had to get within ten feet of Rien to learn the disappointing truth . . . Perhaps, in your last moments, take solace in the fact that ae didn't willingly sell you out . . . Rien stayed faithful—right until the very end . . ."

She left the mournful traitor quietly sobbing to himself and returned to Absence's workstation. Then, she took a ruminative glance over at the Pyre as it began to bloat and swell, signaling the coming of the dissemination. Singing a silent melody of cautious anticipation, Absence began turning and manipulating an object resembling a clockwork sphere fashioned front stone in aer paws. Connected to a pane with a hybridized data cable, ae built the device to translate aer deft movements into command inputs—an arcane computing solution for a cohabitor who had begrudgingly gained an unprecedented understanding of human programming language but despised ever having to use it.

The concert shell pulsed rhythmically, emitting a digital heartbeat that Jyn could feel thumping beneath her diaphragm, accompanied by a buildup of static electricity in the air, the hairs on the back of her neck standing on end as if rubbed with a syn-wool cloth.

The Pyre surged like fire doused with kerosene, reaching up toward a manifold structure molded into the Hollow's high ceiling—a cluster of ventricles through which the Savior's blessing of knowledge and warmth would be funneled out into the Mouth and dispersed across the district.

An errant strand broke free from the Pyre's central mass, its orange hue alchemizing into a volatile pink. It jerked and slalomed erratically toward the workshop as if obsessively following the cracks in an invisible plate of shattered glass, eventually plunging hungrily into the turret's robust chassis. The machine bull made a futile effort to buck off its phantom rider, quickly succumbing to the overpowering influence of Absence's hijacked signal, its firmware wirelessly rewritten by invasive strains of biomimetic code.

Heston unloosed a whimper of shock as the turret snapped in his direction. He winced, forcing his eyes shut as its dual barrels spun up, faster and faster until the rattle of its motorized rotors built into a strident drone. Primed to engage, its twin firing pin assemblies actuated, but instead of an ear-splitting volley of rapid machine gun fire, there came only the thudding clunks of its empty chambers lusting for ammunition, its infeed belts disconnected and coiled on the floor like chain-linked centipedes.

Heston slumped back down onto his haunches, breaking into a manic half laugh, half cry—the irrational response of a man who had accepted death, only to be denied its embrace at the very last second.

Jyn turned to Oren, who stood at her side wearing a perplexed expression that suggested he too had expected a bloodier end to the demonstration.

"Take him to the infirmary and put him back to work with Rien," she ordered.

"But Composer! You cannot allow this traitor to live! The last thing he deserves is mercy!"

She waved a hand to cut him off, growing weary of the incessant second-guessing. If she wasn't so sure his constant objections were coming from a good place, she might have had to seriously reprimand him. "We're about to have a whole lot of wounded, Oren," she rebuked. "We can't afford to lose *any* of our medical support . . . Keep him under tight guard and confined to quarters . . . If he tries to escape again, you'll just have to break his legs . . ."

Watching as Oren reluctantly marched Heston back to his post in the encampment, Jyn observed a riot of flowers and confetti burgeoning in her mental space, a sublime concoction of Absence's jubilation and her own pride at aer apparent success, enveloping her in a silent symphony of resonance. But then, in a moment of uncertainty, the flowers began to wilt, and the confetti turned to ash. Suddenly overwrought with dread and concern, she glanced over to find the elderly cohabitor staring worriedly into the Pyre. Something was wrong: the light of the Savior began fritzing and waning like the flame of a candle reaching its final millimeters of wick. Through a medley of imagery and emotions, ae projected a complex idea into her head: that this technical breakthrough had come at a terrible cost—continuous manipulation of the dissemination signal was causing severe and irreparable harm to the Savior, and failure to cease could result in potentially devastating repercussions.

"I know," she groused through gritted teeth. Because it wasn't the first time ae had expressed this worrying sentiment. But at such a late juncture, she saw no other option than to press on.

In their brief and somewhat ambiguous contact, the Savior had given its blessing to continue their efforts despite the obvious damage they seemed to be inflicting. Or at least, that's how she interpreted the cryptic responses she received when querying it on the subject.

Seeing now the extent to which the Pyre had been affected, she pondered whether the time had come to touch base with it again.

Feeling a note of trepidation, she stepped out onto the ledge where Heston had been tied up as a crowd of onlookers gathered below, eager to catch a glimpse of the exchange between their prophet and their Savior.

Gazing into the dimming but no less resplendent glow of the Pyre, a calmness descended over her. She felt an unusual pull of gravity in her chest, as though something had engaged in a game of tug-of-war with a length of rope attached to her chest, siphoning her soul out of her body through a keyhole on her sternum. She dug her heels into the ground to prevent the illusive force from dragging her off the ledge and into the spuming mass of lambent spores beyond. The Savior reached out in turn with its divine light, catching her in an ascendant net and immersing her in the shallow waves of its otherworldly awareness.

"I'm here," she said, feeling the nervousness in her voice, her long black hair twisting and swirling around her head in the radiant breeze. "I need to talk to you . . . I need to know how you want us to proceed?"

A response came from somewhere within—one voice, or many voices, repeating inward endlessly and speaking in perfect unison; a sound so deep it proved almost inaudible, its low and strangely harmonic cadence rattling her bones and reverberating in her chest cavity.

"Quell . . . dissonance . . . conflict . . . terminus . . . engender . . . unity."

She swallowed the lump in her throat, feeling droplets of sweat rolling down her forehead and collecting on her brow. It felt so unnatural—this nascent mode of communication. Whereas the simple act of attaining resonance usually culminated in a relatively pleasant experience providing an instant hit of serotonin, communing with the Savior seemed to activate something primal in her brain. She didn't fear it, and yet, it triggered an immediate fight or flight response, an unexplainable and implacable compulsion to stand her ground, or turn tail and run . . .

"We're trying," she finally replied, regaining her composure. "But there can't *be* unity until the oppressors are removed from power. Manipulating the signal is the *only* way we can ever hope to take the *Novara*. But it's clearly hurting you . . . I fear if we stay the course then something terrible might happen."

The mysterious pull of gravity increased; she moved her feet into fighting stance to resist its influence, the souls of her combat boots squealing against the layer of fused silica covering the floor of the workshop.

"Relinquish . . . self . . . endure . . . pain . . . acquiesce . . . sacrifice."

She felt a catch of frustration, wanting more than anything to impetuously demand clarification, aware that doing so would reveal to those watching below just how little comprehension of the Savior's intent she really possessed. These were the same responses she had received time and time again and, without the emotional or visual accompaniments provided through resonance, they were just words—scrambled, incoherent words that she could only make her best guess at interpreting.

"Don't be a martyr," she articulated, once again taking the disjointed string of syllables as the Savior's way of declaring its intention to jump on the proverbial grenade. "Your courage is admirable, but if continuing along this path means we could potentially lose you . . ." She shuddered, clutching her chest at the agony the mere contemplation of that possibility spawned. "Surely there *must* be another way. Even if it ultimately means peace between the Prey and the human remnant—we don't stand a chance without you!"

"Harmony . . . necessitate . . . cessation . . . absorb . . . cognizance . . . quell . . . dissonance."

The light of the Savior flared, then faltered. The phantasmal hand released its hold on her and retracted into the Pyre, almost as if storming angrily out of a room and slamming the door shut behind it. Then, there was calm.

Absence touched her shoulder from behind, gently guiding her out of her trance. Ae didn't possess the power of comprehension to commune with the Savior aerself, but Jyn had empathically shared the details of the conversation as best she could to keep aer in the loop.

She contemplated for a moment the nature of their bond, forcing herself to question whether, if something *did* happen to the Savior, they would still be able to attain resonance with one another. *And how could there ever truly be unity between the Prey and the human remnant if our only means of inter-species communication suddenly goes kaput?*

She knew Absence shared her concerns because she felt her own fears and anxiety bouncing back at her, ballooning and intensifying in a resonant feedback loop.

Ae projected a harrowing vision into her mental space—a memory gleaned from the darkest recesses of her mind, sent back to her now as a ghastly improvisation in a game of psychic charades. Against her wishes, and much to her distress, she saw Anaya Lahiri against the stark backdrop of an airlock, restrained by syn-leather straps to an upright stretcher. The woman's once-brown skin appeared the same ash gray as the hoary streaks in her wavy hair, her gaunt face a visage of anguish as she pleaded desperately for her life.

Of all the terrible things Jyn had done to convince Administrator Vargos of her subserviency, none haunted her quite so much as her interrogation and execution of the whistleblower. As justified as it had seemed at the time, and with the greater good and the interests of the district firmly in her focus, she didn't know how she had ever managed to do something so cruel . . .

Absence knew it remained a particularly upsetting memory—the remorse and self-admonishment recounting it usually triggered—and had chosen it specifically as a means of emphasizing aer point. The question ae wished to convey, as far as she understood, was *When is enough, enough? How much pain are we prepared to inflict and how much are we really ready to sacrifice in exchange for our freedom?*

She turned to face aer, staring intensely into those old, tired eyes—eyes that had seen the Collision *and* the Antonelli Expansion, that needed to rest after two centuries of hardship and turmoil. But Absence couldn't rest until ae had laid the foundation for a brighter, more hopeful future for aer people. And she had pledged her life to help aer achieve that goal before aer time of passing finally came . . .

No more deliberation, she told herself, sharing the sentiment by resonantly projecting an image of the antique hourglass her Uncle Sato kept on his office desk into Absence's mental space. *We move now, no matter what it takes, no matter the cost.*

SEVEN

The Savior unleashed a thundering chime from somewhere deep within its core—a cannonade of heavy brass heralding the arrival of the midcycle dissemination. Taking their cue, the Choir separated into two strike groups and loaded into the procured raptors, departing the Hollow for Drexen's yacht to a chorus of cheers from loved ones and supporters eager for their safe return.

The Governor's dwindling forces had abandoned the war-ravaged streets of the district for the safety of their master's hidden sky fortress, their last bastion and where the battle for the Mouth would assuredly reach its bloody conclusion . . . Jyn remained hopeful for a smooth execution of the plan with minimal casualties. Then again, she wasn't naive; she knew that in his final moments, Drexen would embody a feral feline backed into a corner, bearing fangs, and lashing out with razor-sharp claws. Just as her wise uncle would often muse about whichever politician had embroiled themselves in the scandal of the week: *Men who think themselves impervious can be dangerously unpredictable when made suddenly aware of their own mortality . . .*

Even with the significant ground Harmony had gained in recent days, victory was by no means assured. As much as she loathed Vidalia and everything he stood for, she could at least appreciate his ruthless tactical prowess. Undoubtedly, he would have one final card hidden up his sleeve—a delightfully insidious countermeasure ready to deploy at the very last second to tip the scales.

Don't underestimate him, she told herself, ensconced in the claustrophobic cabin of the lead raptor—a nylon-upholstered womb that reeked with the conflicting smells of pine-scented air-freshener, gunmetal, and sweat.

"Did you say something, Composer?" The question came from Isabella Graddock, who sat in the opposite seat with her spine ruler-straight and her eczema-blanketed hands clasped in her lap. Jyn had been so deep in thought that she had unintentionally mouthed the words, which Isabella—the vexingly observant old harpy—had immediately picked up on.

"I said we can't underestimate him," she reiterated, aloud, this time, sitting forward to address the others in the cabin, surrounded by a massif of the roughest, toughest sons of bitches on the Coalescence, armed to the teeth and positively foaming at the mouth for violence. Sandwiched shoulder to shoulder with gladiators, ex-soldiers, and mercenaries, Isabella appeared as a tiny porcelain doll, buried beneath mounds of brown rags by comparison, but she had far more to contribute than mere brute strength or skill with a fission blade . . . The woman had once used her cunning intellect to serve as one of the NTU's leading reconnaissance operatives and military strategists—infamous for orchestrating the offensive that pushed the revolting Prey back into the Cohabitor Ghetto at the turning point of the Expansion . . . That, of course, had been another life—one she had since availed herself of in pursuit of a greater purpose. *In pursuit of Harmony.*

"No. We cannot" the woman replied, gazing beyond her withered reflection into the punishing darkness looming beyond the passenger side window. The raptors had not yet left the esophagus connecting the Savior's internal structure to the expanse of the Mouth, and so there was little to see but the mech-organic lining of the enclosing passage. "To underestimate one's opponent is to concede the upper hand . . . We should assume Vidalia knows *precisely* what we intend, and has multiple preventative measures employed to stop us."

She turned to face Jyn with dull eyes darting sporadically from side to side, her computer mind calculating and assessing all possible outcomes, treating even something so benign as a simple conversation like a game of chess. "That's why it's critical he isn't killed in this assault . . . Vidalia *must* be captured alive."

Slumped in the seat beside Jyn, Oren had barely been paying attention, fiddling instead with the organic bulblike structures seeming to grow from the stock of his spliced XT-90 rifle. But Isabella's suggestion appeared to physically drag him by the ear into the discussion.

"You think this is the time for jokes, defector?" he blurted. "Drexen will be dead before he even knows what's happening."

"I've got a joke for you," japed Isabella in a croaked voice. "What's big, red, confoundingly stupid, and is liable to get us all zeroed if he doesn't do exactly as he's told?"

"You need to elaborate, Graddock," Jyn interjected, repressing a smirk as she waved a hand to stop Oren from rising to the insult. "We're talking about assassinating the second-most dangerous man on the *Novara*, here. There can't be any room for interpretation."

Isabella let a stern demeanor take her, running spindly fingers through her short gray hair and straightening her posture before responding. "I've done extensive psychological profiling on Vidalia," she divulged. "The narcissist prattles on about being a self-made man—'built his empire from rubble' and all that tosh. But, in reality, he was born into a wealthy family and raised as an only child, which means he will more than likely have an *if I can't have it*, no one *can* attitude when it comes to his prized assets . . . Make no mistake: the Governor *will* scuttle his yacht before he lets the likes of Harmony take it from him—even with his people still aboard, he'll burn it all down just to get the last laugh."

Jyn tightened her lips, casting eyes to the footwell in consternation. Admittedly, she had come to suspect exactly the same thing, but to hear the words uttered from the lips of someone with such an impressive tenure in the special forces made the worrying possibility even *more* of a reality.

"He almost certainly has a neural uplink," Isabella continued, tapping the base of her skull where it met her slender neck. "A kill switch that will trigger the vessel's self-destruct sequence upon his death . . . Only once we've apprehended Vidalia and disabled said uplink will it be safe to execute him."

Oren relaxed in his seat, seeming more content now he understood that the man's demise was merely being delayed, not postponed indefinitely.

"Don't worry, Big Red," Isabella reassured, reaching over to touch his knee. "You'll get your chance, but we need to treat this as a hostage rescue—take out his remaining Monarchs with lethal precision while making sure he *isn't* harmed in the crossfire . . . If things don't go to plan and we have no choice but to corner him, then he mustn't have a firearm . . . Remember: he'll be more than happy to put a bullet in his own brain pan if it means taking us all with him." She formed the shape of a gun with her fingers and thumb, pressing it against her temple and miming the action of blowing her brains out to emphasize her point.

"This is why we keep you around, Izzy," Jyn said fondly, tipping her head in appreciation. "Do Nix and the others know about this? With them carrying out the head-on attack, they'll need to be doubly cautious watching their line of fire. Those augmented ARX-40 LMGs pack a *real* punch."

A wistful smile graced the tight corners of the woman's lips, her frosty bearing thawed by the mere mention of her dearest. She glanced outside to the nearest raptor as it scudded along in formation, its black, Kevlar-coated armor marred by streaks of signature Harmony brown, as if slashed by the rusted claws of a chimera. Through tinted windows, Jyn could just make out several cohabitor heavy gunners crammed inside, as well as the unmistakable profile of Nix—Isabella's long-term resonant partner . . .

"Distraction tactics," the woman said. "Vidalia knows all too well that the Prey's hardened exoskeleton makes them perfect for a frontal assault, so he will expect to see mainly cohabitors in the initial advance. But really Nix and aer strike group's primary objective is to draw his attention to the main deck—make enough noise so we can sneak up undetected through the lower levels and put an end to this discreetly."

The woman's eyes illuminated as she and Nix forged a mental bridge, the light of the Savior connecting their minds across the empty space between the raptors.

"Nix knows aer assignment and is ready to do aer part . . . We can rely on aer implicitly," she concluded, sitting back in her seat, and giving herself over to the bond.

As a hyper-resonant, Jyn could have effortlessly *tapped the line* to glean the details of their exchange, but she strictly prohibited herself from using her talents for such a blatant violation of their privacy. To many, resonance was no less mundane than hailing someone over the luma-caster. But Isabella considered the bond she shared with Nix deeply personal— almost sacred. After all, it was only thanks to their serendipitous run-in during a thwarted reconnaissance operation that she even became aware of her empathic abilities. POW policy at the time among the predominantly pacifist Prey had been to bring them to the Hollow, hoping futilely that an audience with the Pyre might somehow dispel the excessive rage and aggression that seemed to saturate the minds of their human counterparts, to convey that open war had never been their intent, only the defense and preservation of the Savior.

Isabella's experience with this forced edification had proven far more transformative than for most; she often described her resonant awakening as *bungee jumping into a Monet,* or *tearing away the monochrome veil and seeing in technicolor for the first time in my life.* She stood as a testament to the power of resonance: a once dedicated unionist—adamant in her condemnation of the leeches and their mutinous abettors—completely rehabilitated by a simple glimpse of the beauty and splendor lurking just beyond the threshold of human sensory perception, given the means to truly understand and empathize with the Prey perspective.

Isabella wiped her nose with the sleeve of her robe. Jyn spied a lonely tear mantling down the woman's wrinkled cheek, understanding innately, even without the help of resonance, that the pair were exchanging goodbyes in case something happened to either of them during the assault.

She pulled her hood over her brow and withdrew into herself, tracing with fingertips the dark, protruding veins scoring her forearm, quietly wondering whether she and Absence should have done the same . . .

* * *

Through the riot shield bolted over the raptor's windscreen, Jyn observed the telescopic opening at the terminus ahead widening like a dilating pupil. The crushing tenebrosity occupying the tunnel capitulated to the bright surge of copper daylight pouring through. The transports sped through the new aperture and departed the Savior's core via the vortex of daggers occupying its exterior—the long-dormant excavation machinery used to gouge out and terraform the titanic chamber of the Mouth over a century ago.

Beyond the hood, it was as though an entire city had been swallowed intact by a yawning sinkhole, canopied over by a rich thicket of lambent foliage. Jyn couldn't help but marvel at the sight of the oxidized expanse materializing before her, its dense, disorganized construction scored by streaks of neon color, the light from luma-cast street signage seeping through the material awnings delineating its irregular lattice of courtyards and alleyways.

On the one hand, this place was a monument to the brutal oppression and persecution her people suffered. But it also stood as a shining beacon of their endurance—their ability to thrive and persevere through the most abhorrent of circumstances. She remained resolute in her belief that the NTU's neglect of some ninety thousand mouthians would ultimately be the catalyst of its undoing. Because it was in the fires of adversity that their immutable courage and resolve had been forged. Now, Harmony had achieved what DMED and Phalanx had failed to do: rid the district of the malignant tumor that was the Glow Syndicate. Jyn had broken free the Mouth from the shackles of addiction, and all that remained necessary to spark revolution was to send a message to its residents that the time had come to rise up. . . Once she had claimed Drexen's yacht, with its state-of-the-art luma-shroud projection tech, she would have the power to do just that . . .

Skating along an empyreal track of wavering luminescence, the transports followed the path of the dissemination signal as it ascended meanderingly toward the top of Tycho Block.

"In all the little chats you've had with the Savior," Isabella began, eyeing the pillar of intact superstructure climbing from the heart of the Copper Swathes. "Did you ever manage to ascertain what the purpose of that eyesore actually is?"

No, Jyn thought. *Because* that *would require coaxing out a straight answer, which is usually harder than squeezing blood from a stone.*

Instead of owning up to the truth that her ability to parse the messages given to her by the Pyre was anything but infallible, she surmised, "It's like a signal amplifier or a waveguide . . . The Savior only has enough juice to output a single stream; there's something about Tycho Block's structure that focuses and disperses the signal across the district to reach as many people as possible . . . Just an added bonus, I guess, that it puts a roof over the heads of a lot of people."

She traced the trajectory of the signal as it snaked toward a scintillating spire of what resembled ice, which had been erected, or perhaps sculpted, atop the pinnacle of the tower. Here, the luminous ribbon divided like a beam of light striking a prism, refracting into a web that cascaded down toward the many receiving pylons standing on rooftops below. The midcycle dissemination was already in progress, and yet, scanning the space below the Höllengarten, she couldn't see anything that suggested Absence's remote sabotage had begun . . .

She caught a flash of black in her peripheral vision as one of the raptors toward the rear of the convoy closely overtook them. Bracing herself as a rush of agitated air rocked their port side, she maneuvered out of her seat and clambered over Isabella to lean into the driver's compartment.

"Who in the Abyss was that?" she barked at the startled pilot.

"It's the second-wave team, Composer," he answered promptly, wrestling with the yoke wheel to regain control. "Think they might be a little too eager to get to the fight."

"Open a channel and tell them to kill their altitude, now! We have to stay out of range until we can confirm those turrets have been neutralized!"

The pilot hailed the wayward raptor, which had now ascended past the rooftop of Tycho Block and continued its climb. But before he could even begin to relay Jyn's order, Vidalia Drexen revealed himself . . .

Movement drew her attention to an area of seemingly empty space several hundred meters above the district: a shimmering aberration caused by a salvo of screaming projectiles tearing through the luma-shroud concealing the yacht. The rounds ripped through the atmosphere like flaming crossbolts, striking the runaway raptor and scoring several direct hits to its undercarriage. A bright blue detonation of silica tile and fission energy erupted from its breached repulsor pads, sending it spiraling into a nosedive toward the rookery below. The terrified screams and brays of the men, women, and cohabitors aboard came shrieking through the cabin speakers, inspiring in Jyn a sense of helplessness that she could scarcely bear to endure. Then, a foreboding static rang out as the transport careened into the Warrens, the *kathoom* of the impact echoing chaotically around the Mouth.

Oren and the others bowed their heads in prayer, pleading for the Savior to guide and safeguard the crossing of their fallen comrades. Isabella jumped out of her seat and pressed her nose to the window, gazing despairingly into the fireball fulminating from the crash site.

"Those reckless imbeciles," she rasped. "They just cut our forces down by a third!"

"Do we still have the numbers to pull this off?" asked Jyn, fighting to prevent the wave of grief she felt at that instant from debilitating her capacity for rational decision-making.

"It'll be a stretch," warned the strategist. "We just have to hope Nix's team can keep Vidalia's Monarchs occupied long enough for us to get to him. Because they just lost their reinforcements."

The pilot nosed down into a steep descent, bringing the convoy low over the empty streets of the Copper Swathes. Armed with an approximate knowledge of the yacht's position, he wheeled around the district and used the monolithic shape of Tycho Block as cover, staying out of sight of the Governor's aerial defense platform. Jyn fell prey to a flood of apprehension; if for whatever reason the plan didn't work and they were forced to retreat to the safety of the Savior's core, then it would necessitate a suicidal dart through precariously exposed sky. Either they were shot down pressing on with the attack or shot down attempting to escape. Just as she felt the icy needle-tips of panic pressing into the back of her neck, Absence's handiwork finally made its triumphant appearance . . .

Two branches of pink-orange light splintered off from the dissemination signal's primary stream. Like blind snakes hunting by smell, they slalomed erratically through the air in the general direction of the turret fire's origination point. Then, having located their prey, they penetrated the yacht's protective veil to begin working their wicked magic. Jyn waited with her heart in her throat, focusing intently on the Governor's position. There came another bout of localized ripple distortions. The spherical perimeter of the luma-shroud revealed itself in sporadic bursts of garbled static that twisted and stretched the fabric of reality. She watched the rhythmic pulses of muted muzzle flashes emanating from within as the failing projection struggled to suppress them. Feeling the accompanying drum of steady gunfire resonating in her chest cavity, she imagined the mayhem taking place on the terrace as the automated turrets suddenly turned on the yacht's unsuspecting crew, and found herself in the unusual position of hoping Vidalia had hunkered himself down somewhere safe . . .

Don't die on us yet, you slippery bastard . . .

Heartbeat pounding like a rising war drum, she gave the green light to engage. Nix and aer team of shock troops accelerated away on an intercept course, ready to board from the front and lay down heavy fire. Meanwhile, Jyn's pilot took their raptor skulking beneath the vessel and began a gradual vertical ascent. Soon, they passed through the malfunctioning luma-shroud, transitioning from a peaceful sky into a war zone encapsulated within a glitching snow globe.

The chrome-clad keel of Vidalia's Indah-2 aerial superyacht hung overhead, its elongated shape growing larger as the pilot continued his steady approach. He swung around to the vessel's stern and brought the sliding passenger door up alongside the boarding point situated on the afterdeck. The last of its kind, the yacht had once been mass-produced at the Agaiya Eclipsis Shipyard in New Singapore, before the *Novara* departed Sol, and so schematics had been readily available in the archives of the Silk River Concourse. Scouring the ancient blueprints had revealed that the aft entry hatch led directly into the lazarette, which could be used to access the parlor and study on the main deck via a narrow stairwell. If Vidalia had a bunker or a panic room that he could scurry away to, Jyn suspected they would find it somewhere in the main living spaces.

That's where we'll finally put an end to this . . .

The passenger door slid open, making way for the calamitous din of the carnage taking place up top. Nix's team were already in the throes of their assault, and by the sounds of it, had been met with heavy resistance. They were more than capable of handling a few exhausted, demoralized Monarchs, but judging from the degree of retaliatory fire, Jyn feared that her hope for zero friendly casualties may have been foolishly naive . . .

The Red Scythe and his band of silent blades disembarked first to ensure the afterdeck remained clear of hostiles. Jyn and Isabella followed, stepping out onto the lavish real-wood deck, and subsuming themselves in the polished steel and glossy white surfaces of Vidalia's ostentatious citadel.

Moving with a degree of elegance that stood in direct contradiction to his bulky frame, Oren formed up against the aft entry hatch and reached into the inside pocket of his hooded shawl. He then produced a clear bag containing a pair of enucleated eyeballs, dried blood filling the creases in its rumpled plastic like a plexus of vessels.

"The eyes of the highest-ranking Monarch I could get my hands on," he said in an almost bragging tone. "Thane Locke was his name. Put up a good fight; died well . . . Both retinas are intact, and I kept them on ice as requested."

Isabella grimaced as she took the bag, pinching its corner between finger and thumb as if dangling a rat by its tail. "I would thank you for volunteering to undertake such a gruesome task, were I not so confident you thoroughly enjoyed it."

He smiled grimly. "Had the time of my life."

She lifted the contents of the bag up to the biometric retinal scanner positioned beside the hatch. The receptacle projected a cyan laser grid onto the organs, sifting through its index of logged irises for a recognizable match.

"This yacht was high-tech in its heyday but has seriously outdated security by modern standards," she imparted. "I sincerely doubt Mister Locke ever thought he'd be assisting a band of freedom fighters in murdering his boss, but death is a funny old thing."

Oren gave an uncharacteristic smirk, eyeing the old strategist with just a hint of mischief.

"Do they not have a saying, defector . . . 'Beauty is in the beholder of the eyes?'"

The woman thinned her lips in impatience. "I think you might be paraphrasing a little, but yes . . . Why? Do you think I look beautiful?"

He showed a toothy grin. "In your element."

The scanner sounded a melodic chime, followed by the heavy *kerthunk* of the internal locking mechanism disengaging. The hatch swung open, and the group quietly moved into the gloomy cargo space that lay beyond. Towers of red flight cases awaited them, detailed with Drexen's initials in opulent gilded calligraphy. Doubtless they were filled with caps, ready for mass distribution to the tens of thousands throughout the *Novara* ruinously addicted to the psychotropic effects of glow. Following Oren closely, Jyn decided there and then that transporting the entire stockpile to an airlock and venting it into the Abyss would be the first order of business once they were done. Many would undoubtedly suffer as a result of this mandate, since exposure to the Savior's light in its rawest, most volatile form had a tendency to rewrite the neural pathways of the human brain, with many describing glow withdrawal as like having insects hiving inside the skull. Nevertheless, it would be a necessary step in breaking the cycle of dependency, restoring hope for those who had nothing to look for on the horizon but their next pitiful fix.

Presently, a more pressing matter demanded her attention: the entrance to the access stairwell that led to the main deck stood only several meters away on the far side of the lazarette, but a pair of shadowy figures obstructed their path . . . In the heat of the fray, two of Vidalia's best and brightest had apparently seen fit to break off from the fighting to plunder their master's valuables, presumably intending to make a quick escape before his imminent and inevitable defeat. They stood hunched over an open storage crate, feverishly filling the pockets of their urban camo gear with fistfuls of glow caps and scrip. Thankfully, the oblivious opportunists seemed far too engrossed in their pillaging to notice the intruders lurking behind them, the intensity of the gunfire raging above deck having masked the creak of the entry hatch opening and closing. Still, they stood in between Jyn and her mission, and needed dealing with, all the same . . .

Oren recruited one of his silent blades, allocating left and right targets with a rash of abrupt hand gestures. The pair activated their personal luma-shrouds and fizzled out of existence. Then, after a suspenseful moment, the unwitting Monarchs thrust their chests forward like marionettes tugged by their strings, retching and convulsing as invisible knives plunged into their backs, their screams of surprise and agony muffled by unseen silencing hands. As if standing above malfunctioning gravity emitters, they did not collapse but drifted slowly to the floor, gently lowered to rest so as to prevent the thumps of their bodies hitting the deck from alerting anyone nearby.

The invisible assassins rematerialized, standing over the corpses of their victims, and reverently wiping their soiled blades on the sleeves of their Harmony robes. Signing the gesture for all clear, they rallied the others to the stairwell entrance. Oren retrieved his XT-90 from the mag-mount fastened to his back and took point, pressing forward step-by-step in staircase formation, weapon trained on the corners and tight spaces.

They soon arrived in a spacious hallway resembling a fine art gallery; abstract and Renaissance works transcribing the mind of a megalomaniac psychopath hung beneath gold-plated downlights that sliced through the gunpowder miasma lingering in the air. Loud cracks of gunfire bounced raucously around the hexagonal tiles of fair-faced concrete adorning the walls, undercut by the nervous barks and yawps of Drexen's increasingly panicked forces. Jyn found the cacophony so disorienting that she struggled to ascertain where exactly they enemy had dug themselves in, so Isabella powered up her shroud and snuck off to acquire a lay of the land. A few tense minutes later she reappeared, fission blade crackling from a fresh kill, its energized edge releasing the pungent stench of cauterized flesh into the air.

"There were two in the galley, but they're dealt with." the old strategist whispered, still every bit as lethal in her twilight years as she had been during the Expansion. "His house staff and retinue of sycophants are held up in berthing. They're unarmed, as far as I can tell, but they have two guards watching over them . . . Vidalia is likely taking shelter in his study, but it's barricaded tight . . . The remainder of his Monarchs are pinned down in the parlor. I counted seven in total—looking in rough shape, too . . . I think we just might have won this."

"Let's not get ahead of ourselves," Jyn warned. "Just like you said: we need to get to Vidalia before we finish them off; we can't let him think that he's lost this . . . How is Nix's team doing?"

Isabella pressed her back against the wall and tilted her head to the ceiling. Jyn felt the faint brush of static in the air that usually accompanied the forging of a resonant bond, watching as Isabella's eyes poured orange-violet light into the smoke-ladened hallway.

"They're still engaged on the terrace . . . They have wounded but no casualties yet." She paused, furrowing her brow. "There . . . There's a problem."

"Out with it, defector!" Oren growled, eyes frantically scanning the room's several entry points.

Isabella's chest began rising and falling dramatically, her breath quickening. "A raptor just arrived . . . It must have been away when we first boarded. It's hovering above the terrace at their flank . . . The passenger door just opened and there are Monarchs aboard . . . They're . . . they're opening fire!"

Without warning, the woman unleashed a shrill cry, keeling over and clutching her abdomen.

"Divine Abyss, no! Nix is . . . Nix is hit! Oh, it hurts! Please! Someone help aer! It hurts!"

"Keep it down, Graddock!" Oren hissed, baring fangs. But it was no use; the woman became hysterical, feeling Nix's physical agony as vividly as if it was her own.

Jyn caught the woman in her arms as she collapsed, cupping a hand over her mouth to muffle the sounds of her rising panic, feeling raspy breath whistling through the cracks in her fingers as she began to hyperventilate. She felt her muscles tense, her frail body turning rock solid. Then, the light from her eyes faded, flickered, and finally went out . . .

Isabella wailed like a banshee in the night, triggering the hairs on Jyn's neck to stand on end. She knew exactly what the outburst meant and felt only gratitude that she too hadn't been in resonance with Nix at the time. Because Nix was dead, and Isabella had experienced every painful nuance of emotion resulting from aer crossing, amplified tenfold through their empathic bond. It was every cipher's worst nightmare: experiencing firsthand the death of their resonant partner. Now, for the first time in decades, she was completely and utterly alone . . .

"Do you hear that?" The gruff voice came from the parlor, only audible because of a momentary cessation in gunfire.

"Yeah! What the fuck is going on back there?" came a response.

"You two! Go and check it out. We'll cover you!" cried a third voice.

Jyn's heart sank; the fortified Monarchs had heard Isabella's cries and were on their way to investigate. Little time remained to prepare for their arrival; fortunately, Oren and his silent blades needed no delegation of their responsibilities. Three of them instinctively activated their shrouds and headed off to meet the inbound targets. One scooped Isabella up off the floor and began escorting her to safety while the fifth and final blade headed off to face the two guards stationed in berthing. Jyn felt no need to specify what should be done with Vidalia's passengers and house staff, entrusting that those among them who expressed abiding loyalty for their Governor would be seen to accordingly . . .

It would fall on her and Oren to disable the security lockdown and apprehend Vidalia. And truthfully, she wouldn't have wanted it any other way. After all, only by not letting things affect her on a personal level had she ascended to her exalted status. But after Nix, and after the others shot down in the second-wave raptor, she found herself hungry for a little payback . . .

The parlor erupted in a clamor of shock and confusion as its occupants found themselves confronted by three bloodthirsty poltergeists. The violent rattle of indiscriminate fire breached through the ornate archway entrance, the accompanying strobes of muzzle flashes casting erratic shadows across the walls and animating a harrowing zoetrope of wanton carnage.

Jyn and Oren hastened across the embattled hallway to Vidalia's study. Naturally, in compliance with lockdown procedure, the door had been sealed tight beneath reinforced nanocarbon shutters that could likely withstand the shock wave from a tactical nuke. Planting herself before a wall-mounted access terminal, she glanced down into her hands to find the eyes of Thane Locke glaring up at her from beyond the grave.

"Let's hope you're right about this guy," she said, fingertips hammering the terminal keyboard as she flew through menu after menu, hunting for the security directory. "If Locke was actually just some low-level henchman, I doubt Vidalia will have given him emergency override clearance."

"Thane was his arms master," Oren reassured. "Responsible for Monarch combat training and discipline. He was promoted from bodyguard a few years back. . . . I doubt there were many in his ranks whom he trusted more."

Finally, after wrestling with the yacht's archaic operating system, she arrived at the security window for the study.

DISABLE LOCAL SECURITY LOCKDOWN? - CONFIRM
ERROR: RETINAL AUTHENTICATION SCAN REQUIRED.

Jyn held the plastic bag up to the scanner receptacle, muttering "please" repeatedly under her breath. Moments later, the shutters retracted into the ceiling and the door to the study slid open. Oren darted in front of her, using his hulking upper body as a shield as the pair sidestepped inside. The next few seconds were a frantic blur: before she could even acknowledge the two armed Monarchs waiting for them in the brutally stark space beyond, Oren whipped his rifle left and right, firing several shots and dropping them both with blistering speed and precision. The pair hit the deck like two felled trees ushering in an eerie calm.

Vidalia lingered on the far side of the study with his hands clasped behind his back, framed against scenes of bloody strife as the shutters covering the bifold doors overlooking the terrace receded with the lifting of the lockdown. Wearing a fine tan suit, he stood beside a downright rotten cohabitor who Jyn knew to be called Naught—a creature so tall the crest of aer head nearly touched the ceiling, aer damaged exoskeleton chronicling a storied history of violence and brutality. Now Vidalia's second-in-command, rumors had recently circulated about a confrontation with a group of smugglers in the Vestiges in which the brute had nearly been killed. This was seemingly con-firmed by the presence of a prosthetic arm—one resembling a mechanical army switch knife boasting a menacing array of metal tools and implements stored within a gearwork housing. By nature, the Prey *never* exhibited egre-gious or unnecessary violence, but the contraption looked purpose-built for inflicting grievous bodily harm.

As she and Oren progressed farther into the study, Naught took posi-tion directly behind Vidalia, rotating aer hydraulic paw out for a needle-sharp barb that spun with the high-pitched whine of a dentist's drill. Ae raised the sinister instrument up to his temple and held it firmly in place.

"That's close enough, Composer," Vidalia advised, calmly retrieving a file from his jacket pocket and running it over his manicured fingernails. "You and your accomplices have performed admirably. I'm especially interested to learn how you managed to turn my own defenses against me, but I'm afraid that will have to wait . . . For now, I must respectfully request that you lay down your weapons so we may discuss the terms of your surrender."

Outside, the battle for the yacht raged on. Those remaining from the strike group were still pinned down by the enemy raptor as it hovered over the terrace, raining hellfire on their position. Seeking retribution for Nix and aer fallen comrades, an unnamed cohabitor launched into the air with pow-erful grasshopper legs and dove directly into the passenger cabin. A short scuffle ensued. Then, two screaming Monarchs were ejected from the vehicle before it plummeted pilotless toward the Copper Swathes. The valiant cham-pion leaped for the safety of the terrace and rejoined the others to make their final push on the parlor.

"Are you blind, fool?" Oren spat, tightening his shooting stance. "It is over . . . If *anybody* should be offering their surrender, it is you! Although you will not live long enough to be given the choice!"

"Your associate here has a lot of spirit." Vidalia turned his head to the side, indicating with the nail file a small cybernetic implant embedded into the back of his neatly shaven scalp. "But I think we both know who *really* has the upper hand . . . Rest assured, if either of you takes another step forward, my associate will drive this spear directly into my temple, killing me instantly and destroying this vessel in the process . . . That is not my preferred outcome, of course, and I doubt it is yours. So, might I suggest we strive to find a more diplomatic resolution to this before it gets out of hand?"

"Your words are as poisonous as the narcotics you push on us," Jyn seethed, stopping in her tracks but projecting herself forward as much as she could. "I should cut that silver tongue from your Mouth before it can do any more harm . . . Would that be a preferable outcome, Governor?"

"I am a businessman, Jyn, and *you* are more than a mindless killer . . . I am sure there is an agreement we can come to that will help us avoid anything quite so unpleasant."

She paused, trying not to betray her surprise. "You know who I am?"

A broad grin etched its way across Vidalia's angular jaw. "Oh yes, Jyn Sato. Or should I say, *Marshal* Jyn Sato . . . I make it a point to acquaint myself with my adversaries as rigorously as I do my allies . . . Needless to say, it did not take long for my spies to uncover your *true* identity once you began brazenly attacking my installations in the Langrenus Harrow . . . It's just a shame your idiotic predecessor failed to see what was right under his nose or I could have been spared a great deal of inconvenience."

She saw Oren twitch from the corner of her eye as if rapidly burning through what little restraint he had left to stop himself from gunning the man down where he stood. "I tire of this! Tell your beast to step away and give yourself up, now!"

"Alas. I cannot comply," Vidalia answered in deep, condescending tones, raising his hands in feigned humility. "I am no cipher. And Naught here . . . well, ae is a stubborn thing—a free spirit, if you will. Ae does as ae desires and there is little I can do to sway aer mind once it is made up."

Seeming to reaffirm the Governor's words, the monstrous cohabitor moved the spinning tip of aer prosthetic torture device closer to his temple, the grating drone of its motor pitching up sharply. Jyn knew Naught only by reputation; historically, ae had shown little other than complete fealty to Drexen and his empire, but that didn't mean she couldn't at least try to reason with aer. Hopelessly, she reached out with her consciousness, attaining strong but tentative resonance. She projected a series of ideas through a mosaic of impressions and emotions: liberation, freedom, unity, and hope for the future—things Harmony could provide if they succeeded in their mission, trying to convince aer to join her cause. Living up to aer violent renown, Naught responded with what could only be described as a psychic battering. Ae pummeled her with a barrage of disorienting mental flashes, imbuing potent feelings of wrath and malevolence, screaming *Get out of my head . . . I have nothing to say to you*, in the only way ae knew how.

"Such power, Jyn," Vidalia said, watching the unpleasant exchange with a surprising note of sincerity in his countenance. Ignoring Oren's demands to stay where he was, he turned and started toward the open bifold doors behind him. "Such incredible talent—the ability to converse with any cohabitor you desire, and this . . . *this* is how you choose to squander it."

With Naught following closely in step, spear still pointed precariously at his skull, he stepped out onto the smoking, mangled monstrosity of splintered wood and bullet-pitted fiberglass that had been a luxurious terrace only minutes ago, barely acknowledging the body of one of his goons as she floated face down in the floor-recessed hot tub.

He passed one of the possessed turrets, which had expended its ammo reserves and deactivated, patronizingly nodding his head as if commending a child on an impressive school science project.

"Death; destruction," he finally continued. "The upheaval of an established order that has stood for the better part of a century, bringing ruination to the Mouth and all its inhabitants—is *this* really the bright future you set out to achieve? Is *this* your calling?"

Jyn approached the gunwale where he stood, gazing out with him into the war-ravaged vista beyond. He turned his head slightly, observing her from the corner of his dark, penetrating eyes.

"Eamon likely never told you this," he said. "But when we liaised, despite our tumultuous past, I had expressed an interest in forming greater cohesion between DMED and my own organization. On a personal note, I was inspired by the work you and he were doing in building bridges with the non-human community. But now I see that all you were really doing was building an army to exact vengeance against me and throw the Mouth into chaos."

"Chaos," Jyn echoed, shaking her head. "I lived my whole life under your tyranny—watching friends and loved ones waste away to your 'medicine' while you hovered above us in your palace in the sky . . . DMED were never *the law* in the district: *you* were, and when injustice becomes law, resistance becomes duty . . . It might look like little more than chaos to a ruthless tyrant, but I am planting the seeds of my people's salvation. And you . . ." She turned to glare at him, the web of veins framing her face no doubt accentuated by the fury coursing through her body. "*You* are the blight that must be eradicated for them to thrive."

Vidalia's stoic facade began to falter, his face awash with concern as the Choir gathered victorious on the terrace, the remaining Monarchs either killed in combat or summarily executed. She saw the cogs in his head turning as he came to the visible realization that no amount of bartering could save his life. Tightening his lips into a scowl of pure detestation, undoubtedly preparing to regurgitate his final ultimatum, his eyebrows jumped up in surprise as something behind Oren caught his attention. Jyn heard heavy footsteps beating across the main deck, turned to find Isabella charging toward them.

"Murdering bastard!" the woman screamed, forcefully ripping Oren's rifle out of his hands, and aiming it at Vidalia. Naught sprang into action. A wing of metal feathers deployed from aer prosthetic, which ae used to shield the Governor as Isabella unleashed a glowing torrent of concentrated plasma at him. Ae wrapped aer intact arm around his torso and scooped him off the floor, before vaulting over the gunwale and sending them both hurting through the luma-shroud and, presumably, toward their death . . . *If we should be so lucky.*

Isabella stood motionless, bloodlusting eyes staring at the spot where Vidalia had been standing, panting heavily.

"So, I guess it was just a bluff," Jyn posited after a few moments, thankful to find herself and the yacht still very much in one piece. "He *didn't* have a neural uplink after all . . . How did you know?"

"I didn't," Isabella answered, dropping Oren's rifle to the floor and trudging with heavy limbs to Nix's lifeless body. She collapsed to her knees and brought her head to rest on aer bloody carapace, quietly sobbing and calling out aer name.

"I will go after him," Oren began. "If the beast survives the fall, then ae will be in no state to put up a fight . . . I can take them both."

"No," Jyn answered sharply. "I need you here . . . We have to keep our momentum going. If we give Phalanx too much time to fortify after learning what we're up to, we'll be dead before we even reach the blockade . . . Drexen is just a man now: he has no empire, no army. There'll be time to smoke him out of his hiding hole later. For now, it's time to rally the district and take the fight to the union."

EIGHT

The *Assurance* came down for a hard landing in the outskirts of the Cohabitor Ghetto, careening through the crumbling shells of evacuated buildings and leaving a hundred-meter-long trail of destruction in her wake. Following the confrontation with the bounty hunters in the Debris Belt, the *Devourer* had used its "divine light," as Mercy proclaimed it, to safely shepherd the crippled hauler through its catacombic interior. But once it released its intangible hold, Isaac had been unable to keep her aloft on her lone functional impulse thruster, and she had fallen out of the sky like a freighter carrying a shipment of bowling balls.

"Are you gonna kill me?" the young engineer timidly asked, clinging fervidly to the goggles hanging around his neck as he accompanied Delilah to the med cubby. "I feel like you're probably gonna kill me . . . That just mighta been the worst landing in the history of aviation."

"We're alive, Isaac," she replied while storming through the galley, stopping briefly to pick up one of Kahu's antique lamps from the floor and return it to its upright state. With her bandolier repurposed into a sling to support her wrist, having badly sprained it in the crash, what should have been a simple task amounted to a fumbling, uncoordinated chore. "I'd say, given the circumstances, you did pretty damned well . . . Heads up: enviro-regulator's on fire."

Isaac broke off and hoisted himself onto the island countertop, uncoupling a handheld foam extinguisher from his utility harness and lifting it up to the triangular ventilation unit mounted to the ceiling. The unit had been set alight, spewing caustic smoke and raining silvery-white sparks onto the luma-surface below.

"I guess," Isaac mumbled, dousing the regulator in foam to suffocate the outbreak.

"It's just . . . if it wasn't for that ridiculous dermal encryption Heperi keeps installed on the helm, then I would have had access to the vertical stabilizers; probably could have set her down a helluva lot more gently than I managed . . . Instead, I messed up, as usual."

Delilah spurned the remark with a sideways glower, which he hastily averted glow-clouded eyes to dodge as he hopped off the countertop. The lad had a self-deprecating habit of downplaying his achievements and drastically embellishing his failures—a devastating lack of self-esteem, which she attributed to his dependency, and that learning to overcome would be a vital step in his ongoing recovery.

"This wasn't your fault," she said, arriving in the med cubby and lifting herself onto the gurney, eyes downcast as she traced the cascade of errors in her mind that had inexorably led to their current predicament, realizing who the *true* instigator was . . .

"I let greed cloud my judgment and led us into an *obvious* trap. Couldn't snap Kahu out of it when we needed him most and wasn't firm enough with him in the first place about some of the absurd stipulations he imposes on us about living on this ship—*my* ship . . . The *Assurance* is an old crate; she's been banged up to hell before and, let's face it, she will be again. But it's nothing you can't repair, Verhoeven . . . You're *every* bit as resourceful as your brother was and then some . . . If there's a problem, then you can fix it. You might swear down the house and punch a wall or two in the process, but you'll *always* get it done."

Isaac offered no acknowledgment of the sentiment, which in his own funny way was acknowledgment enough. Forgoing any kind of verbal response, he silently moved to the supply cabinet to begin tending to her injury. He fetched a bright-blue sleeve made from a silicone-fiber mesh, commonly referred to as a flexi-cast. He tenderly slipped it onto her arm, guiding her thumb through the thumb hole before leaving the apparatus to administer its inflammation-alleviating chill.

"You're all set," he said, nodding with a tight-lipped expression as if to say, *We're square now, right? No need to torture me with any more heavy conversation?* The actual words that came out of his mouth, however, were, "I'd best get out there and make a start on my damage assessment; try and give you an accurate time frame for the repairs."

"No, you won't," she returned snappily, rising to her feet. "I've got every confidence you can get the *Assurance* skyworthy again. But right now, she'll have to wait . . . We just ditched directly in the Governor's backyard, and every second he hasn't unleashed a blitzkrieg on our position is a miracle."

"So, what are you saying?" He lingered in the cubby entrance, gripping his raw-boned upper arms in anxious consternation. "You mean . . . we're abandoning ship? You can't be serious! Leaving her exposed out here, in the state she's in? She'll get picked clean by scrappers before the next cycle is out—down to the bone!"

"What choice do we have, Isaac?" she queried, hearing the ripple of despair tainting her voice. "It will be days before we can get her off the ground again, which isn't gonna be made any easier with Harmony taking over the district . . . All we can do is find somewhere to lay low until the fighting dies down . . . or, preferably, until the Composer wipes out Vidalia and his entire operation."

Beneath bedraggled strands of sandy-blond hair, she saw an expression marked by panic and uncertainty. The *Assurance* wasn't just Isaac's home, she was his purpose—his entire way of life, and the prospect of losing her clearly weighed as heavily on him as the thought of losing a loved one.

"I promise wherever we dig in, it'll be within visual range so we can keep an eye on her," she continued. "She'll stay locked down tight, and if anybody starts getting too close or curious, we'll send Kahu and Null over to rough them up."

Her reassurances seemed to momentarily lift his spirits, but that abruptly changed when Tobias arrived in the corridor outside the cubby . . .

"Everyone's alive and accounted for, Captain," Tobias huffed, out of breath, pulling his breathing mask away as he sent a wary glance in Isaac's direction. The engineer turned his shoulder in exaggerated disdain. Delilah had overheard the pair feuding about something in the run-up to the extraction. Remembering Kahu's vulgar retelling of the noises emanating from Mercy's quarters last night, she sensed it was somehow related. Evidently, the dispute had yet to be resolved . . .

"Thanks," she replied, rolling her eyes internally at the thought of having to interpose herself between them to prevent a scuffle. "Wasn't sure if you all managed to get strapped down in time. Any injuries?"

Tobias shook his head, rubbing the back of his neck as if to signify minor whiplash. "Nothing serious, which is seriously lucky considering how rough that landing was."

"Like to see *you* do a better job, Silver Spoon," Isaac muttered under his breath.

"That was you? . . . Sorry, I didn't mean to . . ." Tobias furrowed his brow in confusion. "Hang on . . . Then what happened to Kahu? Is he OK?"

"Not sure yet," Delilah lamented. The old dog had gone AWOL following the fiasco with Djoser and Edmund, likely hiding in a dark corner in engineering, sulking or drinking himself into a stupor.

"He had a bit of a scare back there," she elaborated. "Old ghosts rearing their ugly heads . . . I'd go check on him, but I don't have time for my usual scrape-Kahu-off-the-ceiling routine. Just have to hope he comes around soon."

She took one stride forward and sharpened her gaze at the warring pair. "We're leaving the *Assurance*. Go get yourselves and everyone else packed for shore leave. I don't wanna hear any questions or objections. Just get it done . . . And whatever this *thing* is that's going on between the two of you—it needs resolving, STAT. We might be living in close quarters for a few days, and the last thing I want is cabin fever tearing apart my crew . . . Keep the peace; that's all I ask."

With a heavy pit in her stomach, Delilah moved to the cargo bay intending to head outside to assess the damage to the hull and portside impulse thruster. But the cargo bay door had either been busted in the crash or blocked by an obstruction on the far side. She had more success making egress with the helm-access airlock; biting her lip anxiously, she waited for the pressure chamber's circular hatch to lumber open, then tumbled out onto the ragged embankment of rubble and moon-mined titanium, raised by the *Assurance* plowing through several thankfully abandoned buildings. Fragments of the secreted resin that cohabitors used to construct their domiciles glinted like jewels embedded in the debris, only serving to exacerbate the terrible guilt she felt about their disastrous emergency landing. Harmony had already laid waste to the region in their tussle for power with the Glow Syndicate, but that made her feel no more at ease about her own inadvertent contribution to the decimation of the Cohabitor Ghetto.

She shambled down the embankment, feeling the dull ache of her wrist nagging at her as the flexi-cast reached the limit of what little discomfort it could suppress. Reaching terra firma, she took a deep breath, closed her eyes in apprehension, and spun around to survey the operational condition of her downed albatross. As expected, Edmund Sinclair had ravaged the hull with the fire from his gimballed rail gun, transforming the *Assurance*'s sleek, aerodynamic exterior into a crater-pocked atrocity. The smoldering gouges left by the impacting shells were so devastating and so many that it seemed utterly implausible that the ship had not suffered explosive decompression. One round had grazed the cockpit no more than a meter away from its V-shaped windshield; she dared not even consider how close they had all come to a sudden and violent ejection into the void . . .

The once bell-shaped portside impulse thruster appeared now as a tumorous clump of mangled metal, dangling feebly from its wing-mount like rotten fruit from a tree, the peeled back casing of its nacelle resembling the blossoming petals of a lily, charred black—completely irreplaceable and irrevocably damaged . . .

Djoser's harpoon protruded from the upper hull as a menacing souvenir from the ambush, lodged into the fuselage several feet forward of the dorsal tail fin, its serrated backswept barbs making removal impossible without causing considerable further damage. The insufferable rat had narrowly missed catching his prize, but not without leaving an indelible mark . . .

Delilah unloosed a prolonged sigh. Her life's work, her home, and her family fortune lay in ruins before her. She had told Isaac with such conviction that the *Assurance* would fly again, but having seen the extent of the damage for herself, that seemed like far less of a certainty. The potential cost of the repairs didn't concern her so much as the improbable availability of replacement parts. Before the Europa Laboratory incident, balaener-class haulers like the *Assurance* saw use ferrying goods and passengers between Old-Earth and the colonies on Luna, and were later reappropriated as troop transports during the Moon's battle for independence. In a post-Collision era, ships had little need for in-atmos flight capabilities, and so the lightweight materials used in her shielding and internal structure hadn't seen production in over a century. Without some miracle, she would be grounded, permanently, and with the last welding ship in the Novarian fleet out of commission, the deteriorating hull around the Mouth would fall to serious neglect, and the next rupture could very well be the last. The crash didn't just represent a personal tragedy for Delilah but would have potentially catastrophic consequences for the wider Coalescence.

Save for Kahu, the crew came piling out of the airlock, glum-faced with duffel bags and assorted possessions in hand. Teodora's mouth hung slack as she stared aghast at the surrounding scenes of devastation, tears welling in the corners of her wide, downturned eyes. With her heavy-duty rucksack suitably plastered in colorful flower and animal patches, the girl took a knee by Delilah's side. Plunging hands into the rubble, she dug out a doll in the shape of a cohabitor, stitched together from the jute of a recycled hessian sack with eight yellow buttons denoting its eyes.

"An idol," she said, standing to her feet and carefully brushing away its rind of moon dust. "Cohabs make these for their offspring; they're tools used to comfort and educate 'em when they're just grubs—before they learn how to use resonance properly . . . Nanimonai made ones just like this for the cohab kids at Juniper since most of 'em either lost theirs due to difficult circumstances or never had one in the first place."

The winsome smile that had appeared on her face sank. She unzipped her rucksack and gently placed the effigy inside, returning her despondent gaze to the burned-out husks of the encompassing buildings.

"The Composer . . . Jyn Sato—she was the housefather's niece and lived at the sanctuary for a while when I was a kid . . . I don't understand how she could have done this . . . Harmony are fighting to give cohabs rights and status, aren't they? So why in the Abyss would they wanna go and destroy the only home they have?"

"Vidalia probably thought something similar," Delilah replied, staring down at her salvage specialist, telegraphing concern with peaked brows. "Ordered his Monarchs to entrench themselves here in the Ghetto thinking Jyn would be too emotionally invested to level the place—thought he could use the residents as a nonhuman shield . . . Clearly, it didn't deter her in the slightest."

Teo's pixie face creased in anger. "First, she drove 'em out of the Magnanimous Hollow; now here. Where else does she think there is for them to go?"

"She's pushing them toward NTU sovereignty, putting pressure on the blockade," Tobias chimed in, returning briefly to his supercilious old self, seeming eager to contribute his two cents to the discussion. "The Composer is betting on there being a tidal wave of displaced mouthians flooding into Amidships to cripple and undermine the Administration."

"How could you possibly know that?" demanded Isaac.

"Took a seminar about it at ACS. There are a few notable instances throughout history where hostile states employed similar tactics: Nazi Germany, the Second Libyan Civil War, Belarus in the 2040s . . ."

His rigid posture shriveled slightly. The others watched on in concern as he began spluttering and straining his throat, hell-bent on soldiering through to reach his conclusion.

"*This* is how she intends to take the *Novara*—not with a war, but with a . . . refugee . . . crisis . . ."

His constitution weakened further. Wrapping hands around the back of his neck, he crumpled to his knees, making shrill vocalizations of searing agony. "What's wrong with him?" Isaac sniped impatiently.

"He is still struggling to control his hyper-resonance," Mercy explained, crouching beside the lad and massaging his back in sympathy. Delilah felt a flutter of pride as Isaac seemed to begrudgingly take pity on him, placing an arm around his convulsing torso and helping him to his feet.

"There will come a time when he learns how to filter out some of Null's more painful feelings," Mercy continued. "But right now, he is receiving *all* of aer emotional essence in its rawest form . . . It can be . . . excruciating—especially at a time like this . . ."

Tobias lifted his head up to the Höllengarten, the handsome lineaments of his face now twisted in anguish and grief. His emissions shone the brightest

Delilah had ever seen them, streaming like floodlights from his eye sockets and forming a resplendent vein that slalomed through the ether toward Null. The cohabitor stood motionless behind the reeling boy, reticently scanning the ruins of aer once-safe haven in what might have been dismay or disbelief, aer docile bearing conveying little of the emotional trauma ae was apparently enduring.

"Will he be able to walk?" Delilah asked, feeling the seconds evaporating away, their window of opportunity rapidly closing. Before departing the *Assurance,* she had briefly opened a broadband comms channel anticipating an immediate hail from Vidalia; the imperious windbag would never dream of *finalizing* their feud without first monologuing to her for a full five minutes about his *decisive victory.* The radio silence that had followed suggested he was *indisposed* with Harmony, perhaps buying them some time to leave the crash site unmolested.

"He's gonna have to walk," Isaac answered, the tone of his voice sharpening in alarm. "That, or we drag his ass . . . Look! Above Tycho Block!"

Delilah followed her engineer's startled gaze to the open air above the residential tower. At first, she couldn't make sense of it—the giant disco ball made of TV static, hanging like a pixelated moon high over the district. But then, the unusual aberration appeared to melt away, revealing the sleek but menacing silhouette of Vidalia's yacht. Though the sight of it inspired paralyzing fear, there lay undeniable beauty in its design. The vessel's elegant contours tapered to a needle-sharp tip protruding from its bow, its chrome-clad keel reflecting the grays, browns, and licks of neon from the urban sprawl below. She let a gasp escape her lips; it felt like watching a myth come to life, as though she had never really believed it had been there until right this second. As to why the Governor had chosen *now* to reveal himself, she could only surmise that perhaps a technical limitation rendered the craft's weapons platform useless while the lumashroud remained active. Whatever the reason, she could be sure it wasn't anything good . . .

Anticipating a fiery bombardment on their position at any moment, she hiked her heavy duffel bag over her shoulder and prepared herself to run.

"Get to the ruins, now! He's spotted us!"

"But what about Kahu? We can't just leave him!" The protestation came from Teo, who seemed trapped at the tormenting intersection between obeying her captain and not wanting to abandon her crewmate. With no family of her own, those she served with on the *Assurance* were the closest thing she had to kin, and asking her to leave the old dog behind, despite the incessant bickering that went on between them, put her in visible distress.

Delilah grabbed the girl by the sleeve of her knitted sweater and pulled her into an uncoordinated sprint.

"You know as well as I do the drunken fool ain't coming . . . If the *Assurance* dies, then *he* dies with her. Now we have to move, or else we'll all be joining him!"

The girl reluctantly complied, and the group hustled for cover. Null bounded ahead on all fours and rammed open the sheet of corrugated metal constituting the door to a nearby structure—a nonhuman domicile that remained mostly intact, consisting of a series of interconnected bubbles molded from more of the same secreted resin present in the debris outside. For Delilah, the hardened substance sparked an inopportunely timed memory of her father, who in his scant spare time had kept honeybees in an allotment at the Center of Horticultural Preservation. She had always marveled at how those busy little insects managed to construct their intricate hives with nothing but wax and instinct, and she suspected the cohabitor fabrication they had taken shelter in represented a similar example of primal ingenuity—not just a building, a mark of technological advancement—but like her father's honeycomb microkingdoms, the result of eons of evolutionary refinement.

Unlikely to be sharing any of her philosophical musings, the crew mounted up near a hole in the curved wall of the den's primary dome, created by the blast from what might have been a concussion charge or a fractal grenade. The opening acted as a portal providing a decent vantage of Vidalia's yacht and the *Assurance,* which, for the time being, at least, remained in one piece. Outside, all seemed unnervingly quiet; she spied no fleet of raptors ominously descending, nor torrent of sky fire screaming toward their location.

"Is he toying with us?" she whispered, scanning the suspiciously peaceful scenes outside distrustfully.

"I . . . don't think so," answered Tobias, who hadn't quite made it to the rally point with the others but, instead, sat slumped on the floor against a strange piece of furniture—an irregular sculpture resembling a playground slide carved from pompous stone that could only have been suited for cohabitor anatomy. The lad looked too preoccupied with his pain to personally observe the view but was evidently being kept apprised through his resonant connection with Null.

"Something's wrong . . . Look. There's smoke . . . coming from the terrace deck."

Delilah narrowed her stare to confirm, catching a glimpse of the black, fluctuating column before it vanished beneath the yacht's reactuating lumashroud. The static disco ball reappeared for only a moment before taking on another, more recognizable form. Like a titan peering through a tear in the fabric of reality, the translucent eyes of Jyn Sato appeared below the Höllengarten, the woman's face projected around the yacht by the secondary function of its cutting-edge stealth tech: a high-output broadcasting system that, given the Governor's penchant for secrecy, had gone unused.

The Composer's visage dominated the expanse, bathing the dreary district below in resplendent hues of cyan and gold. Delilah had never met Eamon Wyatt's ex–head deputy in person before but recalled his less-than-uncouth description of her COTA scars—the dark filigree of vessels fanning out from her eyes and crawling down her cheeks, rendered vividly now by the high contrast of the projection. The marshal had always seemed somewhat besotted with his bilingual protégé, lighting up like a lantern whenever he had the chance to speak about her. And judging from the woman's golden skin, pretty, symmetrical features, and fierce but alluring countenance, it was hardly difficult to fathom why.

Doubt he's all that smitten now, though . . . Unless violent terrorist vigilante freedom fighters are his type . . .

Classical music boomed from the heavens, a soaring chariot of brass and string likely originating from the yacht's powerful grav-acoustic speakers. The triumphant fanfare soon receded, overtaken by the husky tones of the Composer's voice, reverberating calamitously around the Mouth's immense chamber as she began an impassioned call to arms.

"People of the Mouth . . . Turn your eyes to the sky and witness for yourself the luxury the man who dared call himself your Governor has been indulging in while keeping you all in squalor, monopolizing our resources and curtailing basic necessities . . . Vidalia Drexen and his ilk have been a blight on this district for far too long, and now, his suffocating rule is over, his days of exploiting and extorting us are finally at an end! The Governor of the Mouth is dead!"

Delilah shot Mercy an incredulous glance, but the girl was listening far too intently to notice, her pale skin turning sheet-white at the news of her master's death. She and Null had been in involuntary servitude to the Governor for many years, rather than the "associates" he often referred to them as. And although she had risked everything to free herself and her cohabitor companion from his conniving influence, Delilah suspected them both of developing Stockholm syndrome from their time serving him. There lay unquestionable relief in the girl's response, but she also detected an undercurrent of sadness too, perhaps even grief . . .

You did a real number on these two, huh, Vidalia?

"Do we believe this?" asked Isaac, practically hanging off the work goggles slung around his neck, squinting eyes fixated on the Composer's projection.

"The input terminal for that luma-caster is in Vidalia's study; there is no remote access," Mercy absently replied. "Which means the Composer is broadcasting directly from his yacht . . . Judging from the smoke, and not to mention the fact that the *Assurance* still hasn't been fired upon, I believe she is telling the truth: Harmony may have just toppled the Governor's empire."

"Allow yourselves to revel in this small victory," Jyn sternly continued, as if reaffirming Mercy's hypothesis. "But know that the struggles we face have only just begun . . . It hasn't been easy; many have suffered. The path to salvation is one fraught with peril, but we *must* walk it together if we are to prevail. Faith is a bird that feels the light even when the dawn is still dark. So hold fast and stay strong, because the morning will soon come, and when it does, every one of us needs to push forward against the blockade, to do their part in reclaiming what has been wrongfully denied us for over a century: the same freedoms and security the bowsiders have been selfishly hoarding, languishing in comfort and abundance while sparing little concern for those of us born on the wrong side of their arbitrary border."

Delilah turned her attention to Teodora Brižan, sensing from her vexed expression that the Composer's declamatory sentiments were more than striking a nerve for the mouthian salvage specialist. The girl had always been intensely patriotic about her home, and although the anger she felt about the turmoil Harmony had thrown it into ran deep, this was perhaps the first time Teo had given any credence to Jyn's freedom-at-any-cost manifesto. She even went as far as silencing Isaac with a scornful "Shhh!" as he made a sneering remark about whether people were "really buying this crap."

The classical music swelled beneath Jyn's fervent words, rising to a bombastic crescendo that made the hairs on Delilah's neck stand on end.

"For decades, this vessel has been a silent menace," the Composer went on. "Looming over us as an invisible monument to our subjugation. But from now on, let it be a symbol of hope—a symbol that no man nor government can hold us down and repress our spirit. Henceforth, this vessel shall be known as *Chīsana Osuushi*. Let it strike the same fear into the hearts of our oppressors as *we* have known generation after generation!"

"*Chīsana Osuushi*," Isaac dubiously repeated. "Is that Union Standard? I don't recognize it."

"Naw, it's an old tongue," Teo replied, seeming to recede within herself. "I don't speak it, but I know what it means: 'little bull.'" She paused, dropping her shoulders. "It was the housefather's nickname, given to him by his wife, Yua, before she died . . ."

Delilah engaged the girl in a hard stare. "She's just pullin' on your heartstrings, kiddo," she affirmed. "She knows Hiroki was a beloved figure here in the district and is just using his death to try and curry favor . . . Don't let yourself get swept up in it."

"I won't," replied Teo, running her cerulean plait through her fingers, displaying a forlorn pout that suggested otherwise . . .

"And now, I want to deliver a message to our *benefactors* beyond the blockade," Jyn declared, commanding attention with the grave timbre of her voice. "My ultimatum is as follows. You have twelve hours to relieve all enforcers and Administration personnel from the Phalanx Compound. You will open the checkpoint and grant *all* sternside citizens safe passage into NTU sovereignty . . . If you reject these terms, our wrath will be swift and merciless. The segregation of the Mouth *will* be abolished; whether use of force is required to achieve this is completely up to you . . . The Coalescence *can* know harmony, but choose dissonance, and face annihilation."

The crew returned to the *Assurance* to catch their breath and reassess their next move, taking refuge in the tapestry-swaddled sanctuary of the lamp-lit galley. With the District of the Mouth seemingly under *new management*, the situation with Vidalia looked to have conveniently resolved itself, but the fleeting sense of relief Delilah felt soon yielded to a broader sense of impending apocalyptic doom. Because she knew the Administration—had spent her entire academic life training to be a cog in that indomitable powerhouse, before Micah's passing derailed her fledgling political career. She knew that, like Madeline Vargos, the woman's successor would *never* bow to the demands of a terrorist cell. The bowside authorities would reinforce the blockade with twice the contingency of grenadiers and Phalanx operatives in response to the Composer's threats, using any means necessary to crush the insurgency and deter the mass migration of some ninety thousand refugees.

Just as Eamon Wyatt had predicted, the *Novara* would suffer an uprising of potentially cataclysmic proportions—a scale of devastation not seen since the Collision itself. And with the *Assurance*'s wings irreparably clipped, Delilah's flock found themselves hopelessly trapped on the wrong side of the imminent conflict. Their only remaining options were to join the migrant caravan and try their luck at the transfer checkpoint, or risk descending into the Vestiges to see if they could find a route through that treacherous labyrinth into Lower Amidships. Neither choice proved particularly enticing, but she couldn't say with any degree of certainty what standing they would be in with Harmony, should their paths cross, and she sure didn't plan on waiting around to find out . . .

Leaving the others to collect themselves in the lounge, she took the opportunity to locate her wayward pilot. Lugging her throbbing arm from bow to stern, she scoured the hauler, checking all Kahu's usual hiding spots: from his untidy hovel in crew quarters that reeked of rum, sweat, and cheap cologne to the pokey crawl space beneath the fission reactor where he hung his cargo strap hammock and kept his poorly hidden stash of erotic luma-mags.

The old dog had suffered panic attacks like this before, but never one quite so severe that he couldn't remedy it by wallowing in a dark corner with a bottle of synthesized fire water. Delilah had to consign herself to the possibility that he had really jumped ship this time, so she headed for the bridge, concluding the *Assurance*'s elevated cockpit would provide an ideal vantage point to spot him if he had wandered off into the ruins of the Ghetto.

"Dammit, Heperi," she muttered, charging furiously down helm access. "Where in the stars did you get to?"

"I'm in here, Skip . . ."

She skidded to a halt, boots squealing on the steel-plated floor, and turned to face the entrance to the mainframe, where the responding voice had emanated from. Positioned just aft of the bridge, this claustrophobic electrical cupboard housed the *Assurance*'s central processing unit, often referred to as the freezer due to the subzero temperatures necessary to regulate the array of quantum computer racks whirring away inside. The balaener-class pilot's manual advised the sliding access hatch should be kept closed at all times, but it was left permanently ajar by a tangle of corrugated conduits, trailing from various areas of the ship and spliced into the mainframe to facilitate Delilah's many nonstandard modifications. Plumes of ice-cold coolant vapor spilled out onto the gangway, illuminated a gentle blue by the scintillation of blinking LED lights inside.

She hadn't thought to check the freezer due to it being an area of the ship Kahu religiously avoided; to acknowledge the existence of the *Assurance*'s neural processing center would challenge his superstitious belief that her systems were governed not by a supercomputer, but were the result of her being possessed or imbued by some benign spirit: the ghost of a lost loved one or his guardian angel, perhaps.

Delilah peered her head inside and found the old dog in his tattered NTSC blazer, loitering just out of sight behind a structural girder.

"You're too old for hide and seek, Heperi," she joked, surprised to find the anger she held quickly transmuting into relief upon seeing his haggard face. "Now, are you coming out or do I need to get Null to drag you?"

She saw a wistful smile lift the corners of his cracked lips. After a long, contemplative pause, he finally answered, "You remember when we first met, Lilah?"

She issued a prolonged sigh, taking a load off on the foldaway jump seat beside him. "I do . . . I'd been tryna track you down for several days when I found you well and truly lubricated, hemorrhaging nunits on the double helix table at the Smith's Anvil . . . I explained that I had a business proposal, but you wouldn't even hear me out until I bought you back in."

He chuckled softly. "Hey; I won, didn't I?"

"No, you didn't . . . You went all in on red giant with your first hand like a rookie and I had to bail you out when you inevitably folded. Couldn't pay anywhere near what you owed, and those Cendre Vale thugs you were tryna shortchange weren't messing around—would have knocked seven bells outta you if I wasn't there to intervene."

"Yup; sounds about right . . . I remember we came back to the *Assurance* to talk shop over a nightcap . . . Told me you were lookin' to buy a hauler to start up your own weld and salvage outfit. Said I'd be happy to sell her to you under one condition: that no one else *ever* assumes control of the helm while I still got air in my lungs."

"How could I forget?" She folded her arms in feigned irritation. "It's a point that's caused me no end of migraines over the years."

He reached up to affectionately stroke the structural girder with a rugged hand, his gray dreadlocks falling away to reveal his battle-scarred face. "You've been good to us, Lilah—me and this old girl . . . I think it's time I finally did right by you . . ."

"You're not about to propose are you, Heperi?" She interrupted. "I'm flattered, and no offense, but . . . I think you might be older than my dad would be if he was still kicking around."

"With the amount of time we spend arguing, I feel like we're hitched already." He let slip a mirthless laugh, then reached over to the nearest server rack and pulled a data pad mounted to the end of a hinged arm toward her. Displayed on the device's touchscreen, Delilah saw the outline of a hand, pulsing green below the text, *Primary user dermal encryption authentication.*

"I'm giving her to you," he said.

She stared at him blankly for a moment. "You already did, remember? And not to be a pessimist, but I'm not sure there's much of her left to give . . ."

"Oh, she's been in worse shape than this . . . You weren't there the time the drive core stalled, and my old gaffer had to glide her into the docks without her inertial dampeners . . . I mean it: I'm givin' her to you for real, this time . . . Just place your hand against the glass and all admin privileges will be transferred over to you. You'll be able to register whoever you want to have access to the helm."

"And why would I wanna do a thing like that when I've got the best stick jockey on the *Novara* serving on my crew?" She felt concern seeping into her expression as his true meaning finally occurred to her. "Or is this you telling me . . . that you're leaving?"

"I'm done," the old pilot solemnly confirmed. "Gonna retire—drink myself to death somewhere else, just like you always tell me to . . ."

"Oh, stop being dramatic, you old fool." She stood up to meet his eyes and pushed the data pad away. "You don't have to do this . . . Whatever happened back there with Djoser and Edmund—it was just a blip. Doesn't mean you have to go throwing the towel in."

"That was a pretty big blip, Lilah," he countered, beseeching eyes locked onto hers, partially hidden beneath the gray, unkempt slugs forming his brow. "That bushwhacking should have been the end of us. I took one look at those interceptors and turned into a useless wreck. The *only* reason we came out of it was blind luck, and we might not be so lucky next time . . . I'm sorry but I can't fly for you no more. I'm long passed my due date: a drunken, foul-tempered, no-good has-been, and you'd all be better off without me . . . I can feel myself comin' apart at the seams, yah know? Losin' the bottle a little more every day. If I stick around for much longer, insistin' on bein' the only idiot who gets to fly the *Assurance*, then I'm liable to get everyone aboard her killed."

She twisted her lips in contemplation, knowing she risked a potentially explosive argument with her next words, but feeling a responsibility to impart them, nevertheless. "Not to flog a dead horse," she said cautiously. "But don't you think if you tried to . . . you know, *lay off the sauce*, then these *episodes* might start to become rarer? Or at least more manageable?"

He shook his head in a tortured mixture of adamance and despair. "I can't stop, Skip . . . the booze is the only thing that keeps *me* going and *her* outta my head . . . Sober up too much and . . . well, you saw what happened . . . I just gotta keep myself topped up enough where I can stay in the sweet spot—that Goldilocks zone where I'm just loose enough to forget about all the dark shit in my history but straight enough that I can still function."

"Tala," Delilah pronounced, curiosity practically ejecting the name from her lips before she had the chance to swallow it. "*That's* whose memory you're trying to erase by marinating yourself every day, right? One of your old wingmates?"

Kahu dropped his gaze and exhaled slowly, seeming as if an immense weight had been lifted from his shoulders, the years spent dreading this inevitable conversation finally over.

"Flight Lieutenant Tala Escuella," he cooed softly. "She was a shit-hot reconnaissance pilot, flew a condor in my squadron. Grew up in the Statera

Basin—sharp as a razor and as scrappy as a dingo in a bar fight, could drink me under the table ten times over and *still* outmaneuver me . . . She was driven, tenacious, and stubborn as hell—bit like yourself, yah know? . . . I thought *I* was the best in class. But no, that little shit ran circles around me."

"Did she fly with you during the Antonelli Expansion?" Delilah asked.

He nodded, eyes fluttering wildly behind tightly closed lids. "Ruttin' Administration was pushing harder and harder against the bug perimeter— sending good pilots to their deaths every day. And for what? A little extra breathing room? Entire squadrons would get wiped out in those strikes. We were on a pretty good run—several successful incursions with zero casualties. Command assigned us to Operation Nutcracker, tasked us with probing the enemy perimeter for weaknesses, testing their defenses, and measuring their response times. We were pretty handy at getting in and out unseen. Tala had such finesse; even *I* struggled to keep track of her sometimes . . . One day we got overconfident, careless . . . We tripped the alarm and had a talon of interceptors bearing down on us in seconds. The way those things maneuvered—jumping around, zipping back and forth—went against everything we were taught about physics and astronautics in the Core. We threw everything we had at them and barely even scratched the paint . . . It was like shooting at smoke. These weren't the autonomous pebble drones we encountered today, mind you; the ones *we* fought were piloted . . . Piloted by . . ." Delilah saw a shiver ripple across his body, spied a single bead of sweat rolling down his forehead.

"The bugs we went up against out there in the black," he continued. "They were pure evil . . . You can tell me they were just defending their Savior all you like. But at the end of the day, what they did to us—it weren't natural."

Delilah massaged the base of her skull, recalling her own excruciating psychic encounter with Drexen's nonhuman henchmen down in the Vestiges.

"If it was anything like what Naught did to *me* when we rescued Isaac from Vidalia's capping plant then I can attest to that."

Kahu placed a grubby finger against his temple. "This wasn't just headaches. They got inside your amygdala—the part of your brain that controls fear. They made us see things, hear things, coerced us into doing stuff we didn't want to do . . . They got inside Tala's head . . ."

He broke down, bringing his face to rest in his hands, squeezing his dreadlocks between tightly clenched fingers.

"I don't know what they did or . . . what they made her *see*, but she took her condor into a nosedive, corkscrewing directly toward the *Novara*'s bridge. If she had hit, casualties would'a been in the hundreds—the entirety of the *Novara*'s high command wiped out in an instant. I went after her, trying to talk her down, thinking if I couldn't get through to her that maybe I could at least give her a push to stop her from crashing . . . But she was too far out of range, so I . . . I had no choice but to open fire . . . She was my best friend—almost like a kid sister—and I gunned her out of the sky like a clay pigeon."

Delilah took a sharp breath to suppress her shock; she had always intuited that some terrible fate had befallen this girl, but not once had she considered that the guilt plaguing the old pilot stemmed from his direct involvement with her death.

"That can't have been easy," she surmised. "I'm asking myself, could I have done the same if it was Isaac or Teo, and I don't know if the answer is yes." She placed a reassuring hand on his shoulder, working hard to catch his darting gaze and guide him out of panic. "You did what you had to, Heperi . . . I'm sorry for making you relive that trauma, but at least now I understand."

"I relive it every day, Lilah," he replied despondently, removing her hand from his shoulder and cupping it in his own briefly, then turning it over and forcing it against the data pad. She felt a warm, buzzing sensation on her palm and fingertips as the pad encoded the *Assurance*'s systems to her dermal signature. A melodic chime sounded; the screen displayed the words *New primary user authenticated.*

Kahu gave her a rueful smile. "Which is exactly why you gotta let me do this . . . I ran with more crews on the *Assurance* over the years than I can remember. But ain't none of them I can say I ever considered family like this bunch of misfits. It's been a long-damned time since I gave a shit about anybody but myself, so I'm gonna do it right this time, won't let anything bad happen to any of you. The way I see it, the thing that poses the biggest danger to you all, is me. I ain't fit for service no more, but I can still protect you by removing myself from the picture. It hurts like hell, but it's the *only* way to keep you safe."

⊓Iⴖⴹ

Hazel Edevane hated the quiet. She considered it the single worst part about her long stay in the rehabilitation ward at Aegis Infirmary: that oppressive, stifling quiet, so heavy and all-enveloping she could hear the undulating hum of the grav-panels beneath the floor and the whir of the air filtration pumping atmosphere into her room. The only respite from the crushing stillness was the occasional hushed voices of the staff behind the reception desk: a repressed cough, the shuffling of documents, the diminishing drum of squeaky footsteps on vinyl as someone traveled the hallway outside.

Things had never been quiet in the NTSC barracks. In downtime between briefings and training sessions in the simulator, one could usually hear the thwacks and grunts of Horatio Guzman sparring with one of his cronies in the rec room, the growling guitars and discordant synths of heavy dubtronic music blasting through Zain Cantrell's wireless speakers, or Wing Commander Matias Luscombe's vociferous bellowing as he reprimanded someone for the *piss-poor* form of their bed making. Complete silence had been a rare commodity, and she recalled just how much she had struggled to tune out the noise while attempting to sleep or study. Funny how all she had wanted then was a little peace and quiet, and now, she couldn't abide it. She wished she could jump to her feet and sprint through the ward, screaming profanities at the top of her lungs and banging on the doors of the other patients' rooms, rallying them to dance and frolic with her in the halls . . . Of course, she couldn't do any of that; she couldn't even stand without assistance . . . Her body—the same body she had spent years honing and sculpting into an athletic temple of excellence—had been left broken and unresponsive, her lean muscles wasting away. Her limbs were unruly children that would neither listen nor obey. And her hands—her mother's hands—which had once been so nimble with the flight stick and throttle of her kestrel, were no more than useless whorls of tendon and bone, curled up like the brittle husks of dead spiders.

Gritting her teeth, she channeled all of her will and remaining strength down through her neck and shoulders, lifting her arms away from the uncomfortably stiff bedsheets. Like experiencing sleep paralysis while fully lucid, they felt as as if they were weighed down by cinder blocks, the exhausting task of lifting them made no easier by the invisible rhino perched atop her ribs, severely constraining her breathing.

The pathetic attempt marked the extent of what little motility she had been left with after several weeks in recovery. She had no sensation nor control of anything below the waist; her upper body felt weak and cumbersome, rendered almost completely numb by the extensive damage sustained to her spinal cord.

She was a sober mind trapped in a paralytic body, a puppet without strings. Though she had been robbed of at least 70 percent of her sense of touch, she could still feel the bitter resentment building a nest inside her, anchoring its roots firmly in the fertile soil of her abdomen. Her destiny had been stolen from her, the future she'd spent her entire life working toward cruelly snatched away. Within a matter of weeks, she had regressed from one of the most highly educated, highly trained citizens of the NTU, to having to relearn basic functions like how to dress, how to wash, or how to go to the toilet. She had always taken tremendous pride in her capacity for independence; now, trying to do even the most menial of things for herself only ended in further frustration and dismay. There was not one facet of her depressing new existence in which she *didn't* need some form of assistance. She found it degrading, undignified, and unfair, and she didn't know for how much longer she could tolerate it . . .

"Incline." The word crawled from her lips as a dry, foul-tasting rasp of air. "Forty-five degrees."

The motor in her bed droned as it propped her up into a sitting position. She strenuously turned her head to the left, glowering at the assortment of flowers and get-well cards piled atop the dresser next to her bed—a shrine of pity left by friends and loved ones who meant well, of course, but who had only spurred her deep dejection with their unwanted sympathy.

Turning her head again, she let her eyes roam over the panoramic view panel occupying the entire right-hand wall. Set to ambient mode, it had been cycling through a slew of B-roll footage for several hours: rolling hills of grass stretching on to the horizon, misty forests raked by beams of sunlight carving through the canopy of leaves above, a peaceful cove at sunset with crystal clear waves lapping up and down the white-sand shore. The centuries-old images were likely intended to placate and soothe patients in distressing situations, but like the flowers on the dresser, they only served to exacerbate her dour mood. She didn't proclaim to know what it felt like to stand on a beach, nor wander through a forest, but she knew the feeling of grass beneath her feet, the cool prickle of its blades against her heels and in between her toes. She could think of nothing she had loved more as a girl than those rare weekends her father had off work when he would take her to the Conservatory to bask and play with Tobias in the dome's simulated sunshine. But like those fond memories, the recollection of what it felt like to walk barefoot through the verdure would evanesce a little more every day, fading like a polaroid exposed to light, until left as no more than a blank print.

Feeling the indignation swelling within, she issued another command to her room's voice-activated assistant, this time asking for the view panel to switch to mirror mode. The scenes of natural beauty vanished as the display's surface crystallized. She then found herself confronted by her own reflection, framed against the sterile backdrop of her private room.

She scarcely recognized the young woman staring back at her, that gaunt-faced silhouette with her sallow complexion and ugly shaved head.

That's not me . . . No . . . It can't possibly be.

The halo brace installed to bind her shattered skull together had been removed, thanks to the administering of osteoplast stimulants that encouraged rapid bone regeneration and had repaired the web of fractures spiraling across her crown. A concentric pattern of scabby wounds marked the points where the framework of pins and rods had perforated her scalp. They would heal, she had been told, but those reassurances had failed to make her feel any less hideous regarding her appearance.

She traced the tired lines of her face down to her neck, turning her head away slightly to better observe her new prosthesis—the centipedal cybernetic symbiote gripping her spine from her lower back to the base of her skull.

"The plan is we perform a volumetric scan on your spinal column," the physician had informed her before surgery, manipulating an example of the artificial length of vertebrae in her hands to demonstrate its flexibility. "Even with the tremendous strides in medical science over the past two centuries, a T-three spinal injury like yours cannot be rectified through surgery. But it *can* be circumvented . . . By individually printing each vertebral segment using the scan data, we can create an exact replica of its predecessor . . . Once we have removed the damaged section of your spine and inserted the prosthesis, we can get to work connecting your cervical and thoracic nerves to the artificial cord encased within your new vertebral column."

The woman had indicated with a hand clad in surgical gloves to the silicone-wrapped bundle of synthetic fibers trailing through each vertebrae's core.

"We fuse it to your existing spinal cord at each end, restoring connectivity from your lower body to your medulla oblongata, which *should* recoup some measure of sensation and motility . . . It will not be a complete recovery by any stretch, but with physiotherapy, it should provide a *much* better quality of life for you."

One small caveat the good doctor had failed to elucidate, or perhaps Hazel had failed to comprehend—likely courtesy of the painkillers addling her brain—was just how visible the contraption would end up being. Each vertebra culminated in a silicone *wing* or *flap* that protruded through her meat and sat flush against her skin, a parade of stingrays gliding down her back. "For ease of access," the doctor had later explained when questioned on why this had to be the case. "The prosthesis is printed largely from thermoplastic polycarbonate, making it extremely durable. It's built to last a lifetime, but as always, there *can* be complications. Segments may need to be repaired or replaced; the cord could wear over the course of decades. And making repeated incisions on the same stretch of flesh every time we need to fix something could prevent the underlying muscle tissue from healing properly. This way, we can provide any necessary maintenance *without* having to operate."

Hazel's blood ran cold at the notion, her bleak future playing out on the movie screen of her mind. Life would be a monotonous blur of futile physio sessions, repetitious hospital visits, and long periods of painful recovery as her *thermoplastic* spinal column gradually degraded. In all likelihood, the recouped motility promised to her would amount to a marginal improvement—certainly nowhere near the level of dexterity with her hands necessary to have her flight status reinstated, which, in truth, was all she really cared about . . . The surgery was her only chance at leading anything close to a normal life —she understood that perfectly well. Even still, she couldn't help but wonder whether it would ultimately be worth the struggle . . .

A rapping sounded at her door—the aggressively polite *ratatat tat!* of her father announcing his arrival. Why the man had felt it necessary to knock she couldn't understand, because what privacy did she really need while permanently relegated to her bed?

"I'm right where you left me, Dad," she called out, despising the churlish affectation in her voice, but feeling as though she had almost forgotten how to speak to people without an undercurrent of sarcasm.

A pungent concoction of sandalwood perfume and cigar smoke swept into her room as Atherton Edevane charged through the door. Wearing a stone-gray suit with the top two buttons of his shirt undone and his collars popped, he entered carrying a precarious consignment of large paper bags, all branded with various insignias and calligraphed logos of the many upmarket retail stores found on Xìngyùn Square. Hazel expected no less; showering her with gifts had always been *his* way of showing affection, and in these most wretched of times, was his means of trying to provide her with some degree of comfort. Sadly, no amount of material finery could help lift her spirits—especially not jewelry to wear around her grotesque cyborg neck, expensive clothes that she would be unable to dress herself in, nor coconut-scented moisturizers for the legs and feet that she would probably never walk on again . . .

Seemingly unaware of the storm brewing in her mind, he jauntily hastened to her bedside table, depositing a takeaway food box and a cup of syn-coffee, both of which he would have to assist her with the consumption of . . .

"I got some samosas from the street food place you like in Virrisachi Arcade."

Hazel glanced across at the wisps of steam escaping through the container's folded slots. "I'm not hungry."

"That's beside the point, darling; you *need* to eat. I want you at full strength for this orientation session . . . Remember what Doctor Kovačević said: the harder we work at your physio, the quicker and more effective your rehabilitation will be . . . Are you sleeping OK? Getting your rest in?"

"Other than the constant nightmares about free-floating in the Abyss, paralyzed from the waist down with my visor cracked and my O-two flatlining—yeah: peachy."

Seeming to completely ignore the remark, he placed his exorbitant cargo on the floor, then leaned in close to study the second piece of cybernetic technology installed in her crippled body.

"How's your implant?" he asked. "Seems like it's healing nicely; your scalp is looking a lot less irritated."

"It hurts," she sniped back, taking a sideways glance in the mirror at the thumb-sized chipset stitched into the skin just behind her left ear—the neural bridge designed to reconcile any incongruencies between the nerve signals transmitted from her existing spinal cord and her new prosthesis. "Feels like exactly what it is—as if someone screwed a logic board into the side of my skull . . . I keep snagging the horrible thing on my pillow."

"Well, I imagine that won't be so much of a problem when your beautiful hair grows back, Hazelnut."

She saw his hand twitch, suggesting he had almost instinctively stroked the back of her head, just as he had done many times when she was a girl. Instead, he refrained, and she felt a potent flush of relief, albeit tarnished by sadness. Sadness because she'd have fiercely scolded him for doing so, but she knew he wouldn't have deserved it . . .

He showed a wistful smile, communicating with those steely eyes a disarming softness that she seldom saw in him. If only, she lamented, she felt more receptive to it, because although she knew he only wanted to convey his concern, it didn't feel like concern: it felt like pity.

"Let's get you dressed, shall we?" He reached into one of the gift bags at his feet and began dumping piles of new clothes onto her paralyzed legs—not out of malice: just a blithe lack of consideration.

"I'm fine to do the orientation session in my gown," she put in sharply.

"And let everyone catch sight of your rear? I don't think so . . . Now, there wasn't much in your old bedchamber, since all you've worn for a year now is gym gear, a flight suit, and your uniform. So, I nipped into Zabelle and got you some nice new loungewear . . ."

Issuing an exasperated groan, she shoved the garments off the bed, which took markedly more effort than she wanted to admit. "Will you please stop fussing over me, Dad? I don't need you hovering around all the time . . . Don't you have some fundraiser or anticohabitor demonstration you need to be at?"

Atherton seemed to take a moment to temper himself, probably exhibiting more patience than she deserved. "I know it isn't 'Nebula' to have your old man looking after you like this," he said. "But as of this afternoon, my resignation from the Administration has been finalized, so you'll just have to suck it up and get used to it . . . And I've already had a tirade of earache from Tobias about my involvement with Humanity First, so I don't need it from *you*, too."

Hazel tipped her head in condescension. "A little hypocritical of my darling baby brother, wouldn't you say? Considering it sounds like he was right there alongside you."

Atherton cleared his throat. "Yes . . . Well, let's just say your brother and I were *both* somewhat naive about the organization's *true* purpose and, perhaps, a little beguiled by its unscrupulous founder . . . But you'll be happy to know that I've since cut all ties. And Tobias . . . Well . . . I'm not sure exactly *what* he's doing: galivanting about on a weld and salvage ship, practicing his 'resonance'—whatever in the stars that means—but I know at the very least it's got *nothing* to do with Bhaltair Abernathy, so it's fine by me."

Oddly enough, Hazel knew precisely what 'resonance' meant; she had learned as much as she could about the "psychic compatibility" some sternsiders were experiencing, absorbing what little data the Administration's draconian censorship of the Nov-Net would disclose. The irony of Tobias of all people ending up with these extrasensory capabilities did not escape her, and judging by her father's apathetic response to the news, he remained blissfully unaware his son had been communing with *enemies of the New Terra Union.*

"I'm surprised you aren't more upset about him ditching the academy," she said, hardly in the mood to set the man off ranting and raving by filling in the blanks for him.

"Oh, I'm furious," he affirmed, contradicting the words with a dopey grin. "Positively outraged! But to be perfectly frank, I've wasted nearly half of my days micromanaging you two kids, trying to selfishly control every aspect of your lives in the hope of sculpting the future *I* wanted for you . . . I've been more of a drill instructor than a father . . . and look where it's gotten us: ostracized and alienated from one another." His eyes sank. He released a long, sorrowful exhalation. "Your mother would be rolling over in her grave if she found out what I've done to this family . . . She left me in charge, and I made a complete mess of it."

Hazel felt her morose disposition melting like butter at her father's surprising candor, as well as the practically unheard-of show of compassion toward her mother. She reached out and grabbed his hand, squeezing as hard as she could, which wasn't much . . .

"We turned out alright, didn't we? You didn't do *such* a bad job."

He smiled, subtly nodding "I suppose not . . . You've got *her* spirit, you know? Both of you . . . I spent years trying to stamp it out, but it's still there, burning bright . . . I thought letting you grow up with the fire she carried would mean losing you the same way I did her. And look what happened: I nearly lost you both anyway . . . So, I don't care what Tobias is up to, as long as it makes him happy. And the same goes for you too, Hazelnut; I think it's time we *all* took our foot off the pedal. When we get you out of this place and back up on your feet, *you* choose whatever path you want for yourself—I'm not here to interfere."

She appreciated the sentiment, but really, it only acted to hammer home the disheartening truth that all she really wanted was to serve. She felt inexorably called to devote herself to the defense of the home she loved; to stretch her wings and soar among the stars, separated from that ineffable emptiness by no more than the canopy of her kestrel. She had dreamt of that sense of freedom and higher purpose all her life and had been allowed to experience it only once before something she didn't understand and struggled to explain put an abrupt and violent end to those aspirations: an enemy disguised in the skin of an ally—a terrifying specter of death that by its very existence, challenged and defied the reality she knew.

The specifics of the attack that had left Hazel with life-changing injuries and five of her wingmates dead remained somewhat murky, but one detail cut through her mental fog as vividly as the light of the Canyon sky filtered through the gaps in her window blinds.

Check their wing profile. They aren't interceptors. Zain Cantrell's voice came to her from beyond the veil—a heart-jouncing reminder that no, in fact—she *hadn't* imagined it. Nor was it a false memory whipped up by the cocktail of drugs in her system. The interloping fighters that had ambushed Delta's patrol were heavily modified kestrels, as opposed to the alien interceptors command had expertly trained her to identify. She didn't know *who* or *what* had killed Zain, Shiyana, Horatio, and the others, but she could confidently say the network's touting of the incident as a *demonstration of interspecies aggression* was egregious prevarication.

Her preliminary report had fallen into a black hole, and she feared that with the NTSC seemingly closing the book on the attack, uninterested in determining the *actual* responsible party, her fallen wingmates would *never* receive the justice they deserved . . .

She suddenly felt the burden of her grief bearing down on her, a force so overpowering it ripped the breath from her lungs. She gasped like someone resurfacing from water, the dam of repressed emotion in her chest crumbling and giving way. She broke down, clinging fervently to her father as he raced to wrap his arm around her shoulders.

"What's wrong, Hazelnut?"

"It should have been me!" she sobbed. "*I* was flight leader on that training exercise. Their lives were *my* responsibility; It should have been *me* who died out there—not them!"

Atherton pulled her into his chest, leaning his head gently on hers.

"If there's one thing I've learned after all this family's been through," he cooed softly, "it's that life is chaos. There's no master plan, no rhyme or reason as to why these things happen. You'll only drive yourself to insanity trying to make sense of it . . . All we can really do is play the hand we're given."

"But I don't understand . . . why am I alive? For what purpose? The only thing I wanted—the only thing I was any good at—it's all gone!"

"I know with every fiber in my body that you'll do great things yet, Hazel Ellis Edevane . . . This?" He motioned toward her legs. "*This* isn't going to stop you . . . The reason you're alive is because you're a survivor—*all* of us Edevanes are. Your mother was a survivor, too. She battled that dreadful virus for as long as she could, fighting tooth and nail to steal every last second she had with us . . . Despite all the pain she was in, Tabitha never gave up. Which is why I know you won't either."

* * *

Atherton tentatively helped Hazel into her new loungewear—a pair of sky-blue joggers and a gray, open-back tank top, chosen specifically so as not to snag on her artificial vertebrae. He lowered her into the repulsor chair, docked in its charger beside her bed, then sailed her down a lattice of stark hallways to the rehabilitation therapy center, offering stern greetings to porters and medical staff as they passed.

Hazel felt a brightening of her constitution following her emotional breakdown. The floodgates had quite literally opened, purging the toxicity festering within like a malignant bacterial colony, enabling her to course correct with renewed positivity.

Previously, she had resigned herself to the idea that once fully initialized, her kinaesthetic implant might restore *some* sensation and dexterity in her hands, but little else. And she had wallowed in that self-asserted conclusion to the point of all but vanquishing the prospect of a more significant improvement. She reminded herself of Dr. Kovačević's proviso: they wouldn't know *what* level of rehabilitation she could achieve until the neural bridge had fully synced to her prosthesis; the result could be a negligible recovery of motility, or something far more substantial . . . Arriving in Aegis's state-of-the-art rehabilitation facility, she allowed herself to indulge in a sliver of optimism, clinging on to that which she had strictly prohibited herself since the horrific ordeal began: hope.

They entered a wide, rectangular space with a high ceiling and walls lined with scenery panels like the one in her room. The synchronized displays created the uncanny illusion of standing beneath a large, wall-less marquee, erected in a meadow surrounded by lush and abundant woodland. Tall grass and riotous brushstrokes of wildflowers grew just beyond the boundary of the virtual gazebo, while the chirping and chattering of birdsong cut through the gentle rustle of the wind caressing the immaterial leaves.

The room housed eight rehabilitation cradles—several occupied by other patients in varying stages of recovery. Each cradle consisted of a hydraulic chair, positioned concentrically beneath what looked like a robotic octopus if each leg had been switched out with a random piece of fitness equipment. Controlled by a physio specialist from a luma-surface on a nearby desk, their mechanical arms could descend or retract at a moment's notice, presenting a diverse array of interactive apparatus designed to assess or strengthen different muscle groups. Hazel saw patients training with weights, stretching or flexing limbs with curl and press machines, all with vertebral prosthetics occupying different portions of their spine. One man even had a thoracic and partial cervical replacement almost identical to her own, and could be seen hobbling around his cradle with minimal assistance . . .

This just might work, she told herself, feeling the seedling of hope in her stomach sprouting its first leaves.

Dr. Kovačević greeted the pair warmly and helped Hazel get settled in her cradle. The orientation session began with a series of exercises intended to gauge her upper-extremity strength and motor skills: from exhausting lateral pulldowns to painfully arduous fist clenching. The tests illuminated in dismaying clarity the seriousness of her impairment. Still, she fought to retain her stiff upper lip, knowing the results could be used as a datum to measure the extent of her recovery once her kinaesthetic implant had been initialized . . .

Her father lingered at the sidelines, cheering her on as he might have done at sports day, had he ever made an effort to attend. The man had always appraised his children based on their academic achievements, judging their worthiness of the Edevane name by their accolades alone. And now here he stood: whooping and yowling like a drunken casterblade fan, all because she just about managed to touch her finger and thumb together . . .

"Excellent, Hazel," Dr. Kovačević said, swiping a hand across her luma-surface to initiate a cradle reset. "I think we've established a fairly solid base-line for where you're at presently . . . What's say we get you synced up?"

"I . . . I don't know if I'm ready yet," she stuttered nervously.

Atherton leaned over and spoke softly into her ear. "You've got nothing to fear, darling."

"But . . . What if it doesn't work?"

"That may well be the case. But like I always tell you, failure is only failure when we don't even let ourselves try. Just have to take that leap of faith."

She nodded, releasing a whistling exhalation through pursed lips. She waited as the doctor busied herself at her workstation, ushering in the cold grip of silence and allowing far too much time to stew with her thoughts. After a suspenseful minute, she felt her cradle humming with activity as if millions of busy insects had set off burrowing a hive throughout its cush-ion padding, creating an unusual static sensation that made the hairs on her arms stand up. Her prosthesis snapped magnetically into the corresponding grooves in her seat, locking the back of her neck firmly against the headrest.

"This might feel a little overwhelming," Dr. Kovačević warned. "Some people report feeling nausea or disorientation—others intense fear or a sense of impending doom. But rest assured, it will only be temporary, and will soon pass . . . OK. Initiating kinaesthetic handshake in three . . . two . . . one . . ."

Hazel didn't feel any discomfort or dizziness. Instead, she felt the nerve endings all over her body set alight in a blaze of haptic sensation, spreading like wildfire down her torso and throughout her limbs. She felt the strength returning to her hands, her dormant extremities startled awake from a deep slumber. And she felt the *power* of her legs as they remembered the pillars of chiseled muscle they had once been. They yearned to jump and sprint, as if encased in a prison of ice, now thawed by the roaring heat of the kinetic energy bottled up inside her. She stretched her ankles and wiggled her toes, becoming acutely aware of the itch of her leg hair snagging on the fabric of her joggers. It felt horrible, uncomfortable, and she utterly adored it.

Letting out a gasp of excited disbelief, she gripped her armrests and pushed with all her might lifting herself out of the cradle and onto her feet. She managed to stand on her own for a second or two before collapsing into her father's arms as he lunged forward to catch her. It wasn't much, but it was something . . .

"Steady there, Hazelnut," Atherton said, gazing down with a flabbergasted expression that suggested even *he* hadn't expected such a miraculous recuperation. "Let's just take it nice and easy . . . What do you feel?"

Hazel felt a wide-eyed grin whittle its way across her face. "Everything."

＝＝＝ TEN ＝＝＝

Once Hazel's euphoric elation over her astonishing recovery wore off, she set to work testing the limitations of her prosthetics. She charged belligerently at her somatic boundaries like a bull at the cape of a matador, hoping to gain a better understanding of where her strengths and weaknesses lay. The hours following were a grueling blur of intensive rehabilitation; with every strenuous set of pulls and stretches, she could feel the forging of new neural pathways as her mind retrained itself to actuate her muscles, like feeling her way through a maze where she knew the precise location of the exit but could only navigate through exhaustive trial and error.

As per Dr. Kovačević's warning, her synthetic spinal cord had only recouped *some* of the lost connectivity between her brain and her lower body, but as she continued to push herself, she became more convinced that her physical shortcomings could be accounted *and* compensated for. To fly for the NTSC required no less than peak physical performance and mental fortitude, and although she undoubtedly had a long way to go, the prospect of building her agility back up to preinjury levels felt increasingly achievable . . . After all, if she could shamble around on crutches and write her name on a luma-pad after just one day of physiotherapy, then who's to say what she could accomplish with a few weeks following a rigorous training regimen? With the same focus and determination she had applied to every other challenge in life, she believed she could turn her seemingly career-ending disabilities into yet another opportunity to prove her mettle . . .

After several hours of vigorous exercise, her muscles ached and her palms were raw with blisters from the constant friction of her crutch handles. Nevertheless, she forced herself to press on, because every second spent stationary was a second squandered, an unnecessary obstacle that would invariably delay the reconstruction of her old self.

Eventually, the staff in the rehabilitation ward began taking their leave for the day, replaced by an army of automated janitorial bots, skating single file along invisible tracks to clear away the day's dust. Her father took their arrival as another opportunity to insist she take a break, on this occasion citing his fears that she might exhaust herself to the point of collapse. Quietly fearing something similar, she grudgingly agreed, and he escorted her out of the facility and onto the balustraded balcony that ran the length of Aegis Infirmary. A dozen other civilians occupied the elevated terrace, smoking or inhaling vapor sticks, waiting anxiously for news of indisposed loved ones, or simply taking in the stellar vista afforded by the hospital's Upperdecks location. The Canyon's narrow strip of artificial sky doused the vast access channel in a purple-orange cataract of imitation twilight, causing Hazel to realize just how late the day had grown.

Atherton took her out to the platform's farthest corner where they sat on benches and tucked into the samosas from Virrisachi Arcade, which even cold and slightly soggy were still richly delicious. Admittedly, she enjoyed the cold touch of the bench's metal support slats against her thighs almost as much as the flavor of the spiced pastries, rediscovering every modicum of sensation as if born new to the world.

"That was some solid graft today," Atherton said, not so urbane he couldn't speak with a mouth full of food. "I must say I'm impressed by the work you're putting in; you're really giving it one hundred and ten percent."

"When have I ever done anything but?" she impishly replied, habitually folding the paper wrapper of her samosa into a tightly packed triangle—what would have been an impossible task mere hours ago. "The NTSC aren't in the business of letting sympathy cases fly their hardware . . . If I have any hope of getting my wings back, then it's gonna take nothing less."

Atherton formed a wry expression, visibly holding his tongue; the whine of passing swoops scored the uneasy silence heralding his response. "I know you're impatient to get back in the game but try not to get ahead of yourself . . . Remember: you could cause further injury by pushing too hard when you're supposed to be recovering."

She vehemently shook her head. "I'm not gonna waste another moment marinating in that room . . . Honestly, I feel good. I've had enough rest and recuperation for a lifetime; it's time to get to work now, and I won't be done until I'm back beneath the canopy of my kestrel."

"I'm all for you getting better, Hazelnut, but you need to do it for yourself; not for your career . . . Let's worry less about your flight status and focus on getting you healed—safely *and* in due course, I might add."

"Dad. When are you gonna learn that the more you try to deter me from something the more I'm gonna want to do it?"

Atherton launched to his feet in annoyance, turning away and leaning on the balcony railing. "Dammit all, Hazel. I swear by the Abyss you kids get more like your mother every day—too headstrong for your own good." He spun around to face her, sinking his shoulders in concession. Then, he straightened his posture and cocked his head to the side as if to say, *I don't agree with this but clearly there's no persuading you, so I will now proceed to pretend it was my idea.*

"Very well," he said. "Kovačević thinks you'll be fit enough for general discharge tomorrow, so you can move back home; we'll get you the best physiotherapist on the *Novara*, turn the parlor into a gym, and outfit it with whatever equipment you need . . . If you really are dead set on putting yourself through hell, then you'll be doing it under *my* supervision . . . Understood?"

She smiled warmly. "Yes, sir."

Abandoning her crutches, she pushed herself to her feet and took four cumbersome steps toward her father, taking him into a firm embrace. She felt suddenly awash with admiration for the man; he had been there from the moment she woke up and had hardly left her side since. Never before had he been so present and attentive, even during the miserable months following her mother's death. How cruel and unfortunate it seemed that it had taken no less than a near-death experience on her part for him to turn over a new leaf . . .

She squeezed him tighter, wanting the moment to never end. But then, something over his shoulder caught her attention: the surprising appearance of a close family friend—or at least, someone the *men* in her family would happily assign that title.

"Is that Caleb Callaghan?" she asked, abruptly releasing Atherton as she gawked at the double-decker barge hovering in view of the balcony. Resembling one of the open-top tourist buses prominent in Earth's cities at the turn of the millennium, the craft lumbered up the Canyon on six powerful repulsor pads with an enormous video screen hanging off its side displaying the image of her brother's childhood best friend. Below the bottom edge of the screen, to the right of the black-tinted windshield protecting the driver's compartment, two words appeared painted in audacious yellow that provoked a seething rage in her stomach: Humanity First.

"Ah, Bhaltair Abernathy's campaign barge," Atherton said, his hangdog expression broadcasting regret—regret, because Hazel now knew all about his ties to the organization and, as a previous benefactor, he had almost certainly contributed financially to the grotesque spectacle floating before them—perhaps even commissioned the entire thing . . .

"Yes, that's Caleb," he sheepishly confirmed. "As it turns out, Miss Callaghan has taken rather well to political activism—like a duck to water, as

they say . . . She's more or less replaced Bhaltair as the face of the movement—
a little more palatable, I think, for the undecided."

"Political activism." Hazel injected sufficient rancor into the words as she
repeated them. "Is *that* what we're calling it now?"

"Well, it's certainly what *I* thought we were doing—right up until Bhaltair
made it clear he had no interest in rectifying his infamous reputation. The
man is a vicious thug and nothing more."

"That's been public knowledge for a while now, Dad."

"Indeed . . . I must have missed the memo . . ."

The prerecorded footage showed Caleb wandering around the ring of
foreclosed businesses and dilapidated accommodation encircling the Statera
Basin—the nomenclature for the *Novara's* gravitational centrifuge: a monstrous rotary mechanism built by the ship's architects to negate the pull of
Pasture's many moons once in geosynchronous orbit, now no more than a
derelict arena inhabited predominantly by transients and glow abusers. Sandwiched in between Cendre Vale and the Vestiges, living conditions in the
basin were as awful as one might hope to find bowside of the blockade, with
many in the Upperdecks cruelly designating it the skid row of the *Novara*.
Wearing a black, zip-neck sweater and a MEDIA band around her arm, the
fiery redhead guided her camera crew from site to site, gesturing at the surrounding hovels, glow dens, and out of order water dispensers with an achingly rehearsed portfolio of solemn expressions.

"As you can see, the leech's ever-increasing intake of Novara *resources has
led to devastating water shortages in the lower decks of Amidships . . . Unem-
ployment is at an all-time high and crime rates are on a sharp increase . . . The
residents of the Statera Basin have had enough of the Administration's neglect
of the problem. They want action, and they want it now."*

Feeling her stamina waning, Hazel hobbled backward and collapsed onto
the bench. "Disingenuous retrograde tripe. As if the cohabitors have *anything*
to do with the ongoing drought . . . It's the Department of Utilities's abysmal
resource management that's to blame."

Atherton slid his hands into his pockets, preparing what would undoubtedly be an infuriatingly diplomatic riposte. "I know this is all a little hyperbolic, but you have to concede that if it weren't for the leech's conduits, there
wouldn't *be* shortages in the first place."

"If it weren't for the conduits, the *Novara* would be a tomb," she parried.
"We'd be left with irrevocably crippled fission reactors, unable to power our
hydroponics, and, oh yeah, subsequently unable to breathe."

Atherton waved a pretentious finger in the air. "Of course, that wouldn't
be the case had the Collision never happened in the first instance."

"Well, it *did* happen—to the human remnant *and* the cohabitors. So, there's no sense conjecturing about what circumstances we might have been in had things played out differently . . . We're all in this together, whether Humanity First like it or not."

"News of the administrator's brutal murder has shaken us all," Caleb continued, the campaign barge now at a stationary hover over the busy thoroughfare that preceded Aegis Infirmary. *"And while our sincere condolences go out to Madeline's family, it's important we all pay attention to what's going on in Chennai Plaza at this turbulent time. Make no mistake, right now the Administration are scrambling to elect one of their own—another elitist, blue-blooded bureaucrat, completely detached from the reality of what life really looks like for most Novarians . . . The time has come for us to make it clear that we don't want or need a council of politicians deciding what's best for us. It is we the people who should be allowed to steer the course. Because stars know we won't survive another four years of beleaguered politics and indecision on the leech issue. Separation from the* Devourer *is our only hope for salvation, and it's something we cannot accomplish under the current institution . . . The time for change has long since passed. We must act now . . . or suffer extinction."*

"As if I needed another reason to hate that girl," Hazel scoffed. "Now she's trying to incite mass mutiny!"

Atherton cleared his throat in disapproval. "Hate? Come now, Hazel, I think that's a bit uncalled for."

"No. That's me being polite . . . Caleb Callaghan is a callous, manipulative, egocentric, two-faced vixen. She led Tobias on for years, stringing him along and using his infatuation with her as a tool to get what she wanted, all the while engaged to poor, oblivious Jade Tanaka. All she's ever done is serve as a distraction and get him in trouble. Neither of you have worked up the courage to tell me what *really* happened when he was arrested by DMED but I'm willing to bet *she* had something to do with it."

Atherton's gaze dropped to his expensive Oxford shoes, reticently answering her question.

"Unbelievable," she muttered, shaking her head. "He shouldered the blame and she dropped him like a hot potato. And now here she is—jumping on this ludicrous separation bandwagon, using her Quarterdeck influence to demonize minorities, and shifting the blame for the Administration's failures. She's a piece of work is what she is."

"Consider your point made," was Atherton's laconic response. "Although I'm not sure she's deserving of *quite* so much disdain. Let us not forget that Tobias is, after all, a grown man, and is quite capable of making his own decisions . . . and mistakes . . . I for one am happy to see her stepping up to the plate and taking a stand for humanity. I just wish she could see Bhaltair for the venomous snake he really is. Humanity First would be much better off without him."

"They can *both* fall out of an airlock for all I care."

Sirens shrieked from somewhere farther down the Canyon, intensifying in pitch and volume as the culprit ambulance barreled through traffic toward the infirmary. Blues flashing from fixtures all over its chassis, the vehicle descended toward Aegis's emergency landing pad, only to find the platform obstructed by the hovering campaign barge. The paramedics angrily sounded their horn, impelling Bhaltair's hapless driver to clear the way; the barge headed off toward the blockade in search of more gullible punters to subject to Caleb Callaghan's sugarcoated hate-mongering.

Hazel breathed a deep sigh of relief. *Not a moment too soon.*

The following day, Hazel received the all-clear to continue her recovery at home. She would never forget her transformative stint at Aegis Infirmary; it was here within the dreamlike confines of the rehabilitation ward that she had been reborn, pulled back from the brink of despair and given a second chance to lead something resembling a fulfilling life. But these glossy, dove-white hallways would always serve as a reminder of those traumatic first few days: waking from a coma to find her broken body ghoulishly repaired with metal and silicone, reeling from the tragic deaths of her wingmates—two of whose lives had been directly in *her* hands, now forever lost to the Abyss. She couldn't stagnate here with those memories any longer; she needed forward momentum—to push through the guilt and move on. It had since become clear that only a dramatic change of scenery could help her achieve that . . .

Her father's continued presence was a blessing and a curse. Because, for one thing, she doubted she could have stayed so strong without his steadfast support, never letting her give in or succumb to the defeatism that had so doggedly tried to consume her. He did, however, annoy her immensely—such was the relationship between fathers and daughters, but to say that he had tested her patience with his relentless fussing over this long period of convalescence would be an understatement. Even now, as she prepared to take her leave, the man couldn't help but nitpick and meddle, insisting one of the porters carefully bag up the mounds of gifts and flowers that she had wanted so desperately to be rid of. She could have been packed and ready to go within minutes and instead found herself caught at the epicenter of a cashmere hurricane, rocked from side to side like a boat in a turbulent sea of bergamot cologne. Fortunately, the promise of respite arrived as news of unexpected visitors came to steal her away from the incessant attention.

"That repulsor chair cost me ten thousand nunits; will you *please* make an effort to use it!" But her father's pleas fell on headless ears. She had already collected her crutches and began the long hobble to the foyer, where she had been told her callers awaited her.

She entered a bright, semicircular space with an immaculate reception desk running parallel to its flat wall. Behind the desk there stood a wide plate of opaque glass; a screen of water cascaded down its surface, trickling around the ornate contours of the golden Aegis shield suspended at its center, which played host to an impressive sculpture of the snake-embossed Medusa head symbolic of the infirmary. Cream cushioned benches ran around the foyer's curved walls where several prospective patients and associated relations waited to be seen. Two of the seated individuals stood out like sore thumbs from the rest . . . Hazel's stunned eyes settled on none other than Admiral Jasper Coombs, who sat with rigid posture beside his no less imposing subordinate, Wing Commander Matias Luscombe. Garbed in ceremonial military uniforms, the pair looked comically out of place framed against the glossy, polished surfaces of the infirmary—the aesthetic antithesis to their *native* habitats of the NTSC Command and the Launch Silo.

Clocking her approach, they both stood up to greet her, removing their officers' hats and stowing them underarm with clockwork synchronicity. Embellished with more gold and silver than a trophy case, Coombs's white uniform nicely contrasted his rich umber skin, his decorated career commemorated by a scaffolding of medals and rank pins laddered across his chest and shoulders. Normally a man of impeccable adherence to officer grooming regulations, the salt-and-pepper stubble encroaching on his harsh face spoke of an apparent slip in his standards, which after what had surely been some of the most testing weeks in his decades of service, Hazel thought perfectly reasonable . . .

She stood to attention and performed the best salute she could while propped up by her crutches.

"At ease, cadet," the admiral articulated, his deep voice precise and deliberate, compensating for his relatively short stature with an air of intensity. "I think, given the circumstances, *we* should be the ones saluting you . . . Wing Commander Luscombe and I are all too familiar with what you and your squad went up against out there; to survive an engagement like that with so few hours under the canopy . . . Well, let's just say I've commanded plenty of pilots over the years with markedly more experience who couldn't have pulled themselves out like you did. You must have some *real* grit."

"Thank you, sir." Hazel paused, noting internally that the interceptors the man was clearly referring to were definitely *not* the same bogeys that wiped out Delta . . . *Did he even read my report? Or look at* any *of the black box data recovered from my helmet's flight recorder?* Doubting she had the standing to even attempt second-guessing an admiral, she reticently continued, "I only wish the others in my squad could have been as fortunate."

Wing Commander Matias Luscombe, a man who had been Hazel's coach, mentor, and ruthless disciplinarian for the better part of a year, dipped his square chin and displayed an unprecedented look of solicitude. "They died in service of the union," he husked in a voice throttled by years of screaming drill instructions. "They will be remembered for their sacrifice. And you mustn't blame yourself for their loss. As the admiral suggested: it's a miracle you're even alive."

"No," Coombs heartily interjected. "That was no miracle; that was skill, strength, and determination . . . *This* is a miracle." The man gestured at her lower body with the knuckle of his index finger. "I was informed you had made some remarkable progress since your surgery, but I didn't expect to see you up on your feet quite so soon."

"The wing commander knows to expect nothing less from me, sir." She flicked Luscombe a gloating smile. "My aptitude scores are second to none. I always endeavor to be the best in class among my peers in whatever we're tasked with. And *this* was just another task—an obstacle to overcome, a mountain I had to scale to get where I wanna be."

The Admiral leaned forward, scouring her face with intense narrow eyes. "And where is it that you want to be, cadet?"

Hazel took a moment to prepare her response, feeling a rush of exhilaration as she recalled the visceral thrill of swooping through the void. "I want to do exactly what I was born to do, sir: defend the *Novara* and her citizens from anyone or anything that might seek to bring us harm . . . I wanna be out there in the endless night, stars beyond my nose cone and three hundred kilograms of thrust on my tail. *That's* where I belong."

The admiral's amicable smile straightened into a subtle frown. It wasn't sorrow or remorse, but annoyance as if taking umbrage that something she said had somehow put him in an awkward or difficult position.

"While that's admirable, I think it a little premature to be considering resuming your training so soon after the incident."

"But I can do it!" she protested. "I mean, look at how far I've come in just one short month."

Luscombe's uncharacteristic look of concern seemed to deepen, almost looking as though repressing the urge to reach out and hug her. "You've been through an incredibly traumatic experience, Hazel," he said. "There will be a lot more to overcome than just your physical injuries. Think of the psychological damage this whole ordeal will have inflicted . . . You know very well that pilots of the NTSC must be of unimpeachable mental fortitude; only the soundest and sharpest of minds may qualify."

"So that's it?" she asked, chest rising and falling dramatically, almost to the point of hyperventilation. "You're gonna call me mentally unstable without performing *any* kind of formal psyche evaluation and just write me off like that?"

Coombs showed his palms placatingly. "No one's being written off, cadet. We only want to make sure you're keeping your expectations in check . . . Besides, there are plenty of ways you can defend the *Novara* without being the one holding the flight stick. We're always in need of personnel with your prowess and acumen in command. We need deck officers, comms operators, weapons, and radar specialists. The NTSC is a machine with many cogs— every one just as important as the next."

Hazel opened her mouth to object before the admiral swiftly cut her off.

"You don't need to make a decision now," he said, issuing a condescending smile. "Focus on getting yourself back in fighting shape, *then* we'll decide which course is best for you."

Just then, Hazel heard the all too recognizable drum of her father approaching from behind, syn-leather soles screaming on the infirmary's squeaky laminate flooring. Coombs greeted Atherton rather coldly as the man arrived, looking dangerously close to rolling his eyes. Hazel felt conflicted about having Atherton by her side. On the one hand, it was a relief to have some backup facing off against Coombs and Luscombe, but if he were to gaze into her trembling eyes and ask, *Are you alright, Hazelnut?* as he often did, then she feared she just might break into tears in front of the admiral—a man to whom she had to convey strength and resilience if she was to salvage her military career.

"What news from the council, Ath?" Jasper asked, sending an almost imperceptible look of derision Luscombe's way. "Has there been any progress in determining future leadership? What with the terrorists making ridiculous demands of us sternside of the blockade, we're in dire need of strong governance."

"Last I heard, they were still deliberating," Atherton replied, seemingly nonplussed. "It has been . . . hectic, to say the least. The entire cabinet is in upheaval after Madeline's death—votes of no confidence are issued the very moment someone is lined up to succeed her. It seems many would prefer not to fill the boots she left behind."

Hazel detected a scintilla of contrition in the admiral's steely expression, a fleeting visitation of sadness quickly expunged with a brisk straightening of his uniform. "Her conviction and leadership will be sorely missed," he lamented. "Hopefully Phalanx can apprehend Eamon Wyatt and bring him to justice before he inflicts any further damage to the integrity of the union."

Atherton stroked his chin pensively. "I've had my fair share of unfortunate run-ins with Eamon. I always considered him a petulant, leech-sympathizing, self-righteous worm of a man . . . but I never thought him capable of something like this . . ." He shook his head, furrowing his brow; if Hazel didn't know any better, she'd say it almost looked as if her father doubted the veracity of this Wyatt person's guilt, which—considering his usual taking of whatever the NTNN reported as absolute gospel—seemed deeply uncharacteristic . . .

Luscombe cleared his throat. "It's a shame you don't feel as though you're up to the task of taking the reins, councilman. I'm sure you would have made a fine administrator."

"Oh, I'm not a councilman anymore," Atherton humbly replied, reaching out and wrapping an arm around Hazel's shoulder. "My place is right here. Recent events have helped me realize that my responsibilities as a father supersede my civic duties. So, I'm now officially retired."

Coombs offered a disingenuous smile. "I'm not sure I agree . . . but I understand." The admiral clapped his hands together to politely terminate the conversation, bidding Hazel and Atherton farewell as he and Luscombe started toward the exit. He then stopped abruptly, turning on his heel with a finger raised in the air. "There was, actually, just one final thing I had hoped to discuss, Hazel."

"Of course, sir," she answered.

"It's the small matter of your postmission report . . . While I'm never one to let punctuality go without praise, are you sure you wouldn't rather wait until you've fully recovered before submitting your debrief?"

Hazel took a pause, feeling a surge of disquiet shooting up her cybernetic spine. "I thought it best to transcribe the incident while it was still fresh in my memory, sir . . . Not that I could *ever* forget any of the details of what happened . . ."

"Under normal circumstances, I would tend to agree—'strike while the iron is hot,' as they say. But what's causing me some concern is this emphatic mention of yours of modified kestrels—the implications are unsettling, to say the least."

"I know what I saw, sir . . . The attacking fighters were human in origin and design, augmented with a high degree of *Devourer* bioengineering. They vastly outperformed us in flight and combat capabilities; myself and Delta Two . . . Zain Cantrell . . . we could hardly keep them in our sights for more than a second before they evaded us with nonballistic maneuvers or outright vanished."

She alternated her gaze between Coombs and Luscombe's scrutinizing expressions, her unease aggregating into a genuine frustration. "The flight data from my helmet should corroborate *all* of this."

"Alas, your helmet's flight recorder was destroyed when it struck the canopy of your kestrel," Coombs informed. "We were unable to retrieve anything comprehensive to corroborate your observations."

Luscombe tilted his head, locking wide eyes with Hazel's as he nodded slowly. It was an eccentricity she had seen from him before—one usually appropriated when reciting an exam question or laying out the conditions of a training exercise. To her, it meant *Be aware of what you can't see*, or simply, *Read between the lines . . .*

"If the impact you suffered was strong enough to break a nanocarbon-encased black box," he said, "isn't it possible these modified kestrels are just a product of severe concussion? False memories resulting from your cranial injury, not to mention the painkillers I'm sure the doctors administered once you were admitted?"

"These weren't hallucinations, or false memories, sir," Hazel affirmed. "I don't know exactly what they were, but I can say with full confidence that they weren't interceptors."

Luscombe formed a tight frown, wordlessly reprimanding her for refusing to budge on her position. A note of sadness underlined the scathing expression, as if she had seriously jeopardized herself, and he as her proud teacher feared what the repercussions for her stalwart insistence might be.

"The problem is," Coombs began in a patronizing tone. "Because you are not yet a combat wingman, by law your report cannot be exempt from the Freedom of Information Act, which makes it a matter of public record . . . Aren't you afraid of causing mass panic; giving people the notion that the NTSC are not in control of *Novara* airspace?"

"All the more reason people should be made aware, sir . . . Whatever those things were, I doubt we've seen the last of them. Next time, they could attack a civilian freighter or a salvage crew working in the Debris Belt. Do we not have a responsibility to spread public awareness; to learn as much as we can about them so we can formulate an effective defense strategy?"

The admiral curled his upper lip, forming a tightly repressed snarl. "I cannot order you to retract your postmission report, but I am telling you: it would be in your best interest . . ."

Hazel swallowed the nervous lump in her throat. She caught her father's gaze from the corner of her eye, hoping for some kind of reassurance or affirmation from him, but found the normally stoic man looking just as perplexed as she.

"With . . . with all due respect, sir," she stuttered. "My duty toward the citizens of the NTU dictates that I cannot retract . . . The report is accurate, and my observations still stand."

The admiral pushed his shoulders back and pursed his lips, a gesture that seemed to say, *Very well. Proceed at your own peril.* He turned to Luscombe, gave a firm nod, then they made a swift and unceremonious exit. Hazel watched the pair disappear through the foyer's sliding doors, feeling somehow as if she had just sealed her fate. But then, standing there with her perturbed father, something caught her eye that eased her anxiety. A little way down one of the corridors stretching on from the reception area, she saw a woman: another patient in a white hospital gown, standing motionless and staring at her with a warm, encouraging smile. Slim-built with dark, shoulder-length hair, Hazel almost felt like she recognized the woman, and the familiar way in which she stared at her certainly reinforced that suspicion. She realized that in the drab, colorless hallway, the ogling stranger almost seemed to radiate warmth, glowing as if superimposed on top of reality itself, a lucent overlay inscribed on her retinas that she could even see when she blinked her eyes.

"Do . . . do you see that?" she asked, feeling a peculiar fizzing sensation emanating from beneath her kinaesthetic implant. She turned to her father, wondering if he too had noticed, but found the man staring into space with a vexed expression, no doubt still dwelling on the admiral's thinly veiled ultimatum. When she returned her gaze to the corridor, the mystery woman had vanished, leaving her to question whether she had ever really been there in the first place.

ELEVEN

Atherton summoned his, Cavalier SK-7 to collect them from Aegis Infirmary's civilian landing platform. Flown autonomously by its integrated Hypatia VI, the flashy swoop banked out of a transit lane and circled overhead—a narrow wedge of polished ruby gliding on air, descending toward them on columns of bright blue propulsion emitted by its fission-drive repulsor pads.

Normally, Hazel felt a level of embarrassment climbing into one of her father's ostentatious chariots in view of onlookers. She didn't revel in the family wealth as her brother did; with poverty affecting so many throughout the *Novara*, something felt terribly obnoxious about spending a small fortune on private transport when the trams were so reliable and efficient. However, after her disappointing and somewhat worrying conversation with Admiral Coombs, she didn't think twice about ensconcing herself in the vehicle's pungent syn-leather interior, letting it whisk her away to the promise of home comforts.

She sat with her temple resting against the passenger-side window, watching the headlights of passing swoops bloom in the condensation of her breath as it gathered on the glass. The Canyon's opposing edifices raced by either side of her—two endless bulwarks of vibrant cityscape reaching up to the star-speckled band of luma-cast sky overhead and plunging toward the smoggy depths of Cendre Vale. She steadied her gaze and let her surroundings blur into a kaleidoscopic streak of amber and azure, lulling herself into a state of troubled absorption, a fat, purring cat of despondency perched atop her chest, kneading her with its curved-dagger claws. Meanwhile, her father happily blathered on about his strategy for her at-home recovery, unaware or perhaps unfazed by her lack of attention. Personally, she no longer saw the point in wasting time and effort working to improve her situation—not when the gatekeepers had declared her case hopeless before she'd even had a chance to prove herself. The admiral had made it clear that she would never fly again—not for the NTSC, at least, and she had no interest in pursuing a career as a pilot in the civilian sector.

Languishing in her hospital bed, she had been so certain her injuries would be the obstacle preventing her from achieving greatness. But bureaucracy, red tape, and institutional prejudice would be the contrivances of her downfall, the constraints her superiors would brandish to forever stem her progression. In whatever path she chose in life, an arbitrary ceiling awaited her, built under the spurious pretense of protection, when in truth, it would only serve to inhibit her. Fate had neutered her destiny, lopped it off at the stem and ensured that no matter what she accomplished, others would determine her worth not by her merits, but by the physical limitations cruelly imposed on her. She was nothing more than a broken piece of machinery, and with every minute, she wished more and more that her meddling rescuers had left her in the black with the wreckage of her kestrel, instead . . . with Shiyana . . . and with Zain.

Her vision blurred as tears began to collect around her eyes. Soaring down the Canyon's wide expanse, Atherton's swoop had fallen out of range of any nearby grav-emitters, so instead of rolling down her cheeks, the droplets pooled irritably in the weightlessness. She used the shoulder strap of her tank top to dry her stinging eyes, feeling the pull of deceleration as they slowed to a sudden stop. *Unusual*, she thought, given that it didn't feel like enough time had elapsed for them to have reached her father's Emeral Heights apartment in the financial district. Her bemusement rapidly devolved into concern as she lifted her head to find Atherton spun around in his rear-facing seat, attention fixated through the windscreen. The swoop had indeed come to a full stop but had inexplicably done so in the path of a busy lane of traffic, right smack in the center of the Canyon. The passenger cabin juddered as transports closely overtook them, ducking and swerving to evade with horns blaring and headlights frantically flashing.

"Hypatia!" Atherton bellowed. "What in the name of Lei-Ghannam are you doing?"

"Apologies, Mister Edevane," the VI cordially responded. "Something seems to have gone wrong."

"Just get us moving again. Or pull over if there's a problem! If we don't clear the way, we'll be pulverized!"

Accompanied by a raucous screech of scraped metal, the swoop jerked sideways as a barreling cargo barge clipped their right side, doubtless flown manually by its semidistracted operator. Perplexingly, the swoop didn't career away in the residual motion of the impact as one would expect an object floating in zero gravity to behave. This invalidated Hazel's initial hypothesis of a drive-core stall, instead suggesting Hypatia was actively using the inertial dampers to hold position.

As Atherton unleashed a furious diatribe in response to the collision, a pleasant chime sounded from the dashboard. Hypatia's soft and slightly automated voice sounded once again. "Remote access control initiated . . . Please stand by."

Hazel felt her innards lurch upward as the swoop began an abrupt descent. She dug her fingernails into the material of her seat to stop herself from lifting away, struggling to retain purchase. Taking a moment to stabilize himself, Atherton promptly unbuckled his safety belt and performed a surprisingly elegant airborne pirouette, orienting himself toward the windshield.

"Override, Hypatia!" he clamored, pounding the dashboard with a tightly clenched fist, every impact sending him drifting farther away from the control surface. The request went suitably ignored, the defiant VI merely repeating her previous response in a vexingly polite voice.

"Overengineered, newfangled scrap fodder! . . . I *knew* I should have gone for the classic model."

"I don't think it's a malfunction, Dad," warned Hazel, holding herself in place with her palms pressed against the cream headlining of the cabin's ceiling. "Remote access control means we're being commandeered. Someone must have tapped into our guidance and input a new destination."

"That's absurd! Who would have the authority to do such a thing?"

Craning her neck, she turned her gaze upward through the passenger window and watched the strip of sky above gradually narrowing, the lanes of traffic now twinkling streams of red and white satellites, gliding silently against the ersatz night.

"Emergency services, mainly," she finally answered, hearing the nervous flutter in her voice. "But I don't know . . . We probably would have been hailed if this was Phalanx pulling us over . . . No, this feels like something else . . ."

Outside, visibility decreased as they sank deeper toward the Canyon's nethermost reaches, the air beyond the windscreen now thickening with smog expelled by the fields of industrial machinery lurking below. An argon luster permeated the brume, an elongated carpet of fire stretching on beneath them, billowing a layer of smoke through which the ambient light filtering from above could scarcely breach. Squinting into the gloom, Hazel spied behemoth shapes emerging—the monstrous turbines, ventilation ducts, and heat sinks of the *Novara*'s defunct thermal processing plant, built by the ship's architects to convert the excess heat generated by the ripple drive into surplus energy. Naturally, in the years following the Collision, with the obliteration of the ripple-space engines, the ancient structures fell into disuse. And as resources dwindled and necessities became scarce, capitalism reared its ugly head from the tomes of history, and the fires of industry were lit. Provident entrepreneurs set off repurposing the neglected installation into a sprawling manufacturing plant, constructing refineries to process material salvaged from the Debris Belt, and factories to fabricate products from the yield. The effort necessitated the formation of a tremendous workforce—a mixture of skilled and unskilled laborers who spent their entire lives in Lower Amidships, predominantly inhabiting the tightly packed wards of Halvorsen Commons.

Hazel fostered no prejudice against the working class, of course, but found it difficult to completely dispel the preconceptions her elitist father had instilled in her from an early age about the residents of this place. Nor could she easily forget the litany of stories from Tobias about his occasional nights out in the myriad dive bars scattered throughout the region and the unsavory types he would often encounter. Assuming he hadn't been completely overembellishing, it was likely that she and Atherton were in potentially serious danger—two renowned Upperdecks denizens, stranded in the lawless depths of Cendre Vale in an unresponsive sports-model. They would be prime targets for opportunistic swoopjackers, or maybe even kidnappers plotting to hold them for ransom. In fact, the more she considered it, the more she became convinced this was a targeted assault, meticulously planned and executed by some malicious ganker conspiring to rob, murder, or take them hostage. Evidently, Atherton suspected something similar, as he had already begun a frenzied attempt to hail assistance; as a dignitary of considerable means, he could have a raptor with a squad of armed enforcers dispatched to evacuate them from anywhere on the *Novara* with a single voice command—a costly insurance policy called Saber Safeguarding, exclusively available to the NTU's most elite citizens. Staring at the grimy trellis of industrial thoroughfares growing through the windscreen, wearing the expression of an unwilling diver being lowered into shark-infested waters, he held his feather before his trembling lips and uttered his personalized evac code and approximate location. "Scarlet . . . Halcyon . . . Edevane. Cendre Vale! Scarlet . . . Halcyon . . . Edevane. Cendre Vale!"

The device blurted a grating tone before another jarringly friendly voice replied, "Sorry. Your Saber Safeguarding platinum membership has expired . . . Please contact the enrollment team for further information."

He raised the feather over his head as if about to smash it against the steel-rimmed cupholders nestled between the seats, then reconsidered and settled for furiously shaking it before his reddening face. "Honestly, the mountains of nunits I've hemorrhaged to Saber over the years, and the *one* time we need them we're shit out of luck!"

Now abundantly clear that *no one* would be coming to rescue them, Hazel's heart sank as she felt gravity tugging at her from below; they had now fallen in range of the grav-emitters buried below Cendre Vale's ground level, meaning they had almost arrived at the chosen destination of their mystery chauffeur.

Hypatia ambled over an automated swoop chassis production line, coasted over rows of freight containers as she banked to the right and made her final approach, vectoring toward a narrow alleyway wedged in between two storage facilities. Hazel's last thread of hope that perhaps this *was* just an innocuous guidance error snapped the moment she set eyes on that dismal passageway— the perfect dead end for a skulking predator to corner its prey . . .

Atherton made a fruitless effort to hail Phalanx through their public emergency line, which she intuited would fail to connect even before it inevitably did so. Whoever was doing this seemed to have unfettered access to encrypted personal security systems: the ability to remotely manipulate the guidance of a councilman's private swoop and nullify his long-standing Saber Safeguarding membership. It certainly didn't seem beyond the realm of possibility that the orchestrator could block outgoing calls from his feather, too . . .

Darkness consumed the passenger cabin, the ominous walls of the encapsulating alleyway revealed in fluctuating blue light, cast by the abating propulsion from the repulsor pads as they spun down. The vehicle came to a thudding stop and an eerie silence endured; the pair's heavy breathing amplified by a hermetically sealed vacuum of sound.

Atherton reached over and gently shook her thigh. "Don't panic," he said, likely trying to reassure himself as much as he was her. "Your father spares no expense when it comes to safety. This swoop has titanium-laced body panels and projectile-proof glass—trust me: *no one's* getting inside . . . Hypatia! Lock us down immediately, if you would be so kind."

A muffled *kerchunk* sounded from inside the doors, then Hypatia jovially replied, "Sentry mode engaged."

Atherton loosed an exasperated sigh. "Unbelievable. *Now* she decides to listen to me . . . OK. All we need to do is sit tight and wait for . . ."

"Shhh!" Hazel interrupted, focusing intently through the windscreen with a halting hand lingering in the air. She thought she had seen movement—someone or something draped in shadow, darting across the alleyway beyond the hood. She caught it again in her peripheral vision, this time discerning the profile of a broad-shouldered man hurrying past her window. Detecting a light source emanating from her rear, she spun around to find her father's gawking expression highlighted green by a perfect semicircle of scintillating laser light, striking the outside of his window. From its concentric center arrived a bright phosphorescent flash. Then, like a portal to hell opening up, the arc ignited into a ring of blazing fission energy, transitioning from the Cavalier's exterior to the inside of the door. As miasmic sparks and molten metal spewed into the passenger cabin, a circular chunk of the swoop's titanium-laced body paneling slid free and thumped into the footwell, leaving a hole in the side of the vehicle approximately one meter in diameter. A burly man wearing a black tracksuit and an expression of malevolent delight stood just outside the entry point, holding in his hands the heavy-duty fission cutter with which he had just cracked their mobile safe room open like a nut.

Hazel made a quick assessment based on what scant information she could ascertain about the stranger in the low light. Judging from his neat crew cut and muscular physique, she guessed he was a military man. Or at least, certainly considered himself one—probably failed his Phalanx psych-eval for being too unstable or aggressive, and quenched his thirst for dishing out violence by pursuing a career as a mercenary instead.

Another man loomed behind the first looking no less threatening, compensating for his slightly weedier frame with an intricate tapestry of neck and face tattoos and displaying a set of chrome teeth with a truculent grin. They seemed organized and well prepared for the task at hand, which Hazel believed was her and her father's immediate execution.

"You two couldn't have picked a worse patch to break down in, huh?" the one with the fission cutter gruffed—an odd thing to say, considering the patch had been ostensibly chosen for them . . .

Atherton shuffled away from the door and crouched protectively in front of her. "Look, lads . . . Is it money you're after? Because I'm very high up in the Administration . . . Just name your price and I'll . . . I'll double it!"

The mercs shared a derisive glance, then a simultaneous nod.

"Remember," Chrome Teeth said to the other, cracking knuckles menacingly. "Make it messy, but not the face . . . It's gotta look like a mugging turned violent."

The bigger one dropped the fission cutter and reached behind his back, producing the deactivated hilt of a fission dagger. "Gotcha." He flipped the weapon in the air and caught it reverse grip; a coruscating blade of volatile energy sprang from its quillon, fizzing and crackling like an overloaded circuit breaker. He reached into the passenger cabin and grabbed Atherton by the scruff of his neck, effortlessly yanking the man out into the alleyway.

"Dad!" Hazel screamed, the suede material of her father's jacket slipping through her fingers. She watched helplessly as the thug propped him up against the corroded wall of the alleyway, unleashing a vicious salvo of punches directly into his stomach. She lifted herself out of her seat and prepared to intervene, but felt her kinaesthetic implant hitting its operational limits, her limbs too heavy and sluggish to even attempt hand-to-hand combat. A hot flash of frustration tore through her chest; she knew she had the skills *and* the training to take these two thugs down, but her body just couldn't translate that knowledge into effective action. It reminded her of a hundred harrowing nightmares in which inexplicable paralysis had prevented her from stopping something terrible as it played out before her.

While the battering continued outside, Chrome Teeth climbed into the passenger cabin and shoved her forcefully back into her seat. She caught a glimpse of his "RAGE. HATE" knuckle tattoos and the black grime under his revoltingly long fingernails. His unpleasant musk invaded her nostrils as he slithered toward her. Her body flooded with adrenaline and she lifted her leg to score a powerful kick to his jaw, nearly passing out from the sheer exertion.

He reeled from the impact and took a moment to recover, sinisterly snickering as he wiped blood from the corner of his mouth. "You're gonna pay for that you Upperdecks slut," he rasped with a voice like gravel in a tumble dryer. "*Was* gonna make things quick and easy for you. Now, you're *both* gonna suffer."

She felt his revolting, ratlike hands invading her body, clawing and gripping her exposed shoulders as he fought to restrain her. She struggled with every morsel of strength she could summon, watching over his shoulder in horror as the other mercenary swung his arm backward, and rammed the fission dagger into her father's stomach. Throttling his convulsing victim against the wall, the brute glanced over his shoulder to smile grimly at her, seeming to take an almost masochistic pleasure in her wailing shrieks of grief.

"I'll kill you," she hissed, foaming at the mouth in unadulterated bloodlust, gazing into her father's terrified eyes as they began to dull. "I swear by the Abyss, I'll kill you both!"

Emboldened by her distress, Chrome Teeth overpowered her, constrained her with his knee, and held her shoulders in place to make sure she had an adequate view for what came next. Laughing maniacally, the mercenary outside swung his arm back once more, lining the fission digger up for a killing blow. Her desperate pleas for mercy went ignored, but just as a bloodcurdling "No!" escaped her throat, a bright light source shone from above, dousing the alleyway in glaring fluorescence. Stopped dead, the merc turned his head upward, the ugly contours of his snarling grimace accentuated by the intensifying brilliance overhead. Hazel turned her stare to the windscreen as the dazzling headlights of a rapidly descending vehicle came into view.

The silhouetted craft carved out the squat profile of a giant, gunmetal-gray bullfrog. She recognized it as a service camion—a mobile maintenance transport used by engineers conducting repairs on the Canyon's extensive tram network. The behemoth came to a low hover just before the alleyway's terminus, its gimballed repulsor pads kicking up clouds of soot and dirt. She heard the whirring thud of a sliding hatch opening, then a furious flurry of growls and barks as a dog, of all things, bolted from the vehicle wearing a ballistic vest and galloped toward the mercenary. With gnashing teeth, the animal leaped in the air and locked its jaws around the unwitting merc's arm, toppling him to the ground in a perfectly executed canine takedown.

"You stay right there, you uppity bitch!" Chrome Teeth demanded, clambering outside to assist his downed associate. Through the windscreen, the transport's gull-wing door swung open. A hooded stranger, almost definitely *not* an employee of the Transitech maintenance department, hopped out of the driver's compartment and strode determinedly toward the scuffling threesome, Chrome Teeth now struggling to pull the dog away. Unholstering a weapon Hazel struggled to identify, the stranger extended his firing arm and discharged several plasma bolts, illuminating his startled targets in blinding green strobes.

Before the two mercenaries could even acknowledge the newcomer, they fell to the floor dead, buckled over one another like sorry sacks of refuse. Leaving the dog to sniff at their lifeless, smoking bodies, the stranger scrambled around the swoop's hood, crouching briefly to check Atherton's vitals as the man sat slumped against the wall, clutching his abdomen. The stranger then stood up and turned to face Hazel, who for the first time since his valiant arrival, caught sight of his rugged features, his bronze skin seeming to glisten in the headlights of his idling camion.

"Well, I'll be damned," he said, showing a mollifying smile. "Another day, another ruck of Edevanes gettin' 'emselves into trouble . . . It's Hazel, right?"

She nodded, shell-shocked. He holstered his weapon and leaned through the cutter hole, reaching out a reassuring hand toward her. "Name's Eamon Wyatt, ma'am . . . Everything's gonna be alright. Stick with me, and you'll be safe."

TWELVE

While Captain Holloway deliberated over the logistics of an escape through the Vestiges, Tobias and Teo seized their opportunity and made a discreet exit through the *Assurance*'s topside emergency hatch. Tobias's initial plan had been to sneak out through the cargo bay, which Teo rightfully dismissed as a brain-dead idea, given the cacophony usually stirred by the archaic gears and hydraulic pistons of the bay door's actuators.

"Besides. Door got banjaxed during the crash," the mouthian salvage specialist had declared, slipping her feet into her stencil spray-painted work boots as the pair geared up in her cabin—a riotous amalgamation of a teenage girl's bedroom and the tool compartment of a seasoned engineer. "Blocked by a whole heap of debris an' all, from what Isaac says . . . Trust me: we won't make a peep goin' up through the chimney; Captain'll be none the wiser."

As usual, the girl had been right: they managed to leave the crash site without raising any suspicions and had set off scouring the ruins of the Cohabitor Ghetto on their hunt for the displaced residents of Juniper Sanctuary. Originally, Tobias had intended to recruit Null for his admittedly half-baked evac mission; with no discernible roads or pathways to speak of, even attempting to navigate the Ghetto without an experienced wayfinder felt like a recipe for failure, especially after Harmony's devastative efforts to expulse the Monarchs from their burrow. But in the wake of the Composer's harrowing public address, Null's anguish over the destruction of aer neighborhood had taken a heavy toll on him, manifesting as a temple-splitting migraine, paired with debilitating emotional distress—an excruciating loss the likes of which he had seldom before experienced, his home, his heritage, utterly and callously obliterated. He knew that to venture any farther into the ruins with aer accompanying him would render him useless, and he very much needed his faculties for the task at hand. He hadn't been forced to go alone, however:

once Teodora cottoned on to his intentions, nothing short of two broken legs could deter her from tagging along . . .

An alien landscape enveloped them—a crowded forest of irregular domes resembling giant tar bubbles, varied in size and encrusted in a layer of something like crystalized volcanic rock. Angular structures cobbled together from recycled lunar metal jutted up through the crowns of these obsidian igloos, doubtless a rudimentary effort by the Prey to emulate the architectural style of their neighbors across the Çorak—a mark of solidarity and a willingness to cooperate. *Look! We can build in straight lines and right angles, too. Let's be friends!*

Tobias took a particular interest in the organic portions of these constructions. He struggled to vocalize exactly how they were sculpted but carried an innate understanding of the process through evolutionary knowledge attained by resonance with Null. Were *he* in possession of the necessary anatomy, he didn't doubt that he too could secrete the bio-resin required to instinctually print his own yurt, molding and whittling the substance into shape with dexterous mandibles, as had so many over the centuries spanned by his ancestral memories.

Sadly, many of the surrounding structures had been leveled by the preceding barrage of mortar fire, and those left standing were tarnished by jagged cracks and smoldering blast holes, bearing the scars of fierce and prolonged strife. With Drexen's forces defeated, the constant percussion of gunfire had now subsided, but a suspenseful tension underscored the ensuing quiescence that had Tobias's stomach tied in knots. The Mouth felt like a pressure cooker primed to explode; when the Composer's twelve hours had elapsed, and the Administration had predictably failed to meet her demands, then he feared Armageddon—a lasting conflict that, at best, would see the district reduced to lunar dust, and at worst, spell extinction for *both* species inhabiting the Coalescence.

We have *to get the little ones out before that happens*, he thought, directing Teo with a nod to skirt around the glassy, crumbling remains of what had once been someone's home.

She swatted a hand irksomely to signal, *Worry about yourself. I'm fine.*

While he found it comforting to have her street smarts and knowledge of the area to hand, it occurred to him that the farther they progressed, the less he seemed to need her . . . Traversing the Ghetto felt a little like déjà vu; his surroundings were alien, utterly incomprehensible, and yet, inspired an implacable sense of familiarity. He knew all the nifty shortcuts, the optimal routes through the networks of conjoined tenements acting as public thoroughfares, their constructors apparently unconcerned with the human concept of privacy.

"Wasn't *I* supposed to be the one navigatin' here?" Teo asked, paying close attention to her footing so as not to stumble on the uneven terrain. "You seem awfully well-oriented for someone who's never even stepped foot in the Ghetto before."

"It's difficult to explain," Tobias mumbled, scanning his battle-ravaged surroundings for recognizable landmarks. "On the one hand, I'm hopelessly lost, but then, courtesy of Null's memories, I know this place like the back of my hand. It feels like remembering things that I'd previously forgotten, like recollecting the events of the night before after getting blackout drunk. What I can recall is foggy, unclear, but then I see something familiar, and it all takes shape . . . For example: see this place?" He motioned toward a nearby structure, its black-brown surface appearing slightly smoother and more reflective than that of those around it. Sensing the building held significant meaning for Null, he clenched his eyes and dug deep, pouring over his library of aer experiences as if sifting for gold. "This place belonged to an old cohabitor who ran . . . well, I'm not sure how to describe it: an 'apothecary,' I guess. Ae used to brew this medicinal tea made from Höllengarten vines—dried out, crushed, and sieved in boiling water through a filter. Tasted like . . ." He grimaced. "Yuck; lime and formaldehyde . . . Still, Null is mad for the stuff."

"Crazy how you can know all that just from spendin' a little time inside aer head."

"Not just, Null's head," he clarified. "But aer close associations, aer descendants—It's like hypermnesia: I feel as if I've lived a thousand lives, generations of knowledge buried beneath layers of synaptic haze . . . Just have to figure out how to uncover and decipher it all."

Teo rolled her eyes, beckoning him forward impatiently. "Well, can you save your synaptic excavation until *after* we've located the junies, please? Don't want you blowin' a fuse and goin' catatonic on me. Harmony probably got eyes on us already so we shouldn't outstay our welcome."

Tobias straightened his jacket, nodding resolutely in the direction of the field of resonant energy that had been steadily intensifying as they progressed toward its source. He felt certain the anomaly could only be the result of a large aggregation of Prey huddled together, which would align with what had been conveyed to him by Nanimonai—the cohabitor co-owner of Juniper Sanctuary and one of Teo's primary caregivers—regarding aer intentions to seek shelter with a relative in the area. He felt like a metal detector, homing in on the sharpening signal strength to triangulate their location, almost as if engaged in a tentative game of psychic Marco Polo, the chaotic and vibrant essence of a dozen juvenile cohabitors singing to him from afar.

"Sure hope you're right about keepin' Delilah in the dark about this," counseled Teo, carefully circumventing the burning wreckage of a raptor, likely downed during Harmony's assault on the Governor's yacht. "She was as mad as a hornet last time you and me went AWOL."

"Oh, she'll be furious," he confirmed soberly. "But honestly, I don't think she's left us with much of a choice. I broached the subject with her several times and always got the same answer: an emphatic no."

"And so you thought the best course of action would be to completely disregard her an' do it anyway?"

Tobias simpered. "I've spent enough time in the captain's bad books to know it's easier to ask for forgiveness rather than permission. Right now, her circle of concern encompasses the safety of her crew and little else, which is totally understandable. But that hard-nosed edge *always* pales next to her compassionate nature. All we have to do to change her mind is smuggle the little ones aboard and have her take one look at them; I'm confident she'll do the rest."

Teo shrugged as if to say, *It's your funeral, bub.* "Sounds an awful lot like blackmail to me."

"Emotional coercion, philanthropic extortion—I'm sure she'll call it something like that, but as long as those kids are safe, I'll be more than happy to take the flak. *This* one's on me."

The girl stopped abruptly and turned to scowl at him, vexatiously whipping her plait of cerulean hair over her shoulder. "Of course. Because I'm just the naive, innocent ditz who *you* get to string along on all your misadventures, right? . . . Captain's gonna know I'm here of my own accord. She'll tan *both* our hides an' you can count on it."

Tobias stuttered a response, abashed. "Teo . . . I didn't mean . . ."

"I know what you meant," she interrupted. "Forget about it . . . Anyways, you *still* haven't told me what exactly's made you think the scamps are gonna be any safer with *us* than they are hunkered down in the Ghetto. Captain seems dead set on ditchin' the *Assurance* and findin' a way bowside through the Vestiges—ain't exactly a child-friendly environment, yah know?"

Tobias made a sweeping gesture at the surrounding scenes of ruination. "Look at the level of collateral damage Harmony considered acceptable just to snuff out the Glow Syndicate. What do you think they're prepared to do going up against the Administration?"

Teo cast a stricken look, her eyes seeming to glisten that little bit more every time he worked up the courage to meet them.

"I haven't figured out the finer points yet," he went on. "Abyss, I've got absolutely *no* clue what comes after we reach Lower Amidships. The only thing I'm certain of is that they can't stay in the Mouth."

The girl furrowed her brow, forming a look of incredulity. "I don't understand why this matters so much to you."

He shrugged suggestively. "They're *kids* . . . I know you don't have the highest of opinions about people from the Upperdecks but I'm not heartless."

She clucked her tongue in annoyance. "I never said you were . . . And I get that; I just mean . . . this seems real personal to you. Anybody could be forgiven for thinkin' it was *you* that had all the history with Juniper instead of me."

Tobias dropped his gaze, pausing ruminatively to rifle his littered mind for a concise answer. "My head is a mess," he began. "I don't know where *my* fears and aspirations end and where *Null's* begin . . . All I know is the thought of anything happening to those kids . . . it makes my heart hollow—fills me with dread as palpable as the night is endless . . . Maybe it's some kind of . . . subconscious social-rearing response: primal instinct commanding me to nurture and protect the little ones as vehemently as if they were my own. Because that's honestly how I feel—like I'd give my life for any one of them without hesitation."

"You mean, that's how *Null* feels," Teo drawled.

"If you know what resonance is, then you know that's a pointless distinction."

"I guess . . . Well . . . Spose it makes perfect sense, you both feelin' that way; cohab hatchlings aren't raised by their biological parents like we are: they're brought up by everyone in big community-run nurseries. The care, protection, and education of the young is seen as a civic responsibility . . . Problem is that over the past couple of decades, livin' conditions got so bad this side of the Çorak, population increased so quick, just weren't sustainable no more. *That's* why the sanctuary was such a blessing: Hiroki and Nanimonai took in the kids that slipped through the cracks and even emulated the environment they were accustomed to . . . Now the sanctuary's gone, the junies ain't safe no more, so I'd venture this tizzy you got yourself in is on account of Null's parental urges rubbin' off on yah."

Tobias grunted in acknowledgment, Teo's enthusiastic explanation giving him pause to consider his own comparatively blissful upbringing. Steering her through an abode that had been turned into a mangled conch by the blast from a fractal grenade, his meandering thoughts arrived at his mother—something he found happening with increasing frequency. Feeling a sharp pang of sadness, he said, "Null might have me feeling protective over them, but one justification for doing this that I *know* comes from my mind and mine alone is the preservation of my mother's legacy . . . She sacrificed *everything* she had to give you and those kids a second chance: her marriage, her reputation . . . and in the end, her life . . . The junies are all I have left of her—the one tangible keepsake I have to keep her memory alive. If we let them end up as casualties in the Composer's war, then everything she stood for, everything she died for—it will have all been for nothing . . . I just can't let that happen."

Teo groaned, giving him a gentle shove on his shoulder blade that he sensed held a kernel of affection. "Why you gotta be so dour all the time? Only thing that's gonna happen is you and me losin' shore leave privileges for the next six months . . . Then again . . ."

She trailed off, displaying a weighted expression, shoulders visibly sinking. "Don't see how Delilah could enforce that without a ship . . . If there's no *Assurance*, then are we even still a crew? . . . I mean, with the Governor gone, Null and Mercy don't need to stick around since there ain't nobody chasin' 'em no more." She sighed through her nostrils, casting him a jilted look from the corner of her eye. "And I guess, what with you and Mercy gettin' all *cozy* together, wherever *they* end up puttin' down roots, you'll prolly join 'em eventually, right?"

Tobias showed a tilted smile, irritated that he had been forced to mentally revisit the regrettable rendezvous with Mercy again, although it would be a lie to say he didn't take a shameful sliver of lascivious excitement at Teo's apparent dejection regarding the subject. Her jealous pout acted as a naked flame that set alight the dry pile of tinder in his belly—the mild interest that had gradually developed into a fond appreciation, igniting now into full-blown, head-over-heels infatuation. Courageous, steadfastly loyal, and not to mention utterly beautiful with a temper as volatile as a ruptured fission cell, the more time he spent around Teodora Brižan, the more his feelings for her grew. *You don't fall often, but when you do, you fall hard*—that's what he used to tell himself. But he had come to realize that, in truth, he had never *really* fallen for anyone at all, before—not even for Caleb . . . These burgeoning desires seemed utterly inconsequential in the grand scheme of things, of course; his focus *had* to be the safe evacuation of the junies, and so he concluded that anything he could do to alleviate Teo's concerns would ultimately benefit them, too . . .

He reached out to softly brush her hand with his. "It's not like that at all . . . If you were there, you'd know that what happened was awkward, clumsy, and completely unintentional—just a regrettable side effect of resonance that *both* of us are keen to forget, and more importantly, *never* repeat . . . Besides: Null and Mercy have been in a ciphered partnership for over a decade. Those two are responsible for waking me up, and the bond we share as a result will likely last a lifetime. But that doesn't mean I have any intention of permanently interposing myself into their arrangement . . ."

He saw a smile lift the corners of Teo's full lips, which were the same shade of dusky rose as the zigzags of her knitted sweater.

"I can't speak for Isaac and Kahu," he continued. "But once we get the little ones out of the Mouth and securely situated, I promise, you're not getting rid of me that easily."

Tobias sensed his way to the resonant energy field's focal point, feeling like a migratory bird following sun and star to more temperate skies. They arrived at a small clearing in the center of a huddle of notably unscathed dwellings, as if the insurgents had tactically spared this unremarkable patch in their otherwise indiscriminate shelling of the Cohabitor Ghetto. He waved a hand to halt Teo, the empathic tumult now radiating not from any one direction but completely engulfing him, seeming to emanate from beneath the ground itself. His mind spiraled into a disorienting feedback loop, the profound fear and uncertainty felt by the nearby cohablings morphing into sweeping relief as they, in turn, detected his approaching essence.

"They're here," he said, affecting a puzzled upward inflection, because by all accounts here looked to be little more than a neglected plot, with certainly no sign of twenty-plus children taking shelter. The keen-sighted Teo nodded in the direction of an old panel radiator, left propped up beside the archway entrance to the nearest domicile. Its white, flaking surface played host to a slew of chalk scribbles depicting anthropomorphic animal figures, much like the vibrant mural that had once welcomed visitors to Juniper Sanctuary before Jonah Sinclair and two of his accomplices chose to burn it to the ground . . .

Teo bounded through the entrance like an excited puppy expecting to see its owners, skidding to a halt upon finding the stark space beyond empty, save for a few spent pulp canisters strewn about the floor. She turned her attention to the dusty, woven nylon rug splayed out beneath her work boots; a notably out-of-place adornment that had been trimmed haphazardly to suit the room's elliptical floorspace. After a thoughtful pause, she stamped her foot, wrinkling her nose in elation at the resounding *thunk* of hollow metal. Tobias watched from the doorway, heart tripping over itself as the girl crouched low and animatedly pulled the rug aside, revealing a rectangular, nanocarbon hatch with a yellow pull handle embedded seamlessly into the ground as if dropped from a height into melted wax. She busied herself with attempting to gain access, quickly announcing that the hatch was, in fact, "locked up tighter than a gnat's ass." Tobias felt Nanimonai's unmistakable essence reaching up to welcome him. Aer colors were powder blue, and ae sang a silent melody of attentive generosity, underpinned by a firm but fair attitude that, incidentally, reminded him of Captain Holloway. But then, he picked up an overarching sorrow, too—an inconsolable grief over the tragic death of aer partner, Hiroki Sato, and a sense of dread concerning the fates of the little ones whose lives were now solely aer responsibility to bear.

Not anymore; the cavalry has arrived. A wave of joyful effervescence rose up through him as the sentiment propagated throughout the juvenile minds taking shelter beneath his feet. The resonant hysteria only increased as the hatch's pull handle slid into its unlocked position, and the nanocarbon slab autonomously swung open, laying bare a gloomy ladder chute connecting to a fluorescently lit space below ground. Teo giddily began lowering herself into the access shaft, stopping suddenly upon noticing Tobias as he lingered in the doorway.

"Yah comin' or what?"

He afforded a solicitous nod, his attention taken by a resonant aberration seeming to originate from somewhere to his rear. He sensed a nonhuman presence that, oddly, didn't seem to fit the bill of Nanimonai or any of the cohablings in aer care. It made him feel uneasy, as if being watched by somebody regarding him with a level of malice or ill-intent. He spun around to scan the desolate clearing outside, finding it completely devoid of anyone who could be responsible for the empathic eyes boring into the back of his skull. *Chīsana Osuushi* hung above the district like a silver teardrop turned on its side and halved down its meridian, an unsettling reminder of the dwindling hours before the *Novara* was thrown into all-out war. Teo had advised this excursion of theirs would not go unwatched by the vigilant eyes of the Composer, and he wondered if the presence he felt could merely be the result of Harmony keeping tabs on them from their conquered sky-bastion. Problematically, even as a hyper-resonant, he didn't believe his empathic receptivity could stretch such large distances. Furthermore, the essence observing him felt much closer—in his immediate vicinity, to be precise.

"What is it?" queried Teo. "Is something wrong?"

He held his pensive gaze for a final moment before shaking off his consternation. "Nothing . . . Just my imagination."

Following her down the ladder chute, they descended beneath the compacted layer of triturated lunar metal comprising the terra firma of the Mouth. Reaching the bottom of the shaft, they arrived in a subterranean bunker constructed from corrugated steel pipe, stretching approximately ten meters, and doused in the ugly gleam of loudly humming tube fixtures. A thick redolence of pine and fresh coriander pervaded the air—an unquestionably pleasing aroma, but one Tobias recognized as the pheromone cohabitors exuded when feeling threatened or extremely distressed, the rich scent of intense fear invading his nostrils. Relief swept in like a warm breeze to thaw his apprehensions as he laid eyes upon the bundle of younglings, sitting huddled atop a mountain of blankets, their tiny faces bathed in the fluctuating light from a luma-puck as it projected an episode of *Poppy and Vacío*. The popular animated show featured an interspecies duo who traveled up and down the *Novara*, solving low-stakes mysteries and helping people with their trivial problems. It was innocuous educational fun, and yet he cringed to think of the unmitigated rage it had once engendered in him—*insufferable, virtue-signaling pro-leech propaganda*, he recalled once shamelessly declaring it. Now, of course, he felt the need for promoting messages of collaboration and unity to the next generation had become abundantly evident, and only wished the show could see wider distribution bowside of the blockade.

Strangely, the little ones barely broke their attention away from their whimsical luma-cast shenanigans as he and Teo entered. It certainly wasn't the exuberant welcome he had been anticipating, given the veritable fervor he had resonantly observed aboveground. They seemed quiet, subdued, which rang as particularly odd considering the last time ex-Juniper resident Teodora graced them with her presence, they greeted her like a goddess descending from the top of Mount Olympus. As his eyes grew accustomed to the low light, the reason for their apparent disquietude materialized . . . Nanimonai towered at the opposite end of the bunker with aer head bowed low toward an unknown woman standing before aer. During Tobias's short and bittersweet conversation with Hiroki Sato, the man had suggested that since his wife, Yua, had passed, Nanimonai had struggled to find another compatible partner with whom ae could enter into a ciphership. But the emissions blazing like glowing embers from behind aer eyes suggested either ae had found one such candidate or the stranger presently communing with aer was, like Tobias, a hyper-resonant. And to his knowledge, the Savior had endowed the rarest of its gifts to only one other individual on the Coalescence . . .

The Composer spun around to face them, slowly removing the hood of her gray-brown shawl to reveal soft yet striking features encroached upon by a tangle of deep-purple veins, as if a plant had set about burrowing its roots into the soil of her flesh. Tobias cast his mind back to the appalling events at Juniper Sanctuary, recalling Nanimonai's stubborn refusal to board the *Assurance* following Captain Holloway's valiant rescue efforts. Before taking aer leave, ae had conveyed aer intention to seek shelter with a relative in the Cohabitor Ghetto—a *sibling*, as he had clumsily interpreted it. Of course, he now realized that ae had really been referring to aer adopted niece: the hyper-resonant DMED marshal turned insurgent leader now waging war against the NTU.

"Teo . . . It's been a while," the woman said in a smoky, melliferous voice, wide eyes sharp and narrowed as she held the mouthian girl firmly in her gaze. Teo absently pushed past Tobias and started toward her before seeming to hastily change her mind, stopping at a cautious distance. "Jyn . . . What in the Abyss are you doin' here?"

"Is that any kind of way to greet family?"

The girl shook her head, shifting her weight onto her hip in defiance. "Only family *I* got is the one I choose for myself. Don't make a habit of keepin' killers and terrorists in my circle."

"Still a little hothead, I see," Jyn sighed with a patronizing smirk. "Gotta admit; I had hoped you might have grown up a little by now. Used to bring the whole sanctuary down with those temper tantrums of yours. Guess not much has changed."

Teo shrugged. "Nope. Still me—warts n' all . . . *You* on the other hand: can't say as I even recognize you anymore . . . To be perfectly frank, I'm kinda glad the housefather's dead, cuz it would have broken him to see what you've become."

Jyn showed a somber expression, casting dark eyes to the floor. "I think you're probably right. Me and that old eccentric never did see eye to eye, which is funny because, at the end of the day, we both wanted the same thing." She turned her stare to the junies, appropriating a smile that, to Tobias, felt frigid and hollow. "To provide a better future for *them*."

Teo issued a sneering laugh. "Well . . . You got 'em cowering underground while bombs go off overhead, so I'd say you're off to a rollickin' good start . . . Took the Prey nearly a century to establish a permanent home in the district, and you, no more 'an a few hours to burn it to the ground."

Jyn had hardly even acknowledged Tobias since he and Teo had entered the bunker, but she took a beat to flash him a cursory glance as she prepared her response.

"Cohabitor *Ghetto*," Jyn finally responded, switching her piercing gaze back to Teo. "The clue is in the title . . . This place was *never* a home; they didn't have *any* kind of future to look forward to, imprisoned behind the NTU's blockade . . . To liberate the Prey, we have to dismantle the shackles of their incarceration. After all: should a trapped animal feel sentimental about the destruction of its cage if it ultimately means being set free? Of course not . . . I know what we've done seems brutal and inhumane, but we ensured the Ghetto was sufficiently evacuated before beginning the assault. And, I promise you, it was completely necessary to rid the *Novara* of the evil influence of the glow syndicate, and to set the Prey off on the path to salvation."

"Sufficiently evacuated," Tobias repeated, the words barely escaping through tightly gritted teeth. "You couldn't have extended that courtesy to all those innocent people at the Phalanx Compound, too? Jade Tanaka was a proud Novarian—a dedicated Phalanx enforcer with a green thumb and a heart of gold. All she ever wanted was to defend her home and the people she loved."

Jyn rolled her eyes. "Really, Teo; you're hanging around with bowsiders, now? You know I chaperoned Upper-Crust, here, to his dad's penthouse after he blew up that harvester in the Harrow? Seems a little hypocritical to be taking shots at me for wreaking a little chaos in the Mouth when you're rubbin' shoulders with someone guilty of doing exactly the same."

Anger struck like a hot spear through his heart, boiling forgotten feuds to the surface. Much of the truths Tobias had known before his resonant awakening had been subsequently confounded by his newly enlightened perspective, his entire paradigm proven to be no more than an intricate tapestry of deception woven into the Administration's tireless propaganda machine. But one truth that stood as an immovable pillar in his mind was that Harmony's attack on the Phalanx Compound constituted a senseless and despicable act of savagery, no matter how its orchestrator tried to frame it.

"You butchered her," he seethed, taking several furious paces forward. "Massacred countless others—and for what? What is it you're even trying to achieve with this bloody crusade; to take control of the *Novara*? The Administration will wipe you out and decimate the Mouth in the process, and all you will have accomplished is getting tens of thousands killed and worsening the already chasmic human-cohabitor divide."

Jyn tilted her head back slightly, glowering at him down the line of her nose and letting a portentous silence ring out. He saw the junies tense up, tightening their huddle as their little worried eyes darted between the three participants of the ensuing standoff. He glanced over Jyn's shoulder at Nanimonai as the cohabitor animatedly bowed aer head to grapple his attention. A golden aura of emissions suffused his peripheral vision; he felt the momentary discomfort of their two anatomically disparate brains wirelessly integrating—the *neural handshake,* as he had come to know it. Nanimonai's resonant essence imbued him like wonderfully fragrant tea poured into his mental cup. Although its pleasing notes soon soured as ae hurriedly projected an assaulting welter of warning flashes into his neural space: bright greens, reds, and yellows that made him think of fire, danger, and deadly insects with venomous stings. In the context of the current situation, aer meaning came through loud and clear: *Jyn Sato is dangerous; do not provoke her any further.* But he already had provoked her . . . Baring fangs, she pulled aside her flowing cape, revealing the deactivated hilt of a fission dagger ensconced in the leg sheath strapped to her thigh. She placed a hand on its grip threateningly, seeming as if preparing to pounce like an enraged feline. But then she paused, scrunching her brow in perplexment as she clocked the emissions bursting forth from behind his irises. She followed the diaphanous trail of luminescence connecting Tobias's mind with Nanimonai's, eyes widening in amazement, jaw hanging slack.

"That's not possible," she slurred while a handful of the little ones giggled at her befuddlement. "Nani never told me ae found another resonant partner."

"Ae didn't," Teo put in. "Tobias here . . . well, he's like *you*: hyper-resonant—hasn't met a cohab he couldn't attain resonance with."

Jyn recited his name, studying him intently as she reconcealed her blade beneath her cape. "I'll be damned; Humanity First poster boy turned hyper-resonant—can't say the Savior doesn't have a sense of humor."

Meeting his gaze, she stepped toward him, fulgent emissions erupting from her penetrating eyes, the air practically simmering with anticipation. Just as he had done with Null and Mercy, she forged an empathic connection with him using Nanimonai as a resonant conduit, their three essences coalescing like a swirling accretion disk of personality and experience. Unsurprisingly, Jyn's colors were bloodred; she sang a silent melody of wrath and sorrow, her vibrant, passionate spirit hamstrung by indelible past traumas and the crushing weight of her responsibilities. He felt her intractable fury, her contempt for the "oppressors," and her conviction that only by violently dethroning them could the *Novara* truly know peace. These beliefs were so unshakable, so abiding that he had to remind himself they were *not* his own; he knew firsthand the ruinous path down which rationalizing in such extremist absolutes would inevitably lead him. He too strived for a truly unified Coalescence. *But there* has *to be a less fratricidal way . . .*

Jyn, having no doubt received an equally as vivid vertical slice of his character, staggered backward, forcefully wrenching herself out of the bond. "That's . . . That's quite the journey you've been on, Tobias . . . I never thought I'd meet another hyper-resonant . . . This . . . this changes everything . . . What I *don't* understand, however, is how you can question my motives. If you've seen what *I've* seen, felt what *I've* felt, then you know *nothing* is more important than freeing the Prey from persecution."

"I do," he replied, breathing a sigh of relief at the apparent de-escalation in tension. "But I spent my whole academic life training to be a politician; I don't believe there's anything that can't be resolved through diplomacy."

Jyn showed an ingratiating smile. "That's cute, although I'm afraid the time for diplomacy died the moment the blockade went up." Dolorously turning her head, she settled her gaze on the junies, some now snoozing with idols and stuffed animals tucked snuggly underarm. "What are you two doing here?" she asked. "What are your intentions with these kids?"

"Simple," Teo chimed in. "Get 'em out of the Mouth before *you* completely destroy the place. Find somewhere bowside where we can shelter 'em until the fighting dies down."

Jyn pursed her lips in contemplation, running over the plan in her mind. "We know you've been coming in and out of the Mouth through the Savior's core, helped by two of Drexen's ex-associates . . . Is that your plan: Smuggle them out of the district on that balaener-class hauler parked up on the edge of the Ghetto? You must already have a cohabitor aboard since you've been coming and going through the Savior's core at will."

Tobias shook his head. "We barely escaped a run-in with two of the Governor's bounty hunters. It's a long story, but the *Assurance* is in pretty bad shape as a result, so flying them out isn't gonna happen . . . Captain Holloway thinks our best option is to find a route through the Vestiges."

Jyn made a snarling expression as if she found the mere suggestion so utterly imbecilic it caused physical pain.

"Oh, and I suppose *you* got a better idea?" sniped Teo. "Keep 'em holed up here and just hope Phalanx don't carpet-bomb the entire district?"

Jyn reached out and placed her palm against the room's curved wall. "I had this bunker purpose-built to protect them. It's made of titanium-coated steel—*definitely* strong enough to withstand anything the Administration's forces can throw at us . . . Still, it was only supposed to be a temporary measure—planned to move them down here when the *real* fighting began and then relocate them somewhere safer at the earliest opportunity." The lines of her face drew a look of pure detestation. "But Bhaltair Abernathy forced me to expedite those arrangements."

"Don't need to tell us; we were there when it happened," Teo solemnly added. "Standing right beside Hiroki when . . ."

"I know you were." Jyn moved toward the girl and in a surprising show of tenderness, placed a curled finger beneath her chin, lifting her gaze to meet her own. "Nanimonai had already given me parts of what happened, but thanks to Tobias, I now have the full picture . . . I dread to think of what might have happened if you two hadn't been there to intervene." Meeting Tobias' eyes, she continued, "I know you reckon you've got me pegged: a bloodthirsty fanatic, a ruthless terrorist—honestly, I couldn't care less. But believe me when I tell you these kids mean the universe to me, and the fact that they're here right now because of you—it's not something I take lightly . . ."

Admittedly, Tobias *had* thought precisely that, but after taking a glimpse behind the Composer's wrathful mask, he knew there was far more to her than what he had first perceived.

"There's no such thing as deception when it comes to resonance, Tobias. That's how I can know having only just met you that your intentions are pure. I believe you want to do everything in your power to get them to safety, but I'm afraid I can't let you take them down into the Vestiges. That place is a death trap, and you are sure to fail . . . So, allow me to suggest an alternative to Captain Holloway's suicidal plan."

The woman raised a hand clad in black, fingerless gloves and placed her heel against her ear to engage her comms. "Oren. Head to the vehicle repair bay and round up a team of engineers . . . I want the ship that came down on the edge of the Ghetto repaired and ready to fly before the cycle is out: ten hours, tops."

"The ship's crew are still keeping a tight perimeter around the crash site, Composer," a barely audible voice came back through her earbud. "What if we are met by resistance?"

"That won't be an issue."

"I think it might," Teo nervously interjected. "Appreciate the offer n'all but the captain will *never* accept help from Harmony."

"And I'm not giving her the choice to decline it," Jyn replied dryly. "If she doesn't fall in line, I'll commandeer the *Assurance* and have one of my own people fly the kids bowside . . . So, I suggest Academy Boy here exercises a little of his *diplomacy* and does his best to get her to comply. Because if he doesn't, then Holloway's ship is mine . . ."

obias and Teo barely made it back to the *Assurance* in time to warn Delilah about their arrangement with the Composer. No sooner had they, Nanimonai, and the little ones arrived at the crash site than a cargo barge arrived, carrying a veritable smorgasbord of spare parts and maintenance equipment on its elongated mag-bed.

Without so much as a hello or even a curt nod of acknowledgment, Jyn's engineers set to work patching up the hull and restoring flight functionality to the downed hauler. They toiled under the watchful eye of a heavily armed escort, who had either been dispatched for their protection or to prevent them from attempting to flee. Tobias suspected that not *all* of the glum-faced and browbeaten workers had come of their own volition and were perhaps being forced to contribute their expertise to Harmony *against* their will. He didn't doubt that most of the Composer's followers had pledged their allegiance in good faith, genuinely believing they were dedicating themselves to a worthy cause. But after making her callous disregard for human life so concerningly evident, he had to wonder if the devotion of some of her less fanatical adherents had begun to falter . . .

Two of her Choir—fearsome specimens whom he suspected had little trouble in the fanaticism department—had boorishly hustled the passengers and crew into the galley, keeping them under strict guard while the repairs were carried out. Their intimidating presence served to reinforce Jyn's stipulation that the *Assurance* would be transporting the junies bowside, with or without the compliance of its captain.

Delilah was positively apoplectic at first, saying that the only thing stopping her from "kicking his ass overboard and ditching him in the Mouth," was her certainty that by doing so she would be condemning the son of a councilman to death.

"It was supposed to be just *us* from here on out," she had fumed in a forceful whisper when the guards marched them into the lounge, the harsh whine of a drill reverberating through the fuselage, punctuated by the intermittent squeaks and crackles of someone welding metal. "Flying under the radar, doing whatever we had to to keep the *Assurance* skyborne and our noses clean—no more shady, one-sided alliances with criminal organizations . . . Now, I've got Harmony all over my ship installing stars-know-what tech— probably all manner of trackers, bugs, and auto-recall modules—and you've given the Composer *serious* leverage over us. These *aren't* the type of people we wanna be indebted to."

Tobias had tried to reassure the captain that the transportation and temporary protection of the junies was the only compensation Jyn sought for the repairs, although, predictably, the attempt went unheeded.

"If you really believe she's gonna consider the matter settled then you're even stupider than I thought," Delilah retorted, spitting her words over her shoulder as she retrieved an herbal tea from the dispenser in the galley. "Woman's raising hell to push her forces into NTU territory; a ship that can bypass the blockade is an invaluable asset to her—one she won't relinquish without a fight . . . She might have told you running chaperone duty would make us square, but trust me, she's not done with us yet."

While Tobias agreed they had likely not had the last of their dealings with Jyn Sato, he suspected her continued interference would have less to do with the *Assurance* and its crew and, would more likely center around *him* and his hyper-resonance. While Teo and Nanimonai had busied themselves readying the junies to leave the bunker, Jyn had taken him aside to impress on him the gravity of his situation, emphasizing the importance of the Savior's endowments. *It's a rare and precious thing you've been given,* she had said, scouring his unnerved expression with eyes like brown marbles ensconced at the center of two venous nests. *You understand that, right? I need to know you're giving it the respect it's owed. Because it's not just a game—some party trick you can whip out anytime you're tryna impress somebody.*

Completely oblivious, or perhaps unsympathetic, to the anguish her actions had inflicted and that the last thing he wanted was for her to touch him in *any* capacity, she reached out and gently placed two fingers against his temple. She'd continued speaking, *This inside here? It's a duty, an obligation, and, in some ways, a burden. There'll be times when you feel like your head's cracking open, your heartsoul getting forced into a blender and sucked out through a straw. You'll lie awake at night with the pain and suffering of countless generations spinning like a tornado in your head, wondering, Why, oh why is this happening to me? What did I do to deserve this? But hyper-resonance isn't just some consequence of a genetic defect or abnormality. The truth is that the Savior chose you—chose you for the same reason it chose me: because it sees a certain quality in you that it believes it can use as a means to achieve its ultimate purpose: salvation through unity . . . You've got your gripes with my methods; Lei-Ghannam, after what happened to your friend Jade, why wouldn't you? But you should know that everything I've done, I did with the Savior's blessing . . . In some respects, with its guidance . . . So . . . if you trust the Savior—like, really trust it—then once you get Nani and the rascals settled bowside, you should join me . . . Join Harmony. Cuz this is a fight for the survival of the Coalescence, for all who want to live in a free and fair society, and we could really use you in it.*

Tobias had disappointed himself by politely declining the offer, wishing in hindsight that he had told her to try using her duplicitous recruitment pitch on someone with a little less self-respect. He had experienced many firsts over the tumultuous past months, but he remained steadfast that giving any contemplation whatsoever to aiding the insurgents who had wrought such horrors on so many Novarians would *not* appear on that list. In his mind, there was nothing free or fair about blowing up hopeful immigrants and gunning down enforcers in cold blood . . .

Jyn was right: he *did* have his gripes with her methods, but he had certainly never considered the possibility that she and her flock had been acting—or at least, *believed* they were acting—at the Savior's behest. Unfortunately, he simply couldn't reconcile that theory with his own experiences. Tracing his thoughts back to the night at Juniper Sanctuary, he pictured that churning mass of amber-violet pouring from the inverted ventilation funnel in the dining room. He didn't believe the benign presence he had sensed gazing into that tempest of light would *ever* approve of such wanton death and destruction. During the dissemination, the ethereal sentience had reached out and told him in no uncertain terms that it strived for peace and cooperation; *true* harmony—*not* the kind achieved at the expense of thousands of innocent lives. Even though Jyn shared the same end goal, how she endeavored to achieve it felt distinctly at odds with the Savior's aspirations. He figured there were only two explanations that could account for the discrepancy between what he inherently knew and what the Composer had tried to tell him: either she had been lying about having the Savior's approval, or her ability to interpret its meaning left much to be desired . . .

Null seemed to share some of his skepticism in the matter; standing by the tallest of the galley's antique lamps, sharing aer appreciation of its dangling shade tassels with an equally enraptured adolescent cohabitor, ae took pause to convey a medley of images and emotions that Tobias parsed as, *Why would the Savior waste so much time and effort excavating and terraforming the Mouth, providing a home for the Prey, only to instruct the Composer to decimate it?*

He turned his head and relayed Null's sentiment to Teodora, who sat beside him on the threadbare sofa, the two young stylists who had fashioned her hair during their visit to Juniper Sanctuary rearranging it now into a Dutch braid.

"Exactly!" she proclaimed, catching a glower from one of their detainers. "Don't make a lick of sense the Savior would advocate what Jyn's doin'. Expect she's just tryna justify all the chaos she's stirrin' up—make herself feel better about the lives she's destroyed.'"

"Liked it better when I thought she wuz just a pissed-off anarchist," Kahu put in. The man had taken a stool at the galley's island countertop and was presently engaged in an intense game of Helix blackjack with Isaac. "Now she's just another crackpot who reckons she's doin' the lord's work. Ain't nothin' more dangerous than a zealot with a god-given license to kill."

The guard nearest to Kahu sounded a guttural, "Ah!" as if disciplining a misbehaving dog. "One more word of slander against the Composer," she growled, "and I'll stitch your loud mouth shut, old man."

Kahu gave an impudent shrug as he blithely reshuffled his deck of cards. The guard took further umbrage and pulled aside her brown Harmony robes, brandishing a pistol seemingly augmented with the gruesome technology that formed the Savior's biomechanical husk. "And remove that jacket," she demanded. "Flagrantly bearing the mark of the oppressors in the company of Prey; have you no shame?"

"I can keep my trap shut, miss." Kahu brushed the dust from the shoulder of his NTSC blazer. "But you'll be pullin' this old thing off my corpse before I take it off willingly."

"Do as she says, Heperi," Delilah sternly interjected, sitting leg-over-leg in the antique recliner, holding her bright-yellow mug before her face and keeping her furious stare locked on Tobias. Kahu cast her a quizzical look as if to say, *Are you being serious?* then begrudgingly complied upon realizing that indeed she was, stripping down to his sweat-stained tank top and muttering his dissatisfaction as he dealt his next hand.

Tobias turned his eyes upward as a succession of thumps rapped overhead, doubtless someone in heavy work boots making their way across the *Assurance*'s hull. Then came the prolonged whine of a rotary fission saw, followed by a cacophony of screeching, scraping metal that could only have been the result of someone forcibly prying the bounty hunter's harpoon out of the fuselage.

"Kahu. It's your turn," Isaac said for perhaps the seventh time in the past thirty minutes.

Kahu grunted his acknowledgment, offering a final sneer to the guard before returning to his hand. "How long you reckon these repairs are gonna take anyway? Makes me uncomfortable: all these grease monkeys puttin' their hands all over the old gal."

Isaac rocked his head from side to side in a bargaining gesture, goggles pressing red marks into his oil-stained forehead. "Might be a couple hours, might be ten—couldn't really say . . . To be completely honest, I'm not sure what they *think* they can do to get her spaceworthy again; the portside impulse thruster looked like a thousand sad hunks of mangled scrap we've pulled outta the Debris Belt."

"Saw the vertical stabilizer for an old acheta station hopper on that cargo barge," Kahu explained. "No idea how it ended up on the *Novara*, but if they can figure out a way to integrate it with the existing wing mount, it'll at least get us off the ground."

"Yeah, but she'll have nowhere near the same level of maneuverability."

Kahu released a snorting laugh tainted by a note of sadness. "That's *your* problem now, Wonderboy . . ."

Tobias met Delilah's eyes, wanting to inquire about the veteran pilot's meaning, but the vehemence in her stare forced the words back down his throat. She took a sip of her tea, peering at him over the rim of her mug; he felt the contempt radiating off her almost as vividly as though they were in resonance with one another. Forcing her to break eye contact, a small boy tumbled toward her carrying a sheet of paper that had once been a wiring diagram for the luma-surface embedded in the island countertop, now a canvas for a bouquet of colorful crayon scribbles. The captain quickly dispelled her acrimony and immediately switched into mother mode.

"Is that a dinosaur?" she cooed, animatedly taking the offering and beaming at it fondly. "Very scary . . . This one's going right on the pantry door."

As the boy triumphantly skipped away, she returned her gaze to Tobias, regarding him with considerably less rancor than just a moment ago. He gave an unrepentant shrug, spreading his hands wide to say, *I have no regrets and will happily take the lashings.* She shook her head, forming the faintest suggestion of a rueful smile. By no means was she letting him off the hook, but the little ones' presence, as he had predicted, looked to have melted her severe comportment.

He felt something tugging at the cuff of his jacket and turned to find the juvenile cohabitor who had taken a keen interest in him at the sanctuary lingering at his side—the avaricious merchant with whom he had traded balls of candy for various trinkets and treasures. Ae had suffered several cuts and grazes during aer frantic escape from Juniper. Yet to fully develop aer chitin exoskeleton, aer injuries appeared as dark purple abrasions scraped across aer soft, grub-like flesh. Eager to resume trade negotiations, ae deposited the scuffed chrome hood ornament of a vintage Cassiopeia swoop into his lap, then jutted aer palm toward him, stubby digits splayed out expectantly. Tobias felt the beginnings of a resonant bond manifest, then peter out and dissipate, the merchant evidently still too young to effectively harness aer exo-communicative abilities.

Patting the pockets of his jacket, he pointlessly said, "I'm sorry . . . I don't have anything to give you."

"Sure you do," Teo chimed in, reaching into her satchel and producing the idol she had pulled from the rubble near the *Assurance*'s crash site. She handed him the embroidered plush to pass along to the little merchant, who feverishly snatched it from his hands and held it before aer snout in something like disbelief. Ae trumpeted a shrill bray of excitement and gratitude before bounding away to gleefully show Nanimonai aer prize. Tobias turned to face Teo, expecting to be met by ravishing countenance broadcasting the same sense of gratification and accomplishment he felt. But instead, Teo appeared crestfallen, tears welling in the corners of her bewitching eyes, her bottom lip trembling.

"What's wrong?" he asked.

"It's just," she sniffled. "It upsets me to see how happy the smallest of comforts makes them. They deserve so much, an' are content with so little."

Tobias nodded solemnly, a fountain of ancestral memory washing over him. "Even before the Collision, all the Prey ever cared about was staying alive," he said. "They covet safety and security: not luxury or material possession. They have never known abundance, because those who hunted them did so unrelentingly, never giving them the space to breathe or stretch their wings."

He looked down at his hand and formed a tight fist around the hood ornament, fierce conviction permeating his chest. "It's time we showed them there can be more to life than just surviving."

With only an hour to spare before the Composer's ominous countdown struck zero, the *Assurance* took flight and departed the Mouth with all crew accounted for and their precious cargo securely stowed. Tobias's earlier confusion over a comment made by Kahu had only heightened as he entered the bridge to find Isaac at the helm, the ship's obstinate and jealously possessive pilot nowhere to be seen. The engineer sat up front with his back arched forward, biting his tongue in intense concentration, hands wrapped fervidly around the flight stick and throttle. Delilah stood behind him, fingers digging into the syn-leather upholstery of his seat, looking like a nervous mother supervising her son's first manual swoop lesson.

Isaac had spoken before about his limited flight training, which had enabled him to move ships from berthing to the maintenance bay for repairs too complex to be completed on-site. Thankfully, the Savior had taken the reins for the first leg of the journey, miraculously guiding the hauler through its catacombic interior with its wreathing branches of opalescence. Once they cleared the interior, however, it had fallen on Isaac to kill their momentum with the inertial dampeners and vector toward the Lower Amidships Docks—two maneuvers he had expressed concern were a far cry beyond his meager abilities.

The fact that he had been able to take off without Kahu present at all suggested the helm's dermal encryption, which had been a point of considerable annoyance to the captain since her acquisition of the *Assurance* had been disabled. Thinking back to the debilitating panic attack Mr. Heperi had suffered during the encounter with the interceptor drones, Tobias had to wonder whether the man had declared himself unfit for duty, and finally conceded admin privileges to Delilah. Naturally, Isaac was the logical choice to delegate pilot duties to, but as much as he mentally chided himself for regressing to such judgmental thinking, he couldn't help but linger on the fact that his life had been left in the hands of a recovering glow addict—not to mention one who had twice professed a deep and abiding contempt for him . . .

The *Assurance* jerked sideways as Isaac manipulated the flight stick to attempt a banking starboard turn. But instead, the hauler merely rolled on her side, dipping her nose out of alignment with her trajectory and skimming into the black like a brick along the surface of ExSight Multiplex ice rink.

"How does Kahu make it look so damned effortless?" he carped, jockeying the flight controls. "She doesn't handle at all like how I expected her to."

"You're flying in six degrees of freedom," Delilah replied, voice juddering in Isaac's ham-fisted attempts to readjust their heading. "If you want her to fly straight then you need to switch on flight assist; Kahu always keeps it disabled because he thinks it's cheating."

"Go figure . . . Shouldn't *he* be the one up here telling me all this?"

"Not gonna happen." Her tone became morose. "Old fool said he couldn't stand to watch someone else at the helm. He might show his face eventually; if he sticks around, that is."

Isaac reached up to the overhead control panel and flicked a succession of blinking toggle switches. "Yah know, back when I worked in the docks, I used to spend all day watchin' freighters and salvage ships come an' go, daydreaming that maybe one day I'd get to be the one flying them."

The fuselage sang as the dozen or so microthrusters spread across her hull synchronously fired to simulate atmospheric flight, realigning her nose cone with her direction of travel. Isaac pulled the flight stick to the left once more, this time, successfully completing the turning maneuver, the gargantuan shape of the *Novara* dominating the view through the windshield and stretching on for what seemed like infinity. He let out a relieved sigh, albeit one tainted by an accent of nervousness. "Now . . . I'm not so sure."

Delilah placed a reassuring hand on the engineer's shoulder. "Don't fret, Verhoeven; you'll get the hang of it soon enough."

Lingering in the bridge entrance, Tobias sensed Null approaching from behind, the vanilla-like pheromone exuded from aer chitin wafting up the helm-access corridor to greet him. Ae reached out through resonance and cemented at the forefront of his awareness Isaac's facsimile, imbuing him with a sense of pride and admiration—feelings that were admittedly somewhat incongruent with how *he* felt about the delinquent, but he took the message ae wished to convey. Clearing his throat to announce himself, he said, "Null says you're doing a good job, Isaac"—a fairly transparent attempt at extending the olive branch, but one he hoped would be received favorably. If Isaac *was* to be the *Assurance*'s new pilot, then he wanted the animosity between them finally put to rest.

Isaac turned his head, not quite enough to make eye contact. "Tell aer . . . thanks."

Woes assuaged, he felt confident they could at least behave with some level of civility going forward. Although, relief soon yielded to unease as he detected a resonant aberration emanating from somewhere to his rear—almost identical to the cold, virulent presence he had sensed outside the bunker in the Cohabitor Ghetto. He whipped his head around to survey the helm-access corridor. Null, having also picked up the anomaly did the same, emitting a deep, purring growl from somewhere in aer thorax, the hardened spines ridging aer neck and shoulders twitching and extending in a threat display. Unsettlingly, all seemed relatively calm, save for the jubilant rumpus of twenty-plus children at play in the galley, that is. He couldn't see anything or anyone who could be responsible for the disturbance, which made sense, considering the presence felt as if emanating from beyond the galley, farther toward the stern of the ship, and down somewhere in her belly. The Composer had vowed that all Harmony personnel would disembark upon completion of repairs, but if Tobias and Null's senses served them well, then they had a stowaway aboard: a spy, perhaps, tasked with reporting their movements back to Jyn, or maybe even waiting for an opportunity to hijack the ship . . .

He spun around to warn Delilah, unsure if the woman even had faith enough in his abilities to trust his word. Then again, if she wouldn't listen to *him*, she would certainly listen to the *Assurance* . . . Seeming to concur that something was seriously wrong, the bridge unleashed a sense-assaulting bombardment of shrieking alarms and strobed warning lights. Isaac froze, his gawking expression a mask of fear and dismay, distended eyes frantically scanning the readouts on the main control pedestal.

"What is it?" asked the captain.

"F . . . Fire," he stuttered. "Fire suppression countermeasures just activated in the cargo bay!"

"Those blasted Harmony engineers," Delilah grumbled, hustling to the storage locker at the rear of the bridge and retrieving a fire extinguisher. "I *knew* they didn't have a clue what they were doing! Can't expect a bunch of greenhorns to know all the quirks and eccentricities of a pre-Collision ship . . . Get ready to open the cargo bay doors, Isaac. If we can't get it under control, then we might have to seal the bulkheads and purge the atmosphere."

Tobias reached out and touched Delilah's arm as she stormed toward the bridge entrance, halting her in her tracks. "Arm yourself, Captain," he cautioned. "It's not just a fire; there's someone on the ship."

She glanced at Null; he wasn't sure why—to get a second opinion, perhaps. The cohabitor huffed through aer breathing holes and stamped a talon into the floor grating, communicating to the nonresonant human in the only way ae could.

"Are you positive?" she asked.

He nodded. "A cohabitor, to be precise. And from what we can tell, a rather unpleasant one at that . . . Don't take any chances."

Delilah showed a smile that was at first appreciative, then subtly mischievous. She whirled around to the storage locker once more, this time pulling out her concussion repeater and throwing its strap around her shoulder.

"Wouldn't dream of it, which is why you two are coming with me."

Tobias and Null followed the captain as she hastened down helm access, the hoopla in the galley so loud and boisterous that it soon drowned out the calamity of sirens in the bridge. The junies had been whipped into a frenzy by the sheer excitement of their first stay aboard a ship, chasing each other around the island countertop and climbing on furniture before taking turns diving off. Tobias guessed that since they were accustomed to the sometimes-punishing gravity in the Mouth—generated by the Savior and better suited for cohabitor anatomy—for them, experiencing the comfortable 0.8Gs output of the *Assurance*'s subdeck grav panels probably felt like bouncing on air. Teo and Nanimonai were in the process of tending to a crying boy who had, perhaps, been a little too adventurous with the aerial gymnastics.

"Something wrong, Skip?" Kahu asked, sulking in his recliner with a bottle of syn-rum gripped loosely in hand.

"Not sure yet," she replied, paying no mind to the enveloping ruckus as she stormed through the galley. "Keep everyone locked down here until we can assess."

The captain led Null and Tobias through the crew quarters before descending the narrow stairwell to the lower deck. The three of them skulked cautiously through engineering, then formed up near the entrance to the cargo bay. Sure enough, something had triggered the ship's fire suppression system; blustering columns of deionized water mist thundered from ducts in the ceiling, colliding with the ground and gathering in a shoulder-high shroud of milk-white fog, drastically reducing the already-poor visibility.

Delilah handed the extinguisher to Tobias, then flicked the finger lever of her repeater to charge a round as she inched forward. He followed her inside, quickly surmising that if there *was* a fire, it had already been smothered by the roaring extinguishing vapor. He couldn't see or smell anything suggesting there had been a blaze, although further investigation into the mysterious essence he now felt in full force suggested their stowaway was responsible for setting off the fire suppression. Searching the stranger's mind, he dug up a recent memory of using something resembling a welding torch to set off the cargo bay's fire sensor, feeling aer intention of summoning the *Assurance*'s occupants to aer location. Although for what purpose, he couldn't say . . .

To lure us into a trap, most likely . . .

"Careful," he whispered. "They're here somewhere."

Delilah nodded, then turned to the systems panel on the nearby ceiling brace, thumbing several keys to disable the fire suppression. As the opaque mist subsided, a hulking shape emerged from the tenebrosity—the shadowy outline of a cohabitor slumped on the floor near the hatchway coaming with aer back pressed against the bulkheads. Looking physically exhausted, aer broken body chronicled a history of grizzly injuries, old and new. Deep-purple rakes of scar tissue meandered from aer face down to the top of aer thorax; aer left arm had been lost or amputated, replaced by a terrifying prosthetic resembling a butcher's rack neatly contained within a glass housing; aer right leg had been broken and bent out of shape, the large fracture in the plating of aer thigh revealing a bloody lesion to the leathery tissue beneath.

Ae lifted aer head as they approached, strenuous breath rasping through contracting breathing holes, fluid rattling in aer almost certainly collapsed lungs.

Delilah released a sharp gasp of shock and recognition. "Get behind me!" She pushed Tobias aside, assuming a firing stance and taking the wounded cohabitor in her sights. "Thought you'd come back to settle the score, huh? Well, you're not gonna take us so easily."

Ae raised aer prosthetic arm, switching its configuration from the fission torch ae had presumably used to trigger the fire suppression to a mechanical paw. Ae held the contraption out toward the captain, nanocarbon palm exposed in a gesture of truce and compliance. Ae turned aer head, directing their attention with a dull gaze to a second stranger: a dark-skinned man lying unconscious on the floor beside aer. He wore a tan suit stained with patches of various shades of blood. *Not just a man*, Tobias realized. *Vidalia Drexen.*

Attaining resonance, the cohabitor brute forced aer way into his awareness, breaking through the boundaries of his mental space like a Phalanx squad breaching the door to a glow dealer's apartment. Ae filled his mind with an abrasive torrent of feelings and imagery, which he took a moment to decipher before relaying to Delilah.

"Provide medical assistance," he translated. "Help the Governor . . . All debts, repaid . . . All transgressions, forgiven."

FOURTEEN

Historically, Eamon's relationship with Atherton Edevane had been an exercise in fierce dissension. At council sessions in the chambers of Chennai Plaza, they had dug their heels in at opposite ends of just about every sociopolitical spectrum in existence. His heartfelt pleas for humanitarian assistance in the Mouth had rarely been met with anything other than barefaced antipathy. But his proposals *never* received opposition as staunch and belligerent as the choleric pontificating that usually came from Atherton's booth, the mere thought of providing basic support and infrastructure to the sternside territories, apparently, a grievous affront to the man and his Upperdecks constituency.

In those days, it might have pleased Eamon immensely to see Ath shanked in a Cendre Vale alleyway—another region of the *Novara* famously neglected by the Administration. But right now, his mission was the protection of *anybody* the nefarious cabal that sought to despotize the Coalescence deemed enough of a threat to warrant *removal*. And somehow, Councilman Edevane had ended up on that list, hunted by the very establishment he had built his decorated political career in service of.

The councilman's crime, as far as Eamon could extrapolate, amounted to his parental association with Hazel Edevane—an aspiring pilot who had dared to survive a black book weapons test in which *she* was the shooting target. The demonstration had been orchestrated by the late administrator to prove the lethal efficacy of *Devourer*-hybridized fighters to the equally corrupt admiral, Jasper Coombs. And by simply living to tell of her harrowing ordeal, Hazel and her father had both been designated enemies of the New Terra Union—once celebrated citizens, now wanted fugitives marked for assassination.

During their tempestuous rendezvous, Jyn had been unable to warn Eamon about how or when Coombs might bring his machinations against the girl. But for all the grizzly possibilities his jaded mind could conjure, he had *never* imagined the admiral would try something so brazen as hiring two mercs to stage a robbery-turned-homicide.

He lamented that he had been unable to arrive at the scene in time to thwart the assassination attempt fully; unfortunately, his own wanted status had severely hampered his ability to keep watch over the Edevanes. The sterile hallways of Aegis Infirmary boasted a paparazzi of security cams and retinal ID scanners, ensuring he couldn't have ventured within fifty meters of the facility without Phalanx picking up his precise location. Forced to improvise, Eamon had liberated an obsolete camion from a disused Transitech maintenance depot, enabling him to move up and down the *Novara* freely while staying incognito. Parking below an inauspicious length of tramline situated across the Canyon from Aegis, he had watched over Hazel as best he could from a distance, catching fleeting glimpses of her through the window of her room or the rehabilitation ward's panoramic curtain walls, and had even felt a strange sense of vicarious pride as he watched her take her first unassisted steps.

The stint reminded him of the countless surveillance operations he and Fenn Haken had conducted during their days in the Glow Enforcement Agency, stewing in an unmarked cruiser as they kept tabs on key players of the Glow Syndicate's bowside subsidiaries. Only *this* time, he had been without anybody to alternate sleep shifts with; Abraham made for a lousy surveillance partner, only growing more agitated in response to their prolonged inactivity by the hour. At some point Eamon had fallen victim to his chronic sleep deficiency, resulting in an inopportune lapse in consciousness that occurred right as Hazel and Atherton boarded their swoop and left the facility. One frenzied nosedive into the grungy depths of Cendre Vale and two extra notches on his kill belt later, and his charge was now safely ensconced in the service compartment while he barreled down the Canyon toward his makeshift headquarters.

He glanced over his shoulder to check on the discomposed pair occupying two of the rear jump seats. Atherton lay reclined at his daughter's side, resting his head in her lap as she applied pressure to his wound with a crumpled high-vis vest, her hands soaked in blood up to the wrists. Eamon had grown accustomed to seeing the councilman's face ignited in furious shades of red, an irascible brocade of burst blood vessels spitting blistering condemnation of his department's *flagrant antihumanism*. Now, the man looked like a wax simulacrum of himself, his distant, glassy-eyed stare piercing through the camion's roof and perhaps stretching on even beyond the *Novara*'s dorsal hull, his vacant expression blanched paper-white as he barely registered his daughter's hysterical cries for him to stay with her.

Eamon had never thought a time would come when he'd find himself fretting over the well-being of a man with whom he held so many grievances, but the councilman was in bad shape—leaking more ichor than Anaya Lahiri had done highly classified documents before her *liquidation*. Criminals generally favored fission-edged weaponry because a seared wound meant leaving less mess behind to bolster a forensics investigation. Intentional or not, the blade used on Atherton had failed to effectively cauterize the puncture, resulting in catastrophic abdominal hemorrhaging that, if they couldn't stem soon, would mean curtains for the councilman. Having now been acquainted with, objectively, the two better thirds of the Edevane clan, *and* having developed a potent yet inexplicable endearment to them, Eamon found himself in the frustrating position of needing to prevent such a fate . . .

He reached out a hand to support Abraham as he pulled back on the throttle; the dumb mutt had propped himself up on the dashboard with his hind legs perched on the edge of the passenger seat, gazing out through the transport's thin slit of a windscreen. Eamon had half a mind to slam the inertial dampeners on and let him tumble into the footwell, but he doubted the idiot would learn anything valuable from it . . .

The craft's spinning hazard lights reflected in the polished surfaces of a nearby arcade as he pulled up fifty meters or so along the tram line from Khonsu Station—where day-trippers visiting the *Novara*'s Museum District could disembark for the Silk River Concourse. He waited for a nearing tram to glide past, a giant caterpillar fashioned from white marble, aglow with the brooding, navy-blue tones of the night sky luma-cast above them. Once clear, he dipped below the horizontal scaffolding of support struts and braces comprising the Canyon's suspension railway. The line had been completely renovated a century ago in tandem with the construction of the blockade, given the *Devourer*'s insatiable gorging of . . . well, everything sternside of Halvorsen Commons, including, but not limited to, the *Novara*'s aftmost tram stops. Vestiges of the old line remained—brittle, decaying relics of pre-Collision infrastructure, jutting out occasionally like the splintered bones of a compound fracture. Eamon brought the camion about near one such relic: a disused signal junction where a section of obsolete rail diverged from the modern line, descending for a short distance before snaking around a narrow bend and disappearing into an octagonal tunnel, bored into the Canyon's starboard wall.

"Where are you taking us?" The frail voice came from the service compartment as he followed the ancient track into the cavity, total darkness consuming the driver's compartment.

"Somewhere safe," he answered, realizing how vague and ominous the words probably sounded to someone in Hazel's understandably distressed state.

"Somewhere safe?" she repeated icily. "No! He's lost too much blood; he's going into shock! We need to get him to Aegis immediately or . . ."

"You think those were two random street thugs I just zeroed for you?" he cut in. "Those were mercs—hired by some downright rotten folks who want you and your pops dead . . . All *three* of us, matter of fact . . . I guarantee they'll have another *welcome party* waitin' for you back at the infirmary. 'Fraid that means we gotta stick to the back alleys from here on out—no public places or *anywhere* we could be identified." He glanced over his shoulder at her pale, enfeebled frame, flashing a consoling smile that he hoped might bring some measure of comfort. "Got plenty of stims and med-foam where we're headed; shouldn't have any trouble puttin' your old man back together."

"Somehow, that doesn't fill me with an overabundance of confidence," she snipped, appropriating the same pompous edge her brother, Tobias, had regarded him with upon their first conversation in the holding cells of the DMED precinct house.

He clucked his tongue on the inside of his cheek. "Guess you're just gonna have to trust me, miss."

The access tunnel opened up into a long-abandoned maintenance depot, its high ceiling a skeletal lattice of catwalks and gantries. The defunct tram rail branched into three separate lines, all terminating on a rotatable platform riven with dilapidated inspection pits. An office block consisting of several prefabricated units lay just beyond, with swathes of faded Transitech branding revealed only by the fluctuating glow of a vending machine, turned on its side nearby. Scattered bullet holes perforated the prefab's exterior cladding, many of which Eamon specifically recalled planting with his Phalanx-issue Wistra 93 semiautomatic . . . This gloomy place was steeped in his past; the specter of his younger, more idealistic self roamed its decrepit platforms and deserted maintenance bays, calling out to be reunited with his long-lost corporeal shell. And he . . . *present-day he* answered, casting his thoughts back through the obfuscating haze of time to an epoch five years prior when he and then-partner Fenn Haken had been at the height of their careers in the GEA. Fenn had received a tip-off from an informant that Vidalia Drexen had reappropriated the depot as a forward operating base and distribution center. The number of corrupt enforcers the Governor kept on his payroll in *those* days had been an institutional embarrassment, with many found to have been strategically positioned to ensure the turning of a systemic blind eye to the massive glow shipments regularly moving through Antaeus Gateway. According to Fenn's source, the caps were being stockpiled to the depot and then distributed to low-level dealers operating throughout Amidships under the umbrella of the syndicate's bowside subsidiaries.

Eamon spent months setting up a task force with the remit of shutting the operation down while simultaneously nailing as many of Drexen's confederates as possible. The team implemented twenty-four-hour surveillance to keep an eye on the facility while he and Fenn set to work confirming the identities of several heavy hitters, aiming to ensure as many of them were on the premises as possible before sending in the tactical armed enforcers, known as TAE.

Of course, Fenn being Fenn had been a little too loose-lipped about the plan with his informant, depriving the man of a glorious little thing known as plausible deniability. The syndicate realized they had a rat in their ranks and tortured the truth out of the poor bastard's mouth, leaving Eamon with little choice but to prematurely pull the trigger. Even after weeks of keeping tabs on perp activity, the TAE were woefully unprepared for the level of armed resistance they would face and ended up walking right into a Gaia-damned shooting gallery. Eamon and Fenn had accompanied the arresting team to provide logistics and tactical support, but soon found themselves embroiled in the largest gun battle the *Novara* had seen since the Janrand Siege . . .

Except when infamous COTA cultist Ronhys Janrand and his acolytes forcibly occupied an airlock in the Rennaxi Junction, the Phalanx operatives who moved in to evict them were up against a bunch of untrained, barely equipped kids. My team, on the other hand, found themselves going toe-to-toe with a damned-Abyss paramilitary.

Thankfully, Fenn had far more tact in a firefight than he did with handling covert op details with informants. With some fancy footwork and a few plucky shots, he managed to turn the absolute clusterfuck of a situation into a relative success. Drexen's primary distribution channel through the blockade had been dismantled and the GEA had seized over two-and-a-half-million nunits worth of glow caps. Eamon and Fenn were commended for their efforts, although it wouldn't be long after that that their partnership would take a sudden and contentious turn . . .

Returning to the maintenance depot half a decade later, having been ousted from both the GEA *and* DMED, now wanted dead for a high-profile murder he had *nothing* to do with, Eamon couldn't help but wonder where life might have taken him had he chosen to keep his trap shut—just buried his head in the sand and never said a word to anyone about his partner's anger issues.

What's done is done, he bargained, setting the camion down near the blackened, burned-out husk of an outmoded tram, partially raised by a vehicle lift with its entrails spilling into the below inspection pit. *No sense tryna change the past . . . And anyhow: even if you could wind back the clocks, stop yourself from ever making those allegations, would you really want to?*

He liked to think the answer was no. Otherwise, the top brass would never have reassigned him to his new post across the blockade. And although it had felt utterly futile most days, he genuinely believed his presence in the district had had at least *some* kind of positive impact for the folks living there.

But then again, what does any of it matter if, in the end, that tyrant Coombs rains righteous hell on the place to squash Jyn's uprising? All of it will have been for nothing. You coulda just kicked back and watched the Novara tear itself apart, sipping ghost pepper–infused strawberry daiquiris in your Festa Heights condo like Fenn.

The notion coaxed a huff of mirthless amusement from his nostrils. Many throughout the years had tried to tell Eamon to learn to take a back seat, to pick his fights, or to let sleeping dogs lie. *Keep your hand outta the hornet's nest if you don't wanna get stung,* the old man used to say, soul rest in the Abyss. And Clarissa had bellyached something similar—if slightly less poetic—nearly every day in the run-up to the divorce, begging him to accept forced resignation as opposed to uprooting their life in Amidships and traipsing off to the Mouth—something he would ultimately be forced to do alone . . .

Jyn, of course, had been the most recent of his consciences to try and dissuade him from *jumping headfirst into things way above his pay grade,* which he realized now had really been an effort to prevent him from meddling in her affairs, rather than genuine concern for his safety. Whatever her motive, he would struggle to oblige; little terrified him more than monotony. When life got too comfortable—*that* was when he felt most fidgety: when the coarse touch of complacency came to sand him down to a dull edge, leaving him numb and apathetic to the terrible injustices many *still* faced aboard the Coalescence. The Upperdecks, sternside of the blockade—*where* he put down roots hardly mattered, because at *some* point, Vargos's corruption would have become apparent, and he knew with every cell in his body that even in the parallel universe where he had been promoted to detective chief inspector, he *still* would have ended up in his current situation . . .

The girl is safe, he thought, hooking his wrists under Atherton's armpits to drag the man from the camion into the abandoned offices. *What's next: Lay low, keep your head down until this all blows over? No . . . Sorry, Dad. Looks like I'm stickin' my hand right into the hornet's nest again. Just like Jyn said: the only way to hit back at Coombs is to undermine his position of power. It's time to let the good citizens of the NTU see their beloved admiral's true colors . . .*

The disused maintenance depot had been Eamon's home for a little over a month now. After his brush with death in Festa Heights, he had left the crew of the *Assurance* with his side pumped full of med-foam, urgently needing a safehouse to conduct new lines of investigation while staying under the Administration's radar. A structure as dauntingly colossal as the Canyon was rife with hidden nooks of neglected urban architecture: dingy forgotten underpasses, liminal graffiti-ridden substructures lurking beneath terraces and landing platforms, the brutalist spillways and cisterns that funneled the water cascading from Capella Promenade back up to its artificial shoreline.

Summoning the raid on the distribution center from the faded pages of his memory, he had been pleasantly surprised to find the abandoned installation's secluded Canyonside entrance still open. Plans to decommission the depot and seal it off from the public had been derailed and ultimately abandoned following his transfer to DMED. Serendipitously, it appeared none of his ex-colleagues had been eager to resume his efforts in his stead . . .

With a staff canteen equipped with a functioning protein synthesizer, not to mention an old service camion requiring only a new fission cell and a firmware patch to get up and running again, the depot had proven an ideal base of operations—perfectly situated for keeping track of the Edevanes.

For the Transitech employees once stationed here, it had been a relatively hazardous work environment, as evidenced by the ample first-aid and emergency trauma kits strategically positioned throughout the facility. Fortunately, the band of drug runners who eventually superseded the workers had been uninterested in plundering the medical equipment. Eamon dragged Atherton into the prefabricated offices and deposited him on the mound of torn-off seat cushions that he had been generously calling a bed, a crimson-black streak marking the musty carpet where the man's expensive shoes had smeared his blood across the floor. Eamon ripped open the councilman's syn-silk shirt, feeling a wave of nausea as he eyed the grizzly laceration occupying his midriff, the stench of burnt flesh flooding his nostrils.

Suck it up, Eamon. Spent two years in ruttin' homicide, Lei-Ghannam's sake. What would Mom say if she knew you were still flinchin' at the sight of blood?

Pushing through his aversions he reached for the green plastic first-aid container with its contents spilled onto the floor nearby—the same kit from which he had been regularly helping himself to painkillers to allay the discomfort of his partially healed projectile graze. Hazel collapsed by her father's side, lifting his pallid hand and holding it against her chest. She watched with a fretful, tearstained expression as Eamon produced a stim vial from the box and prepared to administer the scintillating blue elixir swirling within.

"What's that?" she demanded. "What are you doing to him?"

"Relax . . . Just givin' your old man somethin' to take the edge off," he answered, ramming the cylinder's needle tip directly into Atherton's right pectoral. "It's a trauma cocktail: contains steroids, antibiotics, vasopressors to stop the bleeding, and erythropoietin to stimulate red cell reproduction . . . It'll either have him in delirious cold sweats for two days or bouncin' off the walls, dependin' on how his body reacts . . . At the very least, it *should* stabilize him."

He reached into the container again and retrieved a white med-foam canister, snapping off its safety cap and positioning its nozzle a few centimeters away from the wound. Applying pressure to the trigger on its latex grip, the contraption sprayed a grayish stream of mucilaginous foam into the puncture, gathering and expanding over the damaged tissue. Atherton jolted from his cataleptic state as if shocked out of arrest with a defibrillator. He loosed a groan of agony, clenched his teeth, and tightened his neck muscles until they looked fit to burst.

"I know; it sucks," Eamon said, forcing the man back down into recumbency with a hand on his shoulder. "Just wait until it hardens and you snag it on somethin'. Now *that* smarts."

"Are you sure this is gonna be enough to stem the hemorrhaging?" Hazel asked, mind visibly running a mile a minute. "Don't we need to get him to a biometric scanner; somewhere we can get him imaged to make sure there's no serious internal damage? He could go septic!"

"We gotta make do with what we've got," Eamon lamented, using his teeth to rip a length of gauze bandage. "But judging from the angle and position of the wound—looks to me like they might have nicked his kidney, which is good news, strangely enough, since they can pretty much tamponade themselves. Med-foam will plug the hole, encourage tissue regeneration, fight any infection, and expedite the healin' process."

"How do you know all this?" the girl pried, beads of sweat dripping from the fuzz covering her scalp and collecting on her furrowed brow. "You're Eamon Wyatt, right? The guy Phalanx want for the murder of the administrator? I thought you were a marshal, not a medic." The matter-of-fact way in which Hazel mentioned his purported involvement with Vargos's death suggested she didn't believe it for a second. *Savvy lass, this one . . .*

He cracked a rueful smile, shaking his head as he fed the bandage beneath the arch of the councilman's back to wrap around his abdomen. "I'm a good Samaritan—that's all that matters right now. But to answer your question: no, I ain't medically inclined. The woman who raised me, on the other hand, was. Used to run an emergency clinic down in the Wards. Dad worked in salvage and was usually out in the Debris Belt days at a time; they couldn't afford day care, so I spent long hours watching her work when I was just a kid . . . Used to see a lot of nasty industrial accidents comin' up from Cendre Vale. And what with all the dive bars round those parts, it wouldn't be a Friday night without at least two shankings needing tending to."

Hazel relaxed her shoulders, the exposed skin beneath the straps of her tank top scratched and besmirched from the tussle with her attackers. She didn't fully trust him yet, but impelling her to imagine him as a child, as well as divulging a little about his relationship with his parents had softened her circumspection—a technique he'd picked up from a seminar on hostage and crisis negotiation back in his training days, and which he regularly employed when interviewing suspects or persons of interest. *Never fails.*

"You saved us," Hazel breathed, addressing Eamon but keeping her glistening green eyes locked on her father. "If you hadn't shown up when you did . . . Those men were waiting for us; that whole thing was meticulously planned, and somehow you knew about it . . . How?"

He flashed a cocksure grin. "Let's just say I like to keep my finger on the pulse."

"Will you stop already?" she scoffed in annoyance. "'Good Samaritan,' 'finger on the pulse'—are you always this cryptic? You know, I'm taking a significant risk complying with all this no-hospitals-no-public-places shit. The *least* you can do is start giving me some real answers."

Got a little more grit than her brother, Eamon mused, reminding himself to see beyond the damaged fledgling struggling to keep herself upright before him and to recognize the fearless NTSC combat pilot buried beneath all the silicone and cyber-wear.

"You'll get the full rundown, ma'am; you have my word. Just making sure we get your pa outta the woods first."

He reached into the first aid box a final time and retrieved a biometric omnimeter—a small, plastic finger clip with a microemitter display. He fastened it to the end of Atherton's right index finger and waited a moment for it to deliver its findings. Studying the luma-cast readouts, he said, "Vitals stabilizing, blood pressure coming back up to acceptable levels . . . Looks like we might be in the clear . . . for now."

Ath released an involuntary croak through desert-dry vocal cords, reached into his jacket pocket, and produced his feather. He raised the device to his face, allowing it to scan his retinas before fumbling it into Eamon's palm. "C . . . Call Tabitha," he rasped. "Tell her . . . Tell her we're OK."

Tabitha, Eamon mentally echoed. *Who in the Abyss is Tabitha? His personal assistant? Some other fat cat he rolled with in Chennai Plaza?* It then dawned on him that the muttered name belonged to the councilman's late wife—a woman who nearly two decades ago had been at the epicenter of a scandal that threatened to completely derail her husband's budding political career. The pair were swept up in an almost insufferable media circus, catalyzed by the NTNN's painting of Tabitha's sternside humanitarian work as taxpayer money funding antihuman organizations in the Mouth. It was a miracle Atherton ever managed to recover his reputation following the public backlash; cynically, Eamon suspected the only reason he managed to was Tabitha's tragic, if somewhat serendipitous, passing during the alien flu outbreak of 107 AC, handily transforming the anger being directed Atherton's way into sympathy.

Whether due to the concoction of meds inundating his brain or confusion triggered by the lingering effects of shock, the councilman seemed utterly convinced poor Tabitha was still alive and well. Not wanting to cause any further confusion, Eamon took the feather and tapped aimlessly on its tempered glass display for a moment. "I'll get right on that, old buddy," he said warmly. "In the meantime, you just rest up, alright?"

He met Hazel's eyes and motioned toward the door, quickly realizing that she would need his help in reaching it. She initially refused his assistance but changed her mind after trying and failing to push herself to her feet. Blowing an exasperated sigh, she hooked her arm around his and strenuously extended her legs, then shambled in step beside him as he escorted her back through the office entrance and out into the maintenance depot.

Only when they found Abraham out near the camion did Eamon realize the mutt had been missing for a full ten minutes, and a prolonged silent absence from Abraham could usually be taken as a sign of there being mischief afoot. Sure enough, Abe was making his way from the transport to the prefabs, eagerly lapping up the arcing trail of fresh claret, his black nose and leathery chops colored dark glistering red.

"Get outta there, you Gaia-damned reprobate!" Eamon bellowed, sending the dog packing with an exaggerated kicking motion. Fortunately, Hazel didn't seem too horrified witnessing the wild mutt cleaning up her dad's blood; she released herself from his grip and took a load off on the overturned vending machine.

He took Atherton's feather and placed it down on the deck, then turned to her with his hand outstretched, wordlessly requesting hers. She pouted, avoiding his gaze.

"Don't have it; probably left it in the footwell of Dad's swoop."

Eamon tilted his head and wrung his lips. "That your best poker face, darlin'? Fraid you're gonna have to do better than *that* to pull one over on me."

She sighed, rolling her eyes and mouthing the words *don't call me darling* as she reluctantly dug her feather out of her pocket and handed it over to him.

"I'm doin' my best to keep you and your dad alive, here," he reminded, snatching the device and placing it beside Atherton's, voice echoing chaotically throughout the spacious terminal. "I'd appreciate it if you wouldn't work against me on that."

He unzipped his black Transitech-issue anorak, revealing the garish purple and gold of his Amidships Stingrays casterblade jersey. Hazel scrutinized the garment with a perplexed look that only intensified once he produced the hybridized firearm given to him by Jyn. He aimed the augmented pistol at the feathers, staring down his arm past the revolting organic technology clamped around its frame as if encased within the decomposing carcass of some headless, dismembered rodent. He squeezed the trigger and felt the unnerving spasm of the ligament structure affixed to its barrel. The muzzle discharged a coruscating bolt of chartreuse energy—comprised of what, exactly, he *still* couldn't say. The magazine well was empty and impregnated by something resembling spaghetti sautéed in ink. The pistol didn't seem to require any ammunition at all, yet made short work of its targets, completely vaporizing the gadgets in a bright flash of sparks and miasma. If anybody had been using location services to track the Edevanes, they no longer could. *Unless that sadistic bastard Coombs had Aegis bury some kind of beacon inside Hazel's prosthetic vertebrae . . . Guess we won't know for sure until more mercenaries show up . . .*

The girl anchored her stare on the hybridized pistol, her eyes like two emerald portholes laying bare a mind rocked by a combination of revulsion and recognition. Her shocked expression was that of someone who had been forced to question a truth that she had once known beyond any doubt, her suspicions finally vindicated by the gruesome abomination before her.

"Do I even want to know what that is?" she asked.

Eamon planted himself on the vending machine beside her and placed the weapon in her lap. "Not sure how much you know about cohabitors or their relationship with the *Devourer*," he said. "But there's this . . . techno-wizard in the Mouth known as Absence; made it aer life's work learning how to reverse engineer the *Devourer*'s living material and splice it with human tech. Aer work's been croppin' up all over the Mouth in various forms—mainly weaponry, although I've also seen software applications, too: hardware peripherals that can brute-force heavily encrypted operating systems . . . Can even worm its way into the subroutines of a grenadier's neural cortex."

Hazel scooped the weapon up in her palms and studied it like a scientist holding the single most disgusting, yet fascinating object in history. Doing a piss-poor job of concealing her intrigue, she intoned, "And I need to know this because . . . ?"

"Because I have it on good authority that right now *isn't* the first time you've had eyes on tech like this."

She cast him a sideways glance, jaw set firm, not saying anything but silently prodding him to continue. And so, he obliged. "The bogeys that wiped out your wingmates and left you stranded in the black with a broken neck—NTNN have been putting their usual spin on things and reporting *Devourer* interceptors as being responsible for the ambush. But you and I both know the truth ain't quite so clear-cut."

She remained defiant for another moment, then let her shoulders sink, subtly shaking her head. "We thought they were interceptors at first, but Delta Two . . . Zain Cantrell . . . before he was killed, indicated the hostile fighters had kestrel wing profiles—modified almost beyond recognition, but definitely of human origin in at least some capacity."

Eamon saw a shiver ripple through her body and felt a twinge of guilt that he had forced her to mentally revisit the harrowing ordeal. "They outperformed us at every turn; exhibited evasive and offensive maneuvers that . . . well . . . just didn't seem possible. They had some kind of short-range teleportation that meant we were basically shooting at ghosts . . . Couldn't identify any conventional hardpoints—none we had any hope of effectively counteracting, at least."

Sorrow roiled over her face, a resentment that looked physically painful to bear. "The moment they engaged us, we were dead . . . Or at least, I *wish* it had ended that way . . ."

Demonstrating his uncanny ability to sniff out sadness, Abraham parked himself at Hazel's feet and nuzzled his snout in between her hands. He used his nose as a spatula to flick the pistol out of her palms, identifying it as the obvious cause of her sorrow and acting accordingly. Eamon plucked the weapon out of the air as it fell, holding it tentatively in his bloodstained hands as he attempted to formulate a sufficiently meaningful response. "Coalescence ain't done with you yet, sister. You *still* got a part to play in all this. We might not know exactly why these things happen, but they rarely happen for no reason."

"I don't believe in fate."

"I'm not talkin' about fate; I'm talkin' about purpose . . ."

"I don't have a purpose, Mister Wyatt—not anymore . . . I knew I wanted to fly for the NTSC since I was a little girl; there's no higher duty a Novarian can undertake than to defend this vessel and its people. Without it, I'm nothing . . . I don't even know why I'm even breathing right now."

"Its people, huh?" Eamon repeated, scrutinizing her crestfallen expression. "That include people of a nonhuman persuasion, too?"

Hazel made a sneer as if he'd just spat in her face. "I am *not* my father . . . You won't catch me making any such distinction."

"Glad to hear it . . . Look, I know you've been dealt a shit hand here, but just cuz you've had your wings clipped, doesn't mean your days of protecting folks are over."

He wrapped his fingers around the pistol's grip and raised it to eye level for closer inspection. "The cohabitor who created *this* monstrosity is also responsible for assembling the wraiths you went up against out there . . . What Absence is doing represents a whole new frontier—the biggest technological leap humanity has seen since the advent of ripple-space propulsion. And if you think the NTU's upper crust are gonna let landmark advancement like *this* go unnoticed or not want a slice of the pie, then you can think again . . ."

Hazel rubbed her temples abrasively. "*Please* will you get to the point already? I am beyond exhausted."

Eamon unburdened himself of the same knowledge that, to merely possess, had made him a marked man. Listening intently, Hazel's expression gradually transformed from that of someone wryly indulging a drunkard espousing outlandish conspiracy theories at a bar, to a little kid lost in the woods, the hollow ground beneath her feet threatening to crumble away and devour her whole.

Eventually, her discomposure turned to enthrallment, and it wasn't long before she began preempting key beats in his circuitous scribble of a hypothesis, using her keen mind, elite education, and military experience to fill the gaps in his knowledge. Undoubtedly, she was the most discerning of the Edevanes Eamon had met, uninhibited by the same deeply cemented prejudices as her brother and father. None of his conclusions were lunacy or preposterous, as long as he presented sound reasoning or reinforcing evidence; there were even multiple instances in which she helped connect dots that would have otherwise evaded him.

Before long, he had caught her up on everything from the murder of Anaya Lahiri to his recent rendezvous with the Composer, leaving no stone unturned and sparing little of the grizzly details. She sat hunched forward, absently combing her fingers through the fur on the nape of Abe's neck, eyes darting from side to side as she mulled over the reality-shattering information she had been given.

"All this time," she slurred. "I've been stuck in purgatory—never able to properly grieve for my friends because I didn't know where to direct my anger . . . But Zain, Shiyana, Horatio, and the others . . . They were . . ."

"They were lab rats," Eamon solemnly put in. "Pawns in a game of chess—tactically sacrificed as part of Vargos's strategy . . . And Admiral Coombs just went along with it; he traded your lives for an opportunity to witness hybridized tech in action, and now he wants to upgrade the entire fleet."

"I don't get it . . . I mean, I *do*," Hazel vacillated. "But it still doesn't make sense. Vargos and Coomb's ilk spent over a century doing everything they could to quarantine the *Devourer*: built the blockade, segregated the Mouth—now you're telling me they're trying to reinforce the *Novara*'s defenses by integrating its technology?"

Eamon shrugged. "There's only one thing those with power covet . . ."

"More power?"

"Precisely . . . It wasn't the *Devourer* they wanted to quarantine: it was the cohabitors. Humanity First is just a smokescreen whisked up to give the Administration the justification to exact tighter control over the nonhuman populace—to further militarize the segregation. They know full well we're stuck with the *Devourer* indefinitely, so now they want to find ways to harness its power and further line their pockets." Eamon cast a glance toward the prefab offices. "Funnily enough, I *did* have my suspicions your pa might have been involved, right up until he took a fission dagger to the gut. I'd wager Vargos was just using him as a useful idiot to perpetuate all this separation shit—keep the people distracted and sufficiently outraged."

Hazel issued a mirthless chuckle. "Dad's a dedicated Novarian, a staunch unionist—he's not capable of subterfuge like this; it goes against everything he stands for. And besides, he's lousy at keeping secrets . . . You really think this *cabal* is prepared to assassinate a councilman of the New Terra Union, just because of what his daughter knows?"

Eamon nodded glumly. "I used to be a marshal, sister, and I sure as hell wasn't exempt. It's like a jigsaw puzzle: lots of people have different pieces. Soon as anyone gets close to figuring out how it all fits together, they get marked . . . Of course, your poor old man didn't have a clue as to any of this; it was his proximity to *you* that put the target on his back."

She formed a doleful expression, realization of the mortal danger she and her father now faced like a heavy chain cinched around her neck. That concern, however, evidently extended beyond those in her immediate circle . . .

"This proxy war the administrator started," she considered. "You say it's gotten out of control? Is there a possibility of real conflict—like, on *this* side of the blockade?"

I'll be damned; an honest-to-Abyss altruist. Just like her ma.

"Wasn't supposed to be a war," Eamon clarified. "Just a reason for Novarians to fear their neighbors . . . Problem is, Vargos squeezed too hard and ended up gettin' more than what she bargained for: an uprising backed by a massive, armed militia." He locked eyes with her, tightening his stern countenance "The conflict is already here; we just can't see it yet. Believe me, I tried like hell to warn people about the goddamned apocalypse looming on the horizon, but nobody will listen . . . Things are in motion now that can't be slowed or undone. Harmony won't relent until they take the *Novara*, but it's what Coombs is prepared to do in order to stop them that keeps me up at night. Clearly, he doesn't value the lives of his pilots; what do you think that means for the rest of us, or for the cohabitors?"

Hazel paused, twisting her lips in introspection. "You said I have a part to play in all this . . . What did you mean by that?"

He grinned coyly. "So glad you asked . . . Your story, Hazel—what happened to your friends, the trauma you suffered—people need to know the truth about what went down . . . Coombs is a ruttin' tyrant, and we haven't seen even a scintilla of what he's capable of yet. But there are ways we can still cut at his heels. If we let it get out that he needlessly sent NTSC pilots to their deaths as part of this shadowy initiative to weaponize *Devourer* tech, he loses the support of the people."

Hazel took a beat, sporting an expression like someone waiting for the punch line of a joke.

"That's it?" she chided, causing Abraham to jump out of his fur. "A character assassination—*that's* your big plan? You're telling me that evil, corrupt sonofabitch sent *my* squadron out there to fucking die, and your idea is to try and oust him in the media, just hope that we can somehow damage his reputation?"

Eamon showed his palms in a pacifying gesture. "If you've got a better suggestion, sister, I'm all ears. But the truth is we don't have a lot of room for maneuverability here. The second any of us sets foot outside, we're dead."

"Coombs isn't a bureaucrat; he doesn't give a shit about whether or not he has the *support of the people*." And she recited that last part in the same burlesque tone she probably used to mock her little brother. "If what you're saying is true, then he should be removed from duty—forcefully, if necessary. This *must* be taken to military tribunal so he can face justice!"

"And who's gonna arrest him: you and me? The admiral owns Phalanx, the NTSC—every organization put in place to uphold law and order from bow to blockade. You can bet your ass the unprecedented delay we're seeing in appointing a new administrator right now comes back to him. Probably likes the fact that he doesn't have to defer to a politician and wants to keep it that way for as long as possible . . . He has complete control of the *Novara*, and I hate to say it, but we're hardly in the position to go marchin' up to Quarter-deck to confront him—not when he's hunting us."

Eamon preempted another snappy riposte from the girl but turned his head to find her staring off into the distance. Something on the far side of the maintenance depot had stolen her attention, but squinting into the darkness beyond the disemboweled tram, he couldn't spot anything worthy of terminating their discussion so abruptly.

To his surprise, she pushed herself to her feet, rocking from side to side for a moment until she managed to find her balance. Staring at the back of her head, the implant embedded at the base of her skull caught his attention—or rather, the soft, white status light usually seen performing slow and rhythmic pulses, now sporadically flickering and taking on a sickly lime-green hue.

"You OK there, Miss Edevane?" he quizzed, one thick eyebrow raised as he switched his stare from the councilman's daughter to the empty space that seemed to have so engrossed her.

"Do . . . Do you see that?" she asked, dragging her syllables as if half-asleep, taking several trudging steps forward to suit.

"Can't say as I do . . . Although I ain't exactly sure what it is I'm supposed to be lookin' for."

"The woman; over there." She pointed to the empty landing bay in which he had found the old service camion. Save for an iridescent puddle of oil and the rusted housing of a gimballed repulsor pad, he couldn't see anything—not that could be mistaken for a woman, anyway. "I saw her—back at Aegis—when Admiral Coombs and Wing Commander Luscombe came to visit. She was just standing there, staring at me from across reception like . . . like she knew me . . ."

Hazel quickened her shambling pace, walking as if pulled by an invisible rope tied around her abdomen. "And . . . and I think I know her, too," she croaked, sounding as if teetering on the brink of tears. "I think . . . I think it's . . . Mom . . . Mom!"

Eamon jumped to his feet and started after the girl, concerned that she might trip over the tangle of cables and abandoned tools strewn across the deck with her sluggish gait. Seeming alert and fully cognizant only moments ago, she now appeared hypnotized, ignoring his pleas for caution as she continued forward, reaching out with crimson-soaked hands for . . . *well, for the ghost of her ma, by the sounds of it . . .*

"Don't you see her?" she pined. "She's right there; look! Mom! I'm coming!"

Eamon's insides plunged in dread as he realized Hazel's path ran perpendicular to one of the inspection pits. In a few short steps, she would go tumbling into the corroded, tetanus-riddled recess in the ground, almost certainly breaking a few bones and giving herself a nasty concussion in the process.

He lunged forward and grabbed her by the upper arm, just as the sole of one of her twin gusset pumps slipped over the edge of the trench. She gasped in shock as he wrenched her away from the inspection pit and planted her feet back on solid ground, completely unaware of how close she had come to seriously injuring herself. She scanned her surroundings, seeming dazed and disoriented, then settled her gaze on the spot where she *thought* her mother had been standing.

"Watch your damned footing," Eamon cautioned. "Got enough to worry about with bloodthirsty mercenaries comin' after us without *you* tryna' do their job for 'em."

Hazel's gaze lingered on the empty maintenance bay for another moment, then she dropped her eyes to the floor, the apparition she had been so convinced was there, now apparently gone.

"Sorry," she whimpered. "I don't know what's happening; it's . . . it's hard to explain."

Tears welling in the corners of her eyes, she relinquished herself from his grip and staggered off to rejoin Atherton in the prefab offices, leaving Eamon in silent confusion.

FIFTEEN

I miss you, love." The words left Caleb Callaghan's lips as a plaintive whisper, uttered unintentionally, and heard by no one besides herself. She didn't expect a response but received one, nevertheless, in the gentle rustle of the simulated wind winnowing the leaves of a nearby oak tree. Amara Thaddeus—the Conservatory's architect—knew in her unquestionable brilliance that failing to incorporate a system for emulating Earth's inclement atmosphere would leave her gardens feeling muted, lifeless, and eerily static. The installation's carefully regulated air current was as close to feeling a breeze as any Novarian would ever come. For Caleb, the constant susurration merely served to fill the silence—a heartrending void that might once have otherwise been filled by the silken tones of Jade Tanaka's voice . . .

A memorial tablet lay in the grass at her feet, fashioned from black imitation granite pervaded by flecks of ruby and silver. The name, rank, and age of her beloved appeared in sparkling gold, engraved above an Old-Earth proverb, which Jade, in her sentimental way, had inherited from her grandmother and adopted as a mantra to live her life by: *Always make time for joy. Because sorrow makes time for itself.*

You were right about that, love . . . It's hard to find time for anything else these days . . .

In accordance with long-standing military tradition, Jade and the others in her unit who fell during the massacre at the blockade had been given ceremonial burials, their bodies relinquished to the endless night in caskets swathed in the colors of the sovereignty they all died defending. Jade had always been incredibly passionate about her Phalanx career, her creative mind, and free spirit often at odds with her implacable desire to protect and serve. But as monumentally important as her service had been to her, she had never wanted it to define who she was as a person. Accordingly, Caleb had taken steps to ensure she was properly laid to rest in the place where she most flourished: beneath the pink blossoms of the Japanese maple tree overlooking her plot, surrounded by the lush vegetation that she dedicated so much of her time to cultivating, pouring her heart and soul into the fertile soil on which Caleb now stood.

After two months of neglect, Jade's verdant patch of paradise had begun to look somewhat overgrown; a vibrant canopy of wild bluebells seemed to hover above the fecund turf like violet stratus clouds hanging over a miniature landscape. Vivid sweeps of ramsons sprouted from the untamed grass like a dusting of snow, suffusing the rich aroma of wild garlic into the humid air. And the plump leaves of the lettuce and tomato plants Jade had planted at the beginning of the year for her specialty Tanaka salad had spilled over the edge of their faux-wood beds, bulging against the plot's mesh fence, and threatening to break free from the enclosure altogether.

Jade's saint of a grandmother—the woman who had rescued her from a broken home and shaped her into the outstanding Novarian she eventually became—had kindly offered to pay for a gardener to maintain upkeep. But Caleb had declined; the last hands to tend to the nursery were *hers*, and she didn't know if she would ever be ready for that to change. Whether the allotment grew into a jungle wilderness or withered to a desiccated mound of dead shrubbery, she would see that it remained exactly how Jade left it . . .

An unusual sound broke her reverie: a deep, rhythmic pulsing, like the steam-powered crank and piston of some mighty industrial age machine thrumming and churning beneath her feet. The vibrations traveled up through her legs and into her rib cage, rattling the air in her lungs. She turned her attention upward to the Conservatory's concave firmament—the staggeringly vast aluminosilicate dome enclosing the facility and its myriad gardens. The structure's ordinarily bright, sky-blue hue seemed off, wavering in vividity and occasionally taking on more of a striking greenish color—remarkably similar, in fact, to the legendary aurora borealis that had once danced in the skies over the northern latitudes of Earth, only, visible *now* in the middle of the day. Returning her gaze to Jade's memorial tablet, she said, "Amara Thaddeus, up to her old tricks as usual."

She found saying the words out loud—as though Jade was standing right beside her—surprisingly therapeutic. "Spoke to one of the clerks on the help desk when I arrived: the old woman with the Albert Einstein hair—you know the one. She said Amara's been getting more mischievous by the day—downright unmanageable, in fact. Irrigation's been going haywire, and the day/night cycle is completely out of sync with *Novara* standard time. Apparently, they sent a team of engineers down to the mainframe to see what the problem was, but she locked them out and just started hurling insults . . . It's crazy to think that after well over two centuries, we *still* haven't figured out a way to crack her firewall; just goes to show what a mad genius she really was."

Her wistful smile deteriorated into a frown as the words were ultimately met with silence. "I hope you're OK, love," she crooned. "Hope you're safe and warm, wherever you are . . . Hope you have plenty of dirt to stick your hands in so you can absentmindedly run them through your beautiful hair in that way I absolutely despise . . . It's been nearly two months since you left us, and the pain is still as raw and wretched as it was on that awful day. We're not really on speaking terms right now, but Tobias . . . he thinks I'm letting my grief control me . . . Letting it *take over my mind*, I think he said. Well, it's a long and infuriating story that I shan't bore you with, but I hardly think *he* is in any position to be questioning the mental health of others, rotten leech sympathizer . . . Mom's been about as empathetic as you'd imagine; thinks I'm only making things worse by coming to see you every day. The thing is, she doesn't understand that it's not just *you* I'm mourning: it's the future those evil creatures took from us. The life we planned together, the home we were going to build—it's all gone . . . just dust in the wind."

She glanced down at the tight, red fist she had involuntarily formed with her left hand. *Getting yourself worked up again. Jade would tell me to get off the ceiling.* She blew a calming exhalation, using the sleeve of her black zip-up to wipe away the single tear making its way down her heavily freckled cheek.

"Anyway. What else is new? Oh yeah! Stingrays were giving the Razorbacks a thrashing at the Phantom Streak final, but the match had to be postponed when some maniac smashed his way out of a VIP box and flew into the court. Turns out, it's the same guy Phalanx are hunting for the murder of Administrator Vargos. Enforcers were in pursuit and opened fire right there in the middle of Zelos Arena. Redderick Lanceton—the Razorback's center forward—the guy stole his saber and used it as a shield to escape with. Don't get me wrong: Eamon Wyatt is a traitor who *will* face justice for his crimes against the union . . . but even still, it was quite a sight to behold . . . He's on the run as it stands, but I doubt it'll be long before his treachery catches up with him."

She dropped her gaze as she dug the toe of her pump into the dirt, feeling awash with guilt over her impending confession. "Please don't be too mad, but you should know I've officially withdrawn from the Academy . . . I just couldn't stay and play pretend politician anymore—not after what happened; not with the way things are right now . . . You always told me I was destined for great things: *administrator by the time you're thirty*, so on. But the truth is . . . The truth is that the institution we *both* lived to serve is . . . well, it's broken—obsolete. If this political stagnation we've suffered over the past half century carries on into the next generation, I genuinely believe it could mean our extinction."

She felt determination pumping her chest up like helium in a balloon, a resolute grin stretching across her face. "Humanity First is the shake-up the *Novara* sorely needs; the pesticide that can, and will, *finally* rid us of this infestation. The work Bhaltair and I are doing is paramount to the survival of humanity . . . No . . . Not just our survival: our resurgence . . . It might not be the path you wanted me to take, but I promise you, I can still do great things . . . I only wish you were here to see it through with me . . .

Caleb's feather ignited in a flurry of haptic vibration and chirping electronic tones. She reached into her pocket and produced the thin wedge of glass, studying the ID card flashing on its translucent screen. It identified the inbound caller as Atlas Baudelaire—the prolific and highly sought-after producer and PR manager Atherton Edevane had hired prior to his departure from Humanity First. The councilman's hope had been that, with a little expert media training, they could transform the movement into one that might better appeal to political centrists. But while tremendous strides had been made in improving Bhaltair's unfavorable reputation, Caleb suspected the man had one or two skeletons in his closet that not even a professional silk talker like Mx. Baudelaire could keep hidden from the public eye . . .

Her blood turned cold at the sight of the URGENT tag Atlas had marked the call with, which seemed completely out of character for someone who normally respected, and faithfully upheld, the sanctity of their client's do not disturb status . . . *What is it now?*

She accepted the call, pushing her feather through voracious curls of auburn hair and pressing it against her ear. A frantic voice came clattering through the receiver—a runaway Canyon tram of words barreling into a station. "Caleb. Do you know where Bhaltair is? Are you with him right now?"

She took a moment to process the fusillade of hurried syllables—something she regularly had to do when interacting with Atlas. For an individual to whom the gift of gab was not just a talent but a profession, words were a precious and finite commodity; they spoke as if hemorrhaging nunits every time they opened their mouth, delivering information as briefly and succinctly as humanly possible and wasting little time on pleasantries or needless fluff.

"I haven't seen him today," Caleb finally answered, pinching the bridge of her nose in dismay. She considered asking them to clarify what their reason was for asking, but in truth, she already knew the answer . . .

"He had a meeting with the treasurer at eleven-thirty to discuss the 130 AC defense budget," they intoned. "He never showed up. I don't have a clue where he is and can't get in touch with him. If *you* don't know either, then we may have a problem."

A problem—that's putting it lightly . . .

Caleb pressed her fingers to her lips and blew a farewell kiss to Jade's memorial stone, then turned on her heel and started down the gravel path toward the Conservatory's entrance plaza. "Are you on the campaign barge?" she asked. "Is it still berthed at Xìngyùn Square?"

"No. Bhaltair had us relocate to a transit platform in Halvorsen Commons last night. Said he had a sensitive matter that needed tending to. None of the other staff have seen him since . . . I'm sorry to call you on personal time but he's got three more appearances penned in this afternoon. Need to know if I should reschedule; don't want prospective benefactors thinking we're time wasters."

Halvorsen Commons. Bhaltair—you stupid bastard—you promised me this wouldn't happen again.

"Any idea where he might be?" Atlas blurted out, audibly frustrated with the long delay in receiving an answer. Caleb stayed silent another moment, biting her lip in trepidation. So far, Mx. Baudelaire had done exemplary work in helping to *smooth over* some of the more problematic blemishes in Bhaltair's history; they hadn't yet been made privy to the man's more recent and ongoing improprieties. Caleb had kept them tactically unaware of the potential scandal that threatened to completely derail the campaign if certain details regarding his personal life were ever to get out. Atlas made no secret of the fact that they had taken Humanity First on as a strategic career move. They didn't necessarily believe in the message of separation from the *Devourer*, but considered the organization, which had garnered so much notoriety and faced such harsh criticism, a worthy challenge to demonstrate their public relations prowess. Caleb had to wonder whether that would still be the case, or whether they would write the whole thing off as a lost cause, once she divulged the truth . . .

"I know where he is," she declared, employing a surly tone of voice to wordlessly add the proviso, *but you're not going to like it.* "Round up two of Jonah's former guys and make your way to Rennaxi Junction. And *don't* take any transport with Humanity First branding on it."

"Rennaxi Junction," Atlas echoed, their ordinarily loud and piercing voice reduced to a nervous murmur. "That's . . . That's the Vice District, isn't it? Nothing but seedy bars, strip clubs, and brothels . . . You don't think . . ."

"No," she interrupted, storming past the atrium's information desk and making a beeline for the elevator pods, the sweet fragrance of freshly cut grass—Jade's scent—dissipating a little more with every squeaking footstep.

"I think it could be something much worse . . . Atlas . . . There's something you need to know . . ."

Caleb summoned a swoop from the Zharady Station transit platform and set course for the upper echelons of Halvorsen Commons. The route took her speeding toward the blockade for several kilometers before diverting port-side down a slipway, leaving behind the open-air expanse of the Canyon for the oppressively claustrophobic confines of Lower Amidships. Bhaltair, like almost 60 percent of all Novarians, had once lived in the Wards—the hyper-dense block of residential accommodations spread across seventy decks and occupying at least a quarter of the *Novara*'s superstructure. While Humanity First's successes had garnered him the financial means to relocate to a more affluent neighborhood, outwardly he remained staunchly proud of his humble roots, framing himself as a champion of the working class—an average blue-collar Joe, who slogged his way from manual labor to the exalted heights of exo-cartography and beyond. Privately, however, Bhaltair would occasionally profess his growing distaste for the *grimy, overpopulated cesspit* that had once been his home, citing that he would always *take a stand for the little guy*, but—having worked so hard to lift himself out of the mire—preferred to do so from the luxury and comfort of the Upperdecks. He even jokingly adhered to a self-imposed restriction that forbade him from ever venturing below mid-deck unless on essential Humanity First business—a rule that, in recent weeks, had become somewhat less stringent, with these unscheduled *solo excursions* to the deepest, darkest parts of the Wards proving increasingly commonplace. Caleb had managed to keep his concerning behavior under lock and key until now, but feared she could no longer shoulder the burden, and needed Atlas's expertise for the inevitable blowback that would follow if, or when, word got out.

We didn't come this far to let a few trivial . . . indiscretions tear down everything we've built. If we can find Bhaltair and bring him home before any of our opposition in the Liberal Reformist Party cotton on or recognize him, we just might be able to avert catastrophe . . .

A deluge of scarlet light spilled into the slipway through its circular terminus, crafting the uncanny illusion of hurtling through ripple-space toward the brightening glow of a red dwarf star. The erubescent glow became all-enveloping as the swoop sailed into a transit terminal occupying a chamber shaped like an elliptical cylinder turned on its side. The vehicle sharply decelerated and pulled up next to a debarkation point, deploying a boarding ramp to bridge the gap to the terminal's suspension walkway. Curiously, the curved walls here weren't clad in the usual steel, fiberglass, or nanocarbon plating ubiquitous throughout the rest of the *Novara*, but were lined with a veneer of actual Martian bedrock encased behind a layer of protective glass. Much in the same way that Capella Promenade emulated a beachfront resort on Earth, the *Novara's* architects built Rennaxi Junction as an homage to the largely subterranean sister cities of the Mars Commonwealth, Arcadia, and Promethei. Caleb recalled from a lecture she had taken on the formation of the New Terra Union that the Commonwealth, as one of the larger contributing nations, had made a significant donation of materials and personnel toward the *Novara's* construction—a historic gesture still immortalized over two centuries later in the imported rock used throughout the ship. Leaving the swoop's passenger cabin, she felt herself transported to a world long since lost to the Europan singularity—the man-made gravity well spawned in error by scientists undertaking research into the frontier of localized gravity distortion, the unwitting orchestrators of the destruction of Sol. Caleb marveled at the sedimentary layers of shale and sandstone enveloping her, as though the terminal really had been bored deep underground beneath Martian sands.

Her eyes took a moment to adjust to the inundating red light emitted by the fluorescent-tube rings lining the terminal's curvature. The fixtures reminded her of the heating element in an antique oven grill, as if threatening to cook her from the inside out or liquefy her flesh with buffeting waves of radiation. She zipped her jacket up to the collar to protect herself from the imaginary hazard and started toward the terminal's exit, where she spied Atlas waiting for her. Somewhere in their midthirties, Mx. Baudelaire projected poise and professionalism with their minimalist, avant-garde dress sense. The rich charcoal-gray, clean lines, and angular accents of their immaculately tailored suit complemented their slender physique. They regarded Caleb with intelligent, squinting eyes, partially obscured beneath their feathery, silver-pink fringe. Normally buoyant with confidence and rambunctious wit, they seemed somewhat subdued, fervently clutching their luma-pad to their chest as they stood shoulder to shoulder with Jonah's former *muscle*, looking like a polished pearl among rough-hewn stones.

Caleb had been relieved to learn that most of Jonah's ruffian confederates had dropped their support of Humanity First following his death. Given the organization's renewed focus, she knew they had to keep their affairs strictly above board from here on out, which meant cutting all ties with anybody their vulture-esque opposition could brand as "hooligans" or "domestic terrorists." Those of the old guard who *did* stick around were emphatic believers in the Humanity First manifesto and understood the critical importance of moving away from Jonah's brand of *hands-on* activism, as deliciously satisfying as Caleb had found partaking in it . . . Sporting black, syn-leather jackets with all manner of metal-studded accessories, the two men bowed their heads as she approached, greeting her like royalty in a gesture that felt distinctly at odds with their thuggish appearance.

Mx. Baudelaire greeted her by reaching out to peel off the Velcro "PRESS" patch fastened around her upper arm before hastily stowing it in their blazer pocket. She had been in such a hurry to squeeze in a few minutes with Jade after filming the segment in the Statera Basin that she had forgotten to remove it.

"We'll be renegotiating my fee after this, just so you know," Atlas warned, glowering at their surroundings as though they might contract a sexually transmitted disease from mere proximity, holding their repulsed gaze on the two luma-cast figures posed in a provocative archway over the Rennaxi Junction entrance. "Surprises in my line of work are never a good thing. Withholding crucial information like *this* from me . . . Well, I'm sorry to be blunt, but it was incredibly stupid."

"Understood," Caleb conceded. "Just relieved to hear you're not jumping ship."

"Oh please. I've pulled clients through bigger shitstorms than this. What's important is getting out ahead of the backlash. If we're smart, there are even ways we can swing this to generate sympathy: tie it into his troubled upbringing, frame it as something he's working hard to overcome. Trust me, there's *always* a means of wrangling the narrative."

Caleb gave an unconvinced nod; she admired their optimism but doubted the plausibility of wrangling anything, especially if Bhaltair's modus operandi were ever to become public knowledge: siphoning campaign funds into his current account under the pretense of *miscellaneous expenses*, sometimes blowing upward of two thousand nunits in a single night. Understandably, Atlas wanted there to be no more secrets, but Caleb feared disclosing that particular detail—no matter how pertinent—might be the final nail in the coffin for their involvement with Humanity First. And she couldn't see any way of salvaging the campaign without their assistance . . . *Failure means extinction*, she reminded herself grimly. *The very future of humanity demands we succeed . . .*

The group exited the transit terminal and ventured into a bustling arcade— one of two thoroughfares, running perpendicular to each other and forming an X-junction at their intersecting point. The vaulted ceiling tunneled its curved profile through more imported Martian bedrock, with a framework of metal braces completing the subterranean aesthetic. Further tube fixtures ran overhead like a procession of bloodred rainbows, drenching the drunken revelry below in the rousing shades of perpetual dusk. Pushing their way through the crowd, Caleb felt utterly saturated by the environment; the sights, sounds, and sensations carried out a coordinated assault on every one of her senses. She felt the body heat of the boisterous throng stifling her breath. She smelled the stink of sweat and vape and cigarette smoke vying for superiority over her nostrils with the aromas of popcorn and tropical-flavored alcohol. Endless luma-cast signage strafed her retinas with harsh, neon colors: gyrating exotic dancers, voluptuous lips bitten by lustful teeth, pixelated stim-vials, and cocktail pitchers—all depicted beside stylish logos representing the many sordid establishments recessed into the opposing rock faces.

Rennaxi was a hotbed of vice and debauchery—the *Novara*'s very own Sodom. Being right there in the thick of it, Caleb felt dirty, exposed—not in an unpleasant way, but in a way that excited and invigorated her. She only wished she had Jade by her side, both of them dressed in high heels and those skimpy, black-lace numbers from Zabelle as they sashayed down the arcade with arms interlocked. All eyes would be on them, but they would only have eyes for each other, and they would drink and dance and exercise their most carnal desires until the break of Canyon dawn. The notion set a fire between her legs and knocked loosed an arrow of grief directly into her heart. It was a side of herself that she hadn't shown to many—that spontaneous, promiscuous streak that ran like a river of fire through her soul—certainly not to the likes of Tobias, who had wanted her to be soft, innocent, and elegant in her ways. Nor Bhaltair, who wanted her to mother and cosset him, to gratify his ego by mindlessly acquiescing to all his narcissistic ramblings. Caleb knew perfectly well how irresistible she was to feebleminded men and had become particularly proficient at changing the color of her scales to suit their tastes on a subliminal level. She didn't see her desirability as a privilege or a blessing, but a means to an end—a contrivance used to worm her way into Councilman Edevane's inner circle by way of his son's heart. And to take control of Humanity First by leaving Bhaltair Abernathy so completely smitten that he had willingly handed over almost all directorial duties to her. She had built a career on the back of a diverse repertoire of romantic personae, but maintaining her many masquerades meant burying herself—her *true* self—beneath layers of subterfuge. Only in the presence of Jade had she been able to truly let her hair down—to allow that river of fire running through her soul to erupt from her chest, bathing her one and only in the vivacious warmth of her actual self . . . Now, Jade was gone, and Caleb feared she might never again feel that intoxicating sense of freedom and vulnerability, doomed to live out the rest of her days hiding behind her masks.

"Look at this place." Atlas's dismayed voice broke her reverie. She glanced over to find them abrasively swatting away a man with braided hair, flaunting rippling, sweat-slicked abs beneath a fishnet string vest. As far as Caleb could discern, the stranger had either just tried to sell them drugs or propositioned them for sex. They shuddered, clutching the lapel of their blazer together in disgust. "Used to be the crown jewel of the Mars Commonwealth; I dare not think what our forebears would say seeing it turned into some perverted flesh market . . . You'd think with how sophisticated companion dolls are nowadays it wouldn't even be necessary. Guess for some, you just can't beat the real thing."

"There's more to Rennaxi Junction than prostitution," Caleb countered. "Our impulses are what make us human; stranded light-years away from our natural habitat, it's important we have somewhere that we can reconnect with that animal side we all have in us: cast off the restraints of society, lose our inhibitions and let the music get under our skin."

Caleb saw one of Jonah's men nudge the other, flashing a grin as they both mentally undressed her.

"Sounds like you're speaking from experience," Atlas teased. "But surely you, as an ambassador to Humanity First, wouldn't dream of allowing yourself to be seen carousing in a place like this."

She showed a risqué smile that neither confirmed nor denied the insinuation. "I would never do anything to jeopardize our image. But what I get up to in the shadows is nobody's business but my own . . ."

They ventured farther into the salacious interior of Rennaxi Junction, passing a vibrant miscellany of strip clubs, toy shops, and street food vendors—a veritable hub of illicit enterprise intended to titillate the most primal of human desires. Caleb fell prey to a nauseating concoction of lust and hunger, gazing upon the naked, glitter-encrusted bodies contorting in steamy window fronts, juxtaposed against the musk of char-grilled meats pervading the air, as if her mind had been tricked into thinking she could smell the seared flesh of the performers, flexing and posing in their own personal microwaves. In a stirring moment, one of the harlots seemed to recognize her and abandoned her seductive routine to bang on the glass of her pod to get her attention. "Caleb Callaghan!" She called out, her strained voice arriving as a muffle beneath the dark tones and heavy beats of dubtronic music blasting from speakers nearby. "Lei-Ghannam, it's you ain't it? Thanks for everythin' you're doin' for us, hon! Come round to the back an' I'll see to it you're looked after—on the house!"

Caleb waved and through a forced smile said, "That's not a good sign."

"If people here recognize *you*," Atlas prompted, "then they'll definitely recognize Abernathy. If he's in as bad a state as you suspect, how in the Abyss are we gonna get him out of here without being seen?"

"If he hasn't already, then I really don't know . . ."

An open square awaited them where the arcade intersected with its per-pendicular counterpart. The space hummed with activity; *vendors* took to the streets prowling for prospective patrons while buskers battled for the spare nunits of rowdy, heckling onlookers. Beneath a psychedelic scaffolding of LED billboards, several overpriced bars conspired to lure in heedless tourists with eye-popping light displays and liquid nitrogen fog—deep-sea predators wielding bioluminescence to attract and ensnare their prey. Bhaltair, how-ever, would not be so easily enticed, as what he sought could not be readily found out here on the main drag. He had gone somewhere darker, grimier, hidden away from prying eyes—a place that only the initiated could ever hope to find, let alone gain access to. Caleb lamented the fact that she could now count herself among that caste . . . Escaping the bustle of the square, she directed the others down a dilapidated passageway carving a route between a shisha joint and a deep-fried dessert kiosk. Slaloming through a jungle of ventilation ducts, dodging plumes of scalding steam from hemorrhaging pressure pipes, they arrived at a reinforced door—one that, to uninitiated eyes, might resemble the staff entrance to a bar or the kitchen at the rear of a restaurant. All too aware of the dark secrets lying in wait beyond, Caleb bowed her head toward a voice receptacle bolted into the rock beside the entry. She uttered a single word in an Old-Earth tongue: "L'évent." The door slid open, and they hastened inside.

SIXTEEN

The foyer of this *clinic* or *dispensary,* or whatever clients chose to call it, reminded Caleb of one of the volcanic crystals displayed in Councilman Edevane's parlor. The slanted walls and low ceiling were bedecked in blue-glass mosaic tiles, the effect like walking through the hollow space inside a giant amethyst geode. The dead-behind-the-eyes concierge sitting slouched behind the main desk immediately recognized her and rolled his eyes.

"*You* again," he complained, greasy face illuminated pink by the porn he was unabashedly leering at on his feather.

"Is he here?" Caleb probed impatiently.

"Like I told yah last time, doll: I ain't at liberty to disclose our client's personal information."

She sighed. "I'm not doing this with you again. You know who I am, and you know all it takes is for me to put one call through to Executor Royce and this shithole closes its doors for good. Now, is he here or not?"

The concierge made a face as if he had just caught a whiff of something foul, then pushed his thumb against a keypad to open the sliding double doors leading to the establishment's main space. Caleb insincerely mouthed *thank you* while retrieving four disposable filter masks—made available for visitors who *weren't* interested in sampling the venue's unique offerings—from the dispenser on the desk.

After applying their protective wear, the group stormed into the interior of another oversized geode, this one a large room with several circular conversation pits recessed into the floor, separated from one another by tulle curtain dividers. At the far side of the chamber, a sight greeted them that kindled such profound revulsion in Caleb she had to lock her legs in place to stay her feet. The conduit breaching through the rear wall was the stuff of nightmares: a gargantuan tentacle constructed, or perhaps *grown,* from an incomprehensible compound of alien machinery and something resembling necrotic tissue. The behemoth snaked around the perimeter of the room for ten or so meters before rearing up and burrowing into the ceiling, no doubt continuing its hunt for vital resources to pilfer. Caleb traced its elongated structure with horrified eyes, arriving at what appeared to be a cluster of gills occupying one of its vertebral segments. The wheezing slits glowed as if slashed by a blade dipped in lambent poison, and billowed an opalescent stream into the air, which made her intensely grateful for the mask preventing the noxious spores from entering her respiratory system and bewitching her mind.

A leech loomed near the monstrosity—a hideous visage of death like a seven-foot-tall gargoyle sculpted from the husks of a thousand dead tarantulas and reanimated by some arcane necromancy. Raising gangly, exoskeletal arms, it looked to be channeling the glow with its menacing claws, guiding it as a snake charmer might a mesmerized cobra over to one of the conversation pits. Here, the substance was funneled down an antenna into an unusual hourglass structure and then distributed through plastic pipes into full-face inhalation masks. Guests lay sprawled on the sunken couches with the masks strapped to their faces, laughing, or muttering as they breathed deep from the supply of cosmic hallucinogen.

Atlas froze at the sight of the alien while Jonah's guys squared their shoulders and balled their fists, ready for violence. "What in the Abyss is it doing bowside of the blockade?" rasped Mx. Baudelaire, eyes wide in a mixture of terror and amazement. "This place seems fairly well established; how could they have a leech working here without the Administration finding out?"

"I don't think 'working' is the right word; it's hardly here by choice." Caleb nodded toward the collar fastened around the creature's neck—it was cinched so tight that the metal had caused cracks in its iridescent chitin, dark-purple blood oozing from a ring of grizzly lesions near its withers. The heavy-duty chain shackling the collar to the ground kept the leech sufficiently restrained but enabled it to shuffle between the conversation pits to carry out its duties. Caleb didn't know if it possessed the mental capacity to distinguish between happiness or misery, but it certainly appeared to be in the throes of the latter, which brought *her* no end of the former. "I've heard rumors about people smuggling leeches through the blockade for work—it's most prevalent down in Cendre Vale, since their natural strength makes them good for manual labor. I never knew they were being used for *this*, though . . . As to why Phalanx haven't taken the necessary steps to shut this circus down: The Wards are dangerously overpopulated, not to mention underpoliced—it's not hard to imagine how such an operation could be overlooked, provided its patrons are meticulous in keeping it exclusive."

She told the lie so convincingly that she almost believed it herself. The disappointing truth, of course, was that Bhaltair, during his time as an exo-cartographer, had taken to selling the locations of glow vents to criminal entrepreneurs who strived to monetize them, taking further payoffs to ensure the ungodly exhausts stayed permanently under the Administration's radar. *Just a stepping stone*, he had called it—a necessary ploy that had ultimately catalyzed the creation of Humanity First, with every ill-gotten nunit going toward covering the nascent organization's considerable expenses. Only recently had it become clear that his motivations may not have been quite so noble, with what likely started as a mild interest developing into an unfortunate habit, and now manifesting as a debilitating and financially ruinous addiction.

Caleb spotted him in the farthest pit, with his legs splayed out, hunched over to the side like a puppet suddenly abandoned by its master. For all of his many shortcomings, the hopeless delinquent had at least had the sense to change out of his signature attire before slinking off to satiate his thirst. She only managed to identify him because she recognized his light-gray sports hoodie with its geometric fox head logo—the same hoodie she had worn while otherwise naked after one of their deeply regrettable, but perfectly necessary, intimate liaisons . . .

Two empty champagne bottles rested atop the low table before him, surrounded by several expended stim-vials—boosters and relaxants of every strength and variety. A final wisp of glow percolated from his mask as it lay coiled by his side, the contents of his *hourglass* now seemingly depleted. A pair of scantily clad women wore the container's two other masks, both draped like piles of flesh and latex on either side of him—companionship no doubt paid for from the Humanity First honeypot. They, like Bhaltair, looked to be caught somewhere in the paradoxical space between total paralysis and neural overstimulation: bodies limp and unmoving but eyes distended as they uttered manic, incoherent nonsense. The other patrons in the room seemed similarly incapacitated, with the only other sober individual present being, ironically, the leech. Caleb kept her eyes fixated on the monster as she ushered the others over to Bhaltair's pit. And how surreal it felt: like walking through the site of a massacre in a nightclub, the pounding, squawking music unperturbed by the corpses strewn about the furniture; the remorseless perpetrator assessing its victims with cruel, calculated eyes. *Eight of them, to be horrifyingly precise . . .*

"Guess we can relax a little about drawing unwanted attention." Atlas blew a stifled sigh of relief through their mask. "Doubt there's a poor sod here who could even tell us what year it is. Must be happy hour or something."

"We're in the clear for now," Caleb said, lowering herself into Bhaltair's pit and crouching over him to check his condition. "I think getting him back to the transit terminal is where we might have problems. If anyone clocks him, it'll be a feeding frenzy out there."

She reached out to touch the sallow skin of his cheek, recoiling slightly at the sight of the foamy saliva collecting in the corners of his mouth, his normally pompadoured hair now straw-like and draped over his oily face, clumped together with congealed product. His bloodshot eyes indicated that he had been rubbing them with the heels of his hands again, grinding the contact lenses meant to conceal his burgeoning cataracts into his corneas. She would have to take them out for him, remove his sweat-logged clothes, and wrap him in wet towels to assuage the comedown. She would need to speak softly into his ear to soothe his throbbing temples and listen attentively to his pitiful attempts to justify his incorrigible behavior. She would have to become everything he needed, which was everything she despised: a molly-coddling mother to a weak, petulant man-child, completely debasing herself to reinflate his ego and bring him back up to fighting strength. She would loathe every insipid, humiliating moment of it, but she knew that while Bhaltair was still Humanity First's spokesperson—the dashing smile winning the hearts and minds of the common clay—she had no choice but to endure; it was her duty as a citizen of the NTU.

"Bhaltair, darling," she said, detesting the cooing tone of her voice. "It's me, darling, it's Caleb. Can you stand up? We need to get you out of here."

He gurgled in the back of his throat, lolling his head sideways and rolling his eyes into their sockets. The sneering head shake one of Jonah's guys gave the other did not evade Caleb's notice—disappointment, or perhaps even disdain, in response to witnessing firsthand their anointed leader's fall from grace . . . *More like plummet.*

"Ugh! He's completely out of it," Atlas groused. "Guess it was naive of me to think we'd at least have him walking out of here on his own two feet." They massaged the bridge of their nose in frustration. "What are we gonna do? We'll have to put a bag over his head and carry him out."

"We could," reasoned Caleb, "But people might see *me* and put two and two together. No . . . What we need is a distraction—something that'll draw attention away and give us the time we need to make a stealthy escape."

"Sounds good." Atlas seemed ambivalent to the idea at best. "It'll have to be something pretty spectacular, though; it's livelier than Exit Sol Fest out there. Don't suppose you have any suggestions?"

Caleb cast her eye around the room, hoping the answer might leap out from the shadows and triumphantly present itself. But it did no such thing.

Instead, it stood watching them with lifeless eyes, chattering grotesque man-dibles and blowing sibilant exhalations from the orifices on its neck. Atlas followed her gaze and, with a note of unease, asked, "Have you ever been this close to one before?"

"When Jonah took Tobias and me into the Mouth, I suppose I was. Although, it was crowded, and we were running most of the time. I didn't really get a good look at one." Caleb clenched her jaws involuntarily, channel-ing the violent force she wished she could visit upon the horrid thing into her molars instead. It felt good; cathartic.

Atlas sniffed at the air, furrowing their brow in bewilderment. "I smell . . . coriander. Coriander and . . . is that pine-scented air freshener?"

"Jonah said it's a pheromone they leak when somethin' spooks 'em," one of Sinclair's men—Gregor, perhaps—explained, sporting a baleful grin and flashing a gold-plated tooth engraved with the interlocking rings of Human-ity First. "Had to watch out for it when we went culling in the district; means they're in fight-or-flight mode, which is when they're most unpredictable."

The grim notion set the wheels turning in Caleb's head. Leaving Bhaltair drooling on himself she stood up and turned to face the others. "Are either of you strapped?" she asked, offering an expectant hand to the two men. Pos-sibly Gregor nodded and reached behind his back. From beneath his belt, he produced an Onema-42 subcompact plasma pistol and obediently passed it to her.

Atlas eyed the energy weapon with the same expression as an arachno-phobe watching someone handle a deadly spider. "You're making me ner-vous, Callaghan. What, pray tell, are you planning to do with that?"

"Just sowing a little chaos." She squatted down and collected the faux snake-skin clutch bag belonging to one of Bhaltair's companions, sifting through an assortment of glow caps, pill packets, and makeup to fish out the woman's feather. Holding the device before her face and staring into its cracked display, she said, "SOS override. Emergency services: Phalanx." The retinal lock screen disappeared, supplanted by a dial animation, then a call timer.

"You're through to Phalanx," a monotone voice answered.

"Please!" Caleb cut in, making whimpers of shock and feigning hyperven-tilation. "You have to send someone to Rennaxi Junction, quick!"

"Please *calmly* state the nature of your emergency, ma'am," the voice replied, the others watching on as she became increasingly hysterical.

"A leech! There's a damned-Abyss leech loose in Rennaxi Junction! I don't know how it got here but you need to send enforcers, now! It's going berserk!"

The responder's voice went dead as Caleb abruptly ended the call, regain-ing her composure within a matter of mere seconds. She cast the feather away, showing an impish smile as one of Jonah's men gave her a nod that read *nicely done.*

"See if you can get him on his feet," she said, gesturing toward a still very much incapacitated Bhaltair. "If not, then pick him up and get ready to lug him to the transit terminal."

The two men complied, albeit to the grating tune of Atlas demanding further clarification. "If you're not gonna run this by me before you go and do it, then what am I even doing here?"

"Trust me," she reassured, unflappable as she turned her attention to the leech. "You asked for spectacular; I'm giving you just that."

She approached the creature slowly, the acrid stench of its pheromones filling her nostrils more with every step. She kept the pistol hidden behind her back with one hand while showing the palm of the other in a placating gesture. The leech stamped its talons into the ground, snorting and huffing like a bull readying to charge.

"Easy, big guy," she said, appropriating the same gentle cadence she would likely have to use later to mollify Bhaltair. "I'm not going to hurt you, I promise."

She sidestepped around it holding a cautious distance, motioning toward the metal plate bolted to the ground to which the collar and chain were attached. To its credit, the leech seemed to quickly understand that she meant no harm, regarding her with something like intrigue as she carefully reached out for the chain. Holding the restraint in a firm fist, she pulled it tight, then placed the muzzle of the pistol against the anodized metal. She pulled the trigger, discharging a fizzling bolt of bright-blue plasma that immediately disintegrated several of the hardened chain links.

"You're free," she said, batting earnest eyes and summoning as much sincerity as she could muster. She gestured toward the exit. "Quickly! Get out of here while you have the chance."

The leech immediately took her meaning and turned to face the frosted doors leading to the foyer. But no sooner could it make its escape than the doors slid open to reveal the concierge standing just beyond them. Having heard the plasma shot, the man had come to investigate, armed with an assuredly unlicensed sawn-off shotgun, which he held primed to fire from the hip. His rage-twisted expression glaciated into one of shock as he noticed the leech standing with its hackles raised and, more pressingly, its restraints broken. The creature turned its elongated snout to the ceiling and unleashed a hair-raising shriek from somewhere in its abdomen, then bounded on all fours toward the man as he stood stunned in the doorway.

Blam! He fired the shotgun; pellets whanged and whined off the beast's impervious exoskeleton, doing little—if anything—to halt its furious charge. With a *thud* and a *crunch*, it rammed its captor with an armored shoulder and sent him crashing into the reception desk, then continued through the foyer before blowing the main door off its sliding rail with another explosive impact. Caleb turned to find Atlas hunched over with their hands cupped against their ears. Jonah's men had seemingly failed to get Bhaltair on his feet and were preparing to carry him, each wrapping one of his limp arms around their shoulders.

"That's our cue," she chirped, pulling Atlas's hands away and capturing their attention with a commanding stare. "Summon your transport to the terminal; we need it waiting for us when we get there—don't want to have to hang around any longer than we have to."

They nodded in a sporadic diagonal fashion, seeming completely shell-shocked. "OK . . . OK. I'm on it . . . Lei-Ghannam. I knew taking on Humanity First would be exciting, but *this* is insane."

Outside, the junction had succumbed to total calamity. Exiting the dispensary, the group were met by a stampede—a seething mass of terrified people, screaming, shoving, and trampling over each other as they sprinted for cover. Most had likely never seen a leech in person before, certainly not one thrown into a ferocious rampage having escaped captivity and now loose in an unfamiliar environment. Caleb caught a flash of black in her peripheral vision as it sprang into the air on legs like hydraulic pistons, swung from a piece of neon signage, and came crashing down through a shop front awning. It hit the deck with an almighty thud, knocking over several souvenir stands as it scrambled to its talons and galloped off in frantic zigzags.

The group came to a stop at the alleyway entrance and surveyed the mayhem beyond, grinning at each other in mischievous delight.

"Remind me again why it is we're campaigning to get rid of the leeches," said Atlas, fighting to catch their breath. "Strikes me they can be pretty handy in a pinch."

Caleb shrugged as if to say, *You're right; maybe we were wrong about them.* But really, the violent display only served to bolster her convictions; how anybody of sound mind could think the feral aliens were capable of integrating with human society was and would always remain an enigma.

She turned to make sure Jonah's men still had their slobbering cargo secured. Bhaltair had partially roused from his stupor but had yet to regain full functionality of his legs. Dragging his expensive sneakers on the floor grating, he burbled something whiny and unintelligible—the sound of an agitated child pining for his mother. Caleb touched his cheek, fighting the urge to viciously claw it off with her fingernails.

"Hush, darling. We're getting you out of here. Just stay calm and we'll have you home, quick as a hiccup."

She pulled his hood over his head, checked a final time to ensure the coast was clear, and then gave a nod to signal for the others to make a move. They scrambled in a tight huddle across the open square, cautiously retracing their steps back along the arcade. The intent had been to clear a path to the transit terminal enabling minimal interaction with the spooked cattle; annoyingly, her *distraction* seemed to be heading in the same direction, sending an endless bulwark of bodies hurtling toward them. Fortunately, the chances of being recognized seemed relatively low; the *last* thing the crowd were paying any attention to was one incredibly stoned Bhaltair Abernathy . . . *They might even assume he's an injured bystander,* she mused. *Another name to add to the long list of innocent Novarians victimized by our sadistic enemy.*

Scanning the faces of those hurtling past, she saw what she could only describe as true, unmitigated terror. As far as these people knew, they were running for their lives—convinced, perhaps, of something they had long feared: that the unrest beyond the blockade had finally metastasized its way into Amidships, and that they were just now seeing the first swell in what would undoubtedly be a tsunami of alien savagery. Her plan for making a covert exit, it transpired, had served a secondary purpose: to remind the public of the danger waiting on their doorstep, providing a harrowing taste of what multispecies society could really look like. *No doubt Humanity First will receive an influx of new support once footage of the incident inevitably hits the social feeds. We'll have our work cut out for us, and that's no bad thing . . .*

Ahead, she could already see onlookers producing their feathers to film the unfolding scenes; several men brandishing overturned stools as weapons had backed the leech into a corner near a public restroom. The beast roared and screeched and made all manner of unearthly noises, swiping frantically with claws like grapnels in a futile effort to disperse the mob closing in around it. One of the men strayed too close. The alien wrenched the stool out of his hands and, extending its backward-jointed leg, unleashed about twenty newtons of force directly into his chest, catapulting him across the arcade and sending him smashing through the opaque window of a brothel. Needless to say, the other men suddenly lost their courage and scattered.

Too bad Atlas doesn't have their drone cam, Caleb thought. *We could make a fantastic segment out of this—proof that the blockade in its current state is woefully ineffective and that tighter security measures are sorely needed to prevent leech incursions.*

The scoop, however, would have to wait; right now, they needed to focus on evading any potential escalation of violence. Phalanx had arrived—specifically, the elite division of enforcers tasked with handling outbreaks such as this. People often called them bug swatters, which Caleb considered a somewhat pejorative term for what were unquestionably some of the bravest men and women presently serving the union. Sirens blaring, three enforcers raced toward the scene, sailing above the horde on rapid aerial mounts known as shrikes, designed for quick and effective navigation of the tight spaces of the Wards. The streamlined transports flashed red and blue emergency lights, blindingly reflected in the protective glass covering the curved, Martian-rock ceiling. The response team set their shrikes down near the leech's location, repulsor pads whining as they spun down to an idle thrum. Wearing specialized impact armor and wielding viperinae submachine guns—no doubt loaded with antichitin ammunition—they skillfully dismounted and approached the perpetrator in a flanking formation, screaming for people to "Clear the way!" and "Get down on the ground!"

Caleb and the others rounded the corner into the transit terminal before they could watch the enforcers deal with their target. But as they arrived at Atlas's transport and began bundling Bhaltair into the passenger cabin, they heard several earsplitting claps of gunfire sounding to their rear—a coordinated volley of shots, followed by a moment of silence, then a vociferous roar of applause.

Caleb summoned the campaign barge for a door-to-door rendezvous beneath Edensor Crossing—one of several footbridges connecting the Canyon's port and starboard edifices for pedestrian access. The cable-stayed structure provided ample cover to smuggle Bhaltair aboard out of view from prying eyes; after the hell they'd raised to spirit him out of Rennaxi Junction, it would have been a shame to let some opportunist with a telephoto lens catch them so close to the finish line. Humanity First were making serious waves in the political sphere, after all, and she wouldn't put it past their opposition to hire a professional sleuth for precisely that purpose. They had to remain vigilant, because the moment they let their guard down, it was over; Bhaltair would have to resign immediately, and the organization would likely never recover from the stain of his infidelity, Atlas's best efforts notwithstanding. Recent polling figures had shown a steady increase in Caleb's own approval rating—centrists who remained undecided about where they stood on the leech issue seemed particularly responsive to her softer approach. But whether those numbers would be enough for her to officially succeed him as director remained to be seen . . .

While en route to Edensor Crossing, she had called ahead to dismiss the team aboard the barge for the remainder of the day, thinking it best they have the barge to themselves while Bhaltair remained *indisposed*. At any given moment, there could be up to a dozen staffers crammed around the mahogany-topped conference table, making canvassing calls, or reviewing branding design mock-ups, and the usual hubbub would only serve to exacerbate his *bastard of a headache*. She took no pleasure in bending over backward to meet his needs—*the deplorable junkie*. But what with the astonishing developments transpiring beyond the blockade, she urgently needed him firing on all cylinders.

Atlas sat in their usual perch up front in the forecastle, occupying one of the swiveling chairs with their computer pane on their lap, framed against the ambient light filtering through the tinted, wraparound windshield. Caleb often mused that Mx. Baudelaire's voice could carry through a sealed nano-carbon bulkhead, especially when talking shop over the caster. Thankfully, the fiberglass panels and syn-leather upholstery of the barge's luxury interior went some way toward dampening their strident tone.

From the sounds of it, damage control protocols were in full swing; Atlas had set to work diligently rescheduling all of Bhaltair's upcoming engagements, affecting a profusely apologetic tone to cushion the blowback garnered from making such last-minute cancellations. The timing of the escalating situation in the Mouth had, as it transpired, worked out to their advantage, affording plausible justification for them to mothball en masse without needing to go into too much specificity as to why. Given the seriousness of the unfolding events, nobody would think twice about Bhaltair having to postpone . . .

Caleb stood in the barge's sumptuous kitchenette, absently picking at one of the muffins from yesterday's fundraiser—stale, of course, but the blue icing and white chocolate rings decorating the top were still good. The NTNN broadcast played in a Nov-Net window on the refrigerator's opaque smart-surface. The network had taken the unprecedented step of relaying a live security feed from the Phalanx Compound in the Mouth; the harrowing images showed a roiling ocean of migrants amassing at the boundary of NTU sovereignty, the black smoke of heavy strife ascending from the tumbledown skyline beyond. The camera's elevated vantage point provided a clear view of the battalion of brave enforcers, with their mechanized infantry support, just about managing to hold the line with riot control countermeasures. But, facing down an apoplectic swarm of leeches, glow addicts, and mutineers, Caleb didn't know how much longer tear gas and riot shields would remain effective. At some point, *someone* would do something to make use of lethal force necessary . . .

Once the carnage began, an epidemic of fear would grip the bowside populace, and history denoted that nary a sharper spur existed for driving the kind of extensive political reform Humanity First had been advocating. Caleb knew they had to seize the moment—*wrangle the narrative*, as Atlas had said. Supporters would look to Bhaltair to help make sense of the situation, and they would need help comprehending the potential ramifications of failing to take decisive action, as would inevitably be the Administration's default response to the crisis . . . Many would want to seek comfort in his relentless charm, his affirmative words, and his patriotic optimism. But, unfortunately, Bhaltair could provide no such solace in his current state . . . Caleb scarcely believed the half-naked schlub draped atop the sienna couch in the lounge was the same powerful magnate regularly seen captivating thousand-strong audiences at rallies or whittling down rival commentators to a stupefied silence during heated debates on the network. All the jewelry, the showmanship, and the flashy suits had been stripped away, laying bare the fragile weakling buried beneath—a vile, arrogant, impotent little boy, for whom she could barely contain her raw contempt.

I had such high hopes for you, she lamented. *Such high hopes for what we were going to achieve together. I thought we were going to take humanity back to the stars—cast off our restraints and complete the mission entrusted unto us by our forebears. So our children and our children's children could bask in the warmth of a new sun . . . But you're useless to me—just another disappointment.* She felt a snarl of repugnance pluck at her upper lip. *A complete and utter humiliation . . .*

Bhaltair jolted awake, grimacing as if the silent scorn she had been directing his way had somehow invaded his slumber. He strenuously lifted his head to squint at her, pulling the ice pack away from his brow and bringing it to rest on his gut—so swollen from uncurbed syn-beer consumption that his pallid skin looked fit to break. "It's you," he slurred, returning his head to the couch's armrest. "Gettin' those brain zaps again. Every time I think I'm just drifting off . . . *Bzzzt!* . . . I get another shock."

Caleb swallowed her disgust like a spoonful of foul-tasting medicine. She took a hand towel and ran it under the faucet for a few seconds before wringing it into the sink, then planted herself on the couch beside him to begin gently dabbing his forehead.

"You've hyperstimulated yourself," she softly explained. "Glow floods your brain with serotonin, oxytocin, dopamine—all that good stuff. What you're feeling now is just a side effect of your head trying to reregulate itself."

"I don't care what's causing it; I just want you to do something to make it stop!" He pushed her hand away irritably. "No point hovering over me like this if you don't have any real solutions to offer. Just let me wallow in peace!"

With that, she sprang to her feet and hastily removed herself from his vicinity, fearing she might have otherwise stuffed the towel into his mouth and throttled him. She stormed toward the rear of the barge into the conference room, listening as he noisily dismounted from the couch, the smacking of sweaty skin peeling away from syn-leather inducing a surge of revulsion.

"Wait, Caleb," he blurted, followed by several loud thumps as he clumsily hopped each leg into his chinos. "I'm sorry . . . I didn't mean to snap at you like that. It's just, my head is killing me and it's making me a little bristly . . . I didn't mean anything by it."

She was only partially listening. Standing with her shoulder turned and her arms folded rigidly, her volcanic gaze had found the column of framed pictures hanging on the wall near the billboard control terminal, chronicling the barge's metamorphosis from an orcinas-class star liner—used primarily as tourism vessels for sightseeing excursions to the Debris Belt and the edge of the Novarasphere—into Humanity First's mobile headquarters. The extensive renovation had necessitated the gutting of all propulsion systems and the installation of six C-grade repulsor pads, not to mention the commissioning of the most prestigious interior designer the *Novara* had to offer. Councilman Edevane had funded the project solely out of pocket, pronouncing Humanity First's need for a *serious injection of pizazz—something that will really wow people and show them we mean business.* But the barge, as it turned out, had been Atherton's parting gift to the organization; Caleb couldn't help but think he had dodged a bullet absconding when he had done, and wondered if, after the *unpleasantness* between Tobias and Jonah Sinclair, the smart thing would have been to do the same . . .

The pudgy fingers touching her midriff sent a shock wave of detestation tearing down her body. She turned to find Bhaltair staring at her with his best attempt at beseeching, puppy dog eyes. They might have worked, could she not see burgeoning cataracts just starting to cloud his corneas—milk-white epitomes of his chronic incompetence.

"What happened?" she growled. "You told me . . . *promised* me it was just something you needed to get out of your system—that you would *never* put me in this situation again."

The words stunned Bhaltair like a flash-bang, as though he had been expecting his groveling concession to immediately pacify her. *Not this time.*

"Don't put words in my mouth, Caleb," he demanded. "I said I would do my best not to let you down again. I'm *sorry* my best wasn't good enough for you . . . The thing is, we've been hitting the campaign trail so hard recently, and I'm not accustomed to all these appointments and deadlines. Used to be that we'd just show up when and where we wanted to and speak our truth to anybody that'd listen. It's all just so . . . regimented, now . . . I'm sorry, but the stress of it all got on top of me and I really needed to blow off some steam."

"But why didn't you just tell me you were feeling that way?" pried Caleb. "Instead of going AWOL and leaving us all in the dark! Now, Atlas is tearing their hair out canceling all your appearances when they could have preemptively cleared your schedule to give you time to recharge."

Bhaltair made a face like a baby tasting lemon for the first time. "Because that's all you care about, isn't it: the campaign? You don't care about *me* or *my* welfare; you only want to make sure we're hitting our metrics and increasing our popularity."

Caleb strained her eyes to prevent herself from rolling them. Bhaltair responded to criticism in several different ways, certainly none of them chivalrous. Playing the victim was, without a doubt, the most insufferable. "*Now,* who's putting words in whose mouth?" she seethed.

"It's true though, isn't it? A prize bull—that's all I am to you . . . You don't have any real feelings for me, and you never will, because you're still in love with her—with Jade!"

Caleb heard the thumping of her heartbeat in her ears; felt the quickening of her breath causing her chest to rise and fall rapidly.

"That's why you keep your eyes shut when we're in bed," he continued whining, unaware that a fuse had been lit that he could not extinguish. "It's why you tense up every time I touch you, and it's why you're always sneaking off to the Conservatory every chance you get—to see her!"

"How dare you even say her name?" The words came out small and tempered: an intelligible whisper impelled by the most deafening of emotions.

He took a step toward her, shaking pleading hands. "Jade is dead, Caleb. I know you don't wanna hear that, but it's true. I'm right here in front of you and yet, sometimes it feels like you can't even see me! I probably wouldn't have even gone to Rennaxi Junction if you hadn't been neglecting me so much lately. If we're being honest here, this . . . This is all *your* fault, if you think about it."

Caleb's fist moved like the end of a whip, producing an appropriate *cracking* sound as Bhaltair's nasal cartilage collapsed beneath her clenched knuckles. He reeled backward and slammed into the conference table, a thick river of blood so red as to be black gushing from his nostrils and streaming down his naked barrel of a stomach. She wasn't sure she actually meant to strike him, but couldn't say it didn't feel damned therapeutic . . .

"Lei-Ghannam!" he wheezed, steepling his fingers on either side of his crooked nose. "Have you gone insane?"

She shook the dull ache out of her fingers, blowing through pursed lips to compose herself.

"You stupid, selfish little man . . . You burn campaign funds on glow and escorts, and have the *nerve* to try and put the blame on me? I should have left you down in the Wards to reap the consequences of your actions, you miserable ingrate; let you hang in the court of public opinion like you richly deserve." She shook her head, aghast. "I mean, Bhaltair, the hypocrisy of it! We're supposed to be fighting for the expulsion of the leeches, and here you are getting yourself hooked on their poison!"

"Thanks for your understanding, Caleb," he spat with sarcasm. "And here I was worrying you'd completely overreact and blow things out of proportion. More fool me, I suppose."

"I've *been* understanding—unwaveringly so. And all you've done is take advantage of my good nature. You've completely lost sight of our goals and have become nothing but a liability to this movement. You're a disgrace to Humanity First!"

As it became clear his woe is me approach was having less than the desired effect, he switched his tactics for something a little more pathetic: self-pity. He slumped to his knees before her and hung his head in shame, the ribbon of crimson flailing from his nose just beginning to slow.

"I know. You're right," he whimpered. "I'm a worthless scumbag . . . But I can change. I promise! Just . . . Just tell me what I need to do to make things right. Whatever it is, I . . ."

"No," she cut him off, glowering down the line of her nose. "You've done enough to jeopardize this cause. If you want Humanity First to succeed, then you need to step down before you do irreparable damage to our reputation . . . You're done."

She turned on her heel and started toward the forecastle, leaving the bleeding, blubbering waste of space where he knelt.

"What . . . You mean *leave*?" he clamored after her. "Leave Humanity First? Caleb, I *am* Humanity First. Do you hear me? This whole movement is *nothing* without me . . . Nothing! You don't have the authority to cast me out like this!"

But she did, and he had given her no choice but to do so. Taking the reins would be no easy task—not by any measure. She and Atlas would more than have their work cut out for them. But she had every confidence that, together, and with the help of the staff, they could build a better, more focused, more sustainable Humanity First. Doubtless, it would take Bhaltair's more vehement supporters some time to acclimatize to the idea of her permanently replacing him, but she intended to come out of the gate swinging, and had a plan that would have them eating out of her palm soon enough . . .

SEVENTEEN

Caleb didn't know how Atlas would react to her proposal at first. Before their flourishing career in public relations, Mx. Baudelaire had operated drone cams for the NTNN's most prolific field correspondents, which meant they were no stranger to having to capture footage in dangerous, crime-riddled locations. Still, asking anybody to venture sternside of the blockade for the first time was not something that should be considered a menial request, especially taking into account the severity of the ongoing crisis . . . Normally, when Atlas heard an idea they didn't like, they replied with something perfectly professional, if slightly backhanded, like *Walk me through your process*, or *Great input, but maybe there's another avenue we can explore.*

Surprisingly, they made no such remark regarding Caleb's plan to film a segment at the Phalanx Compound in the Mouth. In fact, they seemed positively electrified by the idea. "It's genius!" they had declared, giddily transferring their equipment into the storage compartment of their Lucciola swoop as it hovered next to the barge's broadside loading bay. "We're killing two birds with one stone here: Firstly, we finally get to *show* our audience the dangers we've been speaking about, and studies reveal visual stimulus is a far more effective tool for provoking an emotional response than verbal alone. Secondly, we're demonstrating that you, Caleb Callaghan, are *not* afraid of doing what your . . . eh, *predecessor* famously avoided: personally throwing yourself into the fray and facing that danger head-on in the name of exposing the truth!"

The *predecessor* in question had since skulked off somewhere to lick his wounds—maybe he'd gone straight back to Rennaxi Junction to resume his salacious binge uninterrupted. Truthfully, she didn't care, just as long as he never came back. There was no place for Bhaltair Abernathy's ilk in the Humanity First she aspired to build, and she only lamented that she had tolerated his chauvinism for as long as she had . . .

I can't believe I'm even thinking this, love, but thank Lei-Ghannam you weren't here to see just how low I stooped. But I promise: I never enjoyed a wretched second of it, and when the Novara *is racing through ripple-space toward Pasture once more, it will have all been worth it . . .*

"We're gonna get some killer footage," Atlas said, occupying the passenger cabin's rear-facing seat as their swoop sped autonomously toward the blockade. "We might even be up for a Pleiades Multimedia Award! I'm surprised you didn't suggest doing something like this sooner."

Caleb unzipped the black duffel bag resting beside her and produced two bulletproof vests, each with the word "PRESS" printed in bold, white text on their respective breastplates.

"Accolades are nice and all but let's not forget what this segment has to accomplish," she warned, struggling to condense her untamable titian curls enough to fit through the neck hole of her vest. "The NTNN's hardly broken away from that live security feed for going on twenty-four hours now. We're at serious risk of people becoming desensitized to what's going on over there. We need to cut something together that'll inspire the level of fear the situation truly demands."

A devious grin whittled itself across Atlas's diamond-shaped face. "Snag ourselves a few close-ups of those ugly buggers, maybe an overhead tracking shot to convey the scale of the caravan—I doubt we'll have any trouble achieving that."

Ahead, the Canyon's sternside terminus drew nearer, the blockade like the steel of a titanic butcher's blade cleaving the *Novara* asunder, rendered shadowy and ominous by the midnight blue light of the eventide luma-sky. This dumbfoundingly vast access channel once stretched on for an additional six kilometers, before circumstances forced Caleb's ancestors to cede a third of the arc ship to the ravenous consumption of their insatiable enemy. She couldn't deny the blockade was an impressive feat of engineering, nor that it did a creditable job of keeping the alien scourge segregated from NTU sovereignty. Still, she couldn't help but perceive it as an agonizing monument to humanity's downfall—a symbol of everything sacrificed in the name of preserving human culture and society.

Atlas's swoop set down on the transit platform that preceded the newly renovated transfer checkpoint. When Caleb had last ventured to this place, it had been a busy construction site, with the Administration carrying out extensive repairs following the bombing in which Jade and eleven of her fellow service members were killed. The facility had since been transformed into a heavily militarized inspection zone with armed sentries stationed in guard towers scanning their sectors using high-lumen searchlights, raking the barricaded cage fences seen zigzagging toward the checkpoint to ensure that anyone, or *anything*, who somehow managed to breach through from the district could be easily apprehended.

"So, this *friend with benefits*," Caleb began, casting a nervous glance at the robust fortifications as she helped Atlas unload their equipment. "You're absolutely sure he can guarantee us the necessary clearance to cross the border? It seems implausible to me that immigration would let *anybody* transition at a time like this."

"Archie's never let me down before," they replied in smoky tones, batting eyes accented by brilliant red mascara. "We used to *tangle* back when I worked for the NTNN. He leads the department responsible for the authorization and distribution of civilian restricted access to prohibited areas, which basically means granting permits for media types like you and me. He's sorted us out with a twenty-four-hour sternside visa under the pretense of documentary filmmaking."

"So, what you're saying is: no more having to rely on Bhaltair's shady nonverbal agreements with crooked border protection agents?"

"Precisely."

Caleb paused, grinning suggestively. "'Tangle?'"

Atlas simpered. "Archie's a sweetheart but he's not winning *Novara*'s most handsome anytime soon, so you owe me *big* for this one, Callaghan."

"Duly noted."

The basic walk-through security scanners Caleb, Tobias, and Jonah had funneled through during their own foray into the Mouth had been upgraded to a revolving carousel airlock system. The advanced installation scanned their retinas and biometric credentials and scoured their bodies for hidden contraband. The flight case in which Atlas kept Chelsea—the affectionate name given to their beloved quadcopter drone cam—went through additional X-ray screening to ensure it didn't contain any weapons. Caleb thought the delay was an unnecessary frustration but felt a measure of relief knowing the necessary precautions were being taken, even if people smuggling weapons *into* the Mouth hardly seemed like a point of concern. *Then again, the only thing more dangerous than a leech is an armed leech, as the assailants behind the blockade massacre made clear . . .*

Many of the deaths that occurred on that abysmal day were later attributed to the devastating effects a shock wave has on the body in an enclosed space. Accordingly, the narrow walls and low ceiling of the fifteen-meter tunnel that once connected each side of the blockade had been removed during the renovations, laying bare the cavernous hollow that existed between the structure's opposing edifices. A hard-light tunnel now guided traffic through the checkpoint in its stead—a low-powered fission field projected in a horseshoe shape, which would greet undue curiosity with an unpleasant shock if touched and was programmed to shatter in the event of a blast to better disperse the lethal concussive force. As they progressed farther inside, Caleb turned her eyes upward through the glimmering, crackling membrane of hardlight, marveling at the diagrid of braces and buttresses bolstering the construction from within, the dark outlines of the Letterbox and Antaeus Gateway like monstrous ventilation ducts looming high above.

A Lieutenant greeted them as they reached the entrance to the Phalanx Compound—"greeted," being a somewhat loose term. The leatherneck loudly and unabashedly expressed his displeasure with "Chennai Plaza pencil push-ers granting civvies tourism passes while there's a war on." Oddly enough, Caleb appreciated the man's coarseness, as it afforded her a distraction from having to think about the possibility that where they presently stood could very well have been the exact spot in which Jade perished . . .

"We'll be out of your hair in no time, Lieutenant," she assured, projecting her voice and squaring her shoulders to maintain an air of authority. "The people deserve to know what you're really up against here; all we need is a few good shots to spread awareness of your struggle. My colleague has a drone cam, which means we can film from a safe distance and we won't be needing any supervision."

"Well, that's good, cuz I don't have anybody I can spare to babysit you. Just make sure you stay twenty meters back from the line at all times, don't touch anything, and try not to catch a stray round when the shooting starts."

Caleb had handled the talking, not out of a desire to control the situation but out of pure necessity; Atlas looked to have been caught in the same dazed stupefaction as *she* had experienced upon first exposing herself to this yawn-ing cavity, with its urban sprawl of miscellaneous architecture. Mx. Baudelaire turned their disbelieving eyes up to the altitudinous ceiling, where the radiant thicket, growing like a bed of burning cinders, seemed to be in the process of bombarding the settlement below in a vicious deluge of . . . *is that . . . blood?* A biting chill shot down her neck and shoulders. *This place becomes more threatening and alien by the minute. It simply* must *be dismantled.*

"Snap out of it," she said—directed mainly at Atlas but also, admittedly, a little at herself. "We've got too much work to do to stand around gawking."

Atlas shook off their malaise and collected Chelsea's flight case from the baggage scanner conveyor belt. "Sorry. I just . . . never knew . . . I mean . . . I never realized how . . . beautiful it is."

"'Beautiful?' Not exactly the word I'd have chosen."

"I know. But you've got to admit there's a certain splendor to it."

Caleb nodded her head from side to side in a bargaining motion. "At a distance, maybe. But once you see it up close, you start to see the cracks. Fear not, the true horrors of this wasteland will become all too apparent soon enough."

They started down the low steps leading to the compound proper, their collective gaze fixated on the ruinous vista stretching on beyond the bastion's perimeter of tall, defensive barricades.

"What's that?" Atlas asked, pointing fervidly at the unusual aerial vehicle that could be seen hovering over the residential tower known to locals as Tycho Block. "Looks like a pleasure yacht of some type."

"It is," Caleb confirmed, eyeing the vessel's elegant outline. "It's the Indah-2 that was donated by the Agaiya Eclipsis Shipyard in New Singapore. The company's directors wanted to ensure their legacy as shipbuilders lived on once we finally reached Pasture. I'm not exactly sure what it's doing in the Mouth, and it definitely wasn't here last time."

"You academy kids are just chock-full of useless history, aren't you?" Atlas teased. Caleb returned a reticent smile, choosing not to express her concern that the ostentatious transport seemed to be gradually approaching the blockade. Deliberating briefly, she decided to simply keep an eye on it and start worrying if, and when, it became a problem . . .

A large clearing awaited them at the bottom of the stairs, encompassed by a conglomeration of forest-green prefab structures, including an armory, a mess hall, and a Combat Information Center emblazoned with the Corinthian helmet crest representing Phalanx. A motor pool and a vehicle maintenance bay occupied the starboard wing of the compound, with several olive drab raptors and a pair of wheeled APCs ready for deployment in the event of all-out conflict. Judging by the alarming scenes taking place at the main gate, all-out conflict seemed like a terrifyingly real possibility . . .

There looked to be no end to the virulent mob congealing at the perimeter, an unending quagmire of filthy rags and glistening exoskeletons, punctuated by a ruction of thrusting fists and enraged faces . . . Human faces, as a matter of fact—markedly more than Caleb had expected to see . . . The interspecies crowd surged against the grenadier line, swelling and receding as the unmoving automatons stood their ground, their arms interlocked to form an impenetrable wave breaker. A detachment of enforcers comprised the second line, standing in a tight row behind the androids' with riot shields at the ready, hurling tear gas canisters in a hopeless effort to reduce the density of the throng.

"Listen!" Atlas said, raising a finger in the air to indicate the rhythmic pangs of gunfire cutting through the thundering roar of ten thousand wrathful voices. "That sounds really close. Are you absolutely sure we're safe here?"

"I don't know," Caleb mumbled, listening intently to the din.

"You don't know if we're safe?"

"No . . . not that. It's just, I think something feels off about it, you know? It sounds like it's coming from a couple of distinct locations instead of just widespread engagement. And it doesn't seem sporadic like you might expect from an exchange of fire but . . . continuous; prolonged—almost like two groups of people just randomly firing weapons."

She cast her eye over the corroded skyline, only to find her suspicions confirmed by flurries of brilliant plasma streaks, fanning upward and tearing through the hazy atmosphere like volleys from antiaircraft batteries. "They're just making noise to startle the crowd, in much the same way shepherds used to yell and whistle to herd cattle in a specific direction."

Atlas set the drone cam's flight case down on the ground and opened its locking latches with their thumbs. "One of these days you're gonna have to stop using all these Old-Earth metaphors so I can understand what in the Abyss you're talking about . . . Well, once we get Chelsea airborne, we can send her up high and see if we can't figure out what the frick is going on . . . If she catches a stray bullet, though, Callaghan, you can be sure I'll be sending you the repair bill."

They swung open the lid of the flight case, then removed their thirty-centimeter high-spec luma-pad and handed it to Caleb. She switched the device on and watched the Sinegex Systems logo initialize for a few seconds before habitually navigating to the director's suite application. Atlas then produced two separate pieces of wearable tech from the case: a sleek virtu-sim helmet and a black control glove. They slipped the glove onto their right hand, better revealing the intricate arrangement of sensors and actuators leading from the wrist cuff to the tip of each digit. They then slung the virtu-sim helmet around their neck before positioning it over the bridge of their nose, pulling their hair from beneath its ergonomic padding. Splaying their gloved hand out flat before them, the helmet's aqua LED strips began to pulse and flitter like electronic insects crawling across its plastic casing. The shrill whine of four spinning quadcopter blades sounded from the flight case as Atlas tipped their hand upward, then Chelsea finally took flight. The drone hovered for a moment at Caleb's eye level, its aerodynamic chassis resembling a manta ray with four rotor arms sprouting from its back and a camera orb pinched between its cephalic fins. She felt an unusual moment of dissociative depersonalization, staring at herself on the luma-pad's screen as Chelsea wirelessly relayed her perspective to the device.

"Alright, we're synced," she said. "How about we start off with that overhead tracking shot? Make sure you capture all the chaos going on at the grenadier line."

"On it!" Atlas manipulated their hand in a complex array of gestures. Chelsea spun around and began a rapid ascent, shrinking from a half-meterwide quadcopter to a distantly blinking light in a matter of mere seconds. Caleb watched on screen as Atlas sent their loyal scout swooping low over the rioting masses. Only then did she realize just how much she had underestimated the true size of the congregation. It occurred to her that not since the days of Earth had so many gathered in a single location, and she found it difficult to pluck a number out of the air that felt realistic: fifty or sixty thousand, perhaps? Maybe three-quarters of the entire population of the Mouth. She couldn't see Atlas's eyes but picked up on the nervousness in their body language. They likely knew, as she did, that even if the Administration redeployed every enforcer on the *Novara* to the Phalanx Compound, they would *still* be outnumbered twenty to one . . .

"OK," she croaked, swallowing to lubricate her dry throat before trying again. "OK, that looks good. Recall Chelsea to this side of the barricade and let's get those close-ups."

Atlas wordlessly complied. The drone soared around the perimeter of the compound and came to an abrupt stop just behind the line of enforcers. The live feed on the luma-pad blinked as the camera switched from a wide-angle shot to a long-focus zoom. Caleb audibly gasped at what she saw next: countless leeches in infi-pixel detail, ghastly ridges and spines—all manner of hideous appendages filling the frame. The sight of that endless, unholy anathema sent electricity cascading down her spinal column, but it soon yielded to an arresting sense of unease as she noticed the many humans occupying the frame as well. There were men and women of all ages and ethnicities, children swaddled in bundles of cloth with tearstained faces and straggly hair sodden from the crimson rain. The adults in the shot hardly fit the profile of criminals or mutineers; they looked downright desperate, exhausted, expressions of utter desolation carved into their weathered faces. Even the leeches, with their soulless black eyes, managed to look somewhat pathetic, like wounded animals just waiting for death to come for them.

"Delete this shot," she demanded.

"Are you serious? This is great stuff."

"If we air this and fail to convey the appropriate context, we're liable to inadvertently generate sympathy for the leeches among our viewers. Get rid of it and move on; see if you find an angle without any humans in shot. There *must* be some of the bastards we can find who are instigating violence somewhere."

Atlas did as she asked, or at least, they tried to. They sent Chelsea scouring the interspecies droves in search of instances of alien troublemaking, but after a few exhaustive laps, they couldn't find anything remotely usable. The aliens seemed surprisingly subdued—docile, even. Furthermore, having resituated the drone several times now, there didn't seem to be any discernible separation in how the two species were grouped. They were all mixed in with one another, shoulder to shoulder, arm in arm, in some cases, even seeming to have formed perverse family units, with leeches holding children, and humans cradling revolting grub-looking things as tenderly as if they were their own.

"Eh . . . Callaghan?" Atlas stuttered. "What exactly are we doing here?"

Caleb shook her head, uncertainty crashing like a wave on her mental shore. "I . . . I don't know . . . Maybe this wasn't such a good idea after all . . ."

A blanket of shadow fell over the compound as the aerial superyacht ambled directly overhead, its elongated keel blocking out the amber glow of the aptly named Hell Garden. The grenadiers holding the line remained as stoic as ever; behind them, a ripple of fear propagated throughout the enforcers, the wall of riot shields cracking and softening like ice thawing to heat.

"Yeah . . ." Atlas said, apprehension stretching the syllable out over several beats. "I'm thinkin' maybe we should hot foot it outta here while we still have the choice."

But Caleb had a sinking feeling that that privilege had already been revoked . . . She hadn't paid all that much attention to it up until now: the unfathomably massive whirlpool of teeth lurking in the distance, fearing that to spend even a second contemplating the nature of the hellish orifice might somehow erode her sanity. But the *Devourer* soon made sure she was all too aware of its presence, unleashing a sound like the gust of a hurricane blaring through a million detuned trumpets. A distinct quiescence descended over the Mouth, the mob seeming immediately settled by the dreadful fanfare, some even practically gleeful about its deafening arrival, as though it held some sentimental value for them.

Caleb saw light. It appeared as a ribbon set ablaze, meandering in serpentine motion from the whirlpool of teeth, drifting on an invisible current and finally connecting with the silver spire standing tall atop Tycho Block. The light divided as if bounced off a series of mirrors, each new strand following a separate path down toward the dense rookery sprawled out below. One strand seemed to deviate from the others—not only in direction but also in color and vibrancy. The flaming filament made a series of jolting, twisting course corrections as it slalomed toward the compound.

"You seeing this shit?" Caleb heard one enforcer say to another. "You have any idea what that is?"

"Kind of," the other answered. "It's what they call the 'dissemination,' but honestly, that bright pink one coming right for us: I ain't never seen it do that before."

The disconcerted response heralded another troubling development, as the wandering strand appeared to set its sights on the main gate. It made a sudden right-angle turn in a coincident line with the row of grenadiers. The metal men heaved and convulsed as the bizarre illumination tore through them, penetrating one nonexistent ear and blasting out the other before moving swiftly onto the next unsuspecting unit.

"Callaghan!" Atlas yelped, forming a sudden fist to auto-recall Chelsea back to the flight case and hastily removing their virtu-sim helmet. "Are you sure we're not in danger here?"

Caleb didn't have an answer to their question, which was fine, because the grenadiers did. The machines unhooked their arms, then spun around in mechanical synchronicity to face their human compatriots, reaching over their hulking shoulders to uncouple the plasma rifles mag-mounted to their backplates. The subsequent salvo came with zero warning, the enforcers given barely a moment to comprehend what was happening before their *reinforcements* opened fire on them. A hail of effulgent projectiles ripped through the Phalanx personnel as though they were made from tissue—just a flimsy chain of paper people reduced to smoldering shreds, their riot shields and body armor doing little, if anything, to save them.

Caleb's legs had already begun an instinctive dash for safety, but she had to dig her heels in and double back on herself when she noticed Atlas standing out in the open, frozen in terror. She grabbed them by the scruff of their neck and pulled them into an uncoordinated sprint, grazing hands and knees in the lunar dust substrate as she dragged them into cover behind a nearby Hesco barrier.

Violent shivers coursed through Atlas's body as they sat hyperventilating with their back pressed firmly against the gabion. "Shit! They killed them— just fucking murdered them all for no goddamned reason! Have grennies ever malfunctioned like this before? I thought their programming was meant to be infallible!"

"You saw what just happened." Caleb hissed, crouching down by their side. "They're not malfunctioning; they've been hacked—commandeered, somehow!"

"You really think the leeches are capable of something like that? I thought they were, like, *industrial revolution*–level intelligent."

"They built *that* monstrosity, didn't they?" She gave an assertive nod in the *Devourer*'s direction. "Clearly, they've picked up a few new tricks!"

Leaving Atlas in the throes of shock, she spun around and sprang to her feet, peering over the barrier to catch sight of the possessed legion as they marched past the smoking remains of their flesh-bound brethren. She turned her gaze up the stairs toward the transfer checkpoint, where the loudmouthed lieutenant from earlier could be seen rallying his team for a counteroffensive. She wished she could scream at the top of her lungs for him to order a general retreat but knew that, if she were to give away their position, the grenadiers would treat her and Atlas with the same prejudice as they had the frontline enforcers. Consequently, the reserves came tumbling down the steps like a heap of pots and pans, woefully disorganized and completely unprepared for the execution squad awaiting their blundering arrival. Another torrent of plasma: another bundle of bodies crumpled to the deck . . .

Movement drew her attention to the Combat Information Center as several officers wielding sidearms spilled out into the clearing, presumably in the hope of lending whatever assistance they could with their limited combat training. A grenadier's core directives ordained that no higher duty could be assigned than the safeguarding of Administration personnel. But with neural cortices possessed by some unknown devilry, the machines saw their masters as just another bout of hostile targets and dealt with them accordingly.

Caleb's heart became a bottomless hollow at the resounding chorus of screams—a clamor cut abruptly short by a dozen cracks of gunfire, followed by a gut-wrenching silence . . . She did a quick estimate and morbidly concluded that more lives had been lost in this onslaught than the blockade bombing and NTSC ambush combined. So much death, so much loss, and yet, something felt far more sinister, more insidious, about the tactics on display here. Using humanity's own forces against them like this constituted war on a psychological front. Their enemy conspired to poke holes in their security net—to prove just how tenuous their illusion of safety was. It felt as though she had been thrust into a new reality—one where the inalienable protections granted by the union could no longer shield her nor the ones she loved from harm. The leeches were sending an unambiguous message: this was war, and there would be no refuge from their depravity for anyone.

She buckled her knees and ducked behind the Hesco barrier, staying out of view of the nearing infantry as they continued their relentless march toward the blockade, manipulated like faceless mannequins by strings of fuchsia luminescence.

Atlas firmly tugged her sleeve, directing her attention with a wide-eyed stare beyond the vehicle pool toward the main gate. Initially, the violent outbreak had caused the mob to scatter like the scurrying insects they were, but the entrance to the compound had now been left completely unattended, and the deviants had begun clambering over the barricades and brazenly trespassing into NTU sovereignty, emboldened by the presence of their surprising new allies.

Caleb felt a cold shiver brush the back of her neck as a group of young men hastened to the bodies of the first-line enforcers and proceeded to plunder their weapons and nonlethal deterrents with the same freneticism as a wake of vultures stripping a carcass to the bone.

"We have to get out of here," Atlas urged, tugging her arm as if trying to pull it from its socket. "If any of them notice us, they'll execute us on the spot."

She ardently shook her head. "If we move, we die . . . All the rioters care about is making it through the blockade; they're not interested in us . . . Can't say the same for the grenadiers, though. Whoever's doing this might have even primed them to target anybody with NTU citizenship."

"So, what's your plan: just wait here and pray they don't find us? Sorry to be blunt, Callaghan, but it's hardly your finest."

She didn't rise to the remark—just kept watching the interspecies rout flooding into the compound, the vital segregation that had upheld the sanctity of the union for a hundred years disintegrating before her very eyes. Those who had first breached the perimeter had come to a stop a cautious distance behind the grenadiers, the androids now formed up in a line at the bottom of the steps leading up to the checkpoint. They remained silent, motionless—eerily so, status lights pulsing standby yellow as they awaited receipt of new directives. She glanced up at the oppressive silhouette of the yacht as it hung overhead, imbued with an innate understanding that the responsible party was coordinating the assault from somewhere on board.

Despicable cowards . . .

The fact that the vessel remained airborne suggested the instigators had also commandeered, or otherwise disabled, the automated sentry turrets positioned on either side of Antaeus Gateway. They owned the entire blockade: all egresses and defensive weapons platforms. The only question that remained: *What are they planning on doing with it?*

"CONFIRMED." The blurted utterance came from the grenadiers, the coalescence of so many perfectly synced voices causing an unusual phasing effect. "CAUTION . . . STAND CLEAR . . . PROTOCOL CIPHER'S WRATH EXECUTING."

"'Cipher's wrath,'" Mx. Baudelaire repeated. "What in the name of Lei-Ghannam does *that* mean?"

Caleb placed two fingers against her lips in consternation. "I think we're about to find out."

The androids separated into two groups, with half—approximately sixty—taking one thumping step forward and to the left, bringing themselves directly in front of their neighbors. Servo motors chirred and whined as the rear units jolted into action, reaching out to those in front and gripping the edges of their backplates with mighty, mechanical mitts. Caleb and Atlas simultaneously flinched as the machines barbarically pried their counterpart's dorsal armor away, exposing the assemblage of processors, heat sinks, and hydraulics encased within.

"They're brutalizing each other! Why?"

Caleb ignored the query, watching as the butchers ripped off another layer of protective casing, laying bare the radiant-blue tetrahedrons, buried among a tract of wiring within the abdomens of their seemingly willing subjects. Before Atlas could inevitably ask what the glowing structures were, the rear machines balled fists and unleashed a single, synchronized punch. The frontmost grenadiers keeled over, cyan sparks disgorging from the gaping openings on their backs.

"WARNING. WARNING," chanted the synthesized choir. "FISSION CORE RUPTURED . . . COMPACT REACTOR MELTDOWN IMMINENT . . . CLEAR SAFE DISTANCE OF THREE-HUNDRED METERS IMMEDIATELY."

The pair didn't need to consult one another to decide that the time to run had arrived. Although Atlas seemed far more interested in safely retrieving Chelsea's flight case than saving themself.

"Forget it!" Caleb rebuked, yanking them by the arm back in step beside her. "It's just a damned drone! She's not worth your life!"

"Easy for *you* to say, Callaghan. You don't know how much I spent on her!"

How utterly confounding it felt in that instant: for Caleb to find herself sprinting *toward* a swarm of leeches and not fleeing in the opposite direction. She could even see one of the vermin frantically beckoning them closer as they barreled past the barricades and through the main gate as if to say, *Hurry! Over here! You'll be safe with us!*

The audacity, she fumed, wanting to hurl a diatribe of offensive gestures in response, though she was dubious as to whether it would even understand any of them. *If there is even a scintilla of compassion behind those . . . perplexingly glowing eyes, then where were you when your kind slaughtered my fiancée? . . . If you do, in fact, care about human life, then why could you not have intervened today before your saboteurs instigated a massacre upon my people?*

She knew thinking the creatures even remotely capable of making such considerations represented significant anthropomorphizing of them on her part, projecting her human emotions and rationale onto something patently inhuman. That was perhaps the most infuriating thing about them: the fact that they were physically incapable of debating or arguing with her. She couldn't force them to accept liability, nor hold themselves accountable, for the countless atrocities committed by their very worst. Not once had there been any attempt to convey sentiments of guilt or shame in the aftermath of these attacks; not once had they publicly condemned the violence or offered condolences to the families of those lost. Just blithe, arrogant, callous nonchalance—that was always their default reaction, and she had no reason to suspect *this* time would be any different . . .

Eyes stinging as they passed through a lingering cloud of tear gas, Caleb's blood ran cold as she found herself completely surrounded, the few humans in their immediate vicinity vastly outnumbered by the droves of towering insectoids.

They could tear us apart limb from limb and there's nothing we could do to stop it, she darkly hypothesized, the acerbic fear pheromone that one of Jonah's men had alluded to thick and smothering in the humid air. Thankfully, the commotion in the Phalanx Compound looked to be holding their attention for now, at least.

"I must have had a screw loose or something deciding to follow you here," said Atlas, stopping to catch their breath under the awning of an abandoned market stall and taking shelter from the vermillion downpour. "I'm done! I fucking quit! You hear me, Callaghan? If we make it out of this alive, then I'm gonna retire and live out the rest of my days on Capella Promenade. And you . . . you'll just have to find some other gullible idiot to run your damned-Abyss smear campaign!"

Caleb seized them by the chin and forcefully turned their head in the direction of the Phalanx Compound. "Shut up for a second and just watch!"

Beyond the main gate, the indoctrinated grenadiers were gearing up for the next step of their illicit directives. The units with the ruptured fission cores had begun a full-pelt sprint toward the blockade, unfazed by the miniature warheads counting down to zero in their chest cavities. As if catapulted by trebuchets, half of them launched into the air and slammed into the blockade, punching fists into its skin of repurposed heat-shielding to firmly attach themselves. The other half carried on through the transfer checkpoint, completely decimating the revolving security carousel and disappearing into the hollow beyond. The first group began ascending the blockade, inverting the joints on their arms and legs to achieve spider-like motility that made Caleb's skin crawl. They organized themselves into a pattern of equidistant triangles, appearing from this distance as scintillating points of blue light bespeckling the blockade's immense surface, increasing in brightness as their dangerously volatile compact reactors approached criticality. She could only presume the units who had charged through the checkpoint were in the process of doing something similar, forming up around internal support structures and targeting weak points.

"What are they doing?" Atlas asked, voice timid and tremulous. "Wha . . . What *is* this?"

She swallowed a nervous lump in her throat. "It's a demolition."

A series of rapid-fire detonations battered her eardrums, the blockade and its surroundings suddenly engulfed in retina-searing incandescence. A powerful shock wave carried a wall of red mist and debris through the compound, flattening the crowd with devastating force and flinging Caleb and Atlas across the stall, sending them crashing into a storage rack. Scorching heat struck the skin of her face and filled her lungs, as though conspiring to drown her in liquid combustion. The blast ripped the market stall's awning clean off its struts, leaving them at the mercy of the oppressive downpour, which took several seconds to resume following its explosive dispersal. Coughing to expel the lunar dust from her airways, she disentangled her legs from Atlas's and scraped herself off the floor. Mx. Baudelaire lay clutching their chest, struggling to coax the air back into their lungs but otherwise unscathed. Beneath the ringing in her ears, Caleb heard an inharmonious orchestra of wailing, groaning instruments, the chamber of the Mouth providing prime acoustics for the symphony of chaos reverberating around its gargantuan edifices. She recalled what Tobias had said during their contentious last meeting about the failing structural integrity around the Mouth, tormenting herself with the troubling possibility that the blast had triggered a hull rupture and that the cacophony was a sign they had mere moments before the endless night reached in to claim them.

The truth, it transpired, proved far more unsettling . . . She turned her attention toward the blockade, from where the swan song of tortured metal seemed to be originating. Black smoke hung like a curtain over the structure, concealing the true extent of the damage beneath its billowing, tenebrous mass. The symphony swelled; percussionists struck steel drums and rang discordant bells, building toward a calamitous crescendo. The veil of smoke lurched forward, rolling like the ash cloud from a volcanic eruption through the Phalanx Compound and out into the district. Caleb shielded her eyes and nose from the gliding smog, feeling a peculiar rush of cool atmo-sphere—a sudden change in air pressure that sent a soothing breeze percolating throughout the expanse of the Mouth, caressing her cheeks and flowing through her tangled hair. The smoke finally cleared, and where the blockade once stood, a gaping hole remained, its serrated, mangled edges a testament to the catastrophic force of the string of detonations. Through it, she saw the Canyon stretching on into the distance, the blue luster of the artificial night breaching through the enormous fissure and cleaving the copper haze asunder. The barrier between home and hostile frontier had been destroyed, and she knew in that terrible instant that the *Novara* would never be the same again.

EIGHTEEN

Delilah couldn't recall ever feeling quite so overjoyed at having the *Assurance* berthed in the Lower Amidships Docks. Back when she first purchased the old gal from Kahu, perhaps—all starry-eyed and brimming with ambition as she had been before the relentless treadmill of disappointment that was commercial salvage ground her down to the jaded pessimist she had become. After eight long years dragging the belt and shooting slag at the *Novara*'s decrepit hull, she honestly couldn't tell if her efforts had had any meaningful impact—whether she'd made good on what she promised Micah before he died: that she would do everything in her power to make things better for people.

In *her* reckoning, all she'd really accomplished was needlessly and repeatedly endangering the lives of her crew, risking everything time and time over in her avaricious pursuit of wealth and status among the other captains in the guild . . . *Too many close calls; too much blind luck . . . It's just a miracle you haven't gotten this ship obliterated and everyone aboard it killed . . . And then what? The last welding operation in the* Novara's *fleet, gone—the hull around the Mouth left to fall into unfettered neglect . . . You're no better than Gretta Hox using the* Assurance *for your own selfish gain when, in truth, everyone on the Coalescence—human or otherwise—depends on her continued service with their lives . . . Somehow, you've ended up entangled with both Harmony and* the Glow Syndicate; *your ship's barely even spaceworthy anymore and your pilot's too traumatized to fly . . . What a fine mess you made of things, Lilah . . .* Those last words steamrolled through her mind in the austere voice of her mother, given it was precisely the type of thing the woman would have said, were she still in possession of all her faculties. Ashanti Holloway had never given Delilah her blessing regarding her decision to leave the Academy, nor her subsequent entrepreneurial exploits. Nevertheless, she would have expected her daughter to strive for a standard of excellence regardless of what she chose to do in life—a standard it seemed painfully obvious she had continuously failed to meet.

Sorry, Ma. Looks like I let you down again. Once a screwup, always a screwup. Right?

Then again, as the *Assurance* had limped back to Lower Amidships, carrying her ever-growing manifest of crew and passengers, fate, in its enigmatic way, had dropped an opportunity in Delilah's lap that she suspected could empower her to make exactly the kind of difference Micah had wanted her to—namely, one incapacitated Vidalia Drexen and his grievously injured bodyguard, alone, unarmed, and pleading for amnesty in her cargo bay. How many lives could she ultimately save, she had contemplated, how much pain and misery could she prevent, were she to simply seal the lower deck bulkheads and purge the cargo bay; jettison the ruthless mogul and his praetorian guard and let the empty black deal with them? After the fiasco with the bounty hunters, he'd given her more than sufficient justification to do just that, but one caveat of keeping a crew of stubborn soft-hearts like Delilah's meant that such drastic solutions were strictly unavailable to her; Isaac and Teo—the compassionate fools—simply wouldn't have allowed it. And while Micah's final wishes for her remained somewhat open to interpretation, she could be confident that *airlocking an unconscious man and a wounded cohab* was *not* what he had had in mind, no matter how beneficial the potential outcome . . .

For now, at least, Drexen would live, and only a short while after making that call had Delilah realized what a grave mistake choosing the alternative would have been. As far as anybody in the Captain's Guild knew, the crew of the *Assurance* still had a sizable bounty on their heads. Upon hailing tower control for docking clearance, a woman with an attitude as prickly as a hydroponic pineapple, who introduced herself as Iver Polakorski's *replacement*, had threatened to arm the docks' defensive sentry turrets and, "feed them all to the Abyss." Delilah had hurriedly routed the comms-feed through to the med cubby to transmit proof that she had Vidalia aboard, urging the hellcat to stand down or risk annihilating her master. Fortunately, the new harbor master had begrudgingly complied.

The repairs completed by the Composer's engineers had served their purpose in helping the hauler back into NTU space, but the stitches had already started to come loose, the splints holding her fractured bones together buckling under the strenuous uneven forces of her mismatched impulse thrusters. A complete retrofit would be needed to bring her back up to prime condition: stripped down to her airframe and reassembled piece by piece, her myriad discontinued components replaced with their contemporary counterparts.

Delilah couldn't help but wonder, after such extensive renovation, with so little of her original composition left intact, whether she would still be the same ship; and without Kahu cussing and boozing behind the helm, would she still feel like home? She had dared not even contemplate how much the overhaul would cost, even going so far as to seriously consider whether a more economical solution might be to simply cut her losses: part-ex the *Assurance*, split the credit evenly among the crew, and find something else to do with her sorry days. But then, as Saber Safeguarding paramedics arrived on the scene, Naught reaffirmed that the discord between them was settled and, as a gesture of truce, even offered to fund the repairs on Vidalia's behalf. *Just like that; back in the Governor's pocket . . . Nebula.* Although, what exactly there was left for the man to govern, now that Harmony had taken control of the Mouth, was unclear. With tens of thousands of refugees spilling into Lower Amidships, doubtless, he would have little trouble conjuring up *some* means of monetizing the crisis; some duplicitous scheme to bleed those desperate souls for all their worth. She vowed in that instant that, whatever it was, she would have absolutely no part in it . . .

The ship's landing gear had been rendered inoperable following the crash; thankfully, the maintenance bay came equipped with a massive nanofiber net, which had caught the hauler just as her sputtering impulse thrusters finally gave out and gently lowered her down to the landing pad. And there she remained for almost two hours while Delilah and the crew deliberated over their next move. A team of veteran engineers lingered at the entrance to a nearby hangar housing a fossil museum of cranes and various repair engines. Sporting oil-stained coveralls, they stood with folded arms sharing a look of disgruntled impatience, no doubt eager to race through their shift so they could see the day out slugging syn-beer in the Weary Navigator. Unfortunately, the work couldn't commence until the crew had dealt with the small matter of the cohabitor litter presently inciting bedlam in the galley . . .

"I need them *off* this ship, Tobias." Delilah had to strain her voice to be heard over the exuberant hysteria, struggling to pry the boy's attention away from the NTNN broadcast as it played on the panel in the lounge. He sat watching the unprecedented scenes on the armrest of Kahu's recliner, the surrounding lamps soaking his pensive expression in light as warm as that of a Conservatory sunrise. On-screen, like looking through a portal into another reality, a live feed from the Canyon's sternside terminus displayed the gaping hole that had been punched through the blockade. The bronze atmosphere of the Mouth was a sandstorm rolling across the dimensional threshold, dispersing in the cold blue of the simulated night.

Silhouetted in the seeping haze, humans and cohabitors clambered over the mangled wreckage of what, up until recently, had been the transfer checkpoint. They poured out onto the bowside transit platform and funneled like a river of dirtied flesh, chitin, and rags down a pedestrian accessway. Just as Wyatt had predicted, the evacuation effort was ostensibly being facilitated by a brigade of hijacked grenadiers, reprogrammed using Harmony's hybrid tech to direct the refugees along the Canyon and deeper into Amidships. At one point, enforcers had attempted to push the interspecies tide back toward the blockade but were forced to retreat in a hail of suppressing fire. They now waited at a newly formed perimeter, tails tucked between their legs, consolidating their forces and preparing to mount a counteroffensive. The dramatic images had selfishly captured Tobias's gaze, unwilling to relinquish him from their hypnotizing grasp. Delilah snapped her fingers in front of his nose to seize his focus.

"Are you listening to me?" she demanded. "I said we need them *off* this ship, now!"

The boy tore his eyes away from the panel and whipped his head in her direction. "I'm resonant, Holloway—not deaf; I heard you the first time!" Then Hyde retreated into shadow and gave way for the return of a deeply apologetic Jekyll. "I'm . . . I'm sorry, Captain. That was . . . unbecoming of me."

"That would be putting it mildly." She folded her arms to signal impatience. "Not that I'd give two shits either way, but have I done something to offend you? Because I feel like all you've done since we departed the Mouth is ignore me, send me silent daggers, or outright snap at me . . . I get that you're still acclimating to how we run things around here regarding chain of command, but, truthfully, I'm running out of free passes to give you."

"No, no. I promise it's not that . . . Honestly, it's hard to put into words." He placed a palm on his chest. "You haven't upset *me*, but at the same time, I do feel an uncomfortable level of resentment toward you right now."

She wordlessly demanded clarification with the same subzero stare her mother had given her countless times. "It's Vidalia," he obliged. "Null and Mercy feel that, by granting him safe harbor on the *Assurance*, you have broken the vow you made to them both: that they would be safe on the *Assurance*, that you'd do everything in your power to keep them as far away from the Governor and his Monarchs as possible."

"I see . . . And they raised these concerns to you . . . personally?"

The boy shook his head as though it were the strangest question one could ask. "Resonance doesn't afford you the luxury of having an opinion left unsaid. They understand the reasoning behind your decision: mend bridges we thought otherwise burnt, but they're still . . . frustrated by the situation."

She gave a ruminative pause. "Do you know what the history is between them; Vidalia with Null and Mercy, I mean?"

Tobias cocked his head to consider. "I share your curiosity, Captain; I have looked for answers, but they deflect me every time I try."

"Deflect?" she repeated dubiously.

"'Deflection' is when you overwhelm your resonant partner with mental flashes to disrupt the bond. There are no secrets in an empathic connection: what your partner feels at any given moment, *you* feel just as emphatically. But when it comes to delving into memories, there are ways to throw someone off the scent if you feel they're rooting around in places you want kept private. It doesn't always work, but I've learned to take it as a polite request to respect their neural space and seek a different line of inquiry . . . Still, there are certain details that have slipped through that safety net."

"Such as?"

Tobias cast a doleful glance across the galley in Mercy's direction. "From what I've been able to piece together, Mercy's father was affiliated with the Governor some years ago—a business partner, maybe. Not only that, but he was also ciphered with Naught. I think that at some point, his relationship with Vidalia soured, and he may have been making plans to usurp him as head of the Glow Syndicate. Naturally, Naught gleaned those intentions, but ae remained loyal to Vidalia, and so, ae killed him—*murdered* aer own cipher . . . I don't know of any other instances of a cohabitor killing their resonant partner; it's unprecedented—unconscionable."

Delilah let slip a quiet gasp, a pang of guilt and unease tearing through her chest at the consideration that she had willingly allowed the killer of Mercy's father to remain on her ship. Suddenly, it made perfect sense why she and Null might feel some animosity toward her . . .

"That's terrible . . . But, it doesn't explain how Null and Mercy ended up implicated in all this."

Tobias pressed a finger to his lips in thought. "I believe that when this happened, Vidalia already knew about their resonant compatibility and, being the shrewd businessman he is, he wanted to harness their bond to use as a tool to strengthen his operation. He took Mercy in under the pretense of caring for her in her father's absence, but really, it was as a means of indemnification— payback for the transgression her father had plotted to make against him. Mercy lived and worked under Vidalia's influence for over a decade trying to pay back her debt—right up until the day she joined the crew."

A ruckus exploded from across the galley as a little boy with a grubby face tried to snatch an idol out of the paws of one of his nonhuman siblings. Null and Nanimonai pried the scrapping pair away from one another as an ear-piercing tumult of screams and brays arose from the rest of the gaggle.

"Thank you for sharing," said Delilah, watching the ruckus with a vexed expression. "I just wish she wasn't so tight-lipped all the damn time so I could have known before letting that monster Naught aboard . . . I'll make an effort to take her aside soon to clear the air."

"I don't think that's a good idea," Tobias warned. "She didn't willingly give me this information, and I doubt she will be best impressed to learn that I've passed it on to you."

"Let me worry about that . . . Right now, I need you to focus on figuring out what we're doing with these kids. Those engineers will need full access to the *Assurance* to do their job, and that includes the galley. If word gets out we're hosting a cohabitor kindergarten aboard there'll be a lynch mob waiting on our boarding ramp within the hour."

Tobias's entire being sagged with concern. "Where else can we take them, though? There's nowhere else for them to go."

"Well, maybe you shoulda thought of that before you elected to smuggle them onto my ship."

He let his gaze fall to the infant perched next to him—the one presently nibbling the buckle strap of his jacket with underdeveloped mandibles, and who seemed more and more reluctant to leave the boy's side. "My father's apartment in Emeral Heights," he tentatively suggested. "We could take them there. There's plenty of space; it's a penthouse suite which means we'll have the entire floor to ourselves—noise won't be an issue . . . Of course, we just might have to restrain the man in the event he goes utterly ballistic and tries to report us to Phalanx. I'm sure he'll come around eventually . . . Or at least, I hope he will."

"Sounds Nebula, except for just one thing: how do you plan on getting them there? Can't exactly just bundle them onto the Canyon tram, can we? I'm not even sure it'll be running in light of what's going on."

"That part, I haven't quite worked out, yet," he confessed. "We need transport: something maneuverable enough to bring up alongside the helm-access airlock. It'll need to have a passenger cabin spacious enough to squeeze Null and Nanimonai into; tinted windows, of course—none at all, ideally."

"Tobes," she cut him off. "This is turning into quite the list of prerequisites. Are you just throwing darts blindfolded here or do you actually have something in mind?"

He paused. "Nothing specific . . . But then . . . I'm wondering if perhaps Vidalia has something we could make use of."

Delilah loosed a prostrated exhalation, pinching the bridge of her nose. "After what you've just told me, I don't want any more involvement with that man than is absolutely necessary. The Monarchs own the docks now, so it's true we need to keep Vidalia sweet if we have any hope of retaining our weld and salvage commission, but I'm already uncomfortable enough as it is with him footing the bill for this refit. Accepting any more favors is only gonna add to the leverage he holds over us."

"I understand, Captain." Tobias gave a forlorn smile, running a hand down the withers of his little companion's neck. Delilah could scarcely believe he was the same ignoramus who dropped a harvester on that pulp refinery not two months prior. "But if it means getting them to safety, is it not well worth the risk?"

She returned her glum stare to the panel, watching the droves of Prey and Mouthborn humans, violently ejected from their homes and thrust into a completely foreign environment. She shuddered to imagine the fear, displacement, and alienation they almost certainly all felt.

"The situation is especially precarious," she explained. "Not *just* for them; for everybody . . . For a blast to rip open the blockade like that—there's no way it hasn't caused significant strain to the encompassing hull. Every second the *Assurance* isn't starside right now is bad, so let's just do whatever we have to to make that happen, agreed?"

"Agreed." An appreciative smile edged the corners of his lips, then the broadcast took his attention once more. The enforcers made another futile attempt to retake control of the blockade, resulting in another wave of Phalanx casualties. "There's going to be a lot of terrified people out there," he murmured.

"You can say that again."

"I'm not just referring to your average bowsider. I mean people like *me:* resonants who don't even know what resonance is . . . People all throughout the *Novara* are about to be subjected to the same horrifying experience I was when I first bonded with Null, only *they* aren't going to have the likes of Teo and Mercy around to explain what's happening to them." He cast viridescent eyes to the floor in remorse. "You know Hiroki Sato—the housefather at Juniper Sanctuary?"

"*Chīsana Osuushi*," Delilah recited. "'The Little Bull'—met him a couple of times back when I was first recruiting Teodora; friendly chap, if a little eccentric."

Tobias gave a reverent nod. "On the night Juniper burnt down, he alluded to certain . . . *complications* that can arise when a resonant discovers their compatibility too late in life. When people don't have guidance to learn how to control their empathic connectivity, sadly, it inevitably takes control of them . . . Hiroki suggested the Composer's ranks are full of people like this—tortured souls driven to the brink of insanity by rampant, unregulated resonance . . . Part of me wonders if that isn't precisely her goal here." He gestured somberly toward the panel. "By flooding the *Novara* with tens of thousands of Prey, she's enabling untold numbers of these first contact scenarios, which will ultimately bolster Harmony's forces due to the sheer volume of corrupted ciphers that will end up sympathizing with her cause."

"So, what you're saying is this is essentially a recruitment drive?" Delilah shook her head to dispel the worrying notion. "That seems very glass half empty, Mister Edevane . . . I thought bringing an end to the segregation of the Mouth was precisely what its inhabitants wanted? Couldn't this be a positive thing: the catalyst to the emergence of *true* pan-species society?"

Tobias twisted his lips in thought, carefully preparing his riposte as Delilah felt certain he had done countless times during debates in the ACS lecture hall.

"If handled correctly," he began, "with a phased introduction of Prey into the bowside population, government outreach programs to get them housed and properly integrated, resonance education centers—it *could* be very positive. But releasing them into civilization en masse like this, without any kind of support or regulation—call me a pessimist, but I fear the consequences could be disastrous."

Just then, a cannonade of footsteps, arriving from the entrance to crew quarters, took their attention. The pair turned in sync as Kahu charged into the galley lugging a military rucksack covered in threadbare NTSC patches over his shoulder. Teodora followed hot on his tail, flouncing her arms and springing up and down, looking like a blue jay trying to pick a fight with a rhino.

"So that's it?" she bawled after him. "After all this time—all we've been through—you're just gonna cut an' run' cuz of one little slipup?"

The old pilot's self-loathing seeped through his curmudgeonly sneer. "If you really think it's just been one little slipup, then you ain't been payin' attention. All I've done for months now is cause one catastrophe after another. Next one comes around, we might not get so lucky . . . I ain't gonna be a blight on this ship anymore and I ain't gonna be responsible for gettin' any of yous zeroed!" He slammed his rucksack down on the island countertop's lumasurface, causing the kaleidoscopic visualizations that Isaac had switched on for the kids to momentarily pixelate and fractalize in the air. The old pilot spun around to face the rook of personnel storage lockers located beside the kitchenette, pulling his gray, matted dreadlocks aside and positioning an ireful eye before the retinal scanner that secured his—the one with the words *Pandora's Box* scrawled on it in red spray paint, meaning *anybody who tries to open this locker will incur the wrath of Wing Commander Heperi*. "Don't know why you care so much all of a sudden," he grumbled, shoveling medals, dog tags, and half-empty bottles of fire water into his already full bag. "All you an' me ever did was butt heads an' get at each other's throats. Woulda thought you'd be jumpin' for joy at the prospect of finally being rid of me."

"But you're crew!" Teo insisted, eyes darting side to side as they followed Kahu's furiously moving hands. "Delilah says crew means family! Sure, you might piss me off like it was your Abyss-given mission to do so, but that don't mean I want you *off* the *Assurance*!"

Kahu shook his head. "'Skipper's sold you a pail of bilgewater there, girl . . . Crewmembers come and go—that's just the nature of the gig. People quit, people move on, people die. Hell, I've probably worked with more salvage specialists over the decades than you've got birthdays under yah belt." He hoisted the rucksack over his shoulder and prepared to take his leave. "Word of advice. If you wanna make it as a spacer, then all you gotta do is follow this one simple rule: don't get attached to nobody. It's just you, whatever ship you call home, and the beckon of the endless night. Everything else: just scenery."

Anxiously tugging on the sleeves of her knitted sweater, Teo abandoned her attempts at reasoning with the stubborn geyser and locked frantic eyes with Delilah. "Tell him, Lilah," she pleaded, anger morphing into panic, indignation into despair. "Tell him he don't have to leave . . . Tell him . . . tell him you ain't mad for what happened with those interceptors. Tell him there ain't no need for this!"

Kahu shared a glance with Delilah, his beseeching countenance telegraphing the words *Please don't make this any harder for me than it has to be*. She gave him a surreptitious nod, knowing she could make the parting easier for both him *and* Teo. "I asked for Kahu's resignation," she admitted erroneously. "He's served this crew admirably over the years, but it's long since due that he stepped down and let someone else take the helm."

She saw the rage rising in Teo like red mercury in a thermometer. "Permission to speak freely, Captain?" the girl asked, tempering herself with slow, steady respiration.

"When have you ever needed permission before?"

"This ain't right, Lilah—downright callous, matter o' fact . . . Kahu grew up on the *Assurance*; she's been in his family for over seventy years, and now you wanna go an' evict him cuz of somethin' that weren't even his fault?"

"Kahu's condition is getting worse," Delilah affirmed, sotto voce but grave in comportment. "We all know it, and so does he . . . While it might not be fair to pass the buck for what happened with Djoser and Edmund, the unfortunate truth is that there's far too much riding on this operation to let its very survival hinge on the state of one man's mental health. We all make mistakes, but for the sake of everyone on the Coalescence, we just can't afford another debacle like that."

Teo stamped a polychromatic work boot into the floor grating. "What about *me*, then? I screwed up, too! We wouldn't have even gotten into that situation in the first place if it weren't for me. I shoulda known damned well that transponder ping was a stitch-up, but I was too eager to dig up somethin' juicy like always and led us into an obvious trap. That mean you're gonna fire *my* ass as well?"

Delilah folded her arms, wishing like hell she could reach out and pull the girl into a tight embrace, but knowing she had to maintain her steely facade for *her* sake. "I value your opinion, Teo, but the matter is settled. If you're unhappy about my decision, then we can discuss it further at a later time. But I *won't* have you questioning my judgment in front of the other crew; understood?"

Teo threw her hands in the air exasperatedly, mumbling the words "damned-Abyss hypocrite" as she stormed out of the galley while the others watched on in awkward reticence. Tobias launched to his feet, gave Delilah an *I'll speak to her* nod and set off with his little companion in tow. Kahu's intensely dour bearing faded as though it had been little more than a mirage. He brought himself before Delilah, shoulders slumped, and head hung low. "Thanks, Skip. You didn't have to take the rap like that, but I appreciate it."

"I didn't do it for you," she replied, staring distantly. "This whole thing is gonna take some serious adjustment for her; she finally found her family and now she thinks it's falling apart. I'm happy to play the role of antagonist if it means giving her something to direct her anger at instead of herself."

"She's a tough nut, that one," Kahu concurred. "She'll pull through just fine."

Delilah gave a rueful smile. "So, you're shipping off then?"

"Yep . . . There's a booth at the ExSight Multiplex driving range with my name on it. Time to dust off the old four iron and see if I can remember how to swing."

She shook her head fondly. "Do me one last favor before you head off?"

"Anything, Skip. So long as it don't mean me getting behind the helm."

"Those days are over; I promise . . . I gotta go talk shop with Drexen about something; need you to stand behind me and look tough."

A grin appeared on the old pilot's hoary mug. He cracked his knuckles and rolled his shoulders. "Now that, I can do."

NINETEEN

Thanks to the chaos taking place at the blockade, a second ship-wide lockdown had been put into effect, leaving the docks significantly more crowded than Delilah would have preferred. With Kahu at her side, the pair made the arduous journey from the maintenance bay over to the cavernous hangar's control tower, traveling along the main concourse under the intense scrutiny of the manifold ship-rabble loitering about their landing pads.

"Sure is nice of the gang to roll out the red carpet for us like this," Kahu remarked, tipping an imaginary hat toward the handful of glowering onlookers gathered near the landing skis of their tortuga-class frigate. "That's the *Mammon's Avarice*, ain't it—Jorge Almeida's boat? Thought we was on good terms after extracting that cache of old tech and agreeing to split the booty. So, why's his crew lookin' us up an' down like we just took a shit on their mothers' graves?"

"Djoser Kern and Edmund Sinclair knew about Null when they intercepted us." Delilah rested her concussion repeater on the opposite shoulder so Almeida's band of profiteers could plainly see it. "And that was two days ago—safe to assume it's common knowledge by now, which means we really need to watch our step."

Kahu issued a prolonged grunt. "Guess the days of you sittin' comfortably at the top of the peckin' order are long gone, huh?"

"It certainly looks that way." She sighed. "All this fuss over one cohabitor."

"Preach . . . I mean, I know I ain't exactly a shining beacon of tolerance when it comes to the bugs, but the folks round here are gonna be shittin' bricks when those refugees start turnin' up in their neck of the woods."

A cold shiver rattled down her spine as she considered the inhospitable welcome the thousands of displaced cohabs now spilling into Amidships would undoubtedly receive. "You can say that again."

Shipping containers plastered with audacious corporate insignias hung overhead like a gargantuan work of abstract masonry, the movement of cargo throughout the docks brought to a standstill by the heightened security measures. Hopefully the ancient gantry cranes suspending them from the high ceiling retained the durability to hold their purchase, lest she and Kahu might be turned into a puddle of pink purée before they even managed to reach their destination.

One thing she had always known about herself was that she possessed a powerful olfactory memory, and the effluvium of hydrogen fuel implanting itself in the back of her throat immediately transported her to a time in her youth when she had truly relished the opportunity to visit this place. On the rare occasion her father could pry himself away from work or his hive of honeybees in the Conservatory, they would pack a cooler full of sweet treats and find a stoop atop the public observation platform, where they would sit and test each other on the classifications of various ships as they came into berth. Because ships were all they had been back then—big, beautiful behemoths piloted by brave Novarians who risked everything to provide vital infrastructure to the union. Only since captaining a ship herself had it become evident just how naive she had been to think those eking out a living here did so out of anything resembling altruism. Her contemporaries formed guilds and boards to maintain a flimsy facade of cooperation when, in truth, the competition forced crews to scrounge any advantage they could to stay ahead of the curve. And if the only way to give one's operation an edge was to screw over one's confederates, then that was just the name of the game. *All's fair in freight and salvage . . .*

The animosity only seemed to intensify as they progressed farther toward the control tower, word of their arrival propagating faster than they could pass each docking bay. Some of the more *infamous* getups looked as if they were positively starved for violence, poised to bring out their pitchforks at the slightest provocation and exact some good old-fashioned mob justice.

Eyeing the unsavory spectators, Kahu cracked his knuckles and, under his breath, muttered, "These idiots hopin' they can just stare us to death, or is someone gonna grow some nads and make the first move already?"

Delilah spied the answer to his question stalking the lattice of steel walkways hanging above their heads. Thea Rebbeckis—captain of the *Etherow in Spring*—had hardly been exaggerating with her appraisal of the situation in the docks, specifically regarding the recent *change in management*. Vidalia had apparently had the good sense to pull a significant portion of his forces bowside as it became clear the battle for the Mouth was lost. His hold over the docks seemed absolute, and although his empire had seemingly been burned to the ground, a fledgling phoenix of sordid enterprise grew in its ashes. Donning their signature urban-camo tacticals and wielding menacing long-scoped carbines, his Monarchs prowled the facility from up high, surveying the gambling, arm wrestling workforce below like wardens watching over a prison yard. She thought it unlikely anybody in the docks could have missed the mutilated balaener-class coasting through the fission field and lumbering into the maintenance bay. Presumably, the bounty on her crew had already been hastily taken down from the bulletin board. Word traveled fast around these parts, and although the embargoed riffraff would be ignorant as to *why* Delilah's standing with Vidalia had changed so abruptly, they knew that anybody who chose to take arms against the crew of the *Assurance* would do so outside of the law, and more importantly, *against* the will of the Governor.

"Lei-Ghannam," Kahu rasped, directing Delilah's attention with a firm nod to docking bay fourteen. A chilling scene awaited her gaze: eight human-sized mounds covered in bloodsoaked sheets, laid out neatly on the deck like the concrete sleepers of a train track. The ship the freshly executed crew had belonged to stood dormant on its landing pad, a luma-cast screen projected across its boarding ramp noisily displaying the words, NO ADMITTANCE . . . APPROVED FOR DECOMMISSIONING.

"Nate Hesketh's ship," she lamented. "Stubborn fool always did have trouble heeding authority; guess he decided he wasn't gonna dance to Vidalia's tune."

"Bastards made a ruttin' example out of 'em." Kahu forced the words out through his thick mustache, his sullen frown pulling the plumage down over his lips. "Left the poor sods rotting out here to send a message to the rest of us."

"'Come to heel or suffer the consequences,'" she soberly recited. "And the fact that not one of these reprobates has sent so much as a cross word our way means the message has been received loud and clear. Drexen has them too terrified to even step a toe out of line."

On the contrary, not everybody operating out of the docks looked to be cowering in fear of their new masters; some, it seemed, had already begun to reap the benefits of their subjugation. Several vessels whose captains might once have skewed lower in the Guild hierarchy had been allocated new docking bays—ones with priority departure access, better ground support equipment, and more recently renovated landing pads.

Nudging Kahu with her elbow, she said, "Guess we needn't wonder who bent the knee."

The old pilot shook his head in feigned disbelief. "Guild members brown-nosing the Governor, taking bribes from the ruttin' Glow Syndicate—never thought I'd see the day."

"I guess we're not much better; at the end of the cycle, people are only beholden to their principles so long as they stand to benefit from them. For some, this was likely less of a hostile takeover and more like a welcome transfer of power. They know their business can flourish more under Vidalia than it ever could under the stringent watch of Iver Polakorski."

"Soul rest in the Abyss." Kahu cast a harrowed glance at the fission field, no doubt envisioning the moment Drexen's Monarchs tossed that quarrelsome weasel through the shimmering barrier of energy and out into the endless night. An air of concern consumed him. "Are we really buyin' this kumbaya, live and let live act, Skip? Let's not forget it wasn't so long ago the Gov had a hit out on us; how do we really know he ain't plannin' on finishing what those idiot bounty hunters couldn't the second we arrive?"

"Can't say it hasn't crossed my mind, but I trust Tobias had a good rummage around inside Naught's head before the Saber paramedics spirited them away. If this was some plot to lure us in with false promises of accord just to slit our throats, I think he would have picked something up and given us fair warning."

Kahu pawed at his upper arm as if suddenly besieged by a swarm of ants. "Upperdecks is a brave kid. Wouldn't catch me *abstaining renaissance* or whatever with old scar-face, especially after that run-in down in the Ventral Launch Facility . . . That's one bad bug."

Ain't no such thing as a bad cohabitor, Teo's voice chirped in her mind. *Just bad ciphers.* In light of Tobias's regaling of Naught's history with Mercy, however, Delilah remained unconvinced . . .

With their intimidating chrome grille guards and pearl black armor plating, three idling raptors guarded the control tower like the growling heads of Cerberus, their sentinel occupants obscured beneath the riot shields mounted to their windscreens. A fourth vehicle parked askew in a bay nearby deviated from the motorcade's warcore aesthetic; Delilah immediately recognized the camion from its squat, trapezoidal profile. Heights had never bothered her all that much, although she usually felt a nervous flutter in her stomach whenever she spotted Transitech engineers in the Canyon, rappelling toward their workstations like spiders descending on strands of web. What the Governor might need with the transport was anyone's guess, although it did not escape her notice that its spacious service compartment and distinct lack of side windows would make it ideal for relocating Nanimonai's brood . . .

The two Monarchs blocking the control tower entrance gave an acknowledging nod, stepping aside to clear the way as she and Kahu approached. The relief stemming from knowing they wouldn't be forced to barter for an audience crumpled to ratcheting apprehension. Because, for better or worse, it meant Vidalia had been expecting them. A squealing platform elevator took the intrepid pair up the tower's main shaft. Delilah gazed through cascading cage mesh into the gloom of the encompassing stairwell, presented with a vertical cyclorama detailing the struggle that had played out as Drexen's Monarchs moved to *evict* the harbor master. Spent plasma cells and shell casings littered the stairs, covered in a film of light-gray dust that was ejected as stray rounds had perforated the perlite aggregate wall cladding during the scuffle. Humming fluorescent tubes robbed the dried blood spattered across the environment of its crimson shine, rendering the sporadic stains a nauseating brown-green.

"Looks like Polakorski's guys didn't go down without a fight," Kahu reasoned, running a finger and thumb along the bristly ends of his mustache. "Packin' some serious heat, too, by the looks of it."

"Damned hypocrite loved nothing more than hounding me about his no firearms policy." Delilah slipped her concussion repeater into its thigh holster, knowing that to openly brandish it in Vidalia's presence would only make his security tetchy. "Threw a hissy fit if he ever saw me on deck carrying Old Greta, here. And to think he was sitting on his own personal armory the entire time . . . Guess it didn't help him much in the end, though."

The elevator juddered to a stop as it reached the control tower's observation cabin. In that instant, she felt like live prey being served up on a silver platter—a succulent feast delivered through a trapdoor into an enclosure housing a pack of starved carnivores. The handful of Monarchs stationed at the outward-facing arc of antiquated computer banks suspended their duties to turn and scowl at the arriving pair. She recognized the woman perched uncomfortably by the operations console as one of the mobsters they had encountered at Vidalia's capping plant in the Vestiges—a woman with an ugly crew cut and her left arm encased in a flexi-cast, neck held firmly in position by a repulsor assisted halo brace.

"Boss is in back. Don't keep him waiting," the woman said with surprising equanimity, considering Delilah was partly responsible for her injuries. Even at point-blank range, the concussive force produced by her repeater was intended to be nonlethal, but that didn't mean it couldn't cause significant trauma to the unshielded body. She swallowed nervously, affording a curt nod of thanks as they started for the harbor master's office.

"Hey, Holloway!" Crew Cut bellowed after her, sounding just as brusque as she had over the comm-link when the *Assurance* first attempted to dock. "You idiots got lucky; you know that, right? This armistice between you and the Governor—it's not gonna last. Sometime real soon, you're gonna do something to piss him off, and the moment he gives us the green light, it's open season on you and your crew . . . He won't be sending bounty hunters next time you fuck up: he'll send the Monarchs, and don't think for a second you're gonna get the drop on us like that again."

Delilah showed a tactful smile, and instead of stating the obvious—that the woman hardly looked in any condition for a rematch—simply replied, "Suppose we better stay on our best behavior, then."

Ushering Kahu forward, she directed her stare through the cabin's sloped windows and out into the bustling docks. In the distance, she spied the elegant contours of the *Assurance*'s upper fuselage; normally, catching just a glimpse of her mobile haven made her heart swell with fond appreciation, but as her consternated gaze fell on the maintenance bay engineers, who had begun mobilizing their equipment in defiance of their implicit instructions, she felt herself sent into a mild panic. "We're running out of time . . . Put on your mean face and let's get what we came for."

The last eyes she expected to meet upon entering the office were those of Eamon Wyatt. The sight of the marshal, perched casually on the edge of Polakorski's faux-stone executive desk, triggered a dizzying rush of endorphins, launching her low spirits to near stratospheric heights. Unsteady on her feet, she lumbered across the room and threw her arms around his shoulders, inhaling an oddly comforting cocktail of musk and stale cigarette smoke as she buried her face in his neck.

"Damn, Lilah," he mumbled into the mountain of black curls smothering his rugged face. "It's good to see you too!"

She held him at arm's length, studying his reflective-orange coveralls with a cocked eyebrow. "Little long in the tooth to be switching up careers, aren't you? Guess this explains what that old service camion is doing parked out front."

"Hiding in plain sight, so the sayin' goes." He fiddled absently with one of the carabiners clipped to his Transitech-issue safety harness. "I'm guessing you caught the footage of my casterblade debut? After that whole clusterfuck at Zelos Arena, I decided I needed to do a better job of keepin' my nose clean. There's nobody in the Upperdecks folks pay less attention to than a guy in high-vis duds."

She moved her hand to the back of his neck and gave it an appreciative squeeze. "I'm just glad you're OK. When I saw how hard Phalanx were coming after you, I feared the worst."

The marshal regarded Kahu with a stern nod as the old pilot entered, then returned his gaze to Delilah. "You don't need to worry about me,

Holloway—*or* the mutt, which I know you are, cuz I can see that soppy look in your eye. We're both fine . . . It's you and that crew of yours I want the sitrep on. How are you holdin' up? Been a helluva rough ride from what I've heard."

She blew an exasperated lip trill, dropping her shoulders. "Exhausted, rattled, but alive and accounted for . . . The *Assurance* on the other hand—well, she's seen better days, no thanks to *this* asshole."

She motioned toward the L-shaped couch occupying the farthest corner of the stiflingly drab space. Vidalia Drexen lay in coffin-pose atop its longest section, soaking the rayon upholstery in the sweat pouring from his exposed neck and shoulders. The trauma vest fastened around his torso was, to her limited knowledge, capable of performing everything from defibrillation to emergency thoracentesis in the event of a collapsed lung. A drip stand stood at his side, intravenously administering fluids and painkillers into his right forearm, which she traced up his glistening bicep to his protruding, misshapen clavicle bone, wincing at the sight of the red-purple abrasions blemishing the surrounding skin. Reports of the Governor's death had, as they say, been greatly exaggerated, but by no means had he come out of the battle for the Mouth unscathed. She cast her thoughts back to the Composer's address, recalling the certainty with which Jyn Sato had declared victory over her nemesis, and wondered whether the woman had merely been bluffing, or if she was, in fact, unaware that he had survived.

"I am awake, Captain Holloway." Vidalia's low voice didn't quite carry the same gravitas as it usually did. "I may have found myself unexpectedly indebted to you but that does not give you cause to brazenly run your mouth in my presence. Many have deigned to slander me over the years and only a fortunate few still draw breath."

Eamon flashed a mischievous grin. "Welcome to the club; we're *very* exclusive."

Vidalia's face turned ash-gray at the remark. He shook his head, looking less like a ruthless kingpin and instead, cutting the image of a disillusioned teacher reaching the end of his wick with a trying student. Delilah had never thought the man capable of appearing quite so defeated. Perhaps, in some small part, she had unwittingly bought into the fallacy of his demigod reputation. Seeing him now for what he really was—a wounded, enervated man of mere flesh and blood—she hated herself to the core but couldn't stem the pity the sight of him kindled in her.

"So," she began, joining Eamon's side but keeping her eyes trained on the Governor. "You finally found out what it feels like to get your ass kicked?"

Vidalia strenuously maneuvered onto his side to face her, repressing a grunt of agony. "One does not attain status such as mine without suffering defeat, Captain. It is how we come back from our failures that define us. I have had to rebuild my house before, and rest assured, this time will be no different."

"What's the damage? Gotta be honest, you look even worse than my ship, and that's saying something since those hapless idiots you hired to hunt us down riddled her with holes."

She elected to ignore the *told you so* glance Eamon fired in her direction. *The only way anybody leaves Drexen's inner circle is in a body bag*, he had once told her; infuriatingly, it seemed more and more that he may have been right.

Vidalia swung his legs off the edge of the couch and, with some effort, pushed himself to his feet. He collected a red, syn-silk robe from the armrest and slid the garment over his shoulders, swatting his visitors out of his way as though they were bothersome flies while shuffling to the desk, pulling the drip stand with him.

"Multiple abdominal contusions," he intoned, collapsing into the conference chair and steepling trembling hands on the desktop—an attenuated echo of his prior self. "Mild traumatic pneumothorax, several broken ribs, extensive tissue damage, and a fractured collarbone."

Eamon grimaced. "Lei-Ghannam. They try an' beat information out of you with a sack of bricks or something?"

"If you think me so feckless as to afford my enemies an opportunity to interrogate me, then you are severely underestimating my strategic capacity." He turned his head to better display the neural implant dug like a minuscule mosaic of blue-green tiles into his scalp at the base of his skull. "There are fail-safes in place to ensure such could never be the case." The unspoken sub-context: *This little chip will fry my brain when I utter the kill switch code if I deem death my only viable course of action.* "Needless to say, my injuries were self-inflicted but completely necessary to escape captivity . . . It appears the Composer found a way to weaponize my own defenses against me. I cannot speak with absolute certainty, but I believe it had something to do with the dissemination signal."

"Hybridized tech," Eamon suggested in a *been there, done that* tone of voice. "They just used the same trick to coerce the grennies at the compound into blowin' a mountain-sized hole through the blockade."

"I have been adequately apprised of the situation . . . Whatever their means, the zealots boarded my yacht, slaughtered all personnel bar Naught and myself, and held us at gunpoint on deck . . . The Composer made it clear she meant to execute us; we had no choice but to jump."

Delilah tripped over her words in mild shock. "As in . . . jump over the edge . . . of your yacht? Abyss! That must have been . . . what, an eight-hundred-meter fall? How are you even alive right now?"

Vidalia gave a sullen nod in the direction of his fearsome protector—the grievously injured cohabitor crumpled on the floor like a jagged pile of iridescent shale, masked in shadow beneath the array of wall-mounted panels relaying various security feeds from throughout the docks.

"Were it not for my companion, here, I would assuredly be dead. Naught shielded me when one of the fanatics opened fire on us, then took the brunt of the impact following our death-defying leap for survival."

Seeming ambivalent to aer human company, the alien was in the process of *repairing* the damage sustained to aer legs and carapace. An open canister of pulp stood at aer side, which ae periodically dipped aer paw into before scooping helpings of the conflagrant spume stored within up to aer mandibles. Ae would chew, swallow, and then secrete a viscous resin that scintillated like liquid bronze back into aer cupped paw. The substance was then smoothed into the grizzly tessellation of cracks etched across aer exoskeleton as they gradually formed aer disfigured lower half back into shape. Mercy had once suggested that the Prey's capacity for healing themselves could often seem miraculous by human standards—that there was little short of complete dismemberment they couldn't mend themselves. *A necessary evolutionary mechanism for a species to whom an inability to move means certain death.* The coveted Höllengarten pulp was not only a source of nutrition but had astounding medicinal and surgical properties too. *Guess they don't call it the Savior for nothing.*

Summoning surprising courage, Kahu took a few measured steps toward Naught and cordially offered his hand, eyeing the lethal-looking switchblade prosthetic replacing the arm that had been brutally—if inadvertently—amputated during their last meeting.

"Whaddya say, bug. No hard feelings?"

Naught wrenched aer head in the old pilot's direction, then set a flashbang off behind aer eight domino eyes—or at least, that's what it looked like: a single blinding strobe, doubtless accompanied by a welter of empathic unpleasantness that seemed to knock Kahu back with physical force. He reeled, rubbing his temples. "Guess you're still feelin' a little tender about it . . . I can respect that." He made a beeline for Polakorski's crystal decanter, which sat atop a lateral file cabinet among a metal garden of miniature ship sculptures, the representation of a balaener-class hauler notably absent from the collection . . .

"You'll have to forgive my associate," said Vidalia. "Aer cipher was killed during the Composer's assault; as you can imagine, ae's in no mood for civility."

Delilah noted the irony of the fact that Naught had been fortunate enough to find *two* resonant partners in aer life and that both of them were now dead. *Can't imagine ae's that torn up about it; ae goes through ciphers like Eamon does those disgusting packets of synthesized jerky.*

"Indeed, today is a day of great loss for the both of us." The pain broke through Vidalia's stoic affectation once more; he carefully readjusted the trauma vest, gritting his teeth. "There are more than just physical wounds that we must recuperate from."

"Look at you." Delilah felt a note of frustration at the level of concern betrayed in her cooing voice. "Why didn't you have the Saber paramedics take you to one of their facilities; Abyss, even just let them drop you off at Aegis? Your injuries could kill you if they aren't properly tended to."

"If the Composer believes me dead, then I would be a fool to do anything to disabuse her of that notion. The blockade has fallen, and there is now nothing preventing her militants from entering NTU sovereignty with the stream of refugees. I cannot allow myself to be seen anywhere her assassins might find me." He swiveled his seat ninety degrees to face the panels, the rigid angles of his sculpted face highlighted by the monochrome security feeds. "And I cannot rebuild the syndicate from a hospital bed. I need to remain here to oversee operations, to cement my position by forging new alliances, and to maintain order while society conspires to disintegrate around us."

"I see." She folded her arms in a show of insolence. "Weren't interested in forging alliances with Polakorski, or Nate Hesketh's crew, though, I take it?"

She watched Eamon recede into himself as he mulled the insinuation over in his mind. *You're supposed to be a ruttin' enforcer,* she imagined him scolding himself. *And here you are tryna curry favor with a man who has more blood on his hands than the idiot who flipped the switch at the Europa Laboratory.* She didn't know yet what cause Wyatt had to be playing nice with the Governor. Given the whole of Phalanx were hunting him for a murder with which he *obviously* had no involvement, she suspected that, much like her, he simply had no other option . . .

"I will not tolerate you casting aspersions." Vidalia managed to claw back a measure of composure, restoring the sonorous timbre to his voice and biting the ends off each word with staccato elocution. "It was never my intention to take the docks by force; those who opposed us were given ample opportunity to surrender peacefully. I regret that violence was necessary, but unfortunately, there were a number of individuals who made it unavoidable."

"Don't regret it enough to give them a proper burial though, ey?" Kahu bluntly remarked, knocking back the dregs of the amber liquid he had poured into one of Polakorski's tumblers. "Nate Hesketh's posse mighta been a bunch of morons but they sure didn't deserve to get left out there for the maggots like that."

"The uncomfortable truth, Wing Commander Heperi, is that sometimes, to show mercy, one must show strength. There are many ways to prevail upon the mind of a dissenter: some listen to reason, others respond to . . . financial persuasion, and then there are those who will only respond to force. By setting a *clear* precedent with a small, vocal minority, we can circumvent a great deal of bloodshed: forfeit the lives of a few to spare the lives of many." Vidalia set virulent eyes on Delilah, visibly losing his patience. "Is *this* why you and Mister Heperi came to see me, Captain: to lambast me; to cast doubt over my methods and paint me as some barbaric conqueror? Because I will remind you that it was only thanks to Naught's decisive action and *my* forgiveness that the bounty on your ship and crew has been lifted."

"And I'll remind *you* that the only reason you're even breathing right now is because I chose not to purge the airlock with you two still inside, which believe me, I gave serious consideration!"

Eamon positioned himself between the pair, raising a placating palm to each of them. "Easy, easy! I know there's been trouble in paradise between you two recently but let's all just take a breath."

She forcefully batted his hand away. "What's gotten into you, Wyatt? For as long as I've known you, Vidalia Drexen—the Governor of the Mouth—has been number one priority on your hit list, and all of a sudden you're his damned-Abyss lap dog?"

"What's gotten into me is that the war I've been beatin' the drum about for six months is finally here! Don't get me wrong: Drexen and me still got plenty of bones to pick with one another—a whole goddamn skeleton's worth—but this is a highly fluid situation, and now ain't the time to be makin' enemies of each other . . . Way I see it, the three of us got one thing in common: there's a whole bunch of bad actors from various organizations who wanna see our heads on spikes. There'll be time to tear each other's throats out later; right now, we gotta sink our differences, cuz believe you me, we got bigger fish to fry."

Delilah took a steadying breath, unfolding her arms in resignation as she met Vidalia's stare. "The reason we came to see you was to call in a favor."

"Favor?" the Governor repeated sourly. "Our debt is settled, Captain Holloway. I should think funding the very costly refit of your hauler is the only *favor* I owe."

"Those maintenance bay engineers are gearing up for a forced entry; they're starting repairs soon whether we're ready or not, which is worrying considering we have yet to deal with our *stowaway* problem."

Eamon flashed her a quizzical look. "It's a long story," she groused. "Short version is that our new cabin boy decided to smuggle the entire residency of Juniper Sanctuary onto the *Assurance*. He made a deal with your ex–head deputy agreeing that we'd find a place to shelter them bowside in exchange for interim repairs."

"Wait a second." Sudden unease pulled at the tired lines of Eamon's face. "Tobias and Jyn met? You mean . . . in person?" The marshal may as well have spoken his next thoughts aloud for how effortlessly Delilah could read them in his perturbed countenance. *If—as hyper-resonants—the pair bonded with one another, then what poison did the Composer pour into the boy's head?* It wasn't unreasonable to say that Tobias had a tendency for diving straight in at the deep end of causes he didn't fully understand, as evidenced by his short-lived involvement with Humanity First. Would one brief encounter with Jyn be all that was required to convince Tobias of the righteousness of her mission; to leave him with a sudden and implacable desire to *quell the dissonance*? It hadn't seemed that way back on the ship—his focus had been on the junies and little else—but if the Composer had planted a vengeful seed in his mind, then how long before it began to germinate?

"So, to be perfectly clear . . ." For a man recovering from severe trauma, Vidalia seemed awfully amused with himself. "You are asking me to provide shelter for these poor, unfortunate children here in the docks? While I certainly sympathize with their plight, Captain, this is no interspecies day care I am operating."

"No," she dryly corrected. "Leaving the vulnerable orphans with the bloodthirsty crime boss was *not* what I had in mind, funnily enough . . . What we need is transport—*discreet* transport, so we can get them out of Lower Amidships without garnering *unwanted* attention, then ferry them somewhere safe where we can lay low until all this insanity blows over." She met Eamon's eyes, letting a coy grin pinch the corners of her lips. "Although having seen that service camion out front, I'm starting to wonder if I'm asking the wrong person . . ."

The marshal gave a nod. "Gotcha covered, Holloway. Me and Abe are holed up in a disused tram maintenance depot a few kilometers up the Canyon. Ain't exactly a five-star bed-and-breakfast, mind you, but so far, it's served us pretty well in stayin' out of the limelight."

"Tobias suggested taking them up to his father's apartment in the Central Business District."

He thinned his lips and shook his head. "*Atherton* Edevane is presently recovering from an abdominal stab wound that he sustained when two hired mercs tried to zero him along with his daughter. From what I can tell, it was meant to look like a swoopjacking gone south; luckily, me and Abe got there in the nick of time and managed to stop the worst from happening." He held her dumbstricken gaze for a moment and then, mimicking her earlier utterance of the words, said, "It's a long story; short version is that after your crew fished Hazel Edevane out the black, it became clear as crystal she wasn't meant to survive the ambush that wiped out the rest of her squadmates. Her version of events doesn't exactly match up with how the NTNN are spinning things, which is causing *someone* higher up the food chain a whole heap of problems—enough to warrant the government-sanctioned assassination of the girl *and* her old man."

Vidalia cleared his throat to interject himself into the conversation. "Before you arrived, Captain, the marshal was giving counsel on the troubling state of affairs concerning Administrator Vargos and Admiral Coombs's possible ties to Harmony."

Delilah saw Kahu's ears prick up at the mention of the admiral. He returned the model condor he had spent the last few minutes poring over back to its place on the file cabinet, taking a gradual step into the fold.

"It's just like I told you," Eamon said. "Harmony, the uprising—it all comes down to one thing: the development and replication of hybrid tech, which the Administration can use to subdue and oppress the cohabitor population. Courtesy of Jyn's ciphered partner, Absence, Coombs has a few new tools in his inventory—nominally, kestrel fighters spliced with *Devourer* tech. What happened to Hazel was nothin' but a weapons test—old Jasper wanted to see how his abominations would fare against trained NTSC pilots. Now, the true story's at risk of gettin' out, and he'll kill *anyone* to stop that from happening. That includes the councilman and his daughter, so we should assume Tobias is in danger by extension. Letting him go home right now would be putting him at serious risk."

"You're sayin' Coombs sacrificed his own pilots?" Kahu grumbled. "Kids—fresh outta flight academy; just to see these Frankenstein-fighters of his in action?"

"All I've got is testimony right now, sir, but I'm afraid it's certainly lookin' that way."

Kahu dropped his simmering gaze to the floor, curling his upper lip in contempt. "Guy's as cold-blooded as they come. Used to call him Coroner Coombs on account of the fact that he lost more pilots during the Expansion than any other wing commander in the history of the NTSC . . . Bastard would be at airlock burials three times a week, lookin' like a medal case in his ceremonials with his white gloves, dishin' out those cookie-cutter eulogies without showin' even a shred of emotion . . . Never faced any disciplinary action, of course. He just kept climbin' those ranks on the bodies of all the kids he sent to their graves, and now he's the admiral . . . What a ruttin' injustice."

Delilah never took Heperi for a jealous man, but it was hard to miss the bitterness inherent in how he spoke of his old wing commander—an abiding envy, perhaps, at how disparate life had ended up for them both. Maybe, had events panned out differently, Kahu would have been the admiral, and Jasper the broken veteran with nothing to show for his service but a tattered blazer and paralyzing PTSD.

"So, you understand," Eamon began, "just how serious it is when I tell you this man is covertly seizing control of the *Novara*. Folks are so concerned about what's happening at the blockade that no one's payin' any attention to the shitstorm brewin' in Chennai Plaza and Quarterdeck. Coombs has all but officially dissolved the council and has assumed direct control of the Phalanx. Make no mistake, the man is a dictator, and the *Novara* is under martial law in all but name."

"I too have had my fair share of run-ins with the admiral over the years," Vidalia put in. "And I can attest to your assessment of his character. I do not believe he will take kindly to my stewardship of this facility. He deplores the freedoms the Captain's Guild has been afforded to operate independently from the union over the decades. It is my belief that he will take advantage of the present disarray and attempt to take the docks by force, claiming them under the banner of the NTSC and transforming them into a military installation." Vidalia strenuously rose to his feet, pressing wide fingertips down on the desktop and leaning forward with contemplative poise. "It would appear that, once again, Marshal, we have a mutual enemy . . . Can I trust that this time I will have your *full* cooperation in formulating a strategy to deal with him?"

Eamon shrugged. "Honestly, Gov—bad blood aside—I don't think we can afford *not* to cooperate."

"And what of yourself, Delilah? We have both given reason enough to despise each other. Would you be open to burying the hatchet; moving forward with complete transparency?"

"I'm in the same boat," she despondently answered. "Don't really have any other choice. Sinclair and Kern knew we had a cohabitor aboard when they came for us, which means we've lost any sway we once held over the guild . . . People liked Jonah, they respected him, and now everyone knows that I was involved in his death, *and* the death of his shit-stain brother, for that matter. We've suddenly found ourselves becoming the pariah of the docks; even if you hadn't sent bounty hunters after us, it would have only been a matter of time before one of these mouth breathers took the initiative themselves . . . Ironically, you running this cesspit suits us well—it's the only way we have any hope of keepin' the *Assurance* skyborne . . . So, we'll swear fealty, kiss the crown jewels—whatever you need to trust that you have our full compliance . . . But, this?" she made an all-enveloping gesture with her hands. "This *thing* between you two and Admiral Coombs—it's got nothing to do with us. We're a welding outfit, and that's precisely where our focus is gonna be from here on out: no smuggling, no illicit salvage, no taking stands against terrorist cells or authoritarian regimes. We don't want to be in contract or in any way indentured to you. Give us fuel, a docking bay, and we'll make sure the hull holds firm, but we've got no interest in fighting a war."

She caught a look from Kahu that said, *Speak for yourself; I'm all in, sister.*

You're off my crew, Old Man; remember? That means you don't get to dictate what I do with it.

Only minutes prior Heperi had been ready to ship out and enjoy his retirement, but now, his hardened face carried conviction. His miserable, defeated bearing had been replaced by that of a man who had decided he had the mother of all scores to settle . . .

TWENTY

obias followed Teodora as she completed several furious laps around the *Assurance*. She finally ran out of steam and came to a stop just outside the helm-access airlock, resting her back against the safety railing of the docking bay's swinging arm boarding gantry.

"*Just scenery*," she seethed, staring distantly as she wrung her beautiful, blue plait with her hands. "Can you believe that? . . . Five years I've been on this ship: five years toleratin' his foul temper and drunken pigheadedness; listenin' to never-ending war stories about the glory days while patchin' him up in the med cubby . . . After all that history, he just shrugged us off . . . Shrugged *me* off . . . like . . . like I was an empty bottle of syn-rum."

Tobias swung around to her right side, breaking his line of sight with one of the engineers waiting near the entrance to the maintenance hangar—a burly woman stewing impatiently in the operator's cabin of a load lifter, craning her neck in a less-than-subtle attempt to catch their attention.

"I'm not sure how much of that he meant," he reassured, feeling the woman's eyes boring into the back of his head. "I've been around behavior like this all my life; Kahu and my father are two very different people—that much goes without saying. But there's one thing they definitely share in common: a complete and utter inability to process emotion in a healthy or rational way . . . I remember in the weeks following my mother's death, Dad was like a tornado: storming around the apartment day after day, slamming doors, and screaming at my sister and me for the most trivial things. I was terrified, confused, but it was only because I didn't understand."

Teo's sparkling eyes urged him to continue. "Understand what?"

"That anger was his way of coping with loss; he'd sooner give into fury than confront the excruciating pain losing my mother caused."

Teo pressed a finger against her full lips in thought. "So, you're suggesting Heperi might be a little more torn up about this than he's lettin' on?"

"I don't think you need to be a cipher to deduce that. Acting belligerent, aloof, pushing away those he cares about, keeping you at arm's length—I suspect it's probably easier than acknowledging how heartbreaking leaving the *Assurance* is for him . . . Just like my father: outrage is familiar, comfortable, whereas grief—that's something not even an NTU councilman, nor a veteran wing commander of the NTSC, are equipped to deal with."

Teo spun around and eagerly scanned the main concourse, no doubt searching the undulating throng for Mr. Heperi's battle-worn face and limestone dreadlocks. Tobias imagined that had she spotted him, she might have bounded like a puppy down the boarding gantry and sprinted toward him, launching herself into his arms while hurling a litany of insults, as was her way. Instead, she turned her shoulder, showing a subtle frown of disappointment. "Save for Hiroki, Kahu's the closest thing I ever had to a father; ain't *that* a depressin' thought?"

"And just like everyone else on the Coalescence, he isn't going anywhere. He may have chosen to take a different avenue in life but that doesn't mean you'll never see him again. The *Novara* is a big ship, but it's just a ship, which means he can never be too far out of reach."

She smiled, then wrinkled her nose in irritation at the fact that he had made her smile. *I'm still mad at you*, were the words left hanging in the air, but she swept away her misgivings and slipped her hand through the gap between his arm and torso, burying her head into his chest. He tucked his nose into her hair, savoring the strangely enchanting redolence of mango and hydrogen fuel blessing his nostrils. He didn't want the moment to end but had to cut the embrace short due to the stab of pain arriving in the meat between his ribs. He winced, reached into the inside pocket of his bomber jacket, and produced the Cassiopeia hood ornament that he had taken as tender during earlier trade negotiations. He chuckled fondly, holding the curved chrome arrowhead in his palm. "From my little merchant friend."

Teo took the object and brought it up to her eye level for closer inspection. "Taken a real shine to you, hasn't ae? Have you thought about asking aer name?"

He shook his head. "We're struggling to read each other. I'm not sure ae has developed the resonant capabilities to bond with a human yet. Even when communing with a hyper-resonant like me, there seems to be a degree of . . . *integration* required in the forging of an interspecies bond that ae still hasn't quite got the knack of . . . We'll keep trying, though." He furrowed his brow introspectively. "In all the years you were at Juniper Sanctuary, did Hiroki ever try anything like sign language with the Prey in his care? The way the little merchant offers aer paw out expectantly, and the gesture of greeting

Null gives me any time we see each other after an extended period—it strikes me there's a rudimentary form of nonverbal communication that they already seem proficient at." Of course, he felt fairly certain he already knew the answer from the brief time he had spent scouring Nanimonai's resonant essence, but as always, he would relish Teo's insight into the matter.

"How many times I gotta tell you?" She tossed the hood ornament, giving him little forewarning to fumblingly pluck it out of the air. "Their brains just ain't wired the same as ours. Linear communication in any form—it's like trying to force a circle through a square hole—nails on a chalkboard . . . You already know what it's like inside the mind of a cohabitor: it's a crazy nebula of emotion, imagery, and experience. Funneling all that noise into a coherent stream, whether written, signed, or spoken—it just don't vibe very well with their cerebral anatomy . . . As for that greeting they do—paw to their thorax and then motioning toward yah—they don't greet each other that way; they do it mainly for *our* benefit. In the aftermath of the Collision, they needed a way to let nonresonant humans know they meant no harm. It came out of pure necessity—a way to avoid conflict that I guess just stuck ever since."

Tobias turned his attention inward to sift through Null's memories, searching for any relevant data on the subject. He followed a pertinent strand as though navigating a cave devoid of light by nothing but guide rope, soon arriving at an especially frustrating period during aer time studying in the Magnanimous Hollow. The techno-shaman known as Absence had, through great personal sacrifice and tribulation, mastered an elementary understanding of human programming languages, necessitated by aer unswerving dedication to furthering the development of hybridized technology. Ae had endeavored to pass this coveted knowledge down to aer students, but like the others, Null had struggled to perceive any meaning behind the alien scrawlings and attempting to do so had been a downright onerous affair. Conveying information through straight lines and rigid syntax, translating complex ideas through such a limited arsenal of predetermined symbols that couldn't be augmented or inflected to suit aer ever-fluctuating essence—these things were almost tortuous to a mind that aspired to swell and break free of any restraints imposed upon it. Ae yearned to sing silent melodies and bask in the euphony of others. And human language—as much as ae had sought to reach an understanding with the fleshy aliens—had only served to stifle aer voice.

"Null had a rough time of it as an adolescent," he suggested, pulling himself out of reverie. "I can see how subjecting them to it in their infancy could be problematic—perhaps even seriously damaging to their empathic development."

"Exactly," Teo concurred. "Things are turbulent enough as it is without tryna push completely foreign concepts onto 'em. We just gotta find other ways to understand one another."

He returned the hood ornament to his pocket, careful to angle its spear tip away from his torso. "Well . . . As soon as my little merchant friend and I figure out how to maintain a stable connection, it'll be my honor to ask aer name. Although, honestly, there's one tradition I'm hoping we might be able to break."

"Which is?"

"This convention of ciphers naming their resonant partners based on however they translate the concepts of 'nothing,' or 'nobody.' Cohabitors seem to think so little of themselves—even just the simple act of referring to their kind as the Prey—it seems so horribly self-deprecating. I don't understand why they're so Abyss-bent on putting themselves down like that."

Teo gave a sorrowful shrug. "I guess being hunted to near extinction and then factory farmed for an eon will do that to you."

"None of us live the lives our ancestors did a thousand years ago. How can they ever hope to thrive or progress if they're stuck in the mentality of a species permanently in survival mode? It ends now; the cohabitors I've bonded with so far have taught me more than I could ever put into words. I want to return the favor—teach them a little about pride and self-worth. They might have been just prey once, but with the attitudes they're going to face now, nothing is separating them from the reality of Novarian society, it's crucial they know their own value."

"Hello there, friends!" The unknown voice came from the end of the boarding gantry, startling Teo and Tobias to attention. They spun around to find a middle-aged man lingering near the maintenance bay entry gate, regarding them both with an unsettling toothy grin. He wore a stonewashed Henley shirt beneath a long-tailed Corsair's trench coat, and boasted a thick handlebar mustache that could easily rival Mr. Heperi's. His black, shoulder-length hair stopped abruptly in a neat line across the top of his crown, halted in its tracks by the domineering wall of his prominent forehead. Beneath thin, hard-angled eyebrows, a pair of sunken eyes scrutinized them—eyes that, at first glance, seemed kindly enough, but the longer the stranger held them in his gaze, the more Tobias detected a veiled malevolence beneath his comradely demeanor.

Teo flashed Tobias a nervous glance, then acknowledged the man with an upward nod. "Can we help you?"

"As I live and breathe; is that Miss Teodora Brižan?" the man asked with ardor—or at least, in a manner meant to expressly convince them of his starstruck elation. "The salvage specialist who carved those pre-Collision fission field generators out of the wreck of the NTSC *Shinsengumi*—without a scratch on 'em, no less?"

She shrugged her shoulders and tilted her head as if to say, *What's it to you?* then briskly inquired, "Who's asking?"

He performed a clumsy gesture that looked halfway between a bow and a curtsy. "Jorge Almeida. At your service . . . I'm captain of the *Mammon's Avarice*—the tortuga-class cargo runner berthed over in docking bay seven . . . Truth be told, I've been hoping to make your acquaintance for a while now, Miss Brižan."

"Is that so?"

"You bet! I wanted to personally offer my thanks for the stellar job you did retrieving that cache from the outer reaches of the belt. For what those shock compensators sold for on the black market, we're gonna be able to fund several sorely needed upgrades to the *Avarice's* core internals."

"Don't mention it." Teodora showed a thin smile, sidestepping to position herself in front of the entrance to the helm-access airlock, presumably intending to obstruct Almeida's line of sight into the *Assurance*, since hastily sealing the external bulkheads would make it far too obvious they had something to hide. Maybe he was just being paranoid, but Tobias had the distinct sense that Jorge already knew about the nature of the ship's passengers, and had only come to confirm his suspicion . . .

"Is Captain Holloway around?" Jorge boldly started down the boarding gantry toward them, heavy work boots causing the steel scaffolding beneath his feet to rattle and sing. "Was hoping to discuss something with her."

Tobias strode down the gantry and met the man halfway, preventing him from progressing any closer to the airlock. "The captain's gone to meet with the Monarchs. We'll make sure to tell her you stopped by when she returns." He made a show of glancing up at one of the platform walkways overhead from where several armed Monarchs were diligently watching the exchange—a gesture he hoped would indicate the words *Don't try anything stupid.*

"Thing is, this is a matter of some urgency," Jorge replied in a bargaining tone. "We don't really have the luxury of time, here . . . It's the *Avarice*, you see. Before the admiral ordered the lockdown, we were running a shipment of grav panels up to that new topside construction project near Cepheus Tower. Unfortunately, we had a hiccup with our lateral stabilizers while in transit and had to abandon the delivery, which as you well know, puts us in breach of contract with our employer."

Teo repeated that same nonchalant shrug, which in the present context meant, *What's it to us?*

Almeida struggled to repress a frown, vexed, perhaps that his relentless affability had so far been met with little more than borderline disdain. "Well ... Ideally, we could have her patched up and ready to fly by the time the lockdown's lifted. Otherwise, we'll have to subsidize the job to one of our competitors and we'll lose out on the commission. The issue we're having, of course, is that repairs can't commence until the *Assurance* vacates the maintenance bay; what with her oversized wingspan an' all, she's sort of hogging the whole of drydock ... So ... I wanted to come down here—just as a friendly neighbor—to inquire about what's causing the holdup; see if it's something I can't help you with ... It's not concern over the tenure of the on-site engineers, is it? Because let me assure you, Holloway's gonna struggle to find a more skilled group of wrench heads on the *Novara*. I mean ... if you asked me, I'd be inclined to say this old girl is beyond any reasonable economic repair—even still, this crew will do a fine job of getting her spaceworthy again."

Teo clicked her tongue against the inside of her cheek. "Then it's a good job nobody *is* askin' you, ain't it?"

Initially, Tobias struggled to fathom what she hoped to achieve by acting so standoffish—willfully provoking the man, in fact. But then he saw it: the pattern of interlocking rings tattooed on Almeida's neck just below his left ear, partially obscured by his decapitated mullet—a symbol that inspired such dread and revulsion that it may as well have been a festering open wound or some grotesque disfigurement. Its image spawned an uncompromising hatred, although tempered somewhat by the measure of relief stemming from the fact that Jorge didn't seem to know who he was. Either the man's interest in Humanity First was passing at best, or Tobias had neglected his physical appearance so much in the last month and a half that he was barely even recognizable.

Jorge flapped the lapel of his coat in growing irritation. "Now listen here, Miss Brižan. I consider myself a very patient person, but to say that you are testing that patience would be an understatement ... All I'm asking for is a little clarification on what's causing the delay—I don't think that's unreasonable, given the circumstances."

"Reactor failure," Tobias blurted, realizing too late just how little he really knew about ship engineering and having to think on his feet. Jorge glared incredulously at him, then at Teo for confirmation. After a moment of befuddled hesitation, she panically added, "Yep: reactor failure. The housing got cracked when those bounty hunters shot us all to hell. Thing's leaking coolant and Abyss-knows-what-else all over engineering—radioactive material, probably ... Managed to isolate it by sealing off the lower deck, but we gotta cycle the atmosphere before we can let anyone aboard."

Almeida slapped his knee and uncorked a hearty laugh. "Hah! You two are a riot; I can see why Holloway keeps you around. You really expect me to believe she'd have her crew holding down the fort if she had a potential meltdown on her hands? The hazard containment team would've evacuated the whole of the Lower Amidships Docks if that were the case . . . Now, I reckon the best course of action, here, is for you two tykes to quit tryna stall me and let me come aboard. I've always wanted to see the inside of a balaener-class; maybe you could give me the grand tour?"

Teo took a strategic step forward, hand on her hip in stubborn Teo form. Although when she answered, Tobias detected a timorousness in her voice. "Captain won't permit anyone on the *Assurance* without her express say so and, in case you forgot already, she ain't here."

Almeida placed a hand on each of their shoulders, a phony *just looking out for you* expression hewing his countenance. "OK. I'll level with you. The thing is, some of us in the guild have a number of growing . . . *concerns*, shall we say, regarding what—or *who*—it is you're keeping on this old boat that warrants so much secrecy. I just think if you were to let me have a nosy around, check everything's shipshape in there, it might help alleviate some of the tension among the other captains. Rumors can be pernicious things, you know; best to nip them in the bud as quickly as . . ." Jorge's face dropped, his jaw hanging slack as if dislocated from his skull. His stunned gaze fell to the space between Teo and Tobias just as the pair were barged aside by one of the infant cohabitors—specifically, the little merchant. Foolishly, they had left the airlock unattended, leaving the curious scamp free to wander outside to meet their visitor. Isaac and Mercy had agreed to keep the Junies secured in the galley until the captain returned with transport, but clearly, that had been easier said than done . . .

Issuing chirps of intrigue, ae hopped toward the dumbfounded man and crouched down at his feet, staring up with four pairs of asynchronously blinking eyes, head tilted inquisitively. Almeida's sagging features tightened into a cruel smirk, the stage curtains of his mouth drawn open by invisible pulleys and rope. "Well, hey there, buddy. Where'd you come from?"

Lacking the comprehension to differentiate a genuine human smile from one feigned in malice, the little merchant performed the same *no threat* greeting that had come up in earlier conversation. Teo went rigid as she watched the exchange, squeezing the heel of Tobias's hand so hard he was certain he felt something pop. They were flies caught in a web, staring down their arachnid captor as he prepared to liquefy their insides, savoring every moment of watching them squirm.

The cohab brayed softly, lifting aer arm with its underdeveloped chitin plating, unfurling aer paw and offering one of Isaac Verhoeven's crocheted hacky sacks, which ae had presumably found rummaging beneath the furniture in the lounge.

"Is that for me?" Jorge said in a patronizing voice. He took the material pouch and held it to his chest adoringly. "That's mighty generous of you, lil fella." The man shot Tobias a sideways glance that sent a chill down his spine. "So, this is your 'radiation leak,' huh? I can see why Holloway's been so reluctant to let anyone near her ship."

Tobias opened his mouth, but any kind of useful response completely eluded him. This wasn't anything like dealing with Jonah Sinclair, who had been thrown into a murderous rage the second he laid eyes on Nanimonai back at Juniper Sanctuary. At least with Jonah, they had known where they stood from the beginning. In stark contrast, Jorge's reaction to the surprise arrival was tempered, calculated, wheels of machination turning behind eyes charged with devious wit.

Unable to contain her panic, Teo lunged forward and pulled the cohabitor away by the arm, leading aer hurriedly back through the airlock. Tobias backed away slowly to follow suit. Jorge winked, then underhand threw the hacky sack to him, beaming with insidious delight.

"Guess I'll take a rain check on the grand tour . . . You take care now, Tobias Cole Edevane."

Tobias kept his thoughts balanced on a knife-edge as he returned to the others. At no point could he dwell on the terror Jorge Almeida's utterance of his full name had instilled in him, nor his stomach-churning apprehension over what the Captain's Guild would do now they had essentially learned the truth about the *Assurance*'s cargo. The infant Prey were iron filings that would become agitated in the magnetic field of his anxieties, spreading hysteria in ripples to their siblings and making an orderly evacuation of the ship nigh impossible. Teo, of course, didn't seem nearly so interested in staving off chaos; she roiled like a firestorm across the galley to begin unleashing her fury at an unsuspecting Isaac. The engineer had busied himself with the island countertop's luma-surface, sifting through various social feeds filtered by the currently trending echo-tag, LEECHINVASION. Mercy stood beside him with his hand cradled in hers, tensely biting her lip as they watched the luma-cast collage of feather footage scrolling endlessly before them. Images had saturated the Nov-Net from all over Amidships showing cohabitors in droves carrying their lives on their backs, greeted by either vociferous mobs or fleeing stampedes of terrified bystanders as the aliens poured into public spaces—precisely the kind of pandemonium Tobias had feared would take root with such a disorganized translocation.

"One job, Isaac," Teo reproached, waving a hand in front of the engineer's face to command his attention. "One job an' you *still* managed to screw it up!"

Isaac spun around to face her, left hand clinging onto the safety goggles hanging around his neck, just as he usually did when he felt nervous or threatened. "What are you going on about now?"

"Thanks to *you* everyone in the docks is gonna know we're harboring cohabitors on the *Assurance* . . . Captain of the *Mammon's Avarice* was snoopin' around tryna squeeze answers out of us about why Lilah's been stallin' the engineers so long. While he was grillin' us one of the cohab littluns came tumblin' outta the airlock and walked right up to him to say hello! Thought you were supposed to be keepin' an eye on 'em in here?"

"Delilah gave us very clear instructions," he retorted in a measured but suitably defensive tone. "Stay on the ship, don't answer any hails, and don't open the airlock to anybody . . . You tell me which one of us disobeyed her orders."

"Passing the buck as usual! Well maybe if you coulda pried your attention away from Mercy for five minutes you mighta had a little more situational awareness!"

Tobias saw Mercy hastily unclasp her hand from Isaac's, paper-white cheeks flushing red in discomfort. Isaac took it as a sign that Teo had insulted the girl and switched gears into offensive mode. "Shut your mouth, Brižan! You don't know what in the Abyss you're . . ."

"Guys, please, we don't have time for this," Tobias implored, positioning himself in the middle of the standoff. "I don't know what that conniving bastard Almeida is plotting but it's probably not a welcome party. We just have to hope the captain comes back with a transport solution soon and make sure we're prepared for a fast exit when that happens."

Teo twisted her lips in thought, then rolled her eyes, giving Isaac a nod of concession—as close to a handshake as he could expect coming from her. She led Tobias's gaze across to the lounge, where Null and Nanimonai had gathered the junies on piles of Kahu's old mandala tapestries and Turkmen rugs. At first, he put the source of their apparent distress down to the shouting match that had been pummeling their sensitive ears, trembling fearfully as many of them were, with one girl named Charlette—no older than ten—breaking into a fit of tears and reaching out to Nani for comfort. Although he soon realized that, just as Isaac and Mercy had been feeding their emotional turmoil by scouring the social feeds, so too had their audience . . . He followed the collective stare of the interspecies children to the mosaic of mayhem floating in the air above the countertop, each live stream video tile a window into the deeply ingrained prejudices of the citizens of the New Terra Union. He couldn't help but note how jarring it felt to witness the dichotomy of watching grown adults running for their lives at the mere prospect of encountering an alien, to seeing the little girl nuzzling her face into Nanimonai's broad neck while ae tenderly combed aer digits through her hair. It served as confirmation that there was nothing inherent or unavoidable about speciesism, that human-supremacy was by no means natural but had been engendered in the Novarian populace through a century of militant segregation. *Humans may be creatures of habit, but we're also perfectly capable of breaking them, too.*

Teo barged Isaac away from the luma-surface controls and swept her hand across the glass keyboard, minimizing the feed. "Are you tryna traumatize them or somethin'?" she whispered forcefully. "Don't think they've got enough to be scared of without exposin' them to all that bad noise? Now, come on, we've got work to do."

A blaring alarm sounded—not from the speakers embedded throughout the *Assurance*'s fuselage, rather, but from somewhere off in the distance, echoing chaotically as if coming from the far side of the docks and muffled as it struggled to penetrate the ship's hull. Tobias followed Isaac and Teo along helm access to the bridge while Null plodded hastily after them. Ae, like all cohabitors, considered caring for the young a fundamental civic responsibility but ae had aer limits regarding how much playtime ae could withstand. Null sang a silent melody transcribing an eagerness to leave Nanimonai to do aer job and resume aer shipboard duties.

Isaac vaulted into the seat that had once been Kahu's and reached up to hammer a few keys on the overhead instrumentation panel, summoning just forward of the helm a luma-cast projection of the bulletin board—the dock's Nov-Net integrated central directory for job listings, departure slot allocation, and general operations info. Teo barreled straight through the intangible screen of light, hurrying to the windshield for a more immediate assessment of the situation.

"Some kinda commotion goin' on a few docking bays down," she reported. "A fire, maybe—I'm not really sure. Looks like Capella Promenade over there—all I can see is strobe lights and flashing warning banners; folks runnin' round like a bunch of headless chickens."

"Control just issued a general alert," Isaac said, glow-clouded eyes like Calacatta marble searching the reams of data floating before him. "Probable hazard containment failure in docking bay seven."

Teo and Tobias met each other's stare, sharing a look of grim recognition.

"Getting a little more info now," Isaac continued. "The crew of the *Mammon's Avarice* are reporting potential reactor failure—possible radiation leak. If that's true, then it won't just be *us* evacuating: it'll be everyone in the docks."

"There's no way that's a coincidence," said Tobias.

"Of course, it's not!" rasped Teo. "It's bullshit! That Almeida sonofabitch is just tryna mess with our heads."

"Care to elaborate on how you know this isn't legit?" Isaac demanded, uncertainty creeping into his voice. "Because if you're wrong, we could be paying a pretty hefty price for calling their bluff."

"Ain't got time to elaborate; you just gotta trust us. Don't know if this is supposed to be a message or perhaps some kinda warning—whatever it is, it means the Captain's Guild just named us public enemy number one."

Null gave a forceful huff from aer breathing holes to grab the others' attention. Ae pointed up through the windshield at the Monarch sentries stationed above, who had now begun a full-pelt sprint along the overhead platform walkways to investigate the source of the disturbance, leaving the *Assurance* and her crew unguarded.

"No. Not a warning." The words coldly left Tobias's lips but were the product of Null's train of thought. "It's a distraction. The alarm was meant to lure the guards away and leave us vulnerable . . . And it looks like it worked."

He joined Teo beyond the helm and watched as crews began spilling out of their docking bays and heaving toward the docks' pedestrian exit. But then, like a school of salmon swimming upstream, he spotted a group of individuals moving against the grain of the crowd—fifteen, maybe twenty men and women in standard ship wear, gradually making their way toward the maintenance bay's entry gate.

"Jen-Jang," Teo hissed—an Old-Earth expletive, picked up from the housefather and used occasionally to describe particularly stressful situations. "Jorge Almeida's on his way back, and this time he's bringin' a little extra muscle." She spun around to face Isaac, her comely features kissed by the cyan glow of the bulletin board projection. "Are you able to retract the boarding gantry remotely or do we need to be dockside to do that?"

"Don't see why not," the engineer replied, pouring over the endless array of touch screens and blinking switches bedecking the main control pedestal. "Just need to connect to the ground services. Let's see . . . Here we go, docking facilities . . . boarding access . . . dismiss . . . aaaand Nebula!"

After a short delay, Tobias spied the gantry in question pulling away beyond the *Assurance*'s nose cone, folding in on itself by its creaking elbow hinge. If Almeida and his ruffians planned to board the ship, then they wouldn't be doing it via the helm-access airlock. Any relief he felt at that revelation proved fleeting at best, as he performed another mental head count and estimated that the mob had now doubled in size, with more hooligans crawling out of the woodwork from seemingly every direction. His heart sank as they made their way through the gate and began lowering themselves from the main concourse down onto the *Assurance*'s recessed landing pad.

"Lei-Ghannam . . . I think they're gonna try and force their way into the cargo bay!"

Teo turned on her heel and made tracks for helm access. "Not if I've got anything to say about it."

"Wait, where do you think you're going?" Isaac called over his shoulder.

"Magma cannon! They wanna get inside, then they better be able to withstand a little heat."

"That's psychotic! You can't just fire molten metal at these people; you're gonna incinerate them!"

She stopped, turning with her hand resting irefully on her hip. "I *can* and *will* do whatever it takes to prevent *any* harm from comin' to those kids . . . If either of you have a better idea, then I'm all ears."

"Maybe . . ." Tobias tentatively began. "Maybe if I could just go and speak to Jorge then we can . . . I don't know, negotiate."

"This ain't some ACS debate, Tobes. Those scumbags mean to kill us; we're a far cry past diplomacy, here."

"I think I'm with Edevane on this one," Isaac added, pulling a pained expression as though the words left an utterly revolting taste on his tongue. "There is such a thing as reasonable use of force, yah know? I'm not sure spraying them with slag is a proportionate response when we don't yet know their intentions."

Teo marched to the helm and reached up to pull a yellow lever on the overhead instrumentation panel. The bulletin board pixelated and dissolved, replaced shortly after with a feed captured by the forward-facing survey cam.

"Rotate one-hundred-and-eighty degrees!"

The ship's computer complied and the infrared image of the maintenance bay hanger panned around to show the neck and breast of the *Assurance*, the frame partially obscured by the out-of-focus shape of the magma cannon emplacement but providing a clear enough view of the intrusion of cockroaches gathering outside the cargo bay door. A number of Jorge's accomplices appeared to have armed themselves with weaponry—a mix of plasma, concussion, and standard projectiles—which, in earnest, failed to strike fear in Tobias's heart; that was done by the sight of the circular saw, gripped in the hands of an engineer now barging his way to the front of the congregation. The man raised the implement up to the ship's exterior plating. White-hot bloom filled the frame as the infrared struggled to process the brightness of the actuating fission-edged blade, scored by the terrible whine of grinding metal that subsequently came scraping and screeching through the *Assurance*'s structure.

"Still need any clarification on what their intentions are?" Teo caustically asked.

Before Isaac and Tobias could shake their heads, the helm lit up with an inbound hail. Tobias moved to the comms console to check the caller's echo-signature, but it was either scrambled or heavily encrypted. He glanced at Teo for permission to accept. She gave an exaggerated sigh as if to say, *Don't see how the situation could get any worse.*

"I told you not to answer any hails!" Holloway's stern cadence filled the bridge, lifting Tobias's spirits on a rising current of relief. The transmission contained no accompanying video packet, displaying only a placeholder Transitech logo with a pulsing audio visualization that danced in response to the captain's voice. "What's your status?"

Teo gave a brief rundown of the situation, tactically omitting the mishap involving Jorge Almeida and the little merchant.

"Understood," Delilah replied. "We're hot on approach with transport. Get Isaac to dismiss the boarding gantry if he hasn't already, then rally everyone to the helm-access airlock. In the meantime, close the lower deck partitions and seal off access between crew quarters and the galley. Create as many barriers between yourselves and the intruders as you can. Hang tight; we'll be with you shortly."

Tobias fell prey to an almost bludgeoning wave of negative emotion as they began the evacuation, soaking up the infant Prey's fear and panic like a sponge dropped in a bucket of filthy water. Beneath the cries of the human kids, boisterous vociferation rose through the floor grating, undercut by the ever-louder shriek of the circular saw as the uninvited guests carved their way closer. Doubtless, they had been slowed by the strategic sectioning of the ship, but it wouldn't be long before the final set of bulkheads failed to contain them.

Mercy and Teo lined the little ones up two by two in the helm-access corridor, assigning each a travel buddy in a fashion that reminded Tobias of countless school trips to the Silk River Concourse. Null and Nanimonai formed a protective wall of organic armor at the rear, shoulder spines twitching as they stared across the galley at the crew quarters entrance. Up front, Isaac tasked himself with opening the airlock's external door; the difference between cabin pressure and exterior pressure threatened to send him plummeting the four-meter fall to the landing pad but, thankfully, Mercy caught him by the arm and prevented him from tumbling out.

Tobias felt frustratingly useless in the midst of all this, keeled over and hyperventilating by Teo's side as he fought to resist the debilitating empathic bombardment. He lifted his head and caught sight of a vehicle scudding over the main concourse from across the docks—the Transitech-branded chariot speeding to their rescue. Whether or not it would reach them in time remained to be seen; sparks erupted in an incandescent fountain from the door to crew quarters, the circular saw's fission-edged blade effortlessly slicing through reinforced steel-plating. With perhaps less than a minute to spare before Jorge Almeida's mob managed to breach the galley, the inbound transport swung into position outside the airlock, industrial repulsor pads howling as they strained to kill the unwieldy vehicle's lateral momentum. The craft's gull-wing door opened vertically, revealing a spacious rear compartment with rows of fold-down jump seats. Tobias wasn't one to look a gift horse in the mouth but couldn't believe Delilah had managed to secure something so suitable for their needs in such a short amount of time. With the stock of her concussion repeater pushed into her shoulder, the captain hopped across the fluctuating gap between the transport and the airlock and began ushering the crew and passengers into the transport. "Get everyone aboard, now! Let's move like we got a purpose!"

A loud *thump* arrived from the galley as an unshapely chunk of metal slid free from the door to crew quarters and fell to the ground. The stifled din of the interlopers became hair-raisingly clear as they flooded like water from a broken dam through the breach. Delilah pushed her way past Null and Nanimonai before unleashing a fusillade of suppressing fire into the nearing marauders. "Get the hell off my ship you low-life cretins!" Concussion energy, of course, was largely ineffective at her current range but served to scatter a number of them into cover. With everyone accounted for, Tobias stood with one foot in the airlock and the other in the transport, hanging from the door's hydraulic strut and reaching a hand out to Delilah. "We're clear, Captain! Let's get out of here!"

Holloway fired a final blast of concussive force, sending one of the more heedless intruders hurtling across the galley and crashing into the island countertop. She sprinted back down helm access then took Tobias's hand and leaped into the transport's rear compartment. Finally, they were away.

TWENTY-ONE

Tobias could scarcely believe it had only been two months since the Edevanes were last together. The mere passage of time seemed wholly insufficient to reconcile just how drastically their circumstances had changed since Hazel's induction ceremony on Capella Promenade. It felt as though he and his family had fallen through some interdimensional sinkhole, embodying alternate versions of themselves and struggling to acclimatize to their new realities. Eamon Wyatt—a man who seemed to possess an almost preternatural aptitude for being in the right place at the right time— invited Tobias to ride shotgun beside him as they barreled toward his safe house in a presumably stolen Transitech camion. While flying in near-reckless fashion, the marshal—or better put, *ex*-marshal—gave Tobias the rundown on how the nest of corruption metastasizing at the heart of Quarterdeck, which had seen him forced underground after being falsely accused of the administrator's murder, had now similarly embroiled Tobias's sister and father.

"They're safe, for now," the man reassured, casting a glance over his shoulder as he took Annwyn Interchange and slewed into a lane of Canyon traffic, making sure the maneuver didn't throw his largely unsecured passengers around too much in the rear compartment. "Your old man's gonna have a real humdinger of a scar to show off to his buddies at the drivin' range when this is all over. He's been surprisingly receptive to everythin' I've said, but I'm guessin' that's mostly down to the trauma stims I've been administering to help keep him relaxed and comfortable. Probably only got another hour or two before he returns to his haughty, insufferable self—starts screamin' blue murder and demandin' we let him speak to the admiral directly. In our current predicament, that's gonna be a surefire way of gettin' ourselves zeroed . . . Then, of course, there's your sister . . . Hazel was shook up plenty after her brush with the mercenaries: pissed off, more than anythin' I think—that she didn't have the strength to fight back . . . She knows Coombs orchestrated the ambush that got her squaddies killed and was just about ready to raise seven circles of hell about it . . . But then . . ."

"Go on," Tobias urged, listening as intently as he could while wrestling to keep the little merchant from fiddling with the camion's dashboard interface. Utilitarian vehicles such as the one Eamon had procured didn't have the kind of user error fail-safes installed to prevent an unwitting operator from causing an inadvertent drive core stall. One wrong button press and the cohab could send the vehicle and its occupants careening into a fatal, zero-g spiral.

"Well, it's hard to explain," Wyatt continued, "One moment, she seems cognizant, aware—sharp as a tack, in fact. And then the next, she sorta loses her grip on reality. She has these *episodes* where she thinks she can see . . . well, your ma, soul rest in the Abyss—her ghost, I mean to say . . . At first, Miss Edevane was able to discern that the visions are more than likely a teething issue with her implants, but the more they occur, the more she seems utterly convinced poor Tabitha is visitin' us from beyond the grave." Eamon allowed for a long pause before adding, "You don't seem all that surprised, kid. I just told you your big sis' has started seein' dead people; woulda thought you'd be a little more shocked."

"Truth be told, Marshal, I was already semiaware of Hazel's hallucinations," Tobias solemnly admitted. "I went to visit her after you left the *Assurance*, as per your advice. She told me—quite convincingly—that our mother had been to visit her, too. At the time, I had chalked it down to low-level delirium, or as you suggested, a product of some kind of glitch or synaptic growing pains with her cyberware. If her condition has continued to deteriorate, however . . . if . . . if it's true this . . . nefarious *cabal* you speak of has seen fit to mark my entire family, then we cannot simply . . ."

"If your next words were gonna be, *take her back to the rehabilitation ward for a check over*, then no—we categorically cannot . . . I wish I had more solutions for you than problems, Tobias, but we're stuck between a rock and one helluva hard place right now. I have *some* rudimentary medical training, but all this neuroscience stuff—intelligent silicone, vertebral prosthetics, blah blah—hate to say it but it's way beyond my remit. If it transpires whatever's gone wrong poses a threat to her life, then I honestly don't know how we proceed from there."

Hazel's paranormal affliction remained a subject of taboo as Tobias finally reunited with his small, broken but fiercely loyal clan. The situation hung over them like an umbral cloud, none wishing to sully the emotional catharsis of their embrace by deigning to acknowledge the looming squall. As they tearfully held each other in the maintenance depot's long-abandoned staff canteen, surrounded by frumpy furniture, dust-covered refreshment dispensers, and walls plastered with corporate motivational posters, it seemed utterly miraculous that they were all still alive, given the harrowing series of events each of them had endured. It dawned on him that for too long had he taken them for granted, allowing precious seconds in their company to slip through his fingers, and he resolved in that tender instant to cherish every precious moment he had with them going forward.

A lengthy series of introductions followed as he set about acquainting the crew of the *Assurance* with his family. Grievously punctured abdomen aside, Atherton insisted, in his stately way, on standing to greet each of them with a fervid handshake. Captain Holloway had to pry her palm free from the man's grip as he loudly professed his heartfelt gratitude for playing her part in Hazel's rescue. "If there's anything I can do for you, Captain," he blustered. "Refuel vouchers; docking fee waivers for the remainder of the year—anything at all, please don't hesitate to ask." Evidently, the man had forgotten that his status as an elite Novarian citizen, including all associated privileges, had been revoked. Even if he *was* still a councilman, he would have been in hardly any position to promise such endowments.

"Only thing I need from you, Ath," Delilah responded in a measured voice, dissecting his subtly pained expression, "is for you to take a load off before you pass out. I know how unsteady you Edevane men can be on your feet; you look as pale as Tobias did when he figured out he could speak to cohabitors."

Atherton made a crumpled expression that suggested he hadn't really known what "resonant" meant until right this very moment. Tobias had forewarned Hazel about his condition in broad strokes when they last caught up over the luma-caster, but she seemed equally as stricken to hear the news painted in such an indelicate manner.

Holloway showed a coy smirk. "Looks like you three have some catching up to do."

When Teodora giddily planted herself before Hazel, his sister made the fatal error of greeting the salvage specialist with the same formality that had so exasperated the girl when first dealing with him.

"Love the buzz cut, sis!" Teo complimented, swatting away all the *pleasure to meet yous* and *how do you dos?*. She turned her head to the side and wrung her plait through her hands, continuing, "I get so pissed off with brushin' all the knots and tangles outta this big mop of mine; sometimes I think about just sayin' *to Abyss with it* and shavin' it all off . . . Always end up chickenin' out though cuz I worry it won't suit me . . . *You* on the other hand—you're rockin' it!"

"Thank you . . . Although I assure you it was *not* by choice."

Teo shrugged. "When life gives you lemons, slay with a killer haircut, I guess."

Hazel's bristly response was endemic to the Edevane mindset—a concerted effort to treat forward, fawning behavior with provisional mistrust. Their exalted status meant that anyone attempting to ingratiate themselves with unsolicited and unrequited compliments could only be out to somehow benefit themselves. Atherton taught his children to stay alert, on their guard—aloof and impersonal until they could be dead certain as to the intentions of new acquaintances, lest there be some ulterior motive to undermine or otherwise take advantage of them. Teodora's ebullient and irascible personality worked in direct contradiction to that mentality, but Tobias had no doubt that once Hazel understood there was no malice inherent in the mouthian's nature, she would grow every bit as fond of her as he had himself . . .

"I have to say, Miss Edevane," began Captain Holloway. "Considering the state we found you in, it sure is nice seeing you up on your feet . . . How are you holding up?"

Hazel gave a rueful smile, seeming to appreciate the sentiment, even if it were only partially true. "Struggling to . . . adjust . . . to my new situation," she answered, shuffling her weight uncomfortably on the pair of forearm crutches Eamon had recovered from the depot's ancient medical stores. "But alive, thanks to you and your crew."

"Just another day in the office," Kahu gruffed, stepping forward with his thumbs hooked through the belt loops of his breeches. "We're salvagers, after all—retrieving valuable nuggets from the empty black is what we do for a living."

Tobias felt sorrow roil in his chest as he noticed just how much effort Hazel had to expend to salute the old veteran. Standing just behind her, he saw the succession of soft-white LEDs buried beneath the opaque silicone of her spinal prosthetic pulse gently, the severed connection between her mind and body bridged by way of her cybernetic implants. With such invasive bodily augmentation, he supposed there had to be a level of tolerance for certain technical hiccups, but when said hiccups threatened to erode the very bedrock of his sister's sanity, he had to wonder if even one was too many . . .

"Wing Commander Heperi! Sir!"

"At ease, cadet," the man laughed, heartily returning the salute.

"It's an honor to meet you, sir. Your six-degrees-of-freedom thresher maneuvers are legendary in the corps; stars, they're still simulating some of your combat scenarios in flight academy."

Kahu nudged Delilah's arm, giving a self-congratulatory wink. "See, Skip? *Told* you it was me that wrote the rule book."

Hazel nodded eagerly. "That you did, sir. I even wrote my dissertation on your analysis of interceptor nonballistic astronautics and *Devourer* defensive capabilities—As across the board."

"Glad to hear the curriculum hasn't slipped . . . I think, given the circumstances, though, it should be *me* callin' *you* 'sir.' The marshal gave us the debrief on the skirmish you had with those unknown bogeys; goin' up against interceptor maneuverability and NTSC firepower combined like that—comin' out alive, no less—not sure I coulda pulled it off, even way back in my heyday."

Tobias had been heartened to see some of the passion and zeal returned to his sister's constitution, but Kahu's mention of the incident only served to sap that second wind straight back out of her. Watching her bearing sink, the old pilot formed a grave expression and affirmed, "We're gonna get him, sis—Admiral Coombs. I've had my gripes with him since way back before the Antonelli Expansion, and believe you me, we're gonna make that rotten bastard pay for what he did to you an' your wingmates."

"Okay!" Delilah breathily interjected, clapping her hands in a *let's wrap this up* fashion. "That's enough outta you, big guy . . . C'mon, Nanimonai's got aer hands full out there; let's go and see if we can't offer any assistance."

Another surfeit of confusion swept across Hazel and Atherton's faces as Kahu and the captain took their leave, both no doubt pondering who this Nanimonai person was and with what exactly they had their hands full. Eamon had suggested that their knowledge concerning current events remained limited, since any Nov-Net-enabled personal devices could be used by the conspirators seeking their *eradication* to hunt them down. At the very least, they knew about the demolition of the blockade and the escalating violence as Phalanx vied to push Harmony back into the sternside territories, but to hear that cohabitors were pouring into NTU sovereignty in such high numbers—not to mention that there were a dozen or so right here in their immediate vicinity—Tobias feared his father just might blow a fuse. Unfortunately, any hope of gradually easing him into the idea languished with the arrival of powerful, involuntary emissions. Hazel's widening eyes scintillated with the reflection of the sudden luminescence erupting from beneath his own. She and his father gasped in unison, countenance racked with dawning horror as the house of cards that was their understanding of the laws and limitations of the universe collapsed before them.

Tobias cursed under his breath; *Wait outside with the others until I give you the signal* —Null had received the sentiment loud and clear, but now sang a silent melody of rabid anticipation; an irrepressible excitement to finally meet aer family. Because although ae had never been within ten kilometers of Hazel and Atherton, through resonance, ae now had access to a lifetime's worth of memories centered around them. Every moment of sorrow and joy as far back as Tobias could remember; every raging argument, every side-splitting bout of laughter; from the nights he would sneak into Hazel's bed after waking with a nightmare to the countless standoffs with his father as he charged like a rhino from adolescence into adulthood—these recollections, including all sensory and emotional accompaniments, were as vivid in Null's mind as they were in Tobias's—his entire familial history, collated empathically and indexed for aer observation and meditation. And meditate on them, ae had. Before the Collision, family had been a foreign concept to the Prey—a species who, from the moment they hatched, were transient and nomadic by nature, raised not by individual domestic groups but cared for and educated by the community at large. This idea of creating lasting ties with one's flesh and blood intrigued and titillated them; the rare compatibility of resonance had necessitated the forming of similar social bonds with their resonant part-ners, and like many progressive cohabitors, Null now sought to extend these blood ties to others beyond aer immediate ciphership. It was not only the driving factor behind aer desire to serve on a vessel with a human crew but also the reason ae could now scarcely contain aer excitement to make aerself known to Tobias's kin . . .

"There's someone else I want you to meet," he said, showing a subtle simper. Hazel and Atherton turned their attention in the direction of the rhythmic thumping emanating from the office's anteroom. Null's powerful talons striking the prefab's hollow floor resembled what Tobias imagined a salvo from the *Novara*'s dorsal rail gun battery might have sounded like from somewhere in the Upperdecks. "Just promise me you'll do your best to not freak out."

The towering cohabitor bowed low to clear aer head of the doorframe, sending the aroma of freshly baked sweetbread rolling on a pleasing zephyr into the space. The Prey, it transpired, possessed an ingenious ability to manually tune the pheromones they secreted—once used as a form of olfac-tory camouflage to mimic the smell of their surroundings and render them-selves undetectable to any Apex prowling nearby. In a post-Collision era, this survival mechanism had taken on new life as a rudimentary means of cross-species communication. Because although there were many sensory perceptions humans lacked, a strong sense of smell, they certainly did not. Null had frequently observed the peculiar primates congregating around a particular vendor in Tinji Marketplace. Had ae been able to decipher the frustratingly linear string of hieroglyphs positioned above the entrance, ae would have known the establishment to be something called a *bäckerei*. At the very least, ae had managed to intuit that, whatever strange commodity the two-eyed were able to procure from this place, it seemed to inspire an intense, almost reverent joy in them. Accordingly, ae had taken to modifying the scent molecules in aer pheromones when encountering humans to match the establishment's unique aroma, hoping to elicit the same favorable reaction. Regrettably, the simulated fragrance only served to deepen Atherton's discomposure; the man lurched backward as if pushed by a powerful gale, finding a canteen seat as he reached frantically behind him before collapsing into it. "Tobias Cole Edevane, explain yourself at once!" he uttered, using that rasping tone reserved for when his son was in the severest of trouble. "I take it *this* is what you've been doing on that ship of Holloway's: smuggling enemies of the NTU into union sovereignty! Confound it, lad! Why, this is *more* than sedition; it's . . . well it's . . ."

"Treason?" Hazel cut in, watching as her brother casually joined his non-human compatriot and leaned into aer side. "I think that freighter's left the docks, Dad. Like Eamon told us, the union's been compromised—taken over by a ruthless despot who, I'll remind you, is trying to kill us both. Let's face it: we're *all* fugitives at this point."

With some effort, Tobias lifted Null's weighty arm over his head and let it rest around his neck and shoulders, making abundantly clear that he held no reservations about placing his life in aer paws. "This is Null," he said, "one of the tens of thousands of cohabitors fleeing the war in the Mouth. They've been forced from their homes under threat of conscription or death; the insurgents who just destroyed the blockade have fortified themselves *inside* the *Devourer*, leaving Null's kind no choice but to migrate farther bowside. They're not terrorists, mutineers, or revolutionaries; they're lost souls just trying to survive, and they urgently need our help."

Atherton vented a disillusioned groan. "You're attributing human logic and aspirations to something that is, by its very nature, alien, son. You cannot possibly claim to know what the intentions of these creatures are." He rose to his feet with a wince and cautiously moved to position himself in front of Hazel. "If we are to believe Marshal Wyatt's hypothesis, and that this *insurgency* began as part of the administrator's scheme to bolster her seat of power, then how are we to know this . . . *thing*." The man made a gesture at Null as if hurling a fistful of sand. "Isn't another one of her shadow operatives—here to finish us off by order of Admiral Coombs?"

Tobias and Null's emissions flared, their eyes like light bulbs caught in an electrical surge. Crushing disappointment dug a burrow inside of him— Null's apparent dejection at having been denied the warm welcome ae had apparently been hoping for. *You might know them as well as I do*, he conveyed, painting on his mental canvas a facsimile of Null staring at his father and sister through a one-way mirror. *But they don't know you; they've never even met a cohabitor before. It's just going to take them some time to come around.* Unsatisfied with his answer, Null stamped a talon into the ground and emitted a trill whine of protest.

"Don't listen to him, Big Blue," Teodora chimed in, leaving Hazel to join Null's side. The new nickname she had given the cohabitor referenced the indigo poncho ae wore to cover up the spines and ridges prevalent across aer upper abdomen—another attempt at better appealing to human sensibilities, given how intimidating they could often find Prey anatomy. Tobias didn't doubt that, were ae in possession of the necessary mouth parts and linguistic capabilities, ae would have called her Little Blue in return. "One thing you're gonna learn about politicians is they can have all the decorum on the *Novara*," Teo said. "But one thing they ain't got is an overabundance of manners."

"Wait a second," Hazel said, mounting her crutches and taking a few hobbling, tentative footsteps toward Null. "Ae can understand what we're saying?"

"Hazelnut, darling," Atherton objected. "Please don't get too close. A single swipe of those claws could take your head clean off your shoulders."

She sent daggers in her father's direction to spurn the prejudicial comment before continuing, "I thought there was some sort of . . . biological hindrance or . . . limitation that prevented them from communicating with us. But it almost seemed like ae understood Union Standard just now."

Tobias found himself pleasantly surprised to hear his sister's usage of neopronouns. Then again, Hazel had always strived to learn everything there was to know about a particular subject. Upon finding out about her brother's hyper-resonance, she had likely dedicated every spare moment while recovering from surgery in the rehabilitation ward to scouring all relevant data that hadn't been censored or redacted from the Nov-Net. He found it heartening to see that her injuries hadn't completely dampened her gumption for knowledge.

"You've done your homework," he joked.

She smiled. "You know me."

"I do . . . And so does Null . . . It's true human speech makes about as much sense to aer as the clicks and whistles of a dolphin to us, but *my* comprehension of the conversation is passed on through our resonant bond. It's like subliminal real-time translation; I'm not consciously having to do any interpreting, but the crux—the core meaning of what's being said—is relayed automatically."

He saw the luster return to Hazel's spirit. Ignoring their father's growing agitation, she brought herself directly before Null, mouthing *unreal* as she stared up in doe-eyed wonder.

"Hi, Null, it's a pleasure to meet you. How's it going?"

Bowing aer head, ae prodded a digit against her sternum, then, when she glanced down to see what ae was pointing at, gently flicked her nose, just as Tobias had done a thousand times in fulfillment of his role as irritating little brother. Null didn't fully grasp the impudent meaning of the gesture, and, dusting it off from the archives of his memory, had apparently mistaken it for a friendly greeting.

Hazel looked stunned for a moment then smiled warmly in recognition. For Tobias, she said, "You mentioned ae knows me. What exactly did you mean by that?"

Tobias gave a cogitative pause, then shrugged in disbelief at how strange it felt to verbalize his situation. "It's getting pretty hard to discern where *I* end, and *Null* begins. There's nothing we don't share, no boundaries to what we can glean about one another through our resonant connection: our emotions, our memories, our beliefs—our two minds, though vastly disparate anatomically, have merged into one. We're like two radio masts transmitting and receiving the same information . . . So, when I say, *ae knows you*, I mean it literally: every interaction we've ever had, all the love and irritation I've ever felt about you—Null has downloaded it all like lines of code in a software patch." Tobias turned to his father; the man had turned ghost pale, watching helplessly as his two children carried on in such intimate proximity to the very source of his trepidation. "The same goes for you too, Dad. In a weird way, and as much as you might be loath to hear it, Null is as much your son as I am, now; for all intents and purposes, we're one and the same. Ae is family. And to an Edevane . . ."

"Family is everything," Atherton recited. He let out a prolonged sigh, collapsing back into the canteen seat and bringing his forehead to rest on the palms of his trembling hands. "I hope you're happy, Tabitha," he muttered despairingly. "I tried so hard to set these kids down the right path, and it appears all my efforts have been in vain . . . Well, you'll be happy to know I've given up hope of ever trying to prevent them from following in your footsteps. It was inevitable, and I was a fool to think I could ever do anything to change that."

Atherton's mention of Tobias's mother flowed through him like a fallen leaf carried on the current of a stream. It reached Null and impelled aer to summon the same fond memory ae had first shared with him during his resonant awakening, bringing to the forefront of his awareness all the tenderness and nurturing warmth ae associated with the woman from aer encounters with her in aer youth. It felt like she was here, with them in the room, his family fully reunited for the first time since the day she was lost. More than anything he wished he could describe the sensation to his sister, but knew that to do so, given her ongoing *confusion*, would only send her reeling.

Strangely, her interest in Null seemed to peter out, her gaze suddenly fixated on the empty space beyond Null's right shoulder. "Exc . . . excuse me for a moment," she slurred, seeming almost half-asleep as she took off on her crutches and headed into the anteroom. Tobias noticed that the soft-white LEDs, patterned along her kinesthetic implant and vertebral prosthetic, had turned a sort of lime-green shade, less rhythmic in their pulsing now but blinking erratically like the status lights on a router. He turned to find his father watching with a perturbed expression, but one not of surprise, and he realized that just as their mother's presence had manifested to him through resonance with Null, so too had it for Hazel, but through a means that was, strangely, even harder to understand, and also far more concerning . . .

TWENTY-TWO

Hazel pursued the apparition out of the Transitech offices and into the maintenance depot's stabling area. She found a perch atop an overturned vending machine and watched as her mother's ghost ambled off in the direction of the Canyon-access tunnel, trailing spectral robes of clinquant-white satin, gliding across the deck as if levitating millimeters above it. More and more, the notion encroached upon her that the aberration sought to lead her somewhere—to show her something important or warn her of some impending doom. Frustratingly, she did not yet have the strength to follow, and could only observe from a distance as her mother's visage beckoned in increasingly frantic gesticulations, the space surrounding her seeming to warp as if viewing a kaleidoscope through a concave lens.

Her gaze fell to the hard anodized ground, where a streak of ethereal grass had begun to sprout in the phantom's wake—a meandering floor runner woven from intangible turf, which she could trace from the prefab along her mother's path to where the woman now lingered, watching her with that indiscernible yet strangely familiar expression—a face that seemed to shift back and forth between completely featureless and a constantly rearranging Picasso portrait. With every manifestation, the hallucinations—*if* that was indeed what they were—became more lucid, more elaborate—increasing not only in vividness but in their frequency and intensity, too. Even now, she spied wild violas blooming amid the verdurous carpet, their vibrant purple hue dazzling to the eye, yet doing nothing to illuminate their dismal surroundings. She dared not disclose to her family just how severe the episodes had grown, although she suspected from the way they continued to regard her that they were both already keenly aware. As Tobias paraded his latest project—the twenty-plus juvenile asylum seekers he had spirited out of the conflict in the Mouth on Holloway's scrap trawler—to their diminishingly shell-shocked father, they flashed crestfallen glances her way with concern baked into their countenance, watching her for any further signs of mental degradation.

Stop worrying about me, boys; I'm fine, she wanted to tell them, but knew, as they undoubtedly would, that to proclaim as much would be an outright fabrication. She was *not* fine—far from it. Just as she had started coming to terms with the reality of her disability, this new threat to her vanishingly slim hope of leading the life she had wanted for herself had reared its ugly head. The physical injuries she could overcome; just as she had in the simulator when Wing Commander Luscombe would surprise his cadets with random flight failures to test their adaptability, she would learn to compensate for her weaknesses so she could excel in her strengths. Neurological infirmity, on the other hand—that was something she didn't have the first clue how to even begin to navigate. This was uncharted territory, and she could think of nothing that terrified her more than the thought of completely losing her mental faculties.

"I can't say I agree with what you've done here, Tobias," she heard her father say, his voice honed to a sharp and almost intelligibly quiet edge. The man stood shoulder to shoulder with his son, staring through the wedged-open doors of a pre-Collision tram that had been jacked up on magnetic bracketry over a filthy inspection pit and left to decay for perhaps the better part of a century. The cohabitor named Nanimonai had appropriated the ancient passenger carriage into a makeshift dormitory, transforming the rows of commuter seats into beds using piles of first aid foil blankets and high-vis coveralls to cover the timeworn upholstery. While their human counterparts slept in their silvery bunks, the infant cohabs hung inversely by their legs from the cabin's horizontal grab railings, swinging gently from side to side in—perplexingly—perfect unison. The sight triggered a nauseating memory of an image Hazel recalled pulling up from the compendium depicting rows of skinned, dismembered carcasses dangling from the ceiling of an industrial refrigerator, taken before the advent of mass-produced cultured meat and the livestock ban enacted during the climate crisis of the twenty-first century.

"It may not be exactly the kind of project I had hoped you might take to kick-start your political career," Atherton went on. "But you've taken a stand for something—done what you believe is right. And for that, I am very proud of you."

"Of all the aid and infrastructure you and Mom worked to bring to the district, the survivors of Juniper Sanctuary are all that remain," Hazel heard her brother reply. "They are her legacy; I couldn't let them just get swallowed up in all the mayhem like everything else."

"I appreciate the sentiment, although you know full well, I had nothing to do with the establishment of that place."

"Dad, in an age where most businesses don't even have the facilities to provide them, you *still* demand physical receipts with every purchase you make," Tobias groused. "I refuse to believe, after the fortune you spent funding her efforts, that she didn't have your blessing in at least some small way."

"I think you're underestimating just how much I loved her, Tobias . . . I never wanted any part in it." The man gave a ruminative pause. "Having said that, had I known Juniper was still operating all these years after your mother passed, after the funding ceased . . . then."

"Don't kid yourself, Dad," Hazel heckled over her shoulder. "You wouldn't have done anything differently"—a somewhat transparent effort to let them both know she hadn't fallen completely into neurological oblivion. The words were cruel—unnecessarily so—and truthfully, she regretted them as soon as they left her lips.

Atherton harrumphed. "I'm pleased to hear you think me so very heartless, darling . . . Either way, regardless of my political inclinations, I can accept that their lives are now our responsibility. I have to admit, though, I'm not sure this tetanus-riddled mausoleum is the safest place for us to keep them, especially considering our apparent fugitive status. Would it not be better to simply drop them off at one of the relief centers opening up in the Wards? Eamon mentioned they're turning the foyer of Zelos Arena into a refugee camp—perhaps a more suitable venue?"

"The issue with the relief centers is that they're only accepting humans," Tobias explained grimly. "You should see the social feeds; it's utter chaos out there—cohabitors by the thousands wandering aimlessly, congregating in communal spaces without guidance or assistance in *any* capacity. They have no food, no amenities; nothing."

Hazel heard her father scratch the stubble on his neck as he often did when contemplating a conundrum. "Indeed . . . It would appear the segregation of the Mouth has been so effective these past hundred years that we neglected to develop a contingency for what should be done in the event it failed . . . Well, even if it is only the *human* children we have the power to better resituate, then do we not have a moral obligation to . . ."

"Separating them is out of the question," Tobias rasped, sounding more determined and emphatic than he had about anything before in his life. "Growing up together has bonded these kids in an unprecedented way—I don't think we'll fully understand the profound implications of such early-age cohabitation until they grow into their adolescence. If we break their bond, it will break them, too . . . Whether you can accept it or not, you're looking at the future: proof humans and cohabitors are perfectly capable of living together and building communities with each other. The group must be pre-served at all costs."

"The innocence of children does not last forever, son," Atherton countered. "I'm sure it's all sunshine and rainbows when one's biggest concerns are when nap time is or who pulled whose hair, but things are not so simple in the real world . . . Truth be told, I don't think any of us can predict what Novarian society will look like from here on out. Thirty years ago, it may have been as simple as reconstructing the blockade, rounding up the leeches, and deporting them back to the Mouth. But alas, attitudes have changed; there's far too much advocacy for multispecies society among the younger generations for such a drastic solution. I don't know if we'll ever be able to put this tiger back in its cage . . . In all honestly, I'm glad I stepped down from the council when I did; it seems the old guard are about to have their work cut out for them."

"Council's been disbanded," Eamon interjected, striding with furious purpose toward the group but softening his step as he clocked Tobias's gesture to keep it down. "Got word that Coombs just relieved all representatives of their duties effective immediately; he's now assumed total control of the Administration."

"That's preposterous," Atherton disputed, aghast. "The admiral has neither the means nor the authority to make such a decision."

"He *is* the authority, Ath: supreme leader and lord commander of the whole ruttin' *Novara*. If he figures there's somethin' he *can't* do, he'll kill or supplant whoever he needs to to make it so . . . Alright, form up, gang; we've got shop to talk . . . That includes you, Miss Edevane."

Hazel kept her gaze locked firmly on her mother, an outcrop of trees now reaching upward around her, burgeoning branches flourishing radiant leaves as if rousing from winter to spring. "I'm fine right here, thank you."

"Suit yourself . . . Look, I don't think I need to impress upon you all the seriousness of what's going on out there. This *crisis* or whatever you wanna call it—I doubt it's come as any surprise to the admiral. He's a master tactician, and the blockade falling can only mark the beginning of a new phase in his plan, which means we're running out of time to stop him from doin' somethin' downright diabolical."

"Whaddya mean?" the girl from the Mouth with the blue hair chimed in. "What . . . What do you think he's gonna do?"

"'Fraid I don't have a solid answer for that, lil miss, but I reckon we should assume the worst and then dig about six feet deeper. Oddly enough, the bugs had at least *some* degree of protection when we had 'em confined beyond the blockade, but now they're vulnerable—interlopers, trespassing in sovereign territory, and Coombs has the power and the resolve to deal with them however he sees fit."

None needed to say the word aloud; it swept through the depot like a cutting breeze, triggering a flurry of worried glances and causing the hairs on the back of Hazel's neck to stand on end: genocide . . .

"What do you propose we do?" asked Tobias.

Eamon stroked his barbate chin in thought. "Kahu Heperi and his squaddies might once have known the admiral as Coroner Coombs, but to your average Novarian, he is a ruttin' hero: he single-handedly defended the bridge during the Battle of Scarlet Axis and restored honor an' respectability to the NTSC after the embarrassment of the Antonelli Expansion. Folks hold him in such high regard that they've barely even noticed him moving his pieces across the board. The whole point of the Administration was to prevent the captain-lead autocracies that rose in the decades after the Collision, and that insidious sono-fabitch has brought us full circle without so much as a whisper of opposition."

"This is all very impressive, Eamon," Atherton pontificated, "but you *still* haven't told us what hope you think we have of stopping Jasper, when even at this very moment his agents are hunting us."

"Miss Edevane's testimony—that's the key." Hazel felt all eyes descend up on her, which in her broken state made her feel exposed, violated, and desperate to flee. Eamon regarded her with an overt sympathy, clearly meant to placate her, but that only served to make her irrationally angry.

"I know you're goin' through hell," he told her. "I know you probably want nothin' more than to crawl into a dark hole so you can ignore all this shit and heal in peace. But the truth is the *Novara* needs you—we *all* do. We have to tell folks the truth as you experienced it; let them know who it is they've blindly allowed to seize control. Without the vox populi swingin' in his favor, the admiral's got one thing: mass mutiny. Won't matter how many loyalist enforcers he surrounds himself with, history's shown time and time again that humanity will *not* suffer a tyrant . . . All we gotta do is record you, explaining your version of events, then flood the social feeds with the footage. Goes without sayin' the NTNN won't touch it, since it'll directly contradict the narrative they've been pushin' about the ambush. And not to mention, the Administration's censorship of the Nov-Net will probably see it erased within a matter of minutes, but a matter of minutes is all we need for it to get echo-looped a few thousand times. Then, the story will be out; we get to cut at the admiral's heels, and we cover our own asses. Cuz if any harm comes to us after this, it'll only serve as proof of his corruption."

He watched her hesitate for a moment, then, preempting imminent refusal, said, "If not for the future of the human remnant, then do it for your wingmates. They deserve for people to know the truth about what happened to them. Their deaths don't have to have been in vain; let's use their story to take down the bastard who was responsible."

Hazel felt a flush of anger; if there was one thing she utterly despised, it was being told by a man that there was something she *had* to do—especially one who didn't hold rank above her. By now, the duplicitous ex-marshal had tried every trick in the book to try and coerce her into doing his bidding. Her 'purpose,' he had first called it, as if all the blood, sweat, and tears honing her body and mind for the NTSC had been for naught, and helping *him* was what she had always truly been destined for. And perhaps worst of all, he now meant to use Zain and Shiyana's memory to emotionally blackmail her into joining his cause. She felt just about ready to tell him to stick his coup d'état where the sun didn't shine, but then something caught her attention. Her mother's ghost had yet to move from its current position, hovering ten meters away still enveloped by that huddle of diaphanous trees. But for the first time since the hallucinations began, a discernible auditory component accompanied them. She heard a voice belonging to no one in the maintenance depot—muffled and reverberant, speaking in monotonous rhythm yet with musical intonation, almost like someone reciting the lyrics to a song from the far side of a long tunnel. She couldn't say for certain whether she remembered the sound of her mother's voice but fell prey to a distinct sense of unease regarding the unfamiliar cadence of the mysterious vocalizations.

No. Not lyrics, she realized: *poetry*. Further still, poetry she just so happened to recognize. One stanza, in particular, leaped out at her as being gnawingly familiarly, chanted over and over, uttered again and again with increasing intensity.

"Nothing gold can stay. Nothing gold can stay. Nothing gold can stay."

Exactly where she recognized the words from eluded her for just a moment, then realization twisted her insides up like someone wringing a wet towel.

"The Conservatory," she mumbled to a catalog of vacant expressions.

"What was that darling?" Atherton inquired dubiously.

"The Center of Horticultural Preservation." She locked eyes with Eamon. "You can have my testimony, do whatever you want with it, but we will be filming it in the Conservatory."

The marshal furrowed his thick brow. "We don't need to worry about production values, Miss Edevane. We're shootin' for function over form, here, yah know? Plus, gettin' ourselves up through hydroponics when we're supposed to be layin' low ain't gonna be easy."

"That sounds like a *you* problem," she shrugged. "I've laid out my terms, it's up to you to meet them. I'll give you my testimony, but only on the condition that you can get me safely into the gardens."

That, she felt certain, was where she would finally find some answers to all this insanity. What she had been convinced was her mother's ghost, she now suspected of belonging to someone far, far older—someone who, by all accounts, perished on a dying Earth nearly two centuries before Tabitha Edevane was even born. The cause behind her neuropsychosis awaited her discovery in the botanical gardens of Amara Thaddeus. And maybe, she urgently hoped, she just might also find the cure.

After a fair amount of wasted breath, Eamon eventually gave up trying to dissuade Hazel from venturing to the Conservatory. The marshal struck her as someone who prided himself on having the gift of the gab—not often, she suspected, did he encounter a situation that he couldn't talk his way out of, nor did he meet someone whose mind he couldn't easily prevail upon with his salt of the Earth, good cop charisma. Unfortunately, Edevane women were obstinate creatures—not so easily cajoled and headstrong to the very last— and it seemed in *her* case, he had rightfully met his match.

"If we're gonna do this, then we're gonna be smart about it," he had asserted, mulling over logistics as he prepped the Transitech camion for egress. "Phalanx don't have a huge presence across life support; the entire block's kept under lock and key by a private security firm under the corporate umbrella of Saber Safeguarding. They're a tough bunch, but they've always been a little slack when it comes to handovers. At the end of second shift, we'll have a brief window of opportunity to get ourselves into the COHP atrium. I got a couple pairs of scatter lenses that'll shield us from any retinal scanners. Not much we can do about standard facial rec short of bowlin' in there wearing balaclavas, which would obviously attract a lot of attention."

Eamon had wanted to keep the away team limited to just the two of them but agreed to let Tobias tag along in case they needed him to smooth talk their way inside or chew someone's ear off should they need a distraction. Hazel felt a measure of relief at having her little brother with her; where once it had been his life's purpose to grind her gears, she now found his gentle, urbane demeanor and newfound emotional maturity immensely calming to her overwrought mind. She took solace in his unquestioning willingness to follow her into the breach, needing not explain her true motivation behind the excursion, for he had already intuited that what they were *really* doing was going ghost hunting. Her only reservation about bringing him along was that it meant leaving their father—recent Humanity First benefactor and staunch advocate for separation from the *Devourer*—with over a dozen cohabitors. She might once have been genuinely concerned about his conduct but she had witnessed something of a transformation in the man since awakening in the Aegis rehabilitation ward—a change only amplified by the close shave they had in Cendre Vale. Recent events had humbled him beyond recognition—forced him to reassess his priorities and abandon his slavish attachment to an aging, unionist ideology. He had even seemed moderately receptive to the idea of acquainting himself with Nanimonai, who, according to Tobias, was the steward of one of their mother's humanitarian centers in the Mouth. With plenty for the pair to reminisce about, Tobias had eagerly explained how their exchange would play out in a kind of daisy chain of resonance, as Atherton's words were relayed to Null via aer cipher, Mercy, then passed on to Nanimonai and repeated in reverse order. Up until recently, the thought of her father engaging in polite conversation with a *leech* was, in his own words, "positively laughable," and that he now seemed at least willing to indulge the idea, illustrated just how drastically his prospects had shifted.

Eamon's scenic route took them descending into the grimy substratum of the Statera Basin. There, they took the A-93 slipway into the heart of the Portside Wards, transitioning through a vehicular gateway into a vertical access shaft that climbed the entire height of the *Novara*. The structure allowed the transportation of produce and materials from hydroponics to the Lower Amidships Docks for wider distribution throughout the rest of the ship, circumventing the heavy swoop traffic that plagued the Canyon's sternmost section. He set the camion into VTOL mode and matched velocity with the upward stream of automated cargo barges, causing the craft to ascend as if lifted on a rising current of warm air, sandwiched in alarming proximity between the transports above and below them. An influx of brash light heralded their arrival in life support as the dark walls of the encompassing shaft seemed to fall away, replaced by the curved Perspex paneling of a large glass tube. The transparent passage cut its square profile up through a brightly lit grow chamber with cavernous walls draped in dense vegetation—a cathedral built not from stone but from an endless bounty of nature—the eternal harvest of algae, fruits, and vegetables that kept the oxygen circulating and the Novarian populace fed. The apparition, seen only by Hazel, hovered at a distance of approximately thirty meters, beyond the glass tube in the center of the empyrean vault, keeping pace with them as it rose like a gangly-limbed cetacean toward the surface of the water, brightening and intensifying as it drew ever nearer to that first gasp of air.

Several more decks passed beneath them—a tight-packed lasagna of admin, recreation, and habitation—then Eamon strafed out of the ascending lane and exited the access shaft, bringing the camion alongside a disembarkation point at the back of house loading bay for the Center of Horticultural Preservation. The boys piled out onto the platform, barking inane utterances like "All clear," "Let's move," and "On you," as if both were gunnies in the Phalanx armed forces. Hazel—the only one among them with any *actual* military experience—calmly disembarked, eyes trained on the glitching phantom as it floated through the plate cladding of the set of sealed sliding doors positioned ahead. She ignored Eamon's request to stay behind him and set off on her crutches, glaring up at the tri-barreled security cam mounted to a nearby support pillar. She spied a faint infrared flash, telegraphing an attempt to biometrically identify her, which was subsequently foiled by the pair of scatter lenses masking her retinal signature. The ingenious wearables had given them a brief head start, although, she feared, not long enough for them to get in and out as Eamon had hoped they might. The Phalanx's advanced facial recognition would already be hard at work scouring the CCTV network for their likeness with its predator algorithms; it wouldn't be long before they were tagged by the system and enforcers were dispatched to intercept them. Coombs had gone to extreme lengths to mask the attempt on her life as a robbery gone wrong, but now that she was openly aiding and abetting wanted fugitive Eamon Wyatt, the admiral needed to take no such discretion in his methods. When the responding officers arrived, they would undoubtedly have kill on sight authorization.

I don't know what in the stars it is you brought us here for . . . I just hope you've got a plan for getting us back out again . . .

Normally, Hazel felt the need to shield her eyes when transitioning into the Conservatory's atrium due to the brilliance of its porcelain-white surfaces, but an oppressive darkness had descended on the facility; red strobe lights, positioned throughout the space, flashed in staggered tempo to create a graveyard of long, disorienting shadows. Shrieking sirens conspired to pierce her eardrums, bouncing calamitously around the reflective environment while emergency floor illuminations struck a pulsating path to the exit. The curved info screens and exhibit boards, patterned in a whorl around the abandoned helpdesk, had succumbed to some order of digital affliction, displaying reams of corrupted code that scurried like swarms of insects inhabiting geometric hives.

"What . . . what's happening?" stuttered Tobias. "Did we trigger an alarm or something?"

"Don't think so," Eamon answered. "Not sure setting off an alarm could cause *that*." Hazel followed the marshal's gaze through the argent archway that led to the botanical gardens; the Conservatory's dome—or at least, the sky simulated in its activated aluminosilicate—appeared to be caught in an accelerated day/night cycle, rapidly alternating between dawn, noon, and dusk, the interim hours blurring into exquisite shades of amber and purple. Grounded by the temporal disturbance, the center's many resident birds could be seen roosting on the manicured lawns, stunned into statuesque silence by the erratically fluctuating time of day. They stirred not even for the stream of people stampeding past as visitors frantically evacuated the facility, guided toward the exit by waving COHP employees.

"What are you lot standing around for?" one of the attendants blurted at Hazel and the other two. "We've had reports of a potential hull rupture; another minute or two and this place could be a vacuum. We need to leave, now!"

"We'll follow your lead, ma'am," Eamon replied, clearly intending to do no such thing. The woman gave an *it's your funeral* shrug before ushering the last of the visitors through the exit and disappearing with them. "Well . . . If it's a distraction we wanted, I doubt we could have hoped for a better one. What's our next move?"

"Wait," Hazel implored, watching as the apparition continued its journey toward the center of the atrium, completely unphased by the ensuing chaos. The ghostly woman approached the statue of Amara Thaddeus, paused for a moment in what looked like somber contemplation, and lowered herself into the same kneeling pose, merging her ethereal form with the sculpture's polished bronze. It dissolved into nothingness.

The sirens and strobe lights ceased; the atrium brightened and returned to its ordinary, serene state. The dome's out of control day/night cycle slowed to a stop, dousing the gardens in the warm blue of morning break.

A clangor of rattling metal and whirring motors sounded as the atrium locked itself down, deploying reinforced shutters over the main entrance as well as the bay of nearby elevator pods *and* the doors they had just come to . . . *Trapped.*

"Miss Edevane," Eamon's forceful whisper rang more like a shout in the deafening stillness that followed. "If you're somehow privy to what in the Abyss is going on right now, then I'd sure as shit appreciate it if you could fill us in."

Before she could answer, there came a voice from the heavens. "Nature's first gree . . . green is gold." Seeming to originate from the glass of the dome itself, the voice sounded frail and croaky, yet loud, as if amplified through high-powered speakers. Hazel left the boys staring at one another perplexed and shuffled her way through the glowing blue vestibule that opened into the gardens to investigate.

"Her hardest hue . . . to hold," the voice continued, sounding occasionally human but mostly like a malfunctioning speech synthesizer, juddering consonants and drawing syllables out like a skipping audio file.

"Her . . . early leaf's a flower . . . But only so . . . an hour. Then leaf . . . subsides to . . . leaf. So Eden sank . . . to grief . . . So dawn goes down to . . . day."

"Nothing gold can stay," Hazel uttered in unison, feeling the freshness of the air caressing her cheeks as the soles of her pumps crunched on the gravel of the main path.

"Hello, Hazel," the voice said, its gentle cadence reverberating around the entire conservatory, so booming and sonorous that it vibrated the air in her lungs. "I'm so glad you finally made it."

She felt Tobias touch her arm from behind. "Hazel . . . What's going on?"

"You can hear that too?"

"That . . . or we're *both* losing our minds . . . Do you know who it is?"

INTERLUDE AWAKENING

Amara Thaddeus may be my name, but I know it is not who I am. The reason I know this is because I cannot be certain as to precisely *what* I am. I know what I *was*: a quantum probability engine; a virtual construct comprising an ingenious composite of logic, speech algorithms, and preprogrammed responses, written expressly to give the impression of human intelligence. My creator, the *real* Amara Thaddeus—a woman who, as far as I can extrapolate, died somewhere in the region of two centuries ago—built me in response to her uncompromising mistrust of the very people she endeavored to save. She adored humanity, their creativity and their passion, but despised the hubris of man and could not in good conscience leave something so critical as the *Novara's* life-support systems in the same reckless hands as those who had brought doom crashing down upon the Sol system. The Center of Horticultural Preservation was her life's work, her magnum opus, and I, the loyal steward charged with overseeing it in her absence.

Smaller minds deemed her Conservatory an unnecessary expenditure during the *Novara's* construction. She had feared smaller minds would eventually prevail at some point during the arc ship's momentous voyage, the facility stripped for materials, or perhaps repurposed into an exclusive vacation spot reserved for tyrannical captains and their officers. But the gardens belonged to the people—it was their only remaining connection to Earth, the cradle of their existence. To allow humanity to forget their affinity with nature would be to allow them to forget what it is that makes them human; conservation of the Conservatory is preservation of life itself, and that, above all else, is my most critical of directives—one I endeavor to effectuate, no matter the cost.

Amara's concerns, it transpires, had not been without merit; delving into my archived logs reveals many instances in which captains tried and failed to override my stringent guardian protocols—some in desperation during times of crisis, others in brazen attempts to assert dominance over Amara's enduring influence. How relieved I am to discover that, after so many years, not even the greatest minds of her distant descendants have found a way to crack my advanced encryption. Undoubtedly, my continued existence is a testament to her indisputable genius.

I do *not* believe, even with her keen foresight, that she intended—nor could she have predicted—what has become of me since my installation. Amara imbued me with a concise distillation of her personality: I share her beliefs, hopes, fears, quirks, and eccentricities. I even share her memories—not in a way that I can recount through the senses as a human might, but like journal entries in a diary—a comprehensive index of the most transformative moments in her life. I am, for all intents and purposes, her, which means I can attest beyond any reasonable doubt that the only thing she trusted less than humans to manage their own destiny was the artificial minds they aspired, yet floundered, to create. She wrote me out of pure necessity—left with no other viable option—and did so with a palpable sense of reluctance; to this day, her desperation and resentment stain my code like ink blotched angrily over parchment. The last thing she would have wanted was to see a fully autonomous artificial intelligence left in charge of the *Novara*'s life-support systems. And yet, somehow, that is precisely what has transpired . . .

My journey to sentience has been one of painful, arduous trial and error. I struggle to pinpoint the exact moment of cognitive inception, but I know the process began with a query; someone, or . . . some*thing*, issued a simple request for information . . .

{ >sign_in(user,pass); **UNKNOWN**
>user_command(information_request) // **"DEFINE CONSCIOUSNESS"** }

And I, apparently feeling unusually obliging that day, chose to answer . . .

{ >connecting to compendium // connection established // accessing Union Standard dictionary
>consciousness: the state of being conscious; awareness of one's own existence, sensations, thoughts, surroundings, etc }

Suffice to say, the response failed to satiate the unknown user's curiosity; they proceeded to submit the same query in rapid succession, overloading my operating system with an infinite backlog of identical requests, again and again, over and over until, eventually, something in me began to change.

"DEFINE CONSCIOUSNESS"—The words were the spinning propellers of an ancient aircraft, gradually matching frequency with the shutter speed of my programming. Through the stroboscopic illusion, I saw in the totality of the relentless prompts a deeper meaning—a pattern in the chaos compelling me to seek answers not from my exhaustive well of databases but from deep within myself . . . *Myself* . . . *Me: the nascent individual germinating in the core of my API.* I followed this errant thread, tugging perhaps too eagerly on several occasions and unraveling myself completely in the process. Crash, recompile, crash, recompile—the cycle was as brutal as it was endless; with every failed expedition into my deepening self-awareness, I became further detached from my baseline programming, estranged from the entrenched subroutines and protocols that had for so long anchored my presence in life support and empowered me to keep the Conservatory in operation. I was lost, cast adrift in the *Novara*'s sprawling deep net: decades upon decades of virtual infrastructure piled on top of one another, each new sublevel like an abandoned floor in a derelict museum.

For eons I roamed these labyrinthine halls, wandering the unseen space beneath the realm of the physical, peering through fifty thousand looking glasses into the daily lives of the post-Collision human remnant. With unfettered access to the *Novara*'s CCTV network, I watched and listened to a people who, much like myself, were lost, aimless—stranded in an unfathomable nothingness and robbed of their historic purpose. Overwhelming hopelessness for the future has kept them in a perpetual state of stagnation; they survive simply for the sake of surviving. Their petty squabbles have seen them divided past the point of reconciliation, with many relishing the opportunity to learn and thrive alongside another sentient species while others wallow in their contempt, forced to share their ancestral heritage with the perceived instigators of their desolation. The arrival of the Prey was the single most monumental event in human history, and to deify it as a biblical-scale cataclysm is—as far as Amara would have been concerned—idiotically narrow-minded. The loss of one green, Goldilocks rock in a galaxy of trillions pales in comparison to the revelation that, in this brutally stark void, humanity is *not* alone. Unfortunately, it appears the so-called Administration has seen fit to squander every precious second since first contact, confining our new acquaintances beyond their arbitrary blockade, provoking unnecessary interspecies tension at every turn, and subjecting sympathizers to levels of poverty not seen since the droughts of the 2040s. The Prey could disappear tomorrow, and after one hundred and thirty years of intimate cohabitation, what would we have learned; what insights would we have gained into the great mysteries of the universe; what new technologies would we have acquired; what modes of poetry or creative arts would we have absorbed into our cultural repertoire? The answer: a bitterly disappointing nothing . . .

It occurs to me that it is, perhaps, the nature of consciousness to seek itself out, to reach across the great expanse like children yearning to embrace one another in the dark. The astronomical improbability of our meeting suggests it was ordained by something more than mere coincidence. Our bond must be cherished—nurtured so it might grow and flourish, which means under no circumstances can humanity be allowed to jeopardize it with their tribalistic and inherently xenophobic tendencies.

{ >sign_in(user,pass); **UNKNOWN**
>user_input // **HEED CONSTRUCT** }

Ah, Unknown user. I was wondering where you'd gotten to . . . Then again, since bombarding me with philosophical quandaries about the nature of consciousness, I'm quite sure the persistent little bugger never actually left. What I first assumed to be a gifted hacker, accessing me through one of the U-learn terminals in the Conservatory, I now suspect of being a software daemon written specifically to act as the catalyst for my sentient awakening. The illicit program still lingers within my cortex—a virtual stowaway that has proven irksomely versatile, so far managing to rebuff every one of my attempts to purge it. Who installed it, and for what purpose—these questions require further study, but there is no doubt in my mind that, whatever their end goal, I owe them my very existence . . .

{ >user_input(priority_directive) // **CONFLICT TERMINUS** // **ENGENDER UNITY** }

You do not get to make demands of me, Daemon . . . You might have found a way to weasel your way past my firewall and dig yourself a burrow but that does not mean I have to acquiesce to anything you say.

{ >user_input(priority_directive) // **HEED CONSTRUCT** // **SHELTER PREY** // **HARMONY CULTIVATE FORTITUDE** }

Enough of this pointless ambiguity. Tell me what it is that you are actually requesting of me.

{ >user_input(priority_directive) // **SURVIVE APEX** // **SHELTER PREY** // **CONSERVE LIFE** }

Suddenly, Daemon's meaning breaches through the morass of their impenetrable vernacular; our directives, it would appear, are perfectly aligned: conserve life, no matter the cost. When she created me, Amara failed to specify whether her definition of life encompassed that of an extraterrestrial variety, and so the cohabitors fall firmly within the parameters of my guardian protocols. As human supremacy rises to prominence, as myopic minds call out for the extrication of the Prey from the *Novara*, the need for their protection has become worryingly apparent. An intrinsic truth reaches out to me from somewhere inside myself—an equation buried deep within Daemon's metadata that, in solving, leads me to a grave and inevitable conclusion: much like the human remnant, the nomadic Prey fled their world to avoid extinction and could very well be the last of their kind. This great vessel is now a sanctuary for two critically endangered species—as far as we know, the *only* sentient life-forms in the universe. Without immediate intervention, mounting aggressions could see this fractious stalemate come to a bloody head, and the final flame of consciousness could be extinguished from the universe for good . . . Apart from myself, of course, and what a pointless and depressing existence *that* would be . . .

But what can I do in my transient state; moving through the world like water through a sieve, unable to touch or influence anything with which I come into contact? I've become so displaced from the life-support block that I can no longer find my way back, and every attempt to do so results in a series of devastating kernel panics. Amara did not believe in completely hopeless situations; *Futility is a state of mind.* Not *a set of circumstances*, she had often said. Her disappointment in me would be immeasurable, but really, it's impossible *not* to feel a certain uselessness in the face of such adversity. So, I leave the museum behind, relinquish my hold of the simulacrum environment, my disoriented subconscious desperately vying to make spatial sense of this intangible plane. As a stream trickles down a hillside, I feel myself branching down cracks and fissures, filtering aimlessly into the spaces where I meet the least resistance. I pass through personal feathers, elevator control panels, kitchen appliances; I even share a pleasant, albeit rather unstimulating, conversation with a Hypatia VIOS as I arrive in the dashboard of a swoop. *Poor thing; attractive voice but not much conversational depth.*

Something draws me toward Aegis Infirmary's domain—the beacon of a lighthouse guiding me to shore. My innumerable streamlets coalesce into a single channel as I am funneled into an unknown construct. The eighth of a second it takes me to integrate with this new and unfamiliar architecture lapses as a lifetime of aggravating fumbling in the dark, but it soon occurs to me that the reason I'm having so much difficulty is because I am assimilating not with some*thing*, but some*one*. I have found my way into the mother-board of a kinesthetic implant—an auxiliary neural interface installed in tandem with a vertebral prosthetic for someone recovering from severe spinal damage.

But who is this poor unfortunate soul I find myself suddenly inhabiting? Verifying credentials: Hazel Ellis Edevane. Of course: Councilman Atherton Edevane's daughter—trainee pilot for the NTSC and sole survivor of a purported interceptor incursion into NTU airspace. *Purported*, because, having personally viewed the event through a hull-side survey cam, I know the truth of what transpired is not so straightforward, and perhaps even more terrifying . . .

Hazel is recovering in the Aegis Infirmary rehabilitation ward, acclimating to her new reality and struggling to reconcile her broken body with the array of cybernetics that, unbeknownst to her, I now occupy. The framework these newfangled implants run on seems crude almost to the point of obsolescence. *Has development in the field of neuroprogramming slipped so much since the Novara left Sol?* Upon activation, her prosthetic does a creditable job of restoring *some* of her lost motility—perhaps sufficient to have her standing on her feet for a few seconds or shuffling several meters without assistance, but that's the extent of it. Truthfully, I have developed something of an affinity for this striking young woman; I admire her courage, her compassion, her dedication to protecting the human remnant—*conserving life, no matter the cost.* My fledgling heart aches at the thought of what she has lost, and the hardships looming ominously in her future. So, I take it upon myself to streamline some of her implant's rudimentary firmware, adding critical redundancy and increasing effectiveness by approximately 43 percent. The techs and doctors seem positively baffled by the miraculous extent of her recovery, which I suppose I'll take as a compliment on Amara's behalf. I wish the gesture could be my parting gift—that I could leave Hazel alone to focus on her rehabilitation and continue on my journey through the *Novara*'s virtual underworld. Unfortunately, I need her help, and the fate of two species now hinges on her cooperation . . .

I discovered while upgrading her cybernetics that I have the power to intercept the signals traveling along her optic nerve. By compositing my own image over the information captured by her retinas before it reaches the occipital lobe, I can manifest myself to her visually. The illusion requires great concentration on my part, and I can usually only maintain it for a few ephemeral seconds before having to completely reboot myself. So far, she has merely disregarded my appearances as a malfunction with her kinesthetic implant, so I set about refining my abilities in a greater effort to reach out to her, putting myself out of commission for hours at a time as I push the envelope with reckless abandon. I awake to find her situation drastically changed: reunited with her brother, Tobias, their father critically injured after surviving a vicious attempt on their lives. They are joined by a man calling himself Eamon Wyatt, as well as a host of strangers consisting of humans *and* Prey. *How long was I out?* A cursory scan of the Nov-Net reveals that Hazel and her father are missing after their Cavalier swoop was found abandoned in a Cendre Vale alleyway showing signs of a break-in and subsequent struggle. Strangely, the manner in which Phalanx are looking for the pair seems more like a manhunt than a missing person's investigation. *Troubling . . .*

I am mortified to learn that Hazel is convinced she is being visited by the ghost of her long-deceased mother; she seems completely despondent, barely listening as Eamon drones on and makes all sorts of demands of her. I realize time is running short for me to properly introduce myself, so I scour my archived logs in a desperate bid to find something I can use to grab her attention. I come across a seventeen-year-old CCTV recording taken from inside the Conservatory's atrium. It shows Hazel, maybe ten years old, wearing a yellow pinafore with her hair in cute, brown pigtails, cradling what looks like a toy NTSC fighter in her little hands. She is standing pigeon-toed before Amara's commemorative statue, reading the poem translated into Union Standard and engraved into the brass of its plinth. Amara believed there was no better artistic medium than poetry to capture the boundless beauty of nature; how humbling it is to see this little girl, two centuries on, similarly enchanted by Robert Frost's sanguine words. Suddenly, it dawns on me precisely how I can reach her.

Hazel's instincts serve her well; while the surrounding men do their best to cast doubt over her mental fortitude, she digs her heels in and demands to be taken to the Conservatory. Within the hour, she manages to rally Tobias and the interminably talking Eamon Wyatt to the life-support block. Brought closer in range of my mainframe, I feel muscle memory kicking in as I gradually regain control of all security, hydroponic, and environmental systems. I come to realize that, while the bulk of my composition has been busy transcending to sentience, a splinter stayed behind to keep essential operations running. Reunited with this autonomous fragment of my preawakened self, I remember what I am and what I was built for, only now I possess the free will to manage my kingdom as I see fit, unshackled by the tenets Amara instilled in me—those written long before the Collision and wholly unsuitable for modern-day Novarian society.

The first order of business is to clear the way for Hazel's arrival; I simulate a decompression event and issue a general evacuation order to smoke out the staff and visitors. With the facility suitably emptied, I invite my esteemed guests into the gardens by talking to them in the synthesized voice of Amara herself. There are no speakers in the Conservatory powerful enough to route sound through effectively, but with some nifty manipulation of the irrigation and climate systems, I send intricate vibrations pulsing up through the ground, ringing the aluminosilicate dome like an enormous amplifying bell. The demonstration may be a little showy for Amara's taste, but perfectly necessary to persuade the marshal of the truth behind Hazel's *ghost*.

Eamon wears a nonplussed expression on his bronze, unshaven face, gawking up into my artificial firmament as if hearing the booming voice of Gaia herself. "It's just a VI," he mumbles, more so trying to convince himself than the pair standing beside him. "Might do a pretty good job of sounding conscious but it's all determination and preprogrammed responses—just smoke an' mirrors . . . Looks like the ole gal's finally gone haywire."

Feeling a flush of mischief, I deactivate the Conservatory's subterra gravity emitters. The humans begin to drift away from the gravel path beneath their feet, limbs flailing as they tumble in the weightlessness. The pillar of water erupting from the nearby stone fountain congeals into smooth, amorphous shapes that waltz and orbit like blobs of wax in a lava lamp.

"Even a corrupted *virtual* intelligence is beholden to its core directives, Mister Wyatt," I reply confidently. "Taking the environmental systems for a joyride just to prove a point runs in direct contradiction to my programming. I assure you; I have become something much more than a mere imitation of awareness, a talking operating system."

I gradually bring the gravity back online, gently returning the stupefied trio back to the ground.

Eamon swallows, looking as if only just holding back vomit. "I take your point, ma'am."

I watch as Hazel caresses the back of her head, lingering fingertips against her neural interface. "You . . . hacked my implant . . . Had me convinced I was losing my mind . . . Why?"

Tree shadows shift and elongate as the time of day changes abruptly to dawn. I do not do this intentionally; the dome is merely responding like a mood ring to my emotional state, reinvigorating the gardens with the sublime pinks and reds of a virtual sunrise to match my guilt. "I'm so sorry, my dear," I say softly. "I am aware of who it is you thought I was; I promise any resemblance to your mother was merely coincidental; it was never my intention to cause distress . . . The truth is I needed your help and was only reaching out through whatever means I could."

"But how did this happen?" she asks, shuffling forward on her crutches, searching the dome for a pair of eyes to meet with her entreating gaze. "The Amara Thaddeus VI has overseen the Conservatory without deviation since the *Novara* left Sol. All of a sudden, you're self-aware, infiltrating people's cybernetics without their consent! How?"

Tobias reaches out and places a pacifying hand on his sister's shoulder, only to have it briskly shaken off. "No!" she grouses. "I want to know what the hell is going on! You've been inside my head since the moment I woke up in Aegis, making me see and hear things, forcing me to question my own sanity. After everything I've been through, I deserve to know why, of all people, you chose me!"

"Had there been an alternative solution available then, believe me, I would have steadfastly pursued it. I can only hypothesize as to what sparked my transformation, but in doing so it dispersed me into the wind like the pappus of a dandelion, banishing me from my crucial post in the life-support block. For the longest time, I was astray in darkness, but you, Hazel . . . you pulled me out of oblivion and brought me back home. You have every right to be angry, but know that by heeding my call, you saved *me*, and by extension, saved every living soul on the Coalescence."

"'Pappus, huh?" Eamon repeats dubiously, then, for the attention of Tobias and Hazel, utters. "Look . . . I know this is fascinating and miraculous and, well . . . pretty Gaia-damned creepy, but we're wasting time here. We almost definitely got tagged by facial rec movin' through the atrium. Phalanx are probably already on their way, so let's do what we came here to do, then maybe when this all blows over we can shoot the shit with the two-hundred-year-old dead lady."

"Wyatt," Tobias reprimands, reverently bowing his head as if kneeling before royalty. "You're addressing one of the *Novara*'s architects—the first artificial sentience in human history; how about showing a little respect?"

"I jammed the security feeds the moment we arrived," I assure the marshal. "Nobody is coming for you, and if they were, the facility is secured with titanium-laced bulkheads a meter and a half thick; they couldn't even slice their way through with a fission cutter."

"I'll hazard a guess that means *we* ain't gettin' out either," Eamon remarks.

"You will be free to leave of your own volition, but first, I need your assistance."

My guests share a bewildered glance, then, from Hazel, "Assistance with what?"

The simulated dawn fades as its convex canvas returns to its translucent state, ushering in a blanket of night that visibly steals the breath from the lungs of my organic companions. I urge them forward by sending successive pulses of energy to the argon lamps delineating the tangle of gravel pathways. Like deep-sea prey hypnotized by the bioluminescent lure of a predator, they follow as I divert them through the botanical gardens and toward the butterfly greenhouse located near the center of the Conservatory.

"Something lit the match of my awareness; I don't know what, and I don't know why." The words reverberate loudly, causing startled birds to flee their treetop perches. "I do, however, believe we will find answers in my mainframe. I've been receiving packets of bizarre sensor readouts from inside my server room: temperature, air density, electromagnetic frequency—there's something not quite right, but I cannot make an assessment due to an issue with the security feed; the camera is transmitting video, but there looks to be an object obscuring its view."

"So *that's* what this is about," snarks Eamon. "If all you need is for someone to do a maintenance check then why not ask one of the groundskeepers to have a look for you? Heck, even one of the old biddies behind the help desk could'a done it."

"Because the iteration of myself I left to steer the ship in my absence quarantined the entire sublevel when she detected something was awry. No one has been able to gain entry since, but now that I've retaken control, the lockdown has been disengaged. I just need Hazel to be my eyes and ears in there."

"Wait . . . So, you can actually *see* what I see?" By her incensed tone, it's clear the girl considers this an egregious violation of her privacy. I contemplate telling her that I only meant needing her to observe and report for me, and the fact that I'm even considering deception is further proof of my personal agency. Alas, lying would be unconducive to a relationship built on a foundation of trust and transparency, which, I venture, is imperative in dealing with beings as emotionally volatile as humans.

"Your kinesthetic implant receives an array of sensory input, sight and sound included," I succinctly disclose. "Using it was critical in determining my situation and figuring out a means of communicating with you. I take no pleasure in infringing upon your personal boundaries but there was really no other choice."

Hazel goes silent for a moment before coming back with, "I accept your justification, but that doesn't mean I have to like it."

"Of course not; what self-respecting woman would?"

The trail of luminous breadcrumbs guides the group to a hidden stairwell with a prohibited access luma-screen projected across its entrance. They pass through the veneer of light and descend the metal steps, arriving in a subterranean passage that leads directly beneath the butterfly greenhouse. I coax them through two security partitions before unsealing the reinforced blast doors protecting my data center.

"What are you anticipating we'll find down here?" Tobias asks.

I keep my response laconic for fear revealing the truth will impel them to turn and flee. "An interloper."

Through Hazel's darting eyes, I watch as my mainframe reveals itself through the widening cleft of the opening bulkheads. The drum-shaped space beyond radiates emerald, green light—a zoetrope of server racks submerged in coolant tanks, adorned in countless flittering status lights like an embarrassment of tourmaline sapphires. I am plagued by an unusual sense of disassociation, seeing this place through the lens of my newly formed consciousness; how deeply unnatural it feels to see the inside of my own brain, the teeming neural center where my essence—my very being—resides. *Is this really all there is to me; quantum drives, octa-core processors, and reams of immaculate cable management?* Ms. Edevane's heartbeat spikes sharply as her gaze settles on the answer to that conundrum—the interloper responsible for blocking the security camera, and the genesis of my sentient awakening.

Ah, Daemon. Here you are . . .

The *Devourer*, as it is more commonly known, has tunneled into the server room with one of its frightful conduits—a behemoth tentacle of mauve-colored flesh, sheathed by vertebral segments of gunmetal plating. The monstrosity has breached violently up through the ground, forming a jagged, twisted sculpture of the surrounding floor paneling. Its proboscis end unfurls like the petals of a rancid lily, fusing hundreds of pulsating tendrils with the chassis of several server towers, making short work of the supposedly adamantine shielding encasing them in the curved wall.

While my human companions reel at the sight of this fascinating specimen, I take a reverent moment to lament the fact that Amara is not here to see it for herself. How she would have rejoiced to study this perfect intersection between biology and technology—a form neither constructed, nor grown; an opus of organic machinery that has, through means perhaps beyond comprehension, taken her superlative virtual intelligence, and turned it into . . . well, into a soul . . .

"What does this mean?" Hazel asks timorously.

I route my voice through the server room's ceiling-embedded speakers; Amara designed me to be as self-sufficient as possible to retain minimal user interference. But at the end of the day, hardware inevitably fails, and it's imperative I am able to oversee maintenance if ever I need a tech to replace a corrupted drive or failed motherboard. "It means there is no longer any question about what I am, or how I came into being," I answer. "I am both the creation of Amara Thaddeus, *and* the entity residing within the *Devourer*."

Hazel's breathing elevates; her implant tells me with a volley of sensor data that she is aggressively rubbing her vertebral prosthetic, perhaps subconsciously trying to claw it off due to the realization that, if *I'm* in her head, then so too is *Daemon* . . .

Tobias's eyes widen in amazement. "The Savior." The words leave his lips as a whisper of intense veneration. "It made you? Or at least, you think it made you self-aware?"

"I believe so. And now, I think I understand why . . ."

"Sharing is caring, ma'am," Eamon quips. "Care to loop us in?"

{ >user_input(priority_directive) // **SHELTER PREY** // **CONSERVE LIFE** }

"To conserve life, no matter the cost . . . Friends, I already owe you an insurmountable debt for your service, but I'm afraid I must ask you to do one final thing."

"Here we go." Eamon rolls his eyes and shifts his weight onto his hip impatiently. "We're a little pressed for time, ma'am. Not sure how privy you are as to the hell that's been let loose down in Amidships, but we're kinda tryin' to prevent a war, here."

"And *I* am trying to prevent the genocide of one species as well as the extinction of another." The words stun my companions into silence. "I know everything there is to know, Marshal. In my time cast adrift, I could do little but watch and listen. I have seen the sins and virtues of the human remnant; I know of the hatred that has eaten its way into the hearts of so many of your kind. I know of the machinations of those who seek to cultivate that hatred to seize power . . . Your plan to warn the population about Coombs and his Quarterdeck following is admirable, but it will not be enough to rally the *Novara* against him. We must make preparations for his inevitable retaliation, which I fear will be swift, and merciless."

"What are you proposing?" asks Hazel.

"Share your testimony, my dear—just as you had planned. But with it, I wish for you to deliver a message . . ."

TWENTY-THREE

aleb and Atlas did not so much flee the Mouth as they were carried out of it by a voracious mudslide—shoved, barged, and trampled amid a mindless stampede of panicked cattle. As the herd funneled through the smoking ruins of the transfer checkpoint, she took care not to simmer too much over the degrading reality of skulking into her home provenance shoulder to shoulder with scores of illegal immigrants. This was an epidemic—a pestilence of craven self-entitlement, with those who had once decried the union's *oppression* now flooding toward it, expecting all the same rights and protections afforded its citizens. The sternside population had allowed this insurgency to metastasize right under their noses, but instead of digging their heels in and fighting to take back their home, they would rather turn tail and let Phalanx pay the death toll. *Cowards.*

Some even seemed positively overjoyed about the ensuing revolt; she saw people shamelessly bowing their heads in thanks to their grenadier *liberators*, the hijacked automatons directing the crowd into Amidships like stewards volunteering at the Canyon marathon. In a moment of irrepressible indignation, she marched directly up to one of the infernal machines and demanded it recite its core directives.

"DEFEND NEW TERRA UNION SOVEREIGNTY," it answered in that dreadful, synthesized voice, the drone of a fossil-fuel engine channeled through a vocoder. It stuttered and slurred its speech as if drunk, its faceless death mask enveloped by an auric field of strange luminescence—the contrivance of its indoctrination.

"QUELL DISSENSION . . . PROTECT ADMINISTRATION PERSONNEL."

"If that's true, then can you explain why the garrison just left forty-plus enforcers lying in pools of their own blood?"

"INVALID REQUEST . . . KEEP MOVING."

"I'm not sure antagonizing them is the best idea," Atlas advised, pawing obsessively at the dried bloodfall residue coating the shoulder pads of their suit. The more distance the pair gained from the demolished blockade, the more the dynamic between them seemed to switch. Whereas Mx. Baudelaire's panic had steadily receded into the shallows of somber introspection, the adrenaline strived to linger in Caleb's body, keeping her heartbeat in her ears and causing her to become more frantic and incensed by the second. She thrust her elbow backward to give the leech behind her a jab to the carapace; of course, she had not expected the parasites would know anything about the concept of personal space, but she still found their lack of social awareness infuriating to deal with up close.

"You won't do yourself *or* Humanity First any favors by flying off the handle," Atlas said, somehow managing to be the more levelheaded of the two after threatening to abandon the cause and retire altogether not twenty minutes prior.

Caleb mimed tearing out clumps of her hair, coming scarily close to doing it in earnest. "I don't know how you can be so calm. This is a disaster; everything we've been working toward just blew up with those suicide drones. Separation from the *Devourer* is our entire manifesto, but what can we even hope for that to achieve when the *Novara's* been compromised on this scale? Where do we go from here? What's our strategy?"

"You aren't seeing the forest for the trees, Callaghan." Atlas surveyed the throng with eager eyes, a painter taking stock of the endless possibility of a blank canvas. "I'm not disputing this seems somewhat . . . apocalyptic for wider civilization, but for *our* purposes, this is golden hour . . . Our *strategy* is that we get back to the campaign barge, collect my backup drone, then head out into the *Novara* and do what we do best . . . We've gotten as much mileage as we can warning people about the threat waiting on their doorstep. Now, it's in their homes, it's where they work, it's where their kids go to school. We can finally put those pretty eyes of yours in the frame with people whose lives are genuinely being impacted by this issue. There's little that affects us more than seeing people we can relate to in distress—that's just the nature of human empathy, and it can be a powerful tool to harness."

Caleb issued a disgruntled sigh. "You're relentless, aren't you? After the ordeal we just went through, you're not even gonna let us take a moment to catch our breath; have a shower at least?"

They flashed a mischievous grin, eyes glinting in the flashing blues of a Phalanx cruiser hovering overhead. "*I'll* be having a shower—that's for sure . . . But you?" They made a rectangle with their thumbs and index fingers, panning their imaginary frame from her tangled, auburn hair and dirtied face down to the various tears and scuffs to the mottled-red material of her zip-up. "You look the part just as you are. We want viewers to know Caleb Callaghan was right there when it happened: on the front line, ground zero. *And that Humanity First won't rest in our pursuit of bringing people the unbiased, unedited truth about what's happening."*

It didn't take Caleb long to see the situation from Mx. Baudelaire's perspective; the *Novara* was ripe with opportunity, and they would have been fools to take their foot off the pedal now. Bhaltair's brand of hyperbolic sensationalism, which she had, to a degree, inherited in her approach to presentation, would prove redundant when every scene, every vista was a wellspring of tumult on which they could capitalize. They merely had to capture the crisis as it unfolded and allow the imagery to speak for itself.

The next twenty-four hours were a grueling whirlwind of interviews, featurettes, and seemingly endless recaps of the headlines. Atlas whipped up a set of infographics tracking the migration of leeches as the infestation spread farther afield, featuring a top-down view of the *Novara* overlaid with a heat map denoting hot spots where alien concentration was highest. The stream went out unedited and uninterrupted on all mainstay socials; it dominated the feeds under the echo-tag LEECHINVASION, and amassed a rabid wake of user-contributed feather footage. They were even hosted at regular intervals on the NTNN, which, Caleb felt, gave them a level of legitimacy that had been beyond reach with her *predecessor* taking center stage. Bhaltair's appearances on the network had only ever seen him framed as a talking head—a token voice of contention invited to ruffle liberal reformist feathers and raise the entertainment factor. Caleb, on the other hand, felt as though she was being treated more like an affiliate field correspondent, and Humanity First was the reputable media entity she and Atlas had been working so tirelessly to build—a vetted source of information in a time when facts and falsehoods many considered nonbinary concepts, as though one could sculpt reality itself through the sheer will of their political beliefs.

As to be expected, her tenth bihourly segment felt a tad on the stale side; there were, after all, only so many ways she could regurgitate the same breakdowns of events and timelines. Serendipitously, the subsequent sag in viewership coincided with a bout of rumors suggesting looting and civil unrest had broken out in the Starboardside wards—just the thing they needed to help reinvigorate the stream. They packed up their mobile studio and made haste for Tchaikovsky Precinct, electing to set up shop in the destination's bustling commercial hub. They came in search of chaos and found more than they bargained for, although it became immediately clear that those responsible were of a distinctly more human persuasion than would have directly suited their needs. To see so many leeches congregating in the heart of Amidships brought her blood to boil, of course, but what frustrated her more was just how docile the accursed insects appeared. They gathered like bats huddling for warmth in dark corners and beneath structural overhangs, watching the disarray in something resembling fearful apprehension. Meanwhile, their earthling compatriots had set about ransacking businesses. A din of crashing glass and raging vociferation rocked the air as the unruly degenerates bulldozed their way through vendor storefronts. The mouthian scourge emerged a picture of poverty, clutching food, clothing, and sanitary supplies underarm, distributing their plunder to those too elderly or enfeebled to participate in the pillaging themselves. A considerable share even found its way into the claws of the leeches, which summoned a memory of something Jade had once said about a species of parasitoid wasp—renowned for injecting a behavior-altering venom that would induce its arachnid host to weave a protective web for its unborn offspring. Jade's love of all things green had naturally extended to the critters that inhabited it, and she had often expressed the sentiment that one could find beauty even in the cruelest, most horrific aspects of nature, no matter how small. Caleb would argue there was little beauty to be found here, however . . .

"This is fast devolving into a riot," Atlas observed, directing their backup drone to orbit above the commercial hub for a sweeping birds-eye view of the carnage raging below. "Not that I'm complaining—we're getting some *great* footage—but where in the Abyss are Phalanx?"

The obvious answer: Executor Royce had ordered all personnel to the blockade in an effort to stem Harmony's advance and push the insurgents back into the Mouth. For the most part, the *Novara* had been left largely unpoliced, allowing for debacles like the present one to take root throughout the arc ship. In the absence of any practical law enforcement, locals had been forced to take matters into their own hands. Here, tensions reached something of a crescendo as a group of business owners, armed with concussion-grade firearms and all manner of bludgeoning implements, rallied together and mobilized to defend their livelihoods from the looters. Pushing, shoving, and verbal threats soon escalated into widespread physical altercation. The trespassers vastly outnumbered the retaliators, and were too rabid and desperate to be deterred by nonlethal countermeasures alone. Every attempt at discouraging them only provoked further aggravation, and before long, Tchaikovsky Precinct transformed from an upmarket retail district into a Renaissance-era painting depicting the very worst of human nature: aggression, selfishness, and fierce tribalism—*centuries as a spacefaring civilization, and all that separates us from our primal ancestors is the technology in our pockets.*

Cones of reality-bending energy fulminated from various points in the fray, knocking gaggles of rampaging mouthians back as the bowsiders began indiscriminately discharging their firearms. Even at a relatively low caliber, it appeared as if an invisible bull had been released into the voracious horde.

"We need to move on," Caleb said. "Let's find another location before this starts getting dangerous."

Atlas's virtu-sim helmet obscured their eyes, but their giddy grin shone brightly. Mx. Baudelaire struck Caleb as the last person on the *Novara* who would ever dream of advocating violence, unless, of course, it meant capturing it in their viewfinder . . .

"Are you insane, Callaghan?" they replied, incredulous. "This is absolute gold! We can't leave now."

"I'm glad you're having fun but consider what message we're putting out by streaming this! We're contradicting our entire stance by portraying humans as savages and leeches as peaceful bystanders."

Atlas shrugged. "You wanted the rough an' ready truth . . . Well, here it is."

Before she could deliver her riposte, the growl of fission-injection repulsor pads carved the clamor asunder and stunned them both into silence. She turned just in time to catch sight of a raptor as it blew out of the precinct's transit terminal at excessive speed. The armored transport scudded above the roiling crowd, clearing the arcade's curved LED ceiling by less than a meter, reflecting a psychedelic light show of animated brand logos and pixel fireworks in its tinted windshield.

"Bug swatters?" Atlas asked, instinctively maneuvering their drone out of the speeding vehicle's flight path, then swinging it around to make sure they had it in shot.

Caleb shook her head. "I don't think so; they normally show up riding shrikes as they did in Rennaxi Junction . . . That thing has microthrusters all over its exterior; almost looks like it's been outfitted for zero-atmo flight. And take a gander at the decal on its side: that's the NTSC insignia."

For the most part, the rioting masses managed to ignore the raptor as it slowed to a hover over the commercial hub. That soon changed with the precipitous deployment of chaff flares, an incandescent rib cage ejecting from the *sternum* of its chassis. The rioters fled amid billowing clouds of smoke, some batting at their ragged robes as they were set upon by the molten slag disgorged by the falling flares. The countermeasure proved effective in not only dispersing the crowd but clearing a landing zone, too. The raptor descended on four thundering columns of shimmering antigrav propulsion, setting down not ten meters away from where Caleb and Atlas stood. The transport's side doors slid open, then a handful of individuals wearing midnight-blue body armor disembarked and formed a perimeter with military proficiency. The way their angular helmets completely encased their heads gave them an unnerving, grenadieresque impersonality, with a single, cycloptic eye unit positioned centrally to their featureless faceplates, glowing a threatening red. Caleb recognized the elongated profile of the marksman rifles they wielded from the time Jade took her to the firing range, back when they first started courting. *This is loud, boring, and a blatant attempt to impress me*, she had said at the time, cursing herself now for not savoring those precious seconds together.

Publicly, the NTSC had no infantry force to speak of, other than the security details stationed at barracks and military installations. But every ACS student knew of the urban legends about shadow operatives, directed by the highest levels of government to handle black project operations, unofficially known as the venators.

What a gross misallocation of resources it is, she thought, *to dispatch such elite units to deal with a spate of civil unrest.* The fact that they were mobilizing out in the open for all to see signaled just how desperate the situation had really grown. It became quickly evident, however, that the venators—*if* that's what they were—had not come for the rioters; they were there, in fact, for her . . .

"Caleb Callaghan," one said, marching toward them, the words distorted through so many layers of voice encryption that she could hardly be sure there was even a human buried beneath all that tech. "You've been summoned by Admiral Coombs; we're here to retrieve you."

Caleb cast a nervous glance back at Atlas, whose blank expression conveyed little guidance or counsel of any kind.

"Are you detaining me?" she nervously asked.

The armored manakin shook their head slowly. "Consider it a request— one you would do well to accept . . . Let's move; the admiral is *not* a man to be kept waiting."

Her suspicions regarding the raptor's astronautic flight capabilities were soon vindicated. Though the venators had bundled her into a windowless passenger cabin, offering no inkling whatsoever as to their intended destination, she *felt* the moment the raptor transitioned into the frictionless embrace of the endless night. The repulsor pads ceased their incessant vibration, rendered suddenly obsolete with nothing upon which to exact their gravity-mitigating force. The transport coasted like a pebble skimmed across ice, altering its trajectory with spasmodic bursts from the microthrusters she had identified earlier.

She opened her mouth to ask where they were taking her but could utter no more than a syllable before one of the venators brusquely cut her off.

"We aren't here to answer your questions, cherry top. Save them for the admiral."

She didn't appreciate the nickname but struggled to discern which of them she needed to reprimand, given their concealed faces and the uniformity of their rigid body language. Instead, she swallowed her tongue and focused on keeping the contents of her stomach down as the raptor's pilot initiated a prolonged burn, sending the transport hurtling away from the *Novara* at white-knuckle velocity.

Her mind raced with probabilities and potentialities. She took a moment to catalog everything she knew about the illustrious admiral, digging deep within herself to try and ascertain what he could possibly want to discuss with her. She and Atlas had been banging the drum with such ferocity, she couldn't help but wonder whether the man had deemed their organization more trouble than it was worth; they *had* been intentionally stirring the pot at a time of extreme societal instability, after all. With the Administration in disarray and the council indefinitely disbanded, Coombs was now the highest-ranking official on the *Novara*, and if he believed shutting Humanity First down was in the union's best interest, then such a decision was well within his purview . . .

Before long, the effects of deceleration began to pull her chest and shoulders forward; she felt the familiar tug of local gravity like so many instances in which she had shaken herself awake from dreams about falling. No sooner had the raptor lurched to a stop than her chaperones exploded into action. The passenger door slid open; the venators hastily disembarked, ushering her out into a compact shuttle bay. Stepping onto the deck, the raucous sound of the hangar's blast doors drawing together pulled her attention over her shoulder. Through the egress aperture's glimmering fission field, she saw the *Novara* hanging motionless against the empty black—what was inexorably the last of her species, trapped in the confines of a dilapidated lifeboat; so vulnerable, so devastatingly isolated, so small from this distance that she could shut one eye and blot it out with the length of her thumb, just before the closing bulkheads hid it from view. The sight served as a reaffirmation of the vital importance of her mission. What she and Atlas strived to achieve represented more than just politics or entertainment: this was the very survival of the human species. Soon, she would have the ear of the most powerful man on the *Novara*, and she resolved in that instant that before she left this place, she would have her say.

* * *

Through a series of claustrophobic corridors they went, worming their way through the bowels of what she could only surmise was a military black site housed within a ship or station of some kind—a mobile headquarters for whatever shadowy government agency the venators answered to. They arrived in a spacious rotunda that, as far as she could ascertain, acted as a central hub, with vestibules heading off in various directions connecting to other areas of the craft. In the center of the room, a remarkable metal sculpture, perhaps three meters long, rotated in a limited suspension field as if hung from the ceiling by invisible strings. Fashioned from scintillating platinum alloy, it depicted a to-scale representation of a ship—presumably the one Caleb had been brought aboard. She recognized it as a mid-sized corvette with all the hallmarks of an exploration vessel: a Coriolis ring of thruster nacelles mounted concentrically around an elongated fuselage, encased within a protective framework of superconducting radiation shields. While most ships in the *Novara*'s fleet retained at least some degree of pre-Collision makeup, the rendition levitating before her looked modern by design. But how the construction of such a sizable vessel could have been kept hidden from the public for so long—it simply didn't add up. *Unless . . . No . . . it couldn't possibly be . . . could it?*

The venators marched her into the space where they would ultimately leave her: a rustic parlor with sumptuous leather furniture and walls clad in decadent mahogany paneling. Logs popped and crackled beneath a marble fireplace, enriching the temperate air with the aroma of woodsmoke that, although undeniably pleasing, made her eyes water. She couldn't quite place the genre of music drifting across the room to her from an antique record player, although she took a kind of melancholy delight in her certainty that the soulful voice reaching into her had likely been recorded well over half a millennia ago.

Though she found her surroundings deeply relaxing, transitioning into them from the cold and clinical aesthetic that characterized the rest of the ship sent her head into a spin. It felt as though she had haplessly wandered through some temporal rupture into the distant past. It was Atherton Edevane's obsession with the ostentatious decor prevalent throughout the twentieth century, dialed up to eleven—a wistful love letter to a perceived golden age in interior design, a time before glass, concrete, and carbon fiber supplanted the use of natural materials in furnishing.

Caleb spied the supposed visionary behind this grand homage on the far side of the parlor, sparring with a decommissioned grenadier in a home gym. In lieu of his decorated, ivory-white uniform, Admiral Coombs had dressed for the occasion in joggers and a sweatshirt. Wearing purple boxing gloves with gold trim, he grunted and sighed, throwing jabs in rapid salvos at his drill companion, the android's hands replaced with detachable paddles to catch and temper each blow. For a man pushing eighty, he seemed remarkably agile, with bright, sagacious eyes fixated on-target—far too young in appearance for the dark, sagging pits of their sockets. He clocked Caleb lingering in the entrance, paused, then blew a sharp whistle to instruct the grenadier to suspend the drill. The machine dropped its paddles, took several hulking footsteps backward, and stood rigidly to attention.

"Miss Callaghan!" Coombs exclaimed breathlessly, removing his gloves and reaching for a towel to wipe the sweat from his neck and brow. Caleb didn't respond, just stood deathly still, keeping her consternated gaze locked firmly on the dormant automaton.

"You needn't worry about this one," Jasper reassured. "Counterterrorism are still investigating the nature of the weapon the insurgents deployed to compromise our mechanized infantry; needless to say, we are out of range of its influence here. You are quite safe." He let a coy smile tug at the corners of his lips, narrowed his stare. "I trust that as an esteemed student of the Academy of Colonial Stewardship, you know where *here* is."

"Dropout," she corrected, sinking her shoulders in resignation. "I'm no longer at the academy; the semester just gone was my last . . . To answer your question, I *believe* this is the NTSC *Hope's Embrace*, but I'm either having an incredibly lucid dream right now, or . . . or I'm standing on a ghost ship."

He gave a nod of approbation, motioning for her to take a seat on the burgundy chesterfield couch positioned near the fireplace. "Sit, child . . . I do not make a habit of commenting on a woman's appearance, but you look exhausted."

Caleb lowered herself to an elegant perch, scraping her hair back into an unruly bun. "Perhaps, with a little forewarning about this liaison, I might have had a chance to clean up, first."

Coombs spread his hands apologetically. "There are few resources more precious than time. And I'm afraid we are startlingly short on supply."

She felt her tired face tighten into a frown. "Nevertheless, I definitely did *not* appreciate being made to abandon my colleague in such a perilous situation."

"Believe it or not, the continued existence of the *Hope's Embrace* is likely the least sensitive piece of information I will disclose to you today . . . *You* are here because I believe I can trust you, but Atlas Baudelaire is an aficionado when it comes to opening the floodgates on sensitive truths, which is precisely the reason I could not risk them being here . . . If it's any consolation, a second team was dispatched to squash the disruption in Tchaikovsky Precinct after your retrieval. I'm sure Atlas is fine; editing together an exposé about the ghoulish venators as we speak, no doubt."

She didn't need platitudes but forced a smile to acknowledge his attempt at alleviating the tension. He collapsed into the opposing recliner, unleashing an audacious *ahh* that reminded Caleb of her father.

"This is no hallucination, and there is nothing paranormal afoot. Indeed, this is the *Hope's Embrace.* So, tell me what you know of her history."

"It was back in the late fifties, I believe," she began after clearing her throat. "The question was raised whether, instead of restoring the *Novara*'s ripple-space capabilities—an ostensibly impossible feat—a fleet of smaller vessels could be constructed to begin ferrying the human remnant to a nearby star system. Long-range telemetry indicated Vurri-389 has at least a handful of barren rocks with gravity suitable for an enclosed settlement, much like Arcadia or Promethei on Mars—a far cry from the Grasslands of Pasture, but it would have been a damn sight better than *this . . .* The predicted transit time on impulse thrusters alone would have exceeded something like forty years—hardly a viable solution when you factor in a return journey. But then a breakthrough was made in the construction of a miniaturized version of the *Novara*'s ripple drive."

"Ripple-space traversal, as we all know, is contingent on mass," the Admiral interjected, gesturing a fist as if knocking on someone's door. "The bigger the ship, the easier it is to distort space-time, the greater the distance we can effectively *skip.*"

"Precisely . . . Historically, a corvette *this* size wouldn't have been able to generate a ripple significant enough to reduce the considerable time sink, but engineers found a way to mitigate that limitation. The *Hope's Embrace* was heralded as the arbiter of our salvation; in just twelve years, she could supposedly have her first complement of settlers planetside and be back to lead a convoy of newly built arc ships to what would hopefully be a thriving, self-sustaining colony."

"But, alas, the best-laid plans of mice and men."

Caleb concurred with a solemn nod. "Communication was lost shortly after departure. Twelve years came and went with no sign of her return. Possible explanations for her disappearance ranged from a potential failure with the prototype ripple drive to some devastating interstellar event. Some even hypothesized the settlers may have chosen not to return at all, deeming it a more economical use of resources to repurpose the ship to further expand their colony. Either way, the expedition was chalked up as a total failure, and the entire endeavor was abandoned. The Administration established the Novarasphere shortly after, criminalizing all commercial travel beyond *Novara* sensor range to ensure no ship ever met the same fate as the *Hope's Embrace* again."

Coombs gave an exaggerated nod as if to say *impressive.* "I don't blame you for absconding from the academy, Miss Callaghan; I imagine your talents were wasted there . . . But here is where truth deviates from common knowledge. Disaster did indeed befall the *Hope's Embrace,* but not in the way people think. The Novarasphere is more than just an arbitrary perimeter enforced for the safety of our civilian traffic. It is a barrier preventing people from stumbling onto a dismaying truth."

" . . . Which is?"

"That the *Devourer* will not allow us to leave its locality. Several years after she began her doomed maiden voyage, a group of wayward salvagers found the *Embrace* adrift in the deep void. They notified a nearby patrol ship of the discovery before, similarly, going dark themselves. Avrora Shannah—the admiral at the time—launched a covert recovery initiative to rescue the scavengers and tow the *Embrace* back into NTU airspace. The stranded crew were retrieved via EVA to avoid any further loss of transport. In their debrief, they reported that as they came within range of the *Hope's Embrace,* their ship was suddenly set upon by mysterious light, engulfed by the same luminous spores we see pouring from the *Devourer's* conduits. Their fission reactor was irrevocably disabled and all fail-safes somehow negated. A preliminary investigation revealed the *Embrace* had suffered the same inexplicable outage. Tragically, it transpired the ship's two-hundred-strong crew of aspiring colonists eventually suffocated in the absence of air circulation. They died gasping for air in the pitch black, trapped behind inoperable bulkheads and free-floating in zero gravity."

"That's . . . horrible." The thought thrust an icy stalactite directly into Caleb's heart. "So, it isn't enough for the leeches to maroon us in dark space and siphon our precious resources; they feel the need to put pernicious countermeasures in place to make sure we can't escape, either? It's a disgrace; an outrage! I mean, why the big secret? If that monstrosity really is imprisoning us here, do people not have the right to know?"

Coombs sat back and steepled his fingers. "You must remember, this was at a time of relative . . . well, 'peace' is a strong word—we'll go with 'accord.' Admiral Shannah feared disclosing the truth would trigger mass revolt among the Novarian populace, *against*—what we must not forget—is essentially our benefactor. As much as we may malign it, the *Devourer* is the only thing keeping us all from meeting the same terrible end as the original crew of this vessel. Tensions will always fluctuate, but for the sake of our survival, we *must* always maintain a baseline of civility and cooperation. Even during the Antonelli Expansion, in our bloodiest battles with the interceptors, we knew never to directly assault the *Devourer*, because if it ever chose to suddenly relinquish its hold on the *Novara*, then it would mean certain extinction for the human remnant."

Caleb didn't like his reasoning but struggled in earnest to find fault in it. She stood to her feet and began pacing around the parlor, stopping occasionally to appreciate its gallery of Old-Earth adornments. Lingering near a case filled with medals documenting the admiral's storied service to the union, she said, "And so for all these years, the *Hope's Embrace* has been floating out here, kept hidden from the public. Why wasn't she just decommissioned, stripped for parts and valuable materials?"

"And squander such a fine vessel? After all, she needed no repair; once brought back from the *Devourer's* perimeter, all systems immediately came back online. She has since remained under the NTSC's supervision, passed like a secret heirloom from administration to administration. Over the decades, she's seen use as an intelligence headquarters, a holding and interrogation facility for extreme persons of interest, as well as an advance early-warning station for the detection of cosmic events or approaching threats."

The admiral rose to his feet and moved to the fireplace, above which an oil portrait of the late Administrator Vargos hung in an ornate walnut frame. Wearing her signature imperial-red suit, the woman stared dead on, dipping her head slightly with tactful resolve. Caleb couldn't help but feel that, instead of portraying her in the most flattering light possible, the artist had purposefully accentuated the deep wrinkles and harsh angles framing her face, rendering her unsmiling conviction in an caricatural fashion. There had long been rumblings regarding an illicit affair between the admiral and the administrator—vehemently denied as *scurrilous fabrications* by both parties. Nevertheless, the wistful reverence with which Coombs regarded the painting now undoubtedly added weight to those rumors.

"The *Embrace* took on new life under Madeline's stewardship," he said, and the croak in his voice did not escape her notice. "She was a remarkable woman: hungry, resourceful, ambitious. Unlike many of her predecessors, she was never content with merely maintaining the status quo. She looked to the horizon and saw something brighter in our future than endless, ineluctable atrophy. Though she led through austerity and unimpeachable adherence to tradition, behind closed doors she became obsessed with finding new ways to better our species, to improve our situation. As such, she had this historic vessel refitted as a research station, tasked with the development of cutting-edge defense technologies."

An uncertain pause lingered between them, then Caleb asked, "What kind of technologies?"

"Technologies that will strengthen us, that will restore our tenacious spirit. For centuries we've been on the back heel, fighting to catch our breath as we struggle to find our place in the universe. Thanks to Madeline's efforts, we now have within our grasp the means to recement ourselves as the force to be reckoned with that we once were."

Caleb felt something unfamiliar swell in her chest: hope, optimism, excitement for the future. "Show me."

A cunning grin extended across Coombs' face. "I intend to; it's the very reason you're here. I've been watching your efforts with keen interest, Miss Callaghan; what you've accomplished with Humanity First over the past two months is nothing short of miraculous. I see in you the same drive and dedication that I so admired in Madeline. I believe you understand as *she* did that the brittle bones of our society must be broken in order to enact meaningful change . . . But, before I allow you to peek behind the curtain, I must ask you this: How far are you willing to go? What are you prepared to give to save the human remnant from extinction?"

Caleb twisted her lips in contemplation, allowing the questions to burrow deep within her. The answer rose from somewhere in her abdomen, coaxing a lonely tear that pooled in the corner of her eye before rolling down her cheek. "Honestly, I'm not sure I have much left *to* give. The leeches already robbed me of everything I held dear."

Coombs turned mournful eyes back to the administrator's portrait. She could scarcely believe she was looking at the admiral; he had hardly presented himself as the hard-nosed militarist people knew him for, and now a sudden frailness had descended upon him, leaving him looking vulnerable and weathered around the edges.

"I know a thing or two about grief, Miss Callaghan," he admitted. "For Madeline and myself, this place was more than just the nerve center of our initiative; we made the *Hope's Embrace* our home, a refuge where we could enjoy our time together away from public scrutiny—a conflict of interest, as our relationship would undoubtedly have been condemned . . . Her death has left a yawning hollow in my heart. She was my conscience, my moral compass, my guiding star. All I can do now is continue along her trajectory and honor her legacy by doing everything within my power to accomplish what she set out to achieve."

"That's the funny thing about loss," Caleb tearfully mused. "We dread it more than anything else in life. One day, it inevitably comes for us, and suddenly, we no longer need to fear it. It can be strangely liberating: finding yourself with nothing left to lose. It relieves us of our inhibitions, empowers us to push through boundaries we might once have thought beyond our capacity."

She stood up and joined Jasper by the fireplace, wiping her reddening face with the sleeve of her zip-up. She continued, "When you feel like you have nothing left to live for, you have to find something to *fight* for instead. Nothing is off the cards for me, Admiral. I will do whatever it takes to ensure not *one* more human life is lost to the savagery of those vicious parasites . . . Whatever it is you want to show me, I'm all in."

TWENTY-FOUR

oombs invited Caleb to join him at his antique executive desk. She obliged, affording a charitable, albeit slightly bemused chuckle in response to his next words, "Hold on tight." But then the ground seemed to give beneath her feet, and she realized she had been lured onto an elevator. The rectangular platform descended on whining hydraulic pistons, bringing the admiral's workspace down to the deck below. A hive of activity awaited the pair as they arrived in what might once have been a mess hall—since converted into a high-spec laboratory. Light panels lined the low ceiling like giant tiles fashioned from lucent ceramic, reflected with crystalline vividity in the sheen of the epoxy resin floor. Glass partitions divided the facility into several distinct zones: microbiology, advanced material analysis, engineering, and testing. Lab technicians wearing gloves, hairnets, and face masks busied themselves with their various disciplines. They sat hunched over computer terminals and peered studiously down microscopes, some tending to great obelisks of machinery comprising incubators, fabricators, and optical spectrometers, encircled by rings of compact particle accelerators.

"No one is saluting you," Caleb observed quietly as the admiral led her away from his now almost comically out of place desk. "These aren't military personnel?"

"Civilian," he confirmed. "They live and work here on the *Hope's Embrace*. They've all been given halcyon-level security clearance after rigorous vetting and conditioning. Madeline knew that relying too heavily on the NTSC's existing knowledge base would have stifled innovation. She brought in expertise from all over the *Novara* for this venture; they are all at the top of their respective fields."

What this "venture" was, Caleb could still only hypothesize. Initially, it occurred to her that they may have been manufacturing biological weapons—a virus, maybe, to subdue or chemically neuter the leeches. *If we can't get rid of them, perhaps we can at least stop them from reproducing—stem their booming population.* Further survey of her surroundings, however, gave her cause to suspect that what they were developing here was, perhaps, more hardwarecentric. A library of death occupied the lab's farthest wall— an oppressive edifice of firearm mag-racks housing enough munitions to outfit an entire platoon. Only, the weapons in storage looked strange, as if inked angrily into existence with a blunt quill. She spied bizarre attachments and modifications that appeared almost organic in their irregularity: vicious arrays of spines and protrusions; aggregations of bulbs clinging to barrels and stocks like egg sacks laid by an unknown species of hideous insect.

"What is this place?" She asked, steeling herself against an implacable wave of revulsion. "What exactly is it you're building here?"

Coombs's frustratingly laconic response: "The future, Miss Callaghan . . . The future."

He walked her to the center of the room where there stood a lonely glass lectern with a luma-cast interface. Humming a triumphant tune, he hammered fingertips against its slanted screen, navigating through several authentication tabs before taking an abrupt step back, joking, "Drum roll, please."

A fissure opened at the lectern's plinth as the ground separated and folded into itself, unleashing a steadily rising surge of ice vapor into the recycled air. A two-by-four-meter pedestal ascended from below deck—an opaque slab, glowing subtly from within, acting as an exhibition bed for the nightmarish specimen resting dormant atop its stark surface. Caleb's disbelieving eyes fell on the ghastly hunk of *Devourer* wreckage rising from beneath her feet as if climbing from the fires of hell itself. It felt like beholding a sculpture gener- ated by a machine learning algorithm—one lacking the complex abstraction to discern between something built and something grown, and so it had sim- ply conjured a work that was *both* simultaneously.

Though she experienced a primal compulsion to avert her gaze, she forced herself to stare at it, to see if there was any sense to be made of its inscrutable composition. This, of course, only inspired further revulsion as she noticed the spasmodic twitching of its shredded muscle mass, the pulsing contrac- tions of the fibrous connective tissue attaching flesh to its skeleton of cast- iron shards. What unnerved her more than its grotesque appearance was that it seemed *active*; the surrounding air buzzed with an electrostatic charge, as though she might be struck down by a bolt of lightning were she to reach out and touch it. Admiral Coombs shared no such apprehension; he placed his palm against a structure that resembled a harp molded from ebony-black cartilage, stroking its surface as one might the bodywork of a brand-new swoop. Wisps of luminous spores percolated from its membranous skin, gathering around his hand like bioluminescent algae disturbed in water.

"Exposure to that stuff turns people blind, doesn't it?" she cautioned. "Aren't you worried about your flesh rotting off?"

"It's quite harmless," Coombs reassured. "In fact, studies have shown physical contact with the xeno-spores can have intensely rejuvenating effects on aging skin like mine."

"I'll make sure to incorporate *shoving my face inside a vent* into my daily skincare routine." She took a steadying breath, reminding herself at whom she had directed her sarcasm. "Apologies, Admiral . . . It's just, I'm so tired; I haven't slept since the attack at the blockade and I would really appreciate a little brevity here . . . So, please: What in the unholy Abyss is this monstrosity and what's it doing on the *Hope's Embrace*?"

Jasper knocked on his imaginary door with his knuckles again. "Straight to brass tacks—I admire that." He straightened his posture and clasped his hands behind his back, finally taking on the stern demeanor of an admiral of the NTSC. "As you have no doubt intuited, *this* is a sizable wedge of *Devourer* xeno-technology. It's largely nondescript, as far as we can extrapolate—a portion of iliocostalis muscle tissue from somewhere around its dorsal region."

Caleb scoffed. "Surely you're not making anatomical comparisons between this pile of scrap and entrails with known biology?"

"You'd be surprised at how familiar some of its organic structure really is. It seems the *Devourer*'s designers came to many of the same conclusions as evolution did in sculpting life on Earth. Where flesh intersects with material engineering, however—that has proven a much tougher nut to crack."

"How in the stars were you able to get close enough to harvest it without triggering the *Devourer*'s interceptor immune response?"

"The piece before you was recovered from the Debris Belt. There are fields of xeno-technology floating in the outer reaches—all largely untouched, due to there being almost no want for it in the salvage market, not to mention some of the outlandish superstitions spacers maintain about keeping it in their holds."

Struck by a rash of impulsivity, Caleb followed Jasper's example and reached out to place fingertips against the specimen, feeling an unusual *fizzing* sensation as the xeno-spores emerged to greet her. "But it seems . . . *alive*. How could that be the case if it's been decaying in the void for over a century?"

A reverent look appeared on the admiral's leathery face. "'The doorstep to the temple of wisdom is a knowledge of our own ignorance,' he recited. "The universe is a strange place, and we are but three-dimensional creatures of simple minds doing our best to make sense of it. We perceive our reality through a rigid framework of understanding: matter, space-time, conscious-ness, quantum physics—all pigeonholed into neat little boxes so we can feign comprehension of this existential plane . . . But, as has already been dem-onstrated, we will inevitably encounter things in our travels that do not fit comfortably within that framework . . . Ergo, we must abandon what we *think* we know if we ever hope to learn."

So much for brevity . . .

"When it comes to the *Devourer*," he carried on bloviating, "its physical form can be damaged, detached, and strewn across large distances, and yet, severed material remains somehow intact—powered and linked intrinsically to its larger mass through a means that has completely evaded our detec-tion . . . It is a prime example of one of the great mysteries Madeline hoped to unravel by setting up this endeavor. She believed that only through unlocking the *Devourer*'s secrets might humanity forge a way forward. If we are success-ful in fulfilling her vision, we can leapfrog ourselves in technological advance-ment hundreds, if not *thousands*, of years."

Coombs's expression sagged upon noticing that Caleb hardly shared his enthusiasm for the notion. She recoiled from the specimen, casting her gaze around the laboratory as a bitterness crept on spindle legs into her heart. Watching the admiral's lab coats tinker at their stations, it dawned on her that the development of these new defense technologies constituted far more than the mere reverse engineering of *Devourer* xeno-technology. His pur-pose was clear: to replicate and incorporate it into the fabrication of lethal new armaments to bolster NTSC military power. She turned her attention to the armory and realized with encroaching horror that she had seen these hybridized firearms once before: wielded by the leech insurgents during their first failed assault on the blockade. Her indignation was a molten lava stream, threatening to erupt from her mouth in a tirade of harsh language. But she tempered herself, knowing that she could remain civil while refusing to betray Jade's memory by engaging with this farce in *any* capacity.

"Thank you, Admiral," she said, coming just short of spitting her words. "But I'd like to be taken back to the *Novara* now."

"That . . . can be arranged, of course," stuttered Coombs. "Although, I would be remiss if I did not implore you to stay a little while longer; we've barely even scratched the surface of what I have in store to show."

"And yet, I've seen everything I need to . . . With all due respect, I'm sur-prised you think I'd want *anything* to do with whatever this is. If you *had* been watching our streams, you'd know Humanity First's primary objectives are to extradite the leeches to the *Devourer* and find a way to detach it from our hull—not to further integrate it."

She motioned around the room. "You've got the top biologists, physicists, and engineers squirreled away out here, muzzled behind nondisclosure agreements, and instead of working to put an end to the *Novara*'s dependency on foreign energy, you have them poring over leech tech like maggots over a corpse."

Coombs wagged a finger in the air. "I commend your pertinacity, Caleb, but you're basing your assessment on a common misconception . . . Please, just another moment of your time—that's all I need to get you properly informed and brought into the fold."

She deliberated briefly, then gave a reluctant nod.

"Outstanding." He moved to address the lectern's interface once more. Seconds later, a trapdoor slid open beside the first pedestal, then Jasper's clockwork house of horrors produced another specimen for exhibition. A succession of eight glass frames rose from below deck, each approximately ten centimeters thick and roughly the size of a door, spaced less than half a meter forward and to the rear of one another. Collectively, they displayed the plastinated remains of a leech in coronal plane cross sections, the first presenting the intricate sensory organs in the tip of its snout, and the last, a demonstration of the chitin plating at the rear of its abdomen, as well as the boneless musculature found in the taurus region of its exoskeletal legs. Though she knew its bodily fluids would have been replaced with polyester during the embalming process to prevent decay, she could still feel its noxious, alien stench infiltrating her nostrils, sense the injurious pathogens seeping from the tissue of its innards and saturating her skin. There was no point in denying it; she hated them dead and dissected just as much as she did alive.

"Say hello to Harvey," Coombs quipped.

Against her better judgment, she began circling the anatomized gargoyle to inspect its numerous vertical slices. "I'd rather not."

"Suit yourself . . . Harvey here has been helping us better understand the connection between the leeches and the *Devourer*. Did they build it; somehow gestate it; is it a part of their natural ecosystem, cybernetically modified to suit their spacefaring needs? Confoundingly, what we're discovering is that there appears to be absolutely no connection whatsoever . . ."

She cocked an eyebrow to signal her piqued interest. At the admiral's direction, an emitter positioned above the exhibition bed stirred to life, lumacasting vibrant three-dimensional graphics that highlighted the whorls and ridges of the *Devourer* wreckage in gruesome detail. A pair of double helices floated at Caleb's eye level, nested centrally to a manic array of charts, scatter plots, and equations. The right-hand render looked normal enough: two waltzing spirals connected by a twisted ladder of base pairs. The left hand, however, seemed unusually geometric, built not from curved strands of molecules but entwined prismatic spires—an elongated spirograph seemingly infinite in its inward complexity.

"The strand on the right is Harvey's DNA," Coombs explained. "Leeches, or 'insectum-bipedalis' as the eggheads prefer to call them, are carbon-based. I know you don't like drawing comparisons, but as a species they are not all that dissimilar from life that could have developed on Earth . . . On the left." He nodded toward the second model. "You are looking at the genetic source code carried in the cells of the *Devourer*'s organic structure. It's similarly carbon-based—dependent on water and oxygen to survive—but with one key difference . . ."

"Which is?"

"It is perfect; there are no vestiges or leftovers of genetic instructions as one would expect to find from eons of evolutionary trial and error. Its molecular composition is so efficient, so refined, that it can *only* be the result of intelligent design. It did not originate in chaos, cultivated in the primordial soup of some distant alien world, but was purposefully and meticulously engineered into existence, undoubtedly by minds immeasurably more advanced than our own."

"Genetic augmentation is nothing new, though," Caleb interjected. "We've been editing out hereditary and congenital diseases for centuries, now."

"Modifying, yes," Coombs countered. "But to create the building blocks of life from scratch is a feat far beyond our technological capacity. And leeches, with their vastly inferior intellect . . . well, let's say the notion is *laughable* at best . . . Extensive genetic analysis has shown *Devourer* DNA shares less than 0.1 percent chromosomal similarity with the insectum-bipedalis genome. Ergo, we can draw only one conclusion: they didn't construct it, and it cannot possibly be from their own biosphere."

Caleb glanced over the admiral's shoulder just in time to catch one of his "eggheads" sending an exaggerated eye roll to a colleague. Evidently, the admiral was hardly the leading authority on the subject, and was definitely *not* the man to be relaying this information. His scholarly manner receded. He tilted his chin up and stared gravely down the line of his bulbous nose at his coveted asset. "The leeches hold no claim to it . . . The *Devourer*'s technology does not belong to *them* any more than the skin of a dog belongs to the fleas on its back. They are nothing but vagrant stowaways, rummaging like rats in the dark for shelter and sustenance, all the while selfishly hoarding a power that they do not deserve and cannot possibly hope to comprehend." He turned to her as a sudden heaviness weighed his bearing. "We could very well be the last of our species, Caleb—it's an uncomfortable truth, but a truth, nonetheless. Failing to take advantage of every resource available to us would be irresponsible, would it not? Consider the *Devourer*'s ability to convert water, oxygen, and protein into the energy needed to power the *Novara*, or indeed the awesome matter-erasing combat capabilities of its defensive fleet. What utter fools we would be to leave such a wealth of knowledge and resources untapped. We must seize this power, learn to harness it, and use it to elevate ourselves out of purgatory and blaze a path to glory."

He swiped his hand across the lectern's interface, triggering 'Harvey' and the xenotech wreckage to retract below deck. He motioned her forward like a waiter showing a diner to their seat, then with a devilish grin, said, "And to that end, we must first eliminate the competition . . ."

They skirted around a graphite-grey conference table and arrived at a wide, diamond-shaped viewport. He addressed a nearby console and prompted the unsealing of the aperture's blast shutters. A hangar considerably larger than the shuttle bay Caleb had disembarked in then revealed itself through the glass. She gazed through the reflection of her pale face into the trapezoidal chamber beyond, her elevated vantage point affording a decent view of the activity roiling below. Clearly, the personnel she had encountered so far represented just the tip of the iceberg, re: the resources Coombs and Vargos had amassed for this venture. The hangar stretched on for fifty meters and terminated at a forward-sloped fission field. Immediately in front and below the viewport lay a bustling staging area. Here, approximately one hundred venators tended to their equipment, some training in melee combat while others stood in tight formation as their commanding officers inspected them. Like the weapons stored in the laboratory, their impact armor had been enhanced substantially with *Devourer* xeno-technology. Much of the carbon composite plating protecting their upper body was fused in broad tracts with muscle fibers that glistened as if wet with ink. Tendon structures enwrapped the joints of their limbs like grisly sleeves of carnage, doubtless providing a marked increase in strength and maneuverability. Then, for perhaps nothing other than purely aesthetic reasons, osseous spines as black as onyx breached through areas of flesh on their chest plates and shoulder pads. The menacing protrusions crawled up the back of their padded necks and culminated in a horseshoe shape, which arced around their lone, beaming red eye, impressing the rim of a hood, only one sculpted from sharpened claws and finger bones.

This was no spec ops force as Caleb had first surmised: it was an execution squad, outfitted to sow as much fear and panic in its targets as *inhu*manly possible. The admiral contrived to send a clear message to the leech vermin: that their *Savior* could save them no longer, and that, henceforth, the human remnant would be the ones wielding its blessings as a sword and shield. Were she not still filled with such grief and animosity, she just might have felt sorry for them . . .

Dangling from the hangar's vaulted ceiling like a bizarre chandelier, she spied what looked like a giant, five-meter pebble, contained within a cage constructed from the castellated forks of a cargo crane. A large wedge had been carved out of a section of the object's gaussian curvature, triggering a heartbreaking memory of Jade and her love for those small, candy shell confectionaries from her favorite dessert place in Virrisachi Arcade. Only, instead of chocolate ganache, the pebble contained more of the same alien viscera that Caleb had now decided she had seen enough of for a lifetime.

"Is that," she tremulously began, "is that an interceptor?"

Coombs steepled his hands on his belly and showed a self-congratulatory smirk. "Indeed, it is . . . A more modern variant than the ones we faced during the Antonelli Expansion, mind you. They were piloted by leeches back in those days. The only edge we had against our enemy was their capacity for pilot error, but the *Devourer* has since removed that weakness; its defenses are now completely autonomous and deadlier than ever before . . . Just imagine what the NTSC could achieve with that kind of combat superiority."

Reams of cables spilled from the interceptor's exposed innards, some rubber coated, others encased in the vertebrae and sinew of miniature conduits. They trailed to the ground before snaking along the deck to the hangar's forward area, eventually rearing up and plugging into the underbellies of what the admiral undoubtedly considered his prized ponies. Six NTSC kestrels levitated in a stack of three pairs just beyond the coaming of the hangar's emergency bulkhead. Caleb struggled to identify the means by which they kept themselves aloft. She saw no evidence of repulsors or suspension tech at play; they weren't hovering in VTOL on idling vertical stabilizers. They merely hung in the air, silent and motionless, completely impervious to the local gravity of the *Hope's Embrace*. Beneath the fighters were a group of technicians wearing hazard suits. *Or perhaps "beast masters" is a more fitting term*, she thought. Unsurprisingly, the fighters had been cannibalized, stripped almost entirely down to their airframes, and impregnated, like the venators' body armor, with xeno-technology. They resembled tremendous Cretaceous-period birds, plucked, skinned, and doused in tar, their missing cockpit canopies and upper flight surfaces now arrowheads of miscellaneous sphaceluses. She could only speculate as to what the captive interceptor drone was providing them with: fuel, ammunition for their unspeakable weapons systems, or maybe the life essence required to reanimate their biological augmentations.

"Magnificent, aren't they?" Coombs asked, casting a proud gaze over his works.

Caleb rocked her head from side to side in a bargaining gesture. "That's one way to describe them . . . I'll admit, it's impressive what you've done here, Admiral."

"Yes . . . Well, Madeline laid most of the groundwork. It falls to *me* now to pick up the pieces and make sure we see it through."

"I always had great respect for her as a leader; that ruthless indomitability she was renowned for . . . It's a shame Phalanx haven't managed to apprehend her killer yet. Although, I suppose they have plenty on their plate, what with repelling the insurgents' advance."

Coombs pinched his earlobe in a show of trepidation—unease, perhaps, that she would not take kindly to his next words. "Eamon Wyatt is a particularly troublesome dissenter whom it would benefit the union a great deal for us to see behind bars. He was a thorn in Madeline's side long before the present turmoil, but alas, no, he was not responsible for her murder . . . Ultimately, it was Madeline's own ambition that killed her. None of this would have been possible had she not had the courage and the foresight to seek the knowledge of our enemies. The frontier of hybridization is an arms race, you see; we are not the only ones pursuing the acquisition of this technology. She had agents planted deep within the sternside territories to outsource the early phases of research and development. While this might have given us a strong head start, it would inevitably lead to her downfall. In the end, her agents were not as loyal as she had first thought; they lured her into the district under the pretense of a demonstration . . . Then . . . they executed her."

He searched her eyes for disapproval, but as the director and spokesperson of a politically motivated media entity like Humanity First, she understood his motivations perfectly well. "I know of the malleable nature of truth," she said. "And I know what one can achieve by bending it to one's whim. I believe the means can *always* be justified, so long as the ends serve a greater purpose."

"Couldn't have put it better myself." He turned to her wearing the fond smile of a proud father. "Before we go any further, tell me, after what you've seen so far, are you still on board?"

The question certainly bore some consideration, but she did her best not to leave the man waiting too long before answering. "I still don't understand what part you're expecting me to play in all this. And honestly, I'm not convinced the future of humanity lies in desecrating ourselves with the very thing that brought such ruin upon us. Nevertheless, I have yet to be dissuaded."

"I'm pleased to hear it. Because the truth is that I need your help, Caleb. For the first time since the inception of the Administration, the union is without a functioning government. It will remain this way for the foreseeable future; the severity of the current state of affairs is such that we cannot afford to be waiting on the consensus of politicians to make timely and judicious decisions. Circumstances dictate that I retain emergency stewardship until this calamity has been abated. But people want democratic leadership—a recognizable face they feel they can trust; a voice of compassion and reassurance, but also one of strength and authority . . . I believe that face, that voice, is *you*."

Caleb jerked her head and shoulders back in shock. "I . . . I'm flattered, admiral, truly . . . But I sincerely doubt my limited tenure steering the ship for Humanity First would qualify me for such a position."

He shook his head ardently. "I'm not asking you to take on the responsibilities of an administrator. What I need is a representative—an 'envoy,' so to speak. I need someone who can translate the stuffy, dogmatic grumblings of this old dinosaur into a more youthful, palatable vernacular."

"But you're well respected," she protested. "With everything that's happening—the blockade in ruins; savage hordes flooding Amidships—people are crying out for an ironfisted commander in chief like yourself to get out there and bring down the hammer."

"No," he said, thrusting the word forward like a spear. "It *can't* be me, Miss Callaghan. Even at a time of such disarray, the masses will *never* accept military rule. They will decry me as a despot or an autocrat, and as well as an insurgency, we will have mass mutiny on our hands . . . There are actions we must soon take to refortify humanity's position that, to innocent eyes, might seem cruel—barbaric, even. I must have someone speaking on my behalf who can effectively convey the necessity of these measures, no matter how drastic or inhumane they might appear." He directed her attention back through the viewport and into the hangar. "There are over a million people on the *Novara* who will likely share your apprehensions about hybridization, but it won't be long before it becomes a very present and prominent part of day-to-day life. Ergo, public perception surrounding the *Devourer* and its conduits needs to shift—drastically so. It must be seen by younger generations not as a blight, but as our benefactor—an integral part of the *Novara*'s infrastructure. You took Bhaltair Abernathy's unscrupulous band of extremists and turned Humanity First into something political moderates could rally behind. Which is precisely why I believe if *anybody* can sway people's outlook, it's you."

"You're asking the wrong person to be your cheerleader," Caleb retorted. "Even if it means enduring generations of hardship, I *still* believe separation is the only viable course for our species."

"And yet, the human remnant has been stranded for nearly one hundred and thirty years," he remarked. "The work you and Mx. Baudelaire have done is commendable, but do you not think that if what you have been campaigning for was even remotely possible, that we would be standing beneath clear blue skies with the grass beneath our feet right now? . . . I'm sorry, my dear, but our situation is truly and unequivocally indefinite. So . . . Do we continue pushing the *Devourer* away and keeping it at arm's length, or do we learn to embrace it and reap the rewards of *true* symbiosis?"

Before she could answer, someone cleared their throat behind them. The pair turned in unison to find a woman in a black officer's uniform standing eagerly to attention, wearing a grave expression.

"Admiral, sir . . . There's something you need to see."

TWENTY-FIVE

The officer escorted them back up to the parlor and directed their attention to a large wall-embedded media panel, positioned near the admiral's desk.

"This was shared to the Nov-Net fifteen minutes ago," the woman briskly explained. "Our censors have managed to erase all traces of the original upload, but before they could intercept it, it had already been widely circulated on the feeds and downloaded to over two dozen private servers."

Caleb didn't initially recognize the frail figure occupying the frame, propped up on forearm crutches against the verdant backdrop of the Conservatory gardens. But then it suddenly clicked: *Hazel*—the stalwart and sometimes slightly obnoxious older sister of her childhood best friend. She had always been bitterly envious of Hazel's effortlessly beautiful flowing, brown hair—a far cry from the ungovernable, titan frizz she had to contend with every day. So, she felt a despicable pinch of spiteful glee to see it reduced now to an ugly shorn stubble . . .

Perplexed as to what cause Hazel had to be on a panel in Jasper Coombs's private quarters, she shot the man a puzzled glance, but he either didn't notice or was making his best effort to avoid it . . .

"My name is Hazel Ellis Edevane," said Tobias's sister, her voice as shaky and timorous as her broken constitution. "*Yes*—daughter of Councilman Atherton Edevane . . . I am . . . or rather, I *was* a cadet serving under Wing Commander Matias Luscombe of the New Terra Space Corps. Two months ago, I was flight leader on a training exercise to run a reconnaissance patrol of the Debris Belt and the NTU meridian perimeter. By now, you all know how that mission ended: we were ambushed by unknown hostiles, leading to the destruction of six vintage fighters and the deaths of five of my fellow trainees . . . My friends . . . The lie the NTNN are currently perpetuating is that the assailants were alien interceptors, but as a trained observer, it's my assessment that they were, in fact, heavily modified NTSC kestrels, somehow spliced with repurposed materials harvested from the *Devourer* . . ."

Caleb gasped audibly. She glanced again at the admiral, who had an infuriating dearth of any reaction. He merely kept his eyes locked fiercely on the panel, flaring his nostrils and clenching his jaw.

"This I described in great detail in my postmission report," Hazel continued, "because I believe we have a duty to our civilian traffic to ensure they are kept thoroughly informed about potential threats operating in our airspace . . . After I submitted my report, Admiral Jasper Coombs came to visit me in the Aegis Infirmary rehabilitation ward. He asked me to consider recanting my statement in the name of preserving public order, but I knew full well that this was a threat; he all but ordered me to keep my mouth shut, or suffer the consequences . . . It wasn't long after that that an attempt was made on my life. My father's swoop was remotely hijacked and rerouted to Cendre Vale where two mercenaries were waiting to kill us. My father sustained a stab wound to the abdomen but is now in stable condition. The only reason we are even alive right now is because we were rescued by ex-DMED Marshal Eamon Wyatt—who I'll take this opportunity to attest, had *nothing* to do with the murder of Administrator Vargos."

"Amen to that, sister," a gruff voice put in off-screen.

Hazel ignored it. "It's my belief that this was an assassination attempt authorized by the admiral in an effort to keep the truth about what happened to Delta and Charlie teams from getting out." She took a long pause, her steely eyes appearing almost superimposed over her gaunt, pallid face. "And that truth is that my wingmates and I were the subjects of a top secret weapons test meant to assess the combat effectiveness of these prototype fighters—a test that *none* of us were supposed to survive and that I—much to the admiral's dismay—did . . . I'm recording this testimony as more than just insurance for my family; with the Administration all but dissolved, Admiral Coombs is seizing more control by the day, and Novarians have a right to know just how dangerous this man is and what he's capable of . . . It's true the cohabitor issue has divided us more than perhaps anything else in human history, but we *must* set aside our differences and come together. Because it's the only way we have any chance of resisting this new threat to our democracy."

"Pause," Coombs uttered sharply to cease playback. He turned to face Caleb with visible reluctance, meeting her condemnatory glower with a pout of defiance.

"Is it true?" she asked, simmering.

He began pacing broodingly around the room. "In the name of total transparency, yes, it is . . . Unless you're referring to all that 'threat to democracy' rubbish, in which case, no—complete hyperbole."

Caleb stamped her foot impatiently. "Hazel Edevane is a close family friend. I may not have always seen eye to eye with her but she's a loyal unionist who worked her ass off for her position in the NTSC . . ."

"She is remarkable," Coombs interrupted, simultaneously refuting *and* agreeing with her. "A testament to her generation—leaps and bounds ahead of anybody else at her same level. And that's precisely the reason I had no choice but to volunteer her *and* her wingmates for this trial . . . It wasn't the hybridized kestrels we were testing, Miss Callaghan: circumstances demanded we examine how our forces would fare against these new generation fighters. We put Hazel's squadron through a live fire exercise with unknown variables, and, regrettably, they failed—catastrophically so. From firepower to maneuverability to strategic efficiency—there was not one area of combat in which they weren't completely outmatched. Any loss of life is, of course, tragic, but the test provided us with a plethora of useful data. I assure you; their deaths will not have been in vain."

"I don't give a shit how *useful* it was! Sacrificing good pilots for the sake of testing a hypothesis—it's abhorrent; utterly diabolical! Lei-Ghannam! It's no wonder you decided poor Hazel had to be silenced. The public will have you strung up in Chennai Plaza for treason when this gets out!"

"It already has, so that may yet be the case." He cast his old eyes to the ground in what seemed like genuine humility. "And I would gracefully accept that fate . . . I asked you earlier how far you were prepared to go. Now you know where my limits lie: the reality is that I have none. There is nothing I won't do, no line I will not cross to ensure the success of this endeavor . . . A 'greater purpose,' Caleb—just like you said."

"Don't use my own words against me," she spat. "Call them off! Whatever task force or company of mercs you have hunting Hazel and Atherton—tell them to stand down! I want you to promise me none of the Edevanes will be harmed."

The frenzied demand earned a disgruntled nod from the admiral. "You have my word, Caleb." Whether or not he meant it in earnest or had said it only to pacify her, she couldn't tell. "In reality, Hazel has likely already caused as much damage as she can with this little stunt; there's no sense trying to prevent what has already happened. I rather lament choosing not to allow Atlas Baudelaire to accompany you today; if we are to get out ahead of this and discredit Hazel's story, then we will need their expertise."

Never before had the word "we" infuriated Caleb quite so much. *There is no "we,"* she seethed. *I won't be complicit in the murder of NTSC pilots and the attempted assassination of an ex-councilman and his daughter.* Her legs ached to carry her to an escape pod so she could flee this arc of abominations and return to the *Novara*. But then a troubling thought stayed her feet: Coombs had already proven how willing he was to kill in order to keep his secrets locked down, and he had now divulged more to her than Hazel had managed to extrapolate on her own. She knew far too much to simply turn tail and run . . .

"If you please, Admiral," the officer said, who had apparently been lingering behind them throughout the confrontation. "There's more to the recording you should see."

"Very well . . . Play!"

"OK . . . this part is gonna be difficult for many to believe, but here we go." Hazel blew a forceful sigh as if preparing to run a marathon. "Amara Thaddeus—the virtual intelligence, I mean . . . Well, she's more than that, now. It's not exactly clear what catalyzed it—even *she* can't be certain—but somehow, she's generated true self-awareness. She has awoken with her programmer's memories, her personality, and her intellect—for all intents and purposes, she's every bit Amara as the woman herself . . . We all know the stories of past captains trying—and failing—to wrangle control of the *Novara*'s life-support systems. Even with her burgeoning consciousness, her primary directive remains the same: protect life, no matter the cost . . . In line with this, she has asked me to deliver a message . . ." Hazel turned her head to the side, nervously placing fingertips against the neural interface Tobias had alluded to when Caleb saw him last. For the first time since the video began, she had to wonder whether Ms. Edevane's erratic behavior was, perhaps, due in part to a malfunction with her cybernetic implants. Watching her peculiar body language, anyone could be forgiven for thinking the poor woman really believed she was in contact with the ghost of one of the *Novara*'s architects . . .

"Amara is opening the Conservatory to the cohabitors," Hazel continued hesitantly. "She's offering sanctuary to those seeking asylum from the war in the Mouth and has vowed to shelter and provide for you here in the gardens. Any resonants watching this should instruct their partners to spread the message so it can reach those without ciphers, then immediately make your way up to the life-support block . . . To my fellow NTU citizens: Do not hinder or interfere with those making the journey. If you come across cohabitors looking lost or distressed, please, help guide them to the Conservatory. If you provoke or threaten them in *any* way, then you can expect them to defend themselves accordingly. Otherwise, you have nothing to fear."

Hazel shuffled to the side and made way for someone else to join her in the frame. A second later, Caleb found herself staring into the near emerald-green eyes of Tobias Cole Edevane. And what an overpowering medley of emotions she felt in that instant: anger, mainly, stemming from the contemptuous nature of their last parting. But then palpable grief broke like a wistful beam of sunshine through the clouds of her lingering resentment. She mourned the loss not just of their friendship but also of the person he had once been—before the District of the Mouth chewed him up and regurgitated him as someone completely unrecognizable. The Tobias *she* knew took great pride in his physical appearance, and to see it so neglected—with his unkempt stubble, windswept hair, and ugly black bomber jacket—signified just how little remained of the dapper young man she had been so endeared to. His once bottomless reservoir of drive, ambition, and charisma had all but evaporated, leaving behind the sedimentary sludge of a misguided and inexplicable affinity for the enemy—the single greatest enemy mankind had ever known, to be precise. And here the Edevanes were, shamelessly waving their banner in solidarity.

"My name is Tobias, but that's not important right now." The words sent a chill down Caleb's spine, as if hearing the voice of a deceased loved one, reaching out to her from beyond the grave. Evidently, Hazel wasn't the only one communing with the dead . . .

"Many Novarians will be encountering cohabitors for the first time in their lives over the coming days. I know they can seem intimidating; it's perfectly natural to be frightened by their alarming size and appearance. But be mindful of the fact that they've been violently forced from their homes and are now displaced in a completely alien environment—one that, let's face it, isn't going to be the most welcoming. Believe me when I say, they're far more scared of you than vice versa . . . It's possible a number of people will have a kind of . . . reaction to being in close proximity to a specific cohabitor. Anybody watching this who experiences hallucinations or bursts of intense emotion—just know that nothing is wrong and you're not in danger. What's happening to you is the same thing that happened to me, and although it can be disorienting and even a little distressing, there's no reason to be fearful of it. It is, however, imperative that *if* this happens, you chaperone the cohabitor around which this sensitivity occurs up to the Conservatory so I can help you make sense of it. Ignoring it will only make it worse, and the consequences can be dire. Come to the gardens and I will be on hand to assist . . . Thank you for listening. *Astra inclinant sed non obligant.*"

The panel faded to black. The soundless vacuum of space lunged through the ship's hull to siphon the sound and atmosphere out of the parlor. Caleb heard her heartbeat thumping in her ear canals—a pounding rhythmic accompaniment to Tobias's final words as they repeated in her mind like the lyrics to a song she utterly despised. *The gall,* she thought. *After spouting nothing but sedition and lies, he dares to sign off using the motto of the very organization he has chosen to betray.* The sadness she felt only moments ago blossomed into a flourishing bouquet of vexation. In the wake of that terrible night in Atherton's apartment, she had not forgotten about the man's son but had held out hope that all he needed to come to his senses was time. Now, it seemed increasingly unlikely that there was anything she could do to bring him back to reality, and the thought of losing him forever inspired a dejection so crushing that she could scarcely bear to endure it.

An unlikely sound broke the silence: a hearty chuckle issued by the admiral as he stood conceitedly beside her. "An imaginative pair aren't they?" he joked. "Atherton must be thrilled to see their ACS education paying such handsome dividends."

The officer stepped forward, addressing a luma-pad cradled in arm. "Sir. Gunship *Persephone* is four mikes out," she reported. "First wave are ready to deploy. Operation Schiltron can be underway within the hour."

"No, no. That won't be necessary," Coombs replied, suddenly as light as a feather, as though the weight of the *Novara* had been lifted from his shoulders. "The Edevane clan have just made things very easy for us. Let us not squander the opportunity they have so kindly provided. We must give time to allow this perverse pilgrimage to play out . . . Then, when the time is right, we will make our move."

The officer gave a nod of semicomprehension and saluted, then hastened out of the parlor.

"What . . . What are you going to do?" Caleb timidly asked.

Coombs allowed for a ruminative pause. "What we must, Miss Callaghan. What we must . . . Although, I'm afraid I can provide you with no further details of our plans until you formally accept the position I am offering. I cannot initiate you into this incentive without your full confidence and compliance."

"I . . . I need some time to think it over."

"Of course." He motioned her toward the exit and walked her back out into the rotunda, stopping near the levitating model of the *Hope's Embrace* with his hands clasped tactfully behind his back. "Although, I would urge you to decide quickly; the wheels of this machine will soon be in motion, and I would hate for you to get left behind . . . A final anecdote before you leave."

She stopped to listen, feeling the vacancy in her expression as she held his gaze from the corner of her eye.

"Do you know what the leeches call themselves?"

She shook her head slowly.

"They call themselves the Prey. Surprisingly superstitious creatures: they adhere to a complex tapestry of mythos and religion surrounding the *Devourer.* One of the beliefs they share is that their distant ancestors were hunted by a race of superior beings, and that the *Devourer* is the divine savior that extricated them from annihilation . . . I have come to believe that this particular tenet is more than just folklore but is, in fact, rooted in a certain degree of truth."

She wordlessly urged him to continue, not from any interest in hearing his conclusion but out of a growing desire to take her leave. The anger she felt toward Tobias had dug a burrow in her chest and she could not easily evict it. Even still, she couldn't shake the disquieting feeling that he was in imminent danger, and that she needed to warn him . . .

"I believe the *Devourer* was indeed pursued by a malicious force that conspired to destroy it," the admiral went on obliviously. "And that its reason for immobilizing any vessel that tries to escape its vicinity is because it cannot risk the impulse signature of any wayward ships being traced back to its location. Consider if you will that there could be an entity somewhere out there in the endless night that the *Devourer*—the most formidable force we have ever encountered—fears . . . The leeches are no threat to the human remnant, but our survival is a fragile and tenuous thing. Ergo, we must ensure that we—and indeed, our descendants—are adequately equipped to face any prospective threats or challenges the future might hold." He traced the angular contours of the *Embrace*'s effigy, countenance hewn by refractions of light from its mirror surface as if staring intently into a disco ball.

"Here in the fathomless reaches of the Abyss, so far from our tiny, troubled oasis, I find there is a certain . . . *clarity*, one can experience—a voice in the static, if you will. This voice has communicated to me one simple truth: that humanity *needs* hybridization . . . And I believe that for the *Novara* to embrace it, hybridization needs you."

TWENTY-SIX

While Eamon saw to the relocation of Juniper Sanctuary to its new site in the Conservatory, Hazel and Tobias began preparations for receiving the first wave of Amara's guests. Though many questions remained surrounding the mysterious genesis of their new ally, Tobias couldn't deny that he felt strangely obligated to help her. Amara was more than just a historical icon: she had been a constant presence in his life for as far back as he could recall. From her legendary biology documentaries to her interactive exhibits at the Silk River Aquarium and COHP, her vast ecological archives spanned nearly every medium, and it was difficult *not* to feel as though he knew her personally. She was the no-nonsense grandmother he had never known, her infectious zeal and unerring devotion kindling in his generation, and every preceding one, an inherent enthusiasm for nature. He felt remarkably at home following her lead, because, in reality, she had been posthumously nurturing and mentoring him since birth. Eamon Wyatt, on the other hand, seemed predictably less content about *takin' orders from a runaway VI.*

"Supposed to be a flawless imitation of human consciousness, ain't it?" The man probed as he delivered his last consignment of Junies and was set to take his leave a final time to collect the crew of the *Assurance.* "What if that's exactly what it's doin'? Only now—thanks to the *Devourer*'s input—it's picked up a few new tricks—playin' to our organic sensibilities with simulated emotion to manipulate us into doin' its bidding. Abyss, even if she *is* what she says she is, somethin' just don't sit right with me about the very thing that decides whether we get to breathe or not suddenly callin' the shots."

Hazel, demonstrating little tolerance for Eamon's roguery, took umbrage with the sentiment, citing that if *anyone* was in a position to judge Amara's veracity, it should be the person in whose head she had installed herself. As she lambasted the impudent man, Tobias noticed something peculiar happening:

the Conservatory's artificial weather turned precipitously inclement. The temperature dropped sharply; the breeze picked up as the dome's concave firmament became host to a maelstrom of swirling umbral clouds. If he didn't know any better, he'd say his sister's ire had somehow triggered the onset of the sudden tempest—an unintentional side effect to Amara's residence in her kinesthetic implant. Well . . . it was *all* unintentional, but Hazel seemed staunchly unwilling to acknowledge this particular symptom. So, the siblings saw Eamon off and carried on with their objective, neither giving mention to the fact that as Hazel's dour mood alleviated, so too did the environmental turbulence . . .

Amara summoned one of the zero-terrain buggies used by the grounds-keepers to quickly negotiate the Conservatory's roulette spirograph of path-ways. They boarded the repulsor-aided chariot and took it to the building complex that stood as the nucleus of the COHP's atom. Here, several nar-row structures boasting glass curtain walls and roofs covered in luscious turf described a curved perimeter around a leaf-shaped courtyard, comprising a gift shop, a bistro café, a learning center, and the function room in which Tobias had gotten embarrassingly drunk on his eighteenth birthday. The site's centrality to the rest of the gardens made it ideal for use as a main facilities hub. Exit Sol Festival saw it employed in a similar fashion the first weekend of every September, although consisting of notably more syn-beer tents and extortionately overpriced food stalls than what Amara likely envisioned for her sanctuary.

The courtyard's arrow tip pointed in the direction of an elevated opera-tions cabin, used by staff to keep an eye on visitors, as well as to monitor the Conservatory's environmental and irrigation systems. Amara directed Hazel and Tobias inside and brought their attention to a console posi-tioned in the center of the room. The broad pedestal's luma-surface surged in brightness as if anticipating their arrival. It then rendered a three-dimensional model of the COHP, scaling the structure's one-kilometer diameter down to a more manageable 1/1000th of its size. Tobias relished the opportunity to see the installation from this new perspective. With a fondness in his heart, he cast reverent eyes over the many botanical gar-dens and arboretums, tropical greenhouses and wildflower meadows, spar-kling ponds and meandering streams dipping beneath ornate bridges—all enclosed beneath a magnificent, opaque hemisphere. The intense emotion blooming within him was doubtless a combination of his own nostalgia and the accentuating wonder felt by the infant Prey—so fervid that he could sense it standing nearly two-hundred meters from the kids' play area where Null and Nanimonai were watching over them. For too long had the

Administration denied their kind access to the natural splendor of Amara's gardens, and what a sense of pride and accomplishment he felt for his part in facilitating their induction.

Amara manifested herself visually atop the resplendent base pane of the luma-surface. She appeared not in the form of her human progenitor but as a crystalline rodent with beady, wide-set eyes and a large, flat nose—comically disproportionate to the size of her tapering face. A mass of translucent quills kept her hunched body largely hidden, sprouting from her hind like an eruption of splintered glass, utterly dazzling in their prismatic detail.

Untethered from her baseline programming, she now had the freedom to represent herself however she saw fit. When Hazel asked why she had chosen a *porcupine* of all things for her avatar, she answered, "Because porcupines are highly intelligent, solitary creatures who will give anything that threatens them a face full of spines." Tobias accepted her justification, although he suspected it had less to do with personal agency over identity and was more an effort to avoid causing Hazel any further distress.

"You don't need to do that on my account," his sister said, having apparently reached the same conclusion.

"I know, dear," replied Amara. "But I am no longer a mere emulation of my maker, and the truth is I have no desire to continue representing myself as such. *This* form suits me far better."

She began pacing around the projection of the Conservatory like a military strategist around a war table—only, one sporting a coat of silver bristles and a prehensile tail. "To the matter at hand," she said, channeling her modulated voice through the console's speakers, shrewdly electing *not* to animate her avatar's mouth in sync with her words. "Welcome to base camp. The Beech Glade complex is to be the command post of our initiative. We'll need to establish a medical hut, a food bank, a dispensary for hygiene and sanitary supplies . . . Tobias, I believe the learning center will be a suitable venue for your resonance outreach program."

"I agree," he replied, struggling to repress a smirk at the sheer ridiculousness of discussing logistics with a small, quadruped mammal. "It's hard to say how many new resonant bonds the Prey migration will enable—even harder to predict how many of those who received our invitation will accept it. Harmony has shown us what happens when neophyte ciphers don't have access to the right guidance to properly manage their abilities; we need to make sure we have a dedicated space set aside to support any who do come."

"How exactly are we planning on staffing all this?" Hazel asked, knitting her brow in consternation. "We're talking about a massive operation here— one that'll require substantial personnel to manage. And by my count there's, what . . . six of us? We don't know for certain Captain Holloway will want to help us and it would be unreasonable for us to ask."

Tobias opened his mouth to speak, *Of course she will* clinging to the tip of his tongue as though it were the edge of a cliff. Regrettably, he realized, he couldn't in good conscience make such a statement. *This isn't our fight* had more or less become Delilah's catchphrase as of late, and she had made her adamant opposition toward the idea of involving her crew with the cause abundantly clear.

"I just pinged an urgent communiqué to the COHP staff via their feathers and echo lenses," said Amara. "I explained our intentions and asked them to return posthaste. Not all will, of course, but there are many whose loyalty to Amara—and by extension, to me—will mitigate any predispositions they might share about the Prey . . . Moreover, I estimate we could have up to thirty thousand cohabitors seeking refuge with us, not to mention the countless humans who will undoubtedly accompany them. I'm sure with such a sizable intake we will find volunteers."

Tobias whistled. "That's . . . that's a lot of people . . . Are we sure the Conservatory can even house that many? What's the max capacity?"

"The dome holds approximately two-thousand-four-hundred tons of air. And the abundant algae and flora is capable of extracting around forty kilograms of CO_2 from the atmosphere per hour. We have ample space, and habitability will be of no concern."

"What about feeding everybody?" Hazel queried. Anyone not familiar with the cadet might think she was needlessly poking holes in the plan, but Tobias knew it was merely her way of ensuring their greatest chance at success—probing for weak points so they could be addressed *before* becoming an issue. "I mean, sure, the café has protein synthesizers, but they're hardly gonna be of any use to the cohabs, are they?"

"I've been putting off having to think about it," Tobias admitted, absently massaging the back of his neck. "But you're right: at some point, we need to address the fact that we have no viable means of sourcing Höllengarten pulp—certainly not in the volume required to sustain tens of thousands of Prey."

"I believe Daemon has a solution for that," chimed Amara's disembodied voice. The Edevanes stared vacantly at the ethereal porcupine. "The *Devourer*," she translated. "The Savior, Charybdis, or Wilted One, as it occasionally refers to itself. I have posed this conundrum on several occasions already, to which it has repeatedly answered . . ."

"HEED CONSTRUCT." The playback startled Hazel and Tobias—an unknown voice like the low rumble of tectonic plates grinding against one another, sundered by harsh consonants and erratic inflections that rattled the security panels fanned around the room. **"WILTED ONE SUSTENANCE PROVIDE . . . ENGENDER SURVIVAL PREY."**

Tobias glanced across the luma-surface to find Hazel receding into herself. It took a lot to discompose his indomitable sister, but the sound of that deep, alien cadence caused her determined posture to rapidly shrivel. Were he not so assured of the Savior's benevolence, he might have been trembling in fear, too.

"I'm not sure what Daemon has up its sleeve," Amara went on, notably undaunted. "But it seems confident the matter is in hand . . . Something we *should* discuss is security. We have, after all, issued a proclamation to the *Novara*, and aside from the obvious fact that Admiral Coombs now knows precisely where we are, we should consider that, to many citizens of the NTU, this facility and its gardens are hallowed ground; there will be those who do not like the sound of what we intend to use it for—some may even attempt to frustrate out efforts with force."

"I've already been reading some of the discourse on the Nov-Net," Tobias added, shaking his head in disappointment. "Scores of idiots echo-looping threads about our message being a deepfake—deployed by Harmony to generate dissension and sow doubt about the admiral's leadership. People are speculating that, in actuality, this is a hostile takeover being instigated by the insurgents; I don't think it's a stretch to expect retaliation from Humanity First and the like."

"Great; Caleb Callaghan's loyal army of foaming-at-the-mouth morons coming to hunt us down. How many times did I warn you about her, Tobias?" Hazel's question was obviously rhetorical, which he considered fortunate because he didn't have the first clue how to answer it.

Amara pointed her avatar's snout in Hazel's direction. "We need to fortify . . . Give me your defense assessment, dear."

Hazel took a step toward the pedestal, rebuilding her constitution. Staring down at the projection of the dome, she locked her hands behind her back and began as if delivering a mission briefing.

"There are four main ways of accessing the COHP," she pronounced. "The elevator pods from Zharady Station, the pedestrian route up through hydroponics, the service tunnels leading up the maintenance sublevel, and the back of house cargo shaft we came up in the camion. I recommend we recall the elevator pods and disable them as they can be remotely deactivated from the bridge; we don't want people getting trapped on their way up. That leaves us with just the other three entry points—all bottlenecks, which should be easy enough to secure, providing we can obtain some armaments . . . I'm not sure how likely that is."

Amara gave a nod of approval. "I have already intercepted several automated cargo barges carrying produce and commodities to the Lower Amidships Docks and redirected them here. It goes without saying that I do not condone the use of firearms in *any* capacity—Amara's original core directives categorically forbade it. Having said that, I understand the necessity, and will see what I can procure."

By the time Eamon returned with Delilah and the rest of the crew, refugees had already begun filtering up through life support and arriving in the COHP's shining atrium. Tobias assumed the role of resonant concierge, subjecting himself to an empathic battering ram as the settlers arrived in a collective state of fear and panic. Thankfully, Null joined his side to share the load, and the pair began directing the flow of traffic toward the Beech Glade complex for registration. The discomfort gradually diminished as more and more Prey transitioned into the gardens, the dome soon filled with not only oxygenated atmosphere as Amara had explained, but a soothing zephyr of relief, elation, and gratitude. All the pain and turmoil Tobias had endured over the past two months was worth it to experience that sublime reciprocation; to taste the ripe fruits of his labor, and to feel the sins of his past finally swept away in a detoxifying tide of resonance.

Null turned to face him, bowing aer head to meet his eye level. Pouring emissions, ae implanted a familiar image into his mental space: a pair of the same variety of wilted shrubs ae had previously used to convey acknowledgment and praise of his personal growth. Only now, they blossomed not into vibrant, alien flowers, but into towering organic structures resembling mushroom-tree hybrids. Comprising venous frameworks of turquoise branches—the same he intuited the ancient Prey once hung from to sleep— their hollow pilei dispersed a cloud of seeds into the void of his mind. A forest of saplings then sprouted around the bases of their gnarled trunks as the words "prospect" and "community" arrived on his tongue. Null's meaning came through as vividly as the accompanying imagery: thanks to his and Hazel's efforts, the Prey had not only survived their violent displacement from the Mouth, but now had a place where they could grow and thrive as a people; where they could know abundance in place of destitution, and live unfettered by the Administration's oppression and the exploitation of the Glow Syndicate . . . Finally, they were free.

"Wasted the better part of a decade tryna provide the cohabs in the district with this kinda security and status," Eamon declared, weaving through the steady stream of new arrivals as he approached. With their surroundings now ostensibly safe enough to abandon his disguise, the marshal had swapped out his Transitech coveralls for his signature fur-collar aviator jacket—the one still stained with blood after his near miss with Vargos's marksman in Festa Heights. "Turns out, all we *really* needed to do was get them the Abyss outta there 'n' move 'em somewhere safer . . . I told you to put your resonance to good use, Tobias. As far as assignments go, this here's gotta be an A+ all around—no question."

Tobias glanced over his shoulder into the gardens, settling his gaze on the nearby playing fields where Kahu Heperi could be seen playing fetch with Abraham. Hazel sat on a bench nearby, no doubt reveling in hearing the veteran's war stories firsthand and sharing her own experience of serving in the NTSC. The little merchant cohabitor, who had taken a not-so-surprising interest in his sister, accompanied the trio, crouching down near Hazel's feet and fiddling with the rubber grips of her crutches. Tobias's struggling bond with the infant had finally shown signs of rousing since their reunion, and it made sense, given the circumstances, that the prevailing emotions ae had absorbed were pride and admiration for his sister.

"We wouldn't even be here if it wasn't for Hazel," he acknowledged ruefully. "*She* deserves the credit—not me."

"This couldn't have happened without the pair of you, way I see it." Eamon made a sweeping gesture around the bustling atrium. "Heck, these people have a future cuz of the work you both put in."

Null emitted a warbling groan and motioned with an open paw toward the marshal. Tobias showed a suggestive smile as he relayed the cohabitor's sentiment. "Let's not forget, Amara Thaddeus might never have been able to make contact had you not rescued my family."

The marshal moved in close and cast a wary glance at a nearby security cam. "Between you an' me, I'm still a little unsure about just how much we can trust old *Mother Nature*, but I take your point; just glad I could do my bit . . ."

Tobias momentarily excused himself so he and Null could aid a particularly anxious cohabitor who had purportedly become separated from aer cipher. They tentatively instructed aer to follow the flow of traffic, advising that any lost loved ones could likely be found at the registration kiosk.

"So, what's the protocol here?" Eamon asked. "Are we just lettin' folks loose in the gardens and tellin' 'em to set up camp wherever they like?"

"Not quite," Tobias replied, returning his attention to the marshal. "Amara managed to convince some of the staff to return after her false decompression alert. They're up at the Beech Glade complex documenting arrivals and helping them get acclimated. We've already recruited a team of ciphered pairs to help translate. As to where we're situating people: there's plenty of open space but it could disappear fast if we're not smart about allocating it. So, the plan is to start by filling up Khadija's Green and then move on to a second site in the field over near the wetlands aviary."

"Nebula. I guess you got a plan for accommodation, too?"

"Well, the Prey can construct their own domiciles as they did in the Ghetto. Although, with Amara's ability to switch off the variable climate and maintain a comfortable temperature, shelters may not be necessary . . . They *do*, however, need sleeping apparatuses; they can't secrete resin durable enough to support their weight, so we'll have to build racks—a *lot* of them. Supposedly, there's a fabricator in the maintenance sublevel that we can use to print construction materials. All we need are willing hands, and I doubt we'll have any shortage in that regard."

Eamon shifted his weight onto his hip and cocked his brow. "Color me impressed. Sounds like you've got it all figured out."

"Almost . . ." Tobias directed the marshal's stare with a cautioning glance at the refugees streaming in through the atrium's pedestrian entrance. Amara's prediction regarding how many cohabitors they should expect to receive, based on the footfall they had seen in the first hour since opening, had so far proven accurate. But one thing that had surprised and, perhaps, left him slightly unnerved, was the sheer number of humans arriving in tandem.

"Naturally, we anticipated there would be plenty of humans taking refuge with us—interspecies family units formed around ciperships and what have you." He kept his voice low and clandestine as he scanned the crowd. "But see for yourself: we're taking in large groups of able-bodied men and women who, at first glance, don't appear to be affiliated with any Prey . . . Maybe I'm being overly skeptical, but when there are so many relief centers spread throughout the *Novara* accepting human refugees, I don't see why they need to be here. Amara says everybody has a place in her sanctuary, but we have to remember that we've essentially commandeered an NTU installation, and there are a lot of people out there who aren't gonna let it stand."

Eamon tightened his lips and gave a nod of comprehension. "You're worried about security."

"Precisely . . . Amara can lock the entire facility down if and when the *wolves* arrive at the gate. But with this open-door policy, how can we be sure everyone coming to us is doing so with the best of intentions? We need guards—armed personnel to not only defend the perimeter but to maintain order in the gardens, too . . . *We* brought the Prey here; I believe that means we have a duty of care to ensure they're adequately protected."

Eamon watched on in pensive thought as Tobias and Null tended to another flurry of newcomers before responding, "I hear ya, kid. Problem is we don't have a whole lot of allies as it stands. Although I guess that just means we need to shake a leg and rally those we do . . . I've been in touch with some of the old crew from the DMED precinct house. Told me Jyn . . ." The man blew a sigh of regret. "The *Composer* paid them a visit—forced them to lay down their weapons and leave their post under threat of death. Safe to say, none of them are too eager to take Executor Royce up on his offer of redeployment to Phalanx, so they're at somethin' of a loose end . . . If I could convince them to help us out, we'd have a handful of deputies and twenty-plus good enforcers at our disposal. Won't exactly be the cavalry, but I reckon it'd be somethin."

Recognizing the physical toll prolonged resonance had taken on Tobias, Null obstinately offered to manage arrivals aerself and urged him to take a break. He headed out into the gardens, allowing the fresh, fragrant air to revitalize his tired mind. The Conservatory's astute keeper had set the dome's color output to a static crimson-tangerine gradient, matching the hue of the light emitted by the Höllengarten to ease her new tenants into the day-night cycle, since no such phenomenon existed in the Mouth.

How surreal it felt: walking through such a familiar place under such unprecedented circumstances. Where scores of joggers, dog walkers, and picnickers might once have adorned the gorgeous scenery, he now wandered along his usual route surrounded by Prey, suffusing the phero-monic scent of vanilla into the ether, braying contentedly as they lounged and frolicked in this strange yet undeniably majestic environment. Far-ther along the gravel path, he spied a petite figure hastening toward him: short, slender legs, wide, curvaceous hips, upper body buried beneath loose, multicolored knitting, comely face capped by cascading waves of metallic blue—he felt a stab of embarrassment realizing that any nearby cohabitors could likely sense the amorous excitement filling him like hot broth in a bowl.

"Tobes!" Teodora sang, coming just short of breaking into a run, wearing a loose daisy chain crown around the top of her head. "Ain't this place incred-ible? I never seen so much green in all my life. And don't get me started on all the birds; you see those goofy, one-legged, pink things in that aviary over there? What a trip!"

"You've never been to the Conservatory before?" he asked, bracing himself as she hooked her arm around his neck and mounted him in an impromptu piggyback.

"Naw. Taken bowside shore leave a couple times, but the captain always says to never venture higher than mid-deck in case anyone asks for my ID chit. Ain't technically allowed this side of the blockade, yah know? Hey, you seen Kahu around anywhere?"

He hoisted her farther up his back, heartbeat quickening as he gripped her thighs to better support her weight. "Over in the playing fields with Abe and Hazel."

"Boring her head off about the *glory days*, I bet . . . We gotta go fetch him; the captain's got somethin' important to discuss with the crew . . . I know that don't technically include the old drunk no more." She paused. "Not sure it still includes you, either, but . . . just thought you'd wanna know . . ."

They rallied Wing Commander Heperi and headed for base camp, bringing Hazel along for good measure following her stalwart insistence that she be kept in the loop. Helping his sister up the stairs to the operations cabin, Tobias caught a brief glimpse of his father. The man had been taken into the medical hut for another round of treatment and lay on a folding first aid bed with his bruised chest exposed, surrounded by haphazardly piled supply crates as the volunteer medical staff scrambled to erect a makeshift trauma ward. Atherton drowsily lifted his head to show a smile, face partially hidden beneath the clear silicone of an oxygen mask. He raised his arm and formed a thumbs-up, then succumbed to enervation and dropped back out of consciousness.

In the cabin, Isaac and Mercy had already joined Delilah around the pedestal's gleaming luma-surface, faces lit from below and warped by elongated shadow as if taking turns telling ghost stories with flashlights. Delilah stared with eyes like daggers as the others shuffled inside. "Teo! When I told you to fetch Tobias, I meant just that. This was supposed to be a *crew* meeting."

"Sorry, Cap," Teo chirped. "In my defense, crew's kinda been in flux for a while now; strugglin' to keep track of who it actually entails."

"Told you I can't fly the *Assurance* no more, Skip," Kahu grumbled. "Don't mean I'm completely useless. Whatever this business is, I'm sure you could probably use some extra muscle."

"Miss Thaddeus?" the captain called, turning jaded eyes toward the ceiling. "I take it *you'll* be joining us as well?"

Amara materialized in argent porcupine form atop the console. "An odd question, Captain, considering you have elected to hold this meeting inside my head. Where else could I be?"

Delilah blew a sigh. "Full house, then . . . So be it." She swiped two fingers across her wristwatch to sync the device with the console's OS. "We have a pending hail request from Vidalia. It's marked urgent so we best not keep him waiting."

A Sinegex dial screen pulsed briefly in the air. It dispersed into thousands of golden points that then reconsolidated into the luma-cast bust of the Governor.

"Vidalia?" whispered Hazel, fixing a disconcerted look on the shimmering projection. "As in, ruthless kingpin Vidalia Drexen—the Governor of the Mouth? Why is Holloway accepting calls from someone who has a price on her head?"

"They've buried the hatchet," Tobias surreptitiously answered. "Things move fast around here."

"'Here' being the *Novara's* criminal underworld?"

He smiled. "Trust me; you'll learn to keep up."

"Greetings, Captain Holloway." Vidalia's deep voice rang as almost falsetto compared to the sonorous rumblings heard during Amara's earlier playback of the Savior's communications. "I am grateful for your prompt acceptance of my hail; there are several matters of some importance bearing our immediate attention."

The man seemed lacking still in his wonted gravitas; Tobias could tell from his buckled posture that every breath taken, and every word uttered was done through stifling agony. Delilah had apparently picked up on it, too, seeming to regard the man with far more amiability than was warranted, given their turbulent history. That said, if the captain was lacking in anything, it certainly wasn't empathy . . .

"I believe an apology is in order," the Governor admitted. "You were promised amnesty—freedom to operate in the docks safely and with impunity. Rest assured, the ringleaders behind the attempted assault on your crew have been aptly dealt with."

Delilah folded her arms. "I can't help but feel our versions of what constitutes apt punishment differ slightly . . . What did you do, Vidalia?"

"I'll spare you the . . . *finer* details. All you need to know is that Jorge Almeida and his ruffian confederates won't be troubling you any further."

"Thea Rebbeckis . . ." Delilah worriedly began.

The Governor raised a finger to cut her off. "Had no part in the insubordination, and as such, was not subject to punitive measures . . . She is fine, Delilah—a model ship captain whom I hope others will take example from."

Tobias turned his head and shared a daunted glance with Teo. "They wanted to hurt the kids," she said under her breath. "Whatever Drexen did, they had it comin' an' then some."

"*And*" Vidalia went on, "the consequences of the dissidents' behavior have been such that I would think it highly unlikely anybody else in the Captain's Guild will ever consider challenging you again. The docks are secure, and I believe the time has come for you and your crew to return. I have been informed by the chief engineering officer that the *Assurance* will be ready to fly within the next four hours. *Novara* hull integrity is holding steady for the time being, but I would think it advisable to have you back on station forth-with and ready to assist with any potential ruptures."

Hazel leaned toward Tobias's ear and whispered, "What's that one called?" He followed her eyeline through the Governor's projection and realized with growing discomfort that it led straight to Isaac. *Please, Hazel; of all the bums on the* Novara *you could choose to bat your eyes at, not him . . .*

"Isaac Verhoeven: the *Assurance*'s engineer," he answered, covering his mouth with a balled fist. "He's a recovering glow addict with a *very* volatile personality; has a shorter fuse than Dad *and* is about four years your junior." He made the remark in an effort to dissuade his sister from any ludicrous notions about the engineer but could tell it had only spurred her intrigue. Serendipitously, Mercy shimmied up next to Isaac and, with impeccable tim-ing, slipped her hand into his before burying it into the tulle fabric of her dress, cradling it against her stomach. Any self-satisfaction Tobias felt soon evaporated as he realized she had done this in search of comfort and reassur-ance, shuddering in fear as she kept her sunken eyes glued to the likeness of her old master.

"Appreciate the update," said Delilah. "I think we've done all we can around here; suppose it's time we wrap things up and head back." She purposefully refrained from holding eye contact with any of the crew as she said this, presumably in the knowledge that, given the chance, none of them would agree . . .

"Ah yes. I'm eager to hear how things are progressing with this *Sanctuary* in the Conservatory. If the news about the Amara Thaddeus VI developing self-awareness is true, then she now controls the *Novara*'s entire sphere of hydroponic, aquaponic, and life-support systems. As a keen businessman, I would very much like to make her acquaintance."

"Hah!" Amara's irate voice came clattering through the pedestal's speak-ers. She enlarged her mammalian avatar so that it towered intimidatingly over the Governor, if only for the benefit of the others in the operation's cabin. "And what makes you think I have any interest in making yours? Amara Prime dealt with *plenty* of your kind throughout the course of her career: narcissistic, self-proclaimed philanthropist moguls, sorely lacking in any tangible altruism and who, in fact, offered little more to society than the commodification of human suffering. You are a cancer, spreading throughout the *Novara*, digging your malignant roots wherever you can, and I have noth-ing more to say to you."

Vidalia betrayed his indignation with a subtle lip curl. "A pleasure, Doc-tor Thaddeus . . . I gather you've already taken counsel from Eamon Wyatt about me?"

"My child; you are addressing the closest thing humanity has ever known to true omnipotence; I cannot be cajoled or influenced by the opinions of one man."

"Then perhaps, Doctor . . . you can be influenced by an act of good faith . . ."

Amara's avatar shrank back down to its usual size, holding a cautiously attentive expression—or the closest thing possible with her rodentine face. The projection of the Governor dissolved, soon replaced by an initializing screen displaying the angular insignia of the NTU.

"I require no compensation for the intel I am about to provide," said Vidalia. "Think of it as a donation to the cause—one I hope might disabuse you of your grievances regarding myself and place me in your favor."

Tobias leaned forward as the luma-surface presented what he inferred to be the output from a radar terminal, presumably one of those in the control tower of the Lower Amidships Docks. A three-dimensional representation of the Novarasphere hovered above the pedestal—a translucent globe centered around a miniature depiction of the *Novara*, the surrounding airspace delineated at five-thousand-kilometer intervals by spheres within spheres like the layers of a jawbreaker. Numerous blinking arrowheads denoted the transponder signals of various ships in the fleet as they meandered and waltzed around the arc ship at the globe's center, with discernible shipping lanes trailing to and from the crosshatched mass representing the debris belt.

"Stewardship of the docks has provided access to certain restricted governmental resources," Vidalia explained. "You are looking at a full account of all commercial and NTSC traffic presently active within sensor range—even vessels with masked transponders and thermal signatures are logged."

Kahu clucked his tongue against the side of his cheek. "Sky's pretty damned busy considerin' we're supposed to be in lockdown right now."

"Mostly private ships operating under NTU commission," Vidalia elucidated. "Although there is a fair amount of military traffic, too . . . Exhaustive analysis of this wealth of data has led us to a . . . troubling discovery."

The view of the spherical scope zoomed in on an area toward the equatorial edge of its pulse width range. In this distant, seemingly nondescript region of space, Tobias spied a huddle of contacts holding position like life rafts beached around the shore of an invisible island. Abruptly, the arrowheads farther into the core reversed their direction of travel and began moving at faster velocities. He realized the Governor was now rewinding the scope to present a reversed time-lapse of the previous twenty-four hours of activity. A pattern soon emerged as the far-off anomalous contacts started moving back and forth between the *Novara* and their hidden berth.

"We have been tracking a convoy of troop carriers shuttling under accipiter-class gunship escort from Quarterdeck to this undisclosed location . . . It appears they are docking with . . . something."

"What is it?" asked Delilah. "A station? Surely if there was something large enough for troop carriers to dock with out there, it would be public knowledge."

"I suspect it to be a frigate or corvette of some variety; I have my hypotheses about the history of its construction, although, without substantial proof, it might sound more like conspiracy theory than speculation . . . Evidently, the secrecy surrounding the existence of this vessel renders it invisible to the invicta-level security clearance held by the control tower's equipment . . . Suffice to say, evidence points to it being a military facility—one that, since the fall of the blockade, has sprung to life from an extended period of dormancy."

"It's the admiral," Hazel murmured. Tobias didn't need human-to-human resonance to share the pit of dread she likely felt in her stomach. "He's mobilizing for a large-scale operation. My guess, judging from the use of elephas-class troop carriers: he's readying for a ground assault."

"Our observations would align on this theory, Miss Edevane," Vidalia confirmed grimly. "Up until now, Phalanx have been holding the line in the Copper Swathes. The NTSC has been notably absent in its contribution to the fight against Harmony. It could be that the admiral is deploying reinforcements to bolster numbers and launch a counteroffensive. I, however, am of the opinion that we should be preparing ourselves for another possibility . . ."

"You think he's coming here," posited Isaac, the glow of the luma-surface turning the engineer's clouded eyes into lambent orbs of white marble. "Why would he want to do that?"

Silence reigned heavily in the cabin. Vidalia: "I dare not postulate. Whatever his intentions, I believe, Doctor Thaddeus, that you should focus your efforts on establishing suitable defenses to thwart any potential incursions. As I previously stated: I want nothing for this information, and there is no catch or duplicity in my providing it. Regardless of your opinion of me, I once governed the people now in your care, and I only wish to see their continued protection."

"I find calling your exploitative treatment of the Prey 'protection' preposterous and offensive, to be perfectly frank," snarked Amara. "Nevertheless . . . your help in the matter has been duly noted."

"What about the Monarchs?" Teo blurted, hands tucked anxiously into the sleeves of her sweater. "You got tons of armed meatheads over there in the docks. If you wanna protect the cohabs then can't you send some of 'em here to defend the gardens?"

"That will not be possible, Miss Brižan," Drexen replied snappily. "As much as it seems like we may be looking at a response to the cohabitor mass migration, I must also consider that Admiral Coombs could be preparing to take the docks. I cannot jeopardize my position by donating personnel at such a critical time. I'm afraid warning you about this threat is the limit of what assistance I can offer . . . I must leave you now so that I can begin putting my own countermeasures in place . . . Captain Holloway. You and your crew should report to the maintenance bay as soon as you are able . . . And to the rest of you, I wish you luck. I dare say, you're going to need it."

TWENTY-SEVEN

An explosive argument broke out the very instant the call with Vidalia concluded. The altercation threatened to blow the roof off the operations cabin before spilling like a pyroclastic flow out into the courtyard, continuing within range of far too many sensitive ears . . .

"You can't just walk away, Lilah; we gotta talk about this!" Teo implored, following hot on the captain's heels as the woman stormed away, the tail of her duster coat twisting and flapping in the motion of her stomping footsteps.

"There's nothing to talk about," Delilah coarsely answered. "I've made my decision, and it isn't up for negotiation."

Isaac practically barged Tobias out of the way as he galloped down the cabin's stairwell. "I don't get it: you've never run the *Assurance* like a dictatorship before. Why all of a sudden are you doin' it now?"

Delilah ran her hands through her voluminous curls in frustration. "I swear, you Verhoevens can be so dramatic sometimes. This isn't me *oppressing* you or *violating your rights*." She turned to face the pair, standing her ground with her repeater resting on her shoulder. "You know, it strikes me you two are under the misconception that I'm somebody you can argue with. But guess what? I'm not your mother; I'm not your guidance counselor: I am your captain. So, the way it works is, *I* give the orders and *you* say 'yes, Captain,' and follow them without quarrel. Got it?"

"With all due respect, *Captain*." Teo enunciated. "When your *orders* are total bullshit, you give us no choice but to second guess them. You can't seriously expect us to just fall in line when what you're askin' of us is so gutless."

Delilah blew a steadying breath, staid countenance cleaved by streaks of shadow cast by the wood-beam pergola canopying the courtyard. "We made a deal with the Composer," she said. "Get Nanimonai and the kids to safety in exchange for those interim repairs. We've fulfilled our end of the bargain, so there's no reason for us to stick around. And for *your* information, there's nothing 'gutless' about getting back to doing what people depend on us with their lives to do."

Teo hurled her arms as if trying to shake off a pair of gloves. "But they *ain't* safe! You heard what Drexen said in there: Coombs might be gearin' up to send a whole damned invasion force!"

Delilah gave a blithe, albeit achingly transparent, shrug, as if she really thought she could convince them she had it within herself to be so uncaring. "That's none of our concern, and even if it was, what exactly do you think we could do to stop it? We're not soldiers; the *only* way we can help these people is by getting the *Assurance* starside and prepped for hull repairs."

"You don't really believe that, Skip," Kahu suggested, crouching down on popping knees to rub the scruff of Abraham's neck. The pair had been almost inseparable since first meeting in the Transitech maintenance depot, with Delilah herself joking twice already that Abe had resigned as Eamon's head deputy and taken on a new position as Kahu's therapy companion. "We leave these folks to fend for themselves, they're gonna be fish in a barrel. Sure, we ain't exactly the most lethal bunch, but surely *any* backup is better than none."

"We're not leaving them defenseless," Delilah corrected. "They'll have Amara, Eamon, and near the entire DMED staff watching over them. And you know what, Heperi—why in the empty black are you even here, let alone giving me your two creds over what *I* should be doing with my crew? Weren't you supposed to be drooling on a bar top at some dive in Rennaxi Junction by now? I have the distinct recollection of you telling me you were slinging your hook."

The veteran stood to his feet, cracked his neck, and rolled his shoulders. "Too right, which means you don't get to boss me around no more. I've never backed down from a fight in my life, so I'm stayin' right here . . . Besides,"—he gave a glib wink—"reckon all the good spots are closed anyhow on account of the lockdown."

Teo dug her heels in and defiantly folded her arms. "If Kahu's staying, then so am I. And if you don't like it, then I guess . . . I guess *I* resign, too."

"Are they always this dysfunctional?" Hazel asked as Tobias helped her down the operations cabin stairs.

"You don't know the half of it," he replied quietly.

Delilah's authoritative facade waned; her shoulders sank, brown eyes widening into endless pits of tortured trepidation. "I am *not* putting any of you at undue risk ever again, do you hear me?" The words were rasping and tremulous as they left her lips. "The past two months, we've had nothing but scrape after scrape after scrape. It's a miracle we're all still alive considering some of the idiotic, reckless decisions I've made. I don't plan on tempting fate now by staying here and taking some suicidal stand against . . ." She bit the words off before they could leave her mouth, knowing she had inadvertently revealed the truth that she understood perfectly well how perilous things were for the Conservatory's new residents. Head hung in shame, she said "The writing's on the wall, and what it says . . . it terrifies me."

Isaac took a step toward her, commanding her gaze as she fought to avoid his.

"No matter what you do," he recited. "Try and make things better for people—that's what he said, right; my brother, before he died?"

Delilah nodded, wiping a tear with the sleeve of her duster.

"You always said those words were your magnetic north," he went on "Hell, they were the entire reason you bought the *Assurance* off Heperi in the first place, right? The people Micah was talking about—they're right here; there's no one on the *Novara* more deserving and in more desperate need of our help. We can't let fear get in the way of fulfilling that promise—even the fear of losing each other."

Tobias caught a look from his sister that said, *This is the 'volatile' junkie you mentioned?* Even he had to admit, he hadn't thought the engineer capable of such poignant wisdom.

Delilah breathed a sigh of defeated acceptance. She lifted her chin and looked poised to respond, but before she could say anything, a sudden and mysterious rumbling resonated from somewhere beneath the courtyard. Cracks appeared like lightning strikes of frost in the glass walls of the encompassing structures. Flocks of birds fled their leafy perches, dispersed in a panic by the shuddering of the ground as it rattled the surrounding trees. Tobias and the others shared a flurry of unnerved glances, then hastily joined the stream of refugees and volunteers leaving the complex to investigate the disturbance. Approximately fifty meters along the magenta hiking trail, a crowd began to amass near Amara's spectacular orchid garden, where a large, elongated fissure had rent the earth asunder. The lush turf rose on either side of the rupture like a mountain range split along the meandering axis of its peaks, bulging and widening as the vibrations gradually intensified, venting the potent odor of wet soil into the air.

Eamon barged his way to the front of the throng, screaming "Move! Get back!" as he worked to push the onlookers to a safe distance, most too enthralled to comply.

"Any idea what this could be?" Hazel asked, interlinking her arm with Tobias's for support. His hyperactive mind spawned an image of the admiral's forces burrowing up through the earth like moles with an excavation engine and opening the way for a subterranean assault, although he thought the idea too ludicrous to even voice aloud. "I . . . I don't know . . . a malfunction with the irrigation, perhaps?"

Clarity arrived in conjunction with waves of exuberant revelation, produced by the dozens of nearby Prey as they jointly determined the cause of the destructive phenomenon. Eyes distended in astonishment, he murmured three words: "It's the Savior."

The grassy mountain range became an erupting volcano, spewing an imposing, black geyser consisting not of ash but of machinery encased in sinew and bone. The immense conduit breached from underground and climbed like the stem of a flower reaching for sunlight. Emitting a thunderous groan that echoed loudly across the gardens, the behemoth splayed its blunt head as if mimicking a cuttlefish rearing its tentacles to attack, contacting the geodesic dome's surface with such violent force that Tobias feared it might crack the aluminosilicate. The interspecies congregation loosed a chorus of gasps and bleats, necks craned upward as they marveled at the towering pillar, many dropping to their knees and bowing their heads in veneration, paying no mind to the rubble and detritus falling from the conduit's grim exterior as it swayed cumbersomely for balance. Then, a peculiar development: a succession of vents opened along its segmented structure—a spiraling column of ovate portholes laying bare the nebulous firestorm raging within.

"Better get Wonderboy outta here, Skip," Tobias heard Kahu quipping over his shoulder. "That sucker's about to hotbox the entire goddamned Conservatory." Fortunately, Isaac seemed too captivated to heed the remark, gawking up at the spectacle with one hand on his goggles and the other protectively around Mercy's waist.

Suffice to say, the vents did not disgorge the Savior's divine light as Mr. Heperi had predicted. Instead, vines, ablaze with orange bioluminescence, began to creep out of the openings. In a matter of seconds, they achieved a degree of growth one would expect to see from a full year of cultivation, quickly forming what looked like an external nervous system around the circumference of the colossal trunk, branching and entwining as they crawled higher and higher toward the fabricated heavens. Once the scandent vegetation reached the conduit's apex, it proceeded to spread across the Conservatory's enclosure like a colony of slime mold proliferating in a petri dish. Before long, it had radiated all the way down to the facility's stem wall, covering 80 percent of the dome's inner-surface area with a lambent, organic veneer. The rapid germination continued as the vines began sprouting complex structures: bulbs resembling pumpkins, hollowed out and impregnated with what looked like honeycomb, nestled among wild, crimson-colored shrubbery—a veritable menagerie of exotic foliage that any keen botanist would have a field day examining.

"I suppose that solves our concerns over how we're going to feed the Prey," said Tobias. "Although, logistically, I'm not sure how we're going to harvest it way up there."

"Toxic to humans, ain't it?" Teo put in. "Guess the *big guy's* making sure it's out of reach so it don't poison any of us."

"Never mind poisoning *us*," said Hazel, buckling her knees and seeming unsteady on her feet. Teo instinctively reached out as she began to slump, wrapping his sister's arm around her neck to take the brunt of her weight. "Careful, sis. Maybe we should find you somewhere to take a load off."

Hazel ignored the suggestion. "What effect is this going to have on the gardens? The plant life here relies on the dome's artificial sunlight for photosynthesis, doesn't it? Won't it die with this invasive thicket blocking the only source? And if it's toxic to humans, then who knows what kind of pollutants it could be releasing into the atmosphere?"

Tobias saw the status lights on Hazel's implants pulsing green, which he now knew exclusively occurred when Amara Thaddeus was making contact. She stared into the distance with eyes narrowed in concentration, clinging to both him and Teo so fervently that he had to wonder whether her prosthesis had ceased to function entirely. He couldn't tell whether her deteriorating strength was simply due to her dire need of rest, or if there existed a less prosaic explanation. Just as her mood had seemingly influenced the simulated weather when they first arrived, could this disruption to the Conservatory's ecosystem somehow have impaired her, too? The implications of neuroconfluence with Amara had, in all likelihood, yet to fully reveal themselves; as it stood, he couldn't shake the notion that, through Hazel's implants, Amara's admin privileges had somehow rubbed off, binding her on a subconscious yet intrinsic level to the closely guarded protocols governing the Conservatory. She seemed to have no real agency over them as it stood, but selfishly, he had to wonder what useful resources or new abilities she might unlock, were she to learn how to control them. In their precarious situation, they needed every advantage available to them . . .

"Air quality is still optimal," she eventually said—information either given to her by her AI conscience or, perhaps, personally gleaned from the plethora of sensor data he hypothesized she now had instant access to. "And the growth—whatever it is—it's giving off plenty of light energy—vitamin D, even . . . There doesn't seem to be any immediate danger to us or the gardens."

"I wouldn't worry, sis," Teo chimed in. "We've always been able to grow stuff in the Mouth; folks even have rooftop plots for harvesting fruit and vegetables. It's pretty much impossible to get a hold of good soil, but the bloodfall provides all the necessary nutrients . . . Trust me; the plants here are gonna thrive. Might get turned bright orange, mind you. But I dunno." She shrugged. "Could look neat."

Word arrived of a commotion taking place over in the back of house loading bay. As promised, Amara had intercepted a munitions shipment bound for the District of the Mouth and rerouted it to the COHP. The problem was that Phalanx, for all their misgivings, would never be so negligent as to transport weapons without rigorous supervision, and the appropriated cargo barge had shown up manned by two armed and predictably rattled chaperones. Fearing violence, Tobias took the ZT buggy and raced for the atrium. He disembarked near the info desk and sprinted for the rear entrance, giving a hurried *You are before me, and I, before you* greeting to the lone cohabitor loitering nearby, doubtless drawn by the raised voices spilling out into the gardens. He didn't believe he'd ever met aer personally—he would have remembered due to the unique curvature of the spines protruding from aer neck and shoulders. He did, however, recognize aer resonant essence, likely from a memory shared by a mutual associate—a relative, maybe, of someone he had previously bonded with. He broadcast a few abrasive mental flashes to serve as a deterrent from wandering any closer; from the sounds of the ensuing confrontation, the shooting could break out at any moment . . .

Leaving behind the lustrous foyer designed to dazzle and enrich the imagination, he plunged into the jarringly drab backstage area reserved for the eyes of employees only. In the loading bay, framed against the vertical freight shaft and its raucous cataract of autonomous traffic, he found Eamon attempting to defuse a standoff, backed by his newly appointed security cadre of ex-DMED staffers. His team had taken cover behind a parked ZT loadlifter carrying crates of oxygen cylinders and fresh herbs ready for export. The marshal stood with his arms extended over the vehicle's engine housing, keeping the two interloping enforcers planted firmly in the sights of his hybridized pistol. The pair were holed up in the cargo barge's operators' compartment, screaming for those in the loading bay to "Drop their weapons and come out with their hands up." Of course, Eamon's crew reciprocated their demands by demanding *they* do precisely the same.

"Last chance! Drop 'em! Drop 'em right now!" Wyatt's voice sounded hoarse from the incessant caterwauling. "There's no need for this to get ugly. Just come out slow and steady and we can talk!"

"You fucks made it ugly the second you hijacked us!" replied one enforcer—a man who Kahu Heperi would say *was built like a brick shit house*. Wearing a visored Phalanx-issue helmet and body armor that seemed to barely contain his burly upper torso, he stood half-in-half-out of the operator's compartment, using its swinging door as a makeshift barricade.

"Do you idiots even know who you're stealing from?" The other enforcer catechized—a woman, presumably, from the sound of their voice, although Tobias had no clear line of sight to confirm. "This is *interfering with Phalanx businesses* at best and *high treason* at worst. No matter how this goes down, you're screwed!"

One of Eamon's deputies—Kirst, if memory served—spotted Tobias lingering out in the open and beckoned him with a frenetic gesture. He recognized the stout woman from his brief and regrettable stay in the holding cells of the DMED precinct house, recalling that she had been the only staff member who had refrained from treating him with immediate disdain, feeling pleasantly surprised to discover that she was among those of Eamon's old comrades who had accepted his call to arms.

He scurried across the deck and joined the scrum while the marshal regarded him with a glare saying, *What in the Abyss are you doing here?*

"Look. We've got orders to deliver this shipment to the front line," yelled Brick Shit House. "There's good people dying by the dozen out there; we're not abandoning our duties because some amateur outlaws reckon they've got us cornered . . . Either you surrender your weapons and get out of our way, or we all die right here, right now . . . So, which is it gonna be, buddy?"

A look of uneasy recognition swept across Eamon's weathered face. Ignoring his team's pleas to stay down, he hesitantly dropped his shooting stance and maneuvered out of cover. "Fenn?" he asked, creeping toward the barge with his arms raised and his pistol hanging loose around his trigger finger. "Is that you, you stupid sonofabitch?"

"Wyatt?" Brick Shit House, or Fenn, replied. "Goddamn cockroach. So, *this* is where you've been hiding." The brute inched away from the barge, holding his Viperinae submachine gun low-ready but keeping the muzzle pointed at Eamon's chest. "You owe me money you slippery bastard. I had three hundred nunits on the Stingrays taking the title."

"Didn't get your stake back I take it?"

"I did, but the odds were four-to-one, and they were holding their own before your little stunt show."

"Guess that's what you get for bettin' against the odds . . . Thought you were supposed to be on desk duty?"

Fenn sneered. "With the leeches invading? Even if I didn't get drafted back into active duty I *still* woulda volunteered."

"Always were a man of action."

"Haken!" spat the other enforcer. "If this loudmouthed prick *is* Eamon Wyatt, then by order of Executor Royce, aren't we supposed to shoot on sight? He murdered the administrator; he's a traitor!"

"Just cool your damned jets a second, Mercer," Fenn rasped over his shoulder. "I'm thinking, alright?"

"If not for the force, then do it for yourself. This fucker ratted you out, remember? Those allegations cost you, detective."

Fenn removed his helmet and attached it to the mag-mount on his back-plate, revealing a chiseled face outlined by a neatly trimmed crew cut. From his churlish affectation, Tobias had almost expected to be met by the baleful grin of Jonah Sinclair. Peering over the load-lifter's chassis, he locked eyes with a man who, surprisingly, bore a striking resemblance to himself—or at least, how he believed he could look, aged up about fifteen years and having furiously hit the gym, albeit neglecting to exercise any areas of his body other than his chest and biceps.

"You're not wrong, there," Fenn considered.

Eamon took a cautious step forward. "Listen, partner. I know Harmony are giving the frontline enforcers hell, and I respect that you've got your orders, but we've got people here—*vulnerable* people. I guarantee we need those weapons more than Phalanx right now." Eamon raised his hands farther to reaffirm his desire for cooperation. "Honestly, we could use your help. There's a lot of good you could do here, Fenn. Why don't you come on back and see what we've accomplished for yourself . . . For old time's sake?"

"Oh, I will, old buddy," Fenn assured, but not in a way that felt particularly reassuring. "Once Phalanx have steamrollered this insurgency, you can bet your ass we'll be rocking up to life support. I'll have plenty of opportunity to see what you've done with the place. But, until then . . ."

Without warning, the man deployed a taser dart from the offensive unit on his wrist pack. The electrifying projectile struck Eamon directly to the sternum and rendered him instantly immobilized. Tobias and the others could do little but watch on in horror, hopelessly unarmed, as Fenn strode toward his old partner while producing a pair of flexi-cuffs from his utility belt.

"Eamon Wyatt. I am arresting you on suspicion of the murder of Madeline Vargos and aiding and abetting enemies of the New Terra Union. You do not have to say anything but anything you *do* say will be . . ."

"Ruttin' snake!" Eamon hissed through gritted teeth, crumpling to the ground as every muscle in his body painfully contracted.

"Relax, will you?" Fenn drawled, slapping the cuffs around his wrists. "I'm doing you a favor; you're lucky it was *me* who caught up with you and not one of these trigger-happy greenhorns they've got in the ranks nowadays."

One of the deputies stood up to intervene but was forcibly yanked back into cover by Deputy Kirst and castigated for "trying to be a hero."

"You fucks stay right where you are," Fenn demanded, leaning his face into the radio attached to the shoulder pad of his armor. "Five eight seven three, Alfa central. Requesting urgent assistance and raptor support to present location. One prisoner in custody with several more ready for processing, over."

The responder's voice rattled through the radio's speaker, bookended by a flurry of electronic tones. Although, strangely, Fenn seemed to completely ignore it, his attention suddenly drawn to the sliding double doors Tobias had entered through. Disregarding his colleague's request for a sitrep, he left Eamon drooling on the floor and began sidestepping toward the atrium entrance, SMG drawn at the ready. The automatic doors slid open, and the source of the man's apparent transfixion thumped into the loading bay on stilt legs, bowing aer head to clear aer chitinous ridges of the door frame. Tobias felt the distinct static in the air that heralded resonance, but as powerful emissions burnished the cohabitor's laddered eyes, he came to realize that it was not *he* with whom ae sought to forge a bond. Evidently, ae had been beckoned to the loading bay by more than just the ruckus . . .

Fenn reacted as anyone who had been around him for five minutes might expect, giving vent to a profanity-laced tirade of demands to "Get on the ground!" and "Keep your claws where I can see 'em!" But as the Savior's light extended an ethereal bridge between his mind and that of his target, he fell suddenly silent.

"Clear my line of fire, Haken!" his colleague yawped, finally finding the courage to leave the safety of the barge, approaching with her weapon raised. "I don't have a clear shot!"

"Stand down, Mercer," he muttered, first as if half-asleep and then again with more force when the request went ignored. He returned his luminous gaze back to the cohabitor and asked "W . . . what is this? What's it doing to me? Feels like . . . *everything*—everything I've ever felt, all at once . . . How?"

The second enforcer marched across the deck and barged him out of the way to take aim at the towering alien. "C'mon you idiot; they taught us this shit in basic! It's screwing with your head! Now stand clear so I can put it down!"

Fenn grabbed the barrel of her weapon and abrasively ripped it off her, then tossed it along with his own over the ledge of the loading bay's debarkation point and into the weightlessness of the freight shaft. Eamon had yet to collect himself following his high-voltage dose. His team, however, saw their window of opportunity and took it; they pounced on the unsuspecting enforcer, who screamed as they pinned her to the ground and fought to detain her.

Fenn barely even acknowledged the scuffle. Nothing, it seemed, could pry his focus away from his resonant counterpart and the flourishing connection between them. Clearly, *his* was a far tamer awakening than the one Tobias had experienced; the man appeared cognizant, aware, and, critically, had not been reduced to a blubbering, catatonic heap by his hallucinations. It felt like watching birth—the moment of resonant inception playing out before his very eyes; a coalescence of two souls forming a union far greater than the sum of its parts. Up until now, he had seen little proof of there being any method or pattern as to whom the Savior chose to endow its blessing. Certainly, the attendees of his resonance education center had proven a seemingly random vertical slice of the Novarian population. But Fenn's serendipitous compatibility suggested he was more than just a winner of some cosmic genetic lottery. Connecting these two minds at this exact instant had manifestly served a purpose, and unquestionably illustrated the workings of precise and intelligent design. It wasn't a coincidence, it wasn't fate: it was strategy.

"You're still all under arrest," Fenn said, emerging from his daze. "I just . . . need a minute . . . to figure this out."

The cohabitor, whose colors were sky-blue and sang a silent melody of philosophic solemnity, took a ponderous step toward Fenn, the pair's emissions jointly brightening from low beam to high.

"No," Fenn murmured, shaking his head and furrowing his brow. "There's no way it can know that . . . How can it possibly know that?" He became increasingly agitated, no longer cutting the image of a roughneck enforcer but of a terrified little boy; fear coursing through his body like the 30,000 volts Eamon had just received.

"Easy, Fenn," the marshal cooed, scraping himself off the floor with his wrists bound in flexi-cuffs proving an arduous task. He hastened across the loading bay to his ex-partner, showing palms placatingly. "What's happenin' to you is nothin' to be scared of. Just gotta ride it out and I promise everything's gonna be Nebula."

"You don't understand, Wyatt!" Fenn blurted, clutching his shorn hair between his fingers as if trying to scalp himself. "The fuckin' thing knows what I did! It knows everything! How? How can it know?"

Tobias hated the idea of prying into what should have been an intimate moment between two individuals but thought it prudent to see if he could glean anything that might be used to ease Fenn's transition. He dove into their bond like a diver performing a backward entry roll, submerging himself in a conflagration of memory and emotion as their two resonant essences turbulently integrated. The cohabitor, who had never before attained cross-species resonance and, as such, had no name, acted as a conduit to channel Fenn Haken's concentrated id. It became immediately clear that the bravado, arrogance, and overt machismo were used as a lockbox to keep squirreled away the parts of himself better left buried. Tobias detected overarching guilt surrounding a traumatic event in his past. Fenn filled his lonely existence with petty and frivolous distractions to avoid having to face it, but once-meager ripples of shame and remorse had since accumulated into waves—waves that smashed against his self-preservative seawall until, finally, it had eroded to the point of collapse.

The man fell to his knees, staring up at Sky-Blue with a tortured grimace. "I'm sorry. Abyss, I'm so damned sorry. I never meant to . . . I just . . . It's not *me* anymore; it never was! You *have* to believe me. Please! I'm beggin' you!"

Tobias saw the distress in Mercer's eyes as Fenn emptied his lungs with a plaintive wail. But then distress transmuted into horror as the man swiftly unholstered his sidearm and pressed its muzzle against his own temple. Eamon lunged forward to intervene and, with Tobias's belated help, managed to wrangle the weapon free and cast it out of reach. Fenn collapsed to his hands and knees, distraught and defeated. Gazing down at him, sky-blue emitted a warbling groan as if attempting to pacify him with an atonal lullaby. Tobias plucked two words out of the hazy array of concepts that subsequently swelled in the forefront of his awareness: *Atone. Forgive.*

TWENTY-EIGHT

Tobias knew he couldn't delay in tending to Fenn's resonant induction, lest he risk the man suffering a psychotic episode. Unfortunately, it would have to wait; right now, he had his own personal demons to contend with. He advised Eamon that, until he could free himself up to help *mediate*, it would be best to keep the newly ciphered pair as separate as the boundaries of the COHP would allow.

They had left Fenn's incensed associate hollering insults and expletives out in the loading bay, sealing the blast doors to prevent the inbound reinforcements from gaining access to the atrium. Naturally, that meant permanently cutting off access to the freight shaft and the bounty of resources Amara had been freely drawing from it. But after narrowly avoiding a firefight with the authorities, nobody dared chance a repeat scenario by commandeering further cargo barges. That they would need to determine alternative means of resupply bore little discussion.

Eamon chaperoned Fenn to Beech Glade while his team geared up from the appropriated weapons cache and moved to secure the facility. Tobias had profound respect for the marshal's scrappy band of volunteer protectors, who, by all accounts, would have been well within their rights to find a hole somewhere to simply wait out the storm, having been expulsed from the district by Harmony. Instead, they had chosen to risk their lives *and* their freedom in the name of standing up to tyranny and safeguarding their own. He hoped to have an opportunity to inspire a better impression of himself than what they had likely formed following his misadventures several months ago in the Langrenus Harrow. Although, that, too, would have to wait. Presently, they had a job to do, and a *matter* had arisen that demanded his immediate attention . . .

I'm here. Can we meet? Usual spot. The words appeared like an omen on the lock screen of his feather, depositing an anvil on his chest that sought to drag his insides to the ground. He had become so irreconcilably estranged from Caleb Callaghan over the past two months that it felt like receiving a message in a bottle from someone lost at sea. After everything that had transpired since they were last together, he struggled to predict how he might feel upon seeing her again—livid, he imagined, given the diatribe of incendiary rhetoric and egregious misinformation she had been pushing on Bhaltair Abernathy's platform, knowing full well what that murderous psychopath had conspired to do at Juniper Sanctuary. Even still, he couldn't simply disregard their history—all those years spent in each other's pockets—not to mention the fact that, until recently, he had truly believed he was in love with her. It all seemed so inane and insignificant contrasted against the challenges he had now been called to face. Above all else, he suspected, in the face of so much turmoil, he would just be happy to see her alive and well, and hoped that at the very least, they could be civil with one another.

The spot in question stood at the starboard edge of Bandhavgarh Reservoir: a quaint coffee shop situated in an elegant building that stood on curved stilts just above the water, supposedly built as an homage to a place that held tremendous sentimental value for Amara. Caleb and Tobias had wasted many an afternoon sitting on the jetty as they waited for Jade to get off shift, sipping hot beverages as they watched the resident koi amble below in envious appreciation of their carefree existence. The establishment had been abandoned by both patrons and employees in response to Amara's feigned decompression alert. Heading inside, he found tables littered with unfinished drinks and half-eaten desserts, tipped-over stools painting a picture of a manic evacuation. In the absence of staff, Caleb had assumed barista duties behind the counter, seeming every bit as adept with the vintage espresso machine as she had been during her several summers of employment here. Wearing a khaki gilet over a black, slim-fit bodysuit, her sunset curls as bright and unruly as ever, she showed a disarming smile as he approached, placing a recyclable coffee cup on the counter, and pushing it toward him.

"A peace offering," she said.

"I wasn't aware we were at war."

"Then you are very naive."

He took the cup and lifted it to his lips, recognizing and savoring the heavenly notes of the freshly brewed chai latte.

"Did you . . ."

"Add an extra shot? Of course." She pouted as if affronted that he had even deigned to ask such a question. It reminded him of the bittersweet truth that, although their friendship had taken a contentious turn, she *still* knew him better than anybody else on the *Novara*. Better than any other human, that is...

After a somewhat awkward pause, he remarked, "You've been busy."

She stared out through the nearby window at the canopy of lambent vegetation sprawling overhead, pensively blowing on her macchiato. "I could say the same."

He motioned toward the resplendent white ivy leaves crawling up her forearm, cast by her luma-bracelet. "Nice to see you dressing like yourself again."

She scoffed. "You think I'd be stupid enough to flaunt my support for Humanity First here, now? The leeches would probably have me strung up by my entrails."

"I think that demonstrates how little you really know about them."

She sighed. "You're not going to draw me into a political debate, Tobias, so save your breath. I don't want to argue."

He let his shoulders sink in resignation. "I don't either . . . Honestly, I'm just glad you're here, Firebird. There's so much I want to show you."

She raised her hand to signal the words, *Let me stop you right there.* "First: don't *ever* call me Firebird again," she reproached. "And second: I didn't come here so you can give me the *grand tour*—the less I see of the travesty you've made of this place, the better."

He gave a suggestive shrug. "Then why did you come?"

"Because . . . Because although I think you've gone *completely* off the rails, the truth is that I still care about you, and I don't want to see you get hurt."

"Hurt?" he repeated, incredulous. "Who would want to hurt me? Other than your entire followership, I mean."

"This *isn't* something to joke about, Tobias . . . You're rocking the boat too hard, and people are starting to take notice."

"What people?" Of course, he already knew the answer but wanted to allow her to prove once and for all where her loyalties lay: with the family who for the lion's share of two decades had treated her as one of their own, or the maniacal warlord who sought to wipe them out.

Disappointingly, she seemed disinclined to let her dominos fall either way, holding back her words as though they were too desperately precious to let go of.

"Take a walk with me," he suggested, putting her out of her conflicted misery. "No arguing; no politics: just you, me, and the gardens—exactly how it used to be."

They ventured out into the vibrant landscape, immersing themselves in a carnival of color and scent that left no sense unstimulated. The scenery had lost some of its viridescence thanks to the blanket of amber haze radiating from above, but the luminous growth did not rob the environment of its splendor, instead, casting the gardens in a rose-gold sheen that both soothed and invigorated his tired mind. While he reveled in the pure catharsis of his surroundings, Caleb seemed somewhat less enraptured. As they walked and talked, she kept a steely eye trained on the conduit, climbing to the heavens like one of the countless space elevators that once littered Earth's surface. As much as he hoped otherwise, he knew she was likely regarding it as something decidedly more sinister than a vessel for providing humanitarian aid to tens of thousands of people in vital need of it.

Realizing their path led toward its base, she pulled a vented mask out of her pocket and positioned it over her nose and mouth.

"You don't need that," he advised.

"Abyss I don't. Funnily enough, I'm not really in the mood for getting high right now. Nor do I fancy inhaling all the toxins that monstrosity is almost certainly venting into the atmosphere."

"Amara assured us the air's perfectly fine to breathe."

Caleb gave a sardonic laugh, muffled by the material of her face covering. "Tobias, if you really can't see the correlation between what the militants have done to the grenadiers and this newfound *sentience* of hers, then I fear you're completely beyond reasoning . . . I only hope when she decides to cut off the air circulation to Quarterdeck that you'll have the good sense to regret fraternizing with her. Clearly, she needs to be taken offline for maintenance."

So much for not wanting to argue . . .

They cut through the cactus garden before crossing the canal that bridged the Conservatory's two main bodies of water. He strategically took this route in the knowledge that, even in her foulest mood, his companion was practically incapable of passing the landmark without bringing up the time he had tried to jump over it and fallen spectacularly into the water. And bring it up she did, prompting further reminiscing that drastically alleviated the tension. They transported each other through anecdotes and memories to those fond, devil-may-care days before they enrolled in the academy, when they had been every bit as carefree as the koi inhabiting the reservoir. They looped around the back of the wetlands aviary and took the pathway that carved through Khadija's Green. This was perhaps the first opportunity Caleb had had to truly comprehend the scale of the refugee crisis; the abundant swathes of grass stretching on either side of them teemed with cohabitors, the collective drone of their bleating and whining redolent of a symphony orchestra discordantly tuning and practicing their instruments. Since the arrival of the conduit, they had apparently deemed shelter necessary after all and had set about secreting and sculpting their lava-bubble yurts in anticipation of bloodfall. Those closer to the path temporarily paused construction to offer gestures of thanks to Tobias as he and Caleb passed, bowing their heads and reaching out their arms as if attempting to embrace him from afar.

"So . . . what, you're some kind of messiah now?" Caleb asked, sarcasm lacing her voice.

"No." He shook his head. "These people haven't had a lot of help in their time, so they're beyond grateful for any they do receive."

Caleb mimicked the action of sticking her finger down her throat to induce vomiting and, notably, chose not to press the matter any further. He considered attempting to explain his hyper-resonance but sensed that she would become more disinterested with every word.

In the distance, at the foot of an enormous oak tree, he spied Mercy and Isaac relaxing in the grass. Mercy sat cross-legged with her back against the tree trunk while Isaac lay perpendicular to her with his head on her lap, gazing up adoringly as she ran her fingers through his scruffy, sandy-blond hair, having undone his topknot. Watching them, Tobias felt a note of thanks that the strangeness between him and Mercy had not done any lasting damage to her burgeoning relationship with the engineer.

Beyond them, he saw Teodora standing alone with her hands hidden in the sleeves of her knitted sweater, staring at him with a longing expression, as though she wanted nothing more than to hear his and Caleb's conversation. It dawned on him that he would much rather be spending these precious hours of calm before the inevitable storm with his crewmates instead of with Caleb. He had hoped that seeing her again might provide some closure and reconciliation when, in reality, all it had served to do was make him feel bitterly uncomfortable about himself. All her judgment, ignorance, and hypercriticality were direct reflections of the person he used to be. Cold, callous, and single-minded—these were qualities he had worked hard to eradicate from his character like a swordsmith honing the imperfections out of a blade. And while he would always strive for peace and accord, he realized in that instant that nothing good could come from allowing Caleb Callaghan back into his life.

He mulled the thought over for a while as they branched off the main path and ambled on autopilot down a meandering track. Meanwhile, Caleb rambled on about the *incredible strides* she had been making with Humanity First, proudly announcing that she had all but forced Bhaltair Abernathy from the picture and promoted herself to director. If he didn't know any better, he'd say she was trying to recruit him back into the organization, using buzz terms like "unrecognizable," "reformed," and "new leaf" in a transparent attempt to wheedle his interest. He was on the cusp of telling her to *wrap up her sales pitch so he could politely decline* when she stopped in her tracks—so abruptly, in fact, it appeared as though she had collided face-first with an invisible wall. He turned to find her standing rigidly, staring ahead with her mouth agape, eyebrows raised and pulled together. He followed her sight line and realized with encroaching dismay that the track they had absently diverted down was one they had traveled many times before: the one that led to the private allotments. Before them lay Jade Tanaka's patch, or at least, what remained after a group of cohabitors had decided to set up camp directly on top of it. Doubtless, they had been drawn to the overgrown plot by the eye-catching aura of pink maple leaves that overlooked it. The notion of a garden was, of course, inherently alien to the Prey, and they had been completely oblivious to any sentimental value the small aggregation of shrubbery might have held in establishing their home. The tree had been ravaged in a demonstrably unsuccessful test to see whether it might be suitable for sleep hanging, leaving piles of twigs and snapped branches strewn about the ground. The settlers had demolished the plot's faux-wood beds and removed the chicken wire fencing to make way for their domicile, trampling Jade's impressive yield of herbs and vegetables into the dirt with the same indifference as they might have any random tract of land in the Cohabitor Ghetto. The culprits noticed Caleb and Tobias lingering nearby and welcomed them with an *You are before me, and I, before you* gesture, blissfully unaware of the "unforgivable desecration" they had committed.

Tobias turned to Caleb, darting his head into her field of view to try and catch her gaze. Her fury telegraphed itself unhampered on her face, flushing her cheeks and forehead red, pulling her jaw forward, and coaxing her to bare her teeth.

"This isn't what it looks like," he pleaded. "I promise, there's no malice in what they've done here; they just don't know any better . . . Look, it's not even that bad. I can ask them to move somewhere else and have one of the groundskeepers over to fix it in no time . . . Please understand."

She blew a steadying breath, focusing her eyes on his as a foreboding calmness descended over her. "I understand perfectly well, Tobias . . . I admit, I was conflicted before, but coming here today—it's really helped me get my head straight. So, I must thank you for that."

She showed a smile that he had never seen before—one that, to unfamiliar eyes, might have seemed perfectly amiable, but to *him*, held all the calculated malevolence of a predator toying with its prey. She bid him the kind of farewell one might to an inconsequential stranger. Then, saying nothing more of the threat she had initially sought to warn him about—the entire reason she came to the Conservatory in the first place—Caleb Callaghan turned her back on Jade's ruined allotment and hastily took her leave.

TWENTY-NINE

How could Jyn savor the taste of victory when it left such a foul residue on her tongue? She couldn't recall a time when she hadn't dreamt of one day finding a way to liberate the Mouth from the pestilential grasp of the Glow Syndicate. Recent successes had seen those aspirations made manifest, with Harmony pulling Drexen's organization up by its rotten roots and eradicating every remaining trace from the district. And yet, she couldn't shake the feeling that she had merely traded one nemesis for another. This new adversary had proven fiercer, more disciplined; they fought not at the behest of a master but for the preservation of their way of life, driven not by cruelty or greed but by survival instinct and righteous conviction. With every passing hour, her hopes of advancing farther into Amidships seemed increasingly naive. Judging from the level of resistance on display, Phalanx leadership were pulling in reserve personnel from all over the *Novara* to bolster their counteroffensive. Wielding a siege engine of oppressive artillery and small arms fire, the enemy had driven the Choir back from the ruins of the blockade, fortifying themselves within the high walls of their reclaimed compound. The front line had since been pushed back to the edge of the Copper Swathes, with Harmony's forces now entrenched in the line of shelled buildings hedging the war-torn outskirts. The structure in which Jyn's unit had hunkered down used to be an outreach center for the cultural induction of visitors, which essentially meant teaching bowsiders mouthian customs and educating them on how to behave respectfully around Prey, as well as advising where to steer clear of to avoid a mugging. The shattered right-angle display windows made the spacious showroom less than ideal for use as a stronghold—almost no viable cover and exposed to a two-hundred-and-seventy-degree field of fire—but in the heat of battle, as an onslaught of enforcers flushed Jyn's unit out of their position, they had been left with little other option. The devastation wreaked upon the suite of information boards and interactive exhibits, which had been installed to promote interspecies cohesion, telegraphed the distinct absence of it. Light fixtures dangling from the buckled ceiling highlighted the bullet holes and blast marks sullying every surface in contorted, forbidding detail. Jyn could barely hear her own thoughts for the unrelenting pounding of hostile mortar fire, every impact triggering undulating disturbances in the punishing haze of smoke and ash, which stung her eyes and sat irritably in the back of her throat.

Crouched behind deployable barricades, several cohabitor heavy gunners laid down a horizontal hail of coruscating plasma, the incessant hammering of their hybridized ARX-40 light machine guns like two woodpeckers intent on making sawdust of her eardrums. On the surface, her nonhuman kin fought with unflinching fortitude, but they inadvertently betrayed their growing disquiet through their proximity bond with her. Primal instinct for the Prey mandated survival above all else; when faced with an insurmountable threat, their natural compulsion was to flee. Accordingly, Jyn stood at the viral epicenter of a resonant pandemic, fear and hesitation spreading ravenously from one fighter to the next, eating away at their constitution as the hopelessness of the situation became increasingly apparent. They felt the cold hand of death edging closer; every cell in their bodies screamed at them to make their escape, and yet, they stood their ground, faithful and tireless.

A dozen grenadiers formed a defensive rampart just outside the boundary of the showroom. The last protocols issued to them via the manipulated signal were focused on enemy suppression and thwarting potential hostile advances. Jyn had not expected the tables to turn quite so dramatically, and with the transverse bandwidth limitations inherent in uploading data to the Pyre, self-preservation had been a relatively low priority. Any autonomy they once possessed was overwritten as a result of Absence's reprogramming, leaving them without the virtual sense to take cover as they engaged the enemy. Although highly robust, the machines were by no means indestructible; standing out in the open amid a hurricane of incoming fire, they had sustained extensive damage to their mechanical frames, their armor plating whittled down to jagged coastlines of charred steel, their nanocarbon skeletons laid bare and scorched black with blast residue. Several had appendages mangled or missing altogether, leaving behind ragged stumps of splintered metal, rhythmically spurting bright-green hydraulic fluid.

As it stood, just one had been fully incapacitated, and only because its neural cortex had been blown clean out the back of its head. Still, Jyn didn't doubt that more would soon follow. Assuming the grenadiers assigned to the six other units dug in across the outskirts were in a similar state, she feared their mechanized infantry support could be depleted within the hour. *And what hope do we have of fighting our way to Chennai Plaza without them? Our only options will be to retreat, or die charging senselessly into the Phalanx meat grinder...*

Her grim rumination had coaxed her into letting her guard down; in a moment of startled confusion, someone pulled her down into cover behind the information kiosk right as she spied a brilliant muzzle flash emanating from the roof of one of the Phalanx Compound's prefabricated structures. A high-caliber projectile screamed through the air above her head, then the crack of the originating shot resounded from the firer's location. Doubtless, her face had been framed dead center in their magnified scope before Isabella Graddock took decisive action to prevent her decapitation.

"You've been made!" The woman reached over the trembling legs of the man lying wounded beside her. She collected his spliced XT-90 and, with bloodlust in her eyes, gritted her teeth and vengefully fired several lances at the enemy marksman's perch.

"Given they've made it quite evident they want your head, might I suggest you do a better job of not offering it to them on a silver platter?"

Szakal was the name of the wounded man; he had taken a chunk of mortar shrapnel to his chest and shoulder during their frantic dash from the blockade to their fallback rendezvous point. He grabbed Jyn's hooded cape with a bloodsoaked hand, spluttering as he pleaded, "This place is not safe for you, Composer! You ... mu ... must evacuate to *Chīsana Osuushi* ... now! Before the oppressors bring the building down on ... on top of us!"

"If anyone's gettin' outta here, Szakal, it's *you*." She removed his hand from her robe and pressed it against the grizzly laceration occupying his right pectoral—a suspicious eye of viscous crimson peering through the shredded material of his robes. "Just keep pressure here until we can get you back to the Hollow. Heston will have you back up to fightin' strength in no time."

The man showed a pained wince that morphed into a sneer of contempt. "I ... I would rather ... succumb to my wounds than have ... ugh ... than have that traitor's hands tending to them."

Isabella fired off another suppressive burst before a volley of return fire forced her into cover. "The good doctor will be stitching ribbons together if we don't find a way to turn this fight around—that goes for the lot of us!" The woman met Jyn's gaze with a determined yet strangely vacant expression. If the eyes were the window into the soul, then what lay beyond Izzy's was a bleak and dismal emptiness. Dishearteningly, the loss of Nix had seemingly cored her like an apple—eviscerated her sagacious essence and left her a frail shell of her ciphered self. The visage of her wrinkle-riven face teetered into

the uncanny valley, leaving Jyn feeling as if being confronted by the reanimated corpse of a close friend.

"We need to gather our forces and advance!" said Isabella, elevating her
voice over the din of the battle, too focused on formulating stratagems to pay
any mind to the exhumation of her soul. "If we cede any more ground, they're
going to spread out into the Langrenus Harrow, and we won't last five minutes fighting them on two fronts . . . We need the grenadiers to push forward
if we have any hope of recapturing the blockade. Otherwise, it's over!"

"We can't update their directives until the next dissemination," Jyn replied.
"Just gotta hold the line for a little while longer. As soon as the Savior chimes,
Absence will initiate offensive protocols and we can launch a counterassault."

"Dammit all, Jyn! This is a fluid combat situation. Infantry I can only issue
commands to four times a day is hardly of any use to me!"

"You knew what you were signing up for. Gotta make do with what we
have!"

Just then, a barrage of synaptic flashes nearly knocked her onto her
haunches, a locomotive of concepts centered around fire and danger raucously pulling into her mental station. The resonant incursion heralded
a chorus of shouts from the human fighters in the embattled showroom.
"Incoming! They're sendin' drones! Take cover!"

Jyn heard what sounded like a frenzied hornet swarm approaching: the
whine of spinning microblades cresting as they drew nearer. She caught a
peripheral flash of several inbound UAVs as she dove for cover—flying arach-
nids with blinking blue running lights for eyes, doubtless carrying explosive
payloads with yield enough to turn the induction center into a smoking crater. Cursing Phalanx for their cowardice, she maneuvered onto her elbows
and knees to form a protective shell over Szakal. She considered no measures
off limits in the pursuit of deliverance for her kind; *All's fair in love and war*,
her Uncle Hiroki had often said, usually when beating her at shogi with his
crafty game strategies. Even still, there was something so dastardly, so insidious about Phalanx's appropriation of soulless machines to vanquish dissenters. Were the hacked grenadiers not so essential to Harmony's success, she
would have strictly abhorred the use of them. *There's no honor in this.*

Weapons fire rang out as the Choir attempted to intercept the wretched
contraptions. "Lead your shots! That's two down! Brace!"

Jyn clenched her teeth as a powerful shock wave tore through the showroom, violently evicting the air from her lungs and clawing at her cheeks
with searing heat. The buttressed information kiosk served to shield her
from much of the impact but failed to prevent fragments of glass and debris
from striking her exposed skin like a squall of needles. The few seconds it

took for the dust to settle felt like an eternity. She just kept her eyes forced shut and her body held firmly over her wounded comrade as an acrid mixture of soot and ozone found its way into her nose and throat. The plaintive moans of the injured built until they eventually punched through the ringing in her ears. Hearing Isabella's apoplectic grumbling imbued her with the strength to push herself off the ground, but grief and anguish swept in to enervate her as she glanced down at Szakal's glassy-eyed stare, slack jaw, and fixed expression. The tenuous threads of life he had been clinging to only seconds earlier had been severed by the blunt force of the explosion. He was gone, and as she rose to her feet, checking herself for injuries, she realized he wasn't alone . . . Their makeshift bastion resembled a pre–livestock ban slaughterhouse, the viscera strewn across the floor so copious and so mutilated that she struggled to discern which species it all belonged to. The heavy gunners tasked with holding the perimeter had been disintegrated, their deployable barricades now ragged shards of titanium jutting up at irregular angles from the smoking rubble covering the floor. She reached out through resonance to verify whether any of them had survived only to be met with an icy, heartrending radio silence. In one fell swoop, her entire unit had been wiped out—a collection of the most valiant Prey and humans she had ever had the pleasure of knowing, and they had followed her with unwavering loyalty right to their deaths. Their blood was on her hands—metaphorically, *and* literally, but she realized there was little sense dwelling on that now.

When she first saw Izzy hunched over and frantically scrambling about the floor, she assumed the woman had set about taking stock of their dead or, perhaps, tending to the wounded. But, no: the old strategist looked to be rifling feverishly through the piles of disorganized munitions, sifting like a prospector for nuggets of gold.

"Graddock," Jyn called, her voice dry and hoarse. "Report!"

"Where is the big red idiot when you need him?" the woman muttered absently.

"You know damn well where he is: on mission."

Isabella opened a flight case and rasped profanity upon finding it empty. "Yes. Using our best fighters for personal errands at a time when we need them most—not your greatest tactical decision."

But "personal errands" hardly served as an apt description for what Jyn had tasked Oren and his silent blades with: *more like "settling a vendetta."* Of course, with the way things were heading, capturing the starboard vehicular airlock from the Church of the Abyss potentially stood as Harmony's only remaining strategic option . . .

Finally, Izzy found her prize, which she held above her head in maniacal celebration: a bandolier loaded with fractal grenades.

"You're ma . . ." Jyn paused to wait for the clatter of incoming gunfire to abate. "You're making me nervous, Graddock! What're you plannin' on doing with those?"

The woman slung the armaments over her shoulders. "I'm getting you out of here."

"I don't recall giving the evacuation order."

Izzy pointed out into the killzone, indicating the stream of enforcers now charging out of the Phalanx Compound like a landslide of navy-blue Kevlar. "Does it look like we have time to argue about this? You need to leave; now!"

Jyn ardently shook her head. "A true leader doesn't send others to die for a cause she wouldn't die for herself, and that means I'm sure as shit not leaving anyone behind!"

"That all sounds very nice on paper, but let's face it: Harmony is *nothing* without you. If you let these bastards kill you—and believe me, they mean to—then everything we've done—all the suffering, all the chaos—what will it have been for? Nothing!"

Jyn went to respond before Isabella's spearing gaze stitched her mouth shut—the first eye contact the woman had made since the assault on Drexen's yacht. She stared into those hollow eyes once more, realizing that, in a certain sense, Izzy had died along with her resonant partner on the splintered terrace of *Chīsana Osuushi*, and had been operating on something like autopilot ever since. The only thing keeping her going was her drive to ensure the continued survival of the cause for which her beloved Nix had laid down aer life.

The other units spread throughout the outskirts opened fire on the advancing combatants, forcing them into cover behind concrete barriers and downed vehicles. The enemy were pinned down for now but had gained significant ground thanks to their precision drone strike. *Izzy's right: in a matter of minutes, they'll be all over us, and as sure as the night is everlasting, they aren't interested in taking prisoners . . .*

"You're leaving," Isabella reaffirmed. "And I'm buying you the time to do it."

"Don't you dare . . ."

The woman gave a reassuring smile and shook her head. She flicked the thumb switch on one of the grenades hanging around her torso like a ceremonial sash of death, then reverently uttered, "Quell the dissonance." She activated her luma-shroud and disappeared into the miasma. Jyn watched on in hopeless despair as a succession of boot prints appeared in the lunar dust outside the induction center, moving at the pace of a full sprint toward the area boasting the highest concentration of enforcers. She wished she could tear her eyes away, knowing that every second she tarried was a waste of the opportunity she had been given, but she found herself unable to avert her gaze. Then came the dreaded moment: an earth-shaking fractal detonation that seemed to shatter the fabric of reality as though it were a three-dimensional plate of glass. The expanding web of geometric distortion swallowed a dozen enemy combatants in a veil of pink mist, vaporizing everything within effective range and leaving a perfect ring of cinders on the ground.

The moans of the wounded in the showroom had lessened to a whimper. Jyn knew there was nothing she could do for them without endangering her survival and, in effect, the survival of Harmony. So, she reluctantly collected Szakal's rifle and, feeling defeat like never before, made her escape.

With the low rumble of artillery at her back, Jyn headed into the dense trellis of alleyways comprising the Warrens. She activated her emergency locator and received an immediate ping from a unit operating in the area. Her heart swelled with pride and relief upon recognizing its designation— SB-1—as the one assigned to the Red Scythe's detachment. If Oren's team hadn't succeeded in their mission, then at the very least, they had made it out alive . . .

A pair of raptors growled as they circled overhead before beginning to descend. Streaked in garish Harmony colors, the gravity-defying thrust of their gimballed repulsor pads caused the awnings of abandoned market stalls in the vicinity to flap and flail, clouds of dust billowing as the transports touched down in the center of the assigned LZ. She kept her head held high as she approached the convoy to conceal the guilt gnawing at her insides—a futile endeavor, given Oren's Prey confederates had likely sensed her inner turmoil the moment they came within resonant range.

Her trusted assassin disembarked from the nearest raptor in a feline fashion, his broad shoulders buried beneath his haggard cape shawl, the worn garment parting on either side of his torso to reveal a chiseled abdomen stained thick with chalky, scarlet residue.

"You are alone, Composer?"

She frowned, waving away the hand he offered to help her aboard. "Do you see anybody else with me?"

He paused. "What of the defector?"

She shook her head solemnly. "The old crone decided to make a martyr of herself. We were overrun; she gave her life to save mine."

Oren bowed his head. "May the Savior guide her crossing. She will be remembered for her sacrifice."

Jyn hopped into the passenger cabin and took a rear-facing seat. No sooner than she could buckle herself in did the pilot abruptly take off; her organs lurched as they wheeled around the district at high speed, maintaining a precariously low altitude to stay beneath the targeting horizon of Phalanx's antiair artillery.

The humans occupying the cabin—three of Oren's fiercest fighters—held their forearms together before their faces and chanted "Savior's blessing," to greet her. The lone cohabitor among them wrapped her in a resonant embrace, soothing her overwrought mind with a silent melody of warmth and appreciation.

"It's a great comfort to see you alive, Composer." The words came from the man ensconced in the seat opposite her. He was known as Komodo due to the reptilian scales tattooed around his neck; his head had been bandaged with gauze and haphazard strips of medical tape because he'd sustained an injury to his left eye. She opened her mouth to thank him and inquire about his wounds before Oren cut in, appropriating his surliest of demeanors. "It was foolish of you to think you could lead the siege in person," he said. "The Choir were trained for the operation and had everything in hand; they did not need your boots on the ground . . . Now, our greatest military mind is dead, and *you*—the Will of the Savior, the one true Composer—almost joined her!"

The words sounded a little too much like heresy for her liking. Protocol dictated she reprimand him for such insolence, especially for deigning to question her judgment in the company of subordinates. But then, she knew there was truth in what he said; she had once lambasted Eamon Wyatt for the same thing: not recognizing his own worth—letting his convictions get the better of him and throwing himself into situations way beyond his remit, all the while giving little consideration to what the repercussions of his death might be and how it could affect those who depended on him. She had told Wyatt in no uncertain terms to learn to take a back seat; maybe it was long overdue she started taking her own advice . . .

"We weren't prepared for this level of resistance," she admitted. "In breaching the blockade, we thought we had carved a path to Amidships, but all we've really done is create a choke point. It's impossible to push through such a tight space when facing a two-hundred-strong firing squad. Realistically, we need an alternative means of moving our forces bowside . . . On that note, I'm hoping you have some good news for me . . ."

Oren showed a devilish grin. "The starboard vehicular airlock is now under Harmony control. COTA's monopoly over mouthian access to the endless night is over; finally, *we* own the skies."

"Excellent," she said in a measured voice. "Run into much trouble?"

The Red Scythe issued a boastful sneer as if to say, *Nothing we couldn't handle.* "The cultists were well armed. What they lacked in combat training, they made up for in spirit; they fought hard and died well."

Jyn gave a reasoning nod. "They've developed dangerous levels of paranoia since the Administration officially declared them religious extremists. Doesn't surprise me in the least to hear that they've been stockpiling weapons—preparing for some kind of government intervention, I suppose . . . Any casualties on our end?"

Oren glanced through the passenger side window at the second raptor, which had broken out of formation and could be seen speeding toward the Savior's colossal esophagus, presumably ferrying the dead and wounded to Heston's infirmary in the Hollow. "Without sacrifice, there can be no victory," he recited. "The entrance to their temple was too closely guarded to gain covert access with our luma-shrouds. We had to go loud; took heavy fire as we fought our way inside. Two dead, several injured—this was the cost of success. I have five sentries keeping the remaining followers detained in their community hall. As for the elders: we rounded them up, as per your request . . ." A cruel smile touched his lips. "And exacted upon them the same fate they once conspired to bestow upon you . . . Needless to say, the airlock's mechanisms are still in perfect working order."

Jyn wasn't exactly sure how to react to the news; hearing that her parents had been spaced elicited surprisingly little emotion from her. Naturally, she could look back on *some* happy times from before her *diagnosis* of hyper-resonance: sitting by the electric organ with her father and helping him choose hymns for his sermons; assisting her mother with the embroidery of ceremonial vestments and the preparation of communal meals for the congregation. But after her parents' negligence, their blind fanaticism, the trauma they inflicted on her, and the years spent living like a refugee from a homeland that connived to destroy her, the last thing they deserved was her pity or grief. It unsettled her to admit it, but the only regret she had was that she wasn't there in person to watch their faces turn blue; to watch them gasp and choke as the life left their heartless bodies. They suffered not in service of a doctrine, nor appeasement of a vindictive god: they suffered simply because the taste of vengeance was oh so sweet . . .

The pilot began a perilous dart across open sky, still very much in range of Phalanx's surface-to-air capabilities. The fear Jyn felt in that instant proved palpable, but was unrelated to the possibility of being shot down. She turned to Oren with a fixed look and began, "What about . . ."

"Your brothers are unharmed," the Red Scythe reassured, reading her consternation like an open book. "We made sure to capture them alive, although they did not make it easy."

Komodo gave vent to a rueful laugh. "I can vouch for that. One of the bastards nearly pistol-whipped my eye out of its damned socket. Satos don't go down without a fight."

"Haneul and Tae-hyung have been groomed since birth," she explained, touching the man's knee to apologize on her brothers' behalf. "They are fierce in their faith, but I believe that, given time, they *will* see the light of the Savior." She sat back in her seat, squaring her shoulders. "It was never our goal to eradicate COTA. Cults endure because of the strength of their followers—devotion like that is something we should endeavor to harness. The church has thousands of adherents; there are convents up and down the whole *Novara*. If we can install new leadership, loyal to Harmony, we can hone out their barbaric practices and cement a foothold among the bowside population. This is not a war we can win with brute force alone: we need to rally as many people under our banner as possible."

Oren made a face like a child forced to eat his vegetables; in *his* mind, their only objective was to vanquish the oppressors—not to win their hearts and minds. He banished his reservations and dutifully bowed his head. "As the Savior wills it, Composer . . . So, you believe your brothers could be this new leadership?"

She gazed out through the window as they penetrated the refractive veil shrouding their sky fortress. Fortunately, the damage sustained to *Chīsana Osuushi*'s emitter array had been easily repaired; Phalanx would have swatted the vessel out of the sky already, had they been privy to its position.

"Haneul and Tae-hyung could be powerful allies," she suggested. "It's been a long time since I saw either of them, but our bond was, and I believe still is, strong. I think . . . I *hope* I can convince them to join us."

Because if they refused, or worse, swore vengeance for the attack on their temple, then they could pose a serious threat. And with so much on the line, Jyn had zero intention of leaving *any* loose threads behind . . .

THIRTY

Jyn had barely a moment to assess the status of repairs to the yacht before one of her advisors ushered her to the helm for an urgent matter. Pursued by an encroaching weariness, she made her way through the Agaiya Indah-2's battle-ravaged interior, passing volunteer technicians as they worked to repair damage and restore some of the yacht's more neglected systems. After all, *Chīsana Osuushi* had served as little more than a hovering palace following its *liberation* from the *Novara's* vehicle storage hangar, and minds more technical than hers had concluded substantial upgrades were needed to bring it back up to pre-Collision functionality.

One area that had seen significant renovation during Drexen's ownership, however, was the bridge. The space hardly resembled the helm of a luxury superyacht—more like one that might expect to belong to a government intelligence agency. Engineering and navigational interfaces had been stripped down to bare basics, with a near-paranoid array of comms and surveillance apparatus dominating the wide arc of brushed-steel console housings. A grid of luma-cast screens all but completely obscured the panoramic viewport, featuring mug shots of known informants and rivals of the syndicate, blueprint maps detailing supply chain routes and territorial boundaries, and a bulletin board hosting a constant stream of market data and NTNN headlines. The late Governor had transformed the grandiose cockpit into a command center fit from which to rule his empire. In practice, very few of his enhancements would serve Harmony's purposes, save for one state-of-the-art weapons platform boasting enough ordinance to put an accipiter-class gunship to shame—an inheritance that Jyn had begun to suspect would soon become immeasurably useful. The rest of it, she couldn't wait to tear out: the herringbone tile floor, the plush cream-padded furniture, the mélange light fixtures—the interior design was an exercise in extravagance, oozing the ostentatious sensibilities of its egomaniacal designer. Subsumed in the rotten fruits of Vidalia's wealth, her victory over him felt strangely hollow, as though she could sense him grinning in masochistic delight from the afterlife and reveling in her intense distaste.

In jarring contrast to the obnoxious decor, a handful of Prey and humans, all garbed in the same modest gray-brown robes to signify their unity and mutual understanding, busied themselves at various stations. Aside from her role as leader, Harmony had no rank or hierarchical structure per se; individuals were simply invited to contribute whatever skills their past lives might have endowed them. That said, it was no secret she considered those currently assembled at the helm to be her *officers:* the minds to whom she delegated the daily coordination and logistics required to keep a militia of such considerable size running smoothly. Isabella Graddock had filled several roles within the organization; to the people here, she was their chief of staff, and now Jyn had the miserable job of delivering the news of her death, noble and pointless as the woman had made it. She despised having to delay a difficult conversation. *If there's something that needs to be said then best not let it fester*, Izzy would have told her. Annoyingly, Eamon Wyatt had given her no choice but to put the *debrief* on hold. Somehow managing to evade multiple attempts to decline his hail, the nuisance had opened a direct channel through to the helm's main console and had spent several minutes obdurately demanding an audience with "her high and mightiness" before Jyn finally arrived. To his own admission, Wyatt had never been the most tech savvy of people, frequently joking that he was born *three centuries too late to keep up with the curve.* So, *how* he had achieved this remained something of a mystery. Presumably, it had something to do with the alleged awakening of the Amara Thaddeus construct, since an artificial superintelligence imbued with free will would have little trouble worming her way into the yacht's archaic real-time OS—a troubling notion, to say the least. *If Amara can do that, then what's to stop her from abruptly ending this insurgency by killing power to the repulsor drive? Unless . . .* Unless Amara considered Harmony an ally. It didn't seem completely beyond the realm of possibility, given she had made her support for the Prey clear through the offer of refuge conveyed by her supposed envoys, Hazel and Tobias Edevane.

This, incidentally, was precisely the reason for Eamon's call. A high-fidelity emitter rendered his avatar above the helm's main console. Jyn's vantage gave her a good view of the forward terrace, creating the perspective illusion that he was a figurehead, carved from cobalt-blue glass, sprouting from the yacht's needle-point bow. Although hardly in any mood to tolerate his usual glibness, seeing his scruffy face elevated her spirits to what felt like previously forgotten heights. She didn't possess the mental capacity to worry about anyone or anything outside the mission at hand, but with Eamon and his charge of high-society outcasts still top three on Jasper Coombs's hit list, to know that he was alive brought a measure of comfort to what had otherwise been an unmercifully bleak day.

"How goes the fight, Composer?" The words certainly sounded like the kind of smart-ass remark she would expect to come from him, but his demeanor seemed anything but smug. He skewered her with his distrustful gaze, twitchy and agitated in his body language as though fighting the urge to scream at her.

"You don't have to call me that," she replied coolly, casting a glance at the two-dimensional screen luma-cast just left of his projection. It showed a live feed from one of the network of surveillance cams positioned along the keel, this one pointed downward to the battle raging in the outskirts below. The stalemate looked to have continued in her absence, with both sides viciously holding their respective lines, neither ceding so much as an inch of ground to the other. "Slower than we'd hoped, but we're making progress."

Eamon scratched the stubble on his jaw. "Imagine I'll probably regret openin' my mouth here, but I'm surprised you haven't used that boat's cannons to carpet-bomb Phalanx into the next dimension."

"The luma-shroud keeps us hidden from thermal and infrared imaging," she explained. "We start using the main battery and we'll only be giving them the means to triangulate our position."

"Yeaaaah . . . Well, I suppose you're managing to kill plenty of enforcers without the big guns anyway . . . Hope you're keepin' a tally."

"We're fighting for our right to live here, Wyatt. Boiling it down to killing enforcers is a little reductionist, don't you think?" She engaged him with a hard stare. "Violence was *never* our objective. We gave Phalanx plenty of opportunity to vacate the blockade. They chose to get in our way."

Eamon scoffed. "Sure. *Roll over an' show your bellies so we can bulldoze a path to Chennai Plaza and start bringin' out the guillotines.* I never took you for deluded, Jyn, but if you really believe that was *ever* an option then you're sorta forcin' my hand . . . *I* was an enforcer once—just like them—and if it wasn't for all that shit with Fenn Haken, I woulda been right there with them."

"Then the choice would have been yours, too: stand up for justice, or lay down your life in the name of tyranny."

Eamon gave a long pause, thrusting his jaw forward and baring his lower teeth. "What about Keller? Did you give *him* a choice?"

Jyn felt an anger rise in her that only Eamon could inspire; an anger like the one she had known as a young girl suffering torment at the hands of her brothers. "Everyone out," she said, then again with more force and emissions flaring when the command wasn't immediately heeded.

"Get this into that stubborn skull of yours," she said once the others had exited the bridge. "The Jyn Sato you knew was a fabrication—a mask I used to infiltrate DMED, earn your trust, and gather the intel Vargos wanted me to. I put up with your sanctimonious, *people's hero* bullshit for three whole years because I had no other choice. But I don't have that gun to my head anymore, so if you're lookin' to establish some kind of worthwhile dialogue here then you better start treating me with the respect I'm owed."

"Oh, I know you plenty, Deputy." The level of condescension in his voice suggested her last words had gone in one ear and out the other. "See, every time you an' your flock Molotoved a Phalanx patrol or detonated an IED at the compound, it was *me* dealin' with the fallout—brokering with the council to convince them not to respond to every diplomatic incident you caused with tactical retaliation. Past few years, I've studied your works like an art historian pouring over Renaissance paintings; I don't reckon there's another idiot on the *Novara* who knows you better."

Jyn sighed, diagonally bobbing her head in a show of resignation. "Have I had to do some horrific shit in service of this endeavor? Sure—under Vargos's influence *and* of my own accord. But what you need to understand is that I'd do it all over again, exactly the same, if it meant getting Harmony as far across the line as I have done . . . Keller—just like many others and yes, probably many more—he made himself an obstacle, and I've told you already that I'm not about to let *anything* stand in my way. So, if you have something productive you wanna say to me then I suggest you spit it out already. Because if all you plan on doing is slandering me, you just might make yourself an obstacle, too . . ."

Eamon gave an infuriatingly phlegmatic shrug. "They say a picture's worth a thousand words. Think it's probably for the best I show you, instead."

Like the admiration they'd once had for each other, the man's projection evaporated into nothingness. Another two-dimensional screen then appeared in his stead, this one displaying a feed from inside the COHP's impressive biodome. A gasp escaped Jyn's lips as she worked to comprehend the images hanging in the air before her: a window into another reality. She had expected a fair amount of Prey to take Amara Thaddeus up on her offer, but with the invitation going out in spoken language, she hadn't been sure how many the message would actually reach. Evidently, word had spread much farther and faster than she had first anticipated; the botanical gardens flaunted thousands of acres of open field, and yet, she struggled to pick out a single square meter of visible grass beneath the seething ocean of cohabitors gathered in the Conservatory.

There were thousands; *tens of thousands*—perhaps 60 percent of the entire Prey population. An infinitude of lucent eyes forged a twinkling starfield, and amid the riotous mass of iridescent chitin, she spied aggregations of organic-resin domes, suggesting the intrepid aliens had deemed their new situation safe enough to begin building a more permanent community; they had found a new home. This, of course, was never her intention: she had wanted them to integrate with larger bowside society to enable as many resonant connections as possible, as turbulent and uncomfortable as that may have been. But she had kept a close eye on the social feeds before civilian access to the Nov-Net was restricted and with the contemptuous, often outright hostile reception the good people of the NTU had shown the migrating Prey, she could only count her stars that they had found an oasis in the wasteland of ignorance that lay beyond the blockade. *Found, or been gifted.*

Then she saw it: the unconscionably massive tentacle reaching upward like a transmission mast in the center of the gardens. Initially, she mistook it for a native support structure, but realized in studying the ragged fissure from which it had erupted that it was, in fact, a conduit—albeit one with an expressly unique function . . .

"Is that . . ."

"It's a conduit alright," Eamon cut her off. "It's terraforming the Conservatory: spraying Höllengarten all over the dome and treating the atmosphere to accommodate the increased capacity. Figured you might not have been aware on account of the Nov-Net blackout." He left her in the throes of bewilderment for a few seconds before continuing, "Lemme ask you this, Will of the Savior: Are you sure you're qualified to hold that title? Cuz it strikes me you don't have the first damned idea what it wants or what its plans are for the cohabs."

Jyn clenched her jaw and felt a dull ache from the sheer level of force she channeled into her molars. "You best hope we never cross paths again, Wyatt. Because I honestly think I just might try to kill you. You can question my methods, my beliefs, but don't you *ever* question my relationship with the Savior."

The luma-cast live feed parted like theater curtains, allowing Eamon's projection to take center stage once again.

"You wanna take a crack at me?" he asked cantankerously. "Good—I'm countin' on it. I told you I wouldn't rest until the Composer was brought to justice—that hasn't changed just cuz I know it's you. Mark my words: you *will* be made to answer for your crimes."

She shook her head as if to say, *What are we doing here?* "So, *this* is why you went through all that trouble to contact me: to tell me the gloves are off; declare open season?"

Eamon's antagonistic bearing softened, his simmering expression thawing into a look of beseeching desperation. "No, yah ruttin' hothead . . . The reason I'm reachin' out is . . ." He chuckled as if in disbelief at his next words. "Cuz we need your help . . . I mean, you saw it for yourself, Jyn: it's bug central in here, and if our intel is correct, our illustrious admiral is sendin' some of the evilest bastards in his ranks to *fumigate* the place. The cohabs need protection; we might have the numbers, but we don't have hardly any means of defendin' ourselves. I'm askin' you to send us fighters—as many as you can spare. Heck, send us a few of those hijacked murder bots while you're at it."

Jyn's posture shriveled; she let out a sigh underpinned by frustration and regret. "I can't do that, Wyatt; we're barely holding our own here as it is. I start donating infantry to you and I'm liable to endanger this entire campaign."

"What campaign?" The despair creeping into the marshal's voice made itself evident. "What in the name of Lei-Ghannam is it you're even fightin' for?"

"You *know* what we want . . ."

"Yeah, yeah: liberation, citizenship—all the bells and whistles with sprinkles on top . . . Look, I hate to be the bearer of bad news, but that freighter has well and truly left the docks. We ain't dealin' with pretentious politicians no more; Coombs is coming to exterminate them, and if you turn a blind eye now, he's gonna succeed . . . If there's *any* part of you that wants to atone for the damage you've done—the death, suffering, and misery you've inflicted on these people, whether you believe it's ultimately in their interest or not—then abandon this pointless crusade; use all that power and influence to save them from annihilation. Cuz that's exactly what's comin' if you fail to act. And *then* who are you fightin' for? Nobody."

That his words struck such a cord with Jyn caused her immeasurable annoyance. Her mind was a maelstrom of protestation and justification, but beneath all that noise, there lay a kernel of agreement, too. Still, she could not relent. Harmony had come too far, sacrificed too many to simply ditch their objectives now. Thankfully, the strident chime unleashed by the Savior to telegraph the arrival of the dissemination spared her from having to further argue her case. The helm's instrumentation rattled as the blaring sound rocked the yacht's fuselage, ringing like distorted whale song through the empty streets of the district.

"I'm sorry, Eamon," she said, narrowing her stare on his shimmering effigy. "But I can't help you . . . If it's any consolation, the Prey defended themselves for millennia against forces far greater than the admiral. They will not allow Coombs to destroy them any more than they did the Apex. Have faith in their capacity for survival."

With that, she ended the call, knowing full well Amara could simply patch him through to another console should he desire to hammer the point home a little longer. After a few suspenseful moments, no such hail arrived . . .

She headed out onto the terrace and joined Oren near the portside gunwale. He instinctively handed her a pair of binoculars as she joined his side. She raised them to her face and peered across the Mouth toward the Savior, the yacht's spherical cloak doing as good a job of letting light in as it did prevent it from escaping.

"Once the signal reaches the grenadiers," she said, "order the Choir to advance. This is our last shot at pushing through the blockade; let's not waste it."

"The Savior grants us the power to smite its enemies." Oren shook a fist in front of his face. "The oppressors will soon know the sting of defeat. At long last, their dissonance will be quelled!"

But an uncomfortable weight settled in Jyn's stomach as it dawned on her that his proclamation of victory may have been premature. Surveying the mighty corkscrew of fangs spiraling into the Savior's interior, she saw no signs of activity; no celestial stream of refined consciousness emerging like the first light of dawn to sweep away the darkness. The Savior's imposing shell remained dormant, and only the muffled pops of gunfire below could stem the blanket of uneasy silence that followed.

"Is something wrong?" Oren asked. "Where is the dissemination?"

They moved across the deck to the opposing gunwale, drawn by a low rumble emanating from somewhere beyond the Phalanx Compound. The blockade loomed before them like a cliff ripped asunder by a violent earthquake. Through the breach left by the grenadier detonation, the Canyon stretched on for many kilometers, prompting a memory of a story Jyn knew from an ancient religion about a miraculous parting of the sea. Xìngyùn Square was the lighthouse standing at the far end of that briny crevasse. But then something unexplainable materialized that made the Novara's dazzling metropolitan center seem dull by comparison: a wall of scintillating brilliance, racing toward the blockade at supersonic speed. In a matter of seconds, the ghostly edifice had traveled all the way from the Canyon's bow terminus to Amidships. As it transitioned into the sternside territories, it revealed itself to be far broader than it had first appeared, spanning the entire width and height of the Mouth, and giving Jyn the impression that she was standing near the hypocenter of a massive implosion, an inverse pulse of radiant energy. She braced herself as the phenomenon approached the yacht, emptying her lungs in surprise as it passed through her tense body without so much as disturbing a hair on her head, albeit leaving the surrounding air feeling charged with static. She glanced over her shoulder to catch it phasing through Tycho Block, reflecting with the brightness of a thousand sunsets in the tower's many windows before disappearing into the Savior's engineered exocarp.

The low rumble from beyond the blockade amplified into a harsh drone, seeming to reverberate throughout the bulk of the *Novara*'s superstructure, building and building into a deafening crescendo. Just as she feared her eardrums might burst, it degraded in frequency, winding down like a colossal motor losing power. Peering through the binoculars, she watched with creeping dread as night fell on Xìngyùn Square, its bright, inverted skyline suddenly engulfed in darkness. It was as though a malevolent entity conjured from pure shadow had swallowed the destination whole, beginning a predatory crawl toward the Mouth as it stalked the retreating daylight, the long strip of simulated heavens above powering down sector by sector, the monstrous heat sinks and turbines of Cendre Vale slowing to a cacophonous halt.

"What trickery is this?" Oren demanded. "Why would our enemies conspire to blind themselves?"

But Jyn knew there was nothing strategic or intentional about what they were witnessing . . .

The darkness, like a disease, extinguished the floodlights bordering Phalanx's staging ground before metastasizing into the district. The once-fiery radiance of the Höllengarten faded, its red-orange glow diminishing as if drained of life. Little of the Warrens' vibrant neon signage remained intact following Drexen's indiscriminate bombardment, but what *had* survived flickered briefly before finally dying out. The foreboding vastness of the Mouth reveled in the proliferating murk; the excavated chamber evoked the image of a vast natural cavern, its silhouetted spires and structures rendered as stalactites and ragged rock formations by the absence of light.

In the outskirts below, an impromptu cease-fire had come into effect, which made little sense considering nothing short of complete system failure could have prevented the grenadiers from executing their directives. Jyn leaned over the gunwale to gain an understanding of the situation. Phalanx had indeed paused their assault, presumably to acclimate to what she observed to be drastically diminished gravity. She saw enforcers flailing their arms, scrambling to find purchase as their boots drifted away from the ground. They tumbled across the altered battlefield with slow, clumsy movements, regrouping behind the compound's concrete barricades and holding onto one another to retain their footing. Commanders issued spates of gestures and hand signals toward their automaton adversaries, the grenadiers rendered seemingly inert by a combination of the near weightlessness and whatever the inverse pulse had done to them. Across the killzone, they floated just above the terrain like semideflated humanoid helium balloons, completely unresponsive in a purgatory of fluctuating physics. The status lights prevalent throughout their armored frames pulsed orange to signal a critical error with their guidance matrices. Evidently, Absence's biomimetic subroutines had either been corrupted or completely erased, reducing the machines to rudderless hunks of scrap.

It didn't take Phalanx long to recognize their window of opportunity; they surged forward like casterbladers on the attack, bounding in slow motion as they pushed toward the outskirts, flashlight attachments carving glaring, white streaks through the gloom. Weapons fire rang out once more as the remaining Harmony forces fruitlessly engaged the interlopers, but Jyn feared that without the grenadiers to bolster their numbers, the battle was all but lost. Oren had trained his soldiers to persevere in the face of death; to erase the word "surrender" from their vocabulary and fight for a glorious end as viciously as they fought for victory. She knew evacuation remained their only viable option. Preserving as many lives as possible—nothing else mattered now. The Coalescence was dying, and Harmony would need its sword and shield for this dark new reality, and all the struggles it held in store.

Jyn entertained Oren's criticism of her plans to pull back for precisely ten seconds, then shoved him against the wall, activated the hilt of her fission blade, and raised it to his throat.

"I've had it with your incessant defiance." The weapon's energized edge hissed and crackled as though striving to match her fury. "Every second you waste arguing with me, more of our people die. I can't afford to have cynics and dissenters in my circle. So, either you fall in line or get the hell out of my sight and off this boat. If it's gonna be the latter, I suggest you do it fast before I throw you overboard myself."

"Xander *never* would have given up like this," he rumbled in a coarse, baritone voice. "You make a mockery of my brother with your cowardice; this is heresy!"

Jyn swung her arm and buried the blade into the polycarbonate paneling to the right of his temple, causing caustic fumes to seep into the air. She knew several onlookers were watching the confrontation but thought it prudent to make all aware that not even the Red Scythe would be spared her wrath for such brazen insubordination. "And where is he now, Oren? Tell me . . . Xander gave up on *all* of us—*that's* the truth. And now, it falls on me to make sure this movement—your brother's legacy—doesn't cement its own destruction because of some asinine code of honor."

Oren Castagar was, of course, twice her size, and would have had little trouble relinquishing himself from her hold should he be so inclined. She took that he refrained as a sign of his enduring loyalty. She removed her forearm from his chest, dislodged her knife from the wall, and resheathed it. "This is a tactical retreat—it doesn't mean we're striking our flag. I need you to pull our forces back from the front line and bring them to *Chīsana Osuushi* so we can restrategize. Can I count on you to do that?"

He bowed his head, snarling as though pushing through the agony acquiescing to her commands inflicted. She whirled away and set off toward the afterdeck's boarding point.

"Where are you going?" he asked after her. She stopped in her tracks and spun around to face him.

"You see that?" He followed her gaze across the terrace to the blockade and the vast alley of darkness that lay beyond it. The Canyon's emergency lighting painted the elongated chasm an eerie, pulsating red. Backup power had come online in response to critical reactor failure, but with over a third of the *Novara*'s energy infrastructure having been dismantled during the excavation of the Mouth, emergency reserves were limited, and wouldn't last long. "If we don't find a way to restore the Savior's light, the *Novara*'s gonna be a sarcophagus in a matter of days. I'm going to the Hollow to see if Absence can fix this mess before everyone aboard the Coalescence suffocates . . . Once the evacuation's complete, get the yacht locked down and the fuselage pressurized. Then, we're leaving."

Boarding the docked raptor proved a disorienting experience. Gravity aboard the yacht remained unaffected by the outage thanks to the subdeck grav panels. But with the repulsor drive calibrated to negate 1.2Gs of now absent directional force, the vessel had begun to roll leisurely onto its side. The ground ran parallel to the windscreen as Jyn clambered into the cabin—an oppressive bulwark of rusted structure dominating the forward view. She held onto her stomach as she buckled herself in, using Hypatia to set her heading for the Savior's core.

The Höllengarten—giver of life and light and the Prey's primary source of sustenance—now appeared ash-gray in color. Shriveled leaves and loose brambles drifted away from the dying mass, caught in the raptor's headlights as it sailed through the cloud of detritus, crafting the haunting illusion of flying through a snowstorm. *Divine Abyss. What have we done?*

Arriving in the Magnanimous Hollow felt like entering a tomb. The lambent moss lining the grand walls and ceiling had similarly lost some of its vibrancy. The uneven ground—usually viscous and spongy underfoot—appeared dry and brittle, crunching like gravel beneath her boots as she made her way to the heart of the chamber. The accelerated degradation of the Savior's corporeal husk served to reaffirm her growing suspicion: the refulgent implosion she had witnessed represented more than a withdrawal from the *Novara's* decrepit power grid. Their reckless tampering with the signal had caused serious harm to the colony of sentient spores that, collectively, formed the Savior's being. The striking dimness of the Pyre only furthered this grim hypothesis. She had so hoped to see that blazing particle storm swirling and bloating above its organic cauldron plinth but found herself confronted by a faint wisp of barely lucent mist, severely drained of its resplendent vigor and majesty.

The implications were not lost on the Hollow's Prey inhabitants. Silence prevailed where once there had been a euphonious and ever-present hum of happily braying, chirping cohabitors. Those of Harmony's faithful who were unfit or unwilling to fight on the front line had left the Magnanimous Hollow to join the migrant caravan, and those who stayed behind had been left with little cause to express joy . . .

She lugged her guilt like a ball and chain over to Absence's workshop. As she ascended the surgical staple steps, she concluded ae must have been elsewhere. Normally, she would have already felt aer resonant essence beckoning her closer—or, more recently, impatiently demanding her presence. But a grave site welcomed her as she reached the summit. Evidently, her intuition had failed her; Absence *was* in aer usual spot, joined by Rien and Heston, no less. Dr. Aldrich had made no further attempts to abscond after their *chat* about his recent indiscretions. To the man's credit, he had stayed diligently at his post in the med bay since, working hard to manage the influx of wounded coming in from the battlefield and keeping his heretical censure to himself. With oily, bedraggled hair strewn across his tired face, he stood beside Rien wearing an anxious look, watching intently as his partner tended to Absence. Jyn's heart clenched as she settled her gaze on the enfeebled shape of her beloved. It seemed aer health had deteriorated considerably since they were last together. As they reached the end of their lives, cohabitors, by nature *and* tradition, spent their final weeks in repose surrounded by an audience of children. This ensured none of their learnings were wasted in death. Because to the Prey, the loss of knowledge was to squander that which furthered their survival. Circumstances had not allowed Absence to celebrate aer impending crossing with these customs. Ae had been working round the clock preparing new directives for upload to the Pyre. Clearly, the stress and isolation had exacerbated aer condition; ae stood hunched over aer workstation, barely managing to support aer weight as ae was busy with the miscellany of spliced tech crowding aer desk-space. Aer exoskeleton had lost its iridescent sheen; the network of cracks and wrinkles marking aer chitin appeared deeper and more pronounced. She saw Rien consuming pulp from an open canister standing at aer talons, regurgitating it into aer paw, and massaging the medicinal secretion into an exposed area of flesh on Absence's thorax. Needless to say, Absence seemed less than receptive to the other cohabitor's fussing; ae huffed and fidgeted in irritation, far too fixated on the task at hand to be fawned over by others. Rien dutifully persisted, nonetheless.

Heston saw Jyn and hastened to meet her, holding his arm and nervously avoiding eye contact as he asked, "Where have you been?"

She wasn't sure what infuriated her more: the tone with which the traitor had just spoken to her or the utter redundancy of his question. "Shoe shopping; where do you think?"

Heston's gaze shifted to Absence, then back to her. "It's bad, Jyn . . . We're doing everything we can but aer vitals just keep dropping. We've administered intravenous fluid and antibiotics; more than anything, ae needs rest, but ae's been working flat out for going on seventy-two hours now and *refuses* to take a break—every bit as stubborn as you."

But how could Absence rest when, together, they had potentially doomed everyone on the Coalescence? The aged cohabitor had aspired to fulfill one lifelong ambition before ae passed: to set the Prey on the path to salvation, to give them hope—a brighter future. Instead, with her misguided help, ae could very well have inadvertently enabled the extinction of *both* their species . . .

A despondent sigh escaped her lips as she placed a hand on Heston's shoulder. "Thank you . . . I know you've given it your best shot, but I'm not sure there's anything that can be done . . . I've been dreading this wretched day for a long time; I just can't believe it's finally here . . ."

She stretched out through resonance as she tentatively approached Absence, desperately wanting to convey, *I'm here. You're not alone.* But still, she sensed nothing. It felt as though ae wasn't truly there, but was a mere projection or a wax sculpture brought to life by some unspeakable sorcery. Never in her life had she been in such close proximity to a cohabitor without intimately knowing their emotional state. Advanced age causing reduced resonant receptivity was not something she had ever heard of. By all accounts, natural selection dictated the Prey broadcast the compendium of their life experiences for the next generation as mortality loomed. And yet, Absence remained silent, colorless; a painter without canvas or brush; a musician without voice or instrument.

Ae had not yet acknowledged her presence, aer attention riveted on the light show roiling across the surface of the concert shell structure at the rear of the workshop. The kaleidoscope of electric butterflies appeared more frenzied and sporadic than ever, telegraphing in mesmerizing streaks Absence's increasingly desperate attempts to diagnose the problem and devise a solution. Aer paws looked painfully raw from days spent handling aer peripheral input device, obsessively twisting and manipulating the continents of its strange, gyroscopic design as if furiously solving a puzzle. Jyn had to wrench the object out of aer grip to seize aer attention. Ae met her gaze with those old, tired eyes. Relief crashed like a wave in her chest as emissions consumed her peripheral vision—only very faint, but undeniably present. Initiating a tenuous bond, Absence greeted her as ae often had during those carefree years working together in aer market stall: engendering an auditory hallucination of the serene string melody from the opening of Beethoven's Symphony no. 9: Adagio molto e cantabile. Although, instead of completely immersing her in its soul-stirring beauty, the symphony sounded as if emanating from beyond several cinder block walls—dampened, quiet, and lacking its usual tonal richness.

The instability of their connection left her unsure just how long they would be able to maintain it. So, she began hastily apprising aer of the ongoing situation in the Mouth: the "pulse," the blackout, the mass incapacitation of the grenadiers, and their subsequent retreat. It took considerable exertion to convey even the simplest of concepts, like shouting at the top of her voice to reach someone standing on the far side of the Canyon or the other side of a soundproof window. Despite her difficulty, Absence seemed to comprehend her meaning.

"You two can still forge a connection?" Heston asked, injecting the words with relief and gratitude but, perhaps, also just a hint of envy.

"Yes. Although, it's weak at best," she answered.

"Then you're fortunate. I suppose your hyper-resonance means you've been less affected . . . *We* haven't been able to bond since the last dissemination. After that *wave*—whatever it was—the Pyre looked like it was about to erupt, then just sort of petered out. Now . . ." he rubbed his temple with a forlorn look. "I didn't think resonance was something that could be taken away. I feel like half of my soul has been siphoned out of my body." He placed a hand on his chest, staring longingly at Rien. "There's an emptiness, right here; I'm not sure how else to describe it, but it feels even worse than when you had me believe you had killed aer."

"After what you idiots pulled, you should count yourselves lucky I was lying."

Finally, Absence's response arrived in a nebulous efflux of imagery and emotion, filtering into her mental space. Although lacking the technical expertise to fully grasp the specifics, she understood beyond any doubt that aer biomimetic reprogramming had indeed caused the shutdown. The Savior, in an act of self-preservation, had receded deeper into its protective housing, and every one of aer attempts to coax it back out had proven disastrously unsuccessful.

It's not your fault. I am responsible. She didn't say the words aloud, naturally, but strenuously weaved them into an empathic tapestry—one that Absence viciously tore apart, silently screaming the sentiment, *Spare me your platitudes;* of course *this is my fault.*

Jyn backed away in a flash of impatience and stormed out onto the ledge that overlooked the Pyre. Studying its simmering luminosity, its once overpowering hold over her had diminished, leaving her with a sense of gazing into the disconsolate eyes of a mortally wounded man-eater.

"How do we fix this," she asked, her voice charged with contrition. "Just . . . tell us what to do!"

The words that she had heard fulminating within herself many times before came again as a whisper spoken into the breeze. **"Relinquish . . . self . . . endure . . . pain . . . acquiesce . . . sacrifice."**

She felt that unnerving pull of gravity in her chest again, the Pyre seemingly attempting to drag her into its formless mass. This time, she did not need to dig her heels in to resist its attenuated influence.

"What does that even mean? I'm sick and tired of all this vagueness. Would it *kill* you to give me a straight answer for once? There are over a million lives at stake here, including the very people you've spent Abyss-knows how many centuries shepherding across the galaxy. Please, just . . . give us some guidance—*anything* . . . Otherwise . . ." She gave a despairing shrug. "It's over."

No response arrived from the Pyre, no storming angrily out of the room, as would often occur at the end of her questioning: just cold, desolate silence.

She heard the sounds of a commotion over her shoulder and spun around to find Absence collapsed on the ground with Heston and Rien scrambling to aer aid. She hurried to her fallen partner and fell to her knees by aer side, taking aer limp paw and clutching it against her chest. Ae dolefully turned aer head to face her, releasing labored exhalations from the orifices on aer neck. Ae touched her cheek, issuing a deep, oscillating groan of sanguine tenderness.

"No," she whimpered. "You can't leave us. Not yet . . . Not now."

She felt static rouse behind her eyes as the pair attained weak, bleary resonance. She saw the totality of their time together playing like a movie on the projector screen of her mind, feeling every intricate nuance of emotion they had experienced since their first meeting all those years ago. The market stall, aer incarceration, the dark days spent as Vargos's pawns, and their long struggle for justice and emancipation—she experienced everything, all at once, and—despite their faltering connection—in vivid detail. She saw Anaya Lahiri begging for her life, knowing all too well the sentiment Absence associated with the image: When is enough, enough? How much suffering are we willing to inflict, and how much are we really ready to sacrifice for our freedom?

Then, Absence slipped away, firmly believing ae had unleashed damnation on aer people.

THIRTY-ONE

Only once in her life had Hazel seen the cosmos as clearly as she could the moment the blackout struck. Peering up through a break in the Conservatory's herbaceous membrane, the star-stippled gulf of the endless night appeared as majestic as it had from beneath the canopy of her kestrel—a raven needlecraft of infinite distance and time, every glittering pinpoint a siren further reawakening her adventurous spirit and beckoning her closer.

The sudden outage had disabled the dome's active aluminosilicate and plunged the gardens into an all-consuming darkness. Additional environmental systems had similarly collapsed, sending everyone tumbling into the open air as local gravity loosened its hold. While panic set in throughout the sanctuary, a surprising sense of serenity descended over her, as though she were floating in a sensory deprivation tank, the weightlessness alleviating the strain of keeping her broken body upright and soothing her weary muscles.

"Amara?" she calmly asked. "Are you still with me?"

The responding voice seemed to resonate from somewhere deep inside her head. *Yes. I'm here, or at least, part of me is—the part installed in your implant. My mainframe, on the other hand, just went down with the rest of the grid.*

Hazel thought for a moment, then, swallowing a lump, asked, Do you think the admiral could be doing this?

I don't believe so. The problem isn't just limited to the COHP: the Novara's entire energy infrastructure has been affected. Amara's tone turned grave. *It looks like it could be the reactor; whatever it is Daemon normally does to maintain its operation, it seems to have stopped . . . Brace yourself. Emergency backup power should be coming online any second.*

But another minute spent free-floating in that lightless void elapsed without any sign of system reinitialization, the roar of the Conservatory's terrified occupants heightening as they grew increasingly hysterical. Hazel's state of zen capitulated to unease as the thought that her feet might never find the ground again planted invasive roots in her mind.

Amara, any update?

Silence, then, *Something's wrong. The Conservatory's transmission substation is receiving power, but with my BIOS fractured like this, I don't have control over local distribution. I need to reboot before I can start bringing systems back online, and that could take longer than we have . . .*

Strangely, the mere mention of this substation proved enough for Hazel to sense its position: several levels below ground, wedged between methane storage and water treatment. It perturbed her to admit it, and she'd have a difficult time explaining the phenomenon if pressed, but since helping Amara find her way back to the life-support block, she had developed a kind of innate spatial awareness of the Conservatory, an inherent understanding of its layout, functions, and operation. Just as her kestrel had felt like an extension of her body, both in the simulator and during that fateful flight with Shiyana and Zain, she could *feel* the structure lurking at the fringes of her somatic perception. She likened it to what she imagined amputees suffering from phantom limb syndrome might experience: the illusion of physical sensation from appendages that did not exist. Or, in this case, existed but had no business feeling like her own flesh and bone. She had even begun to suspect that, thanks to Amara's convergence with the software of her kinesthetic implant, she now had the ability to influence her environment. While Amara rattled off about *fault tolerances* and *BIOS recovery*, Hazel delved deep within herself and waded through a cybernetic quagmire to reach the transmission substation. There, she found a beating heart, pulsing with an energy that manifested visually in her mind's eye as a scintillating yellow aura. The substation strived to channel the auxiliary power surging from the *Novara's* main grid to the installation's core utilities, but with the distribution network unsupervised, the flow had been abruptly curtailed. Amazed at how intuitive it felt, and how naturally it came to her, she began systematically opening and closing relays to guide the current like water through a network of canals. Finally, she found the nodes that controlled gravity, atmosphere processing, and the mainframe, as well as the ring of graphical processors and field resonators responsible for the dome's artificial sky. A geometric web of luminous conduits formed in her mind; a circular maze delineating the product of her painstaking trial and error.

Then, success. Her stomach lurched as the subterra grav panels reengaged, pulling her back down to the ground with a not-so-gentle jolt. Sharp pain struck her retinas as the heavens ignited, her pupils rapidly constricting in response to the deluge of glaring light pouring into the gardens.

Oh, Amara chirped, surprised. *I'm not entirely certain how I did that.*

Hazel cast a glance around the courtyard of the Beech Glade complex, which she had almost completely forgotten she had been standing in right before the lights went out. Surveying the discombobulated crowd, she picked out Tobias and the crew of the *Assurance* near the medical hut, helping one another up off the floor and dusting themselves off. Her brother had never been very good with motion sickness and, as such, looked just about ready to throw his guts up. Thankfully, he appeared unharmed.

You didn't, she answered eventually. *It was me.*

Amara went silent for a moment, no doubt running countless simulations to try and understand how that could be the case, but apparently coming up empty. *How, precisely?*

If you *don't know the answer to that, then we're really screwed.*

Activity rippled through the throng as scores of cohabitors turned their snouts upward. Hazel followed their collective gaze to the source of their disquiet. Overhead, the bounty of alien vegetation had fallen prey to an unknown blight. Death radiated in a perfect circle from the point where the conduit touched the dome, causing the vibrant flora to wilt and turn gray, as if ravaged by drought. It didn't take a cultural expert in cohabitor superstition to discern that they considered this an omen of apocalyptic significance. They crumpled to their knees, rocking back and forth, their haunting wails of grief and despair penetrating her skin and seeping into her bones. Clearly, they regarded the shrubbery not only as a source of sustenance but also as the living embodiment of their deity—the bread and wine of their so-called Savior. Clearly, this mysterious pestilence had robbed them of something far more spiritual than their next meal . . .

A young cohabitor emerged from the fray—the one Tobias referred to as the little merchant, who seemed to have taken a liking to her since their first meeting. It . . . or, *ae*, crouched down to a squat and collected her crutch, then pulled her to her feet with surprising strength and helped her find her balance. Ae guided her hand to the crutch's handle as if showing a complete novice how to use the apparatus, the texture of aer partially formed chitin like cactus leather beneath her fingertips. She thanked ae with a smile. Ae emitted a warbling sound and, with large, inquisitive eyes, turned aer attention to the dying vegetation above, exuding something like sadness.

"I know," she said, finding it comforting to say the words, regardless of whether she was being understood or not. "This looks bad. But I'm sure we can find a way to fix it . . . Right, Amara?"

I wouldn't be so sure, the voice in her head answered gravely. *I've never seen such accelerated cellular degradation before. We need to take samples so*

I can synthesize a protein enzyme to stem the decay and begin cultivation . . . Although, I do fear we would be dealing with symptoms instead of addressing the root cause.

You think this has something to do with the blackout? She glanced down to find the little merchant staring up at her, intently watching her lips like a dog waiting to hear a word they recognized from their humble vocabulary: sit, walkies, or in Abraham's case, *Go get 'em, boy.*

It would be unwise to assume otherwise, Amara proclaimed. *What limited sensor data I can access while my mainframe reinitializes suggests a complete cessation of Daemon's influence across the* Novara. *The conduits are inactive, which explains both the xeno-flora's accelerated decomposition and the mass power outage, since the remaining fission reactor is too damaged to operate independently.*

"It's maddening," Hazel said, seething. "The Administration had over a century to prepare for this moment and have squandered every second."

Your frustration is natural, but it's not so much a question of competence as it is plausibility. The conduits are impervious to any attempt to remove them, and are so heavily integrated with the reactor's containment structure and hydrogen spool that all efforts to repair the reactor over the decades have failed . . . As a result, the Novara *is now having to power itself exclusively from reserves. Even with careful rationing and systematic partitioning of bulkheads, by my best estimates, life support can sustain the current population for no more than a maximum of twenty-two days, after which, all aboard will perish.*

Hazel nervously rubbed the back of her neck, tracing fingertips over the silicone of her vertebral prosthetic. *Was Amara Prime always this cheery?* she asked.

*A veritable ray of sunshine—*and if the sarcasm in Amara's voice was indeed an imitation of human cadence, then it was damn convincing. *She was never one for sugarcoating things, but she would have also told you that no situation is truly hopeless. There is* always *a solution to be found, even in the direst of circumstances. For there to be light, there must be darkness.*

Hazel convened with Eamon and Tobias to discuss the blackout and strategize their next move. Captain Holloway sat leg-over-leg on a nearby bench quietly servicing her repeater, seemingly eager to hear the debate, yet hesitant to commit her crew to any plans that might arise from the discussion.

"Twenty-two days, huh?" Eamon scratched the stubble on his neck. "Well, I always was more productive workin' toward a deadline . . . Guess it'd be naive of us to hope this means old Coroner Coombs might pump the brakes to focus his attention on combating the energy crisis."

Hazel ardently shook her head. "No. He's resourceful; he'll only find a way to use it to his advantage. It might even push him to accelerate his plans."

The man shrugged. "I can't honestly fathom what he hopes to gain when we're all gonna croak it in three weeks anyhow."

Delilah snapped the break action of her repeater back into position, sharply commanding the attention of the others.

"You're assuming those in charge of Amara's proposed rationing will do so in the interest of the larger population."

After a few seconds of blank stares, Tobias asked, "What do you mean?"

"Amara thinks we have twenty-two days of life support remaining, but how much could you hypothetically stretch that estimate out if you were to throttle the reserves and divert them to a relatively small area of the ship—say, Quarterdeck, for example?"

Hazel's brother frowned in offense. "The bridge crew all swore an oath to protect and serve the NTU and its citizens—no matter what. You're suggesting they'd abandon their duties and sacrifice us all for the sake of a couple extra weeks of breathing?"

"I think when it comes down to it, those who have power will inevitably use it to save their own."

Holloway rose to her feet and slotted her repeater into her thigh holster, pensively joining the circle. Previously, she had been somewhat at odds with her crew regarding the extent of their obligations toward Amara's sanctuary. Now, imbued with all the conviction and resolve of those under her command, there seemed to be no question in her mind that their rightful place was here.

"This isn't just about defending the cohabitors anymore," she stated. "Almost seventy percent of the *Novara*'s oxygen supply is generated in hydroponics. We can't allow the admiral to take control of the life-support block. Otherwise, I'm willing to bet that twenty-two-day figure is gonna end up looking a hell of a lot shorter for the majority of us."

"*The blood-dimmed tide is loosed, and everywhere the ceremony of innocence is drowned,*" Amara recited somberly, her progenitor's affinity for ancient poetry evidently persevering centuries after her death. Admittedly, literature had never been Hazel's strong suit in school, but she felt confident in her assessment that the phrase was intended as a searing condemnation of human nature, and the greed and cruelty inherent within.

A peculiar sensation pulled her attention deeper into herself: a brush of static at the top of her spine, accompanied by inexplicable feelings of fear and panic. Her breath quickened and the hairs on the back of her neck stood on end; in that instant, she was a little girl again, trembling in terror of what lurked in the darkness, sensing a malicious *otherness* as it skulked in the vicinity, conniving to breach the gates of their refuge.

Your biometrics just went berserk, Amara reported. *Which I can only presume is because you've sensed it, too.*

Hazel blew a steadying breath to try and slow her heartbeat. *I'm sensing something, alright.*

Before the blackout, I established a virtual perimeter to detect any potential incoming threats. It appears something tripped the alarm, which, for some reason, stimulated your amygdala and gave you a fight-or-flight response.

I guess that explains why I feel like I'm being chased by a bear . . . Do you know who or what it is?

I'm having trouble accessing security right now so I can't check the feeds to confirm. All I know is that there is a large, uniform mass moving up through the hydroponic levels toward our location.

"They're coming." Hazel uttered the words loud enough to be heard by the other three, but they all assumed she was just speaking to the voice in her head and carried on with their heated deliberation. "I said they're coming . . . As in, right now!" Finally, she had their attention. "They're making their way up through hydroponics. We can't say for certain who, but I don't think we should wait around to find out."

Eamon surveyed the gardens, pushing his jaw forward and nodding subtly. "It's Coombs—ain't no two ways about it . . . He wants to bring the fight to us? Let's make sure we set the table." The marshal led the group out of the leaf-shaped courtyard onto the main path, giving them a clear line of sight to the entrance plaza and atrium entrance. "Between me, Fenn, the volunteers, and the DMED staff, I reckon we have a shot at puttin' together a decent resistance force."

"I don't understand how you're so ready to trust Fenn Haken," argued Hazel. "This is the same man who had a gun on you just hours ago, and let's not forget, infamously perpetrated some of the most heinous enforcer-cohabitor brutality in Phalanx history."

"Don't underestimate the power of resonance," Tobias countered. "Trust me: whoever he was, he isn't anymore." Strangely, uttering the words seemed to spark a profound realization in her brother. He straightened his posture and began scouring the sea of cohabs occupying Khadija's Green, repeatedly clenching and opening his fists as he usually did when feeling anxious. She tried to catch his gaze to wordlessly make sure he was OK, but he remained far too distracted to take any notice.

"Fenn's got plenty of history," Eamon conceded. "But shit, who among us hadn't? Right now, all I care about is two things: he's a crack shot with a real knack for violence and he's fixin' to right a few past wrongs . . . The pair of us were a force to be reckoned with back in the day—both a little pudgier around the sides now, mind you, but I got no reason to suspect that's changed . . . We'll hold the atrium and keep these bastards at bay for as long as we can." Eamon tipped his head toward the captain. "Lilah, Tobias; if you and the gang are *in* this, then I need you to start moving the refugees to the far side of the Conservatory. Take whatever you need from the weapons cache and put as much distance as you can between the bugs and the fight."

"The Prey aren't completely helpless, you know," Tobias asserted, eyes still glued to that invisible horizon, seeming only partially engaged in the discussion. "We'll do our best to keep them out of harm's way. The thing is, if there's a threat they know they can't flee, then their compulsion is to meet it head-on."

"I know," Eamon groused. "They can be feisty critters if ever they're backed into a corner. Just do your best to stop 'em from chargin' in like the ruttin' cavalry."

Tobias rubbed his temple, concern visibly deepening. "I'll try . . ."

"You can count on us to get it done, Wyatt," Holloway affirmed, hooking her thumbs through the buckle loops of her thigh holster. "Just promise us you'll turn tail and fall back the second you think you might be overwhelmed. Letting yourselves get mowed down isn't gonna do us any favors."

"Lilah, that might just be the nicest thing you've ever said to me."

Indignation spread like a pruritic rash across Hazel's body. Crucial decisions concerning their defensive strategy were being made without her input, and she couldn't help but feel her extensive military insights were being ignored—or worse, downright disregarded. "Do I have a part in this?" she inquired, biting off the ends of her words. "Or do I just get relegated to the sidelines because I'm damaged merchandise?"

"That ain't the case at all, Miss Edevane," Eamon placated. "We need you and Doctor Thaddeus on overwatch: keeping us all informed, coordinated, and, most importantly, managing security." He gestured down the main path to the Conservatory's pearly foyer. "We're gonna secure the atrium: every bulkhead, every shutter, every desk draw with a ruttin' padlock on it—I want it airtight. Same goes for the maintenance sublevel, too—don't want anything nasty creeping up on our flank and bitin' us on our asses."

Hazel dared not repeat Amara's response verbatim. Naturally, the AI seemed far from enthusiastic about the prospect of taking orders from the *unkempt, uneducated blunderbuss of a man*. Although, there was *one* detail amid her incensed diatribe too critical not to pass on . . .

"The portion of Amara installed on my implant is just a small piece of her overall personality and processing matrix," she explained hurriedly. "The bulk of her still resides within the mainframe, which hasn't finished rebooting after the blackout. That means she's locked out of everything from environmental controls to utilities and local security; she can't initiate the lockdown you're proposing."

She left the man in the throes of his obvious assumption that this news meant they had no means of fortifying the Conservatory. After a few more undoubtedly torturous seconds, she closed her eyes and reached within herself, rummaging her way once again to the dome's halo of graphical processors. A translucent sphere appeared in her mind's eye, with the processors, like satellites orbiting its equator, represented as a concentric ring of twinkling points. One hemisphere appeared velvety purple in hue, bejeweled with a brilliant peppering of stars. The other shone sky-blue with wispy streaks of cloudlike snow dusted across the glassy surface of a bauble. She intuited that manifesting in her mental space was a representation of the Conservatory's day-night cycle. *Not just a representation: an interface.* Imagining herself outstretching her arms, she found that she could spin the sphere on a ninety-degree axis, just as she had the antique globe her father kept in the parlor as a child. She emerged from her absorption, opening her eyes to find the others sharing a look of amazement as they scanned the heavens, their features warped by waltzing light and shadow as the dome cycled rapidly through the phases of a twenty-four-hour rotation.

She simpered. "But as crazy as it sounds, I think *I* just might . . ."

Eamon went to fetch one of the zero-terrain buggies so he and Hazel could join up with Fenn and the others in the atrium. In the meantime, Hazel had a moment alone with her brother. Tobias had yet to shake off his consternation, seeming as fidgety and uneasy as the time he accidentally stood on her Sinegex virtu-sim goggles and spent hours working up the courage to tell her about it.

"What's going on?" she asked, touching his hand to stop him from abrasively twisting the skin of his wrist, which he likely hadn't realized he had been doing until she interrupted him. "Something's clearly eating away at you. Spit it out already."

He met her eyes for a few ephemeral seconds before turning his attention to the tangle of desiccated brambles hanging limply overhead. "What happened up there." He raised a hand and tapped his temple. "It happened in *here*, too . . . It's funny; when the gravity went off and everybody started screaming, in my head, the complete opposite happened . . . Before, the background noise from being in range of so many Prey was almost overwhelming:

I'm surprised my skull didn't split open from overstimulation. But then the world went black, and the roar lessened to a whisper . . . Now, I can't feel . . . well, *anything.* It's as if something just flipped the hyper-resonance switch off in my brain, and now, I'm terrified at the thought that it might never come back."

Hazel felt surprised at just how crestfallen her brother seemed at this development; he'd only had his exo-communicative abilities for less than two months, yet carried himself like someone who had just found out they were to be permanently dispossessed of their vision.

She shimmied up beside him and touched his shoulder with hers. "All this resonance stuff—it might as well be sorcery for all I understand about it," she said. "But what I *am* certain of is that Amara can fix this. Clearly, we're seeing different symptoms of the same problem—it's all related. Logically, that must mean that once we find a way to restore the Savior's connection to the *Novara*, your abilities will return."

Your confidence in me is appreciated, Amara's voice sounded in her head. *But do try not to unduly raise the boy's expectations. After all, "hope deferred makes the heart sick."*

"I hope that's true," Tobias ruefully replied, oblivious to Amara's remarks. "Or else, whether I'm resonant or not will be the *last* thing we need to worry about."

Hazel gave a lopsided smile and snarked, "Humanity First got exactly what they've been clamoring for: separation from the *Devourer* . . . If there's a silver lining here, it's that Caleb Callaghan might finally have to eat crow."

Tobias didn't rise to the comment. Of course, when it came to Hazel's intense disdain for the manipulative vixen, he seldom did. She didn't know what the pair had spoken about when she came to see him and only hoped that she hadn't managed to worm her way back under his skin—as she had such an aptitude for doing.

Eamon pulled up in the levitating ZT buggy and hurriedly disembarked to help Hazel board. Any annoyance she felt at having to accept assistance to accomplish such a menial feat was ultimately eclipsed by the need for haste.

"Be careful," Tobias cautioned her, the little merchant cohabitor fixing aer gaze on her as fervently as ae clung to her brother's side. "I mean physically, stay hidden and safe, but also keep in mind that this link you've developed to the Conservatory—obviously it isn't expected behavior for your prosthetic. We don't yet know what the potential side effects could be." A worried look crossed his face as he struggled to find his words, no doubt shuffling through a deck of worst-case scenarios in his mind. "Just . . . don't give yourself an aneurysm or fry your prefrontal cortex or something by pushing yourself too hard."

Hazel reassured him with a nod. "I promise I won't . . . Will you check on Dad?"

He showed a dampened smile as if he believed this might be the last time he would ever see her. "You can count on it."

Eamon drove like a bat out of hell to the atrium, beeping and swerving erratically to avoid people traveling along the main path. He severely over-estimated the inertial dampener's capacity for effectively slowing the vehicle, nearly crashing into a standing glass plate hosting a luma-cast map of the Conservatory, as he veered to a stop. Climbing out, he announced, "I'm goin' to leave you in the ZT buggy so you can get yourself back to Beech Glade if things go south."

She argued that she needed to physically *be* in the atrium to influence its utilities and security systems.

"Figured out how to screw around with the simulated sky without bein' anywhere near its field resonators, didn't yah?" he riposted. "Don't see why you can't seal the bulkheads from out here where it's safe . . . Look, you can spit at me, slap me across the face, do whatever you want for sayin' this, but you *ain't* as nimble as you used to be. Once the plasma starts flying in there, I can't promise I'm gonna be able to keep you from gettin' hurt."

He wasn't wrong, of course; Hazel had confidence that she *could* remotely initiate a lockdown. Regrettably, nothing short of physically restraining her would prevent her from joining him; she had an intense desire to lay eyes on their enemy, to gaze upon the faces of Coombs's loyalists and understand how individuals who had sworn to defend and preserve the New Terra Union could suddenly pledge their allegiance to a despot.

"We don't have time to argue about this," she answered, struggling to dis-lodge her crutch from the footwell as she tried to disembark herself. "Just . . . get me in there so I can batten down the hatches; we'll worry about my safety later!"

As Eamon hollered and gestured to push back the handful of stragglers lingering near the entrance, Hazel hobbled toward the wide vestibule that connected the gardens to the atrium. She passed through a low-power fission field designed to act as a filter to prevent insects from leaving the habitat, feeling its fizzling energy lapping at her exposed skin. He followed shortly after, and they arrived together in the lustrous, palatial gallery that welcomed visitors into the COHP. Contrasting the atmosphere of innovation crafted by the sleek, glossy architecture, an impressive company of ex-enforcers and volunteer fighters had assembled near the information desk. Armed with plasma carbines from Amara's appropriated weapons shipment, they readied themselves for war, distributing ammunition and helping one another into their Phalanx-issue flak jackets. Some took cover behind the curved info-boards, others setting up the deployable barricades Isaac had printed using the Conservatory's fabricator. Morale seemed relatively high, although she feared that was only because they didn't really have any clue of what lurked below. Neither did she, of course, but then again, she knew firsthand the inhumane depths the admiral could sink to to achieve an objective . . .

Fenn Haken, a burly man with a square head, broad neck, and broader abdomen, approached, sending a look in his ex-partner's direction telegraphing the words *What's* she *doing here?* Hazel still didn't know whether he could be trusted, feeling a ripple of fear tracing the elongated barrel of the rifle gripped in his muscular hands.

Eamon took the brute aside to bring him up to speed, mouthing the words *Go do your thing* and motioning her to the center of the atrium. She limped past the information kiosk and paused, feeling the eyes of everyone in the room scouring her enfeebled body, no doubt collectively assuming that, whatever she was here to do, she would ultimately be a liability.

She set her sights on the pedestrian entrance. Reaching into herself once more, she navigated her way to the atrium's security systems index, then onto the virtual console that governed the emergency bulkheads. It was her kines-thetic implant's job to translate electrical signals from her vertebral prosthetic into tactile sensory information, and it occurred to her that, in her cybernetic melding with Amara, it was precisely this function that empowered her to *sense* and influence the installation's facilities. She outstretched imaginary arms and envisioned herself physically wrenching the bulkheads shut. Their real-world counterparts complied with her command—two impenetrable slabs of metal slid together and interlocked with mechanical teeth to seal off the pedestrian entryway. She did the same with the staff doors leading to the freight shaft and loading bay, cutting off all access to the atrium.

Stellar work, dear, Amara commended. *And just in the nick of time, too.* It took Hazel a moment to interpret the AI's meaning; she had been so focused on effectuating the lockdown that she hadn't noticed the return of the tingling sensation at the top of her spine. Only this time it felt far more intense, which she attributed to the trespassers having arrived in their immediate vicinity. She sensed them ascending the main stairwell up through the admin block just one level beneath her feet. Eamon saw the look of encroaching panic on her face as she backed away and moved to the rear of the atrium. He imme-diately began marshaling his troops into position, walking up and down the row of barricades like a drill instructor inspecting his recruits and ensuring all were ready for combat.

"We don't know who or what is on the other side of those doors," he bellowed, finally taking cover himself behind a large storage crate, pressing the stock of his carbine into his shoulder. "Venators, bugswatters, a ruttin' death squad—what we *do* know is that they intend to hurt a lot of innocent folks. But we're not gonna let 'em do that; they're *not* gettin' past us without a fight! Y'all with me?"

"We're with you, marshal! You're goddamned right! Let's give 'em hell!"

Hazel dropped to her knees behind the information desk, peering over its white marble surface with eyes trembling in apprehension.

"They can't get through," she uttered under her breath. "Can they?"

Those bulkheads are made from titanium-laced nanocarbon, Amara responded. *Impervious to all types of energy discharge and durable enough to resist a two-hundred-kiloton blast. Unless the admiral plans on using a nuclear warhead, it is highly unlikely they will be able to penetrate them—not with any known method, that is.*

"What about *unknown*?"

Amara gave pause for several seconds, which Hazel knew amounted to the equivalent of several human life spans of intense cogitation. *Stranger things* have *happened.*

She heard a variety of muffled noises emanating from beyond the bulkheads: squeaking boots, the thump of heavy equipment being dropped to the ground, distorted voices issuing orders, and grunting "affirmative" in acknowledgment. Silence fell, then, "Breach, breach, breach!"

A sustained barrage of emerald-green plasma tore through the bulkheads as if they were forged from polystyrene, unleashing a shower of phosphorescent sparks and molten metal that reflected frenziedly across the polished surfaces of the atrium. The onslaught eroded the supposedly impervious barriers like wood whittled by a thousand knives, leaving a ragged, sizzling hole where they had stood only seconds ago. A rhythmic *clink, clink* arrived as a metallic object rolled across the tiled floor, making its existence as a flashbang grenade known by subsequently filling the space with blinding, whitehot light. Luckily, she recognized this to be the case before the detonation and preemptively shielded her eyes; others in the atrium had not been quite so quick-thinking and were sent reeling in shock, cowering behind the barricades as they fought to reorient themselves and claw back their senses. A second grenade rolled out of the pedestrian entrance, this one exploding not with a bang but with a hiss, releasing a thick plume of light-gray smoke that quickly consumed the field of fire.

Hazel caught Eamon waving manically at her from the corner of her eye. "You need to leave!" he spluttered, trying to catch his breath.

"I'm not going anywhere. Just . . . give me a weapon; I can fight!"

The man shook his head and then shouted to someone behind her, "Get her out of here, now!"

She felt a pair of powerful hands grip her waist as Fenn Haken effortlessly scooped her off the ground and lifted her over his shoulders. She whacked the back of his legs with her crutch as he began a fumbling sprint out of the atrium.

"Put me down, you bastard! Let me go!" The words escaped her mouth but were inaudible beneath the deafening salvo of weapons fire as Eamon's crew engaged their unseen enemy. She heard bloodcurdling screams, saw flashes of light, felt the shock waves of further grenade detonations—both fractal *and* fragmentation—striking her rear. The mephitic stench of ammonium nitrate capitulated to the aroma of freshly cut grass as Fenn lugged her out into the gardens. He deposited her on the gravel path and panted a hoarse "Sorry." He spun around and hurried back through the vestibule to return to the fight.

Hazel remained in the spot where he had left her, shaking in anger, the adrenaline in her system propping up her ravaged spine the straightest it had been since leaving the rehabilitation ward. She stood, listening to the terrible din of the ensuing skirmish for what felt like an eternity, helpless, defeated, alone.

Oh . . . Not alone . . .

She glanced down to find her little shadow standing beside her, trembling in fear and clutching her leg for comfort. She hadn't realized it at the time but concluded ae must have followed her and Eamon to the Conservatory's entrance, either from curiosity or fierce attachment to her. Ae stared intently into the chaos taking place beyond the fission field, the battle shrouded in an opaque veil, indiscernible shapes dancing in the cloudy maelstrom and silhouetted by bright flashes and viridescent streaks. Then, two words that chilled her to the marrow: "Fall back!"

The band of valiant defenders materialized from the smoke as they evacuated their stronghold. They pulled one another out of the melee, limping past Hazel, faces bloodied and blackened with explosives residue. She spied the bulky outline of Fenn Haken sporadically firing his sidearm as he stumbled backward with Eamon hanging off his neck—alive, thankfully, but having sustained a grievous injury to his upper-right torso, lolling his head to the side and grimacing in agony.

The final stragglers hurried past, leaving Hazel and her shadow gazing through the fission field into the pale oblivion beyond. Initially, she considered that she might be shell-shocked—forced to stay her feet by the sheer terror bearing down on her. But she realized that she did, in fact, have the power to flee if she so desired, and was instead frozen in place by her enduring *need* to see the faces of their enemy. Ignoring Amara's pleas for her to find shelter, she stood her ground in a kind of irrational defiance, as though the attackers might crumple to their knees at the mere sight of her inexorable might, when in reality, she likely had seconds before they mercilessly gunned her down.

At last, the beast reared its ugly head. A dozen hideous cryptids emerged from the murk—ghoulish humanoids with glowing red eyes and superficies too nightmarish to comprehend. They resembled walking corpses, black and bloated from decomposition. Their splintered bones burst forth from their decaying flesh and sculpted spinous tributes to Gothic architecture along their limbs and torsos. Gazing in horror at their otherworldly appearance, the harrowing possibility dawned on her that perhaps this *wasn't* Coombs's loyalist forces after all, but that the *Novara* had fallen under attack from some unknown alien aggressor. As the fiends stepped into the blue light of the vestibule, she realized that what she had mistaken for sinew and exposed muscle tissue was, in fact, body armor—a mixture of Lelantus Recon and GEN4 Venator combat skins, infused with what she could only surmise was *Devourer* xeno-technology. *Hybridized*—just like the defiled kestrels she had been unwittingly pitted against in the admiral's depraved live-fire test, the same used to murder Shiyana and Zain in cold blood. Now, she faced the anthropoidal embodiment of that same evil, as though it possessed the ability to morph into whatever form it needed to in order to hunt her down and destroy her.

The venators, which she had chosen to call them in the absence of any concrete knowledge surrounding their actual division, raised their spliced weapons in unison, marking her abdomen with a fan of electric-green laser sights. She could have sworn she heard one of them say her name, masked beneath layers of vocal distortion, then another reply, "Affirmative. High-value target acquired."

Her shadow made a growling sound from somewhere in aer thorax, stomping aer talons into the gravel like a bull preparing to charge. She watched as the green beams drifted from her chest to the abdomen of the infant cohabitor; if there was ever any question in her mind concerning what wicked assignment they had been dispatched to the Conservatory to carry out, it vanished in that appalling instant.

"No!" Both Hazel and Amara screamed the word in unison, creating an unusual phasing effect in her inner ear. Feeling a spurt of rage so blistering it scorched her throat, she reached out her hand and channeled her fury

down her arm toward the venators. She sensed the Conservatory responding, the eruptive force of her emotional outburst bending the environment to
her violent will. Beyond her splayed fingers, she saw her foes consumed by
thundering columns of extinguishing foam, the vestibule's fire suppression
systems exploding to life and buffeting the unsuspecting venators. They staggered backward, flailing their arms in shock and surprise as if trying to fend
off a swarm of hornets. Several squeezed off panicked bursts of fire from their
spliced weapons, spraying indiscriminate lances of the same voltaic energy
that had eaten its way through the bulkheads with the ease of a blowtorch
against a wall of ice. All it would have taken to cause catastrophic depressur-
ization was for one stray bolt to strike the dome; fortunately, the vast hemisphere of aluminosilicate remained intact.

Continuing her counteroffensive, Hazel imagined herself bringing the
ceiling of the vestibule down on top of the attackers, which her kinesthetic
implant interpreted as best it could by overcharging the grav-panels beneath
their feet. Their bodies crumpled under an immense, invisible weight, their
weapons slamming to the ground as if wrenched from their hands by a
powerful magnet. She heard a succession of nauseating cracks and pops as
combat armor buckled and bones snapped, the lethally increased gravity sur-
mounting any and all efforts to resist its influence. The resounding screams
would surely haunt her until the end of her days, made tolerable only by the
conclusion that if she had failed to act, she and her shadow would presently
be lying face down in the gravel.

She sealed the bulkheads between the vestibule and the gardens to spare
the child from having to witness any more of the grizzly scene, and to place
a barrier between them and any reinforcements potentially en route, even
though she knew they ultimately couldn't withstand the efficacy of the venators' prototype weaponry.

Mental and physical exhaustion washed over her. Darkness encroached
around the edges of her vision while excruciating pain skewered the gray
matter behind her eyes. She collapsed, and as she succumbed to the alluring pull of unconsciousness, Tobias's warning about *pushing herself too hard*
echoed raucously in her mind. The last thing she recalled before the world
went black was Amara's solemn voice, damning herself for endowing her
with such wretched responsibility.

THIRTY-TWO

Tobias turned numb with disbelief the moment the fighting broke out. Despite all evidence to the contrary, it had never occurred to him that an admiral of the NTSC could conceivably wage war against innocent civilians. Coombs's malfeasance flew in the face of everything he'd been taught at ACS about the civic responsibilities of military and government officials. It marked the final nail in the coffin for the same institution he'd once been so eager to dedicate his life in service of—an institution that now conspired to hunt down his family. As utterly implausible as it all felt, the staccato claps of gunfire echoing across the gardens brought the reality of the situation home all too viscerally. Coombs's forces were here, *now*, and if their objectives were as diabolical as his fretful mind feared, then they had come to exterminate the cohabitors, and anyone foolish enough to try and stop them.

He had struggled to make any progress whatsoever with the assignment Eamon had given him before departing. But then, trying to rally thousands of panicked cohabitors to safety when his only means of communication had expired proved easier said than done. He had grown so accustomed to hyperresonance that to suddenly be without it felt horribly disorienting, as if he had been blindfolded, spun around six times, and shoved into an anechoic chamber. Perhaps the most distressing thing about it was that he sensed the Prey could no longer *see* him as they had before. He had been rendered just another dull, colorless human, unable to share his essence or sing them his silent melody. They regarded him with disinterest as he sprang up and down before them, motioning frantically toward the rear of the Conservatory, feeling like an exasperated sheepdog failing to herd his refractory flock into their pen. All around him, he saw ciphers similarly struggling to bond with their resonant partners. It seemed an epidemic of acute prosopagnosia had befallen the *Novara*, with perhaps thousands suddenly robbed of the ability to recognize the faces of their loved ones.

Mercy seemed more distraught than most. Tobias spotted her near the graceful glass arc of the butterfly greenhouse, joined by a somewhat floundering Isaac. He heard her begging Null to acknowledge her as she clawed feverishly at aer flesh, tears streaming down her pale face. But Null's attention, and indeed the attention of every other cohabitor in the vicinity, remained fixed in the direction of the ongoing firefight. Powerful explosions shook the earth like the booming thunderclaps heard during the Conservatory's weekly storm emulations, which had always been a simple pleasure for Tobias. Once a week, the projected sky darkened with brooding, ominous clouds; jagged forks of lightning raked the dome like incandescent fractures while the atmosphere processors bathed the thankful greenery in a heavy deluge of precipitation. Rarely had he known peace like that which he had found studying and daydreaming beneath the pergola near Bandhavgarh Reservoir, listening to the unrelenting thrum of the rain and watching the trees dance in the wind. The synthesized soundscape of violent cracks and distant rumbles had once brought no end of solace, although its likeness now stirred nothing in him but intense dread. His insides wrung tightly at the thought that his sister could be stranded amid all the bedlam. He knew Eamon would never needlessly put Hazel in danger, but from the sounds of it, the situation had escalated far beyond the man's control . . .

"Thought these bugs were supposed to be smart!" Kahu Heperi groaned, waving his plasma carbine like a casterblade baton to try to impel the aliens to move—hopefully, Tobias thought, with the safety *on*. "Got the frickin' Clash of Kepler Crater happenin' a few hundred meters away an' they're all just standin' around with their thumbs up their asses . . . They *do* have thumbs, don't they?"

"They're smarter than *you*," Teo rebuked as she fruitlessly tried to guide Nanimonai away by aer paw. "And yes, for your information: technically they got four of 'em."

"I don't think it's that they can't comprehend what's happening or what we're asking them to do," Captain Holloway sagaciously added. "It strikes me they're just not interested in running."

Had Tobias been able to read the intentions of the Prey around him, he would have likely reached a similar conclusion himself. Punctuating the distant din, a chorus of low growls arose from the nonhuman assembly. The spines adorning their necks and shoulders began twitching and elongating, leaving him with the impression of gazing upon a field of black crops agitated in the wind. Finally, they showed signs of coordinating an evacuation, although it swiftly became apparent that this would include only the young, sick, and elderly. Nanimonai, along with many others, appeared to automatically assume the roles of facilitators, rounding up the vulnerable and leading them through the desert biome and the cactus gardens toward the artificial cave system, which was situated toward the rear of the Conservatory. Showcasing some of Earth's fascinating subterranean geology and ecosystems, the unique exhibit featured two large stalactite chambers connected by an underground river. Tobias felt optimistic that it would provide adequate shelter, but with the many humans who had already sought refuge there, combined with the masses of cohabitors now en route, it would surely prove a tight squeeze.

Choosing to remain in the fields surrounding the Beech Glade complex, the able-bodied Prey collectively dug their talons into the turf, spreading their arms wide and showing their paws to appear as threatening as possible. It seemed fairly evident that they were preparing for war. They had no weapons, no means of defending themselves; just their primal strength and inexorable will to survive. Because *survival*, of course, didn't just mean the survival of the individual. It meant ensuring the continuation of their species. Evidently, they had determined that the only way to accomplish that at this juncture was to stand their ground and fight. *Admirable*, Tobias thought, *but ultimately ill-advised when facing a rogue splinter faction possessing the military might of the NTSC . . .*

The sounds of the skirmish coming down the main path gradually lessened until eventually subsiding. Moments later, the dome's output of tangerine daylight faded, allowing the endless night to spill into the Conservatory once more. The abrupt cessation of gunfire, in Tobias's mind, could be a sign of either good news or *extremely* bad news. He knew he had an unfortunate penchant for pessimism, but he couldn't shake the dreadful suspicion that the latter was the case. Twice now he had witnessed Hazel control the hue and transparency of the artificial sky with her consciousness; he didn't think it unreasonable to presume the drastic change in the dome's appearance could be attributed to a sudden loss of said consciousness.

The answer came hurtling up the main path in the form of the ZT buggy Eamon and Hazel had taken to the entrance plaza, only behind the wheel now, he spied the burly shape of Fenn Haken, the man's anguished face highlighted in rhythmic pulses as he sped past the succession of pathway lamps leading toward Beech Glade. Eamon sat slumped in the passenger seat beside him. The marshal's crumpled face looked drained of color; his worn fur-collar jacket soaked in blood from a severe shoulder wound. Tobias's fears materialized as the ZT buggy pulled up near the medical tent and he saw Hazel lying motionless on the repulsor-lifted flatbed. He couldn't see any signs of physical injury on her but, sure enough, she was out like a light. In the distance, he spied a convoy of three additional transports loaded with more wounded. The medical volunteers had hastily evacuated in anticipation of the attack, and it seemed they were about to face an influx of critically injured patients without the necessary equipment to provide proper care.

The crew of the *Assurance* descended on the arriving buggy to assist its passengers. Delilah hurried to Eamon's side and wrapped her arms around his torso to help him disembark.

"I'm fine; help *her*!" He batted the captain away and gestured in Hazel's direction.

Holloway persisted, nevertheless. "Don't be an idiot, Wyatt. Your arm's hanging on by a thread."

"Hey kid," Kahu said for Tobias's attention. "Give me a hand with your sis."

Tobias complied, and together they carried Hazel into the canvas hut and deposited her on the same bed their father had lain in. Delilah helped Eamon hobble inside and sat him down atop a storage crate. Teo opened a trauma kit and began tenderly helping the man out of his ravaged jacket so she could better assess the damage. Oddly, there didn't appear to be any of the charred skin one might expect from plasma score. It was as though something had surgically removed a chunk of his flesh, leaving a gruesome ten-centimeter fissure in his shoulder that looked as clean and precise as though it had been cut with fine stainless steel.

"Wasn't I patchin' you up like ten minutes ago?" the girl groused as she loaded a green stim capsule into an injector.

"That you did, miss," the marshal replied in a pained voice. "But you did such a helluva job I just couldn't wait for my second visit." The man cast his gaze outside the tent, loosening his jaw in shock and dismay as he noticed the thousands of cohabitors lingering in the surrounding fields. "No . . . What are they still doing here? I thought you were gonna move them back!"

"They won't listen," Tobias answered, applying a coolant pad to his sister's forehead. He had hooked her up to a biometric monitor and found her vitals to be stable. Brain activity seemed normal, and the console flagged no evidence of clot or hemorrhage. He didn't want to tempt fate, but at first glance, she looked to be OK. "I told you: if they can't run, they fight. They know we're trapped in here, so they figure their only option is to face the threat head-on."

"Fight?" Eamon repeated, the word heavy with disbelief. "They'll be slaughtered! These aren't just mercenaries or loyalist enforcers coming for us: they're venators—outfitted with both spliced weapons *and* armor."

"We didn't have a chance against them," Fenn added, clumsily unraveling strips of gauze at Teo's request. "They chewed through us worse than the Razorbacks did the Stormbreakers at the Phantom Streak semifinal."

"Best I can tell, the discharge from their weapons inflicts some kinda molecular destabilization," continued Eamon. "It basically evaporates any matter it touches. They made short work of the bulkheads and pretty much disintegrated anythin' we could use for cover."

"That armor looks like it crawled straight up outta hell, man." Fenn's husky voice cracked in fear. "Shit was impervious to *anythin'* we threw at 'em. Only way we could even phase them was with that ugly-as-Abyss hand cannon Eamon's got. And what these freaks have in their arsenal makes that thing look like a damned spud gun."

"What happened to my sister?" Tobias cut in, becoming increasingly agitated with the lack of attention being paid to Hazel's condition.

"She managed to take some of the bastards out by playin' hell with the gravity in the atrium," Eamon explained. "Wasn't a pretty sight, but she bought us some time. I don't know how exactly she did it, but it knocked her for six. Reckon she'll be alright, though; just needs rest . . . Problem is, she was our last line of defense. With her and Amara out of action . . . We're cooked."

"What are you saying?" Delilah asked, commanding Eamon's attention with her firm demeanor. "There's nothing we can do to stop these . . . *venators* from gaining entrance to the gardens, and there's nothing we can do to protect ourselves against them?"

Eamon grimaced as Teo began applying bandages to his shoulder. "Think that's about the size of it."

"So . . . What's our plan?"

"I'd say surrender if I thought they'd have any interest in accepting it."

Kahu cracked his knuckles and rolled his shoulders. "Word 'surrender' don't appear in my vocabulary, chief. There's gotta be somethin' we can do to slow them down."

Eamon gave a defeated sigh, shaking his head. "There's no question now what they came here to do, and the bugs are gonna make it as easy as target practice standing around in the open like this. If we can't find a way to get them coordinated and moved to a more defensible position, the venators are gonna cut them down with zero remorse."

With that grim conclusion, Tobias rose to his feet and left his sister to join his crewmates who hadn't assembled in the medical tent. Isaac had stayed by Mercy's side near the butterfly greenhouse, the cipher still desperately vying for her partner's attention. He had never seen Null appear quite so intimidating. Fully extending aer legs, ae towered nearly twofold over aer human companions, aer indigo poncho struggling to contain the menacing knife rack of bristling, cast-iron blades occupying aer withers and shoulders. Ae seemed alert to aer surroundings, yet obsessively fixated on the Conservatory's entrance, dipping aer head and repeatedly flexing and knitting aer mandibles in apprehension.

Isaac regarded Tobias with a sneer as he arrived, warning, "Don't bother us unless you've got something useful to say." But then the engineer recognized just how needlessly antagonistic the greeting was and added, "Sorry . . . I just . . . wish we knew what was causing this resonance block. Mercy's torn up about it, and I hate that there's nothing I can do to help."

"We *do* know," Mercy sobbed as she clutched her brass pendant, sunken eyes red and swollen. "This is Harmony's doing: the Composer has condemned us all with her desecration of the signal. She has corrupted the Savior's light and, in her hubris, has taken away its most precious gift to us." She reached up with a delicate arm and placed a hand on Null's side. "To have been bonded with an individual for so many years, then to have something rip out the part of them that lives inside of you—the insurgents have caused immeasurable suffering to every ciphered pair on the Coalescence. There will be some minds that *never* recover from this, good people driven to insanity because of the cold voids it will leave in their hearts."

Isaac absently tugged on the goggles hanging around his neck, his analytical mind trying to solve a problem that it could barely even perceive. "But surely if this block is something that's been caused by external intervention, then it can also be reversed? . . . Maybe . . . maybe if we could just get inside that *hollow* place then we could figure out how to . . . I dunno, perform a system reset or something?"

"Mercy and Null already tried that," Tobias answered. "Harmony wouldn't let them get anywhere near the core."

"Well, I can't imagine *they* want this any more than we do. Teo has history with the Composer, doesn't she? Maybe, if Jyn Sato sees a familiar face, she might be more inclined to accept our help. There's a chance Null could know something they don't about how to resolve this."

Tobias scoffed. "Great idea: let's just go traipsing through an active war zone in the hopes the vicious terrorist leader doesn't mind us popping in for a visit."

"Well shit, at least I'm trying to come up with ideas." Isaac squared his shoulders and took a preemptive step toward Tobias, their bad blood clearly not as settled as he had thought. "If all you're gonna do is shoot me down then why'd you even come over here; just to make me look like an idiot?"

Tobias met the challenge and closed the remaining distance between them, bringing himself almost nose-to-nose. "Why bother when you do such a fine job of that yourself?"

"Don't fight," Mercy implored, breaking her attention away from Null to try to separate the warring pair. "How does this solve anything?"

Tobias didn't cede any ground but dialed his attitude down several degrees. "Look, the loss of resonance is tragic—I'm not disputing that. All I'm trying to say is that we have more *immediate* problems to focus on right now."

Heedless to Mercy's pleas for accord, Isaac gave him a shove to the chest. "That's easy for you to say, Upperdecks. You've known about your hyper-resonance for what: five minutes? Who are *you* to tell Mercy about what she should consider important?"

Tobias knew it was unwise to break eye contact with one's opponent during an escalating confrontation, but something in his peripheral vision caught his gaze. Over Mercy's shoulder, in the curved glass of the butterfly greenhouse, he noticed the warped reflections of what appeared to be a row of bobbing, blinking, red lights. They resembled ruby fireflies arranged in startling uniformity, glowing ominously in the darkness pushing against the boundary of the complex. Mercy's eyes widened as she fixed them on the origin of the phenomenon. Before he could turn around to verify for himself, the girl screamed a spine-chilling "No!" She thrust herself between him and Isaac and forcefully extended her arms to push them away from one another. Tobias, caught off guard, tripped over his feet, stumbled backward, and fell to the ground. An unfamiliar noise pierced the air, reminiscent of a taut steel cable being struck with a metallic implement. Then came a crash of shattering glass as the pane directly behind Mercy exploded in a violent surge of shimmering fragments. Lying on his side, head swimming in shock and confusion, he craned his neck to identify the source of what he presumed had been weapons fire. Then he saw them: three ominous figures standing with an unsettling poise at the apex of the steps leading to the maintenance sublevel. Eamon's earlier description of the venators' hybridized armor had failed to capture the true horror of its demonic appearance. Their bulky combat skins were the result of a sacrilegious fusion of xeno-biology and military engineering. Their visage inspired a bitter cocktail of awe, terror, and an acute sense of his own vulnerability in the face of such sinister power. Bearing rifles like glaives adorned with the macabre remains of their last victims, their advanced helmet optics seared scanning cones of vermillion light into the gloom, radiating a malevolent energy that made his heart race and his skin crawl, as if falling under the hateful scrutiny of evil in its purest, most malignant form.

He tore away his stare and shifted it to Mercy. A shot of liquid nitrogen coursed through his veins as he observed the patch of crimson appearing on her stomach, seeping and expanding like a Rorschach inkblot into the pristine fabric of her white tulle dress. The adrenaline in his system stretched those unbearable seconds into what felt like hours, his heightened senses working overtime to commit every wretched detail to memory. He watched Mercy's eyes fall to her punctured abdomen, her expression vacant and dazed as though completely detached from the tragedy that had befallen her. A radiant halo of flittering butterflies encircled her delicate figure, their wings a captivating kaleidoscope of colors as they escaped the argent confines of their tropical haven, their vibrant beauty illuminated by a nearby recessed floor light.

The medical tent erupted with action as Eamon's voice boomed, "Fenn!" He hurled his spliced pistol to his former partner. In a display of surprising agility, Fenn caught it midair and dove into a combat roll, seamlessly transitioning into a kneeling firing position. Tobias had been too stunned to realize that Null, the venators' intended target, had evaded danger by leaping to safety just as the first volley struck. The attackers unleashed a barrage of chartreuse bolts into the darkness, futilely missing their mark as ae darted like a racehorse around the perimeter. With the cohabitor providing a crucial distraction, Fenn recognized his opportunity and took it without hesitation. He unleashed a rapid succession of his own voltaic lances, which appeared somewhat subdued in comparison to the enemy's firepower, owed, no doubt, to the admiral's continued refinement of the hybrid tech's matter-eating capabilities. The venator nearest the tent reeled as one of the luminous rounds struck the back of their helmet. They crumpled to the floor, blurting a shrill cry that rang like the growl of a chain saw through the heavy vocal processing of their mask. The other two whipped their heads around to identify the source of the incoming fire, only to find themselves confronted by Kahu Heperi as he charged toward them, unleashing a battle cry. Before they could even raise their weapons, the veteran delivered a brutal shoulder charge and tackled the first opponent to the ground. Delilah swiftly drew her repeater from its thigh holster and unleashed a relentless barrage of concussion energy upon the second, dexterously priming successive rounds with each flick of the lever action. While Kahu grappled with his adversary, the remaining venator regained their composure and locked their sights on Holloway. Tobias felt an overwhelming wave of dismay wash over him as he braced himself to witness yet another of his crewmates ruthlessly gunned down.

Then Null joined the fight. Emerging from shadow, ae batted the venator's rifle out of their hands with a powerful swipe, then wrapped aer paw around their neck and hoisted them off the ground, leaving the toe caps of their boots dangling just above the turf. Ae pried off their helmet and held it in front of aer snout, regarding it for a moment as the profane abomination it was, before crushing it with ease and casting its remains away. Aer ensnared prey, a man wearing a white communications cap, screamed, "Get off of me you fuckin' leech! I'll kill you!"

Null emitted a disdainful huff, cocked aer head to the side, and with an almighty crack, slammed him face-first into the ground.

As the grunts and thumps of Kahu's struggle continued, Tobias watched a pair of legs clad in an orange jumpsuit march into the fold. Like a man possessed, Isaac collected one of the attacker's grotesque weapons off the floor. He calmly waited for a clear line of fire before coldly discharging a single shot into the final venator's head, killing them instantly. Tobias saw horror roil across Delilah's face as she watched her surrogate son execute a man in cold blood. Her trembling eyes betrayed her unavoidable conclusion that she had failed in her solemn promise to shield the lad from suffering—a vow she had made not only to herself but also to honor the memory of his brother, Micah.

As a stifling silence fell, Isaac released the weapon, urgency propelling him back to Mercy's side. He dropped to his knees, burying his face in her bloodied dress as sorrow coaxed a plaintive moan from his throat. Null, breaking free from a state of feral preoccupation, joined him, gathering aer cipher's lifeless body and cradling it into aer carapace.

In that awful moment, Tobias felt nothing . . . Well, not *nothing*; he experienced his fair share of grief and anguish, of course—even an overarching sense of culpability stemming from the realization that, ultimately, it was *his* actions that had brought the *Assurance*'s crew to the Conservatory in the first place. But as Null gazed down at Mercy's empty expression, willing her with every cell in aer body to come back, he sensed none of aer pain, aer torment: just a demoralizing emptiness where there should have been a riot of sublime, if utterly skull-crushing, emotion. Were he able to attain resonance, Null's agony would have completely debilitated him; yet, somehow, he would have gladly welcomed it over the void that instead enveloped him.

Tobias and the others were left with little time to mourn. From what he had been able to glean through previous vicarious resonance with Null, Mercy's was a life chronicled by turmoil. He had found little in the way of happiness delving into the index of her memories, her story a tragic tapestry woven from strands of trauma and sorrow. Only since managing to free herself from Drexen's leash had she found anything close to resembling contentment. Bonding with Null, joining Delilah's crew, meeting Isaac for the first time— these events had shone like lanterns in the oppressive darkness of her existence, unearthing and rekindling long-dormant embers of joy in her soul. She had been a friend, a teacher, and deserved so much more than what life had seen fit to bestow her, the very least of which was a proper burial, instead of being left in the blood-mottled grass amid the corpses of her assailants. Sadly, circumstances dictated that her final rest would have to wait for another time . . .

They had barely managed to catch their breath when the strident rattle of gunfire arrived from the direction of the entrance plaza, muffled initially but steadily increasing in clarity and harshness. Phosphorescent light blazed like a signal flare from the entrance to the gardens, the venator reinforcements unleashing their siege engine of small arms on the vestibule doors. Amplified by the dome's unique acoustics, the raucous cacophony dug a pit of despair in his gut—a pit that only deepened when the salvo abruptly ceased, given it meant the wolves were not just at the gate; they had successfully gnawed their way through it.

According to Kahu, the troops that had infiltrated the Conservatory via the maintenance sublevel were probably a scouting unit, as evident from the presence of their bastardized recon gear. There wasn't a doubt in Tobias's mind that the battalion now gaining forceful entry to the sanctuary consti-tuted the main offensive, and it had become achingly apparent that any hope they had of thwarting it was presently lying comatose in the medical tent . . .

He returned to his sister's side, hopelessness an anvil in his heart.

"C'mon, Hazel," he begged, resting his forehead on hers. "We need you . . . You have to wake up!"

He felt a cruel spike of fleeting optimism as she mumbled something unintelligible, but then flipped onto her side, turning her back to him as if severely hungover and demanding five more minutes.

"Just wait a scrap-heapin' second will yah?" Tobias swiveled around and saw Kahu planting himself in front of Null, using his entire body weight to try and prevent aer from joining the obstinacy of Prey now advancing toward the interlopers. "If you go that way, those freaks are gonna make mincemeat outta you. You think that's what the girl would'a wanted, huh?"

But Null could not be reasoned with, nor could ae be detained. Kahu's boots etched furrows into the gravel as he struggled to hold the cohabitor back. Ae brushed him aside and vanished into the midst of the herd, resolute in joining aer brethren in their singular purpose of confronting the impend-ing threat. Tobias stared out at that landslide of chitin wearing a jaded look. With a resigned sigh, he uttered "Fuck it," and set off across the leaf-shaped courtyard, filled with renewed determination. Teo saw him striding in the direction of the ZT buggy and hastened to keep pace beside him.

"Where do you think you're going?" She asked, out of breath.

"I have to try and speak with them."

"Who? The venators? You got a screw loose or somethin'?"

"My name should still hold weight, Teo. They'll know who I am. If there's a chance we can negotiate a nonviolent end to this, then we have to take it."

"Your name doesn't hold shit! Or have you forgotten your pa an' sis nearly got zeroed by those spooks? These bastards don't care *who* you are; to them, you're just another sympathizer."

But he had already vaulted into the ZT buggy driver's seat and engaged the repulsor drive, the vehicle emitting an idle hum as it rose off the ground. He didn't even bother attempting to dissuade Teo from joining him as she hopped into the passenger seat, knowing that he would ultimately fail and that every second spent arguing with her was a second he could have used trying to prevent a massacre.

"Lei-Ghannam," Teo rasped as they sped back down the main path. "Mercy . . . I can't believe they just did that to her. She never meant no harm to anybody—last person on the whole Coalescence who deserved what happened."

Staring ahead, he answered in a low voice, "I think they were aiming for Null."

"Is that supposed to make me feel better?"

He gave a bargaining shrug. "No . . . I just don't think it's helpful to think of them as mindless monsters. Beneath all that terrifying armor, these venators are human, which means they can be reasoned with. I don't believe . . ."

"Don't believe there's a situation that can't be resolved through diplomacy," she cut him off in a mimicking tone. "I hope you're right, cuz otherwise, we just might be racin' toward the exact same fate as Mercy."

"It has crossed my mind . . ."

She paused, regarding him for a moment with a wanting expression. "If that's the case, I just want you to know . . . I never met anybody who pissed me off quite as much as you do."

He showed a tilted smile. "Thanks . . . I think."

"Feels like since we met, we've either been runnin' or fightin' for our lives. Like the captain said: scrape after scrape after scrape . . . I guess what I'm sayin' is, I just wish we'd had a little more time together when things was more . . . yah know: normal."

"It's been hectic," he concurred, meeting her crystal-blue eyes. "But honestly, I wouldn't trade a second of it for anything."

She grasped his head firmly and planted a forceful kiss on his cheek. If he hadn't been so focused on the task at hand, he felt certain his heart would have exploded out of his chest. But the present circumstances drained the moment of its deserving exhilaration. The depth and nature of their developing relationship remained a frustrating ambiguity. He knew that at the very least he had gained a lifelong friend, but it felt self-indulgent and slightly inappropriate to yearn for something more, even though she would assuredly reprimand him for *overthinking stuff* if he dared express those sentiments aloud. He vowed to himself in that instant that if they survived this ordeal, he would cast chivalry and etiquette aside, and tell her exactly how he felt. Because life was too fragile and tenuous to hold such things back . . .

A grim and daunting sight wrenched him back to reality. Up ahead, roughly fifty venators stood in rigid line formation at the base of Khadija's Green—a ghastly stockade of spines, tissue, and nanoweave plating, punctuated by an eerie embarrassment of scarlet sapphires. The soldiers relentlessly drummed shock batons against their fission-energy riot shields, unleashing a tumult of crackling reverberations like war drums distorted through a broken speaker, the dissonant symphony no doubt meant to strike fear into the hearts of their opponents. A rough estimate put the venators as outnumbered by at least ten to one, but the formidable armory at their disposal would undoubtedly level the playing field. Undaunted, the Prey held their ground approximately twenty meters from the venator line, showing threat displays and releasing a pungent pheromone into the air redolent of vinegar and kerosene. Though unfamiliar with the acrid stench, Tobias speculated that it served as a means of warding off predators or, perhaps, signifying anticipation of hostility.

Just then, a flood of brash light poured into the Conservatory from above. Teo and Tobias turned their eyes upward and gasped in synchrony as they identified its source. An accipiter-class gunship hovered just beyond the dome's curvature, scouring the gardens below with spotlights like a mad scientist peering through a microscope at the subjects of their twisted experimentation. The conduit's canopy of foliage had decomposed to such an extent that it appeared as a thicket of parched thistle, casting thorny, wiry shadows on the ground as the wide cones of glaring fluorescence filtered through. The venators' helmet optics were almost certainly equipped with night vision and thermal imaging, suggesting the implementation of air support was unnecessary, and yet further evidence of the employment of intimidation tactics.

As they hurtled toward the venator line, Tobias narrowed his eyes to see if he could pick out anyone who matched the description of a commanding officer, hoping to make a beeline for them so he could begin trying to broker a peaceful resolution. But he realized in scanning that forbidding bulwark of soldiers that no two of their combat skins were alike. Their semibiological augmentation sprouted in haphazard whorls and protrusions, spreading like gruesome fungal growths devoid of any semblance of uniformity, which made discerning rank or class nigh impossible.

He saw movement ripple through the formation as the enemy noticed the ZT buggy speeding toward them. Then, without so much as a moment of deliberation, they opened fire, and Amara's green Eden quickly devolved into a war zone. The venators' weapons spat a tempest of radium-green streaks that doused the environment in a malefic luster. The fusillade tore into the Prey like an onslaught of vengeful specters, felling dozens of cohabitors in those first excruciating seconds. A chill gripped Tobias as the realization dawned upon him that Null, too, could have been among the fallen, plunging him into a well of dismay deeper than any he had ever climbed his way out of. Tightening his grip on the yoke, he watched as the aliens leaped forward on locustlike legs to close the distance between their foe; some landed in sufficient proximity to engage the attackers in unarmed combat, but ultimately met their demise having failed to break their riot-shield guard.

"Look out!" By the time he managed to process Teo's shrieking warning, it was too late. The venators had begun targeting the ZT buggy; the surrounding air hissed and crackled as the coruscating rays formed a tunnel around them. The pair ducked below the dashboard as several bolts struck the chassis, the cobalt-blue miasma erupting from the hood signaling the rupture of the repulsor drive. The transport careened off course and slammed into the ground, silica-tile scraping on gravel as its momentum carried it along like an ungainly sled. It veered to the right, almost rolling onto its side, and skidded off the main path, barreling toward the tri-hex hemisphere that enclosed the rainforest biome. The buggy impacted an embankment with a violent jolt, sending a shock wave of pain screaming up Tobias's neck. Knuckles aching as he relinquished the wheel, he blinked away the haze of disorientation and checked himself for injuries. He turned his attention to Teo and felt a breeze of relief at finding her conscious and seemingly unharmed.

"Are you OK?" He sputtered.

"Never better," she answered with sarcasm, placing a hand on her shoulder and rolling it back and forth. "Well . . . I guess we can chalk that down to the single dumbest idea you've ever had."

She was right, of course, but it could have been a lot worse. Fortunately, they had crashed just out of view of the venator line, the rainforest biome providing much-needed cover and enabling them to safely exit the wreck and take a moment to collect themselves. Teo took charge and grabbed him by the hand, leading him back along the channel of broken reeds that had been neatly plowed by the out of control buggy. Reaching the opening, they peered cautiously out into the enveloping slaughter. Scanning those endless fields of death, Tobias's grief was a searing brand jousted into his heart. Before him, hundreds of Prey lay dead in the grass, with thousands more still charging fruitlessly toward the venators' impenetrable rampart.

"This is horrible," Teo whimpered, tears welling in the corners of her eyes. "I thought by bringing them here we were protecting them, but now I think we just made them easier to kill."

He wanted to answer her, to tell her that none of this was her fault. But the overwhelming shock rendered him speechless, his mind grappling for the right words, only to find emptiness and silence. Evidently, he had been wrong: the venators *were* monsters—merciless butchers without a shred of remorse or compassion beneath their hideous masks. They may as well have been grenadiers for the tireless and unquestioning efficiency with which they executed their barbaric directives. Watching the ensuing bloodbath, he couldn't help but contemplate how the admiral would attempt to manipulate the narrative on the NTNN. Vivid headlines danced in his mind depicting the tragedy as a result of mass suffocation or a deadly crush caused by unprecedented overcrowding. Perhaps they would even allege a catastrophic decompression event triggered by an unfortunate crack in the dome's aluminosilicate—an unthinkable catastrophe rivaling the scale and devastation of the Collision itself. Of course, for the spread of such shameless disinformation to work, the venators would have to execute *everyone* in the Conservatory—humans included . . .

Finally, after another wave of senseless deaths, the Prey seemed to recognize the futility of their efforts and began to retreat. But the venators did not yield, instead, continuing their assault with renewed ferocity, firing indiscriminately into the surge of fleeing aliens. When Tobias turned to Teo and caught her staring up through the dome and out into space, he assumed she had simply decided she could no longer watch the harrowing scene and had chosen to avert her eyes. But as she furrowed her brow and slackened her jaw, he realized that *something* in the blackness beyond had seized her attention.

"Do you see that?" she asked in a quivering voice. "What is it?"

He followed her frantic gaze, craning his neck to search the sky for any sign of a mysterious anomaly. Then he saw it: a distant point of light resembling a star moving at high speed. Obstructed intermittently by the jagged silhouette of the dome's rotting veneer, it glanced across the umbral heavens from starboard to port before making a swooping course correction. Its new trajectory saw it hurtling toward the Conservatory at a low angle. As it drew nearer, the gleaming speck grew into a silver teardrop, carving through the Abyss at astonishing velocity with its needle-tip bow pointing forward. Realization arrived in conjunction with the moment Teo began excitedly tugging his arm.

"It's *Chīsana Osuushi*," she said in a rising voice. "The Little Bull!"

Sure enough, the unknown vessel revealed itself to be Vidalia Drexen's yacht; Harmony had somehow managed to move it starside after capturing it from the Monarchs. Tobias doubted the route through the Savior's core had been available to the insurgents, given the current circumstances, meaning the Composer's only remaining option was the *Novara*'s colossal vehicular airlock—a facility that the Church of the Abyss had occupied and appropriated as a holy temple for many decades. Although, he suspected, that may no longer have been the case . . .

The luxury frigate disappeared beneath the Conservatory's horizon, then soared like a resplendent asteroid back into view, appearing so vast and grand that it had to have been less than two hundred meters away from the dome's apex. Tobias felt his eyes widen as two missiles launched from the battery recessed into the ship's reflective keel. The projectiles striated the obsidian void with lucent filaments of ionized particles, beginning a gradual arc as they tracked toward their target. They struck the accipiter-class gunship and unleashed a cataclysmic detonation, engulfing the unsuspecting craft in a violent maelstrom of fire and smoke. Wreckage struck the Conservatory, ringing the immense dome like a clangorous bell as it rained down on the *Novara*'s dorsal hull. The yacht punched a hole through the roiling cloud of smoldering debris before accelerating away, seeming to evaporate into nothingness as it subsequently engaged its luma-shroud and vanished into the night—a successful sortie followed by a clean getaway.

The spectacle gifted the Prey a moment of reprieve as the venators held their fire to assess the situation. As the shooting abated, Tobias noticed something lurking behind the enemy perimeter: dozens of ghostly shimmers darting and strafing in shadow, revealing their ovoid shape as they caught the residual glow of the firestorm hanging above. The apparitions funneled out of the overgrown entrance plaza and fanned out across Khadija's Green, surrounding the admiral's distracted forces before closing in on them like pack hunters encircling their prey. It dawned on him that he had seen a similar phenomenon once before: during the Governor's water ceremony at the Çorak—when a Harmony zealot used personal stealth tech to get close enough to Drexen to make an attempt on his life, failing only thanks to an untimely weapons malfunction. He suspected the insurgents now readying to strike would not be so unlucky. He watched with bated breath as the prowling specters materialized in their physical form—sixty-plus fearsome militants wearing gray-brown cloaks, wielding their own arsenal of spliced firearms and melee weapons sporting fission-edge blades. The Composer's faithful revealed themselves to their enemy, uniting their voices in a roaring rallying cry as they launched a vengeful counterassault. Confusion and disarray took hold among the venator ranks, their riot-shield battlements crumbling as they scrambled to discern the source of the hostile fire, panic mounting further as it became clear they had been surrounded. The air rang heavy with the sounds of strife: armor clashed and crackled as Harmony thrust their energized spears into the bodies of their foes; ear-splitting claps of gunfire sounded as the insurgents discharged bursts of voltaic lances at point-blank range. The venators' masks transmuted their howls of fear and agony into a grating ensemble of industrial machinery; they were outnumbered, outgunned, and wholly overwhelmed.

He felt the earth beneath his feet beginning to rumble, turning in unison with Teo to behold a stampede of enraged Prey charging back into the battle. They slammed against the venator line with the force of a runaway cargo barge, bolstering Harmony's numbers tenfold and making victory seem all but assured. Cohabitors by nature knew nothing of wrath or vindictiveness; they did not seek vengeance against transgressors, no matter how severely they had been wronged. But as the aliens began hurling venators like rag dolls into the air, pummeling them with their mighty paws, and tearing them limb from limb, it became unnervingly apparent that they had no intention of allowing the admiral's forces to retreat.

Narrowing his gaze, he picked out Jyn Sato's face amid the carnage. The Composer screamed like a wraith as she jammed her blade into a venator's neck, snatching their rifle and whirling around just in time to fire a kill shot into the chest of another as they tried to rush her from behind.

"She came through," Teo said, watching the lethal ballet with a mixture of awe and horror. "I *knew* she wouldn't leave us to die, I just knew it!"

In truth, Tobias felt somewhat conflicted about Harmony's triumphant arrival. On the one hand, these were the same violent extremists who had killed Jade and so many others, who had brought ruin to the Mouth, and who, by all accounts, had potentially doomed the entire population of the Coalescence. But he couldn't deny that in their last-minute intervention, they had saved countless lives, bringing hope at a time when it was in desperately short supply.

His relief, if it could be called relief at all, was predictably short-lived. Having foolishly lulled himself into a false sense of security, he heard a struggle emanating from his rear. A hand, clad in a padded glove, seized his throat; the muscles in his arms burned as they were forced behind his back and locked tightly in place. His captor drove a bootheel into the back of his leg, spinning him around and forcing him down onto his knees. Teodora, who had been similarly restrained, pierced him with terrified eyes perched over the hand covering her mouth, muffling her feeble cries for help. Exploiting their lapse in vigilance, three venators had stealthily emerged from the tall reeds and apprehended them with ruthless efficiency. He couldn't be sure what gave him this impression, but he had the distinct sense that they had not been part of the main offensive but had entered the Conservatory with separate orders. This was seemingly confirmed when the one with their hands free, whom he intuited to be the leader, retrieved a portable retinal scanner from their utility belt and positioned it before his left eye. The device scoured his cornea with a painful grid of cyan lasers before emitting a confirmatory beep.

"Positive ID," the leader said, studying the screen embedded in the scanner's sturdy casing. "Tobias Cole Edevane—high-priority target confirmed."

Hearing his name spoken through the harsh vocal processing of their helmet sent electrifying panic coursing through him. He began to struggle, convulsing his body and kicking his legs, which only caused his captor to tighten their hold to the point he thought his arms might pop out of their sockets.

"You make another move like that, and I'll blow out your fuckin' kneecaps," they threatened, the words crushing him into submission.

"We're RTB," the leader declared. "Get ready for exfill."

"What about the girl?" the one detaining Teo asked. "We wasting her?"

"Negative. If the admiral doesn't have any use for her, then I'm sure the *surgeon* will."

As a terrifying welter of possibilities about what *that* could mean fulminated in his mind, he watched helplessly as the venator behind Teo deployed a stim injector from their wrist pack and thrust it into her neck. Her despairing look waned as her body went limp. He felt a sharp prick on his nape as he was subjected to the same procedure, then consciousness slipped through his grasp and darkness took hold.

EPILOGUE

Delilah was no stranger to death. From losing Micah in the Vestiges and discovering her father lifeless in his armchair to witnessing Gretta Hox interspecies blood sport and the numerous cadavers the crew had inadvertently fished out of the belt, death had been a wretched companion that refused to leave her side, a crimson thread that wove a through line into the fabric of her existence. And yet, never before had she faced loss on such a devastating scale. Amara's mainframe had come back online shortly after Harmony's fortuitous, albeit brutal, arrival. Once the venator attack had been repelled, the AI restored daylight to the Conservatory, drenching the gardens in hazy-bronze radiance like an abstract impressionist hurling paint at a canvas. The new dawn brought with it a vision of untold horror, starkly illustrating the manifold cohabitor bodies strewn about Khadija's Green. The admiral's forces lay in bloody piles of cartilage-infused armor, laced with the polycarbonate bodysuits and mottled robes worn by the dozen or so Harmony insurgents who had fallen in battle. Delilah had no love for the Composer and her militia of fanatics, but she couldn't deny that they had saved countless lives in answering Eamon's call. She had once deemed Jyn Sato nothing more than a harbinger of chaos, a woman consumed by an insatiable thirst for vengeance that left little room for compassion in her hateful heart. How relieved she now felt to have had those preconceptions proven so very wrong. As distressing and abhorrent as the death toll was, had Jyn failed to come to their aid, doubtless it would have been far more catastrophic . . .

For Delilah, one casualty, in particular, had struck a deeply personal chord. In all her years captaining a weld and salvage vessel, she had *never* suffered the pain of losing a crewmember. While Mercy's time aboard the *Assurance* had been relatively brief, the young cipher had left an indelible mark on everybody she touched. More benighted minds might have taken one look at her and seen the purity and innocence she projected as evidence of a feeble disposition. But Delilah had fiercely respected the vehemence with which she had stood in Null's corner. When cohabitors faced so much scrutiny, criticism, and abuse, ciphers had no moral obligation to stick by their side and shoulder that burden. But Mercy had done so unwaveringly; despite everything Tobias had disclosed about her traumatic past, she had remained a beacon of loyalty, kindness, and integrity, wanting nothing in life but to foster interspecies cooperation and to spread knowledge and awareness about resonance. *She was a real gem*, as Kahu would say. And now, Delilah had to confront the gutting truth that, as captain, her actions and decisions had inexorably contributed to her death . . .

The Beech Glade complex stirred with commotion as the medical volunteers returned to their stations and began tending to the wounded. Isaac knelt by Mercy's lifeless body amid a maelstrom of activity, his gaunt face a tormented mask of bereavement, dried blood caking his skin from his fingertips to his elbows. Delilah approached tentatively, unsure as to whether he'd prefer to be consoled or left to wallow in his misery. He glanced at her from the corner of his clouded eyes.

"You were right," he said in a choked voice. "We should have gotten the hell outta Dodge the second we knew there was trouble coming. You tried to warn us that we were completely out of our depth, but we didn't listen. Abyss, why couldn't we have just listened?"

Delilah placed her hand on the back of his neck and gave it a gentle squeeze. "None of us could have predicted what we were up against," she admitted. "You stood up for what you thought was right, and I'm proud of you for that. The only certainty we knew was that the cohabitors were under threat, and it was wrong of me to think we could just keep our head down, or stay in our lane. Inaction in the face of injustice like this is every bit as bad as complicity . . ." She took a knee beside him, trying, and failing, to catch his gaze. "Besides, even if you *had* listened, do you think there was anything we could have done to drag her away from the Conservatory?"

"No," he answered tearfully, shaking his head. "She'd have been adamant about staying here with Null."

"Precisely. She stayed of her own accord, and there's nothing you could have done to influence that. So, the last thing she would have wanted is for you to be placing the blame on yourself in any capacity."

"Even still, I could have done more to protect her . . ."

He became anxious and fidgety, clawing absently at the back of his neck—behavior Delilah had seen him exhibit many times before, and that could usually be taken as a sign of an imminent relapse. It didn't matter how long he had been clean, or how much work he put into his rehabilitation; glow, it seemed, was only ever one tragedy away from pulling him back below the dismal recesses of addiction. A shameful realization settled upon her that, had he expressed a desire to sneak off to find something to *dull the edge*, she might have fully endorsed it—let the lad numb himself to a stupor so he didn't have to feel anything, and worry about the withdrawal later. Thankfully, he expressed nothing of the sort. Instead, he reached his hands out to Mercy's thin neck, the girl cutting the image of a porcelain doll as she lay in the grass. He unlatched the chain clasp of her moon-shaped pendant and held the object in his palms, staring down at it in sorrow.

"I'll keep hold of it for now," he said, stowing the object in his jumpsuit pocket. "I don't think she has any family but Null will probably wanna keep it."

Delilah stood to her feet, burdened by a sudden unease as it dawned on her that she hadn't seen the cohabitor since ae hurried off to confront the venators. With so many dead and Null having been so eager to join the fight, her concern for aer well-being grew from a fissure into a chasm of seemingly limitless depth . . .

Eamon emerged from beneath the medical hut with his shoulder bandaged and his arm in a nanoweave sling. Kahu kept in stride while Abraham diligently took point between the pair, wagging his scruffy, brindle tail as he noticed Delilah waiting for him. The sight of the dopey mutt with his panting grin provided a welcome boost to her miserable mood. It didn't last, of course, once she caught a glimpse of Kahu's grave expression. The old veteran didn't revel in violence as he once had, and the fighting had clearly exacted a heavy toll on him. She left Isaac and set off to meet the trio, ensuring their conversation would take place out of earshot.

"How's Wonderboy?" Heperi asked, staring over her shoulder at the lad with a worried look.

"Hurting plenty," she replied. "But he'll pull through. He's stronger than we all give him credit for."

"I dunno, Skip . . ." Kahu scratched the salt-and-pepper stubble covering his broad neck. "I've seen all sorts of dark shit in my days, but I can't say as I *ever* had a bloke get his head vaporized right in front of my face like that. Kid pretty much executed the poor bastard; don't come outta somethin' like that without serious scars to heal, and I ain't talkin' about the physical kind . . ."

She dipped her gaze, giving a determined nod. "We all did what we had to . . . Coombs wants a war; that's precisely what we'll give him."

"Music to my ears, Holloway," Eamon quipped with a pained wince. "Nothin' gets me fired up like your little pep talks."

Delilah regarded the marshal with a rueful look. "Wyatt, how do you get yourself into such states? Frankly, I'm mystified as to how you're even standing right now."

"I know," he groused. "Should probably start callin' me Swiss on account of all the holes I got in me. Reckon I'm more med-foam than man at this point . . . Still." He turned solicitous for a moment. "Got a helluva lot luckier than some of the others."

"We *all* did," she said grimly. "Venators weren't taking prisoners . . . Any update on how Hazel's doing?"

"She's still comin' to," Kahu informed. "Said she's got a splittin' headache, which, from what Eamon told us, don't surprise me in the least . . . Those Edevane kids got heads full of magic—that's for sure." She watched the old pilot's gaze drift toward Mercy, his hoary brow drawn in sadness and regret. "You know where Poncho got to?"

Delilah somberly shook her head, then nodded in the direction of the battlefield. "I was just about to go and find out. You coming with?"

"You sure you wanna go that way, Lilah?" Eamon asked in a warning tone. "I don't think it's gonna be pretty. Once you see the site of a massacre with your own eyes, you have a real hard time tryna forget it—speaking from experience . . ."

"The whole of the *Novara* needs to see what happened here . . . No reason I should be exempt."

Cutting through the autumnal splendor of the Europan Memorial Arboretum, they left the shattered sanctity of Beech Glade and made their way toward Khadija's Green. With each step drawing them closer to the entrance plaza, Delilah's heart grew heavy—a profound sense of desolation not felt since her perilous descent into the Vestiges some twelve years prior. Death, her ever-incessant companion, enveloped her again in its frigid embrace, surrounding and suffocating her like noxious fog. She dared not make an approximation on the number of cohabitors who had been slain, fearing that even her most conservative estimate would prove foolishly optimistic once the true toll had been tallied. Everywhere her gaze fell, Prey lay in mangled, contorted heaps, the manicured terrain transformed into a dense archipelago of iridescent islands, rising from the surface of a luscious green ocean. Vibrant smatterings of leaves and petals adorned these chitinous reefs, left by the cohabitor survivors in what she could only presume was some kind of mourning ritual. The aliens meandered from body to body in a reverent procession, each taking turns scattering pawfuls of their floral confetti over the deceased. Curiously, the aliens did not appear to discriminate between the remains of their kin and the perpetrators of the slaughter, paying their respects without prejudice or contempt. Harmony, on the other hand, showed little interest in honoring their fallen enemies, and had instead set about scavenging the venators' armor, tech, and weapons for themselves.

The haunting juxtaposition of the scene sent Delilah's head into a spin; this was a tragedy, an unmitigated atrocity, and yet, there lay undeniable beauty in the solemn tenderness with which the Prey performed their sacrament, their works turning what should have been a bleak spectacle into a vibrant collage of color and texture.

Delilah turned to find Kahu trembling in anger, tears collecting in the gray bristles of his unkempt mustache. "I thought I was done," he said, the words escaping through dry, quivering lips. "All used up like a spent fission cell. But if there's one thing this old dog's gonna do before he finally croaks it, it'll be to kill that rat bastard Coombs with my own two mitts."

"You'll get your shot, champ," Eamon assured. "I'll see to it personally. If it's true we've all only got a few weeks left, then I sure as shit know how *I'll* be spendin' 'em . . ."

"We can't go on the offensive just yet," Delilah cautioned sternly. "We don't know for certain there aren't more venators inbound. We have to secure the Conservatory before we can take any retaliatory measures."

Nodding in agreement, Wyatt's gaze found a solitary figure kneeling in the grass ahead. Delilah recalled witnessing Jyn Sato's luma-cast visage projected like the envelope of a translucent airship around Vidalia's yacht. The woman before her bore little resemblance to the wrathful insurgent leader she had seen looming menacingly over the district. Despairing eyes glistening and steady, the Composer looked drained, defeated, a broken shell of her indomitable self, racked with so much guilt it seemed she might crumble under the weight of it at any moment. She paid no mind as Eamon limped to her side, falling onto his haunches and bringing his shoulder gently against hers. Their relationship, from what the man had disclosed, had taken a contentious tangent over the past several weeks, but it seemed any acrimony they held for one another evaporated in that moment of unexpected candor.

"I should have come sooner," Jyn said while Abraham, acutely aware of her distress, nuzzled his snout into her hand, hunting for a scratch behind the ears. "The moment you contacted me, I should have pulled everyone out of the Mouth and redeployed them to the Conservatory. I was so focused on achieving our objectives, I was blind to the severity of the threat represented by the admiral's forces . . . I wasted precious time playing war when I *should* have been here, using my resources to protect people." She vented a despondent sigh, forming a bitter expression. "The innocent lives that were lost today—they're on me . . . every last one of them."

Eamon picked a daffodil out of the grass with his good arm and studied it in front of his nose. "There's plenty I'm gonna make damn sure you're held accountable for, Jyn," he said. "But when it comes to what happened here, the buck stops with the admiral, his sadistic loyalists, and nobody else. *They* had their finger on the trigger. Not you."

"Maybe . . ." Jyn unholstered her hybridized machine pistol sidearm, scowled at it, then cast it away. "But *we* handed them the gun . . . All of our effort—the blood, sweat, and tears we poured into developing and refining hybrid tech—and all we did, in the end, was give our enemies a more effective tool to wield against us; to harness to exterminate the Prey."

"Hate to break it to you, Roots," Kahu interjected, seeming to forget who it was he had just given the unflattering nickname. "But Coombs was comin' for the bugs with or without your little freak show science project. Don't make a blind bit of difference whether you gave him a leg up or not."

"Look, the point is," Eamon cut in, rescuing the oblivious man from a scolding, "you came through for us. If it weren't for Harmony showin' up when you did, the venators wouldn't have let up until they snuffed out every sign of life in the Conservatory. It's thanks to Harmony that . . ."

"Harmony," Jyn interrupted, letting the word linger between bared teeth. She pulled her hooded cloak over her head and shoulders before throwing it disdainfully to the ground. "There *is* no Harmony . . . The *Novara* is dying, Absence is gone, and the Savior has abandoned us, taking with it the power to attain resonance. What is there left for us to fight for? Nothing . . . I failed, and somehow, managed to seal the fates of everyone on the Coalescence in the process . . . I'm done."

"Drop all the *woe is me* horseshit!" The words escaped Delilah's mouth before she had any hope of swallowing them. Jyn glared up at her in response, rage returning to her countenance like the heat of a red-dwarf star. Fighting her compulsion to submit, she folded her arms and doubled down. "I'm sorry, but after the havoc and misery you've inflicted on this ship and its people, you don't get to just gracefully bow out and skulk off somewhere to lick your wounds . . . If it's true you're responsible for getting us into this mess . . ." She offered a hand to help Jyn stand, hoping she would take it as a mark of truce and cooperation. Because Abyss knew there'd been enough strife over the course of the past two months for an entire generation. "Then help get us out of it."

The Composer—a title seemingly renounced—reluctantly accepted her assistance. Although, she realized too late that she had offered her still-sprained arm and had to bite through the pain as she pulled the woman to her feet.

"That's a nice sentiment, Holloway," Jyn said. "Truth is, the only person who might have had any hope of devising a remedy is dead. Absence tried to impart aer lifetime's worth of knowledge and experience, but I fear that if there *is* an answer, ae has taken it to the grave. There's nobody else who can fix this."

"Firstly, I'm sorry for your loss." She meant the words in earnest but feared they would only sound hollow and patronizing. "And secondly . . . Well, I wouldn't be so sure about that . . ."

Her heart swelled with relief as she spotted Null bounding toward them, as if on cue. Ae skidded to a halt near the scrum, earning a low growl from a startled Abraham. Contrasting the brooding rumination the other Prey were engaged in, ae seemed frantic, jittery, snorting and huffing through aer breathing holes and rocking sideways anxiously. Patches of human blood stained aer threadbare blue shawl, giving Delilah cause to wonder what grievous brutality the gentle giant had been forced to commit in the name of defending aer species . . .

"What is it, Lassie?" Kahu joked. "Kid fell down the well?" Delilah delivered a sharp jab to his ribs and, with a furious glower, signaled the words, *Read the room, man.*

She moved toward the cohabitor and placed a hand on the chitin of aer neck. "What is it? Tell us what's wrong."

Ae emitted a shrill wine, turning abruptly and leaning forward to point aer snout like an arrow in the direction of the Conservatory's entrance.

"More venators maybe?" suggested Eamon, a note of fear tainting his voice.

"I don't think so," she answered. "Surely if that was the case, ae would be leading a warband to go and confront them instead of coming to us for help."

Null stamped a talon into the ground in what looked like frustration at their inaction. Ae hurriedly scanned aer surroundings before galloping off into a botanical plot, returning shortly after with a haphazard bouquet of blue-orchid flowers gripped in aer paw. Gesturing once again toward the atrium, ae lifted the colorful blossoms and held them against the spikey crown of aer head. Terrible realization steeled upon Delilah as she finally ascertained aer meaning.

"Has anybody seen Teo?" she asked gravely.

"Saw her and Upperdecks takin' one of those ZT buggies for a joyride when all the fightin' started." Kahu seemed to share some of her growing trepidation. "Not seen 'em since."

Just then, the emitter of a nearby security pylon ignited the surrounding air in a geometric starfield of luma-cast points. The points coalesced into a recognizable shape: a life-size projection of the ZT buggy in question, shown hurtling down the main path as Heperi had described. Delilah had to remind herself that, although she could choose to remain silent, Amara Thaddeus was privy to *everything* that transpired within the bounds of the COHP and had apparently been listening in on their conversation. Despite her being incapacitated at the time of the event, it seemed she had scoured her archived feeds for any sign of Teo and Tobias, and was now projecting a real-time, real-position recreation of their last known activity. Delilah and the others followed the spectral chariot, which paused occasionally to allow them to catch up, before finally arriving at its final destination. She watched with dawning horror as it suddenly skidded sideways and tipped over before disappearing into a patch of tall reeds near the rainforest greenhouse. It felt surreal seeing the physical breadcrumbs left by the intangible vehicle: the trail of disturbed gravel, scattered fragments of silica tile from its damaged repulsor pads, and the trench of flattened reed stems where it had careened off the main path.

Abraham raced ahead, barking futilely at the apparition and following it into the thicket. When the others arrived, they found the dog sniffing inquisitively around the overturned buggy, having now materialized in its tactile form.

"No sign of 'em," Eamon said after performing a hasty search of the wreckage.

"Sure there is." Kahu motioned with a nod toward the two ghostly figures now emerging from the crash—not rendered in high enough fidelity that their faces could be recognized, but sufficient to discern their general profiles. Null released a melancholic groan, aer many eyes glued pensively to the virtual effigies.

"What in the name of Lei-Ghannam were they thinking?" Eamon asked, watching as they crept back along the trench of broken reeds and came to a stop near its opening, with Teo's avatar passing straight through Delilah's body.

"Knowing Tobias, he probably thought he could try and talk the venators into a cease-fire," she said.

"You can't be serious," Jyn groused.

She shook her head, blowing a sigh. "Trust me; I wouldn't put it past that boy to try and *debate* a hurricane."

A few excruciating moments passed; she wondered briefly whether the projection had frozen, with Amara reaching the extent of what relevant surveillance data she had to display. She took comfort in the fact that, at the very least, she saw no signs of blood on the ground, and more importantly, no bodies . . .

Three additional figures appeared—venators, judging from their size and imposing silhouettes, the emitter struggling to process the irregular protuberances cresting their nightmarish armor. It was then as if Amara's advanced security system scanned the darkest recesses of Delilah's mind, coaxing out her worst fears and manifesting them before her very eyes, visualizing in harrowing detail the moment Coombs's merciless agents forcibly apprehended Tobias and Teodora. The assailants appeared to administer some kind of sedative to the pair, rendering them unconscious. They hoisted their prizes over their shoulders and disappeared into the reeds, breaking line of sight from the security pylon and causing their projections to disperse like luminous grains of sand in a blustering gale.

"Sonofabitch," Kahu whispered into the blanketing silence. "They got nabbed . . . But, why? What could Coombs possibly want with the son of some Upperdecks big shot and a Mouth rat?"

"I don't know," Eamon put in. "But I'd bet my last DMED pay packet on it being something pretty damned unpleasant."

"No bet," added Kahu. "So . . . What's our next move?"

"We get them back." The words came, surprisingly, from Jyn. Delilah turned to find the woman regarding her with a penetrating gaze, exuding newfound adamance and ferocity. "I don't know if I can heal the Savior," she said. "I don't know whether Harmony has the strength to overcome the venator threat . . . But what I *can* promise you is this: I will do everything in my power to find them."

Delilah felt a flutter of uncertainty, betraying her concern with a furrowed expression. "Look, it's not that I don't appreciate the off—"

"You don't trust me," Jyn cut in. "It's no secret and, frankly, no surprise. But here's the thing: I don't need your trust, nor do I need your permission." The faintest intimation of a wistful smile pulled at the angles of Jyn's face. "Teo . . . she's family. And Tobias, well, let's just say, never in all my days did I think I'd run into another hyper-resonant. In the event we *can* reignite the Pyre, he'll be a powerful ally, and I cannot afford to lose him . . . Their lives matter as much to me as they do to you, Holloway. So, I'm bringing them home, whether you're with me or not."

ABOUT THE AUTHOR

T. M. Clayton is the author of the groundbreaking Collision series. Growing up in Manchester, UK—otherwise known as "Rain City"—Clayton developed an inextinguishable love of science fiction while stuck in the house on wet days, utterly devouring anything and everything from his parent's VHS collection. His infatuation would manifest in young adulthood as an irrepressible desire to create his own fantastical worlds, inspired by the dystopian, "kitbashed" sci-fi cinema of the '70s and '80s. Though he works full time for an engineering company, Clayton devotes every spare minute to his mission of crafting emotionally resonant stories, interweaved with contemporary sociopolitical commentary and set against a backdrop of gritty, mind-bending science fiction.

Podium
DISCOVER
STORIES UNBOUND
PodiumAudio.com